GEARS OF WAR

THE SLAB

THE SLAB

KAREN TRAVISS

Based on the Xbox 360 video game series
from Epic Games / Microsoft Game Studios

GALLERY BOOKS

NEW YORK   LONDON   TORONTO   SYDNEY   NEW DELHI   SERA

G

Gallery Books
A Division of Simon & Schuster, Inc.
1230 Avenue of the Americas
New York, NY 10020

First Gallery Books hardcover edition May 2012

GALLERY BOOKS and colophon are trademarks of Simon & Schuster, Inc.

For information about special discounts for bulk purchases,
please contact Simon & Schuster Special Sales at 1-866-506-1949
or business@simonandschuster.com.

The Simon & Schuster Speakers Bureau can bring authors to your live event.
For more information or to book an event contact the
Simon & Schuster Speakers Bureau at 1-866-248-3049 or
visit our website at www.simonspeakers.com.

Manufactured in the United States of America

1   3   5   7   9   10   8   6   4   2

Library of Congress Cataloging-in-Publication Data

Traviss, Karen.
Gears of war : the slab / Karen Traviss.—1st Gallery Books
hardcover ed.
p. cm.
1. Imaginary wars and battles—Fiction. 2. Space warfare—Fiction.
3. Soldier—Fiction I. Title.
PR6120.R38G49 2012
823'.92—dc23   2011050647

ISBN 978-1-4391-8407-3
ISBN 978-1-4391-8410-3 (ebook)

For my father

ACKNOWLEDGMENTS

My thanks go to Mike Capps, Rod Fergusson, and Cliff Bleszinski at Epic Games, for a wonderful run in their universe; Ed Schlesinger (senior editor, Gallery Books/Pocket Books) and Anthony Ziccardi (VP, Deputy Publisher, Gallery Books/Pocket Books), for making things happen; and Jim Gilmer for always being on hand with a sense of proportion.

GEARS OF WAR TIMELINE

(ALL DATES ARE SHOWN IN THE MODERN SERAN CALENDAR—
BEFORE EMERGENCE OR AFTER EMERGENCE.)

80 B.E. (APPROXIMATE)—A long-running global conflict begins to sweep the world of Sera as the Coalition of Ordered Governments (COG) and the Union of Independent Republics (UIR) fight over imulsion energy resources. This becomes known as the Pendulum Wars.

17 B.E.—Infantry lieutenant Victor Hoffman holds the besieged Anvil Gate garrison against UIR forces and makes his name. Adam Fenix—a weapons physicist—leaves the army to work on his dream of the ultimate deterrent, an orbital laser weapon to end the Pendulum Wars.

9 B.E.—Adam's wife, Elain, a biologist, goes missing in the underground caves of Jacinto, leaving him with a young son to care for—Marcus.

4 B.E.—Marcus Fenix enlists in the COG army against his father Adam's wishes, serving alongside his boyhood friend Carlos Santiago.

3. B.E.—Carlos's younger brother Dominic—"Dom"—enlists.

2 B.E.—Intelligence reveals the UIR is close to building its own satellite weapons system. A commando raid headed by Hoffman is staged to sabotage the UIR research station at Aspho and seize its data. Carlos Santiago and Major Helena Stroud (Anya Stroud's mother) are killed in the battle. Hoffman, Marcus and Dom are decorated for gallantry. The seized data enables

Adam Fenix to perfect his Hammer of Dawn orbital laser, which eventually brings the UIR to the negotiating table.

SIX WEEKS BEFORE EMERGENCE DAY—The UIR surrenders and the Pendulum Wars are finally at an end, although a handful of small UIR states, including Gorasnaya, refuse to accept the armistice and vow to fight on.

EMERGENCE DAY—With no apparent warning or motive, an unknown species of sentient creatures—the Locust Horde—erupts from underground caverns and attacks cities across Sera simultaneously. A quarter of Sera's population is slaughtered in the initial attack. E-Day, as it becomes known, is the start of a fifteen-year war for survival.

1 A.E.—The COG, fighting a losing rearguard action against the Locust, is driven back to Ephyra, the granite plateau where the Locust can't tunnel. In a desperate bid to stop the Locust advance, new COG Chairman Richard Prescott orders the destruction of all Sera's major cities using the Hammer of Dawn. Although civilians are urged to take refuge in Ephyra, few can reach the plateau in time and many millions die in the Hammer strikes.

2 A.E.—The Locust, slowed but not stopped by the global destruction, are back in even greater numbers. The few civilians outside Ephyra who survived the Hammer strikes band together in gangs, living hand to mouth in the ruins. The Stranded, as they call themselves, see the COG as an enemy.

10 A.E.—The Locust attack Ephyra. Sergeant Marcus Fenix disobeys Colonel Hoffman's orders and tries to rescue his father, a decision that leads to the fall of Ephyra. Adam Fenix is buried in the rubble of the Fenix mansion when the Locust attack, and Marcus faces a court-martial. His death sentence is commuted to forty years in Jacinto's notoriously brutal prison, nicknamed the Slab.

14 A.E.—The Locust overrun the prison, and the inmates are set free—except Marcus. Dom Santiago rescues him and Marcus rejoins the COG army. Using Adam Fenix's research notes on the Locust tunnels, the COG detonates a Lightmass bomb underground, but the "grubs" are back in force a few weeks later. The human population of Sera has been reduced from billions to a handful, and the last COG bastion—Jacinto—is now under threat.

14 A.E.—Chairman Prescott plans a final all-out assault on the Locust warrens by tunneling into their strongholds around Jacinto. The Locust in turn begin their push to take the city. The COG finds that the Locust have been waging an underground war with another aggressive species known as the Lambent, and were forced to the surface by them. Marcus and his fellow Gears find recordings by Adam Fenix in the Locust command center, describing how to flood the tunnels, and the COG makes a final, desperate decision to wipe out the advancing Locust. Evacuating the city, they deploy the Hammer of Dawn to sink Jacinto and drown the Locust forces.

14 A.E.—The column of refugees moves from place to place evading the few surviving Locust, eventually settling on a remote volcanic island that the Locust never reached—Vectes, a former COG naval base. The local population has never seen a "grub," but is plagued by Stranded pirate gangs. Forming an unexpected alliance with the last of the UIR's Gorasnayans, the COG newcomers and the islanders drive off Stranded pirate gangs and begin to rebuild civilization.

15 A.E.—The brief peace is shattered when Lambent life-forms appear in the seas around Vectes, destroying ships and sinking a Gorasnayan imulsion drilling platform, the last remaining source of imulsion fuel. Chairman Prescott is found to have an encrypted data disc, the contents of which he refuses to reveal to Colonel Hoffman. The remnant of the COG is now effectively besieged on Vectes, fending off Lambent attacks from the sea.

15 A.E.—Lambent stalks begin to overrun the island. Unknown to Hoffman or anyone else, Prescott has been in touch with a secure COG facility called Azura throughout the Locust and Lambent war, and Adam Fenix—not dead as everyone believes—has been held there since the fall of Ephyra, working on a countermeasure. He's found that Lambency is a parasitic organism that will eventually destroy all life on Sera. While Prescott secretly updates Adam on the increasing rate of the Lambent mutation, Hoffman and his Gears fight a losing battle to contain the "glowies." Eventually Prescott decides to take vital biological samples to Adam to continue the research, but refuses to reveal his reasons for abandoning the population of Vectes. He leaves Hoffman, Michaelson, and Trescu to run what's left of the COG amid bitter recriminations. He isn't heard from again and is presumed dead.

15 A.E.—After a few months, the Lambent have all but overrun Vectes and Hoffman is forced to evacuate the island. With no single safe location where society can be rebuilt, the survivors are split into small groups to maximize their chances of survival. The COG ceases to exist. Hoffman takes one band of refugees to Anvil Gate, the Gorasnayans return home, and the rest find shelter in small settlements on the mainland. Captain Michaelson and a core force of Gears remain at sea in the helicopter carrier *Sovereign*, ready to assist civilians scattered ashore, but by 16 A.E. they've lost radio contact with Anvil Gate, and it's become clear that they're just another band of refugees trying to survive. Everyone is Stranded now.

17 A.E.—The Locust, trying to escape the Lambent and survive at any cost, find Azura and capture it, taking Adam prisoner. Prescott escapes and tracks down *Sovereign* to ask for help in driving off the Locust, bringing Marcus a message from Adam. But the ship comes under immediate attack from Lambent. Prescott is wounded and dies before he can reveal the location of Azura, but he gives Marcus a data key that will decrypt the information on the data disc that Hoffman took with him. Marcus learns that his father is alive and has been a prisoner on Azura since Prescott had him abducted.

17 A.E.—Delta Squad leave for Anvil Gate to search for Hoffman, who turns out to be alive and fending off Locust and Lambent attacks on the fort. When decrypted, his disc shows the island of Azura—concealed by a permanent artificial storm, the Maelstrom device—and how it can be accessed from underwater. The squad sets off for Azura, planning to commandeer a submarine from a COG shipyard, but the journey brings them into contact with Lambent-infected humans and Locust at Mercy, Maria Santiago's hometown. Dom sacrifices himself to hold off the attack and enables Marcus and the others to escape and locate the submarine.

17 A.E.—The squad reaches Azura and disables the Maelstrom to allow former COG and UIR forces to launch an assault on the Lambent. Adam and Marcus are reunited, and the truth begins to emerge: Adam was in contact with the Locust long before E-Day and knew they would be driven out of their tunnels by the Lambent and forced to colonize the surface, but he mistakenly believed he could talk Myrrah, the Locust Queen, out of the bloodshed of E-Day. Adam reveals a targeted particle device akin to a neutron bomb that will kill every Lambent-infected cell on Sera, and that may also wipe out the

Locust. Myrrah makes a final attempt to save her people by stopping Adam from activating it, and her warbeetle is downed as Delta Squad hold off her attack to give Adam time to activate his device.

17 A.E.—Adam has deliberately injected himself with Lambent cells to test the countermeasure on himself, accelerating its life cycle, and the infection has progressed so much faster in him that he knows he will die when the device is activated. He activates the device and Marcus sees his father die along with the Lambent organisms and the Locust now on the surface. Myrrah survives the attack on her warbeetle and returns to confront Marcus about his father's arrogance and humanity's greed. Grief-stricken, Marcus kills her with Dom's commando knife and withdraws to contemplate the near-destruction of Sera. The first signs of recovery begin, but the survivors now face rebuilding their world from nothing.

PROLOGUE

COALITION PRISON SERVICE ESTABLISHMENT HESKETH—
JACINTO MAXIMUM SECURITY PRISON, EPHYRA, ALSO KNOWN
AS "THE SLAB": TEN YEARS AFTER EMERGENCE DAY.

I'm just a regular killer. Nothing exceptional, nothing special, nothing *weird*.

I'm not one of those sick bastards who do it for a hobby. It's just a job. Okay, I've done a few, *more* than a few, and that's how you end up in the Slab. Occupational hazard. I'm not some kind of nutter, although we've got those in here too, the serial killers and arsonists and kiddie fiddlers. And even cannibals. We've got all sorts.

But I had a reason for killing, and I was good at it, so don't look at me like I'm some kind of pervert with a dozen bodies buried under my patio. I had *rules*. Like it or not, some people get what they deserve and they knew the rules going in.

Even criminals have them, buddy. Can't have a world without rules.

The Slab's for what they call maximum security prisoners. We'll never get parole. But that doesn't matter, because the average life expectancy in here is two years, so they might as well stick us up against the wall and pull the trigger anyway. No idea why they don't do it. I mean, in a world like Sera, who's doing a body count? Millions dead on Emergence Day. Millions more dead when Prescott fired the Hammer of Dawn to stop the Locust advance. Ten years since E-Day, and now we're talking *billions* dead. The majority of the world's population. What's left of humanity is mostly here in Ephyra.

So why not just cap us and have done with it, Prescott? What are you keeping us alive for?

Curiosity? Last shreds of the rule of law? Plain bloody-mindedness? God alone knows.

Like I said, we've got all kinds in here, mostly killers. We've got people who don't actually kill but do a whole lot worse. And now we've got a war hero. That's a first.

Everybody knows who he is. Marcus Fenix. They pinned the Embry Star on him, the highest award for bravery. You know who his dad is, don't you? Adam Fenix, the hotshot weapons scientist, the man who created the Hammer of Dawn and got the Octus Medal for services to humanity. Hey, never let it be said that the Coalition of Ordered Governments treats the rich differently. Sometimes they've got no damn choice.

Marcus Fenix abandoned his post during the battle for Ephyra.

Usually, that buys you a firing squad. You have to wonder how he got it commuted to life, but then there's a lot of questions about this war that I don't think I'll live long enough to see answered.

Somebody must really hate that guy. He's going to wish they hadn't commuted his sentence.

(Millton Reeve, currently serving twelve consecutive life sentences for murder: month of Brume, 10 years after Emergence Day.)

CHAPTER 1

We're surrounded on land and we've got our backs to the sea. We might as well be on an island.

(Lieutenant Meredith, Hammer of Dawn fire support team, assessing the situation in Ephyra, last defended area of the Coalition of Ordered Governments: 10 A.E.)

KING RAVEN KR-96, ON PATROL OVER CRESSY ESCARPMENT, EPHYRA: END OF REAP, 10 A.E.

The Coalition of Ordered Governments had bought time. But like time, everything—luck, patience, hope—ran out sooner or later.

Dom Santiago hung on to hope as tightly as he clung to the Raven's safety rail. Rothesay banked the helicopter to get a better look at what had been Estana, then let out a long breath. "Shit. Will you look at that . . ."

Dom knew what he was going to see. So did everyone else, and nobody said a word—not Marcus, not Tai, and not Jace. Even Castilla, Rothesay's crew chief, kept her mouth shut and just hunched over the door gun, chewing mechanically. Dom wondered where she'd managed to find some gum. He hadn't seen any in years.

Estana had been a nice town a couple of hours down the highway from Jacinto, the kind of place to take the kids for the day. Now black palls of smoke hung over it like skeins of filthy wool and the skyline wasn't the way Dom remembered it. The place had been burning for two days.

All he could think right then was that Maria couldn't possibly have been there when the grubs attacked. She was alive. He knew it. He could *feel* it. He'd keep looking, like he'd looked every day for the last eight years, and he'd search every Stranded camp until he found her.

Jace finally broke the silence. "We're fucked, man. They'll be up our asses inside a week."

"Been here before," Marcus said. "Nine years ago. And we're still here now."

"Yeah, because Prescott fried the goddamn planet. But we've run out of places to fry now. It's just us. Just Ephyra. And the grubs keep changin' the rules."

Tai got up from the bench seat and stood at the edge of the crew bay, gazing out. The stiff crest of black hair across his shaven scalp didn't move as the slipstream hit it, but that summed up the South Islander: the world didn't touch him. He moved in it, but seemed somehow to be above it all, cocooned in some weird kind of spiritual separateness.

"Then we must change our ways, too," he murmured.

From anyone else, that kind of mystic shit would have got right up Dom's nose. But Tai made it through the grind of each day by keeping part of his brain in another place, and Dom envied him. Everyone had their talisman, some place or idea they clung to simply to justify trying to stay alive one more day. For Dom, it was looking for Maria. For Tai—well, wherever he went in his mind, it left him serene. There was no other word for it.

Jace was anything but serene. He was angry. Dom decided it was healthier to let rip like that than bottle it up like Marcus.

"In case you ain't noticed, Tai, we've tried it all," Jace said.

Rothesay came back on the cockpit radio. "Don't underestimate the sappers. They'll do it."

"How many cubic meters of sewer have they got to block, though?" Dom asked. "I mean, do the math."

Locust tunneled. Beneath the 10-meter layer of rich soil, Ephyra was a granite plateau, a big lump of dead volcano, too hard for even grubs to dig through, and that was part of the reason Ephyra was still largely intact. If the assholes wanted a piece of it, they had to come up to the surface and face the COG on its own terms, or find a fissure. Dom had bought that impregnable Ephyra crap that Prescott peddled right up to the moment when he realized how much tunneling humans had done here over the centuries.

The plateau wasn't airtight. Tyran engineers had excavated sewers, installed underground cable conduits, and built subways. Any one of those was now a back door for the grub army to exploit.

And if we can tunnel through granite . . . maybe the grubs will learn to as well.

The 3rd Ephyran Engineers—3EE—and what was left of the civilian construction industry were now trying to infill what they could to barricade the plateau. A loud, rumbling explosion shook the air, followed by two more in quick succession. It wasn't artillery and it didn't sound like Locust. It had to be the engineers out there, blowing up bridges and cratering roads to block the grubs' route.

"That's the sappers," Marcus said. "They're cutting it fine. There'll be scouts ahead of the main grub force."

Even from this distance, Dom could see the forward edge of the grub advance. South of the plateau, the vast granite plug that made Ephyra an island in the sandstone and clay sea of central Tyrus, the terrain was a mix of city and forest. Or at least it had been: a swathe of conifers and Tyre oaks had been mowed down like a lawn along with the high-rise buildings. Dom had a clear view—one that hadn't been there before—right down the river.

3EE were out there somewhere, digging and laying charges. *Crazy bastards. Fucking heroes.* They didn't just dig ditches and drive trucks. Rothesay said some of them were undermining the grub positions, actually tunneling under the grubs' own tunnels, which struck Dom as the most insane thing he'd ever heard, and he was commando-trained. He knew what impossible looked like.

"Better check on them," Rothesay said. "I make that grub line about twenty klicks from the edge of the plateau. Anyone mind if we're late back? I know you've got a weekend pass, Fenix."

"Let's get it done," Marcus said. "It's not like I've booked a table at the Segarra."

The Segarra had been a pile of rubble for years, not that Dom had ever earned the kind of salary to eat there. It had become a watchword for all the nice civilized things the Locust had destroyed, all those comforts Sera had lost and might never have again. Marcus was supposed to be spending a couple of days with his father, though, and Dom got the feeling he was looking for an excuse to make the visit even shorter. It wasn't a hostile relationship. It was just an awkward, silent one.

Rothesay took the Raven down again, dropping below the tree line. There was no flurry of birds disturbed by the deafening noise this time. Everything in the path of the grubs that could make a run for it had already left town. Branches whipped in the rotor wash, scattering a blizzard of leaves.

"See anything?" Rothesay's voice dropped off the intercom for a couple of seconds as he switched to the open channel. "KR-Nine-Six to Red-Three—I need a position check, people. I hear you but I don't see you."

Right on cue, another explosion shook the air. Dom caught a glimpse of dust billowing up from the highway like smoke.

"Red-Three to Nine-Six, we're at grid zero-seven-eight-three-three-five." Dom could hear a grinding noise in the background. "You getting anxious?"

"Yes, and so should you."

"We've still got a lot of concrete to pour."

Marcus leaned out of the crew bay, holding on to the rail one-handed to check below. "Not before the grubs get here."

"And it ain't gonna set in time anyway," Jace said.

Castilla stopped chewing. "So much for the granite keeping the assholes at bay. They're doing just fine on the surface. Anyway, they can tunnel through bedrock, so how much is concrete going to slow them down?"

"Yeah, I give it a week before they're in Ephyra," Jace said.

"Like I said, we've been here before, people." Marcus looked as if he was going to turn and give Jace one of his don't-even-think-about-it stares, but he seemed to change his mind. Maybe he agreed with the estimate. Dom certainly did. "We stopped them then, and we'll stop them now."

"It's gonna take more than blocking the john to do it, Marcus."

Dom decided to put a stop to the defeatist talk, even if Jace was damn right. "They're collapsing and infilling sewers." He shot Jace a glance. *Don't. Don't mention the fucking Hammer.* He knew the kid was going to say that it was the Hammer of Dawn that stopped the Locust advance last time. Nobody needed reminding, least of all Marcus. "No point leaving ready-made tunnels for them."

"But even if they get into the main sewer, they'll have to dig through ten klicks of backed-up human shit," Rothesay said. "Which is kind of satisfying."

"I'll do an extra dump for them, then," Castilla said. "Maybe two."

"Yeah, crap for victory, Charlie. The COG expects every Gear to do his lavatorial duty. Or hers. Don't take hours about it, though. Why the hell do women take so long in the bathroom anyway?"

"We meditate," she said. "Or do calculus. Are you meditating, Tai?"

The South Islander was just gazing out of the door with that look on his face, that weird half-smile. *Serenity.* That was it. Dom envied him. How did anyone find serenity in a world that was going to hell in a handbasket? But none of it seemed to touch him. He turned his head slowly.

"I was communing with my ancestors," he said.

"Bit premature."

"We may draw on their wisdom without joining them."

"Glad to hear it. Did they have any suggestions?"

Tai cocked his head to one side. Dom was never sure if he was having a joke at their expense—taking the piss, as Pad Salton used to say—or not. He seemed to have taken a shine to Castilla, though. The smile broadened a little.

"They taught me that the best weapon is the will to survive."

"No, that'd be a door gun with a nine-meter ammo belt," Rothesay said. He changed course and Dom's view of the world was suddenly wide-open sky, a rare patch of blue that made the world look normal and unspoiled for a few moments. "Get on it, Charlie."

Castilla went back to chewing again. Maybe it was jerky, not gum. As the Raven zigzagged to evade targeting, the black silhouette of another Raven tracked across the smoke-filled skyline.

"KR-Eight-Zero to all call signs, grubs on the move." That was Gill Gettner. She'd clocked more flying hours than any other chopper puke and spent most of her free time tinkering with her Raven, as if she couldn't bear to be parted from the thing. "Column of about forty drones heading northeast—about five klicks from the escarpment."

"Nine-Six here, Gettner. We're south of Shenko Falls, hanging around for the sappers. And how are you today, my divine flower?"

"Need some help, Nine-Six, or can you manage it without Mom's help?"

"We'll keep an eye on them. I'll flash you if we hit problems. Nine-Six out." Rothesay turned back toward the Falls. "Think I'm in with a chance there, Charlie?"

"She'll tear you up for ass-paper, Lieutenant."

"I like 'em sassy."

"Yeah, but not homicidal."

"Ah, just semantics." Rothesay's whole conversation went on over the radio, piped down Dom's earpiece whether he wanted to listen or not. "Okay . . . Nine-Six to Red-Three, we've got grubs heading your way. Time to down tools and move out, people."

The radio crackled in Dom's earpiece. "Red-Three to Nine-Six, we didn't come down here for a picnic. Got a job to finish."

Marcus's attention was still fixed on the ground as the Raven circled over the escarpment that marked the boundary between life and death. The plateau had been the only place to escape incineration when Prescott turned the Hammer of Dawn on Sera's own cities. Dom relived the day in occasional nightmares, wading through the frantic rush of refugees trying to get to this one safe haven when Prescott had given the rest of Sera three days to get to the granite high ground or kiss its ass goodbye. Over the years, Dom had swung between horror and relief—the billions dead, humanity split into those who unleashed the Hammer and those poor bastards who were the collateral damage—but now he understood that Prescott had succeeded in a situation where the choice was between bad and worse. He'd bought a handful of people nine more years. The grubs had been weeks away from overrunning the COG, and nobody would have been around now to argue if Prescott hadn't made one of those brutal decisions he was so good at.

He saved his own. The granite barrier that had been his convenient excuse had held out for far longer than Dom had expected. But he had the feeling they'd now come full circle. The grubs were still there, armies of them, Ephyra was under siege again, and there was still nowhere to run.

"Red-Three, the grubs are only a few klicks from you, so better make your way to the fire exits," Rothesay said. "Not a suggestion. An order."

"KR-Nine-Six, this is Captain Shaw, and you're not hearing me, *Lieutenant*. Two more detonations and a couple of pours to go. We're not done."

Rothesay didn't back down. "*Sir,* just leave the machine and get to the extraction point."

"If we don't block that sewer, half of Ephyra's wide open. Red-Three out."

The radio went dead. Dom heard Rothesay shut his mike for a couple of seconds, probably effing and blinding about dumb engineers with a death wish. Marcus moved to the cockpit hatch and stuck his head through the opening.

"Get us down there and we'll drag them out if we have to." He sounded more weary than anything. "That goddamn cement won't even set in time anyway."

"You got it, Sergeant."

Rothesay swung the Raven south again. Another couple of explosions boomed. It was hard to hear what the ambient noise levels were like from inside a Raven with its doors open, but Dom got a sense of a silent landscape, all the birds and animals long gone. Castilla leaned back from the door gun and pulled out her field glasses.

"Brumaks," she said. "Moving up fast."

"Okay, captain or no captain, we're getting them out." Rothesay circled. "I don't know if those concrete trucks can outrun Brumaks."

Dom craned his neck to check out what Rothesay could see. A couple of camo-painted trucks were parked under the trees a few meters away from a crater like an emergence hole. It was only when the Raven hovered almost overhead that Dom could see a churn of bricks, the bright terracotta edges of broken pipes, and the glitter of water. Six sappers in a weird mix of hard hats, helmets, armor, and overalls were guiding a massive chute into the hole while two others jogged around with reels of cable, apparently laying more charges.

"I see them," Jace said. "Wow, that's one big fuck-off hole."

"Nine-Six, you're stopping us blasting." Captain Shaw sounded breathless over the radio. "I heard you. Brumaks. So what's new?"

"Just listen, sir. You've got to get everyone out now."

"Nearly done."

"Good. Because I'm coming in."

Rothesay hadn't even set down fully in the clearing when Marcus jumped down from the crew bay and started jogging toward the hole. Dom chased after him with Jace. The sappers looked up, two of them wrestling with the chute that was spewing concrete into the hole, one of them a big scruffy guy with a captain's rank tab on the front of his filthy overalls. Shaw was definitely a hands-on kind of officer.

Marcus gestured toward the Raven. "Come on, sir, you're not going to make it. All aboard."

"Can't leave it now, Sergeant," said Shaw. "We've collapsed the sewer in three places and now we're sealing it with a special mix. That'll give them a few thousand cubic meters of trouble to chew through."

The concrete glittered. Dom thought it was just the larger pieces of gravel catching the light until he ventured in for a closer look and realized it was small chunks of jagged metal. "What's that for?"

"Corpsers don't like digging through it," Shaw said. "Too sharp for the poor little assholes. It won't stop them, but it'll slow them down."

The Corpsers were big bastards, spider-like animals up to five or six meters tall that the grubs used for excavation, but maybe they weren't as tough as they looked. "You can leave this truck to pour the rest, can't you?"

"And leave it for the grubs? We're short enough of kit as it is."

"We're short of Gears, too, sir," Marcus said. "Let's go."

"Ahhh, *shit*." Shaw paused for a second and looked around. It was just two massive concrete trucks that had seen better days, but they were like priceless limos in a world where almost everything had been destroyed and wasn't going to be replaced anytime soon. "Okay, everybody bang out. You heard the man."

They didn't exactly jump to it. The engineers paused for a full five seconds before following orders, really reluctant to go, and Dom found himself chivvying one of the corporals to get her to move. She was only a little scrap of a kid, no more than eighteen. He jerked his head in the direction of the helicopter and herded her.

"Is that stuff going to set?" he asked.

"Well, they're not going to dig it out in time to stop it, are they?" She ducked under the rotors and climbed into the crew bay. "We've got to buy whatever time we can."

"Hey, Captain." Marcus turned and called out to Shaw. "Come on, sir. Move it."

Dom looked back. Shaw was still messing around with the concrete chute, reluctant to leave the truck until the very last minute. Captain or not, he wasn't going to get much patient deference from Marcus.

"Two seconds," Shaw called. The crater was ragged, and soil and bricks were crumbling into it under the weight of the truck's rear wheels. Shaw was balanced right on the edge as the thick, gravelly gray mass bulged out of the pipe and pumped slowly into the hole. "Where are they now?"

"I think we've got a hundred meters on them." Marcus started walking back to him, shaking his head slowly. "You've really got to shift your ass *now.*"

Dom wondered whether to go back him up. Marcus wasn't above physically dragging an officer out of a tight spot if the guy didn't cooperate without him, and Dom could already hear the grubs crashing through the woods. Rothesay wound up the throttle. Castilla aimed the door gun into the trees, ready to suppress ground fire. Marcus started jogging.

"*Down!*" Castilla yelled. "Everybody down!"

She opened up on the trees with the door gun, sending wood splinters flying everywhere. Dom's first thought was to give Marcus and Shaw some covering fire. He jumped down and ducked under the rotors and Marcus went to grab Shaw, but then the edge of the crater collapsed. Shaw fell, sliding a couple of meters at first and grabbing for the concrete pipe. But there was nothing to grab hold of and his helmet vanished below the edge. Marcus dropped down onto his belly and held out his arm, yelling.

"Captain, come on—I got you. Come on. Grab my hand."

Dom couldn't see how far Shaw had fallen. He ran for the crater as Castilla squeezed off a few more bursts into the trees. The grubs couldn't have been far away now. Shit, this was cutting it fine. Dom reached the edge of the crater expecting to see Shaw standing on a pile of debris and just needing a hand out, but when he got his first look down there, the poor bastard was in real trouble. Shaw was up to his waist in concrete, struggling to get any purchase on whatever was holding him up. There was no way Marcus was going to reach him from the edge.

And the grubs were now right on top of them. Shots ricocheted off the trucks.

Dom crouched on one knee and returned fire. He could see the gray shapes about fifty meters away now. "Marcus, you can't reach him."

"We need a damn rope. He can't pull free on his own."

"Just get out," Shaw yelled. "Go on, *get out.*"

Rothesay cut in on the radio. "*Winch,*" he said. "The only way you're going to get him out is with the damn winch. Fenix, get over here!"

"I'll cover him," Dom said. "Get it."

"No, come on." Marcus grabbed his shoulder. "We need to lift. The goddamn cable's only seventy meters. Captain? You hang on. We'll get the Raven to winch you out."

Marcus got up and ran for the Raven, shoving Dom ahead of him as the door gun hammered sporadically. Once they scrambled into the crew bay, Rothesay lifted and positioned the Raven at a hover over the crater. They were taking fire and there wasn't a worse possible situation in which to extract someone. All Dom could do was hose the approaching grubs while Castilla burned through belt after belt of ammo. It was about more than covering the extraction. It was about protecting the Raven from ground fire. Marcus grabbed the lifting strop and paid out the cable on the winch. It hit the surface of the concrete a little way from Shaw but he grabbed it and managed to get it around his neck and then slip one arm through it.

"*Both arms,*" Marcus yelled. "Come on, Captain. Under your arms, okay? You know the drill."

Dom broke off from the defense and slid across the deck to give Marcus a hand. Shaw was chest deep in the mix now, the rotor wash plastering his overall sleeves to his arms. He was covered in the concrete but he managed to get the strop under both arms.

"Okay, bring him up," Marcus said.

Dom hit the winch control and the cable started cranking in. It was only fifteen meters, no height at all, but the guy was completely helpless on a winch with rounds flying past him. It seemed to take forever. Dom was expecting Shaw to be hit by grub fire any second despite Castilla's efforts on the door gun. Marcus reached down just as Shaw came up to the two-meter mark, fingers almost touching, and then the nightmarish worst happened.

Shaw started to slip.

"Hey—"

"Hang on, Shaw, hang on!"

Rothesay cut in. "Fenix, what's happening?"

"We're losing him."

"You get him inboard, Fenix. Any way you can."

"Shaw, *arms*! Tight at your side!"

"Don't you think I frigging *know* that, Sergeant? Shit—"

The orange plastic strop slid and Shaw's arms flew up for a second, then he dropped like a stone into the concrete below. He didn't even scream. It wasn't like hitting water: he went in completely upright, straight up to his waist, then seemed to go down sharply, like he'd hit a pocket of water or air.

"Lieutenant, we've lost him," Marcus said. Shaw was up to his armpits now with one arm free, and Marcus started paying out the cable again. Rounds were now pinging off the Raven. If they hung around much longer, the grubs were going to bring the bird down in the crater. "Bring her down again. Fifteen meters."

"God Almighty, Fenix, you better get that strop on this time."

"Yeah. I know that."

It was unbearable. All Dom could do was watch. The strop hit the wet concrete again. Shaw struggled to reach it with his one free arm, but he was sinking faster as he struggled. Marcus leaned right over the side, as if that would make any damn difference. The engineers huddled in the crew bay said nothing. There wasn't a damn thing they could do either.

"*Lower*, Lieutenant," Marcus said. "Come *on*."

Shaw was now up to his neck, then his chin, and Dom could see it was too damn late and that there was no way the guy was going to get a strop around his body again. Castilla was yelling for a fresh ammo belt. Dom waited for a grub round to finally puncture a fuel tank. They had seconds left but Marcus wasn't giving up on Shaw any more than Rothesay was. He reached out and tried to flick the cable closer to Shaw. If he got one arm free, they might stand a chance.

"Grab it!" Marcus yelled. Shit, Shaw's head was going under. "Come on! Just get your arm up. The helmet's going to keep your mouth and nose clear for long enough."

Shaw couldn't hear him now. Marcus had to know that. But he kept trying, and suddenly all there was above the level of the concrete was Shaw's right hand. The strop was maybe ten, fifteen centimeters from it.

And then he was gone.

"Lieutenant?" Marcus started winching in the line as fast as he could, eyes fixed on the point where Shaw had gone under, because the second he looked away he'd never be able to find the spot again. The motor squealed. "I'm going down to get him. Hang on."

No, Marcus. You're not.

Dom did what he'd had to do too many times with Marcus. He grabbed him by his belt and yanked him back. Marcus turned to push him off, but Rothesay began lifting clear and Dom shoved Marcus down onto the tilting deck. He landed with a thud. Dom sat on him for a few moments. He'd calm down sooner or later.

"What the fuck, Dom, we can't—"

"Leave it, Marcus. Nothing you can do. You hear me? *Leave it.*"

One day, Marcus was going to explode. He nailed down everything so hard and tight that even Dom was afraid of him finally letting rip. For a second their eyes locked. Anyone who thought Marcus was all ice-cold control had no idea, because they'd never seen that look, those few moments of complete anguish that exposed the raw core of loss and pain inside. Then it snapped off again like a light. He scrambled to his feet and the little girl corporal grabbed his arm.

"Sergeant—"

"I'm sorry." Marcus didn't brush her off. "I am so damn sorry."

Nobody spoke all the way back to base. Marcus leaned against the bulkhead, looking out but obviously not seeing anything. Dom watched his jaw working, like he was arguing with himself, and from time to time he'd glance away and screw his eyes shut for a moment. He thought Dom couldn't see. Oh, Dom could see, all right: he could imagine every thought going through Marcus's mind, and they were all about what it must have been like to drown in concrete seconds from being rescued. In water, you stood a chance. In thick liquid cement—the reality seeped into Dom's mind unbidden and it took all his effort to stop himself from dwelling on it.

It was a fucking awful way to go.

"Fenix," Rothesay said quietly. "We've got to overfly your old man's place anyway. Want me to drop you off? I'll file the reports."

"No thanks, Lieutenant."

"Let me put it another way. I'm going to land there and shove you out the frigging door. I'm the officer and I can do that shit. Got it, Sergeant? Go have a stiff drink with your old man."

"Sir," Marcus grunted. It was his way of saying *fuck you.* Rothesay had the measure of him, though, that he needed a break whether he wanted it or not, and especially now. *But he won't talk it over with his dad. He'll never talk it over with anyone, not even Anya.* Dom watched Marcus edge into the comms compartment in the Raven's tail section and pretended he wasn't keeping an eye on him. A few minutes later, he heard a thud that was all but drowned out by the Raven's noise. Marcus emerged from the compartment and took a few steps across the deck, making a pretty convincing attempt to look deep in thought about anything other than the man they'd just lost, but flexing his right fist slowly.

He'd punched the shit out of the bulkhead. He did that sometimes when he saw one death too many. Dom never mentioned it when he did, but they both knew, just as Dom knew exactly what was playing out in his mind at that moment.

Marcus was watching a Gear's hand being swallowed into a slow-churning sea of cement, blaming himself for not being able to save the world.

HALDANE HALL, EAST BARRICADE, JACINTO—THE FENIX ESTATE.

Fifteen years was a long silence, and the longer it went on, the harder it was to break.

Adam Fenix rehearsed his confession again as he stepped out of the car and stood at the doors of the mansion. The maintenance company had been tidying up the grounds, war or no war; the smell of cut grass and fresh creosote wafted on the breeze. It was the perfume of carefree childhood summers that he would never know again.

"You okay, sir?" The driver lowered the staff car's window and leaned out. "Lost your keys?"

Adam wasn't sure how to tell him he was afraid to walk into his own house and face his son. He made a show of casually inspecting the doors. The deep green gloss paint hadn't been manufactured for centuries, and had to be mixed specially for the estate by restoration experts from the National Museum of Ephyra. Countless layers applied like geological strata over the ages gave the wood the slightly rippled appearance of old glass.

This is what the Fenixes are. History. A museum curiosity. The pretense of stable continuity in a world that's falling apart.

"Could do with a coat of paint," Adam said. "See you next week, Hendry."

"Have a good break, sir."

The tires spat gravel as the car turned around the fountain in the courtyard and headed out of the gates. Adam found himself still plucking up courage to push open the doors. They were never locked. A few billion dollars' worth of art treasures inside, with the enemy nearly at the gates, and still he couldn't find it in himself to give a damn about objects. Who would venture in here? Who would risk scaling the walls?

Locust don't loot. Not art, anyway. Got to admire their pragmatism.

He took a breath, lowered his head, and pushed the door. Marcus should have been home by now. He was such a rare visitor to the house these days that Adam could tell if he was here just by inhaling. It was that once-familiar blend of army soap and rifle lubricant, something he'd once been so steeped in himself that he hadn't noticed it until Elain pointed it out. Now Elain was long dead, his son was a stranger, and the nostalgic scent of army life was more painful than bittersweet.

But Adam couldn't smell anything now except coffee. The noises echoing down the hall were coming from the kitchen.

"Mrs. Ross?" He laid his briefcase on the priceless Furlin lacquer table in the hall. "I wasn't expecting you to stay this late."

The housekeeper stuck her head out of the kitchen door. The corridor was so long that Adam felt like a locomotive approaching a station, boots clattering on the inlaid floor like wheels rattling over rails. The light slanted from the open door behind her, catching a fragment of goldstone set in the marble.

"I wanted to make sure you didn't have to cook for yourself, Professor." She stood back and ushered him into her territory. The two of them had rules; one was that he never entered the kitchen without her permission while she was working, just as she never entered his study or the laboratory in the cellars. It was hardly a crowded environment, but somehow the sheer emptiness of the mansion seemed to demand territorial agreements. "Marcus is doing an extra patrol and he'll be late. Lieutenant Stroud called."

She didn't even raise an eyebrow. A lesser woman would have asked for the hundredth time—quite reasonably—when Marcus was going to settle down, and comment on the extraordinary patience of Anya Stroud. Mrs. Ross just paused.

"Glad we can rely on CIC to keep us updated on his movements," Adam said. "Shouldn't you be home by now? Your grandson's on leave too."

"I have my professional pride, sir . . ." She opened the fridge to reveal rows of wrapped, labelled packages laid out with military precision. Cold air rolled out into Adam's face like a frosty morning. "I've prepared the ingredients and all you have to do is follow the instructions. And I got steak. I know you don't like me using your influence to bypass rationing, but . . . well, how often does Marcus make it home?"

It was only a fifty-two-hour pass but the brief visit had taken on the magnitude of a triumphal homecoming. Mrs. Ross, patient and non-judgmental, had laid on a spread fit for a prodigal son. Adam inspected the packs of meat and prepared vegetables. He'd never needed to cook in his life, not with his wealth and privilege, not with his rank, but it was a matter of pride that he could. When he'd finally accepted that Elain was dead and that he had to bring up a thirteen-year-old boy on his own, he'd taken to cooking Marcus's meals as an act of paternal devotion, nourishing him with food as a proxy for the affection that Marcus already seemed to shrink from. Now, nearly twenty years on, he found himself driven to do it again.

It's contrition. Apology. Except this time, I really do have something to apologize for.

Mrs. Ross was staring into his face. He must have looked like a terrified rabbit.

"It's no trouble for me to stay," she said. No, he couldn't do that to her. She was an employee, not a servant. And with the war almost at the Ephyran boundary, there was always the chance that this would be the last time she ever saw her grandson alive. "Just say the word."

"Go home to your family," Adam said quietly. "If I incinerate this, I can take him out for dinner instead."

"Of course you can," she said. "You're Professor Fenix."

There were few restaurants left in Ephyra ten years after the Locust invasion. A man needed some pull to get a table, and Adam had that in spades. He'd never felt less deserving of it than now.

"Take the steak for your grandson."

"Professor—"

"Please. We won't starve." Adam pulled a cold, heavy packet from the fridge. The steaks must have been six or seven centimeters thick. "And take a couple of the bottles of the vintage Ostri red. Make an occasion of it."

Mrs. Ross paused, expression fixed, then nodded. "Thank you. You've always been very good to me and my family, sir."

"You've stood by us during some very tough times." *I might have avoided those, too.* "It's the least I can do. I'll get you a pool car. No point waiting for public transport."

Adam wanted her to go. He would have welcomed the company at any other time, but not now. He had to prepare for the hardest conversation of his life, harder even than telling Marcus that his mother wasn't coming home. He called the office and ordered a car before taking refuge in his study.

He'd grown up in this mansion, Haldane Hall, like generations of Fenix men before him, but he'd never truly grown used to it. It had always felt empty even when Elain was around. When Marcus left home to join the army, it had become an echoing void. The study was as near to a comforting space as he had these days, a smaller room than most of the others in the house, free of the accusing gaze of ancestral portraits that reminded him he'd fallen far, far short of the standards set for Fenix men, and that not even the Octus Medal and lavish donations to the Royal Tyran Infantry Benevolent Fund would atone for that now. His forefathers had been infantry officers to a man. They wouldn't have understood why he'd resigned his commission, and they certainly wouldn't have understood any of his decisions over the years.

And I'm not sure that I understand them myself now.

Adam leaned against the wood paneling, tracing his fingertip over the map of Sera that covered almost an entire wall, waiting for the sound of the car. Gravel rumbled somewhere in the muffled distance, followed by the faintest *clonk* of the heavy front doors closing. Adam was alone now: alone with his guilt, and alone with his research—the project he couldn't pursue at the Defense Research Agency, director or not. He straightened up and took out a pencil to update the extent of the latest Locust incursions on the map.

They were awfully close now.

And I've looked them in the eye. Can I do that with Marcus?

The heavy paper was covered in scribbled notes, some on scraps of paper tacked to it, some written on the surface itself, many of them decades old, an untidy history of a military career and a war that had claimed the lives of billions. On every city that had been targeted by the Hammer of Dawn, Adam had drawn a red circle. Millions had died in each. He never wanted to lose sight of that.

I made that possible. My vision. My work. My responsibility.

If he stood close enough to the map, he couldn't see the scale of it. Sometimes, though, when he reached the door and turned to look back, the enormity of it caught him off guard. The whole map, the whole world, was a mass of red circles.

I might have stopped it if I hadn't been such a naive bastard. I should have told Dalyell what I knew.

He'd lived with this knowledge for fifteen years and now it was starting to choke the life out of him. Even when he was working on the Hammer in the closing years of the Pendulum Wars, it had played on his mind, and now he wondered why the hell he hadn't just come clean with Chairman Dalyell and told him that the Indies, the UIR, were the very least of the Coalition's worries.

And if I'd told him . . . he would have thought I was insane. No. That's an excuse. He trusted me. He believed me. I just thought I could handle it myself, but God, I couldn't have been more wrong.

Adam couldn't look at the accusing map with its indelible record of his failure and slaughter any longer. He turned his back on it and walked out along the balustraded landing, heading for the stairs. He still had a couple of hours.

The basement laboratory was kept locked, but the cleaning company would never have ventured in there anyway, not with Mrs. Ross on duty. She never asked why. She seemed to take it as read, as everyone did, that whatever he worked on was classified. It was, but what went on in here was a secret even from Chairman Prescott; Adam could honestly say that no other human being knew anything about his work down here. He booted up the computer and sat staring at the screen, wondering if he should simply bring Marcus down here, sit him at the terminal, and show him.

Marcus would ask why and what, as he always did, and that would invite the more important questions: how and when.

The screen began building a three-dimensional model like a structure made of irregular pipes. It could have been anything. A geologist might have seen it as voids left by lava. A mining engineer might have seen it as the shafts and galleries of a pit. A biologist might have thought it was a nest, a warren of some kind.

It was all those things, perhaps, and Adam realized there was no easy way to deal with the most difficult detail of all—not what it was, but when he'd discovered that it existed, and how much it had told him about how little he understood about his wife.

Marcus will despise me. How can he possibly respect me again after what I've got to tell him? What kind of relationship can I have with him after he knows what I really am?

Adam rehearsed every possible outcome, every question and answer, every reaction that he might get from his son, but in the end he knew his only option was to look him in the eye and blurt it out. He stared at the screen for far too long. The shapes began to dance in front of his eyes and he thought he could hear the phone ringing a long way away. Damn it: he *could*. He realized that he'd unplugged the extension in the laboratory, and scrambled to reach the socket before the caller rang off. By the time he shoved the plug in and picked up the receiver, though, it was too late.

Damn. Well, if it was important, they'd call back. He switched off the computer, locked the laboratory, and climbed the stairs back to the ground floor. There was plenty of time to prepare the meal—to heat it, anyway—but he decided to leave nothing to chance that might interrupt a difficult conversation, and put a prepared casserole in the oven on the temperature setting that Mrs. Ross had written on the wrapping.

Marcus, there's no easy way to tell you this, but . . .

Adam sat at the kitchen table, reading a rare item of mail that had been delivered that morning, a handwritten message scribbled on the back of an old tax demand. There was nobody left to write to him at home now except Marcus and the *The Engineering Digest,* and both happened once in a blue moon. A charity—a private effort by some citizens, nothing to do with the refugee administration—was asking him to donate blankets for the Stranded. Adam's urge these days was to give until he bled, but it still wouldn't have been enough to scour his conscience clean.

The sound of a helicopter made him look out the window. King Ravens were an almost unnoticed part of the city's background noise now, but to Adam they still sounded of rescue and triggered a reflex of relief. This one had to be flying very low indeed for him to hear it inside the fortress-thick walls at all. He craned his neck, but he couldn't see the Raven and for a moment he couldn't hear it. It was only when the front doors slammed and he heard heavy boots that he realized Marcus had arrived.

Adam tried not to run down the passage. Marcus was in the hall, Lancer in one hand and looking uncomfortable. He was still in full armor, still wearing that damn do-rag instead of a proper helmet, and he smelled of smoke.

"Didn't have time to change, Dad," he said. "One of the KR pilots dropped me off. Mind if I grab a shower first?"

It was his home. He didn't have to ask. "Go ahead, Marcus," Adam said. "You want a drink standing by?"

"Good idea," Marcus muttered, and thudded up the stairs.

There was still some of the decent brandy left in the cellar. It demanded the best crystal tumblers. Adam poured a decent shot into each under the reproachful gaze of his grandfather, Brigadier Roland Fenix, immortalized in full Royal Tyran Infantry dress uniform by the foremost artist of his day. Adam was still trying to avoid those eyes when Marcus came downstairs again.

Young men usually looked even younger out of uniform. But not Marcus: he looked older than he deserved to be, exhausted, resigned. Adam could see more gray in his hair than he'd noticed before. Marcus rarely smiled, but today he looked absolutely stricken. His face betrayed nothing, but his eyes said it all.

He's thirty-two. He's not a boy anymore. But I wanted better for him than this.

"How's it going, then?" Adam asked cautiously, handing him a glass.

"Lost a guy today."

"Damn, I'm sorry." Adam knew how that felt. But he hadn't coped with it at all. It had driven him from the army on a crusade to build weapons that would end wars forever. He'd failed in that, too. "It's not your fault. You know that."

"I had his hand. I should have saved him."

"Marcus, don't do this to yourself."

Marcus drained the glass in two pulls without even blinking. He seemed to be focused on a point on the far wall behind Adam. "The grubs are going to break through any day now. I think you should get out, Dad. Seriously."

"I've got work to do." *And it's all my fault. I have to stand and take it.* "Where would I run to, anyway?"

"There's an evacuation plan. There always is."

"We'll hold Ephyra."

"We'll try."

Adam didn't know how the hell he was going to break his news now. How many comrades had Marcus lost to the Locust? But it had to be done. He couldn't leave it a moment longer, and perhaps if he showed Marcus how close he was to finding a way to stop the Locust, then his son might judge him a little less harshly.

"Dinner's going to be a while," Adam said. Marcus was still looking at the wall behind him. "What is it?"

Marcus pointed, still nursing his empty glass in one hand. "Why did you take it off the wall?"

Adam glanced over his shoulder. There was an outline on the red brocade panel, a rectangle less faded than the rest. He'd finally taken down a picture that troubled him.

"I got fed up seeing Dalyell every time I came in here." The picture had been taken at the Octus Medal ceremony, the highest civilian honor the COG could bestow, a formal shot of the late Chairman Dalyell presenting the award for Adam's services to humanity in ending the Pendulum Wars. *Services to humanity? I invented a weapon of mass destruction. It killed as many of our own citizens as it did UIR ones. And then I went ahead and let something even worse happen.* "Brought back too many memories."

"Dad, you need to stop beating yourself up about the Hammer strikes."

No, poor Marcus didn't understand at all. When he did, though, Adam knew he would never forgive him. "It's not that simple. There's something I've got to tell you."

"Let's eat first." Marcus wasn't a talker, and Adam knew how hard he found it to discuss anything personal. He clutched at the first diversion he could find. "Then you can tell me."

It was sobering to realize how long an hour and a half at 180 degrees actually felt when it was spent in near silence, sitting at the kitchen table and trying to work out the best time to make a confession.

"So. Anya." Adam forced himself to look away from the oven's glass door. "How are things with her? On? Off?"

"The usual."

Adam wondered if Marcus was a different man with Anya and poured his heart out to her. He doubted it somehow. "And is Dom okay?"

"Still searching every Stranded camp we come across."

"You think Maria's still alive?"

"He's sure she is, and that's good enough for me." Marcus's accent shifted a little. Sometimes he seemed almost bilingual, moving from sounding like any other regular working-class Gear to the educated, patrician tones of his childhood, depending on who he was addressing. He was what Dom called *Posh Marcus* now. He looked Adam right in the eye. "You wanted to tell me something. Looks like it's bad news."

"Yes." *Oh God. Here we go. Don't hate me, Marcus. Please don't hate me. Try to understand. Try to forgive me.* "There's something . . . that I didn't tell you. I've never told anybody."

Marcus just tilted his head back a fraction, that I-don't-believe-you look just like Elain's. "It's about Mom, then."

It was the last thing Adam expected. But yes, in a way, it was: Elain had found the tunnels long before Adam had imagined what might be within them, and it had cost her her life. He couldn't admit to Marcus that she'd even been down there until years later. And here he was again, doing the same thing, clutching information to himself because he didn't have the guts to tell his son *why* she'd been down there.

"Not entirely." Damn, it was even harder than he'd expected. He thought it would come out in a cathartic rush, but guilt choked it all back. "I'm sorry. Do you think about her much?"

Marcus looked away for a moment as if he was trying to remember. "No," he said. "Sometimes I can't even recall her face. Look, just tell me. Is it your project? You know I never ask about any of that. Classified means classified."

It was an opening of sorts. Adam tried to seize it, to make himself do the right thing and finally tell Marcus the whole shameful story, but he looked into his son's face—battle-weary, old before his time, robbed of the life he could have had, robbed even of his closest friends—and simply couldn't force the words out.

Is it about burdening him? Or is it about me, because I can't bear to lose his respect?

If I tell anyone, I have to tell him first. And it's getting so very, very hard to live with it.

"Yes, it's the project," Adam said. He'd try to find his courage again later. "I thought I might be getting closer to a way of stopping the Locust."

Marcus defocused a little and glanced at the oven. He'd been told that so many times before. He might have been a relative stranger to his father these days, but Adam could still read him well enough to know when he was embarrassed.

"That's great, Dad," Marcus said, slipping back into his ordinary Gear voice again. "You sure you should be telling me this?"

Adam couldn't blame him. But how did a man break this kind of news?

How could he explain to Marcus that he'd known the Locust were massing underground, years before E-Day, but that he'd warned no one?

How did he tell him that he'd actually been *in contact with the Locust*, pleaded with them, and knew what was driving them to colonize the surface?

And still he'd warned no one, because he was sure he could build an alliance rather than create an extra enemy in a trigger-happy, warring world where nobody had yet learned to handle peace.

After fifteen years of silence, it was impossible—just as it would be impossible to explain that the Locust weren't now the biggest threat to all life on Sera.

"You're right, Marcus," he said at last, understanding that he would never be the man his son thought he was. "Classified is classified."

SUIZA BLOCK, COG DEFENSE RESEARCH AGENCY (COGDRA), JACINTO.

Nevil Estrom couldn't remember the last time he had two days to himself without Professor Fenix around, and he was determined to make the most of it.

It wasn't that he didn't like the man. He'd worked for Adam for nearly fourteen years, and it was—well, it was more like having a second father. The poor guy had a very awkward relationship with his son, and Nevil was always willing to lend a sympathetic ear. It was a short step from that to being co-opted into the family dynamics.

But now the Fenixes were spending some very rare quality time together, the first days off that Adam had taken since Nevil had joined the Project Hammer team during the Pendulum Wars, and that meant he had the archives to himself. There was work to do. And he could do it without Adam's well-meaning interruption.

"Stop whistling," said a voice. "You're too damned cheerful."

Nevil edged out from between the packed shelves to check who'd come in. It was one of the security guards, Gordie, standing in the doorway with one hairy hand gripping the brass handle.

"Just fulfilled in my vocation."

"I wasn't expecting anyone to be in, Doctor Estrom."

"It's a weekday."

"Yeah, but the Director's not in, so I thought you'd be taking a couple of days off, too."

"In a way, I am." Nevil indicated neat stacks of documents on the floor, each with DO NOT MOVE notes taped to them. "I hate the way he gets behind with the archiving. Don't get me wrong, I'd die in a ditch for him, but we need to have this stuff ready to ship out at short notice if we have to evacuate. I can clear this backlog before he returns."

Gordie chuckled to himself as he backed out, closing the door. "Make the most of it. It'll be another ten years before he takes a day off again."

If we have ten years left.

Nevil paused to watch the dust wheeling in a shaft of sunlight like birds riding a thermal. Even in the muffled silence of the archive rooms, he could hear—and sometimes feel—the *whomp-whomp-whomp* of artillery getting closer. He didn't need to read the daily updates that passed across Adam's desk to know that the grubs were massing south and west of Ephyra. It had the feel of a final push. Sitting on a granite island only bought you so much time, because the grubs weren't confined to tunneling. They were moving on the surface now, and they had squadrons of Reavers that pushed the Ravens to the limit. Nevil had no intention of running anywhere; if his brother had been willing to die as a Gear, then he'd stand his ground too.

"Come on, get on with it," he said to himself. He picked up the next folder in the pile and worked his way along the shelves, looking for the right place to put it in the row of anonymous brown and red cardboard sleeves. The red ones contained classified material, anything from restricted to top secret. This was the COG's most sensitive archived material: every single paper document generated in the DRA was filed here, right down to the scruffiest handwritten note scribbled on the back of an envelope, and even the unclassified stuff wouldn't be released for public inspection for at least fifty years, if ever. Nothing was thrown away, nothing was shredded, and nothing—absolutely nothing—left the building. Nevil opened one of the folders. A cash register receipt fluttered to the floor. When he picked it up and examined it, it turned out to be from a grocery store, forty years old and with prices that seemed almost amusing now, but penciled on the back of it was a long and complicated equation on focal lengths. That was how seriously the DRA took its security. There was also always a possibility that the material would be needed again one day.

Nevil marveled at the idea of a kilo of shrimp for a few cents—or any shrimp at all with rationing getting tighter every week—and worked his way through the stack of folders. He'd cleared two and was about to start on the third when his stomach started growling and reminded him that lunch was overdue. Settling down with a sandwich was still one of life's little pleasures. He pulled up one of the battered leather chairs that still had a pre-Coalition Tyran coat of arms on it and positioned it in front of the window to bask in what sun was available.

The bread was a bit soggy. Rebecca had always made great sandwiches for him, but she was gone now, and that was his own fault. He chewed and wondered if she was happier these days.

So once I've finished that stack . . . well, it's not going to take me two days.

There seemed to be little research work to do now. He thought about the heady days of the Hammer of Dawn project, when resources were unlimited and there was a clear, definable, tantalizing objective—to get a laser accurate and powerful enough to target assets and even cities from planetary orbit. And they'd done it, even if Adam hadn't seemed overjoyed with the achievement even then. Now they were running out of resources, and not entirely sure what would kill the Locust. The global Hammer strikes had just slowed them down for a few years.

Maybe I'm expecting too much of Adam. We're physicists. Nukes and lasers are as far as we can go. We need biologists. Chemists. Where the hell did all those guys go? How unlucky can we get, losing so many researchers?

They'd lost a lot of the senior army command, too. The Chief of Defense Staff was just a colonel, so maybe it was fitting that a physicist was trying to cover all the scientific and technical bases single-handed. Nevil liked the idea of just flooding the grubs' tunnels and drowning the bastards, just like Adam had once said, but it would have meant flooding half of Ephyra too. Just a crazy thought, Adam had said, born of too much coffee and too little sleep. They'd never be able to do it: the COG no longer had the infrastructure to manufacture what was needed, anyway.

How desperate do we have to get before we have to try, though? Nevil's thoughts wandered along two tracks, one focused on some new way to kill grubs that they'd overlooked, the other on what he'd put in his sandwiches tomorrow. He was out of pickles. *We're in a worse position now than we were when we had to deploy the Hammer.*

Gas. Water. *Chemicals.* If the grubs lived in tunnels, that had to be the best place to tackle them, to trap them and poison them like the vermin they were. *Smart vermin, though: look at all the creatures they've bred. Organic weapons, more or less.* Letting them reach the surface and fighting them seemed an insane waste of men and equipment, but the Lightmass bomb was still on the drawing board. It was the only device they had for underground deployment, and the sonic resonator needed to map the Locust tunnels was still in development. Nevil put his physicist mentality to one side for a moment and got up to look for the geological survey section. He just needed ideas. He needed to look at something that would spark some off-the-wall thought and let him see the problem in a different light.

But it's probably already too late. They're on the surface.

The muffled thump of artillery a few kilometers away shook the floorboards under his feet. The front line was getting closer. Nevil knew he was probably wasting his time because experts in fields outside his own had already tried every solution and failed, but he had to lay this anxiety to rest. Ideas born of desperation were sometimes inspired.

Adam's key gave him the run of the archives, the entire floor. Nobody was going to disturb him. He locked the door, shoved the last piece of sandwich in his mouth, and worked his way room by room along the unbroken walls of shelving mounted on runners until he found the ones that housed the geological surveys.

The hand-wheel on the first row was stiff from lack of use. He wound it back until the shelves parted, then edged gingerly between the aisles of tight-packed filing boxes. The air smelled musty and unbreathed.

Shit, I hope these are stacked safely. If all this falls on me . . .

The obvious place to start was at the beginning. The labels on the filing boxes didn't tell him much, so he pulled out the first box in front of him at eye height to get a feel for the contents. It was an envelope stuffed with photographs. When he pulled them out, a musty smell hit him. The images were aerial reconnaissance photos with grid references and the date stamped on the back—Thaw 15, 5 A.E. He stuffed them back in the envelope and moved to the shelf below: more images and rolls of seismic data, this time dated through 6 A.E. So the earliest stuff was at the top. This was going to take a ladder.

Gordie will find my desiccated remains a year from now, squashed flat like a pressed flower under a metric fuck-ton of paper.

This was why you were always supposed to tell a colleague where you were or even have someone accompany you when you ventured in here. It was only filing, but accidents happened. Nevil could have trotted back up to the main building and found one of the technicians, but everyone was always busy, and he was enjoying the solitude. He dragged the integral ladder out on its runners as far as he could and rattled it a little to make sure it was secure, then began climbing.

The rungs seemed to give a little as he put his weight on them. He could have sworn the whole contraption was starting to lean away from the cliff face of boxes.

Come on, don't be a girl. Just take it slowly, pull out the first box, and climb down again . . . one-handed.

There really should have been a pulley basket on this goddamn thing. He tucked the box under one arm. His glasses slipped down his nose as he descended but he couldn't reach up to move them. This was going to be a long, sweaty job.

And I don't really know what I'm looking for. But that means an open mind.

Nevil worked through the first ten boxes, extracting their contents and laying them out on the big chart table in the next room. He checked recon image dates and tried to get a time sequence for each location. The seismic traces didn't give him enough data on their own, and he wasn't qualified to interpret them anyway, so he put those back in their respective boxes and concentrated on photos and reports. When he ran out of room on the table—and he could have landed a Raven on that damn thing—he stopped to evaluate what he had so far. It was going to take a hell of a lot longer than two days to check the whole year. And there were ten of those.

Got to start somewhere. He had nothing to go home for now. He pulled a candy bar out of his back pocket and settled down to stare at the information in front of him and let it speak to him.

There were an awful lot of emergence holes. The recon images were all of the area north of Tyro Station. The pictures reminded him of the aftermath of the Archipelago War, fifty years before the Pendulum Wars, with its images of whole landscapes left holed by artillery shells and every recognizable feature of the landscape from farmhouses to individual trees completely obliterated. Every trace of life seemed to have been swallowed by those holes. At least the Tyro images showed traces of where spur lines had branched off the main railway track, although the grubs had stripped all the rails and sleepers, leaving only an impression where the line to Tollen had been. As Nevil pored over one sequence of grainy pictures, he could almost put together a time lapse sequence over a period of three weeks, from ten hours after the first Locust emergence. E-holes appeared in ones and twos, then peppered the ground, then seemed to be filled in again—the abortive concrete-pouring effort that had lasted only two or three days—before springing up in even greater numbers. Seen from directly overhead, the terrain looked cratered.

Okay. Maybe the tunnel idea wasn't so great after all. Bastards can come up pretty well anywhere.

How about flamethrowers again? No. We'd never have enough fuel for thousands of kilometers of tunnels, and we'd have to trap the things down there as well. And they're on the surface now anyway.

Adam was still working on an energy weapon to deliver massive shockwaves underground. He was working on a lot of things. Nevil didn't doubt his genius, but how could anyone plan when new tunnels were formed every day? How the hell could you calculate force accurately when the parameters changed by the hour? That didn't stop Adam, though, and he was still churning out frenzied sketches and calculations right up to the moment he announced Marcus was coming home on leave and rushed out of the door.

Nevil emptied out another brown envelope secured with a twist of red twine and a metal pin. The issue list pinned to the front showed that nobody had booked it out of the archives since the day it was put into storage. Damn, it looked as if Adam had been working on that same idea for the past ten years. Here it was: scraps of squared paper covered in rough schematics, cross-sections of tunnels with numbers scrawled on them, more recon images taken from low altitude, and even pages torn out of a dog-eared technical journal. The pages intrigued Nevil. The date was ripped so he could only see the year—two years before the end of the Pendulum Wars, a calendar that had been wiped from history now—but the article was about the propagation of shockwaves in underwater explosions.

Can't say the Director hasn't considered all the angles.

Nevil sorted through the rest of pile, trying to put everything in strict chronological order. It was only then that he noticed that the recon images, the ones from a low angle, didn't have a date stamp on them. The darkroom techies generated a date on the front of all photos, and the archivist stamped it on the back of each print, but there was nothing on these.

He studied the image, trying to work out where it had been taken, but it could have been anywhere between the Tyro parkway and the Hollow, and it was hard to see the e-hole at all. In fact, it looked more like a wild animal's lair. The buildings in the distant background meant nothing to him. A few flakes of chocolate fell from his candy bar as he bent over the images, and he pressed his fingertip on them to pick them up, licking off the precious fragments. There was no knowing when chocolate would be on the menu again.

He'd come back to the picture later. It wasn't important.

It was the next envelope that got his attention.

When he pulled it out, it felt unusually light. There should have been eleven items in there, as numbered and listed on the front, but when he tipped it upside down five photos fell out. Six documents were missing. He had no idea what they might be, only that the code indicated text documents with an unclassified rating, and nobody had signed to take them out.

Careless; but they weren't top secret, so . . . no, he'd check. Incompleteness kept him awake at night. It meant hauling out the big index ledgers at the reception desk, but that would tell him what the documents were and if and when they'd been countersigned out. It was all from the first month after E-Day. He wouldn't have many pages to look through.

It was only when he turned around that he realized how late it was and why his stomach felt hollow again. The sky graduated from purple to amber on the skyline, silhouetting the Octus Tower into a tourist's postcard. Distant palls of smoke hung in the air and spoiled the illusion.

At least I won't get locked in. Plenty of people working late. And I've got Adam's keys.

The ledgers were stacked on heavyweight teak carousels behind the front desk, an eloquent embodiment of everything the COG stood for. When they said Coalition of Ordered Governments, they meant it. Order was everything in Tyrus, even before the Coalition. Every act was recorded. The archive manager said there were five hundred years' worth of records stored in a vault below the city, but the library of ledgers from the past eleven years was enough of a library to daunt Nevil. He found the massive leather-bound book covering all documents entered in the first six months after E-Day and heaved it onto the counter. The thud conveyed the weight of history. He was almost afraid to get greasy fingerprints on the pages.

Okay. E-Day . . . here we go.

He wiped his hand on his pants before running his finger down the long list of dates, document titles, and signatures. The missing documents were right there—six postmortem reports on Locust drones. Nobody knew what these damn things were when they burst out of the ground that day: nobody even knew they were there. Recovering grub cadavers was the only way to work out who and what this enemy was, even though knowing more about them proved to be useless when it came to stopping them. Humans had some DNA in common with just about every form of life on Sera to a greater or lesser extent, too, so their origins remained a mystery as well. Nevil couldn't see a note pinned to the page to indicate the reports had been booked out. That meant they'd been taken and never returned.

"Asshole," Nevil muttered. Rules were there for a reason. He looked back up the list and turned the pages back to the start, to material generated on E-Day itself. Raven pilots had been meticulous about logging recon images, and the very first image was noted as being taken within forty-five minutes of the first emergence. It was now archived in box 1–15-A, aisle 12C, shelf A.

That was when Nevil started to realize something was amiss.

He walked back to the chart table and checked the dates. Then he climbed the ladder and looked along the shelf—shelf A. The filing boxes started at 1–15-B. The first box was missing.

"Goddamn," he said aloud. "What the hell do we pay these archivists for?"

He'd talk to the manager in the morning. This was unacceptable. He wondered whether to call it a day and grab some dinner, or just carry on through the night, but his eye was now drawn to those photos that didn't have any ID or date stamp at all. Yes, E-Day had been pure chaos, and nobody could expect a government department to worry about bureaucratic detail when millions of citizens were being slaughtered by an unknown enemy, but it *had*—it really had kept meticulous notes of the events, typically Tyran, typically COG. They clung to order like salvation. Why not with these images, though?

Nevil studied the animal lair photo again and decided to find out what the building was in the background. Gordie was nearly seventy and knew every district in Ephyra like the back of his hairy, gnarled hand. He'd know what it was. He was still upstairs somewhere, doing his thirteen-hour shift before handing over to the night guy, and Nevil went in search of him.

"I thought you'd left," Gordie said, looking up from the security monitors on the front desk. "What can I do for you?"

Nevil held the photo in front of him. "Can you tell me where this is? No damn ident on the image."

Gordie squinted slightly and picked up his glasses for a closer look.

"It's somewhere near the old bronze foundry," he said. "Wow, that takes me back. My uncle worked there for years. See?" He indicated the tallest building in the backdrop with a crooked pinkie. "They had to pull it down because of subsidence."

"What, because of grub incursions?"

"No." Gordie shook his head. "Long before then. This was before the end of the Pendulum Wars. Maybe four years before we knew those ugly bastards were even there."

CHAPTER 2

We have no communication with the Locust whatsoever. How can I possibly give them an ultimatum?

(Chairman Richard Prescott to Professor Adam Fenix, two hours
before the Hammer of Dawn strikes: 1 A.E., nine years earlier.)

SOUTHERN OUTFALL SEWER #2, EPHYRA: LATE FALL, 10 A.E.

"Fenix? Is that you?"

The approaching light wobbled in the darkness, approximately head high, then resolved into two faint patches of blue. The longer Victor Hoffman stared into the pitch-black tunnel, the more tricks his eyes played on him, but he could hear the splash and gurgle of water now as boots waded through it. He kept watching, finger inside the trigger guard of his Lancer just in case. There were two pairs of blue lights heading his way now. It wasn't a Corpser.

"Ain't nobody here but us rats." The echoing voice was Rossi's. The damn radios didn't work down here. "You okay, Colonel?"

"Up to my ass in shit, Sergeant. Never better."

Hoffman waited at the junction of the sewer pipes, trying not to look down at what was flowing slowly around him. The shock of the smell had worn off, but he didn't want to catch a glimpse of anything that would tip his gag reflex over the edge. Drew Rossi emerged from the tunnel a little ahead of Marcus and squinted as his eyes adjusted to the faint light from a line of grimy electric bulbs spaced at fifteen-meter intervals in the vaulted brick ceiling.

"Is this stuff backing up?" Rossi asked.

Marcus looked down at the tide of effluent around him and frowned as if he was checking the tide on a nice sandy beach. "Looks like it's still flowing out. It's on a gradient."

The raw sewage was up to Hoffman's calves and he found himself praying that his boots were waterproof. Further up the main sewer, voices echoed. The manager from Tyran National Utilities was talking to Lennard Parry, the staff sergeant whose miserable task it was to keep basic services running in Ephyra. It was like trying to bail out a sinking ship with a teacup. Parry never complained, though. He just got thinner and more harassed-looking each time the grubs trashed a pipeline or an aqueduct and he had to find a workaround or send repair teams into grub-ridden territory.

Hoffman walked with slow care, anxious to avoid splashes or—worse—slipping and falling in it.

Dear God, Margaret. I'm glad you can't see me now. Wading through shit.

Hoffman found he spoke to her a lot more these days. It was all in his head. They were conversations he'd never have, but he missed her like never before. He wished that he'd kept something of the burned-out car that one of the reclamation teams had finally identified on that terrible road of destruction leading out of Corren six years after the Hammer strikes had burned the coastal cities to a cinder, but he hadn't. He didn't even have her wedding ring. They never found it—just enough of a charred jawbone to do a dental ID.

Maybe I'll be dead in twenty-six hours, Margaret. And I won't mind. I just want to rest. I just want it to be over.

Damn, that was defeatist talk. He was Royal Tyran Infantry, for fuck's sake, the 26th, the Unvanquished, a regiment whose battle honors dated back more than five centuries before the COG had even existed. And he was de facto Chief of the Defense Staff. That was only because he was the last senior officer left standing, though, just a goddamn colonel with a few battalions and a handful of ships and helicopters. Grubs didn't give a shit about regimental pride. They rolled over everything.

But if they wanted to try rolling over him, he was ready for them now. He plowed on toward the sound of the voices like an ice-breaker. Marcus walked behind him with Rossi, creating a wake that lapped against the brick-lined walls on either side.

"You okay, Fenix?"

Hoffman had heard about the incident out at Shenko Falls. Marcus didn't talk much, but Hoffman knew him well enough by now to guess what would eat at him and what he'd bottle up: hard to read, maybe, but not a poker player. Shaw's death had hit him hard and it showed. It was in his eyes: that unblinking, slightly defocused, bloodless blue stare.

"Fine, Colonel."

"You're due a couple more days' leave. Go see your dad." His father was an arrogant asshole. *Another useless scientist. All talk. Royal Tyran officer, my ass.* Hoffman worked hard at not telling Marcus that. "Might be a long time before you get another chance."

"He's a bit busy, Colonel."

There was no way of interpreting that. Hoffman could guess that the gulf between father and son was a goddamn ocean. Rich kid, happy to give it all up to be a grunt and shovel the shit with the rest of the Gears, and an Embry Star for gallantry, *real* gallantry: a father who left the army for a nice office job in weapons research and got the Octus Medal, the gong that the rich aristocratic bastards gave one another for being a member of the old boys' club. The two Fenixes looked alike, but that was all there was as far as Hoffman could see.

"So what can you tell us, Mr. Slader?" Hoffman called, slopping along as carefully as he could.

Parry and the utilities guy turned round at the same time.

"We've still got monitoring equipment in some of the pipe runs, but keeping an eye on this is going to mean sending men to walk the course, I'm afraid," Slader said. "The concrete pours won't stop them forever. They might even come up the metro, or tunnel along gas mains."

"Well, that still gives me a map," Hoffman said. "And it gives me choke points."

It was a matter of geology. The Ephyran plateau was granite, but volcanic plugs had fissures full of softer deposits that those bastard grubs could dig through like sand. The tough bedrock wasn't completely grub-proof. It just slowed them down.

But it also funneled them into choke points, and that meant Hoffman could concentrate his fire. They either had to launch a surface assault, in which case the artillery around the city would blow the ugly gray assholes into the middle of next week, or they'd have to dig their goddamn e-holes where his map said they could. He just hoped the geologists were right.

Scientists. Neither use nor fucking ornament, Margaret. No answers.

"You're a glass-half-full man, Colonel," Slader said.

Hoffman felt something tap gentle against his boot. "Full of what, that's what worries me."

He looked down against his will and common sense. But it wasn't a turd. It was a rat, paddling valiantly with its chin just above the surface and dragging a bow wave like an arrowhead. Hoffman watched it scramble up onto a narrow ledge and begin scaling a cable conduit to the surface. The rat had the right idea. It wanted to get out of this sewage as soon as it could. Hoffman had never realized how squeamish he was about shit until now, but it was all the memories that the stench brought back, everything from the siege at Anvil Gate to that terrible smell when some poor bastard took a shell fragment in the guts.

"C'mon." Hoffman beckoned to them and started wading back the way he'd come. There was a ledge further down the tunnel like a canal towpath. "Rats generally know what they're doing."

The sewers had metal notices bolted to the walls like street signs, indicating the distance to the next junction or manhole and the location above them at street level. ALMAR-CORRELL—50M, the sign said, with a helpful arrow for the hard of understanding. They were heading back to the Almar Street intersection, sunlight, and fresh air.

"I do *not* want to fight down here," he said, catching an echo. "They'll have the advantage."

"Not if we use flamethrowers," Rossi said. "That'll stop a few grubs. Until we run out of fuel, at least."

"Sewer gas," Slader said. "Methane and hydrogen sulfide. Flammable and explosive. It'll launch the manhole covers into the next block."

"So it'll stop a lot of grubs," Rossi said.

"It could collapse the whole system."

"Mr. Slader, you're talking to a government that fried half of Sera to stop the Locust," Hoffman said quietly. *Me. I did that. Me and Prescott and Bardry and Adam goddamn Fenix.* "Destroying a sewer system to defend our last goddamned city is small change after that."

Slader's voice hardened a little. "Let's hear you say that when the civilians have to dig latrines to get rid of their own waste."

They walked on in silence, now on the towpath that was punctuated by dim pools of light from the overhead lamps. Hoffman was sure he could see movement ahead. For him—for any Gear—things that lurked in the dark were always the same real-life monster, usually Locust drones but sometimes other equally foul things from the grub menagerie. Someone had taught him to look slightly to one side in semi-darkness to see more detail. All he could recall now was that stuff about rod cells in the eye seeing better than cone cells, and not who'd taught him that, but it always worked. There was definitely something moving. But it was small-scale and it wasn't lit up or glowing, so he guessed rats again.

Yes, it was definitely rats. He could see them now, huddled on the ledge, reaching up the walls or sniffing around for a way out. The closer he got, the more he could see. Faint splashing and the occasional glop of water made him look around.

"Wow, it's the whole ratty navy," Rossi said. "Do they usually hang around in gangs like that?"

Slader grunted. "Hang on."

Suddenly a beam of white light shot out ahead of Hoffman and he was looking at more rats than he'd ever seen in his life. They were like a moving carpet on every surface, in the water and on the ledge. He stood still, more out of bewilderment than curiosity, and they simply swarmed over his boots or jumped into the water to get past him. Nobody said a word until the rats had moved on.

Hoffman turned. Slader still had his flashlight on the water and Marcus was peering over the edge. Hoffman couldn't work out what had grabbed his attention until he saw something small and brown bouncing up and down and realized it was the whiskered nose of a rat that couldn't get out of the water. It was struggling to climb up the slippery stonework. Marcus dangled his boot over the edge to let the creature scramble aboard, then drew it in so the rat could jump to safety on the ledge. It raced away to catch up with its buddies.

"Guess what's spooked them," Marcus said. From time to time Hoffman got a rare glimpse of a kindlier Marcus under that unsmiling veneer and piratical do-rag. It always surprised him. Few men would stop to rescue a rat. "Got to be grubs."

"They react to vibrations," Slader said. "Might be tunneling further down the line."

"Okay, you keep an eye on the network and flash me or Parry as soon as you spot anything," Hoffman said. "We better get back up top. I've been out of radio contact for too long."

Hoffman could see the shaft of sunlight long before he reached the metal ladder and looked up. It was like gazing on the constellations when lost at sea: salvation beckoned. He climbed the rungs and heaved himself out the manhole on his hands, reassured at nearly sixty that he could still lift his own weight. The sky was dotted with white cloud and dispersing balls of black smoke that could have been from downed Reavers or Ravens. He needed to catch up with that fast.

"You stink, sir." Corporal Aigle, the radio operator, was waiting with a stirrup pump full of disinfectant. He hosed down Hoffman's boots without asking permission and moved on to Marcus and Rossi. "Wipe your feet before you go into CIC."

Hoffman knew he'd shower and scrub himself raw tonight and still not feel clean. He shook off the water and started heading up the road toward the old Bank of Tyrus headquarters, now commandeered as the COG area command center. "Fenix, you and Rossi take your squads and do another sweep for refugees south of La Croix Boulevard. They keep creeping back in and I don't want anything inhibiting our ability to fight, understand? Clear them out."

"Understood, Colonel."

Marcus jogged off with Rossi. Hoffman watched him go and wished he had a whole damn brigade of Fenixes. He could always rely on the man to deliver. Maybe he didn't deliver for Anya Stroud, but Hoffman decided that wasn't any of his business and she was old enough—and tough enough, despite appearances—to look after herself on that front.

Entering the command center was surreal. Hoffman walked past the sentry and a wall of sandbags that looked more like bricks. Out of curiosity, he picked one up and hefted it.

"Fifties, sir," the Gear said. "Best fit. Nice color, too."

Hoffman pulled the drawstring. The rough hessian bag was stuffed with fifty-dollar bills. That was Gears for you: pragmatic and resourceful, and left to their own devices in a bank, they made the most of it. Currency was no use for spending in a world surviving on barter. But bills still made good kindling and wadding.

"Tell me you've done something creative with the bullion bars," Hoffman said.

"Better see Lieutenant Stroud about that, sir. Comes under designer accessories."

Hoffman took familiar comfort from the fact that even staring a grub assault in the face, Gears still had a sense of humor. He made his way up the stairs from the lobby and into the maze of offices on the mezzanine floor above.

There weren't as many personnel about this time. Everyone who could fight and wasn't critically essential in support roles was on the front line now. If anyone got killed in here, then there was nobody to take their place.

We're running on empty. But this place isn't going to be an easy nut to crack.

The bank was as safe a bet as any building in Ephyra. It was designed to be criminal-proof, and that meant it was almost as secure as a military bunker. It had to withstand tunneling, frontal assault, and incursions via the roof. Its windows were toughened glass and the basement was two floors of steel vaults. The layout wasn't ideal for a headquarters, but beggars couldn't be choosers these days. Hoffman pushed open a door with FOREIGN HOLDINGS painted out and COMMCEN stenciled over the raised letters to find Anya Stroud hunched over a leather-topped mahogany desk, one radio headset pressed to her left ear while she listened to another on her right. Somehow none of the frantic activity had mussed her neatly pinned blonde hair.

He gave her a hands-up gesture to indicate he'd wait for her to finish. A pile of papers on the desk was weighted down against the fierce draft of a fan by a single gold bullion bar.

"You need a couple of hours sleep, Lieutenant," he said as she put down the headset. "Nice paperweight."

"You can club drones with it, too, sir."

"I'd rather you had a sidearm."

"I haven't requalified with a pistol for a couple of years."

"You're Helena Stroud's daughter. That competency's genetic."

Anya managed a smile. She was a good-looking girl, just like her mother had been, and yes, at his age, he still reserved the right to call a thirty-something woman a girl.

"Do you want a sitrep now?" she asked. "I've got some gaps, though. Radios are down in one sector and we're waiting for someone to get a message back."

"Give me what you've got."

Anya pushed herself back from the desk and went over to the map tacked to the wall. The colored pins on it looked new, probably another unexpected treasure looted from the bank's stores. Hoffman could see the situation for himself, but Anya was always meticulous about briefings.

"We've got all the potential ingress points covered," she said, "but we've had Reavers targeting the Hammer and artillery positions, so Major McLintock deployed another squadron of Ravens while you were out of contact." She looked as if she was taking a breath to allow him ranting space, but for once McLintock had done what Hoffman would have done himself and he said nothing. "No emergence reports yet."

Hoffman leaned closer and traced his forefinger along the river, reminded how much he was depending on holding the main bridge—Chancery. His forces needed them in one piece to be able to move south quickly rather than detouring more than a hundred klicks north, or else he would have blown them up by now to stop the grubs using them to penetrate West Ephyra. He dragged his finger along the map to Correll Road, the wide street that led into Correll Square and the center of the financial district.

"My money's still on a major emergence here," he said. "All the utility tunnels and the shortest distance to key targets. As long as we can hold the bridges, we can use Correll as a choke point."

"Got you, sir. Major Tomas has Chancery Bridge buttoned down tight."

"He's going to need to keep it that way."

"And you're going to stay at the command post, sir?"

Anya was asking if he planned to do the sensible thing as the Chief of Defense Staff and stay in CIC. She had to know him better than that.

"Until I'm too senile to fight, Lieutenant. Besides, I've got to keep an eye on Fenix."

"Thanks, sir," she said. He could have sworn she blushed. "And you're going to stay in radio range now, aren't you?"

"I'll take that as an order." Hoffman touched the peak of his cap. Marcus really needed to get his shit together where that girl was concerned. "Keep your head down, Anya."

Hoffman walked back to the command post at the junction of Almar and Correll, not only because it was quicker to walk than find a Packhorse, but because his Gears needed to see him out there with them. The post looked more like an oversized stall at a country fair, no real fortification except a sangar made of sandbags and concrete blocks. Aigle had set up a radio desk and a solid fuel stove. Well, there was water, there was ammo, there was space to curl up and get a few minutes' sleep, and there was an empty tin to take a leak in. Hoffman could live here until the grubs came.

"Don't mind me, Corporal," he said, and pulled up an empty ammo crate to sit and stare down Correll Road, waiting for the inevitable.

HALDANE HALL, EAST BARRICADE, JACINTO.

It was too late to make excuses, and too late to talk to Myrrah again.

Adam had to use a smaller-scale map to chart the forward edge of the Locust advance. It was the one centimeter to one kilometer TGS chart that showed street detail, its glazed paper covered in pencil notes and cracked from years of folding and unfolding.

He would never discard it even if it fell to pieces. It had been Elain's. She'd marked all her field surveys on it, every spot she'd visited to take samples and the date she'd collected them.

You knew. You understood, long before I had any idea. You were always smarter than me. More intellectually rigorous.

Just one more minute. Just one more chance to talk to you again. I'd give anything for that.

Did you meet Myrrah? She never said.

Elain had been gone nearly twenty years now. He hoped she'd been dead for all that time, because the thought of her held underground by the Locust was more than he could face. He'd found some of her remains in the tunnels—arm bones and scraps of fabric he recognized all too well. He'd kept what he'd found out about her disappearance from Marcus, at first because it begged too many questions about why she'd gone into the tunnels at all, and then it became a habit because he just didn't have the courage to tell his son. It was a repeating pattern, and Adam accepted that. He'd kept the Locust secret from everyone until it had all blown up in his face.

I thought I was an honest man. A decent man. But I lie by omission. And they're big, big lies.

Marcus never asked questions. Even as a grown man, he seemed to accept that one of Elain's forays into the caverns around Ephyra had ended in disaster because the Locust were waiting down there and nobody knew.

Rock shrews. It had all started with damned rock shrews.

Adam refolded the map for a moment to clear some space on his desk. He needed to look at the creatures again. Elain had been collecting specimens while he was still serving in the Pendulum Wars, and hadn't said a word until she presented him with the evidence—a small, velvet-furred creature preserved in formaldehyde, nothing special until she X-rayed and dissected it, and found the mutations. Like most of the other shrews she'd analyzed, it had an extra pair of vestigial legs concealed under its skin.

We always had secrets. She had hers, and I have mine. What kind of a family are we? No wonder Marcus doesn't talk much.

Adam opened the cupboard and carefully removed the stacks of filing boxes that hid the specimen jars from casual view. He took out a couple and held them up to the light. The sight of the specimens always made him feel sick and breathless, as if they were eternally drowning in the straw-yellow fluid and he was drowning with them. One was the rock shrew that Elain had showed him so proudly before he deployed to the Kashkur front nearly thirty years ago. The other was something else entirely.

It still seemed to be alive.

He set both jars down on the table and let the liquid settle for a moment. The rock shrew rolled slowly and settled on the bottom, a sailor lost to the deep. The other specimen—four legs and two vestigial stumps now clearly visible through its fur—floated before sinking, then flipped over. It twitched a few times. The longer Adam looked, the more he could see the faint yellow luminescence that wasn't a trick of the light. It was real. The mutated shrew was long dead, but the bioluminescent parasite within it was still biding its time, just as Myrrah had said.

It's odd to be on first-name terms with the Locust Queen. Clever woman, Myrrah. Not as clever as you, Elain, but a fine mind nonetheless.

Myrrah was the first to call this organism *Lambent*.

And the name had spread through Adam, just as the glowing material was spreading itself, infecting more Locust drones, and Gears were now reporting seeing them on the surface.

The phone rang. This time he had only to reach across his desk to grab it, afraid to miss a call in case it was bad news about Marcus. He almost knocked over the jars in his haste, steadying them one-handed as he shoved the receiver between ear and shoulder.

It was Nevil. "Just checking you're okay, Adam," he said. "You're normally in early."

Adam glanced up at the clock. Damn, he was over an hour late. "Sorry. I got caught up in some paperwork." *Elain's notes: all we've got that can save us now.* "I'll be in at lunchtime."

"I need to show you something. We're missing some files."

"Oh?"

"Old stuff. I decided to catch up on archiving while you were away, and — well, long story short, we're missing some grub autopsy reports. I know it's not our department, but I'm the monitor-evaluator type, as you know."

Damn. *Damn, damn, damn.* "They'll turn up." Adam knew he should have copied them and brought them back. It was all so long ago. He hadn't thought anyone would go looking that far back. "It's not as if it's information the Locust can exploit."

"And I found a really odd image. I need to show it to you."

"When was it taken?" Adam was expecting something new, something from the Locust advance. He reached into the cupboard and fumbled for a sealed box of glass vials, phone still wedged under his ear. "What kind of image? Diagnostic?"

Then Nevil said something that made his stomach flip over. "Photo. I think it's an emergence hole that predates E-Day. In fact, I know it is."

Adam struggled for words. "Where did it come from?"

"No idea yet. I'll work it out."

"You always were meticulous, Nevil." From the day he'd joined Adam as a shy, awkward research assistant, Nevil had been the one who checked and rechecked every line, every detail, every calculation, the human safety net who caught the errors and spotted the inconsistencies. Without him, the Hammer might have taken even longer to develop. He was exemplary; Adam had been fiercely proud of him when he'd been awarded his own doctorate. Now he was becoming a nemesis. "I'll see you later."

Adam put the phone down. Everything was starting to unravel.

His heart was pounding. He wasn't sure if it was because signs of his deceit were surfacing, or because he knew he had very little time to prepare to move his research to a safer place.

If the Locust penetrated further into Ephyra, they'd destroy everything in their path. His history with them would probably count for nothing now.

"Time's up," he muttered. "You knew this would happen one day."

Adam put the specimen jars and the sealed vials into his briefcase with Elain's notes. She'd been a developmental biologist, and rock shrew cell differentiation had been her specialist area. She'd thought the six-legged shrew was the descendant of a much bigger and extinct animal that had lived on in folk memory as monster myths. She couldn't have known then that it was a much more recent mutation. She simply recorded the cell changes.

This is what Lambency does.

This is all I have to work with.

He was a physicist by training, and a competent engineer. He'd always tried to keep abreast of other disciplines. But now he was trying to be a biologist without any possibility of conferring with scientists in that field. There were no experienced biologists left, and even if there had been, how could he explain to them why he was pursuing this line of research?

I met the Locust Queen, you see, and she told me her species was fighting for survival against a parasitic organism in their tunnels. I promised I'd help her destroy it if she kept her people underground and left humanity alone . . . but I failed. So can you help me out?

Adam tried to imagine the reaction, like he'd tried to imagine Marcus's. Now he tried to imagine Nevil's. Everyone he respected and cared about would spit in his face. He knew it, and he knew he deserved it.

It took him fifteen minutes to pack the rest of the specimens. The tissue samples that Myrrah had given him still showed some bioluminescence after all these years and were sealed as biohazards. He had no idea what to do with them. He couldn't just stroll into La Croix University and ask to borrow their glove box. But he was out of his depth now, and the time had come to share what he knew regardless of the personal consequences.

They'll jail me. Or shoot me.

He realized he was thinking in terms of having to abandon the house, getting ready to withdraw to the center of Jacinto at short notice. The briefcase and folders stacked on his study floor said it for him. What would he do about the art and historical artifacts? Haldane Hall was more a collection than a home. He remembered stumbling over a priceless silver horse statuette in the rubble of a bombed museum in Shavad, and Lieutenant Helena Stroud's reaction to his sorrow at seeing such a rare and ancient treasures waiting to be looted and melted down in a desperate, war-torn world.

Paintings. Statues. Things. Not people.

Adam walked along the landing, gazing at the art on the walls and wandering in and out of the bedrooms while he plucked up courage to do what had to be done. They were snapshots of lives lived. Marcus's room was much as he'd left it—neat, sparsely furnished, impersonal, a few half-read books lined up on the shelf with neatly torn strips of plain paper as bookmarks, pants and shirts arranged by color in the closet. Marcus had never needed to be told to tidy his room. In the bedroom Adam had shared with Elain, perfume and brushes still sat on the exquisite Silent Era dressing table on a glass tray. Adam picked up the bottle to spray a mist on the air and inhale it. It was a carefully rationed act of remembrance. The scent was no longer made and now it was changing, oxidizing slowly year by year, but it was still close enough to the original fragrance to trigger poignant memories that brought the pressure of tears to the back of his palate.

He put the cap back on the crystal bottle, made himself forget again, and went downstairs to the laboratory.

After ten years of destruction, even the university and the DRA couldn't re-place equipment. Food and arms had manufacturing priority. Adam was doing whatever he could with items salvaged from bombed schools and doctors' surgeries, repairing them himself. The lab was a bizarre mix of state-of-the-art computers and jury-rigged test benches.

Just like the Stranded. I go for walks in the rubble at night and loot ruins like a scavenger. Where's your Octus Medal laureate now, Chairman Dalyell? Where's the man who saved the world? Lying, looting, and doing high-school biology experiments on the most dangerous life-form on Sera. God help us all.

A thought crossed his mind, but he knew it was insane. How long had it been since he'd talked to Myrrah? His last visit to the tunnel cities had been just before E-Day. They'd spoken since—if radio transmissions that were never answered or notes left hidden at cave entrances could be called conversa-tion—but the message was always clear. She'd put her trust in him and he'd failed her. She had no choice but to invade the surface and displace humans to save her own species.

You know what we are, Adam. He could hear her voice more clearly than

Elain's sometimes; authoritative, patrician, human. *You know where we came from. We deserve to live, we have the* right *to live, but you'll never let us. Just remember that what's killing us will one day kill you. And I shall be there to see it.*

He pulled open the bottom drawer of one of the filing cabinets. The transmitter sat there, wires coiled around it, looking more like a very old hair dryer connected to a cigar box than a radio set. The Locust had always been adept at recycling human technology. Now they had their own, very often organic. Elain would have been fascinated by their skill at engineering other species into living weapons for their war effort. Perhaps she'd glimpsed some of it before she died. He almost hoped she had, that she'd had at least one final moment of the revelation and discovery that she lived for.

They're a civilization in their own right. They're the enemy, but nobody can deny what they have and what they are.

Adam hefted the receiver in his hand and blew off the dust. He knew it was too late. There could be no truce, no accommodation. Even humanity was divided, COG against Stranded, unforgivable and unforgiven. As many people had been killed by the Hammer strikes as by the Locust.

Maybe even more. Pin a medal on that. Another mistake to atone for.

He set the transmitter on the bench and plugged it into the power supply. If he didn't try, he'd never know. But with every day he kept this to himself, every scrap of research carried out in secrecy, his guilt compounded itself. Could he possibly do any more damage?

He stared at the transmitter for a full minute before flicking the switch. The faint buzz of a circuit that hadn't been used in years suddenly filled the room. There was probably no receiver at the other end now.

"Myrrah?" Even saying the name was an effort. The circuit did sound as if it was functioning, though. "Myrrah, this is Adam Fenix. We need to talk."

When Adam read quotations from the great leaders of history, their words at pivotal moments, he always wondered how they chose them so well. They always had a memorably perfect phrase to hand. Now he realized they did nothing of the sort, and that whatever they actually said had either been written for them in advance, or transformed after the event by publicity experts. They said dull, unimaginative things that weren't the stuff of history.

"The Lambent are going to destroy you, Myrrah," he said. "I know you never found a solution yourself. I can see it. So you need us—you need the COG. Stop this. It's not too late."

Adam stared at the handset for a few more minutes. He could still hear the faint hiss of static. For a moment, he could have sworn he heard a slight pop on the other end, but it could have been anything, and he felt foolish for imagining someone would be there to listen after so many silent years.

He locked the laboratory, put his briefcase in the safe, and took the autopsy files out of the cabinet. Then he phoned for a staff car to go to the office. In the echoing hall, the long case clock ticked so loudly that it sounded like a thudding heartbeat.

Sometimes inanimate objects spoke more eloquently than any statesman.

COG DEFENSE RESEARCH AGENCY, JACINTO.

They said there were remote South Island tribes who were afraid of photographs because they believed they captured souls. Nevil never mocked that belief. He understood it.

He had days when he could face Emil's picture and others when it was too much even five years later. Most of the time it lived in his desk drawer, face-down on top of a dog-eared staff booklet on the DRA pension fund that had vanished along with the rest of the Tyran economy. Today he felt strong enough to take out the framed photograph and position it to the right of his computer screen. It showed Emil in the uniform of the Duke of Tollen's Regiment, a big guy with a big grin, all pride and commitment. Nevil stood beside him in a formal suit, all regret.

Emil had written on it: *My kid brother, the one with the brains.*

It looked like a military medal ceremony, as if Emil was the focus of the event. But it had been taken on the day that Nevil had become Dr. Estrom in a plain suit he'd last worn for their father's funeral. Tyrus no longer made luxuries like academic gowns. Emil had found the phrase *hooding ceremony* very funny, "like some goddamn gang initiation."

Nevil would have traded his doctorate and every useless piece of fucking paper telling him what a clever boy he was for the chance to serve alongside Emil. Today, they were so desperate for Gears that he would have been allowed to. But now he was deemed too valuable to the war effort to do even that.

Safe on my ass. Sorry, Emil.

Mom, as usual, hadn't bothered to show up at the ceremony. Nevil thought that was for the best. He leaned back in his chair and tried to concentrate on the power requirements of a ground-based Hammer laser generator, but all he could think about was Emil and all the things they'd never had the chance to do. Outside in the corridor, the snack trolley rumbled past and shuddered to a halt at the end of the corridor. It was so quiet in the building with so many people gone that the remaining canteen staff didn't need to yell "Tea!" any longer as they went on their rounds. Some routines carried on regardless of grubs. They had to, to give the day some focus, to remind everyone that life was worth carrying on and that one day it might return to normal.

Normal? Just take a look at the news.

The television was never switched off now. It sat on the tall filing cabinet opposite Adam's desk, permanently tuned to the news station that was now pretty well all that was left of Tyrus state broadcasting. Nevil debated whether to step out and get some coffee from the trolley but decided the news was more important for the time being. He found himself watching recon footage from Raven patrols. The southern edge of the Ephyra plateau was a national park, an idyllic landscape he'd seen on picture postcards all his life, and it still looked pretty until the shot swung around with the Raven to show the shattered buildings and columns of smoke that marked the path of the Locust advance. Nobody could accuse the COG of feeding its citizens upbeat propaganda. Ephyra itself was next. The footage said it all.

What are we going to do with all the records if we have to evacuate? We can't move them all. We're five years behind on transferring them from paper to computer. How the hell will we ever start over if we lose all that?

The DRA had contingency plans like every other government department, off-site recovery drills to move essential data and equipment to a safer site and set up again. But they were running out of safer sites. Nevil sometimes wondered if anyone really had a handle on all this. After the first year—the total shock of E-Day, the immediate slaughter, and then the even bigger losses from the Hammer strikes—the war had turned into a slow-burning fire. There was time to move what was left. Nevil tried to imagine a world with no national library and archive, no universities, and no museums. All governments had stashed away what they could, even during the Pendulum Wars, but this was different. This was the final phase of an apocalypse.

Nevil found himself thinking that—surely—someone on a higher pay grade than his had this all under control, and then remembered there was no such concept in government. Not even the COG thought of everything.

And I'm as responsible for the Hammer as Adam is.

Seismology. What were the university geologists doing while the Locust were tunneling all that time?

This war was so full of unanswered questions and things that didn't make sense that people had stopped asking, even those whose job it was to *keep* asking. The why didn't seem to matter half as much as the how these days. Nevil found himself unable to concentrate on power requirements. His attention was too torn between the news, working out what he'd grab first if the contingency plan went belly-up as plans so often did, and the vague, nagging anxieties circling around in his semi-conscious like sharks.

He found himself staring at Emil's photo when the standby fire alarm went off, three short blips that meant they should wait for instructions while some emergency was checked out. It was only when the alarm changed to a single continuous bell that it was time to drop everything and get out. Nobody else seemed to be moving around. Nevil did as the blips told him and waited, but he slid his desk drawer open and took out a few key things—filled notebooks, calculator, the pistol he knew he'd never use—just in case. He stacked them next to the photo, ready to shove them in his briefcase and run.

Leave personal belongings behind—sure. Can't replace all that.

And there was still no sign of Adam. The clock on the wall, its faded cream face marked COLNA BROS., JACINTO in ornate script, showed just past midday, 1306 hours. Nevil checked his watch and forced himself back to the calculations on the screen in front of him, one ear still on the alarm. In the background, the news continued to remind him that things were deteriorating fast.

Okay, concentrate. How do I get that power output up twenty percent? Because that's what it's going to take.

He slipped back into the trance of staring at the figures on the screen until the alarm bell switched to a continuous tone and the public address system burst into life.

"Attention all staff. This is not a drill." It was Gordie, clearly uncomfortable with using the PA. "Please evacuate the building. Off-site recovery procedure. Mainframe shutdown in five minutes." He cleared his throat. "Apologies for scaring everyone with the fire alarm, sirs, but I've only got two signals to choose from, *standby* and *run.*"

Nevil heard a burst of laughter from an office up the corridor and the sound of filing cabinets opening. Yes, everyone knew the drill. And the order to evacuate must have come from Adam, which meant he was in the building somewhere. Everyone was used to running. Every civilian was ready to move out at a moment's notice, every office and business practiced at a hasty exit, because that was how people had survived for the past ten years—by staying ahead of the grubs.

Except this is Ephyra. We always thought we were safe here, more or less.

Nevil logged out of the mainframe before the shutdown and then grabbed everything on his must-take list at a steady pace, knowing he had time. Boots clattered along the parquet corridor. For a moment they were fading, moving away, but after a few seconds' silence, one pair of feet came back down the passage at a brisk stride, and the door burst open.

"Hi, Adam," Nevil said. "Why are we clearing out this time? Precaution, or what?"

Adam looked terrible. It was the only way to describe it. He usually looked tired, but now he looked anguished as well, and it wasn't a look that Nevil was used to seeing.

"Not my call," he said. "Hoffman's orders. He's prepping for a ground assault on Ephyra and he wants all non-military personnel out of here."

"Are you okay?"

"No. I'm not."

"Look, we've done this before. We give it a couple of days and then we roll back in."

Adam looked at him with a frown as if he thought Nevil didn't get it, then hauled a sheaf of folders out of his briefcase and laid them on the desk. It seemed a crazy, confused thing to do when they were supposed to be taking as much as they could carry out of the building.

Nevil stared. So it was Adam who'd taken the autopsy folders from the archives.

"Sorry, Nevil. I should have returned them."

Nevil wasn't sure what to say. It wasn't that Adam had taken the folders that surprised him, but that he hadn't said so when Nevil mentioned it.

"They're not supposed to leave the building." Nevil, ready for this moment, shoved the contents of his in-tray into his case, including his folder with the e-hole image he couldn't explain. "It's academic now, though. Come on, Adam." He indicated the bulging briefcase. "I've cleared your drawer too. Let's go."

Adam stood frozen for a moment, looking around the office. Nevil felt guilty for nagging him. Damn, this wasn't just his boss: Adam was a veteran Gear, a national hero, a man who'd earned the right to break a few bureaucratic rules. Nevil jerked his head in the direction of the fire exit.

"There's something I have to tell you," Adam said.

"It can wait." Nevil shut and locked the door out of habit. Adam walked ahead of him down the corridor but kept half-turning and holding them up. "We've got to get to the rendezvous point."

"No, I mean it."

"Keep moving."

"Goddamn, this is *important*, Nevil."

"Have we left something behind?"

"No. But—"

"Then it can wait until we're out of here."

Adam took the hint and the two men quickened their pace, then broke into a jog that Nevil was determined wouldn't turn into a panicked sprint. They'd been here before. They'd always come back later when the alert was over. But for the time being, they were getting on the transports to the east side of Ephyra, Jacinto itself, the unbroken granite core of the plateau that swept down to the sea.

When they got outside, about fifty or sixty DRA staff were milling around, feeding a human chain with filing boxes to load another truck. It was more than a lifetime's work being saved. It was the labor of generations of scientists. Adam was rooted to the spot, stricken, not his usual focused self.

Poor bastard. He's the Director. He's been under a lot of strain.

Nevil put his hand under Adam's elbow to get him to move. Maybe a military approach would galvanize him. "Mount up, sir."

"No. I need to tell you something. The files. That image."

"So what if you take work home with you? No harm done."

Adam grabbed Nevil's arm and led him a few meters from the evacuation team, none of whom seemed to have noticed that their boss was as close to freaking out as Nevil had ever seen him. This wasn't Adam Fenix at all. He stared into Nevil's eyes, almost nose to nose, grip tight and showing no signs of relaxing.

"You mentioned an image."

"Adam, you're starting to scare me."

"The image. Tell me. *Which image?*"

Nevil had clipped it inside the flap of his working folder. The trucks didn't seem close to moving off, so maybe it would be easier to humor Adam and avoid a scene. "Here. An emergence hole. No date, but it was taken years before E-Day. See the building in the background? Demolished during the Pendulum Wars. It doesn't make sense."

Adam took it and stared at it, anguished, as if it was a picture of a dead relative, then pinched the bridge of his nose. It was his oh-shit gesture. Nevil had seen it all too often when the Hammer tests had been going wrong and Adam had despaired of ever getting the satellite array operational.

"I've been working on something," he said. "I need to tell someone now. I need to tell *you.*"

Nevil's gut flipped over. This was it: this would be the miracle in the nick of time, the brilliant plan or device that would finally see off the grubs. This was Adam Fenix, after all. Nevil started to feel a weirdly excited relief hiking his heart rate.

"You're cutting this pretty damn fine, sir . . ."

"I knew."

"Knew what?"

"The Locust. I found them. I *knew*." His words were perfectly clear but they made no sense whatsoever to Nevil. He had to be mis-hearing all this. "I tried to talk them out of emerging. I tried to stop them. You have no idea what's down there, Nevil, no idea what made them do it." Adam seemed to be waiting for a reaction. Nevil looked around for a moment, expecting the others to be staring at them, but everyone was too busy clearing out. "For God's sake, Nevil, are you listening to me? The Locust. I *knew* about them before E-Day, five years earlier, and I thought I could avoid a holocaust if I came up with a scientific solution."

No, Nevil hadn't misunderstood. He hadn't misunderstood at all. And he couldn't say a word. There was nothing in his brain that would come out as a rational sentence.

He knew. He knew.

"Nevil, we couldn't have defeated them anyway, whether we knew they were coming or not."

My boss knew. The man I trust. The man the Chairman trusts.

"Nevil, *say something*."

No, it can't be. Why would he do that? Why would he keep it to himself?

Adam shook him. "For God's sake, do you understand what I've told you? I never told anyone. Ever. Not even Marcus. I just couldn't. Forgive me, Nevil. *Please*. But I can still stop this. I know I can."

All Nevil could see now was Emil, watching the chaotic, terrifying footage of the Locust invasion on the news flash and saying that he was going to do something about it. He enlisted the next day. He waited in line at the recruiting office for three hours, he said, because there were so many volunteers who wanted to fight.

And now Emil was dead.

Nevil prided himself on clarity. He was a physicist: he saw both the bigger picture of the universe and the sub-atomic detail with equal ease. But right then all he could do was stare at Adam and try to place a few random thoughts together, small thoughts, *fragmented* thoughts, like trying to put a priceless broken vase back together and not knowing how to make the pieces fit again. He couldn't take in the global enormity of a once-heroic man who knew the grubs were coming but said nothing, but he could certainly join up the smaller pieces—his dead brother, a man he'd respected and adored, and the speechless, confused pain that now gripped him.

All your fault, Adam. You could have saved us.

Traitor. Rotten lying fucking traitor.

Nevil pulled away because he didn't know what else to do and his legs had made the decision for him. Adam caught up with him again and tried to turn him around. People were definitely watching now. Nevil didn't care, but he couldn't yell what he wanted to yell because he was too numb, too shocked. His throat had sealed shut. Now he felt physically sick.

"I'm going to put this right, I swear," Adam said. "Give me a chance."

Nevil felt the dam suddenly burst. It all flooded out on a strangled sob. "And what about me? Why tell *me*? You *bastard*."

"Nevil, I'm going back home to get something from my lab. I'll see Prescott. But I've got to do this first."

Adam looked at him for a few moments as if he was expecting something, then turned away and headed out of the compound. Nevil had no idea what to do next. Out of the corner of his eye, he saw Gordie bearing down on him.

"Is everything all right, Dr. Estrom?" The security guard loomed over him. "Where's Professor Fenix going?"

How could Nevil tell him? How could he sum up those few terrible moments? Had he even heard right, or imagined it, or what?

Gordie's expression said he hadn't imagined anything, but that didn't make it possible to share this burden with the man. Half of him was already working out logical reasons why Adam did what he did, but the other half—the emotional part, the part of hurt feelings and fears and grief—was screaming that his brother had died and Adam had kept the grubs a secret from the rest of the world.

Nevil thought he had no idea what to do, but he did. He'd just have to think it over, because it was a terrible and irreversible step.

Unlike Adam, Nevil knew this was something he didn't dare keep to himself.

"Just gone to get some stuff from his home," Nevil said, voice shaking. Gordie looked unconvinced. "Let's get going. He can catch up with us in Jacinto."

CHAPTER 3

They are a divided people, and that is why we will ultimately defeat them.

(Myrrah, the Locust Queen, on the weakness of humans.)

OFFICE OF THE RIGHT HONORABLE RICHARD PRESCOTT, HOUSE OF THE SOVEREIGNS, EPHYRA: FROST, 10 A.E.

Richard Prescott had stood looking out of this office window before, and with an equal sense of the inevitable.

You knew.

The memory came back to him clearly, as if his brain had understood at the time that something wasn't quite right and had filed away the evidence for later analysis. And in the way of all betrayals, the words drifted back to him as well, this time with a new meaning that made his stomach knot. He replayed a meeting in this room nine years ago, when the Locust were about to finally overrun humanity. It had been with Adam Fenix and the defense chiefs, it had been about the last-resort decision to deploy the Hammer of Dawn against Sera's cities to stop the Locust advance, and it had been about deaths: billions of deaths. It had to be a surgical strike. It had to be done fast, to catch the Locust unaware, and most of the population of Sera would never get to the only safe haven in time, to the Ephyran plateau.

But you already knew, Adam. You'd known for years.

Adam Fenix had argued against it. It was his weapon, his ultimate deterrent designed for these doomsday scenarios, but he'd *argued*. Did he have an alternative, Prescott had asked? Fenix's answer came back to him clearly now, each word now tinted with a fresh and shocking meaning.

If we'd had more time . . . there could have been other ways we might have stopped them.

Yes, Fenix had said that. It had sounded like a scientist considering less mutually destructive ways to wipe them out, nothing more, just uncharacteristically indecisive, but that was only to be expected. It wasn't every day that governments took the decision to wipe out most of their own civilization to win a war.

But you didn't mean that at all, did you?

Prescott, like everyone else, had believed the Locust had erupted without warning, an unknown species that had been biding its time unseen and undetected under Sera's surface for years. This morning, he suddenly knew better. And it hurt.

You lying bastard, Fenix. You arrogant, treacherous, lying bastard.

It all made sense now. It all fell into place.

Prescott turned back to Nevil Estrom. The physicist was sitting with his arms folded awkwardly on the table, almost as if this was an interrogation — skinny, bespectacled, visibly crushed by the shame of having turned in his boss. Loyalty was the quality any politician prized most, even if he displayed it the least, but it was wasted on Adam Fenix.

He knew. He damn well knew. He knew they were coming, and he told nobody. And he kept it to himself until now.

Prescott couldn't recall the last time anyone had shocked him. *Events* had, yes: he'd been as stunned as everyone else when the Locust emerged. There'd been classified matters that had sometimes woken him in the middle of the night and left him staring at the ceiling, gut churning and unable to get back to sleep again. There were things he'd quietly dreaded becoming public, background things like the real health risks of imulsion exposure.

But nothing had slapped him hard across the face like this and challenged his view of the world and everything he knew about it.

He thought he knew how low humans would stoop. It was his job to know that, handle it, and even exploit it to work for him and the good of the state.

But he hadn't realized one man would let his own species face extinction for no better reason than conceit.

Adam's a scientist. A former officer. A gentleman. Always the malcontent, always critical of the government, but I never thought of him as a traitor. Just a liability. Not the kind of man to relocate to Azura. He would have talked. He would have objected. All that fine morality from a man who made it possible to burn billions to death.

Prescott decided it was time to throw a lifeline to Nevil. "I realize how difficult it must have been to come to me, Dr. Estrom," he said. "And I won't pretend I'm not shocked. You're sure about this?"

"He told me himself."

"And why do you suppose he did that? And after so long a time?"

Nevil meshed his hands and frowned at them. "I couldn't live with knowing all that and having to keep it to myself. I think that finally overwhelmed Professor Fenix, too, keeping that bottled up for so many years."

Prescott had to know. "To unburden himself to you, and not to his son?"

"Oh, he never told Marcus, sir. They don't talk like that. I always got the impression that Adam feels unworthy of him."

At least Fenix had no delusions on that front, then. He *was* unworthy. Prescott still found it hard to believe that he could have kept it from Marcus for so many years, though. But people hid terrible crimes and dirty secrets from their families for their entire lives. Prescott decided to put that suspicion on a back burner and deal with the immediate problem: his most senior scientific adviser, his foremost weapons expert, had been in regular contact with the Locust, knew their intent, and might still be in league with them now.

Prescott didn't understand Fenix's motive, so he had to treat it as hostile until he did.

So perhaps he still believes he can avert a bloodbath by talking nicely to them. It doesn't matter. It doesn't matter a damn if he's a well-meaning idiot or if he's just doing a deal to save his own skin. The effect is the same. He knew that E-Day was coming, he knew about it for years, and if he'd told Dalyell, we could have been prepared.

He's an enemy of the state.

We could have shipped him out to Azura long ago, but Dalyell . . . my God, did Dalyell know too and not tell me?

The thought seized Prescott and he walked as casually as he could to the window and stood looking out, in case Nevil spotted the turmoil on his face. Prescott's father, David, once Chairman of the COG himself, had taught him from the time he could walk how to behave like the statesman he would inevitably become. He'd schooled his son to hide his feelings and remain detached. But the thought that Chairman Dalyell might have kept the presence of the Locust to himself for so long was a hard idea to swallow without showing some reaction.

Party politics could be insanely destructive. They almost always came before the interests of the state and its people. Prescott knew that. It still made his scalp crawl.

Nevil shuffled in his seat, making the antique mahogany creak. "Do you ever hate yourself, Chairman?"

It wasn't a scientist's question. Prescott rather liked that. He turned, composed and in control again, hands in pockets as if he heard shocking revelations of apocalyptic secrecy every day.

"Do *you?*" he asked.

"Yes, sir. I do. I've denounced a man who's treated me like family, who's given me a career . . . and it doesn't feel good."

"But does it feel *right?*" Prescott was looking directly into Nevil's face now. The extensive security checks the man had undergone to work on classified projects said he'd wanted to serve as a Gear but failed the medical on various grounds. His brother Emil had been killed in combat. A yearning to do the honorable thing showed on his face. "Does it feel *necessary?*"

"I wouldn't be here if it didn't."

"There's no need to be ashamed, Doctor Estrom. Self-loathing is just our consciences trying to get our attention." It was time for a little calculated theater to help Nevil put his actions in context. Prescott put his hand on his shoulder. "I hate myself quite regularly. You can't cause the deaths of billions and shrug it off. You just have to be honest with yourself about why you did it."

The office was suddenly the quietest place on Sera. Prescott could hear Nevil breathing and then the wet click as he swallowed. The sporadic dull boom of artillery fire seemed suddenly louder.

"Shock, sir. Because it's all hindsight. We can't do anything about it now."

"Well, one thing we can do is not compound the deceit. It's much easier to charge a machine-gun position than inform on someone you like and respect." Prescott knew that it wasn't at all, not for most people. But it was almost certainly true for Nevil, desperate to fight for his country but resigned to doing the next best thing. Prescott slid into a more familiar tone, soothing, all first-name terms. "Did Adam tell no one at all? Not even Chairman Dalyell?"

"He says he didn't. That was why it ate at him, I think. It's one hell of a burden to carry alone."

"Indeed. For *fifteen years.* Almost beyond belief."

"If he'd told anyone, we'd have heard by now, sir."

"Oh, I know. I merely marvel at the mind-set that doesn't rush to share that information with somebody. Is he sane, do you think?"

"I'm not a psychiatrist. But he's always seemed perfectly logical . . . reasonable. Perhaps I should have spotted it."

"No, this isn't your fault. This is Adam's responsibility, Nevil—I'm sorry, may I call you Nevil?"

"Of course."

"Then call me Richard. Do you know if Adam's been in contact with the Locust since E-Day?"

Nevil pushed his glasses up the bridge of his nose and looked helpless for a moment. "I didn't ask enough questions. I'm afraid I was too shocked. Not very scientific and rational of me."

"Perfectly understandable. Nobody expects a state hero with Fenix's background to betray humanity."

"He said he thought he could avert a war. I know he meant that."

"Don't make excuses for him, Nevil. He's one of the most intelligent men of his generation. He should have known when he was out of his depth." Prescott sat down at the table, facing Nevil. "A new species. A new *sentient* species. Even thinking as a scientist rather than a soldier—you just can't keep that to yourself and think it's all fine."

"He's not evil or dishonest. He just thinks he always knows best and has to solve every problem himself."

"The road to hell, Nevil. You know what it's paved with."

"But how do I face him now? Are you going to arrest him?"

"You don't have to worry about that."

"Easily said."

There was no way Nevil could be allowed to go back to the DRA after this. He'd have to be shipped off to Azura. He was a valuable asset anyway, a key man in the Hammer of Dawn program, as well as a loyal citizen.

Loyalty. It was priceless.

"Excuse me for a moment." Prescott went to his desk and pressed the intercom to summon his secretary. "Jillian, would you ask Captain Dury to drop by as soon as he's free, please?"

"Certainly, sir. Would you like some tea?"

"That would be very kind, Jillian. Thank you. And one for Dr. Estrom."

"Right away."

David Prescott had taught his young son the essentials of political survival while other fathers were showing their boys how to fish and play thrashball. Richard Prescott had expected to win elections to become leader of the most powerful alliance on Sera, but his final ascent to power had simply been fate; Tomas Dalyell dropped dead almost a year after E-Day, when elections had already been suspended. Deputy Chairman Prescott took his place, surprised but fully prepared. He already had his survival kit. He had a loyal and efficient assistant, and he treated her like the last Queen of Tyrus: he had personally loyal officers in the army, not *too* senior, so that they were both low-profile and had something to aspire to: and he had sufficient dirt on everyone without their having any on him. Acquiring and maintaining loyalty was the hard part, but recruiting the right personality types and applying gracious treatment— honesty, courtesy, making a cup of coffee or remembering a birthday here and there—worked its magic.

Now he had to work that magic on Nevil Estrom. He could have called security and had Nevil bundled into a cell before shipping him out, but the man deserved better, and it was far easier to get work out of volunteers. Jillian came in with a tray of tea, some herbal substitute for the real thing now that supplies had run out. The two men sipped in polite silence as if they hadn't been talking about Adam Fenix fraternizing with the enemy at all.

"You do understand that I can't let you return to the DRA knowing what you know now, don't you?" Prescott said.

Nevil didn't blink. He would have made an excellent Gear if his physique had matched his courage. "Is this where someone from COGIntel puts a round through the back of my head?"

"No. This is where I put you on a helicopter and send you to Azura. I'd better tell you about that, hadn't I?"

Prescott walked Nevil to the window. The smoke that hung like a permanent curtain in the distance was growing denser by the hour. It would focus Nevil's mind, not that the man had a choice.

"You can see how bad the situation is out there," Prescott said. "You really would be much better off on Azura. And I need you there."

Nevil looked blank for a moment. "What's Azura?"

"Nothing to worry about. It's an island facility the COG built early in the Pendulum Wars because everyone was convinced that the conflict would end in global annihilation. Ironic. Anyway, Azura is a bunker of sorts. The Locust are unlikely to ever find it."

"And somehow nobody knows this island exists."

"*Few* know. Anyway, *bunker* hardly does it justice. It's rather beautiful, to be quite honest. Every comfort you could wish for and every facility for your research. If you've ever wondered why all our best minds were lost in the last ten years—they weren't. We shipped most of them out. Biologists, engineers, our senior army officers, all the disciplines required to rebuild Sera after a disaster. And the contents of the museums and libraries, of course."

Nevil just stared at the darkening skyline and seemed to be shaking his head very slowly. After finding that his boss was a traitor, discovering that the COG had a hidden bolthole for the great and the good probably seemed a minor surprise by comparison. "But you didn't relocate the director of the Defense Research Agency."

Relocate. Prescott almost smiled. Nevil caught on very fast indeed. "How do *you* think he would have reacted to finding out about Azura?"

"So you're not actually surprised by what I've told you, then. You never trusted him anyway."

"Nevil, even the Chief of the Defense Staff doesn't know about Azura. It's not because I don't respect or trust him. But blunt people can cause more damage than dishonest ones when they open their mouths. Besides—the Adam Fenixes and Victor Hoffmans of this world are still needed right here."

Nevil was still doing that very slight, very slow head shake. "So I just vanish. What do you tell the people I work with? Or my mother? Missing presumed dead, like the others?"

"Partial truth. That you've been sent to work on a classified project. We can do MPD if you wish, though."

"Adam won't believe that."

"Adam doesn't have to. And if you want members of your family to accompany you, I can arrange that." Prescott knew that Nevil hadn't spoken to his mother in fifteen years, because COGIntel was thorough in its checks. Like so many in Ephyra, Nevil had few relatives left alive to check on. "You don't have to lift a finger. Your belongings will be collected and you'll be on the next flight."

"You could just handcuff me and shove me on the Raven. Or have me shot."

"I don't want to do that to a man who helped develop the Hammer of Dawn. And you *did*, Nevil. Adam got the Octus Medal, but now it's your turn for a little reward, albeit a private one."

Nevil turned and looked him in the eye. If Prescott had passed him in the street, he would have thought he was just a clerk, a dull, weedy little man of no importance. But there was that look: absolute steel, absolute honesty, and a refusal to give in to his fears. He *was* scared. Prescott could see it.

"If there's a job for me to do," Nevil said, "then I'll go. If there isn't, just shoot me and get it over with. That job's my life. I can never do it again, even if you let me walk out of here. I can't look Adam in the eye."

Prescott patted his shoulder and nodded. "Azura may be all we have to rebuild from. We need you there." Nevil didn't move from the window. "I'll have your things picked up and your desk cleared after Adam's left the office. Perhaps you need a few moments alone to think. Let me know what else you need done before you leave."

Prescott walked out and closed the door behind him. Captain Dury was wandering around the lobby, taking slow paces up and down the Furlin rug as if he was marking out a boundary. He had his finger to his earpiece. Jillian was at her desk, still typing as if she was ignoring the fact that the commanding officer of the Onyx Guard was in her office.

"You heard all that, Paul?" Prescott asked.

Dury raised his eyebrows. He was a solid-looking man in his forties, his gray hair cut so short that it looked like bristles. "Yes, sir. You want me to pick up Fenix now?"

"No, I want twenty-six-hour surveillance on him." Prescott had to time this carefully. "I need to know if he's still in contact with the Locust. If he looks as if he's going to skip town, then you take him, but I want to give him a little space and see what shakes out. He might well make a move when he finds Estrom gone."

"On it, sir."

Dury left. Jillian was still typing as if she hadn't heard a word or seen a thing. Prescott found his anger had now not so much cooled as frozen into an assessment of how much use Adam would be to him now.

But he's not going to get away with it. Whatever utility he has, he'll get what's coming to him.

"I'm going to have Dr. Estrom moved," he said.

Jillian looked up at him. She knew what that meant. "It was very brave of him."

"I don't think he sees it that way."

"Azura, sir," she said. "Do I *have* to go?"

"The situation's deteriorating. You really should." Prescott paused a beat. "And of course, you can bring your sister. We have to be discreet, though. We can't accommodate the whole population. But you understand that, I know."

Jillian had known about the global Hammer strikes in advance, said nothing, and simply heeded Prescott's oblique advice to move her sister into Jacinto as soon as possible. But Hoffman had known too, and didn't even share it with his wife. She died in the strikes; he lived with that.

Loyalty. Honor. Duty. Quite stark, pitiless things when you really apply them and mean it.

"Oh, I understand, sir." Jillian smiled. Prescott could count on her to stand by him come hell or high water, and both were very likely now. "Thank you."

Most people's lives were intricately connected to others. It was hard to take them out of circulation without leaving broken links and ragged edges, questions asked and not answered. But in the fog of a chaotic war, all things were possible.

Prescott wondered how long Marcus Fenix would spend looking for his father if he were to vanish like so many others. He suspected it would be a very long time.

EPHYRA, ONE KILOMETER FROM TREASURY ROW.

The inevitable had been postponed for a few years, but the day had finally come just as Dom had always known it would.

He drove the Packhorse down the deserted street, bouncing over potholes and debris. This was the no-man's land between Ephyra and the rest of Tyrus, a couple of kilometers of ghost towns that separated the relatively safe territory from the grub-infested wastelands. Dom accepted it was all an illusion, a false sense of security. Nowhere was truly safe, and nowhere was completely in grub hands. Ephyra was hit by air raids from Reavers, and sometimes raiding parties made it across the invisible line between granite and sandstone. Outside the wire, Stranded settlements somehow managed to survive. The grubs were closing in a meter at a time and picked off humans only when it suited them.

And it sure as hell seemed to suit them now. He passed boarded-up stores that had been abandoned and re-occupied a couple of times over the last few years and spotted a wisp of smoke above the roofline. He slowed the Packhorse for a better look.

"What is it?" Marcus asked.

He was looking the other way, out toward the grub lines, with his Lancer resting on the open passenger window. Dom checked the rearview mirror. In the back, Jace was fidgeting with his Lancer, flicking the catch on the magazine. Tai looked as calm as a statue.

"Just checking," Dom said. "Give me a couple of seconds."

As the vehicle rumbled slowly past the store, Dom could see jury-rigged cables strung precariously between the building and a pylon. A grimy window flickered with dim light: someone was watching a television. It was a miracle the place hadn't burned down. Then Dom ducked instinctively even before his conscious brain registered what had spooked him. *Rifle.* He saw the flash of optics. Suddenly Marcus's Lancer was aimed past him out the driver's side window.

A Stranded guy with a hunting rifle was crouched at the side of the road in the cover of a pile of garbage bins. If the grubs had been patrolling, those tin cans wouldn't have stopped a round.

"Take it easy, buddy," Dom called. He stopped the Packhorse and stuck his head out. "You need to clear out of here. The grubs are coming. Big push on Ephyra."

"Like you give a shit." The guy was maybe Dom's age but thin and deeply lined. He had a firefighter's helmet. Maybe he thought it would give him some protection. "You just cruisin' around lookin' out for us Stranded, huh? Or you wanna bill me for the electricity?"

Dom was immune to abuse after nearly ten years of stopping at every Stranded camp he found. He couldn't blame them for seeing the COG as another enemy just as bad as the grubs. He went through the ritual, fishing the photo out from behind his chest-plate and holding it up for the guy to check out.

"You ever seen this woman?"

"What's she done?"

"Nothing. She's my wife. She's missing."

The guy actually studied it, head slightly cocked on one side. "No. I'd remember *her*."

"Thanks." Dom put the photo away and slipped the Pack into first gear. "You better get moving."

"Yeah, I'll get my chauffeur to bring the limo 'round. Tell you what, maybe I'll just walk out of here because it's terrific exercise."

The Packhorse had four seats, four *occupied* seats, and a space in the back that was full of ammo and supplies. Dom tried not to look at Marcus. He wanted to save everybody even when it was a bad idea.

"It's cramped in the back," Marcus said, "but we can drop you inside the city."

The Stranded guy stared at him like he was considering it, then shrugged. "And then what? I still got nothin' and nowhere to go. Beat it. Go on. I'd rather deal with the grubs."

"Suit yourself," Dom said, and accelerated away, checking the mirror to watch the guy dwindling in the distance. They only got one chance. "Asshole."

The Packhorse rattled along the cracked pavement toward the Ephyra line. Jace leaned forward and crossed his arms on the back of Dom's seat.

"You gave him a choice, man. Don't beat yourself up."

"Yeah, so I did." Dom groped along the dashboard and switched the radio to the speaker. Anya's voice filled the cab. She was talking to the Raven pilots on the comms net and he caught the words *Landa Square*. "And we've got bigger problems."

They listened to the voice traffic between Anya and the Ravens. *"KR-Seven-Five — still awaiting confirmation on Reaver contact . . . wait one — confirmed visual, range three kilometers, bearing one-three-zero . . . Roger that, Four-Nine, Seven-Five. Control to all KR units — Reavers inbound, bearing one-three-zero."*

Marcus was getting agitated. He stared dead ahead at the road, jaw muscles twitching. "Come on, Dom. Better not be late to the party."

"She'll be okay." Dom didn't have to say *Anya*. "CIC's in the old bank HQ. Can't get much safer than that."

"Yeah."

The Packhorse crossed the Ephyra boundary and merged into a river of military traffic. Some was streaming in — Centaur tanks, mobile artillery, open trucks full of Gears — and some was moving northeast toward Jacinto carrying civilian refugees. Dom had to stop for a moment to let a transport pull out in front of him and he found himself staring into the back. Civvies, mainly women and kids, were huddled on benches that ran the length of the truck, clutching suitcases or bags. A little girl with braids caught his eye. Once again, he couldn't really tell the difference between COG citizens and Stranded except by how clean they looked, because the homes inside the wire still had running water. Other than that they all looked much the same. It was just a case of which side of the wire they ended up on.

Somewhere nearby, an arty piece opened up with a ground-shaking *pom-pom-pom*. Dom craned his neck but couldn't see what the crew was firing at until he slowed and turned the corner. A small cloud of black smoke marked where a Reaver had been taken out, but it might have been a Raven and the Reaver could have fled. Marcus leaned forward to stare, unblinking.

"Come on, Dom, we're gonna run out of grubs if you don't pull your finger out . . ." Jace muttered.

"Hey, where do you expect me to go in this traffic? There'll be plenty of grubs to go around."

Dom was heading for Hoffman's command post at the intersection of Almar and Correll. It was almost like the colonel wouldn't start the battle without them, his lucky charms. He'd been Dom's CO one way or another for more than fifteen years, and Marcus's and Tai's for almost as long. Even if the regimental structure of the COG army had long since dissolved, the old ties of the 26th Royal Tyran Infantry lived on.

26 RTI. The Unvanquished. Dom could remember how proud he'd been to get that death's head cap badge when he enlisted. *We better live up to that today.*

"This is as close as I can get." Dom couldn't see a way past the islands of waist-high concrete and rubble that had been dumped in the street as both cover and barriers. They were on South Mercantile Way, a block away from the Treasury and the National Museum of Ephyra, and the sidewalk was dotted with Centaurs. An artillery piece sat at the end of the road. "Everybody out."

"Better to walk into battle," Tai said, sliding out of the back seat. He was a big, heavy guy these days, quite a few kilos heavier than the lean tribal warrior they'd first run into on Arohma during the Pendulum Wars and persuaded to join the COG. "So that the enemy may see the resolve on your face, and the great number of your victory tattoos, and take the opportunity to run away."

"Yeah, Tai, you go and do your tattooed resolve thing," Jace said. "That'll scare the grubs shitless. Me, I'll bank on a full clip any day"

Marcus went ahead. "Full house," he said. "Let's report in."

Hoffman was standing at the control post, looking out down Almar Boulevard over a wall of sandbags and makeshift barricades manned by ranks of Gears with every weapon from .50 cal Stompers to Longspear missile launchers. He had his field glasses to his eyes and one boot on an ammo crate. Somehow, though, he was managing to shave with his free hand, raking the razor over his chin as he surveyed the road. Corporal Aigle, the radio operator, tapped him on the shoulder and he turned around to look at Marcus.

"Excuse the mess, Fenix," Hoffman said. "The help didn't show."

"So how are we doing, Colonel?"

Hoffman turned and walked a few paces down the road. "They've got to come this way," he said, pocketing the razor. "That's the main sewer. Damn Reavers are mopping up a lot of ordnance, though."

He kept walking and Marcus followed. Marcus hated the hero thing, but he had an effect on morale just by being there, and that was probably why Hoffman was taking the trouble to walk him down to the front line. Dom could hear the comments as guys noticed he'd arrived.

"Hey, look who just rocked up."

"Kiss your asses goodbye, grubs. The cavalry's here."

"Nice of you to fit us into your busy diary, Fenix."

Marcus didn't break his stride and settled down behind a barricade right at the front. "Yeah, I had my hair done specially."

He sounded totally in control, but Dom knew he was embarrassed. It was his telltale gesture with the Lancer that gave it away, playing his fingers on the muzzle like it was the fretboard of a guitar and he was trying to remember a difficult chord—just the slightest movement, something only Dom would spot. Marcus didn't want to be seen as the savior who could put everything right just by fronting up.

He wanted to save everyone because he thought he had to. If there was a phrase that summed him up, Dom thought, it was *I must*. He'd been like that as long as Dom could remember, even as a kid—even before his mother disappeared. But Marcus's father's take on life was *I can*. He believed in science and that he could fix everything if he thought about it hard enough. The two men looked alike but thought like strangers.

Nobody could fix this shit, and nobody could save everyone. Dom had decided to save the few he could.

He waited in silence for ten, maybe fifteen minutes. Nobody even coughed. He felt he could hear every breath, every click of metal, every Raven in the air, in that heavy silence. Then his earpiece popped. Anya's voice, calm and steady, gave them all the bad news.

"Control to all callsigns, we have an alert from NTU," she said. "Locust ingress into the sewer system. Estimate now less than one kilometer from Correll Square."

Hoffman, pacing up and down behind the obstacle course of concrete blocks, sounded almost relieved. Dom knew he wanted a fight, and he wanted it over and done with. "You heard the lady, Gears. Stand to."

Jace, squatting next to Tai with his Lancer resting on sandbags, put one hand flat on the pavement.

"Shit . . ."

"What?" Dom followed suit. "What is it?"

"Feel 'em?"

It started as a faint vibration, like someone was pile-driving in soft ground. Then the resonance increased like an earthquake. It was the familiar warning of an e-hole about to erupt, only much stronger. Dom held his breath and sighted up.

There was a manhole cover dead ahead, a big fancy one decorated with ornate, interlocking cog shapes. There were perforations in it. Dom saw something poke up through one of the holes and realized it was brown fur.

A rat popped out like a cork, then another, and another.

"Rats making a run for it, sir!" someone yelled. "This is it!"

"*Steady*," Hoffman barked. A steady stream of rats was now frantically squeezing through the perforations and racing for the shelter of the nearest building. It must have been one hell of a climb for them to get out. "Steady . . ."

The stream of rats vanished. Dom was only vaguely aware of the Ravens circling overhead. His focus narrowed to a tunnel ahead of him, Correll Road, still largely intact except for the old furniture store that had taken a direct hit from a Reaver a year ago and was boarded up and missing its roof. The ground was still trembling.

Oh God.

It wasn't the first time he'd waited for a grub onslaught to begin, not by a long chalk. But this was somehow different. Nobody moved. There was just the click of Lancers around him as everyone kept checking their weapons.

Come on. Come on. Just do it, you assholes.

The vibration was becoming more sporadic. Suddenly he could hear distant cracking and rumbling. He tried to picture the Corpser—maybe more than one—blundering through the sewer at the head of a grub column, smashing the brick lining and picking the spot to break through. Suddenly the pavement a hundred meters ahead of him seemed to bulge upward. Something burst into the air—another manhole cover—and then he was looking at a shockwave, a single rippling movement traveling fast down the center of the road and flinging paving slabs and chunks of concrete into the air like a zipper being torn open. It took seconds. Gears around him didn't even have time to swear. He felt the ground lift under him, and dirt, brick, and water fountained into the air from an instant crater.

"*Corpser!*" someone yelled. "*Fucking Corpser!*"

As the huge spider-like legs groped over the crater's edge, a hundred Lancers, RPGs, and grenade launchers opened up at once, grubs poured out of the e-hole—two arms, two legs, but so gray and scaly and monstrously *ugly* that you'd never mistake them for humans—and hell erupted. From that moment on, Dom was on autopilot. Part of him still had an eye on Marcus, but the rest was doing what it usually did when he was staring into a hail of fire. His body took over and he couldn't tell where his arm ended and his Lancer began. He squeezed off a long burst, spraying rounds left to right, then ducked behind cover and reloaded. It was one continuous wall of muzzle flash. The noise was so loud he'd stopped hearing it. It was only when a Gear to his left—a guy he knew by sight but couldn't put a name to—fell to his knees and slumped over the barrier that he snapped back into the wider picture.

There was a lull, a few seconds, nothing more, a moment of bizarre silence. He saw the pile of grubs for the first time, a perfect ramp of bodies to
the top of the barricade. He was staring into the next ugly rank of motherfuckers, right into their weird yellow eyes. And then they charged, firing, and
then they were over the barricade, crashing through the lines of Gears. One
jumped right over him and caught his shoulder with its boot. The impact
spun him around. The next thing he saw was Tai lunging at a grub to bring
his chainsaw up between its legs. It was impossible to hose the bastards now;
they were too close, right among the Gears, and the only option left was
hand-to-hand. Dom dived in and revved his Lancer's saw. The first grub he
saw tried to dodge him but he had a moment of pure animal rage—not fear,
not reflex this time—and chased it. He caught up with it in just a few seconds
and took a swipe at the backs of its legs to bring it down. Then he jumped on
it, feet first, and sliced through the top of its skull because that was the only
part he could reach right then.

That's for Bennie. That's for Sylvie. That's for my kids, you ugly fuck.

Bone fragments stung his hands even through his gloves. Dead wasn't
enough. He took another slice at it. Yeah, it felt *right* to kill them. It felt like
sweet relief if only for a few moments and he never wanted it to stop.

"*Gas!*" Jace yelled. He was right behind Dom. He seemed to come out of
nowhere, spattered with blood. "Smell it?"

"Shit, you mean nerve agent?" Dom wasn't sure why he said that. Did the
grubs have chemical weapons? "What is it?"

"*Methane* gas." Marcus was suddenly jogging toward him from the other
direction and Dom had no idea how he'd gotten there. "They fractured a gas
main. Or maybe it's sewer gas. Either way, that shit's combustible."

For a moment, the three of them ignored the battle raging around them
and looked back down Correll Road. There it was: at the crumbling edge of
the e-hole, a bright yellow pipe was sticking up at a crazy angle. Grubs were
still clambering out of the hole like the line was never going to stop.

"Jace, I'm out of frags." Marcus held his hand out for a grenade, impatient.
"Quick. Give me one."

It was that simple. Marcus ran a few steps forward, pulled the pin, swung
the frag by its chain and then let go. He always did have a good eye for distance. And it was a damn big e-hole. A couple of grubs noticed the lone grenade arcing through the air and started running, but by then it was too late.

The explosion sent brick and paving high into the air on a column of
flame. The blast nearly knocked Marcus off his feet. Dom ducked, and when

he straightened up the flames were still roaring from the e-hole like a blow torch.

So that was one access point now closed to the bastards.

"That's fucked them," Dom said. He turned and started running after the grubs that were now breaking through to the command post, a lot fewer, but it only took a handful to cause chaos. This had to be the last of them. They were surrounded and cut off from reinforcements now, and Tai, usually the most mellow of guys, went scything through them with his chainsaw, screaming tribal stuff that Dom couldn't understand. Every Gear who was still standing converged on the grubs. It was a bloodbath. Dom didn't manage to get his hands on another one. For a moment, it seemed to be over, at least on Correll Road. It was hard to see anything in the financial district because it was a dense forest of skyscrapers and towers packed so close together that you had to be on the tallest roof to get an overview. But he could still hear the *whomp* of artillery a few blocks away and the occasional rattle of Lancer fire. He tried his radio and got a burst of static and garbled voices.

"Hey, have we got grubs elsewhere now?" Maybe it was just Reavers on an air raid, although that was bad enough. "Listen to that."

"I'm not getting anything on the radio," Jace said. "Where now?"

"Where's Hoffman?" Marcus pressed his earpiece, looking around. "Shit, is the net on the fritz again?"

Marcus started jogging up the road to the command post and Dom automatically followed. It was the obvious point to regroup. Dom could now see Hoffman leaning over Aigle as the corporal wrestled with the portable transmitter. The colonel looked up, not a happy man at all, and now Dom could hear the voice traffic that seemed to be pissing him off.

"Bastards are jamming us," Hoffman said. "But I don't think this was the main event."

". . . *KR-Four* . . . *Reavers, inbound at* . . ." Dom struggled to make out the words, but the signal was breaking up. ". . . *Exchequer* . . . *Prince's* . . . *at least a thousand* . . ."

"*Fuck it.*" Hoffman's lips compressed into a thin line. He wasn't an Academy grad officer like Marcus's dad. "They're not using the sewer. They've found a way into the metro system."

The underground rail network had been shut down a few years ago. It didn't extend beyond the plateau so there must have been another fissure nobody had mapped. Dom was distracted for a moment by a glimpse of more Reavers heading northwest at low altitude and wondered where the Ravens were.

Hoffman took the radio handset off Aigle. "Command to all callsigns, anyone currently engaging grubs, call it in." He waited, staring down the road, jaw clenched. The firefight a few blocks up seemed to be intensifying and the arty boys were hammering something hard, but nobody was reporting in. "Command to all callsigns, report current contacts."

They were on the open net now and it was just a series of staccato bursts of words. Then a stronger signal broke through, a voice that they all knew. It was Anya.

"Control here, sir, they're coming up through the metro." Dom, watching Marcus's expression intently, could hear more explosions in the background, either right outside the bank or inside it. "They've cut us off. They're in the building. We're going to have to—"

The radio went dead. They were all listening to static now, not even fragments of voice transmission.

"Shit." Dom looked toward the Bank of Tyrus tower instinctively. It was the tallest structure in the financial district, a perfect spot for a radio mast, and one of the few buildings he had line of sight with. He couldn't see Reavers, but he could see a pall of black smoke from the roof like a chimney fire that had run out of control. Reavers didn't have the firepower to take out a whole building. They'd taken out the comms aerials on the roof instead.

Hoffman kept trying anyway. "Anya? Lieutenant Stroud, do you read me?"

"Lost everyone, sir," Aigle said, fiddling with the receiver. "All comms are down."

"We need to get to CIC," Marcus said. "Sir?"

"Wait." Hoffman held up a hand. "Check what you're running into first. Aigle, have we got any contact with the Ravens? We don't know where else these fuckers are coming up now. I need aerial recon."

"Some still have the navy comms fit, sir. I'm going to try those channels."

The artillery radio net was down, so there was no sitrep from the gunners either. But you could always rely on a Raven pilot to think laterally. The noise of rotors suddenly blasted the square and everyone scattered as a Raven descended and landed with an alarming bounce. The crew chief jumped out and sprinted for the command post. It was Kevan Mitchell, just a kid who'd been flying for less than a year.

"Colonel, they're coming up through all the central metro stations," he said. "Old Exchequer, Museum Plaza, Prince's Street, and Forbridge. They've overrun the tanks. Best estimate is ten thousand grubs, and more coming."

The blood had drained from Hoffman's face. "Aigle, get those other damn channels working."

"On it, sir, but I'm counting on pilots realizing I'll be trying the navy net and switching channels." Aigle was hunched over the radio. "Wait one."

"Mitchell, did you get a look at Chancery Bridge?" Hoffman asked.

"They're holding it, sir, but the grubs can come up at the metro terminal now. There's nothing to stop them."

"And then they'll be around the back of us." Hoffman shut his eyes for a second. "Okay, we pull back north of Sovereign's Parkway. Everybody—pass it down any way you can. Clear everyone out. Have we got any muster point left for landing birds?"

"We're using the Treasury roof," Mitchell said.

"Fenix, go check if anyone's left in CIC. Then RV with me on the Treasury roof." Hoffman stuffed a couple of ammo clips in his belt and reloaded his Lancer. "How are we doing, Corporal?"

"Got the En-COG net up, sir," Aigle said. "Some of the Ravens have the comms kit to use that, so we've got some eyes in the air again now. I'll work on taking over the police frequency now—most personal radios can switch to that if we get word out."

"Do it, then, people. I'm going to round up whatever armor we've got left."

"You ought to wait for an escort, sir," Dom said.

Hoffman turned and started running for Redoubt Street. "There's nobody left, Santiago. Go get Stroud and her team out. And take the bot—don't lose him."

Crazy old bastard: he thought he was indestructible. Dom was about to run after him when he looked around and saw that Marcus was already halfway up Almar Boulevard with Tai and Jace at his heels.

Dom had his orders. He ran after Marcus, but he looked over his shoulder just as Hoffman vanished behind the Stock Exchange building, and wondered if he'd see his old CO alive again.

BANK OF TYRUS, BULLION DEPOSIT VAULT: FOUR HOURS INTO THE LOCUST ASSAULT.

Anya had no idea how long she'd been sitting here in the pitch blackness with her back against the door, hugging the CBs to her chest.

The operating procedures were clear: keep the confidential books—the CBs, the codebooks containing the COG's authorizations—from falling into enemy hands at all cost. So Anya had done just that when the Locust smashed up through the floor and opened fire on the three Gears unlucky enough to be in the comms room at the time. She couldn't outrun drones, so she did the next best thing. She sprinted out the back door to the service stairs, darted through the basement using the currency stacks for cover, and locked herself in the bullion vault behind not one but two doors.

It would take them days to break in if they got in at all. But now nobody—except the grubs, perhaps—knew she was in here.

She pressed her earpiece and worked through all the comms channels again, but she was sealed in a giant steel box, effectively a radio screen. Getting a signal out meant opening the door.

Were they out there waiting for her? If she found the light switch, would there be a crack in the wall or some other chink of light to give away her hiding place?

Sealed in here, she had no idea if she was the last human left alive in Ephyra. But she *was* alive, and she had an objective: to get out with the CBs, find Hoffman or whoever was now senior commander, and regroup.

Or whoever . . . no, he's not dead. Hoffman's too smart. And Marcus is out there too. He wouldn't get himself killed and leave me on my own. Come on, Mom, what would you do now?

Major Helena Stroud—posthumously awarded the Embry Star, the COG's highest award for bravery—had thrived on impossible odds. One day her luck had run out though, and Anya had been in CIC with no choice but to listen to her mother's final moments as if she were a stranger.

How did you feel, Mom? Were you scared when you charged that tank? You never sounded it. When you realized the blast was going to take you with it, what were you thinking about? My father? Me? Winning? Losing?

It didn't matter. All Anya wanted to know was whether heroes, real honest-to-God, have-a-go crazy heroes like her mother, thought the same small things as lesser mortals like herself when death was imminent.

Marcus won't tell me. He's a hero too. Embry Star. Won't talk about it, won't let me in. Dom and Colonel Hoffman, too—Embry Star heroes who tell me it's just their job when I know it isn't. I need you to show me, Mom. Show me how to be at least half the Gear you were.

Anya wasn't going to get anywhere until she assessed her environment. She'd thought the vault was just a big square room, but it wasn't that simple, and she'd slammed the door to spin the hand-wheel before she'd noted where the controls were or even checked the place was empty. The door had been ajar. Anything could have sneaked in to wait.

This is how you do it. Get on with it.

It was her own voice in her head, she was sure, but it sounded like an order.

She didn't want to put the books down and not be able to find them, so she tucked them under one arm and slid her back up the cold steel door to stand. Then she turned around and groped one-handed along the metal surface to her left until she felt the surface change to warmer, more textured plaster. There had to be a light switch one side or the other. She worked her way along a pace at a time for what felt like meters until she brushed against a corner or a shelf at 90 degrees to the wall, then swapped arms to work her way back again. Her foot hit something heavy and soft—a body?—and she nearly tripped. She stifled a yelp and froze.

Whatever she'd kicked didn't move. She squatted to feel it, heart pounding, and realized it was an upholstered chair lying on its side. *Not a grub, then. Okay. I can do this. Why didn't I make sure I had a pistol?* She felt for the wall again, edged past the chair, and finally felt the raised surface of a switch panel.

One . . . two . . . four switches. Here we go.

She flicked the first switch: nothing. Was it a light at all? Was the power supply cut off? What about air? Was this place airtight? How long could she stay in here? *Damn.* Then she tried the second switch and a harsh yellow light flooded the room. She turned around, half expecting to see a grinning Boomer waiting for her, but it was just an empty vault after all, just steel shelves, a row of deep metal drawers at floor level, a chair, and desk. There were alcoves off it, but she could see into every one of them easily. Perhaps that was a security measure so that no bank employee could take anything without the security cameras seeing it.

The cams were dead. She knew that because she'd tried to get the monitors working from upstairs. Nobody would spot her down here, Gear or enemy. Now she had the measure of her hiding place, she felt more confident and laid the CBs down where she could grab them in a hurry. What she needed now was a weapon. All she had was a pen, and the chair was a box construction type with no handy legs she could break off and use as a club. The desk was too sturdy to break apart, but she marked that mentally as a possibility for later.

You can do better than this. Think.

Anya wandered around the vault, thinking—sharp edge, sharp point, heavy weight. Then she peered into one of the alcoves and saw the four bullion bars.

The bars were marked with their weight, the bank's crest, and the gold's purity. They were ten-kilo bricks, but they were long and narrow, and that made them more manageable than the smaller but chunkier bar she'd been using as a paperweight. She picked one up, surprised by the heft of it, and practiced a few swings that nearly ran away with her. It was a hell of a lot heavier than a Lancer rifle. And that was heavy enough.

Come on, Mom would have cracked a few skulls with this if she had to.

But Mom wouldn't have been in a combat zone without a weapon.

Anya had once felt constantly in her mother's shadow but now that shadow had become a shield, a source of comfort and example. *Both hands free. Come on, find a bag.* She put the bullion bar on the shelf and took off her pullover, knotting the arms to make straps and pulling her belt tight around the open end of the waist. It worked fine. It took the CBs with a little room to spare. Now she had both hands free to wield that bullion bar if she had to.

But first she had to check outside.

She stood next to the door with her eyes shut for at least fifteen minutes, straining to hear any sound outside. The silence meant nothing. The vault might have been soundproofed. She thought she could hear distant booming, but it was hard to work out if she was imagining it and it was her own pulse playing tricks on her.

But she couldn't stay here. Nobody had any reason to look for her. She switched off the light so that she wasn't an easy target when she finally got the door open, and was still working up to turning the wheel when she thought she heard gunfire in the distance, a firefight that went on for what felt like ages.

It could be anywhere. I can't tell. But I have to get out.

She placed the gold bar between her feet and began turning the hand-wheel a little at a time, slow increments that probably wouldn't get the attention of anyone outside. By the time she finished, she couldn't hear gunfire any longer, and wasn't sure if she'd actually heard it at all.

The door groaned a little as she inched it open and grabbed the bullion bar. There was no light outside. She held her breath and listened for movement before squeezing through the smallest gap she could open and edging along the wall.

Then her eyes began to adjust to the gloom. It wasn't pitch black, not quite. She could see denser black patches that were the shoulder-high pallets of banknotes. If anything was lurking there and waiting for her, it had detected her by now and there was no point standing still, so she lunged for the stack, then the next, and the next. She was moving toward where she thought the door had been.

Then a loud metallic clunk shattered the muffled silence.

She was right. The door was ahead of her. But someone was trying to get in. She ducked behind the next pallet, clutching the bar two-handed, ready to fracture the skull of the first grub bastard through that door or die trying.

That's my girl. Anya.

Anya.

Someone was calling her name.

For a second, her hair stood on end. But it wasn't her mother's voice. It was a man's.

It was Marcus.

"Anya? *Anya!* Let's have some light, Jack. We're not leaving until we've checked everywhere." A brilliant white beam swept across the far wall, a bot's tactical lamp. "Anya?"

She was safe now, but suddenly much more scared. Her bravado and her plans to brain a grub with the gold bar evaporated. "Marcus?"

She dropped the bar and stood up. The light shone in her face, blinding her for a moment, then it moved away and she could see Jack, one of the COG's last prototype bots, hovering in the gloom like an oversized egg with his jointed steel arms folded back. Marcus was suddenly right in front of her. For a moment she saw him as a stranger might—big, grim, and lethal, not her lover at all.

"You okay?" he asked.

I was going to fight. I was ready to fight, Mom. Honestly, I was.

Anya found her legs shaking, a tremor that traveled up to her chest and throat, and she hated herself for not being two-fisted Helena Stroud, the officer who embraced death to save her Gears. Her voice shook. "They're all dead. Everyone. I just ran and hid, Marcus—*I couldn't do anything.* I couldn't stop them—"

"It's okay. You did fine." Marcus frowned at her, more inspection than disapproval, but kept looking over his shoulder. The gunfire she'd heard was real, all right. "We've got to RV with Hoffman now on the Treasury roof. Stick close to me and keep moving."

"We're pulling out?"

"Pulling *back.*" She could see Dom, Tai, and Jace covering the outer door. "We're not beaten yet. Come on."

Anya decided there and then that she would never be without a sidearm again. Damn it, if she got out of this alive she'd learn to use a Lancer properly, too. She scuttled behind Marcus, wondering if the CBs on her back would be enough to stop a round, and was suddenly plunged into his world, his daily reality, in a way she'd never been before.

As soon as they emerged into the gloom of the next lobby they came under fire. The noise was deafening. The muzzle flash blinded her for a moment before Marcus shoved her behind the nearest pallet of bills and pinned her there with his bodyweight while he returned fire.

Anya had always experienced combat over the radio or via a bot's video feed. Now she was inhaling it, tasting it, feeling it, *smelling* it: sweat, oil, cordite. And Dom—kind, gentle Dom—was yelling his head off as his chainsaw revved and screamed. "Yeah, bitch, fucking payback time, huh?" But it wasn't the Lancer's saw screaming. It was a Locust drone on the receiving end of it. This was another world, violent and primal. She wasn't part of it, merely trapped in it. It was all happening over her head as if she wasn't there.

"You clear?"

"Clear!"

"Yeah, all down."

"Thin out, Jack. Off you go."

"Goddamn, Jace, *move!*"

It could have been ten seconds or ten minutes—Anya had no way of telling. Her own breath sounded like a locomotive, almost too loud to bear. Then the firing stopped. Marcus grabbed her arm and yanked her upright so hard that it hurt and she found herself running just to recover her balance. Doors crashed open ahead of her and bright light hurt her eyes. They were in the second floor corridor that led to the roof terraces and the Treasury building, a walkway that was all windows on the street side. Her shoes crunched on broken glass. Marcus was shielding her from the window side, blocking her bodily, so she only caught a glimpse of what was down there. But it was enough. A Brumak's head bobbed slowly above a tide of drones flooding into the city.

"Oh *God*," she said.

"It's okay. Just keep moving." Marcus caught her arm again. "Don't look."

Anya found her legs were taking care of the situation for her. She let them. Somewhere ahead, Tai let out one of his roaring tribal cries that merged with the chainsaw and the rattle of automatic fire. She was now so deafened by the noise—or numbed by adrenaline—that she couldn't tell where the sound was coming from. Marcus pulled her along again and she tripped over a dead grub, cut in two from shoulder to hip in a ragged slice. Then cool air hit her face. She realized they were now on an open balcony. She was looking out across Ephyra at roof height. Was she just deafened or was it really that quiet? Raven engines and the sporadic *whomp* of artillery faded in and black smoke bloomed out of instant fireballs as shells hit their targets.

Marcus stood panting, pressing his earpiece, the fingers on his other hand dug deep in her arm as if he didn't trust her to stay alive if he let go. "Fenix to Hoffman—we've got Lieutenant Stroud. What's your position?"

"Hoffman receiving. I've run into some shit. Just get to the Raven. I'll be there."

"*Reavers,*" Jace yelled. "Everybody down."

Anya should have dropped, but she didn't. She was transfixed by the incoming Raven. Maybe the pilot hadn't spotted the Reaver or maybe the Raven just wasn't fast enough, but one moment the familiar black shape was there and the next it was a ball of flame and spinning rotors. That was the last she saw. She was suddenly flat on her back, winded by Marcus crashing down on top of her as something flat and black spun overhead so close that she felt the draft.

"Shit, that was Daniels," Dom said. "Goddamn it, he's gone—where's the frigging Hammer team? What the hell's happened to them?"

"Goddamn it, have we lost them too?" Marcus got to his feet and held out his hand to pull Anya up like any other Gear. "Sorry. Better a few bruises than getting your head sliced off."

Her elbow hurt like hell but she gritted her teeth rather than give in to it. When she stood up, she saw a section of fuselage embedded like a blade in the wall ten meters away. The Reaver was gone. Daniels, and his crew chief, Julia Lawry: Anya knew all the Raven crews by voice if not in person. They were dead and all she could do was put that numb horror to one side and get on with the job. It wasn't even conscious. It was a reflex now. Marcus leaned over the balustrade as Tai and Jace kept an eye out for more Reavers, Lancers raised.

"There's the Hammer," he said. "Shit."

Anya looked down onto the flat roof below. She thought it was just a pile of sandbags at first until her brain made sense of the mess and she realized it was the remains of two Gears. The targeting laser, the handheld device they used to paint targets for the Hammer of Dawn satellites, lay a few meters away. The Hammer net was failing a sat at a time after ten years without maintenance but it still packed a punch, and the handheld lasers were too precious now to leave behind. Marcus clambered over the balustrade and hung there for a moment, looking as if he was calculating the drop.

"We're going to need that Hammer if we want the evac Raven to land," he said, and let go.

He landed with a thud, stood over the dead Gears for a second before taking their COG tags, then picked up the laser and something next to it that he jammed into his belt pouch. Climbing back up to the balcony was a lot harder. He managed to get a grip on the balustrade, boots jammed into holes in the brickwork below. Dom and Jace hauled him in.

He examined the laser and tapped his belt, indicating a pouch. "I need to reattach the front targeting optic," he said, steering Anya by her elbow. "Come on. Keep moving."

The pull-out had begun. Anya could see more Ravens lifting off, some of them rising from the smoke and flames below, packed solid with Gears. By the time they reached the Treasury roof she could hear a Raven close by and realized one was already waiting on the far side in the cover of the radio mast, rotors turning, but there was no sign of Hoffman. Anya had to walk around the edge of the roof to even see the Raven. The pilot, Strachan, looked up and tapped his watch theatrically through the cockpit window. She gave him a shrug and indicated *wait* with both forefingers before ducking back along the roof.

"Where's the Colonel?" Anya eased the makeshift rucksack off her shoulders and rubbed her bruised elbow. It was starting to throb. "Control to Hoffman—we're at the RV point. Strachan's here. Where are you?"

All she got for a long time was the crackle and hiss of interference. Then he responded.

"Right below you, Bravo. Wait one."

Jace leaned over to look. "Shit, the old man's a mess."

"What?" Anya craned her neck to look. "Sir?"

"Go on." Marcus jerked his thumb over his shoulder in the direction of the radio mast and the sound of the helicopter's engine. "Dom, Tai, Jace—you guys buckle in. We'll wait for Hoffman."

"I heard that," Hoffman said. He sounded as if he was running up stairs, catching his breath. Dom and the others jogged away and disappeared behind the base of the mast. "*Mess* my ass. Just shrapnel. Where's the Hammer team, Anya?"

"They didn't make it, sir, but we've got the targeting laser."

"Goddamn." The puffing stopped for a moment. "Well, change of plan, then. Chancery Bridge. Tomas needs that damn laser more than we do. They're going to lose the bridge. We're going to have to blow it."

Anya could hear Hoffman's boots now. The elevator winch room door swung open and he walked across the roof, none too steady. His right sleeve was shredded and dark with blood.

"You better get that fixed, Colonel," Marcus said.

"It's nothing. Don't fuss over me." Hoffman made a bee line for Anya. Her earpiece was stuttering and buzzing as the radio net struggled with the torrent of voice traffic. "Just get that targeting laser to Tomas at Chancery Bridge. Stroud, call in KR-Eight-Zero and get out of here."

"Sir—"

Hoffman was a gentleman despite the foul temper and language to match. "And I need you to reestablish CIC in Jacinto, fast as you can, Lieutenant. Do it."

"You better go too, Colonel," Marcus said.

"Fenix, just do as you're goddamn told for once, will you? I'm coming to Chancery with you."

"Look, Colonel—"

"*You* look, Sergeant."

Anya switched channels and pressed her earpiece. "KR-Eight-Zero, this is Control, come in. Eight-Zero, evac required from the Treasury roof, come in." She was waiting for Gettner to respond when another voice suddenly cut through the static and distracted her.

"Control, this is Adam Fenix. Control—I need to contact Marcus, Marcus Fenix—"

"Say again?" She put her hands over her ears to drown out the noise behind her and walked a few meters away. "This is Control. Say again?"

Anya didn't catch the rest of the conversation between Marcus and Hoffman. She was too distracted by hearing Adam Fenix. He never used the radio net. She wasn't even sure how he managed it, but he could access pretty well anything as Director of the DRA.

"Adam?" She forgot RT procedure for a moment. "It's Anya. Where are you?"

"Anya, I'm at Haldane." Adam's voice was breaking up. "The Locust have broken through in East Barricade. Tell Marcus I'm sorry. Is he there? I need to say goodbye to him."

"Adam, hang on." *Goodbye?* Anya's gut lurched. She turned back to Hoffman and held up one hand for silence. "Sorry, sir—Marcus, you're going to want to hear this. It's your father. The Locust are near the house and he called in to say . . . goodbye. He says he's sorry. He says—" She paused. "Adam? Professor? Come in, Professor . . . damn, I've lost him."

Hoffman froze. Marcus's expression went blank. It was as if everything else had ceased to exist: no Locust assault, no bridge, no evacuation. He turned to Anya.

"I've got to get him out of there," he said quietly, as if Hoffman wasn't there either.

Hoffman looked impatient, lips compressed into a line, nothing more. "Are you going *deaf*, Fenix? I said get that targeting laser to Chancery."

"I'm not leaving my father to die. I've got to get him out first."

There was no eye contact, nothing at all. Marcus was staring past Anya, suddenly focused on something she couldn't see. The shelling and the Raven seemed forgotten. Hoffman looked more baffled than angry. Marcus had never refused an order in his life. Anya stared, thinking she'd misheard.

Hoffman gestured in the direction of the Raven. "Get your ass on that bird, Sergeant," he snapped. "And that's a goddamn *order*. Your father's not the only man who's in trouble—there's a whole brigade of Gears in deeper shit than he is."

Anya didn't even see how it happened. It was too fast. In a heartbeat, the two men were nose to nose and she was looking at a Marcus she didn't know. Hoffman was a big man, but Marcus loomed over him.

"I've put myself on the line *every day* since I was eighteen years old," he growled, so low that Anya could hardly hear him. "Followed every order. Even the half-assed ones. But now I'm going to save my father. So with all due respect, fuck *you*, sir."

"Fenix, *we need to blow that fucking bridge.*" Hoffman paused for a breath as if Marcus was just in need of a good talking-to and everything would snap back to normal. Anya thought that too. "*Do it*, or I'll see you court-martialed, hero or no goddamn hero."

Marcus turned away and started walking. "Fine. You do that, Colonel."

Hoffman would have punched out anyone else by now. But Marcus—he thought the world of him. That had to hurt. Hoffman went after him, grabbed his shoulder, and pulled him around.

"Fenix, your father's been sitting on his ass for the whole damn war, inventing all kinds of useless shit, and he hasn't made so much as a goddamn *dent* in the Locust. He's not worth the life of one honest fighting Gear. He's certainly not worth *yours*."

It wasn't even a shouting match. It was more shock, disbelief, an attempt at reasoning, but this was another Marcus, an instant stranger. When it came to his father, he was one big raw nerve. He didn't even blink. He drew back his fist and landed a right hook on Hoffman, knocking him flat. The colonel hit the concrete with a crack and lay groaning.

Oh my God. This isn't happening. This just isn't happening.

Anya rushed to Hoffman and knelt to lift his head. "Marcus! For God's sake, are you insane? What are you *doing*?" Hoffman struggled to get up, murmuring, "Bastard . . . bastard . . ." Anya managed to prop him up against her knee. Marcus stared at Hoffman, eyes wide as if he suddenly realized what he'd done, and for a moment Anya thought he was going to rush to help the colonel up and it would all be forgotten tomorrow, but he just turned and started striding away.

Marcus didn't look back. "Take him on the other Raven, Anya," he called out.

"Marcus? *Marcus!* You can't just disobey an order." But he wasn't stopping. She needed him to stop right *now*. He *had* to. "*Marcus!* Get back here, and that's an order. Are you damn well listening to me? What do you think you're doing?"

"My duty," he said.

Gettner cut in on the radio. "Eight-Zero to Control, you still need a ride?"

Anya wasn't one of life's panickers. She was used to all hell breaking loose on the radio net and being the calm eye of the storm. But she froze for a moment, almost sick with dread at what would happen next, and it wasn't a healthy fear of the Locust assault. Marcus had abandoned his duty in the middle of a battle. He might have fractured Hoffman's skull. She almost ran after him, but common sense—or her mother's voice, she wasn't sure—shook her out of it and told her she needed to stick with Hoffman.

Hoffman struggled onto his hands and knees, then tried to stand again. Somewhere behind the mast, an engine roared and Strachan's Raven lifted clear, banking away almost instantly over the edge of the roof.

"Easy, sir. Gettner's inbound." Anya grabbed Hoffman's arm to steady him and found it still wet with blood. "We'll get you sorted out."

His cap had gone flying. He managed to bend over to pick it up, and then pressed his earpiece. "*Fenix!* Fenix, you damn well *listen* to me, I *order* you to turn that bird around and get your motherfucking ass back *here*. Fenix? Answer me, goddamn you!" Marcus must have cut him off. Hoffman was cycling through channels, probably blindly, and even if the Raven pilots couldn't hear him, a lot of Gear units could. Marcus's crazy moment was public now. "Fenix? You get your ass to Chancery! I fucking *need* you there!"

Eventually Hoffman's arm dropped to his side and she thought he was going to collapse. His shoulders sagged for a moment.

"Did he leave the laser? Where's the goddamn laser?" He looked around, dazed. The carbine-sized device was still there on the floor. Anya didn't know if Marcus had left it deliberately or if he'd simply lost sight of everything except his father. "Is he out of his fucking mind? Goddamn Fenix, of all people, Anya, he should—"

Hoffman stopped dead, either fresh out of expletives or about to keel over. He struggled to pick up the targeting laser and stood looking at the sky in the direction of the Raven noise. Then he checked out the laser and starting spitting fury again.

"It's missing a goddamn optics piece."

"Sir, you need a casevac."

Hoffman didn't move. "Later. Goddamn, where's the targeting optic?"

"Sir . . ."

"I can't save him now, Anya," he said. He seemed almost lucid again. "And if he's cost us Chancery Bridge, I'll shoot him myself."

CHAPTER 4

It's almost too much to take in. A new species. A new sentient species, right under our noses all these years, sharing Sera with us. You realize what that means for a biologist? It's an unimaginable fantasy. We all dream of some discovery that will change our understanding of the world, and—yes—put our name in the annals of science. I have no idea how to make this public. I have to get my evidence first and make sure it's watertight before I tell anyone else and make a fool of myself. I'm going further into the tunnel today. I'm going to talk to them.

(Last entry in the private journal of Dr. Elain Fenix, senior developmental embryologist, La Croix University: nine years before E-Day.)

HALDANE HALL, EAST BARRICADE, JACINTO: SEVEN HOURS INTO THE LOCUST ASSAULT, FROST, 10 A.E.

Adam Fenix knew he would survive the day, but he might as well have been dead already.

The Locust were coming for him.

He sat at the bench in his laboratory, staring at the dead radio handset in his palm. *Oh God, Marcus. Maybe it's better like this. You'll never know what I did.* He was waiting because he knew how his signal had been jammed, and who was jamming it. His briefcase was packed. He knew what he had to do.

I shouldn't have tried to call. It'll only distress him. Why can't I ever get it right?

He could hear the shelling getting closer and the constant Raven sorties overhead. The Locust were gathering south of East Barricade, moving into position. He could see from the top floor.

They could come and get me anytime now. They think I'm going to commit suicide rather than let them take me. They don't want to spook me. They're work-ing out how to take me alive, because that's something they're not very adept at doing.

But he wasn't planning to shoot himself. Whether he carried out the re-search here or below Ephyra in the Locust caverns, his sole objective was to find a way of destroying the Lambent organism before it spread across the en-tire planet. Surrendering to Myrrah was the best option in a list of bad choices.

Queen Myrrah. It was an odd choice of title. It smacked of termite colonies and ants, an analogy he knew she'd find offensive, but he suspected she'd chosen it in an attempt to make herself feel more embedded in Sera's history, more Seran than the humans who'd long since discarded their monarchies.

You know that's not true, Myrrah. You know all about your origins. But this is no time to argue that with you. Come on. Come and get it over with.

He knew her too well. The quaint radio receiver he'd always used to contact her finally vibrated on the bench, buzzing against the varnished wood.

"Adam, you knew this day would come."

It was a familiar voice: silky, imperial, polished, and utterly human.

"Hello, Myrrah." Adam found himself thinking of the terrible Locust food again. "You got my message, then."

"And how right you were. We *do* need you. And we shall take you. I hope you're not planning anything foolish. You have responsibilities, Adam."

It would be a living death. She'd never release him, even if he developed a countermeasure. But he didn't deserve any better.

"I also have my service pistol."

"And I can take your son at any time."

He had the measure of her, then, and she had his. "You leave Marcus out of this. It's a condition." He opened the desk drawer and took out the handgun, a 9mm officer's weapon. It made a distinctive *clunk* on the wooden desktop as he slammed it down. "If anything happens to him, I don't care what happens to the rest of Sera."

"Ah, no, Adam, you find it easier to care about grand impersonal ideals than the flesh and blood at your side. And you were never very good at threats."

It stung, like all painful truths. And it provoked him. He picked up the pis-tol and chambered a round right next to the mike. Myrrah would hear that and recognize it. He waited.

"Try me," he said.

"You try my patience. Stop this game."

"Leave my son alone."

"If he dies, Adam, it will not be by my order or at my command."

"I'll take that as a deal." Adam put the pistol back in the drawer, safety on. He hadn't carried a weapon on a regular basis in years, but today it made him feel strangely naked to discard it. "You have my word."

"We will come for you when my troops have dealt with the defenses near your home."

"I'll be ready."

The radio clicked off. Adam sat back in his chair, resigned to the fact that he was probably the only human being on Sera who had ever waited patiently for the Locust to come. He was certainly the only one who had any kind of relationship with them.

Imagine how fascinating this would have been in another world, another time. First contact, of a kind. No. More like understanding the full intelligence of another animal.

And whatever Myrrah said in her speeches to rouse her troops, humans weren't to blame. They were just accelerants. That didn't make them any less greedy, violent, and destructive, but nobody could be blamed for Lambency. It simply existed.

And that's what I need to understand more than anything. I wish you were here to help me, Elain. Dear God, I do.

That was something he'd forgotten to pack: her picture on his desk in his study upstairs, so much a part of his day that it sometimes became invisible. He tried not to think that he was killing time while the Locust army was killing humans. The house was more empty than it had ever been before. Mrs. Ross had been evacuated to Jacinto—Adam still had some pull—and Marcus probably wouldn't have a legacy to inherit once the fighting got this far. As for the art treasures, mankind had made them once, and could make them again. The paintings would have to take their chances.

I'm sorry, Dad. I really am.

There were too many ancestors to preserve, almost all of them men and women Adam had never known. He rearranged the tightly packed data discs and notes in his briefcase to make space for a few more items—the picture of Elain with Marcus aged ten, and Elain's journal—and dithered over the Octus Medal. He hefted it in his hand, then placed it in the small box that he would leave for Marcus, along with the certificate and his will. The photo of the presentation that had stared down at him like a rebuke for too many years went into the box. Damn: this was getting to be a lot to carry. And if he took it with him, would Myrrah ever make sure it got to Marcus? If he left it here, would anyone find it?

Too late to visit my lawyer's offices now . . . not that they exist any longer.

And where the hell is Nevil? Okay, he needs time. I should never have burdened him with all that. But better that he knows what I am than he spends his life respecting a man who never deserved it.

The sound of a Raven distracted him. It sounded as if it was right overhead, but that wasn't unusual, and then it faded away again. He was about to sit down and drink in the image of his sanctuary for one last time when a massive explosion shook the room and he heard someone calling up the stairs.

"Professor Fenix? Sir? We've come to get you out."

It was Dom Santiago. And rescue was the last thing Adam wanted.

Now he could hear a firefight outside, and heavy boots thudded up the stairs. The next voice was bittersweet. It was Marcus's. "Tai, Jace, hang on— we're checking." The footsteps were coming along the landing, heading for the study. "Where the hell is he? Dom, go check the bedrooms."

Damn, Marcus, not now.

Adam wanted to see his son again more than anything, but this was bad timing. How could he ask them to go away because he was waiting to take his research to the Locust tunnels? Concealing E-Day had been bad enough, but there was no way of explaining this.

He looked out the window at the smoke rising right across the west of the city, and knew he never could. Then he spotted the Locust drones pouring over the orchard wall and realized that he was staring down at rubble and slates. The explosion had been close. Perhaps a shell had even hit the house. Haldane Hall was so big that he'd have to walk outside and stand back to check for damage.

The rattle of automatic fire and the sound of a Raven answered his question. The house was now the battlefield, and Myrrah's promises couldn't be kept if the COG was engaging the Locust. They'd defend themselves and he would be collateral damage. It was just a matter of who got to him first.

My research. Whatever happens—wherever it's completed—that's got to survive.

Adam grabbed his case, shoved a folder under his arm, and went out onto the landing. Marcus and Dom, Lancers raised, stared at him for a second. All he could do was blurt out a rebuke in the way of all guilty men caught in the act.

"Marcus, what in God's name are you doing here? You're going to get yourselves killed, *both* of you."

Marcus hesitated. For a moment Adam thought he was going to step forward and hug him, but he stopped and just held out his hand as if to take the case.

"We've got a Raven waiting. Let's go."

"Is this Prescott's idea? I didn't want you to try to rescue me. I just wanted to say—"

"Later. We've got to go now."

"There's something I have to collect from my lab."

A window shattered across the landing, showering glass on the carpet. Dom swung around, smashed a pane, and returned fire. "Sir, I don't think there's time for that."

"Look, Dad, there's a goddamn war going on outside," Marcus snapped. "Forget the lab."

"Marcus, you don't understand." *How could you? I did nothing but lie to you.* "You don't realize what this research is. It'll stop the war. It'll—"

"Leave it, Dad. It doesn't matter now."

Marcus was drowned out by another explosion as a shockwave swept up the stairs like a wind and blew out a door. The rattle of a Raven's door gun filled the stairwell. Adam braced for the Locust to pour in. He'd agreed to go with them, but they were now in a full-scale firefight and all bets were off.

"I need your sidearm, Marcus."

"Yeah, you can be a hero later, Dad. Keep moving."

"Damn it, I was a Gear too. Give me the pistol. Mine's in the lab."

Marcus ushered him along the landing, managing not to touch him. Even now, there was still that embarrassed distance between them. "Leave that to us."

Dom broke off from the contact and aimed down the stairs one-handed with his other hand to his earpiece. "Tai? Tai, you receiving?" He was talking to someone on the radio. "What do you mean, they're *waiting*?"

"Who's waiting?" Marcus demanded.

"The grubs. He says they're massing outside."

"What, they're too polite to storm us without a formal invitation?"

"No idea what they're up to. Come on."

Dom went charging down the stairs and ran across the hall to flatten himself against the wall on one side of the blown-out doors. Adam had no choice. What did he do now, tell Marcus he had a deal to go with the Locust? It didn't matter. He'd continue the research wherever he was. He followed Marcus down the stairs and wished he had a damn weapon. He could still hit a target.

"You must have really pissed off the grubs to get a special visit, Dad." Marcus squatted on the other side of the doorway and reloaded. The fight seemed to be going on outside, judging by the noise. A Raven roared overhead spitting heavy caliber rounds. Adam knew that sound too well. "Forgot to send a card?"

Dom gestured frantically. "Did you hear, Marcus? Tai and Jace are roping down."

"For fuck's sake." Marcus shook his head angrily. "Tai? *Don't*. They'll pick you off."

Adam could hear the responses now: Marcus must have had his receiver open. A calm, heavily accented voice was audible even over the gunfire.

"We are a small moving target, Marcus. But you can distract the grubs if you wish."

"Goddamn," Marcus muttered. "Don't get yourself killed. Not now."

"Hey, Marcus, *chill*." That was a much younger man. It must have been Jace. "Here we come—*whoaaaa!*"

Marcus and Dom both burst out of the door before Adam could move. He prided himself on still being combat-fit in his fifties, but he was still the age he was, and his reflexes weren't as fast as a younger man's. He stumbled outside into a firefight and almost tripped over the splintered remains of the ancient green doors that had stood guard at Haldane Hall for centuries, clutching his precious briefcase and flapping papers to his chest with both arms. Perhaps the pistol hadn't been such a good idea after all. He dropped behind Marcus in the cover of the low courtyard wall. Rounds zipped over his head like angry insects. The fire was coming from both directions, focusing on the courtyard. Every few seconds, Marcus just shoved his Lancer over the low wall and fired blindly. Adam could see Dom edging along the base of the wall at a squat, springing up every so often to open fire. Adam risked a look over the wall.

It was a bloodbath. Locust drones lay dead in a pile while others used their bodies for cover like sandbags. Above the perimeter wall of the estate, smoke palls hung like a forest of tower blocks. Suddenly a huge Gear with a crest of black hair and facial tattoos burst over the wall, hosing the drones with Lancer fire as he ran, and vaulted over the bushes on the other side. The air was full of noise, screams, and smoke. It brought back too many memories of a simpler, more solvable war.

"Ah, *shit*." Marcus pressed his finger to his earpiece, frozen for a second. "We've got Boomers inbound, people," he yelled. "Yeah, I hear you, Strachan. You ready?"

There was a brief silence. Adam couldn't tell if the Locust had been cleared out but he took another look. Nothing was moving. He could see the big South Islander with the tattoos kicking over some of the bodies to check if they were still alive, and a young Gear with cornrowed hair was recovering rifles.

The Raven was right overhead now, descending on the rubble and churned flowerbeds of the courtyard. Adam felt the downdraft whipping his face as he struggled to hold on to his papers. It was a very small space to land in.

Imagine Hoffman diverting a helicopter in the middle of a pitched battle just to extract one man. Perhaps I've misjudged him.

The Raven pilot seemed to be having problems setting down. He lifted a little and turned to take another run at it, probably because the tail was perilously close to the shattered fountain that was gushing water. Adam was still watching, adrenaline starting to ebb, when movement in a gap in the thick yew hedge caught his eye. It was gray, it was moving surprisingly fast, and the first one he'd ever met had been in very different circumstances.

"Boomer!" he yelled. "*Down!*"

That was all Adam had time for before the whoosh and the yellow flame streaked upward and a huge explosion knocked him flat. Thick black smoke and roaring flame rolled right over him. The smell of fuel was choking.

"Fuck, it's the Raven." That was Dom. "Now we've got Reavers."

Marcus was calling out. "Dad?! You okay, Dad?! Come on, let's get out of here."

Adam curled up to protect his head as debris rained on him. His briefcase went flying. He could hear the noise of something whirling through the air before it thudded into the ground a few meters away like a javelin, probably a rotor blade, and then another explosion lifted him off the ground. Something very heavy hit him in the back. Everything went dark. He was still conscious but he had no idea what was happening to him, only that he couldn't move and he couldn't see.

But he could hear, and it was Marcus yelling the same thing over and over: "Dad? Dad! *Dad!*"

Then there was a third explosion and Adam couldn't hear a thing. He stopped trying to move. Then he understood that he couldn't. Every breath hurt.

"Marcus?" But there was still no sound, not even his own voice. *Am I dead?* The courtyard wasn't there any longer. "Marcus . . ."

If he'd lost consciousness, he hadn't noticed. But the attack had stopped and something was pressing on his back. At first he thought Marcus was holding him down, covering him, but he realized eventually that it was the dead weight of rubble burying him.

When he managed to suck in a deeper breath, his nose and mouth filled up with dust and the pain brought tears to his eyes. He couldn't cry for help, and he couldn't hear anything apart from distant gunfire—no helicopters, no voices, nothing. He had no idea how long he'd been trapped but he knew he had to try to move or call for help. All he could see was a patch of ground through a gap in the rubble, but he couldn't even move his head.

He tried to call out. It didn't matter who found him now. But the only sound that emerged was a gurgle.

Have I broken my spine?

No, he could move his toes. He could feel that, so at least he wasn't paralyzed. But breathing was an agony. He took short, shallow breaths that set him off coughing, and that hurt like hell.

I'm going to die here. Where's my research? Where's Marcus? Oh God, I should have told him. I should have handed over my papers. Marcus?

Adam stared along the ground at that small patch of gravel. He could feel cool air on his hand and realized at least part of his arm wasn't buried. Maybe someone would see it moving.

Who, exactly? There's nobody out there. You're going to die.

Then the gravel crunched. One, two pairs of boots, maybe three, definitely more than one person. Marcus had found him. Adam stretched his hand as far as he could and tried to shout.

"Oh, fuck. Prescott's going to go nuts." Adam didn't recognize the voice. It certainly wasn't Marcus or any of his squad. "Is he dead?"

"Don't think so, sir. Look."

"Well, damn well get him out of there, then. Jerge? Find his stuff. He had a briefcase somewhere. Then search the house."

"It's on fire, sir."

"So get a move on. See if you can get into the basement. He's got a lab down there."

"I've called for casevac."

"Better hope we don't lose him."

Adam still didn't know who it was and he wasn't sure if it mattered as long as they got him out. The weight started to lift off his back. He tried to speak, but every breath was unbearably painful, and then hands grabbed him and he found himself looking up into a smoky sky as a man in a plain black uniform leaned over him, frowning.

It didn't make sense. Maybe he really *was* dead and he'd been all wrong about an afterlife.

"Okay, don't try to talk, Professor," the man said. Adam's head lolled and his nose was almost touching highly polished black boots, not Gears boots at all. The sound of a helicopter was getting louder. "The Raven's here. You're going to be fine."

Marcus. Adam thought he was saying his name, but he was just thinking it. *Marcus. Are you all right?* Then something dug deep into the back of his hand, making him flinch, and the pain and light and the smell of burning aviation fuel melted into black, blissful oblivion.

RAVEN KR-80, EN ROUTE TO CHANCERY BRIDGE.

It wasn't the first head injury Hoffman had had and it probably wouldn't be the last.

He cradled the Hammer targeting laser in his arms, wondering if he was concussed or shocked. Gettner was going flat out for Chancery Bridge but there was no straight route with that many Reavers in the air. Barber, her crew chief, sat on the door gun, squeezing off a burst every so often.

"Sorry, Colonel," Gettner said. The Raven was jinking all over the damn place. Hoffman thought he was going to puke in a helo for the first time. "One door gunner, Reavers every-frigging-where. I'm trying to keep them on one flank."

Hoffman tried to focus on his watch. They'd lost twenty or thirty minutes. Maybe it wouldn't matter. Maybe he'd get the Hammer there in time and he could deal with Marcus later, man-to-man and no rank, before forgetting it ever happened.

Bullshit. You can't. It's not some error of judgment. He knew what the stakes were. He's finally cracked up. Happens to the best of us. Come on, Gettner. Move it. Fucking move it. Get me there.

He pressed his mike. The Raven sounded even noisier than usual. He hoped it had been serviced recently. "You're doing okay, Major."

Anya hauled another ammo belt across the deck for Barber, all twenty kilos of it. She was doing her damnedest. *I should be doing that.* She tottered back to the seat, struggling on the tilting deck in those dumb high heels—*why the hell do we make our women officers wear those?*—and leaned over him.

"Sir, you're still bleeding. I really should fix that."

"I'm not dead yet, Lieutenant."

"Sir, about Marcus . . ."

Here we go. Poor kid. What the hell am I going to do about him? "Later, Anya."

"It's not like him, sir." She adored Marcus, and despite the fact that Marcus had never shown her the slightest affection in public, Hoffman knew the deal and didn't lecture her on officers fraternizing with enlisted men. "You know he'd never abandon his post."

"Anya, not now."

"Sorry, sir." She got up and took the first aid kit out of its bulkhead bracket. "Hold still."

Hoffman couldn't see what she was doing. Whatever it was, it hurt, and he hated anyone fussing over him. But this was Anya, one of the few people he would never snarl at: loyal, uncomplaining, reliable, unflappable Anya.

"Ah, we've got radio again," Barber said, more to himself than anything. "Well, we've got the Hammer relay, and we've got ten other Ravens."

Hoffman perked up. Maybe Marcus had come to his senses and was on his way back. "Strachan?"

"No, wrong comms kit. Problem, sir? I thought he was evacuating."

"Nothing important."

Gettner interrupted. "I've got a visual on Chancery."

She didn't elaborate. She didn't need to. She banked the bird and Hoffman found himself looking along the glittering path of the river, down into the granite gorge that cut deep into Ephyra from the south. He could see the pillars and suspension cables of Chancery Bridge. On a normal day it was a six-lane highway, but today it was a battlefield wreathed in smoke. For a moment, he thought the carpet of broken gray and black was chunks of tarmac or vehicle debris, but where the haze of smoke thinned out he got a better look.

It was Locust drones, a whole seething column of them. It was hard to see the Gears' line. "Come around again," Hoffman said. "I don't see Tomas."

Gettner lifted out of small arms range and looped back again, this time coming in from the northern pier of the bridge and heading straight down the line of cables. Hoffman leaned out of the crew bay as far as he could. Grubs were already on the northern side of the gorge with Brumaks, crashing through the toll booths a hundred meters up the road. Where were the Gears? He caught a brief glance of a Centaur on its roof in the river below. If bodies had fallen into that torrent, the current would have carried them away by now. But there was small arms fire: he could hear bursts of it. A grenade round shot out and hit something in the center of the bridge.

Then he spotted them. High on the suspension towers, a few Gears were clinging to cables and trying to pick off grubs with Longspears and Lancers. It was valiant but utterly futile.

"Have we got radio contact with Four-ELI?" he asked. "Get on it, Anya. Warn them they're going to run into grubs if they don't swing further north."

Hoffman strained to look at the south pier. There were more grubs advancing. All he could do now was collapse the bridge, and he'd have to do it with men on it.

"Goddamn," he murmured.

Anya was right beside him. He didn't realize that until he pulled back into the crew bay and tried to work out the best area to paint with the laser. Common sense told him to hit the span as near to the southern edge as he could. That would at least stop more grubs crossing, even if most of them had surged across now.

Is it worth it?

Will the numbers matter?

The Gears on the bridge were going to be dead men anyway. There were still a few companies from what he still thought of as the 4 ELI—the 4th Ephyran Light Infantry—trying to make their way to Jacinto, and the grub advance would run right into them.

We should have blown the bridge from the start. Hindsight. Fuck it.

"Get us in close, Major," Hoffman said. "South pier. I need a target."

"I won't be able to hold position long if the grubs spot me. You okay with that laser?"

"Sure." How hard could it be? "Realistically, Major, can we winch those guys off the cables?"

"I'm willing to try."

Once he'd called in the Hammer strike, they'd know the bridge was doomed. Chances were that it wouldn't collapse completely. Yes, Hoffman was willing to try, too. He didn't ask Anya. This wasn't a vote, and things were agonizing enough as it was. He leveled the laser and wondered how the hell he was going to manage without the targeting optic.

"Okay, get me in position, Major."

Anya leaned close to Hoffman. "It's pretty much like a Lancer sight," she said. "You don't need to be so accurate with a big, stationary target."

Hoffman was too fond of her to say he knew that well enough and he didn't have any goddamned choice anyway, because Marcus had run off with a key component. He just concentrated on what he could see as Gettner slowed the

Raven to a hover about a hundred meters above the end of the bridge and held it steady.

Anya fiddled with her earpiece. She was usually the Hammer of Dawn interface at CIC anyway. She worked with this system far more than he did. "Hammer sat online. Ready when you are, sir."

It really was like aiming a rifle. The reticule settled on the tarmac a few meters onto the span but wouldn't lock on. He struggled to hold it steady. But like Anya said, the bridge was a big target and it wasn't going anywhere fast. Hoffman pressed the trigger to activate the laser targeting and waited.

If I could do this to a world, I can sure as shit do it to one goddamn bridge.

He counted. One, two, three . . .

A stream of fierce white light punched through the cloud and held steady on the bridge. Suddenly the surface erupted as if it had been detonated from below and a ball of flame and smoke obscured the target for a moment. When it cleared, there was a thirty or forty meter chunk missing from the span and Hoffman was looking down at the concrete stumps of a pier, bent and frayed metal girders sticking out of it at all angles. On the south bank of the gorge, a blast area had taken out the toll booths and the grub column had scattered.

"Nice shot, sir." Barber fired a few short bursts at something Hoffman couldn't see. "I'll hold them off now while we get those guys off those cables."

All Hoffman could think was that if he'd been here sooner, then he would have been hitting the north side of the gorge and the grubs would have been cut off, or at least held up until the COG forces could regroup. But he was just doing damage limitation now.

Much as he tried to save it for later, he couldn't stop himself thinking about Marcus, still unable to believe it. "Yeah, let's do it, Corporal."

There were still grubs on the bridge itself. Most had now streamed across, but a few were waiting and taking pot shots at the Raven. Hoffman was now in Gettner's hands. She banked again to give Barber a clear arc and went in for a strafing run. Heavy caliber rounds ripped through the road surface and cut some of the grubs in half.

"We're hit," Gettner said. "Nothing serious, though. One more trip around the buoy, Nat?"

Barber slapped in a fresh ammo belt at remarkable speed. "Yeah, let's not risk a perforated undercarriage while we're winching. Bring her around, Gill."

Hoffman hung on to the safety rail and tried to see how many Gears were still up there to be extracted. He could only see two as Barber opened fire. A couple of rounds hit the frame of the Raven's door but Hoffman couldn't tell if they'd passed through or embedded themselves.

"You're going to need me on that gun, Barber," Hoffman said. "I haven't the first idea how to operate a winch."

The automatic fire from below seemed to have stopped. Hoffman peered over the side at two men clinging to a narrow ledge on one of the towers. Judging by the thumbs-up gesture, they got the idea.

"Sure, sir," Barber said, swinging out of the gun seat. "Remember that you've got a blind spot below."

"I'll go nose-in," Gettner said. "Just make it snappy."

Hoffman hadn't used a heavy-cal gun in years. If circumstances had been different—if this had been a small victory rather than the aftermath of the unthinkable—then he would almost have enjoyed it. The Raven hovered with its tail over the river at 90 degrees to the bridge while Hoffman laid down bursts every time he thought he saw something move below. It was only when he heard the sound of a Lancer that he realized Anya had picked up his rifle and was loosing a few off from the other door.

And she's not qualified on a Lancer. Good girl. You'd be proud of her, Helena.

"How're we doing?" Gettner asked.

"Five meters . . ." Barber said. Hoffman glanced back for a moment and saw the two Gears dangling from the same winch line. "Three . . . two . . . one . . . on deck, disengaged."

"Okay, we're *gone.*"

The Raven swung around and climbed in one alarming corkscrew movement as Gettner pulled out of the range of grub fire. Hoffman watched the shattered bridge dwindle beneath him. When he eased himself out of the gun seat, feeling his age as the adrenaline ebbed, the two Gears were sitting on the deck, exhausted and smoke-stained.

One of them was busy patching up a bleeding hand. The other looked up at Hoffman.

"Thanks, sir," he said. "Fucking comm failure screwed us, didn't it?"

"Yeah," Hoffman said. He wanted to believe that. He wondered what it would do to morale when word got out about Marcus, as it surely would. "I'm sorry, son. Gettner, see if you can spot Four-ELI on the way back."

Two men out of ten companies. *Two men.* With the most immediate crisis over, Hoffman had nothing to distract him from the hardest duty he'd ever had to perform. He couldn't sweep this under the carpet.

Marcus Fenix was a goddamn hero. Most Gears were as far as Hoffman was concerned, but Marcus always went that bit further. He didn't need to be ordered to do anything. He'd always seemed to have no sense of personal danger whatsoever. If there was a risk to be taken, he'd be the one grabbing for it, not out of some sense of invincibility but because he seemed to think the world's troubles were his personal burden. And that was the problem. Hoffman realized that, even with his head throbbing and the taste of blood still in his mouth. Marcus would put himself on the line for anyone without thinking, even an ungrateful stranger, but this time his father had been the one who needed saving.

You asshole. Adam fucking God-Almighty Professor Fenix. This all is your goddamn fault. You've destroyed him. Your own son. What did you think he'd do when you called him to say goodbye, you self-centered prick?

Adam Fenix had been an infantry officer, 26 RTI just like Hoffman. He should have known better.

"Have we got comms with Jacinto yet?" he asked, looking at Anya. She was back on the bench seat again, looking ladylike if a little flushed. The Lancer was wedged between the struts. "We need to re-establish CIC there."

"Aigle's working on it. He's good."

That was all she said. All talk of Marcus was set aside. Whatever had happened, 4 ELI was still out of contact, and Hoffman couldn't tell if they'd scattered. He spotted a small convoy of 'Dills and Packhorses barreling down the Jacinto highway at high speed, but he couldn't see any trucks. Half an hour later, as he was wondering if he was so concussed that none of this was actually happening the way he thought, Anya touched his shoulder. Her face was stricken. It had to be bad news.

"Okay, I've got Temp CIC Jacinto," she said. She indicated his earpiece. "Strachan's Raven went down."

Hoffman felt sick to his gut. The thought crossed his mind that fate or divine providence had stepped in to spare the regiment the shame of Marcus's actions, but he hated himself instantly for it and could only think of Dom and the others who'd been on that sortie.

"Colonel? This is Reid. Ephyra's pretty well evacuated now along with South Jacinto, and I'm starting on the casualty lists."

Shit. If he was going to hear this from anybody, it had to be that asshole Reid, didn't it? Hoffman gritted his teeth. "Go ahead, Major."

"We lost the Raven, but Fenix was picked up alive."

"Adam?"

"Marcus."

There'd be no sorting it out privately now with a fistfight in one of the Raven hangars or a back alley, regimental-style. Hoffman had given up the right to that simple and effective summary justice the day he accepted a commission when he should have had the sense to remain an NCO. He was an officer now, not a sergeant. *You're the fucking Chief of Defense Staff. How in the name of God did that ever happen?* The rules were different. He had to be seen to be obeyed, not for his own sake but for all the Gears who followed orders and didn't have a father who was on first name terms with the Chairman.

"Is he conscious?"

"Not yet."

"What about Adam Fenix?"

"Dead, sir. They found his remains in the rubble."

"Who did? You sure?" Even with a cracked skull, Hoffman couldn't make that all fit. And if some Raven crew had pulled Marcus and Bravo Squad out of there, then they'd work out in about two seconds flat that he'd gone to get his father. Plenty of Gears would have heard Hoffman yelling on the radio, too. It would be common knowledge eventually that Marcus had disobeyed orders. Hoffman had run out of choices. "Who extracted them? How? Where's Professor Fenix's body?"

"KR-One-One got to them, sir. On the spot right away. Not sure who called it in, but it's pretty chaotic out there. East Barricade's been completely overrun. So that's most of Ephyra and part of Jacinto in Locust hands."

"How about Santiago?" Dom was special. He'd been with Hoffman since Aspho Point, one of his commandos, just about the last one left, and Hoffman wasn't ready to lose him. "Tell me Dom's okay."

"Yes, he's conscious now. Stratton and Kaliso have minor injuries."

Hoffman had to ask. "Did Santiago give any indication what his orders were?"

"No sir. Just seemed very upset about Professor Fenix and believes the mission to rescue him failed."

Hoffman rubbed his eyes one-handed. That, at least, sounded more typical of Marcus. Even if he'd hijacked his squad and a Raven crew to go off on this goddamn rescue, he still made sure they wouldn't be held responsible. He hadn't told them he'd refused an order and misused COG assets.

But he was still willing to risk their lives, though. *Asshole.* The fact that all of them would have done that for him anyway without a second's hesitation didn't make it okay.

Sometimes you thought you really knew a man, knew him well enough to stake your life on him, and then you found out how wrong you were.

Once the risk to Dom and the others sank in, Hoffman's decision was suddenly much easier. This wasn't about punching out a superior. In a way, it was even more than defying an order and losing Ephyra or Jacinto, although that was what would appear on the charge sheet and what would change the course of the war. At the moral heart of it, lurking in the little sour taste at the back of Hoffman's throat, it was about duping your buddies into taking part in the whole thing.

That was unforgivable, hero or not. But Hoffman had no other option anyway.

"Put a couple of MPs on standby," he said. "And when Fenix regains consciousness, have him detained and charged with dereliction of duty."

He didn't take that thought any further. It hurt too much. The penalty for doing shit like that in wartime—let alone in the middle of a battle—was the firing squad.

Unless Marcus entered a plea of not guilty and had some amazing mitigating circumstances to back that up, then Hoffman had just condemned one of the finest men he'd ever served with to death.

LOCATION UNKNOWN: DATE UNKNOWN.

The light was painfully bright. For a moment, Adam tried to reach out for the alarm clock, not sure what day it was, let alone the time. He'd be late for the office. Then a searing pain stabbed through his chest and stopped him from breathing for a few terrible seconds, an agony that said *thrashball game, bad tackle, my fault.* He heard a yelp and realized it was his own voice.

I've broken a damn rib.

How the hell did I do that this *time? Haven't played for years . . .*

It took his fogged brain a few seconds to start assembling the pieces of reality. *Rubble. I'm not dead. I'm in a hospital. Marcus. Where's Marcus? Is he okay? And Dom. Where are my notes?* Someone was leaning over him. He could smell antiseptic and coffee—antiseptic at close quarters, mixed with something floral, the coffee more distant—and then something pricked the back of his hand.

The fog began to lift. A middle-aged woman in green scrubs peered into his face and then stepped back. *Hospital. Yes, I'm in a hospital.* Crisp sheets felt cool and smooth under his hands. The bright light had resolved into a big window with a white roller blind, not a lamp at all. If this was Jacinto Medical Center, they still had better facilities than he'd realized.

"Is Marcus okay?" The voice that was somehow coming from outside his head didn't say that at all, though. It sounded more like a whimper. "Where is he?"

"You can talk to him now, sir," said a woman's voice. "But if he starts getting agitated, call me."

Sir? *Hoffman.* It had to be Hoffman. Adam struggled to look around, ready for the colonel's surly disapproval, but then he realized that "sir" wasn't Hoffman at all.

Richard Prescott was leaning against the wall next to a gold-framed watercolor of a lake. Whatever had happened in Ephyra, the urgency seemed to have passed.

"Feeling better, Adam?"

Prescott pushed himself away from the wall with casual slowness and went to reach for something out of Adam's field of vision. Water glugged and a servo whirred, then the head of the bed rose slowly and Adam found himself sitting up. It still hurt. He yelped.

"Broken ribs," Prescott said, handing him a crystal tumbler of water. "And a concussion. You're lucky to be alive. Can you manage to hold this?"

Adam wasn't sure, but he was damned if he was going to let anyone feed him like a child. He gripped the glass as hard as he could. The water was icy, the most delicious thing he'd ever tasted, and he gulped it down despite the pain at every swallow. Prescott waited patiently and took the empty tumbler from him.

"Marcus," Adam said. "Marcus was with me when the house was hit. Where is he?"

"He was discharged a while ago. He's fit."

Discharged. A while. How long? "Can I see him?"

"No. I'm afraid that won't be possible."

"Where is he?" *I should have asked about Dom.* "Are we still fighting?"

Prescott tilted his head slightly to one side and just stared down his nose as if he felt sorry for Adam, but that wasn't Prescott at all.

"The Locust took Chancery Bridge and overran most of Ephyra," he said quietly. "We've pulled everyone back to Jacinto."

"God . . ."

"God, indeed. We lost a lot of Gears. Anyway, let's talk about *you*, shall we?"

So Marcus was all right. Adam would get a call to him somehow, but his next thought was his research. How did he ask about it? The problem hadn't gone away. "Did anyone recover my briefcase?"

"Oh, yes." Prescott had adopted that deceptively mild tone that he usually reserved for staff too junior and insignificant to be worth dressing down. "Captain Dury recovered your effects."

Adam had no idea who Dury was. He was more concerned about where that case was and getting it back. He wasn't thinking as fast as he usually did, but even in this state he knew that someone might have opened it and wondered what the hell was in those jars. He hoped they understood what a biohazard sticker meant and hadn't tried to open them.

"I need to get back to work. When are they going to discharge me?" *I can explain this. I have to.* Damn, he needed more water. "Look, I generally try to avoid clichés, but where am I? This isn't JMC."

"No, it's Azura. Some considerable distance south of Jacinto."

"Never heard of it."

"I should hope not. Although your research did enable us to keep it that way. We drown in irony, don't we, Adam?"

The other shoe was slowly dropping, although Adam wasn't sure quite where. "Is this some kind of game?"

"You tell me, Adam. I'm the man who's been kept in the dark, after all." Prescott opened a vent at the top of the window. The air that swept in was the kind that Adam hadn't smelled in many years: warm, clean, oceanic, laden with wet green scents and tropical flowers. He couldn't think of anywhere on the south Tyran coast that was either that warm or that had escaped the worst of the Locust onslaught. "But tell me. How's Myrrah? That *is* how one pronounces it, yes?"

Her name was like a punch in the mouth. It had to be said sooner or later, but no matter how many times he'd imagined this moment, Adam wasn't ready for his stomach to knot so hard that he felt sick. It might have been the medication, but he doubted it. Guilt was a powerful emetic. *Did I write the name down? Have they been tapping my phone?* But at least he didn't have to work out how he was going to break the sordid, shameful truth to Prescott now. He just had to answer the question.

I kept it to myself for a day. Then a week: a month: a year. Then it was too hard to ever share it at all. Why? How did it all get to be so difficult?

Marcus was going to have to live with the shame of having a traitor for a father.

"I'm waiting, Adam," said Prescott.

"Yes. Myrrah. *Meer-ah.*" Adam wondered if he should explain who she was. "For want of a better word, the Locust Queen."

"We're being very civilized, aren't we? No insults, no threats, no outrage. I imagine you thought I'd be asking Dury to increase the voltage to your more sensitive areas by now."

So Dury was a security agent of some kind. "That should tell me something, shouldn't it?"

"I had you down for a security risk, but only because I thought you'd be too outspoken and want to blurt out everything in public. I pride myself on being a good judge of liability. But I was completely wrong about you."

Adam wanted to explain that he'd done it out of a mistaken confidence in his own ability, that he wasn't a collaborator, but it was a very technical distinction right now. "I genuinely thought I could avert a war."

"Oh, I do believe you. What was it? Let's not start a panic? Let's study this? Let's not overreact? I can understand. Academic arrogance, a sense of entitlement, doing what's best for the little people—I come from the same class as you, Adam. I know how privilege can distort our sense of reality. But omitting to mention it after it all goes wrong and for so long—very plebeian. Very ordinary. Very criminal."

"I didn't sell out my species to save my own skin, if that's what you're thinking."

"The end result was the same."

"The difference matters to me, though."

"The Locust could have killed you. What did you offer them?"

"Help."

"*Help?*"

"If I'd thought preparedness would have saved us, I would have warned Dalyell before they emerged. If we'd attacked them in the tunnels, we would have been cut to pieces, and any chance of negotiation would have been lost."

"You were banking on cutting a deal right up to the last minute."

"Like Dalyell did in the Pendulum Wars."

"Don't even start on that line of argument," Prescott said, shaking his head slowly. It was more a show of disdain than anger. He was an actor. He didn't so much as twitch or blink without planning the ideal moment to do it. "That's disingenuous, Adam. Intellectually unworthy. That was never your decision to take, even as a scientist. You're not a biologist. This isn't some kind of eccentric gentleman's hobby. You were dealing with an obvious global threat." He paused. "*Two*, in fact. You knew about Lambency."

"You've read my notes, then."

"Dr. Estrom's assessing them now with the life sciences team, but I've had a summary so far. And they've quarantined the samples. I only hope that your sloppy methodology hasn't spread the contamination further."

Nevil Estrom. Life sciences team. Azura. What in the name of God was going on?

Adam's clarity was returning, painkillers or not. "If I'd been able to develop a countermeasure for Lambency before Myrrah's patience ran out, the Locust would have been a scientific curiosity, nothing more."

For some reason that seemed to irritate Prescott, or at least he made a show of it. "And we'd all live happily ever after. When will you people ever grow up? I can factor in greed or malice, but not naivety."

"You have a lot to learn about the Locust."

"Not as much as you might think."

Prescott didn't elaborate. If there was such a thing as spontaneous reaction from him, that was a rare example. He was an icon of self-control. Adam had rarely been able to read him, and he knew that the only times that he had were when Prescott had allowed him to. There was now a faint smile playing on Prescott's lips, but it wasn't amused or kind or sympathetic. It was reluctant tolerance. He walked slowly across the room to the window blinds, one hand in his pocket, and took the cord in the other hand as if he was about to unveil a dedication plaque.

He didn't say a word. He just pulled the cord.

Light flooded the room, ferocious sunlight, as hot and intense on Adam's face as a day on the beach. He had to shut his eyes for a moment. It took him a few seconds to adjust and start to make sense of the view from the window.

Palm trees rustled in a light breeze. The sky was a searing turquoise but he could also see black cloud creeping into the postcard scene from the far left.

He wasn't in Jacinto, but then he already knew that.

"There." Prescott's voice was so quiet he had to strain to hear it. "We both kept our secrets, but mine were constructive. I'll take you on a tour of the island, when the doctor lets you out. Meet your staff. Get to know your facilities."

Island? For a moment he wondered if this was the biological and chemical research base on Vectes, but the scenery was all wrong and that place had been shut down years ago. "What facilities?"

Adam struggled with the welter of information and tried to fit it into the strange landscape outside his window. He'd been concussed. Prescott had said

so. He'd been medicated. Perhaps this was all part of a richly detailed halluci-
nation. Prescott, still looking out of the window, put his finger up to the glass.
On the other side, a brilliant magenta gem of a hummingbird hovered there
for a moment before darting away.

"You're a traitor, Adam," Prescott said quietly. He ambled back to the bed-
side and reached into his jacket to take out a small notebook, then tossed it
into Adam's lap. "And your wife was a traitor, too."

It was one of Elain's field notebooks. *You bastard. Don't you dare. Don't you
dare insult her memory.* Prescott knew how to goad him. The son of a bitch
was damn lucky that Adam was too weak to land a punch and too much of a
gentleman to use the rich list of obscenities he'd picked up from his Gears in
his army days.

"My wife," Adam growled, "was a scientist and a patriot. She gave her damn
life to get that information. Those goddamn notes may be all we have to save us."

Prescott didn't blink. The hummingbird was back again, zipping back and
forth in front of the window. Adam tried to ignore it. His brain struggled to
focus, torn between worry for Marcus, anger about Elain, and complete helpless disorientation.

"That luminous substance in the jars," Prescott said. "Is all imulsion some
form of Lambency, then?"

"I think so. It seems to have a long and complex life cycle."

"So how much time do we have to beat this thing?"

"I only know that it's spreading," Adam said. "So let's assume we don't have
long."

"Then you'd better get some rest so that we can put you to work as soon as
possible."

Prescott looked at Adam for a few moments as if he'd never seen him before
and was wondering why his face seemed familiar. Adam was beginning to realize he was a prisoner.

"I'm ready now."

"I don't want you dying on me, Adam. And that's not sympathy, by the way."

"Does Marcus know I'm here? Wherever *here* is."

"No. He thinks you're dead."

Adam's gut knotted. He didn't know his son half as well as he wanted to,
but he knew this: Marcus would be devastated, and he would blame himself.
Adam struggled to sit up and swing his legs out of bed. He was going to punch
Prescott into the middle of next week.

"You sadistic *bastard.*" He managed to get his feet on the floor. Pushing up with his arms was another matter. The pain brought tears to his eyes. "Why? What the hell are you getting out of *that*? Are you wiping me off the map? Fine, damn well do whatever you want to me, and God knows I deserve it, but don't make Marcus suffer. Try me for treason, whatever you like, but don't take it out on *him*."

Adam managed to stand up, unable to preserve any dignity in a hospital gown flapping open at the back, but his temper had taken over and he was damned if he'd just lie there and take this. Prescott looked at him, expression hardening.

"Would you rather we get this over with in one fell swoop, Adam?" Prescott watched him totter to the end of the bed, hand over hand on the metal rail. "Because I would. Marcus is in custody awaiting court-martial because he refused an order and assaulted the Chief of the Defense Staff. We lost Chancery Bridge as a result. He cost us Ephyra and a great many lives. Do you understand, Adam? He neglected his duty in the middle of a battle to try to rescue you. Your son. The COG's Embry Star hero. You know the penalty for that."

Adam did. It was a mandatory death sentence: a firing squad.

"Marcus would *never* do that." Adam fought down a rising tide of nausea. "You know he wouldn't."

"He did, and he's pleading guilty."

Adam refused to believe it. It had to be a mistake. The anguish and frustration almost knocked him flat. "And you're telling me this because you're going to use it as a bargaining chip, aren't you?" he said. "Or is this just the only punishment open to you because you need me too badly to put a round through my head, however much you want to?"

"I don't think you need motivation to work on a countermeasure for Lambency." Prescott glanced out of the window. "But I don't want you distracted by anything else, so I'm offering to intervene and have the sentence commuted to life. I want you to focus."

"I want him freed."

"Sorry. It's too late for that. I can't."

"You're the Chairman and we're under martial law. You can do anything you want."

"No, even I have limits. I can't let men be seen to get away with disobedience on that scale. It's bad for morale, bad for discipline, and it undermines my commanders. He punched Hoffman to the ground when he gave him the order, for God's sake. I can't make that go away. I have to back my officers."

Adam was wary of Hoffman, but Marcus always seemed to like and respect him. It seemed utterly out of character. There had to be more to it than that. But perhaps he'd lost touch with the real Marcus so long ago that this was what his boy had become.

"Hoffman's insisting on this, I suppose."

"Actually, Hoffman's mortified. He likes Marcus. He certainly admires him. But there are some things that just can't be brushed under the carpet."

"Then let me speak to him. At least let him know I'm alive."

"And how will I explain your absence?"

"He understands opsec better than anyone."

Prescott did a little contemptuous snort. "This isn't petty spite on my part. This is about Azura. This facility has to remain secret from everyone, even Hoffman. I regret what's going to happen to your son, but he's collateral damage in the scheme of things."

"He's my *son*. Can you understand that? No, of course not, you son of a bitch. You don't have a family."

Prescott blinked, nothing more. "Neither does most of Sera. That's partly my doing, but now we know it's also *yours*."

The bastard never missed a chance. The fact that he was right made each twist of the knife even more painful. Adam was still hanging on to the end of the bed, unable to move forward. If he let go and tried to stand unsupported, he knew he'd collapse.

"Bring him here, then. Use a cover story. I'll do anything you want."

"Justice has to be seen to be done, Adam."

"Prison will kill him."

"And what do you think the shame of having traitors for parents is going to do?"

"Come on, Richard, look at his service record. Hasn't he earned some latitude?"

"Damn it, *he lost us Ephyra*. Why shouldn't he pay the price for all those men's lives? Because he's a Fenix and not just any old riffraff? What would we have done to Private J. Working-Class Oaf if he'd run out on a battle like that?"

Prescott opened the door for a moment and beckoned to someone. Adam heard the soft tread of shoes on tiles and a distant voice announcing something over a PA system, but he couldn't make out the words. He dithered for a moment, wondering if he might make it across the room after all, but Prescott walked over to him and caught his arm. It was a disturbingly helpful gesture under the circumstances.

"We have *lineage*, Adam." Prescott looked him in the eye. His lips compressed into a thin line at the end of each sentence, as if he was slamming a door to stop real, ugly fury from escaping. He'd obviously been raised as Adam had, in that upper-class way that forbade a gentleman to raise his voice anywhere but the battlefield. "We have a duty born of privilege and ancestry. We do *not* have the right to choose to do otherwise."

Adam could hear the purr of rubber tires and a faint metallic noise outside, and then a nurse in a white tunic pushed a wheelchair into the room.

"Come along, Professor." She was about thirty, well fed and tanned, nothing like the hard-pressed, threadbare medical staff in Jacinto. She held out a dark gray plaid garment. "We've got a nice bathrobe for you, too. Can't have you wandering around like that and scandalizing the ladies, can we?"

Adam submitted to the indignity of being helped into the bathrobe and struggled into the chair, ribs screaming. They hurt so much he couldn't even wheel himself along. Prescott took the handles and pushed the chair out into a corridor unlike anything Adam could remember seeing in Jacinto.

This was a state-of-the-art hospital, and relaxed staff in pristine white walked calmly back and forth as if they'd never had to sweat in a blood-soaked ER to save Gears and civilians torn and shredded by the fighting that had been part of Adam's life ever since he was old enough to notice, first the Pendulum Wars, and now something far, far worse.

Prescott pushed him through double doors into a sun lounge tastefully decorated with potted plants and lush upholstered chairs. This was too menial a task for the leader of the last government on Sera. It was also not the gesture of a kind friend. Adam was sure that Prescott was making the point that he was now totally under his control, and that he would go only where Prescott pleased. On the public address system, Adam could hear a soothing voice he thought he recognized, but it was the content rather than the familiarity that shocked him.

". . . *and don't forget that there'll be a guided walk around the forest this weekend in search of our rarer orchid species, as well as a healthy eating seminar at . . .*"

He didn't catch the end of the sentence. Another set of doors opened and he found himself on a balcony overlooking exquisite landscaped gardens, a mass of fountains and flower beds bathed in full sun. Beyond the gardens, a complex of honey-gold towers and ornate buildings overlooked a beach, and men and women in civilian clothes or lab coats walked around as if they had nothing much on their agenda. It might as well have been another world, because it certainly wasn't the Sera he knew.

And then there was the sky, which couldn't possibly be.

It was blue and clear above, but when he looked out at the ocean, the worst imaginable tropical storm seemed to be rolling in and Prescott didn't seem troubled by it. The black clouds were sucking up water from the surface, forming a wall that stretched as far as he could see. It was so shocking that his uppermost thoughts—Marcus, Marcus, Marcus—were forgotten for a moment.

"So you did it," he said. "You got a Maelstrom operational."

"Clever, isn't it? I suppose I should thank you for helping make it possible." Prescott parked Adam's chair and leaned on the rail of the balcony next to him. "A permanent artificial storm. The perfect camouflage and defensive barrier. Welcome to Azura, Adam. The COG's doomsday bunker."

CHAPTER 5

The Slab was like a septic tank. You tipped the shit in, walked away, and for a while it stank, but then it developed bacteria and became a self-sustaining environment. No sane warder would get within punching distance of a prisoner because the inmates had plenty of reasons to kill us and nothing to lose. So when the Justice Department cut our staffing levels, we started leaving the inmates to run the place themselves while we kept a nice safe distance. Okay, there was a lot of bloodletting. I mean, lots of it. But the guys who survived settled down into a kind of scum ecosystem and started looking after themselves pretty well.

(Kennith Heugel, former warder at CPSE Hesketh—aka the Slab.)

HOUSE OF THE SOVEREIGNS, NORTH EPHYRA: BRUME, 10 A.E.

The only part of Ephyra that the COG hadn't lost completely to the grubs was the northern borough, the home of government offices and official buildings, and the irony wasn't lost on Dom.

They still had somewhere to hold a proper court-martial.

He hadn't been allowed to see Marcus since the sortie to Haldane Hall. The last thing he remembered was yelling at him to get down when the Reavers attacked. How the casevac Raven had managed to extract them so fast was close to a miracle. He was still putting the pieces together to work out how he ended up in the hospital, because Tai still swore that neither he or Jace had managed to call for casevac. Right now, though, it was a minor mystery that could wait.

Marcus was in that room at the end of the corridor arguing for his life. Dom had to keep his mind on that. Marcus hadn't been making much sense when they dragged him on board, and then he was knocked out when the medic pumped him full of something, so there had been no discussion. When they landed, Marcus had been put under armed guard in the hospital.

Dom needed to talk to him. He needed to get his story straight, to prepare his defense, but nobody had said a word to him or even to Anya. She was going to be a witness, wasn't she? That was going to be terrible for her. That was probably why she hadn't been allowed to see or speak to Marcus either. She said it was killing her. Dom believed it.

He waited in the wood-paneled corridor, sitting almost on the edge of the bench while he waited to be called to give evidence. He'd already given a written statement about the sortie to Haldane Hall, and he'd asked if he could be a character witness. The last thing he could remember was hearing Marcus yelling for his father and the weird whistling sound as a rotor or something skimmed past his head before he hit the ground hard.

Why haven't they called Tai, or Jace?

Dom had no real idea how court-martials worked. He wasn't even sure that was the right name for more than one. *Courts-martial? Come on, does that shit matter now?* He thought they'd be like civilian trials without juries, like a magistrates' court, except that there'd be officers in place of lawyers for the prosecution and defense. But there was nobody milling around outside the courtroom like in the movies. But the corridor was deserted. Occasionally a side door would open and a female Gear or civilian would come out with a sheaf of papers and vanish through another door. Dom had expected to see some media there, too, but maybe they were in the courtroom. They could hear the whole case if there was no classified information in the evidence. Witnesses couldn't.

Then he heard footsteps, two pairs, one made by heavy boots, one by high heels. He knew who it was without looking up. He stared down at his clasped hands until the steps got closer and waited until the last second to stand to attention as Hoffman stopped in front of him.

It was hard to tell who looked worse and more distraught, Hoffman or Anya. Dom saluted. It was a very formal day today.

"Where *is* everybody, sir?" He wanted Hoffman to look him in the eye. "Is this all being hushed up?"

Hoffman gave Anya a sideways glance. She fiddled with her jacket, picking off imaginary lint.

"Look, you can tell me stuff without . . . prejudicing the hearing, can't you?" That was the right phrase, Dom was sure of it. "I mean, I know I can't talk to Marcus, but this isn't . . . Goddamn it, sir, I expected you to level with me, after all this time."

Hoffman looked up at the ceiling for a moment. It was his embarrassment gesture, not impatience. He really didn't know how to deal with this any more than Dom did. Dom could see it. But he still didn't believe it.

"I didn't want this, Dom," Hoffman said. "But once it happened, it acquired a life of its own. And it isn't going to end happily. I'm sorry."

They were very plain, low-key words, but they shocked Dom to his gut. He'd never heard Hoffman talk like that before, and they'd been in some pretty damn harsh spots over the years. Hoffman walked away in the direction of the men's washroom, very deliberate, leaving Dom with Anya.

"Okay, Anya, *you* tell me, then," Dom whispered. "No evidence stuff. Just tell me. I know I can't talk to him yet, but what has he said to you?"

Anya chewed her lip for a moment, then braced her shoulders.

"I kept asking, but he refused to see me anyway."

"What? Oh, you're a witness. Yeah. Sorry."

"No, he won't talk to me at all. He won't even say why." She reached out and caught Dom's hand, squeezing it. It felt desperate. "He's pleading guilty. There's no evidence to give."

Guilty? Shit, that was insane. "But he didn't *do it*. Not Marcus."

"He did, Dom. He did." Anya's brow creased for a second. She looked like she'd run out of tears. "You know he did. I was there. I saw it, and he was someone I didn't know. Don't you believe me?"

Dom realized he'd been clinging to a complete fantasy for weeks, some stupid childlike idea that all this was a misunderstanding and Hoffman or Anya would come up with a sensible explanation that the Judge Advocate would accept, and Marcus would just get busted down to corporal.

But this was real. Marcus was going to face a firing squad. He'd made sure of that by entering a guilty plea.

"And we're just going to let him die?"

"No, we're going to think of something, Dom. I swear it."

"I'm not taking it. I'm *not*. And he kept us out of it."

"You didn't know what he was doing, did you?"

Dom felt guilty for even admitting he didn't. It felt like he was denying Marcus. "No. But I don't know if I would have stopped him if I had."

They fell silent. It was so quiet in the corridor that Dom heard the toilet flush. Hoffman came out of the washroom a few minutes later. There was nothing they could do but wait, although Dom now had no idea what they were waiting for if all the court had to do was pass the only sentence on the statute books that military law allowed.

They won't carry it out right away. I can ask to see Prescott. Dom's mind was racing. *Who are they going to get to volunteer for a firing squad anyway? No Gear would want to shoot Marcus.*

He looked at his palms, wet with sweat. He couldn't meet Hoffman's eye and now he couldn't look at Anya. When the double doors swung open and a woman lieutenant came out, he was expecting Hoffman to be called in, but she beckoned to Dom instead.

She was a redhead and she had one arm. Dom was completely thrown by that. Why he was surprised that disabled Gears did admin jobs he had no idea. It was just that she was a woman, and it seemed especially tragic for no sensible reason.

"Private Santiago?" she said. He was the only grunt there. "The President of the Board's about to pass sentence. This is when you get to give evidence of character. Come with me. Come to attention at the lectern, salute, repeat the oath, and make your statement when asked to do so."

All Dom could see when he walked in was the lectern, the kind everyone used for briefings, nothing special or grand or ceremonial. Then he took in the rest. The room looked like a school gymnasium that needed a coat of paint. The board—the three officers who were judge and jury—were just sitting at a plain table at the end of the room with a civilian clerk almost taking cover behind a pile of blue, leather-bound books. There were two more tables on each side at right angles facing one another. Marcus—no do-rag, no armor, in his number two uniform that really didn't fall right on him—sat on the left hand side with a pilot officer Dom didn't even recognize, presumably his appointed counsel. To the right, a captain with an artillery flash was taking a great interest in the surface of his table. If he was the prosecution, he hadn't had a lot to do.

Is this it? They decide on a man's life in a scruffy place like this, just these guys, nobody to watch or check on them? God Almighty.

Dom did as ordered and saluted. "Sir, Private Dominic Santiago, 26th Royal Tyran Infantry."

The board president, a NCOG commander, looked awkward. It probably wasn't every day that he got to sentence a Gear with an Embry Star to death, and at least he had the grace to look unhappy about it. It was just a damn formality. Dom was still going to give it everything he had.

"Private Santiago, do you swear to answer truthfully all questions put to you, to conceal no material facts, and to accept responsibility for the consequences of your intervention?"

It was the COG tribunal oath. "I so swear, sir," Dom said.

"Very well, make your submission in support of Sergeant Marcus Michael Fenix."

Dom reached into his jacket for his notes, but stopped. No, he'd have his say. He never had been much good at speeches, but he was just great at explaining why Marcus was the finest human being he knew. What had he got to lose?

"Sir, you know Sergeant Fenix's service record," he said. "He's been frontline since he was old enough to enlist. He's never pulled any crap about being rich or from a founding family, if you'll pardon my language, sir, and he's put his life on the line for us and for civvies more times than I can count. It suited you and the Chairman to use all the smart weapons Professor Fenix developed, so in a way Marcus was just trying to protect your top asset. Now, my brother Carlos was happy to die to save Marcus's life, and so am I, in a heartbeat. Recognize what he's done for the COG. Without him, we wouldn't have the Hammer of Dawn, and half of us wouldn't be here now. Maybe *none* of us. That's all I've got to say, sir."

The room was horribly silent. Dom expected the panel to retire to consider the sentence, but they just sat there scribbling notes to one another. He stared straight ahead until he couldn't take it any longer and had to glance at Marcus. For a second, no more, their eyes locked and Dom couldn't read his expression at all. Marcus looked old and tired and beaten. He looked like he wanted out. That terrified Dom.

Maybe he really had cracked up. Traumatic stress was waiting for all of them sooner or later.

"Thank you, Private," the commander said. It was almost as if he hadn't been listening. "Given the evidence and the circumstances, we rule that the death penalty is inappropriate in this case and we sentence Sergeant Fenix to forty years in prison. This court is now adjourned."

No, that wasn't what Dom was expecting at all. He looked at Marcus and for a second, the horror showed on his face. There was only one prison still running in Ephyra: the maximum security jail, Hesketh—the Slab.

You wanted to die. Forty years in the Slab. That's the same damn thing.

I swore to accept responsibility for the consequences of my intervention. Oh God . . .

Two military police walked in and escorted Marcus out the back door. He didn't even look at Dom. The redheaded lieutenant ushered Dom through the main doors, but Hoffman and Anya weren't waiting outside.

He couldn't leave it like this. "Don't I even get to say goodbye to Sergeant Fenix, ma'am?" Dom asked.

She gave him an embarrassed nod. That was the tone of the whole procedure: embarrassment. An Embry Star hero had lost it and betrayed the trust his comrades had put in him. There was no anger or disgust, just *embarrassment*. The COG was a strange, restrained animal in some ways.

"You got the Embry Star too, didn't you?" the lieutenant said. "For Aspho Point. Special forces."

"Yes ma'am."

"Come on, then. This way."

Dom didn't make a big thing of the medal, but right then he was glad it did the job. He followed her down the corridor and through a set of security doors to a door marked DETENTION AREA. She opened the door and gestured at him to go in. He could already see the thin yellow light of an old tungsten bulb and the shadow of bars on the tiled floor.

"In you go," she said. "Don't hang about too long."

When Dom walked into the lobby, Marcus was staring at the cell floor, hands behind his back, boots a little way apart. He didn't look up. Dom waited.

"Hey, Marcus . . . I didn't know they'd do that."

Marcus's eyes were still fixed on the floor.

"Look at me," Dom said. He felt like shit. He'd never cope if Marcus turned on him. "Come on, look at me. *Please*. Don't you want to see Anya? Goddamn it, Marcus, *talk to me*. What do I tell Anya? She wanted to see you. You can't shut her out like that."

Marcus finally looked up. Dom had never seen that look on his face before. It was total defeat. His eyes were glassy. "Tell her to forget me and get on with her life."

"Oh, that's bullshit. That's total *bullshit*."

"I don't want her to remember me like this. Both of you—just walk away. No visiting, no letters, nothing. Just go."

Marcus rarely talked about his feelings. Dom had always had to guess what he was thinking, and he'd gotten pretty good at it over the years. It broke his heart. "You can stop that shit right now, Marcus, because I'm going to get you out. They've already given you a lighter sentence. There's more room for maneuver."

"Dom—"

"I swear it, Marcus. I'll get a lawyer. I'll—"

"*Don't*. I'm guilty. I fucked up everything."

"Marcus, you can't just give up."

"I can, and you better do the same." He took a step forward toward the bars. "I'm *dead*, like I should have been a long time ago. So get out of here and just look after yourself. That's all I want, Dom. I want you to be okay."

"How the hell can I be okay when you're rotting in that shithole?"

"Because I'm asking you to. Do it. And take care of Anya. Do it for me."

Marcus straightened up for a moment and stared into his face as if it was for the last time and he wanted to remember what Dom looked like. Then he turned his back and rapped on the cell door for the MP to take him away.

"I'm not done, Marcus."

"Goodbye, Dom."

"You hear me? I'm going to get you out of there."

Keys rattled in the cell door. Marcus stood square on to it, arms held in front like he was waiting to offer them up to be cuffed. He looked back over his shoulder just once.

"You and Carlos, Dom," he said. "You were my family. That was the best of me."

The door opened just as someone put their hand on Dom's shoulder. He turned. It was just the JAG lieutenant, the redhead, but by the time he turned around again the cell door was closing and Marcus was gone.

"Oh, goddamn it, no—"

"This way, Private," the lieutenant said, as if he was an asshole for even talking to Marcus.

"I can't just leave it like that."

"You can, and you will."

Dom wanted to make her listen and tell her about every time that Marcus had risked his life for someone, or hadn't given a shit about his own safety, or had plodded patiently around stinking Stranded camps in what little off-duty time he had to help Dom look for Maria. He wanted to remind her that Marcus had the money and connections to make sure he never had to serve at all, but he'd enlisted gladly and never once used his privilege. He wanted to tell her that he loved Marcus every bit as much as he'd loved his real brother Carlos. But there didn't seem to be any point, because one fact was clear and concrete and completely inexplicable: Marcus had gone to rescue his father instead of doing his duty, and a lot of Gears had died because of that.

Dom just started walking down the corridor, conscious of the loud click of unfamiliar leather parade boots on the parquet floor. It sounded a lot like the floors of Haldane Hall, and Haldane Hall was mostly rubble now.

The cool air hit his face as he stepped outside the main doors and waited at the top of the steps, not even sure what he was doing. He heard footsteps behind him. He didn't turn this time.

"Dom," Hoffman said. "Talk to me."

Being numb had its advantages. This was his CO, the man he'd looked up to since he was seventeen or eighteen, not some waste-of-space officer but a real fighting Gear who'd come up from the ranks and knew the score. Dom would have cheerfully died for Hoffman if he'd ordered it. Now he had no idea what to say and decided it didn't matter what came out of his mouth next.

What else could he have done? Seriously, what could he do, put Marcus on latrine duty for a month and tell him not to be a naughty boy again?

"So did you think that was a softer option?" Dom asked.

"What?"

"Forty years rather than a firing squad. You got it commuted."

"That came as a surprise to me, too, Dom." Dom didn't turn around so Hoffman took a step in front of him. "Maybe the Judge Advocate took notice of your letter. I have no idea. Maybe the Fenix name counts for something."

"He'd rather have been shot, sir. You know that."

"Yeah. I do. I damn well *do*." Hoffman looked pretty cut up. Dom thought he looked a little puffy around the eyes, like he'd been awake all night sweating about it or maybe even crying. "Look, if I could have found one single damn reason for *not* having him charged, I'd have grabbed it with both hands. But I couldn't. Make an exception for Fenix, and the whole thing falls apart. Everybody heard what went down on the radio. Where does that leave us if I say it's okay for Fenix to do it, but anyone else gets shot at dawn?"

"Sir, everyone knows he's never done anything like that before."

"Men died who probably shouldn't have. And you and Jace and Tai—what if you'd been killed in this goddamn insanity? You didn't volunteer. Fenix didn't even tell you."

"And if he had, I'd have gone with him."

Hoffman ignored that. A lot of officers wouldn't have. Dom didn't know if he would have knowingly disobeyed orders or not, but it was what he felt at that moment, and Hoffman could ram it.

Hoffman took his cap off and turned it over in his hands a few times, making the leather creak. Then he tapped the colonel's insignia on his collar.

"See this?" He was right in Dom's face now, so close that Dom could smell the coffee on his breath and the faint eucalyptus scent of shaving foam. "It's not a reward or a privilege. It's a fucking *burden*. No Gear gets to do whatever he wants, but this goddamn tin shit says I can't stick by my buddies any longer. It says I've got to see the bigger picture and the greater good and all kinds of cold hard fuckery, whether I want to or not. And I *don't* want to, you know that? I want to be Staff Sergeant Hoffman again, except if they gave me the chance, I'd know I was chickening out and leaving the tough decisions to some other unlucky bastard. So I do it. *It's my duty.* Like it was Marcus's duty to get that laser to Tomas. I bet half the Gears out there would love to go rescue their families rather than fight, but they don't. *That's* why Marcus Fenix is a disgrace to the uniform. He let his comrades down, and that's all an army is—your willingness to stand with your brothers in arms, and die with them if need be."

It was all true and all the more painful for it. Dom felt his eyes brimming and the pressure building at the back of his throat. If he cried, he wouldn't even know exactly why. He didn't want to think any less of Marcus.

"Who are you trying to convince, sir?" he asked.

"No fucking idea, Dom," Hoffman muttered. "But not myself." Then he put his cap back on and stalked off.

Dom stood on the steps until he realized he had no idea how long he'd been there. But the sun was setting behind the Tomb of the Unknowns, and he debated whether to find Carlos's grave and explain the whole shitty thing to him.

He didn't pay his respects half as often as he'd intended. Carlos had been dead nearly twelve years now. Dom couldn't think of anything better to do right then and made his way through the colonnade to the immaculately tended graveyard next to the mausoleum. This was where the COG interred its heroes. Marcus had been a hero once. Carlos hadn't planned to be one, and maybe he'd fucked up too, but at the end he died so that Marcus didn't. That was all that mattered to Dom right then.

The gravel crunched under Dom's boots as he came to a halt at the grave. The inscription on the headstone was as crisp as the day it had been dedicated. It was almost twelve years to the day that he'd died.

PRIVATE CARLOS BENEDICTO SANTIAGO, ES, 26 RTI—FALLEN AT ASPHO FIELDS, OSTRI,
15TH DAY OF BRUME, 77TH YEAR OF THE WAR, AGED 20

All three of them, brothers either in fact or feeling, all awarded the Embry Star for gallantry, and where were they now? Nobody remembered Carlos, Marcus was disgraced, and Dom—he felt like a goddamned ghost. He squatted on his heels, uncomfortable in his formal uniform.

"What would you do, Carlos?" he whispered. "Hey, like I need to ask. You thought he was worth dying for." He wiped his nose on the back of his hand, eyes welling. "I better get him out of there, right? Yeah. That's it. You rest easy, *Carlito.*"

The walk back to the barracks was the longest he'd ever taken. Marcus had been his friend since Dom was eight years old and the world couldn't possibly be the same without him. Dom had spent the last few weeks trying to get used to him not being around but it was impossible. He'd look over his shoulder, expecting to see Marcus, or remember something he needed to tell him, and Marcus simply wasn't there. Now that was going to be permanent unless he damn well did something about it.

I should be out there looking for Maria. Stranded camps shift all the time.

Dom didn't *want* to get used to Marcus being gone. The more pain he felt, the more he was motivated to do something about it.

Like Maria. If I ever stop feeling lost without her, I'll stop looking for her. And she's still out there, I know it. She needs me to find her.

And Marcus needed him, too.

Dom went back to his quarters, hung up his uniform, and started working out what it would take to get Marcus out of the Slab before that place finished him off.

JACINTO MAXIMUM SECURITY PRISON, CPSE HESKETH, AKA THE SLAB.

The dogs were going crazy.

Nikolai Jarvi leaned on the wrought iron rail, arms folded, and watched the lockdown begin on the grimy floor below. There were no prison officers down there. They weren't needed. The gallery that ran around the upper floor of the jail was by far the safest place to be, and it wasn't just because of the prisoners.

The warning siren sounded in a steady pulse. *"Twenty seconds,"* said the public address system.

Frantic barking and thuds almost drowned out the count. The dogs flung themselves against the wooden door like they did at every lockdown, demanding to be let loose. The door was all part of the calculated psychological process. It was the only one in here made from hollow softwood panels instead of heavy mahogany or metal, because the animals could pound against it and make a terrifying noise without actually injuring themselves. It was like beating a drum. The wild noise said uncontrolled savagery could be unleashed at any moment, and it also hinted that one day the dogs would smash the door down before the final siren and start tearing prisoners apart anyway.

It always did the trick. Any prisoner stupid enough not to obey the order to get back to his cell in time knew what would happen when that door opened.

It was the first thing Niko had been told when he was drafted to work here: the Slab ran on three doors—one to the warders' territory, one to the kitchens and latrines, and one to the dogs. The dogs could be released pretty well anywhere in the prison using the remote-controlled portcullis gates in the network of mesh runs along the corridors. It worked a lot better than sending officers down there to sort a guy out. Trap a difficult bastard in one of the mesh passages, open the gates, and suddenly he wasn't in the frame of mind to be a bad boy ever again.

Niko had never authorized that on his watch. What went on when he wasn't there was another matter.

"Ten seconds."

The big, empty floor was already deserted. Every prisoner was back in his cell, willing the bars to slide shut and protect him from the crazed pack.

And they got a psychiatrist to work that out. A doctor. An educated man who's supposed to help people feel better, not terrify the shit out of them. Hypocritical asshole.

It wasn't that Niko had any sympathy for the bastards banged up in here. He didn't; most of them deserved a bullet, not humane care. But that was a separate issue. It was the sadistic creativity of nice middle-class professionals that unsettled him. Sometimes he wasn't sure where the line lay between the criminals he had to keep away from society and the people who told him how to do it.

"Lockdown."

The steel bars on each cell slid shut with a loud clang a second before the wooden door opened and the dogs raced out. It was a daily ritual, although not usually at this time of day. The dogs charged up and down outside the cell doors, snarling and barking in the echoing gloom; the prisoners yelled at them and called them every unholy fucker under the sun. Then everyone got back to normal business.

Most of the dogs were the same breed—Pellesians, tall things with short tan hair and a broad black patch from the top of the head to the tip of the brush-like tail. A couple of the pack were black Tyran mastiffs—big, slow chunks of meat with permanent but deceptive grins that dripped slobber. They were the ones Niko trusted least.

One of the Pellesians sprang back as a stream of piss shot through the bars and drenched him. The dog seemed baffled for a moment, as if this was some attempt to communicate with him in his own language but the mutt didn't understand it because of a heavy accent. Niko laughed his ass off. Then the dog started snarling—yeah, he finally got the message—and the handler, Parmenter, stormed out onto the floor. He went along the cell doors like an angry ticket collector on a train looking for fare dodgers. Then he stopped at the guilty party's cell.

"You bastard, you pissed on my Jerry," he yelled. "I'm going to—"

Parmenter was drowned out by guffaws and whoops of derision from the whole block. He didn't interact much with the inmates, and never quite got the hang of dealing with verbal abuse. It didn't pay to let these scumbags rile you.

"Ooh, *your Jerry*! You two do it doggy style?"

"Yeah, 'cause he got doggy breath!"

"Yo, pooch-shagger! *Goooood* dog! Hey, shouldn't you be doin' it with a *bitch*, you big nancy?"

"I'm going to let him chew on you sick fuckers next time," Parmenter snapped. "Just remember who operates the gates."

Things quieted down instantly. Parmenter put the leash on Jerry, who took that as his cue to go nuts. As soon as the leash went taut, he was up on his hind legs, straining against it and snarling. Yeah, dogs could be just like humans. Jerry was all mouth when there was no chance of getting a kicking. But Niko was never going to turn his back on the thing, no matter how well-trained it was. He watched the dog trot back through the door. Jack Gallego—Gally—walked along the gallery to the metal gantry and joined him, jangling his keys.

"So who's our special studio guest today, then?" he asked.

"They're transferring Marcus Fenix."

"Should I know who that is?"

"Seeing as you're pig-ignorant and never read a newspaper, no."

"He's got to be at least a serial killer to be worth all this security. Maybe a kinky one."

"*Sergeant* Fenix. Hero of Aspho Fields? Ring any bells, Gally?"

"I'm too young to remember that."

"The hell you are."

"What did he do? To end up here, I mean. Don't the grunts deal with their own shit?"

"He slugged his CO and refused an order. Goodbye Ephyra."

"Wow." Gally frowned. "But couldn't they just shoot him?"

"*Fenix.*"

"What?"

"His dad's a hotshot scientist. Old money, ancestry, big estate."

"Oh, too good for us, huh? He's going to have a hard time in here, then."

Gally walked off, whistling. He was the single most uncurious human being Niko had ever met. Niko put it down at first to being thick as two short planks, but over the years he'd been here, he'd worked out that it was how Gally coped with the job. He switched off. It wasn't like he'd had a choice. If you weren't in a wartime reserve occupation—essential factory work, police, firefighter, farmer, merchant navy, imulsion jockey, medic, the kind of job needed to keep the COG running—then you served your time as a Gear, and if you weren't up to that for any reason, usually medical or general fitness, you got assigned where the government needed you. Being drafted as a warder in the last prison left in Ephyra wasn't exactly the top career choice for Niko, and he doubted that Gallego had dreamed of being a screw either. Most guys and an awful lot of the infertile women preferred being Gears, grubs or no grubs. Niko understood that.

He waited, watching the arched doorway at the far end of the floor. This was how they brought in the new boys to break them in.

Any minute now, Marcus Fenix would come through that door flanked by two warders, and get his first taste of what it meant to be stuck here for the rest of his life.

The building still had some of the elegant architectural detail that Tyrus liked even in its public lavatories, but it was crumbling and filthy, and if the smell of mold and piss didn't bring this Fenix guy up short, then the crumbling stone facing on the pillars and the old blood that still hadn't been washed off the walls would tell him everything he needed to know.

Forty years? He'll be lucky if he lasts five. Yeah, it's a life sentence, good as.

Well, it broke the monotony for everyone. There were forty-three prisoners left in the Slab and only a handful had been sent here since E-Day, so a new arrival was a major event for the inmates, even if it threatened to disrupt the settled pecking order of their lives. Fenix would be let out for free association after a day or so. Then he'd be on his own. He'd have to work out how to survive.

The door finally opened.

For a moment, Niko wondered why Will Chalcross and Bradeley Campbell had brought in another prisoner instead of Fenix. He was expecting the son of an old, wealthy family—a guy of average build who'd look around this cesspit and cower, war hero or not, a rich kid fallen from grace into a human sewer. But this guy was *huge*, all muscle in a prison-issue singlet and pants, black hair cut brutally short, with the life-worn face of a man who wasn't afraid to swing a punch or take one. He was too old to be Fenix. And he looked harder than most of the men already in here. This was a guy to avoid in a bar.

No. Shit, this *was* Marcus Fenix.

Niko could only stare. Fenix walked past the cells that formed the walls to either side, eyes straight ahead. The usual barracking and hooting started but died away gradually, cell by cell, as the prisoners saw what they were getting for a new neighbor.

The gantry was about five meters above the floor, so Niko was now looking at Fenix head-on at a shallow angle. The man just raised his eyes and looked at—no, *through*—Niko for a few beats without breaking his stride. Niko was used to eye contact with men who would slit his throat out of curiosity, but Fenix's stare was unsettling in a totally different way—ice blue, unblinking, but not *unfeeling*. The look in them was a distant, distracted anguish, a snatched glimpse through a briefly open door into some kind of private hell.

Chalcross glanced up at Niko and just raised an eyebrow as Campbell unlocked the cell door manually. Then Campbell—a nice guy, really quiet, never voiced an opinion about anything—stepped back with the big bunch of keys gripped tight in his gloved fist, and smashed Fenix across the face with them.

"That's for my fucking son," Campbell said.

Shit, Niko wasn't expecting that from Campbell. But Fenix just took it. He didn't even lose his balance. The look on his face was more surprise and indignation, like he couldn't work out what he'd done, and his fists clenched. But he kept his arms at his side. He had an audience, though, and the yelling started from the cells. It was a really bad idea to take a swing at a guy and make him look instantly unbreakable. It just encouraged the others.

"Hey, screw, you found one you can't knock down!"

"Whoa, you better not turn your back now, Campbell . . ."

"He don't look the forgettin' kind . . ."

Fenix stared into Campbell's face for a few seconds, blood trickling down his chin. Niko had to stop this fast.

"Campbell?" he yelled. He jogged along the gallery to the doors. "*Campbell!* Lock him in and get up here—*now.* That's a goddamn order."

Campbell looked up to the gantry, flexing his hand. The punch must have hurt him almost as much as it hurt Fenix. "Anything you say, sir . . ."

Chalcross shoved Fenix in the back to get him to walk into the cell, then took the keys from Campbell and locked it. The shouting was going from cell to cell now and as Niko watched to make sure the two warders left the floor, he caught some of the approving comments. Fenix had taken a punch in the face and been ready to fight back. The rest of the inmates loved it. Fenix was either going to go straight to the top of the food chain or start a lot of fights. But at least he wasn't young or pretty. Nobody was going to slug it out over whose bitch he was going to be.

Great work, Campbell. You made a hero of him inside five minutes. Terrific.

Maybe it would settle things down faster, though. Niko had to hope. The worst bastards could start worrying about whether Fenix was even more violent and unstable than them, and the quieter ones could make up their minds to be really careful. Keeping a lid on this place was a delicate balancing act: there were only twelve guards, six of those on the day shift, and even with a dozen psychiatric cases locked up in solitary it was hard. How the hell did those assholes at Sovereigns think he could manage that without cutting every corner? Niko did what each senior warder before him had had to do—the Slab was forced to rely on prisoners keeping other prisoners in line. It also relied on prisoners managing day-to-day life down there on the floor for themselves, and that had worked pretty well so far, at least from Niko's end of the deal. The prison ran like an ant farm. The ants were enclosed and went about their business in a sealed ecosystem while Niko and his fellow officers kept an eye on things from a distance and hoped they never had to enter to empty out the container and clean things up.

That meant the floor down there was a no-go zone and the service areas, like the kitchens and boiler room, were a kind of no-man's land that either side could occupy. Without the dogs, without the network of mesh passages that meant they could let the pack loose like a living, snarling moat, Niko wasn't sure if any of his colleagues would risk going down there at all.

Niko got to the stairs just as Campbell and Chalcross were shutting the inner doors behind them.

"Well, that was fucking clever," he said. "Way to give the guy an instant rep. What the hell got into you?"

"My son's a Gear."

"Yeah, we know."

"So he's putting it on the line while that asshole gets the kid glove treatment. They should have shot him, you know that? Anyone else—straight up against the wall. But him, he's too special."

"Well, he's not exactly got a room at the Redoubt, has he?" Niko didn't know if he was more pissed off at Campbell's miscalculation in the mindfuck game or just shocked that a nice guy had smashed a new inmate in the face. Fenix wasn't really a criminal. This was army shit, some technicality or other, nothing that would get a guy arrested in the civilian world. "Let it settle down there, for God's sake, or we'll have a riot."

"So?" Chalcross followed Niko and Campbell into the staff room. "We just let them kill each other and we've got less to worry about."

"We get paid to run this place," Niko said. "We're not here to sit on our asses."

Chalcross started making himself a coffee. It was just roasted barley, utter crap, but nobody recalled what the real thing tasted like now. He sniffed the contents of the cup as if he thought it was going rancid.

"He's a big bugger, though, that Fenix. What did he do?"

"Punched out the Chief of the Defense Staff, refused an order to take some hardware somewhere, and eventually lost us Ephyra." Niko helped himself to the pot. "He went to save his father. The big weapons scientist, remember? Adam Fenix. He didn't dismember and eat anyone. Pretty damn girly by our entrance standards."

"You sound like you feel sorry for him," Campbell said.

"He's not a serial killer. He's just a grunt. Rich boy or not."

Chalcross slurped his coffee. "So, does someone hate Fenix and want him to go crazy in here, or has he got friends in high places who saved him from a firing squad and think they're doing him a favor?"

Niko reached inside his jacket and pulled out the custody sheet, the form that the prison service used to make sure they had the right prisoner and knew his relevant medical status, mental or physical. Warders needed to know if an inmate was likely to infect them, collapse on them, or had a mental condition that made him even more dangerous. Niko read the form again. Fenix was predictably fit and healthy, as he should have been on Gear rations, and he was apparently certified sane, whatever the hell that meant these days. He held up the form and pointed to the section marked SPECIAL NOTES.

"Look," he said. "*Prisoner is not to be exposed to unnecessary risk or privation, at the request of the Office of the Chairman. A weekly welfare status report is to be submitted.*"

"So when did we last do a welfare report for any of these lice?" Chalcross asked. "Who the hell cares about any of them now?"

"Obviously Fenix still has some serious connections."

Parmenter came in with Jerry, but Chalcross gave him a black look and he took the dog outside to tell it to sit and wait. Chalcross didn't like it wandering around the food prep areas.

"Who's got connections?" Parmenter asked.

"Fenix. We've got to make sure he stays hale and hearty. Chairman's orders. Except this genius here just smacked him one but he took it like a gentle tap, so now we've got us a bad boy with a reputation."

"Way to go, Campie. Fuck our lives up some more, why don't you?" Parmenter rummaged through the fridge and took out some slices of raw bacon. He was going to waste them on that damn dog, Niko knew it. "Prescott must belong to the same country club as his father, then."

Chalcross stared at Parmenter until he put the bacon back in the fridge. "If he's *that* well-connected, why is he in here at all?"

"You think he should be in here?" Niko asked.

"What, he's not bad enough to get a suite?"

"No, I mean what makes a guy who's served in two wars and been decorated for bravery suddenly decide he's had enough? I mean really crack up. He hit his CO and went to rescue his father. That sounds pretty emotional and screwed up to me."

"Stress," Chalcross said. "Shell shock. Battle fatigue. PTSD. Whatever they call it now."

"Exactly."

"They're all shoveling the same shit, Niko," Campbell said. "They don't all crack."

"You ever been under fire?"

"No, and neither have you."

Chalcross suddenly got that oh-I-get-it look. "Come on, don't start about your uncle again."

"I've seen it, Will," Niko said. He hated them dismissing it. They hadn't got a clue. "Really. I have. Uncle Josh was as hard as nails until his ship got sunk and he spent two days in the water waiting to be picked up. Never the same since. Even the toughest guys go under."

"Well, you can feel as sorry for the asshole as you want, but whatever he did or didn't do means the grubs are on our doorstep now, and he looks like trouble to me. I'm not going make him a cup of tea and ask him how he feels."

Working the Slab was the last job in the world that Niko wanted to do. There were maybe only three or four guys in here who might be of any use to society or wouldn't offend again if they were let out. There was no rehabilitation or cure possible; there was no point teaching them a new trade, putting them in a nice suit, and expecting them to start life afresh having paid their debt to society. The Slab was here—officially, anyway—to stop the worst of the worst from being among decent people. It was a garbage bin. They couldn't even be trusted to fight grubs, because they'd desert with their weapons in five minutes flat and resume their old habits. This wasn't a place where a prison officer could do something useful and change men's lives, even if any of the staff here had volunteered to join the prison service, which none of them had as far as Niko knew. He certainly hadn't. The guys locked up here had shot people and set fire to buildings and raped and strangled and done stuff that defied human imagination. One of them was an Indie terrorist left over from the last war, and he looked like one of the nicer ones. Most of them were sane but rotten. Most of them were pretty choosy about who they preyed upon.

But none of them were career Gears who'd finally lost it after years of endless, daily, unrelenting combat. Fenix, poor bastard, was probably just broken, not a criminal.

God help me, I'm turning into a social worker. A frigging whiny do-gooder.

"Well, someone's got to fill out the goddamn welfare report," Niko said. He thought of his uncle and how he wanted people to treat him. "Might as well be me."

D WING EXERCISE YARD, THE SLAB: TWO DAYS LATER.

Millton Reeve was minding his own business and taking his mid-morning constitutional around the vegetable beds in the yard when Officer Jarvi stepped out and startled him. The screws didn't have much face-to-face contact with the inmates, and they definitely didn't hang out in the yard.

"I've got a job for you, Reeve," he said.

"How much?"

"Pack of smokes once a week."

"Done. Who do you want given a spanking?"

"No spanking. I need you to look out for someone."

Niko Jarvi was okay for a warder. He quietly despised most of the assholes in here, but then so did Reeve, so that was okay. "I'm trying to guess who, and I'm guessing it's the new guy. Seeing as we haven't had anyone transferred in for years."

"Yeah, it's Fenix. He's had his time to settle in and we're unlocking him now."

"Any special reason?"

"Orders from the Chairman's office. He's connected. Embry Star, founding family, famous dad, the works. Just don't let him get his throat cut. Or let him cut his own. If he's looking longingly at ropes or belts, warn me."

"I didn't see it, but I heard it. Campbell couldn't even knock him down. Maybe you're the ones who need protecting." Everyone was talking about Fenix, taking bets on whether he could knock Dan Merino flat. "Poking my nose through his bars seemed a bit risky. He might be the kind that kicks the cat after a bad day."

"You'll see." Jarvi gave him a just-do-it nod as he left. "One pack a week, okay?"

Reeve stood in the yard, hands thrust into the pockets of his overalls, and looked up at the patch of sky, the only sight he'd had of the outside world since before the grubs showed up. A light rain with the sharp feel of sleet pecked at his face. A helicopter passed high overhead, which might have meant Reavers were around, so he decided to cut the session short. He'd have to pace the floor inside instead.

But it was as good a time as any to go meet this Fenix guy. In fact, it was probably better to do it now before one of the less benign residents decided to roll up with the welcome wagon.

Reeve took pride in his work. He killed people—professionally, no undisciplined personal shit—and he also stopped some from getting whacked. That was his job. He was doing it for a different boss and working for smokes and soap instead of random-numbered untraceable bills these days, but as far as he was concerned, he was still employed and had *purpose*. That was how he kept going. Prison was an occupational hazard. It was no excuse to give up and get rusty. When he got out of here, and he was damned sure he would, he needed to hit the ground running.

D Wing was the last operational block left in the Slab, a vast vaulted hall with a skylight roof and recessed cells set on both sides like a colonnade of shops in an upmarket mall. But that was all that was upmarket about it. The only part that had proper heating was the kitchens, even in the dead of winter, the water supply was almost always cold, and a bunch of men didn't keep things spick-and-span even with Merino around to break their fingers if they messed the place up. There was a level of squalor that they sank to where civilization kicked in and they didn't want it to get any worse, and that was the level they kept it at. The Slab was a slice of Sera, a miniature version of it, with the nice civilized guards living one side of the wire and the inmates, like the Stranded, surviving as best they could on the other.

Reeve remembered the word now: *microcosm.* The Slab was a microcosm.

The rest of the prison was empty now, except for the freaks who were kept locked up for everyone else's good one floor below in the windowless solitary block. Reeve counted his way along the north side cells and passed Chunky.

"Hey, Reeve. Man on a mission?"

Reeve stopped and took a step back. The guys in here could read everyone like a book. "Pays to keep busy. How's the knitting?"

"You going to brief us on our war hero when you're done with him?"

"Who says that's where I'm heading?"

Chunky gave Reeve a toothy grin. Half the little runt's bodyweight seemed to be teeth. "Man's got to have a proper welcome. They say the screws are already shit-scared of him."

"Might be an exaggeration."

"Well, I'm damn glad to see a guy they probably can't break. Not that they won't try if they can."

"We run the floor," Reeve said. "They won't get a chance."

Reeve never expected this to be a private meeting anyway. The trick was to get the job done and not lose face or status. He came to a halt in front of Fenix's cell and found the bars shut but the bolt wasn't slid across, and Fenix didn't look up. He was polishing his boots with a scrap of grubby cloth, hunched up in one dark corner of the cell like a zoo animal that wasn't going to come out for the tourists no matter how many cookies they threw into the cage. The cold didn't seem to bother him. His prison-issue jacket hung on a nail in the wall.

Reeve tapped on the metal frame, because this place had rules. Fenix looked up very slowly as if he had to force himself.

"Hey, I'm Millton Reeve," Reeve said. "Thought somebody ought to say hi."

Fenix just stared. Then he stood up. He took a couple of slow steps over to the door and into the dim light. The guy looked huge sitting down, but seeing him unfold to full height was a bit like watching someone draw a big handgun and then put an equally big silencer on it. His lip was split and his mouth was swollen, but it looked like that didn't bother him either.

"Marcus," Fenix growled.

His teeth were intact as far as Reeve could see. *Marcus.* Okay, Marcus it was. Either he was an informal kind of guy or he didn't want anyone using his surname. Reeve was making notes because attention to small detail could be all that kept you alive in this place.

"You got a few minutes?"

"At least," Marcus said.

He pushed the door open and Reeve walked in, keeping a diplomatic distance. A lot of guys didn't like being crowded. Marcus stood with his arms folded. There was a regimental tattoo or something on his upper left arm, a skull on a pair of crossed rifles with a small motto that Reeve couldn't read without looking way too interested for his own good. A lot of guys put on a tough act to fend off trouble, but Marcus didn't need to. Whether it was genes or a hard life, it wasn't just his size that said it was a bad idea to piss him off. He radiated something that made Reeve want to walk around him. That intense pale stare didn't help.

"You okay? That lip looks sore."

Marcus shrugged. "Had a lot worse."

"You want a quick run-down of the rules?"

"Do I need one?"

"You'll live longer."

"I'll skip it, then." Marcus sat down again and picked up his left boot to resume polishing. "Thanks for your concern."

"No, you don't get it. I need to make sure you're okay."

Marcus did a slow head turn that would have been theatrical in any other guy. It gave Reeve the impression that he was reining in a lethal temper.

"You call me Sugar," he said quietly, "and I'll break your fucking neck."

Oops. Too chummy, maybe. "Hey, I don't get *that* lonely. Just been asked to keep an eye out for you, seeing as I can do that kind of thing."

Marcus's frown relaxed, but only a fraction. "Hoffman's idea?"

"Who's Hoffman?"

"Doesn't matter."

Reeve pressed on. "Okay, so here's a quick guide to not having to pick your teeth up from the yard." Reeve doubted there were more than half a dozen guys in here who stood a chance of even landing a punch on Marcus, but that didn't mean he wouldn't run into other trouble. "Lockdown time—when you hear the count on the PA, just drop whatever you're doing and get back to your cell before they let the dogs loose. Never ask anyone what they're in for. And don't join a gang."

"Dogs." Marcus's tone changed very slightly. "Yeah, I heard them."

"You scared of dogs?"

He just stared at Reeve, unblinking. Ah, so he was. "Should I be?"

"The screws let them loose in the passages. It's like a network of mesh barriers in the corridors. You know, they're separated like those pens and runs in cattle yards, with remote gates and everything. So the warders never need to set foot down here."

Marcus was still staring at him but his expression was now completely unreadable. "So what *are* you in here for?"

Oh, so he's decided to be a handful. Okay. Fine. "I'm not a goddamn nonce, if that's what's worrying you." Maybe he didn't know what that was, being upper crust. "A pedo. Child molester. Kiddie fiddler."

"Yeah. I get it."

"I'm a contract assassin. I'm a pro. Like you."

Marcus said absolutely nothing for a long five seconds. "I'm a *Gear*," he said, so quiet that Reeve had to strain to hear. It wasn't indignation. It was sorrow. "Or at least I *was.*"

Reeve added that to his mental notebook and knew that unraveling all the stuff in those few words was going to take a long time, but would probably tell him every last detail about Marcus Fenix.

This wasn't what Reeve was used to. In the twelve years he'd been here, he'd met every kind of sick bastard under the sun, and had seen most of them die or disappear one way or another, but none of them had managed to disturb him as much or as fast as this guy. He was from another world.

Reeve had to stick with it now, though, and not just because he wanted the smokes. Hanging on to his professional pride was what kept him from going under. "So . . . you're going to look like a challenge to Merino. That's Daniel Merino. He's got a half a dozen guys who break bones for him when they need to. He organizes the place and keeps the inmates under control and the screws don't get involved. Suits them, sometimes doesn't suit us, but hey, we're not here for being model citizens."

"I'm sure he'll introduce himself."

"Bet on it. So seeing as you broke the rules already, I get to ask why a stand-up hero like you refused to fight."

"I didn't *refuse to fight*," Marcus growled. Ah, that was a useful raw nerve to know about, but Reeve decided not to twang it again unless he absolutely had to. "I went to save my father instead of other Gears. But he got killed anyway. So, not one of my better decisions."

"Hey, sorry."

"Well, now you know." Marcus looked like he was making a point of changing tack. He indicated the prison-issue safety razor on the cracked washbasin bolted to the wall next to the toilet pan. The basin looked like he'd actually *cleaned* it somehow. "Can't help noticing that they let us have sharp objects in here."

It was the "us" that struck Reeve. Every other guy who came in spent anything from a month to a year or more saying "you" because he didn't think he belonged here and took some time to get used to the idea. Marcus just took it as read that he was scum now like everyone else. No airs and graces for all that privilege, then.

"They let us have belts, too," Reeve said. "Because if we kill ourselves or each other, it's a win-win for them. They don't even have to come down here. How else do you think this place runs on a dozen screws and a few dogs?"

Marcus went back to staring at the wall. "Smart business model."

He didn't say anything else. Reeve was trying to read if a long silence was his fuck-off signal, but it was impossible to tell. He decided to err on the side of caution.

"Catch you later," he said.

Reeve did a circuit of the cells, checking who had stuff to trade and who wanted it. Twenty-six hours was a long time to fill each day. It had been tedious enough in the early years, before the shortages had begun to bite and the outside world still had a semblance of normal life going on. There'd still been TV and coffee and books back then, and a guy could earn a few bucks to buy basic comforts by making car parts in the prison workshops. But the car work had stopped abruptly because the factories were turned over to arms production, and the TV had dwindled to a news channel, and then it got harder to get food supplies sent in or even medicines. Stuff wasn't being manufactured outside. The criminal scum of the COG were just about the lowest priority there was. Now their time was taken up keeping an obsolete prison from falling apart and growing whatever food they could wherever they had space. They did it themselves, too. Merino might have been a bastard, but he was an efficient bastard, and ran his domain like a business, like the organized crime boss he'd been—with the emphasis on organized.

Reeve was okay with all that. If the warders didn't run the day-to-day life of the inmates, then the inmates had to do it themselves, or sink further into anarchy and filth. Merino's iron fist meant a few clean floors and enough food. An occasional kicking was a small price to pay for that.

If the smell got too bad for him, there was always the fresh air in the prison gardens, a sports field that had been dug up when every scrap of grass or mud in urban Ephyra was reclaimed to grow food. It had its own fish pond, too, and even if the fish tasted like shit—not surprising seeing how shit had to be recycled in this dump—it was a welcome change of protein from the myco crap they fermented in the kitchens.

But gardening had proved more satisfying than Reeve had expected. He went outside to check his personal crop, a few rows of speckled beans. He could dry those and stash plenty away for himself at the end of Bounty. He worked along the rows of poles lashed together like tent frames, picking bugs off the leaves.

They could have just shot us all, any time. Funny where governments draw the line. Fry the whole world and kill millions of helpless citizens, but balk at executing prisoners even under martial law. The Indies worked POWs to death but shipped them out to hospitals when they got sick. Maybe that's the definition of civilization — pretend rules of decency. That, or else they need to keep some deterrent for the thousands of folk they can't afford to shoot: play nice, or we'll stick you in the Slab.

"I've got some real nice lettuce seedlings," said a voice behind him. It was Merino. "Gonna be a good harvest. Is our new boy interested in horticulture?"

A few men in a confined space without a lot to distract them meant that news got around in minutes. The Slab was a village, minus the kindly old ladies and ruddy-cheeked farmers.

Reeve squashed a cluster of aphids between his fingers and contemplated the smeared remains. It was nothing personal, just necessity. "I think he just wants to keep himself to himself."

"You know how it is. Guy with a reputation shows up, and bored assholes want to see if he's going to shake things up a bit."

"Like I said, he's not exactly sociable. You just carry on as normal."

"It's not me who needs telling," Merino said, and wandered off.

Reeve watched him go and realized he was sizing him up. Merino was pretty big and solid, but Marcus was bigger and had fought grubs hand to hand. Maybe Merino would bear that in mind.

That chainsaw rifle was kind of impressive, though. Reeve almost regretted his own career choices. He turned over another leaf, ran his thumbnail along the underside, and wiped out another growing colony of aphids.

CHAPTER 6

Welcome to Azura, a haven of security, stability and comfort for humanity's most precious resource: you. Like all of Azura's citizens, you have been selected for your outstanding contributions to society. This island, isolated and hidden from the troubles of the mainland, was developed to protect and allow society's greatest minds to continue their work, free of fear or peril. You will be the architects of a grand reconstruction. No matter what fate befalls the rest of the world, Azura—and its citizens—will carry on. Your diligent work ensures the enduring survival of mankind.

(Introduction to orientation leaflet given to new arrivals at Azura research station.)

COG RESEARCH STATION AZURA, SOMEWHERE IN THE SOUTHERN HEMISPHERE: BRUME, 10 A.E.

The residents of Azura had counseling sessions to stop them feeling guilty.

Nevil looked at the menu—a *menu*, for God's sake, a menu with a *wine list*—and found he'd lost his appetite yet again. This was all wrong. And if that smarmy recorded voice from the PA system started up again, the one they said was Niles Samson himself, he'd lose it completely.

Counseling sessions? Too right you're guilty. You need to face up to it.

I'm sorry, Emil. I had no idea. Believe me, I didn't know this place existed.

He pushed the plate of lamb cutlets away from him. It was a lovely plate, too, Furlinese bone china with a gilt rim, and the silverware really was silver, hallmarked with the Jacinto Assay Office's winged cog. He picked up the fork and examined it. But he couldn't even bear to drink from the crystal glass, even if it was just full of water.

It wasn't, of course. It was some kind of white wine, and Nevil wasn't a drinker at the best of times. He'd never felt less like drinking in his life.

A waiter darted over to take his plate. Nevil found himself more interested in the lives the staff led and how many of them worked here. He hoped the guy reheated his untouched lamb later and enjoyed it. The thought of throwing it away was disturbing for someone used to rationing.

"Nevil, you really do need to see the doctor." Erica Marling was a molecular biologist and there was nothing wrong with her appetite. "Most of us have been through this. It's hard, I know. You hate yourself. You feel you have no right to be here when everyone else is struggling to stay alive."

Revelation could be ecstatic, like a scientific breakthrough after years of struggle, or an agonizing slap in the face when you realized your life was a charade. All Nevil could see were the lies, the slaps in the face, the insults to the dead. Reality shook him by the collar and laughed at him. *You thought the genetics team at La Croix had been killed in a Reaver attack, did you? Well, they look just fine now. They're having roast quail and a bottle of nice fruity red.* The disappeared, the dead, and the defected were here on Azura, counseled and fed and full of fucking purpose for the future.

But Emil was *really* dead. There was no bringing him back with a nice day at the spa and a bit of psychotherapy.

Nevil had never realized that he had such a bitter, slow-burning temper. It was stoking up to a full eruption. "Oh, I don't hate myself," he said quietly. "I hate you bastards and I hate my government."

"This was built during the Pendulum Wars, Nevil. It was designed to sit out another apocalypse. You can't blame Prescott for making good use of it."

"Yes, some of you have been here since then, haven't you? Never even seen a Locust in the flesh. Bully for you."

She took a sip of wine. "Your department did some of the research used on the Maelstrom project, actually. Professor Fenix is cited. As are you."

Bastards. "If we did, we didn't know what it was going to be used for."

"Exactly."

"No, not *exactly*. Why *exactly*? Ah, damn it. You can shove your need-to-know."

Erica just shrugged and sliced up her pork filet. Behind her, a spectacularly ornate open elevator rose like a monument, bringing more displaced scientists and thinkers to the tower restaurant. Nevil hoped they choked on their duck pâté.

"Where does all this stuff *come* from? All this food?"

"You think we don't have rationing here? There's a lot of food off the menu."

Nevil thought of his precious and very stale chocolate bar back in Jacinto, how he'd harvested every last crumb. "Pardon me while I sob in my napkin."

"We haven't been able to ship in supplies for years. Anyway, Azura's obviously designed to be self-sufficient. So we have intensive agriculture—hence the quail."

"And presumably some *peasants* to do all the work for you. Do we ever get to see them, or are they like the housekeeping staff and stay out of sight in the service corridors?"

"Spare me the theoretical socialism. *Of course* we have support staff. We're supposed to be focusing on research, unless you want the biochemists made to work in the fields like they had to in Furlin . . ."

"I fully understand the logistics of running a community like this, thanks, but that doesn't mean it won't make my flesh crawl."

"Look," Erica said. "The Locust are closing in on Jacinto. You haven't got the facilities you need. And when they finally overrun the city—well, imagine if this facility was there now. We've already lost *years* because Adam Fenix kept Lambency to himself."

But they all knew about the Lambent now, and how it had driven the Locust to the surface. Nevil got the feeling that the biologists here resented a physicist like Adam more for dabbling outside his discipline than for not sharing his discovery. They really had been away from the real Sera for a very long time.

"Do you see any news coverage from Ephyra?" Nevil asked, folding his napkin. *Linen. Real linen.* "Do you have any idea how bad things are? Do you even know about the poor bastards outside the wire, the Stranded? Do you understand how we stay alive?"

"Of course we know."

"I bet you watch it every night when you're having a small brandy to help you sleep."

"Nevil . . . please, take advantage of the counseling. You do need it."

Nevil pushed himself back from the table and walked away. He had to step onto the magnificent elevator to get out of here and it wasn't an express. As the platform slowly descended, he had far too much time to look at the art treasures in the lobby below. This was where all the stuff from the National Museum of Ephyra had been moved, then: they had the resources to save that, but not to save people. He understood. He knew the impossibility of the heavy lift, of finding room for the population of Ephyra on a small island, and the need for a society rebuilding itself to hang on to some scraps of its culture and remember what it could be. But it still felt utterly wrong.

My brother died for this. And I didn't volunteer.

He still hadn't seen a fraction of Azura yet. He had an office and nice suite of rooms. He'd found the library and the botanical gardens. Beyond the careful landscaping, Azura had a fascinating coast of rocky cliffs and sandy inlets, and he was still working out where he could find refuge so that he could have some time alone to think without being surrounded by people who thought—or had been persuaded—that they had a right to be here and sit out the global holocaust.

The ground floor was an interlocking complex of rooms and corridors, all of them beautifully decorated with exquisite inlaid floors, drapes, and gilded console tables. It looked like a cross between a five-star hotel and a spa, which was pretty well what it was if it hadn't been for the research facilities and extraordinary defenses. Nevil found a door leading into another formal garden crisscrossed by decorative canals and dotted with water features, and just wandered around for a while taking in the setting sun and rehearsing what he'd say to Adam Fenix when he finally saw him again.

Eventually he sat down on a decorative wrought iron seat to stare at the palm trees and purple-flowered tropical vines he didn't have a name for. The early evening air was pure perfume. It was all wrong, wrong, *wrong*.

Through an archway, he caught a glimpse of the curtain of permanent tornados and waterspouts shielding the island from the rest of the world. The physicist in him marveled at the scale and ingenuity of it. The rest of him wasn't so sure. He spread his arms along the back of the seat and looked straight up, where the sky was uniformly clear and full of swifts scooping up insects on the wing, not Ravens patrolling to keep Reavers out of Jacinto airspace.

Then that damned voice drifted across the scented air. It was all recorded messages, either playing on a loop or triggered by opening doors or setting off infrared detectors, but it had started to stoke a personal dislike in Nevil. He didn't like the voice, and he didn't like the bullshit it came out with. It was a man's voice, unnaturally soothing and reassuring, telling the cocooned residents about the facilities or the latest recreation being laid on for them.

"*. . . and later this week, you're invited to see the new desalination plant at . . .*"

"For God's sake, shut it," Nevil sighed.

He leaned forward, elbows braced on his knees. A couple of women in dark blue uniform dresses—probably domestic staff—appeared on one of the walkways wheeling a cleaning cart before disappearing behind a cascade of vines. For a moment, the illusion of paradise looked a little more mundane. And he reminded himself this was a prison. He couldn't opt to go home now.

No point hiding here, then. Got to face him sooner or later.

Nevil got up and headed for what he'd come to think of as the center of town. It was another set-piece garden, flanked by the medical center on one side and an office block on the other. It didn't look like an office building. The whole thing was a spectacular piece of architecture, all sinuous organic forms and mellow stonework softened by hanging baskets of brilliant flowers.

A bunker was one thing. This level of excess was something else.

You know the reason.

This was designed with the assumption that the rest of Sera would be wasteland and this would be the place humanity started its recovery. The planners had expected the Pendulum Wars to end in mutual destruction. They couldn't have seen the Locust coming.

I could go up and knock on Adam's door, I suppose.

But Nevil didn't have to. As he was watching the ebb and flow of people in lab coats or tasteful leisure clothes wandering up and down the paths and walkways around him, his eye was caught by someone walking a lot more slowly. It was Adam Fenix. He had two crutches, the forearm kind, and he was trying to negotiate a flight of stone steps lined with flowering bushes in fluted urns. Nevil wasn't sure if the professor had seen him until the man stopped and stared across the gardens at him.

Nevil could only raise his hand. It wasn't a friendly wave. It was just a here-I-am. He waited for Adam to make his way across, determined not to get up and meet him halfway despite his physical condition.

And I was worrying about facing him after turning him in.

Adam stopped a few meters from him and tilted his head slightly on one side. Maybe he didn't know where to start either.

"So who's going to shout at who first, Adam?" Nevil said. "You could start off by telling me what an asshole I am for reporting you to the Chairman. Or I could go first, and tell you that I still can't believe you'd do this to your own people when you've got a son in the army."

"I can't blame you for going to Prescott." Adam fumbled with his crutches and managed to sit down on the seat next to Nevil. "In fact I'm relieved it's over. I suppose I told you because I didn't have the guts to come clean myself."

Nevil wasn't sure if that meant Adam regarded him as someone who would automatically going running to the authorities. It might have been an inuslt or flattery. Nevil decided to think it was the latter.

"So . . . how are you feeling?" he asked.

"Sore. Broken ribs take weeks to heal. I'll live."

"So this place came as a big surprise to you as well, did it?"

Adam nodded. He looked wrung out. All that pent-up energy that had al-ways illuminated him had vanished. "That's an understatement."

"Well, life's full of surprises for most of us."

"Okay, I lied, Nevil. I lied by omission."

"It's a bit more than that. Isn't it?"

"Would you be amused if I told you I found out about the Locust the hard way too?"

"Not really."

"My wife Elain. Well, you know all about Elain. I thought I did too, right up to the day she went missing." Adam raked his fingertips through his beard as if he was tidying himself up before a meeting. "I was frantic. I knew some-thing was wrong. And while the police were looking for a body in the river—I told them she'd never do anything stupid like that—I went through her study, just in case. Never went in there, usually. Private space. And I found it—her journal. She'd gone into the Hollow regularly to look for specimens, those damn rock shrews with the extra vestigial legs, and she found the Locust in-stead. Never told me. Then one day she went down there to make contact with them and never came back. You know the rest."

Maybe he was looking for absolution. Nevil didn't have an answer, let alone a sensible question. He simply let another little bombshell leave his head rat-tling. Elain Fenix had kept a whole species secret even from her old man: did the whole world behave that way and he simply hadn't noticed? It was hard to know where to start on any given day now.

"So she lied to you, and you lied to me and everyone else, and Prescott—well, he inherited a lie and decided to keep it too." Nevil tried to separate his sense of personal betrayal from the global implications, but decided the personal scale was the only thing he could handle right now. A couple of men carrying briefcases slowed down to look Adam's way. He was still a celebrity in these circles. "Am I the only idiot who told the truth?"

"No." Adam shook his head. "You and Hoffman. He's as straight as a die. Not an easy man to work with, but he'd have handled this very differently. Which is why he's been kept in the dark too. We reward the liars, you see."

Adam leaned back with some difficulty and took a slow, cautious breath. He pointed at a group of people coming out of the main office building, a couple of women and three or four men, one in army fatigues. There were quite a few military personnel here, mostly in the black uniform of the Onyx Guard. But men and women in uniform were so much part of the daily fabric of life in Tyrus that Nevil had long since ceased to notice any other kind of uniform.

"What?" he said.

"Recognize the older man?"

"Oh God." The man had lost weight and he was much grayer now, but that profile was distinctive: Bardry. Nevil was shocked, and given the torrent of ugly surprises he'd been subjected to over the past couple of weeks, he didn't expect to be capable of reacting any longer. "He's supposed to be dead. They said he was *dead*."

"Yes. General Salaman Bardry. Prescott needed quite a cover story to explain his going missing."

"You said he blew his brains out because he couldn't live with deploying the Hammer of Dawn against cities."

"Because that's what I was told. I had no idea either."

"So he was brought here?"

"Prescott needs parallel armed forces ready to take over."

Nevil didn't know Hoffman all that well, but he felt instantly sorry for the poor bastard, under siege and holding it together on his own for the last eight years. If he could have picked up the phone to Hoffman and told him right then, he would have. He could imagine the colonel losing sleep over the suicide, maybe even blaming himself in the way that people did when someone they knew did something terrible and without warning.

"You're all lying bastards, you know that?" Nevil said. "All of you. You don't even think twice about it."

"You ever wondered why they didn't ship me out here right away, their head of research?"

"Because Prescott might be a deceitful ball of slime, but he's not stupid. It takes one to know one."

"Nevil, don't think I escaped my punishment." Adam tried to turn to look him in the eye, but Nevil couldn't take it. He just focused on Bardry, alive and well, like so many of the other key people who'd gone missing over the years but turned up here. "They've let Marcus think I'm dead. He's serving forty years in the Slab for disobeying orders to try to save me, as well as thinking he's failed me. So if you think I'm reveling in this, you're very much mistaken."

He'd even brought his son down. *What a selfish son of a bitch.* Nevil could only take this in small doses. He wasn't even sure what use a physicist would be now, given the nature of the real threat facing them, but he didn't have any choice, and he'd have to work with Adam. Right then it was the last thing he wanted to do. He stood up to go. Lights sparkled in the palm trees, some kind of firefly.

This isn't happening. I think I preferred Jacinto. That's reality. That's what we're facing.

"You didn't even tell your own son," he said. "Don't expect me to apologize for turning you in."

"I don't." Adam looked as if he was chewing something over. "No, I never told Marcus. He's like Hoffman in so many ways. Ironic, isn't it?"

"So we're all serving a sentence, one way or another. I think we're going to choke on irony before too long." Nevil found himself groping for what was right. He wanted a moment of clarity, that voice in the back of his head that said *you really ought to do this, however tough it seems.* But there was nothing he could think of except venting his disgust. "You'll have to excuse me, Adam. I can't deal with this right now."

Adam didn't try to stop him. He probably thought he'd come around after a few weeks. Did they even have that much time? Nevil had no idea. He just felt utterly alone, an exile among aliens, and he had no idea how he was going to cope with this enforced stay. It was going to take a hell of a lot more than a five-star restaurant and all the luxuries that the rest of Sera had forgotten even existed to stop him wanting to lash out.

Bardry was still standing on the steps of the office building, chatting in the balmy evening breeze and occasionally flicking away a firefly with a sweep of his hand.

And people mourned over you.

Nevil walked back to his suite, half-expecting to see Emil, *wanting* to see him, but knowing the COG had no reason whatsoever to fake the death of an ordinary Gear.

CHAIRMAN'S TEMPORARY OFFICE, AZURA.

Prescott fully understood Nevil Estrom's reaction to the sheer incongruity of Azura in a world of slaughter, rubble, and famine.

The fresh pot of coffee in the office—genuine coffee, not some ingenious but completely unconvincing cereal concoction—smelled tantalizing, but he had to resist. He didn't want to reek of coffee and invite questions when he returned to Jacinto in a few hours. Nobody forgot what the real thing smelled like.

But it was more than that. Prescott felt uncomfortable enjoying what the average citizen no longer could. His sense of entitlement, that subconscious expectation that his exceptional job demanded exceptional rights, had slowly evaporated year upon year. He clung to that realization. It surprised him that even after nearly ten years, even after giving the order to raze Sera's cities to the ground with the Hammer of Dawn, he still needed reassurance that he had a conscience.

I'm still human. I'm not a monster. I just have unique burdens that I have to bear in unpalatable ways.

He slipped some documents into his briefcase, checking that they weren't conspicuously new paper. Dury was due any moment. Prescott heard footsteps in the corridor, but they weren't heavy and male, and then there was a hesitant tap on the half-open door. Esther Bakos, the head of biochemical research, hovered in the doorway.

"Chairman, have you got five minutes?" She clutched an old folder to her chest. "I wouldn't trouble you, but I need your clearance to share a document with Dr. Fenix."

Esther had been based on Azura since the Pendulum Wars: her children had been born here and had never seen the mainland. They'd never seen a live Locust, and neither had she.

"Come in." Virtually everyone here seemed to have a Ph.D. Prescott teetered on the edge of saying *Professor* but decided he'd stick to first names. "I suspect we're long past the secrecy stage now, Esther."

She laid the folder on his desk. He could see the security stamp on it and the year. It was very old, its red stenciled label faded to a pale orange, but it was still very much a live document:

TOP SECRET

TERATOGENICITY STUDY

(SAMSON)

"We're still working through Dr. Fenix's notes and discs—*Elain* Fenix, I mean—but Adam's already made some very valid observations about the Lambent pathogen's relationship to imulsion," she said. "This research into the teratogenic effects of imulsion was sealed years ago, but I think he should have access to it."

"I agree. Go ahead."

Esther just looked at Prescott as if he hadn't answered her question.

"Is there a problem?" he asked.

"I have a question, sir."

"Fine." Prescott spread his hands. "Ask away."

"We need to know what happened to the rest of Niles Samson's New Hope research. The children with abnormalities."

Prescott watched her expression: a little disbelief, a little fear, and a fair amount of hope. It was hard not to put two and two together, but it was also unscientific, he knew that much. He tried to meet professionals on their own terms.

"If I had it," he said, "I would hand it over. We searched for those children for years."

"We could go back and recover the Sires."

"No. The facility has to stay locked down."

"Sir, we know imulsion can cause changes in human physiology, and I think Adam's established the link between imulsion and the pathogen."

"We've been living with imulsion for more than a century and Samson wasn't the only one looking at its possible toxicity. How did we miss the fact it's alive? If it is, of course. I'm going with Adam's theory for the moment."

"Imulsion itself showed no signs of being *alive*, as you put it. The only evidence of that is Adam's samples, which came from the Locust tunnels. That pathogen has all the characteristics of imulsion, but also of an organism."

"Keep it simple for me. Is the pathogen a form of imulsion?"

"I believe so."

"Will all imulsion . . ." Prescott chose his words carefully but still felt foolish. "Will all imulsion come to life? I realize that's a layman's interpretation."

"We don't understand its lifecycle enough yet to know. But if you take the rock shrew samples and the field reports of bioluminescent Locust, that's strong evidence that it can jump the species barrier. We need to acquire some live test subjects."

"Straight question, Esther. Can we work without the Sires? Yes or no?" Dalyell had always been very cagey about their existence and origin. Prescott had been kept out of the loop: it had suited him not to know about mutated humans, *poisoned* humans, but it was a gap he now needed to fill. All he could do when he took office was keep the New Hope facility quarantined and hope he never had to open the lid. "Transporting them here is going to be difficult to say the least. They might not even have survived."

"They were in suspension, sir."

"Nobody's been inside New Hope for years. Don't you use tissue samples these days? We have samples of Locust tissue, and now we have a viable supply of the Lambent pathogen. *Lambency.* Sorry, I'm really not sure what to call it yet."

"*In vitro* research is no substitute for *in vivo*," Esther said. "A complete living organism, and I don't just mean mice."

"Why? What's the biggest threat to us? Contamination of other forms of life, or of ourselves? I'm still struggling for clear priorities here, Esther. The Locust told Adam they were literally at war with Lambent creatures—they were being killed by them. But does Lambency kill its hosts? Does it just change them? Is it even a *survival advantage*?"

Good grief, why am I asking that? Because I'm clutching at straws. Perhaps I'm not the first to start down that path.

Esther's expression hardened a little. The argument seemed to ring unwelcome bells with her. "The Locust told Adam that some Lambent began to self-destruct—literally *detonate*. If you're thinking it has a future as a defense against the Locust, I suspect you'd have had an interesting conversation with Dr. Samson." She looked down at the faded folder on the desk as if that would give her an answer. "Whether it's the global threat that the Locust and Adam Fenix think it is, or we're mistaken and it's actually a new tactical advantage, we still have to fully understand it first so that we can control it. And given the inarguable evidence of human mutation, this is research we also need to do *in humans*. Not cell cultures."

Prescott thought she was still asking for access to the Sires. It was a massive risk: there were too many unknowns, and the last thing he needed was to unleash any extra problems that he couldn't put back in the box. There was another option he could live with, but he wasn't sure that she could. Scientists had unpredictable ethical boundaries.

"If I can find you a human specimen or two," he said, "would that help? Not a Sire. A basic human."

Esther's face fell slightly. "But who'd volunteer for that, sir?"

"I didn't say *volunteer*."

"Oh, you mean . . ." Her face fell a little further. "Actually, I don't know *what* you mean."

"We've still got a small supply of utterly worthless people I'm willing to use."

"Stranded?"

"Prisoners. From the Slab." He waited for a shriek of outrage, but she just seemed to be listening patiently. "I'm sure they have a few pedophiles or serial killers stashed away who owe society a debt."

Esther didn't react at all. She just cocked her head on one side, looking slightly past Prescott, as if she was debating whether a child molester had the right genome for the job.

"You'll have to run it past Dr. Fenix," she said. "Thank you, Chairman."

She walked out, leaving the file on the desk. Prescott was always wrong-footed by scientists. That troubled him. People thought politicians had no scruples, but at least those missing scruples were easily definable. It was much harder to guess where a scientist might draw the line between acceptable and unacceptable. Prescott tried to unravel it, but every time he settled back into his own default: his line lay at what had to be done for the good of the majority. He would have been paralyzed into indecision otherwise.

I've pressed a Hammer command key and condemned millions of innocents to death. I wonder if that feels any worse than facing an individual living creature and injecting it with a substance to watch and learn from its suffering.

Dury appeared in the doorway. He felt like blessed relief, the reliable and the knowable. "Am I interrupting, sir?"

"Not at all, Paul. I need to leave at fifteen hundred, and then I don't think I can come back here personally for quite some time. I'm going to have to leave Professor Fenix in your capable hands for a while."

Dury nodded. He didn't look happy. "Sir."

"Speak your mind."

"Grubs to fight, sir. Just guilt for doing the spa deployment, that's all."

"I understand. No reason to live on ration packs here, though. Nobody's going to think less of you for it."

"*I'll* think less of me, sir."

Dury was cut from the same cloth as Hoffman, at least where his Gears were concerned. But he seemed to find it easier to accept murky politics. Hoffman functioned perfectly where he was right now, in a different world where the senior command could still concentrate on warfighting—hands-on, immediate, the stuff they signed up to do. He would never have coped with the maneuvering and politicking in the Defense Department, but he certainly had the ruthless skills needed for the top job in a world fighting for its life.

"I don't think a coffee will send you sliding into the abyss of decadence, Paul," Prescott said.

"First it's a coffee, sir, and then it's a fancy pastry, and before you know it, you're griping about the lack of the really good vintages on the wine list these days." Dury dressed it up as humor but he couldn't completely suppress the look in his eyes, which said that he meant it and that it irked him. It was so specific that it was probably from a real conversation he'd overheard. "Human beings habituate fast. I note that you don't indulge yourself, sir."

Damn. He thinks I'm scrupulously principled. No, he's too intelligent for that. "Hoffman can smell coffee at ten kilometers."

"I'll have the boat standing by. Any special instructions regarding Fenix?"

Adam wasn't going anywhere, but Prescott had been hopelessly wrong about the man once and he couldn't risk a second slip. This was one of the most technically able and intellectually gifted men of his generation. Some of the other scientists were like starstruck teenagers at the idea of having the great man working with them. If Fenix put his mind to getting a message out to Jacinto, there was a high risk that he would manage it.

"Just remind him we have his son's life at our disposal," Prescott said. What an extraordinarily lucky break that had been. He couldn't have created better leverage if he'd planned it. "Just make sure he's kept under surveillance. Nevil has sufficient grievance with him to be a useful pair of eyes, and there might well be some malcontents among the biologists who resent him out of vain professional rivalry, so be creative."

"Understood, sir." Dury slowly raised one eyebrow. "May I ask a question?"

"An awkward one?"

"I really need to know at what point you'll agree to leave Jacinto."

"I'll leave," Prescott said, "if and when we have to evacuate the city. I know that's counter to every emergency plan and best practice, but I simply *cannot* be seen to abandon citizens. Whatever Dr. Samson's nauseating cheerleading says, we can't rebuild Sera from the population here alone. We need as many of our less illustrious residents as we can save."

Prescott could have sworn that Dury was on the verge of a rare smile. *Damn.* He hoped the captain didn't have a higher opinion of him than he warranted, because duping honest men wasn't a satisfying sport. For a moment, Prescott missed the thrust and parry of real politics, outwitting other politicians and maneuvering around journalists with a well-phrased denial or elegant omission, but perhaps he would live long enough to see it all return one day.

"No, I wouldn't breed from some of the people here, either, sir," Dury said, and finally gave in to a smile. It was amused, not warm. "The next time I see you will be in Jacinto, then. Safe journey."

Prescott checked his watch and adjusted for Tyrus coastal time. He could fit in a visit to Fenix's laboratory and still be ready for the submarine. It would be a couple of pleasant and much-needed walks, the kind he simply couldn't have in Jacinto. It was almost funny being the most powerful man on Sera and yet the last who could make use of Azura. That was what the place was for—not just classified research and a repository for all that Sera needed to rebuild after a global catastrophe, but the emergency seat of government. Prescott had to tough it out in Jacinto with the rest of them. It was his duty. Politics was a dirty business carried out by even dirtier people—out of necessity, just like warfare—but he had his standards, the standards learned since childhood from his father, and those were clear. A leader had a duty to serve his people, however brutal the choices he might need to make for them.

See, Fenix. I don't cut and run. I can't. This is all I am. No wife, no son. No legacy except history. And perhaps not even that.

Adam Fenix couldn't have asked for better facilities, Prescott decided as he strolled along the flower-lined path to the main lab. The laboratory was bright, clean, and airy, and certainly better-equipped than the one Adam had at the DRA; his suite of rooms had another study, luxurious and wood-paneled, very like the level of elegance he was used to at Haldane Hall. It still baffled Prescott that a physicist could do useful research in biochemistry, but history was dotted with rare polymaths who could find insights in every discipline they touched.

Adam also had his brilliant wife's research papers, though. His brilliant *dead* wife.

Imagine being so curious that you're willing to die to find out something nobody else ever has. To be the first, to have your discovery named after you. Scientists. Such vanity.

And how extraordinary for a man to be willing to work with those who killed his wife. Adam's more of a politician than I gave him credit for. Or perhaps he's just as seduced by the problem solving and thrill of discovery as his wife was.

"How are you today, Adam?"

Adam looked up at Prescott over his glasses. He had those same unsettling pale blue eyes as his son, and he was still a big man, built like the frontline Gear he'd once been. Sometimes that reminder caught Prescott off-guard. "How's my son?"

"Marcus is doing fine," Prescott said. "I'll make sure you get a regular update on his welfare. Now, is there anything you need that's not been provided? I'm heading back to Jacinto shortly. I can't be away for more than a day or so, or too frequently, or else my cover starts to wear thin."

Adam sat hunched over his desk at an awkward angle, probably to relieve the pain in his healing ribs. A cup of tea, milk fat congealing on the cooling surface, sat on a pile of reports and lab tests next to a framed picture of Elain.

She'd been a very pretty woman then: fine-boned and clearly aware of her looks, Prescott decided, not some dowdy absent-minded professor in a scruffy cardigan. The portrait looked on as if Adam needed her there to supervise his efforts or perhaps bless them. Prescott glanced around for a photo of Marcus, but there was just Elain. Perhaps the other pictures were in his suite. Dury had definitely retrieved them from Haldane Hall.

Adam gave Prescott that professorial scrutiny look. "How do you account for the Raven going off the plot?"

"You don't know how you got here, do you?"

"I was unconscious at the time, I believe."

"It's easier to go under than over. Although you can, if your aircraft has the altitude. A submarine dives under the churn of the Maelstrom, and then surfaces near Endeavour Naval Base to rendezvous with a Raven. I'm glad you don't recall being winched onto the boat. Rather too exciting in a high wind. So—do you need anything or not?"

Adam did a slow unblinking sweep around the room, then shook his head. A couple of lab technicians were busy behind the glass wall on the far side. Prescott caught a glimpse of a row of jars holding something yellow and translucent, backlit by a fluorescent strip. "Oh, we've got everything we could possibly wish for, except a solution. Would you like to see what we're doing?" He picked up the cup of cold tea and took a sip, then frowned. "Come on. I'll show you."

He was almost affable now, probably distracted by this new scientific puzzle to solve, but then he was hardly in a position to be indignant. Prescott followed him and stood at the glass wall.

"This is the first time I've worked directly with organic chemists." Adam folded his arms. "Or any biologist, to be exact."

"You didn't work with your wife, then."

"You know she didn't share this with me."

"I meant in general."

"No, I didn't." Adam gave him a quick frown as if he couldn't believe Prescott's ignorance about scientific disciplines. "Anyway, we're propagating the samples here. The Lambent pathogen. Then we can test destructive methods."

"Before you fully understand it?"

"They're two sides of the same coin, Richard. We have to be able to kill it, and that's part of understanding it."

Prescott watched the technicians. They were fully covered in hazmat suits, gloved and masked, despite the fact that they were handling the substance in the safety of a fume box, yet Adam had been keeping it in simple glass jars in his home for years.

It still looked like imulsion, the fuel that had transformed Sera's economy and started eight decades of war.

"Dr. Bakos is going to share some previously classified material with you," Prescott said. "You had your research secrets, we had ours. Were you aware of the health concerns about imulsion?"

"Emissions? Yes. Like any combustible material. Particulates, volatile fractions, that kind of risk."

"I mean teratogenic. Mutagenic. Have I used the correct terms? Causing malformations and changes at the genetic level."

"Oh. We suppressed those findings, did we? Can't upset the imulsion companies with health scares." Adam looked as if he was going to start some sanctimonious lecture, but backed off, shaking his head. "Share prices are hardly our biggest problem now, I suppose."

Prescott debated whether to tell him about New Hope or leave it to Esther Bakos. No, he'd plunge straight in with the most difficult issue and hope he'd picked up enough research jargon to sound in control. "Esther seems to think human tissue would be the best test option."

"We have plenty of that in the medical lab, I'm told."

"She used the phrase *in vivo*." *You can explain yourself to Adam, Esther.* "She suggested I run it past you."

Adam's dark brows knitted in a frown again. "No, I can't accept volunteers. We have no idea what this pathogen can do in a human being. Informed consent would be impossible."

"We know what *imulsion* does to humans."

Adam blinked. "But this isn't imulsion any longer."

"I'll get to the point. If human subjects are needed, I can get them from the prison—"

Adam hit the heel of his hand square on the glass. His face was expressionless but somehow luminous with outrage, intense pure ice. The technicians flinched and twisted around to look, almost jerking their hands out of the fume box.

"Absolutely not. *No.* Absolutely out of the question."

"Your choice. One day you might decide a child murderer's life is worth a world."

"Cheap false equivalence. I will *not* experiment on a human being. *Any* human being."

"Sorry, I forgot. Omitting to mention an invasion force—fine. Building and deploying weapons of mass destruction—fine. Vivisecting the worst kind of criminal—*not* fine. I'll make a note of that."

Adam was staring into the glass. Prescott could see that he wasn't focused on the laboratory on the other side. Yes, it was an obvious shot, and Prescott knew he should have been above taking it, but Adam needed to be broken down and rebuilt like a Gear recruit again. He needed to have his nose rubbed in his little pile of stinking guilt until he lost all delusions of having rights, a guilt so unthinkable that even Prescott was still coming to terms with the enormity of the decision Adam had taken in isolation. His wife had done much the same, although the unlucky woman hadn't known until it was too late that the Locust would be hostile.

I make mistakes. I'm not a saint, much less a martyr. But I would at least have rushed to share the burden of that knowledge with someone who might know more than I did. Chairman or not.

Adam dragged his eyes away from the glass. "As obscene as that sounds," he said, "that's exactly the way it is. If human tissue is necessary, I won't accept a volunteer, and I certainly won't accept a *victim*. I'll find another way."

There was no point trying to win an argument with him. Prescott turned and walked away. It was simple: Adam would do as he was told, and if a live human was what the research required, Prescott would get one and shove a needle in the bastard himself if necessary.

It wouldn't have been the first time, and it wouldn't be the last. With millions of lives on his conscience already, Prescott knew he wouldn't burn any more hotly in hell for a few more.

26 RTI BARRACKS, FORMER WRIGHTMAN HOSPITAL: STORM, 10 A.E.

"Where are you going, Dom?" Jace leaned against the door frame, scrubbing the detached chain of his Lancer with a wire brush. "You want some company?"

It was an unusually mild early evening. Half the company seemed to be doing their cleaning and maintenance outside on the white stone steps. The hospital had been built in the old COG style, like barracks with a central square, and apart from the old metal signs still on walls and washrooms that were a bit more comfortable than the army standard, it didn't feel medical to Dom at all. He squatted beside the motorbike to check the tire pressures.

"It's okay, Jace," he said. "Just going to check out a new Stranded camp."

"Happy to help, buddy."

"I'll be okay. Anyway, Anya's coming along."

No, Dom *wasn't* going to be okay. He knew he'd never be okay again, not until he found Maria, but now Marcus was gone too, and that had hit him even harder than he'd expected. The dead, however much you missed them, didn't beckon all the time. They were in their allotted place and you couldn't do a single damn thing about it except remember and regret. Dom hadn't come to terms with the deaths of his mom or dad, or Carlos, and certainly not Bennie and Sylvie. Maria was probably still out there—his heart said definitely, his common sense said a fighting chance—but Marcus was confirmed and located, there but not there, stuck in a frigging shithole where Dom couldn't even phone him to keep him going.

The dead couldn't suffer any longer. The separated living could. Dom now woke up each day and kept breathing for only one reason, to bring Maria and Marcus back home. The Locust could have the rest of the goddamn world as long as he got to keep the last people left alive that he loved.

"Hey, Dom. Ready to roll?"

Dom glanced up, catching a glimpse of civvy boots and fatigue pants. Anya stood over him, out of her smart gray officer's skirt and woolly pulley for once. She'd made a brave attempt at looking averagely inconspicuous. But she was Anya, and not even scruff rig and no makeup could make her look anything less than luminously beautiful. That wasn't a good idea when venturing into Stranded camps.

"You better put on a ballistic vest or some plates." It was a sensible precaution but it would also disguise her *shape*. Even mentally, Dom couldn't bring himself to say the actual B-word. They were just her . . . *shape*. This was Anya, his friend, effectively his superior officer, and she was Marcus's, so none of the normal, casual, harmlessly natural things a guy thought about women— especially women who looked like Anya—could ever be allowed into his head. "And these bikes kick up a lot of shit, so better put a scarf over your mouth. Oh, and bring your sidearm. I mean it. *Ma'am.*"

Anya nodded and jogged back into the barracks. Jace watched.

"She ain't okay, either, is she?" he said.

"Would *you* be? And stop checking out her ass. You're disgusting."

"Sorry." Jace almost shook himself. "Look, whatever it takes, man. You think of a way to get Marcus freed, you just say the word and I'm in. And Tai. The whole of Two-Six, probably."

"I'm still thinking. I'll let you know." Dom slid onto the bike with his Lancer slung across his back. Anya reappeared, swamped by an EOD blast jacket and a scarf that covered her hair and chin. "If we're not back in a couple of hours—ah, shit, I'll be on a charge by then anyway. See you later."

Anya swung onto the pillion seat. She really didn't have to do this. But she'd always make herself do things that scared her, and that was the definition of guts as far as Dom was concerned. He was damn sure that her gung-ho mom had had to steel herself and get on with it more than once, no matter how confident she'd always seemed and no matter how many medals got pinned on her. Any asshole could be oblivious to danger out of sheer ignorance or cockiness, and maybe that didn't matter as long as they did the job, but Dom knew what Anya saw and heard daily in Ops, the terrible stuff that came over the radio and the video feeds, so she knew damn well what the stakes were. She'd heard her mom *die*, for fuck's sake. Desk jockey or not, she *understood*. And since Marcus had been gone she'd been getting a lot more assertive.

Now she was bending the regs to go out with Dom to pass Maria's picture around some roach-infested camp and ask if anyone had seen her. Hoffman turned a blind eye to it all. Dom gathered all kinds of intel while he was out, Hoffman said, so if Dom wanted to risk his ass and burn a little fuel getting it, it was okay by him.

I can get away with anything with Hoff. I thought Marcus could, too.

The potholes and broken paving began about fifty meters outside the Jacinto wire and Dom found himself weaving around obstacles. Maybe it hadn't been such a great idea to let Anya come after all.

"Okay back there?" he yelled.

The slipstream and engine noise snatched his words. He had to slow down anyway. If he bent the forks on this thing, he'd be in real, can't-get-out-of-it trouble. They'd stopped making parts for the bike years ago. It would cost time and resources they just didn't have these days.

"Fine," Anya said. She didn't sound it. "Kind of."

"Grab hold of my belt." She was gripping the small handle behind her seat, which felt precarious at the best of times. He could feel her knees brushing the back of his legs as she tried to hang on without making a fuss. "Or waist. But for God's sake don't fall off. Marcus will kill me."

It was just a figure of speech. Marcus had never so much as disagreed with him over an offside call in a thrashball game. But Marcus wasn't there, and his absence was an aching void. The guy had been so thoroughly stitched into the fabric of Dom's daily existence that all that was left now were holes—no

Marcus on patrol to keep an eye on, no Marcus to swap rations with, and no Marcus to just give him that it'll-be-okay look when yet another sighting of Maria turned out to be a false lead. And those voids in Dom's day were now filling up with extra fears. Was Marcus getting enough food? Did he have some frigging psycho that he couldn't turn his back on for a cellmate? Was anyone giving him any shit? Was he *scared*?

Yeah, Marcus got scared like everyone else. Everyone seemed to think he was above all that. Dom knew better.

"I put in a request for a visit," Dom said. "They said one visit a month once his first three months is up. I didn't realize you'd written."

"Sorry, Dom." She had a firm grip on his belt but gradually her right arm slipped round his waist. Then she suddenly slapped her left hand over it as if she'd been working up to letting go of his belt, and hung on for dear life. He'd thought he was riding pretty sedately. "I don't even know if he's received it."

"Aren't they supposed to tell us that stuff?"

"I should be finding this out. Damn, I'm supposed to be the admin expert."

"Hey, it's okay. We're both missing him. We're not thinking straight yet."

"He doesn't really mean he doesn't want to see us again. Does he?"

Dom suspected Marcus really didn't, but for very self-sacrificing, Marcus-like reasons. He brazened it out. "No. Of course not."

He tried to concentrate on what was around him. The route past the new Stranded camp had been swept by patrols a couple of times but grubs came up anytime, anywhere. It was a case of maintaining situational awareness and opening up the throttle to get the hell out if anything cropped up. Stranded had their own kind of personal radar when it came to grubs, though, and the fact that there were any left alive ten years after E-Day was proof. They had to stay one step ahead of these assholes. Dom wondered if grubs were just bone-idle and couldn't be bothered to pick off small groups unless it was handed to them on a plate. He kept scanning back and forth, now alert to every shadow, swaying branch, or reflection off broken glass. It was a long, empty highway through a wasteland of burned-out cars and the stumps of buildings, the universal Seran landscape for the last decade, and he was looking for a fleeting landmark of sorts just west of the Ilima off-ramp.

"See it?" he asked.

"What?"

"Smoke."

"Got it."

Stranded were good at digging in. Sometimes he didn't see a camp until he tripped over it. Centaur tanks were a lot higher off the ground and the guy on top cover could see for kilometers on a clear day, but Packhorses and 'Dills were too low on the ground and a bike was even lower. Smoke was usually the giveaway; smoke, or packs of dogs. Stranded who couldn't tap into a power line or fuel a generator relied on wood-burners and open fires. This was one of those. Dom slowed down, giving the sentry plenty of time to check him out—he couldn't see anyone, but there'd be a guy on overwatch somewhere—and rehearsed his opening line again. Gears were rarely welcome. He had to be diplomatic.

Hey, guys. I'm Dom Santiago. Have you seen this woman? She's my wife. She walked out of our home a year or so after our kids were killed and I haven't seen her since.

Mostly people shook their heads. Some didn't, though. Some got that look in their eyes that gave him renewed hope. He heard the barking start up and knew he was in someone's cross-wires now. He was approaching a fuel station—no roof, no pumps, and no doors—with what looked like a junkyard behind it.

"Anya, just keep behind me, okay?" he said. "They don't normally get awkward, but there's always a first time."

"I've got my sidearm."

"Yeah, but can you still use it?"

"I'm requalifying. Rossi's helping me."

"Okay. But leave this to me."

Dom braked gradually to a slow putter and looked for a logical entry point so that he didn't look like he was trying to sneak in the back door. The bike still sounded throaty, like the muffler had blown somewhere, but at least whoever was tracking him knew he was there. Now he saw the first dog. It was a scruffy brown and white thing barking its head off. Then all its buddies showed up behind it to stand in a group, yapping. If they went for him, he'd shoot, but he hoped it wouldn't come to that.

"Anybody home?" he yelled. There'd be a Stranded security party along soon. "Dom Santiago. I'm looking for my wife."

He waited with the engine idling, just in case. He could still hear Anya breathing, taking in the occasional deep breath as if she was getting ready to run. As he stared at the fuel station, he saw the first sign of movement, and a skinny middle-aged guy with a beat-up hunting cap and a rifle to match edged out from behind one of the concrete pillars. The dogs seemed satisfied that their masters had things under control and trotted away.

"And why'd she be here?" the guy asked. More Stranded men started appearing behind him. "Seeing as she's got a soldier boy to keep her fed in the city."

"My kids got killed and she went out looking for them," Dom said. He'd said it so often now that the words blurred into one continuous cadence of sound, stripped of meaning like singing a song in a foreign language and having no idea what the lyrics meant. It helped him stomach them. "She never came back. You know what I mean. Tipped her over the edge."

A frank admission often did the trick. *My poor damn wife went crazy.* Half the survivors out here must have understood that level of despair. Dom studied the grim, haggard, suspicious faces and waited for the lines to soften and become baffled embarrassment, as they sometimes did.

"Nobody here by that name," the guy with the hunting cap said. His rifle dipped just a little and Dom noted one of the guys looking past him at Anya. *Don't even think about it, asshole. She's my brother's girl. You'll be wearing your junk for a pendant.* "Santiago."

Dom held his arms out away from his sides to show he wasn't going to use the Lancer that must have been the first thing they spotted. "Maria Santiago. I've got a picture. Will you take a look?"

The guy who'd been checking out Anya stepped forward while the other Stranded covered Dom. He had a shotgun. "Tell your buddy to keep his hands away from his pistol."

Dom heard a rustle behind him as if Anya had decided to hold out her arms too. The body armor had done a better job of disguising her figure than he'd expected. "No sweat, man. We just want to find my wife. Okay? I can't offer much for the information, but I've got some hard candy for your kids if you want it." Dom waited for the shotgun guy to get within five meters and then raised his hand. "Okay, I'm going to reach under my chest plate and pull out the photo, so *relax.*"

The guy stopped and watched as Dom went through the motion that was automatic by now and slid out the photo of himself and Maria—more tattered every time, showing more creases, threatening to erase Maria completely one day. He held it up so the guy could see it.

"I don't have many pictures of her," he said. "Just look and don't touch. You understand."

"Okay." The guy squinted and nodded. The man with the hunting rifle came over to look as well. "We'd remember her. Pretty lady. Even if she looked a bit different now."

"No luck, then."

"Sorry."

Dom reached slowly into his belt and took out the bag of candy. It was old and sticky, but kids would go crazy for it. "Thanks, anyway. You ever see her, find a Gear and tell him Dom Santiago needs to know. I'll make it worth your while somehow."

Dom was used to abuse because his armor said one thing to Stranded: the COG, the government who'd hung them out to dry, and most of these poor assholes had been COG citizens before the Hammer strikes. So Stranded saw no reason to love Gears, and patrols often got stoned and spat at if they ever got close enough. Gears had an equally low opinion of Stranded, who could have enlisted and had three square meals a day. But Dom was careful to present himself as a guy on his own, worried sick about his wife and no threat to anyone. It usually worked. The shotgun guy took the candy, touched his cap, and stepped back.

"Hope you find her, buddy," he said. "Really."

Dom put the picture away and revved the bike. "Thanks. Stay safe."

"We hear the grubs are all over you in Ephyra. We've seen 'em moving up Corpsers, too. They're still keen on digging around the plateau."

"Yeah." That hurt more than Dom imagined. "Nobody's safe now. Maybe we should learn a lesson from you guys."

Dom turned the bike and roared away. Maybe they'd feel better for knowing that the COG was getting its comeuppance a street at a time. But it happened to be the truth, even for a never-quit guy like himself.

"Are they always like that?" Anya asked. Either he was riding more sensibly now or she was getting used to the bike, because she wasn't squeezing the breath out of him. "The only way I can handle it is not to think about them. I was right there when Prescott gave the order."

She sometimes said that to Dom, almost confessional, as if she'd taken the decision herself. She was the ops room lieutenant. She just happened to be there. Nine years on, she still seemed to feel the need to remind him. He'd never heard her mention it to anyone else.

"They don't forget," Dom said, "and I can't blame them. But some are more polite about it than others." He looked back over his shoulder for a second. "I'm going to ask about a legal appeal for Marcus."

"It'd have to be against sentence, not conviction. He pleaded guilty."

"You know about this stuff, then."

"Basic law's the same, military or civilian. If you admit you did it, you can't

complain that the judge believed you. Unless they find you confessed to something you didn't do."

"Okay, sentence it is."

"The Judge Advocate's officers are mostly doing supply work now with
Major Reid. We don't have courts-martial often enough to keep them busy."

"So I see Reid?"

"You could try. Or I could."

"I'll do it, Anya. I know it's awkward for you."

"Why?"

"You're an officer. Marcus is enlisted."

"He's a civilian by default now. Dismissed the service. Automatically."

"You know what I mean."

"No, Dom, you can't use that excuse for him now."

"It's not an excuse. It's regs."

"Well, screw the regs. I love him and I'm not giving him up without a fight."
Anya had never actually voiced her disappointment that bluntly before. She
sounded angry with Marcus, but that was pretty much like the early stage of
bereavement. "Mom would never tell me who my dad was. I'll be damned if I
become another Stroud girl who's okay to screw but isn't good enough to marry."

"Aw, c'mon, you know Marcus doesn't think like that. It's the whole fraternizing with officers thing."

"He's in jail for dereliction of duty. Nobody gives a damn now who he did
or didn't sleep with."

"And it's the way his upbringing made him. But he loves you, Anya. He's
never looked at another woman, I swear it."

"He never even stays the whole night."

"He has nightmares. I mean *bad.*"

She paused, as if she hadn't realized that. "Who doesn't? I can handle it."

Dom cringed. This was a conversation they had to have well out of earshot
of anyone else, painful private stuff that people probably knew anyway but
nobody dared mention. Dom had known Marcus since they were kids, more
than twenty years, and he'd become friends with Anya—an unlikely friendship, across class divides and across rank—in the last years of the Pendulum
Wars. They'd all been at a medal ceremony, raw with grief and determined to
close ranks against a curious world: Embry Stars for Marcus, Dom, and posthumously for his brother Carlos, and Anya was receiving the Embry on behalf
of her dead mother. It was an agonizing way to forge a friendship. It also made
it rock solid. And Marcus and Anya—that's when it had all started.

Marcus rarely said anything about her to Dom because he wasn't a gut-spill kind of guy. Like Carlos used to say, you had to listen to his silences as much as what he actually said. But he loved her in that weird, distant, upper-class, Fenix kind of way. Maria had said it would never work out. Dom wanted it to work out *better*. But Dom knew it was just Marcus being Marcus — not callous, not unfaithful, not even neglectful, just struggling to cope with intimacy and whatever side of himself that he felt he didn't dare let Anya see. She was right. The officer-enlisted divide was now probably more of an excuse than a reason.

Damn, Anya was *patient*, a saint waiting for crumbs of affection. Dom could only think of it like the Tyran lynx, solitary cats that mated for life but spent most of the year prowling and hunting alone, only getting together in season. Dom was too wary to do anything more than give Marcus an angry jab in the ribs occasionally and tell him to shit or get off the pot in case Anya got fed up and went off with a guy willing to at least admit he was dating her.

She never would, of course. Dom could see her still waiting for Marcus in forty years, if anyone had that long to live these days.

"Anya, he's my brother. He's my *family*." Dom had to get this over with before they got back to the barracks. "I can't sit on my ass. I'm going to get him a lawyer. The army wouldn't give him a really good one, even if we had any."

"How? Lawyers don't do it for free, even these days."

"I'll think of something."

Anya didn't say another word. About a kilometer from the barracks, though, just as they were crossing Timgad Bridge, she patted him on the back.

"You're the best friend anyone could ever have, Dom. We'll get him out. And we'll find Maria. Promise."

All anyone could do in a war was look out for the guy next to him. Dom looked out for Marcus and now he'd look out for Anya, because Marcus couldn't. It was that simple. He dropped Anya off at the mess, returned the bike to the motor pool, and went back to his quarters, a metal-framed bed and a battered locker in what had been a side ward. Wrightman Hospital was where the rich had once sent their lunatic relatives, and some nights Dom lay staring up at the egg-and-dart cornice around the ceiling, wondering what kind of poor tormented bastard had been locked in this well-meaning prison. Everywhere Dom turned, he was surrounded by prisons and madness now.

I must be crazy too. Who gets out of the Slab alive?

He opened his locker. He didn't have many possessions left, but one small item was worth something, a dull bronze medal with a red and black striped ribbon: his Embry Star. Without Carlos and now without Marcus, it wasn't worth shit to him. They said some people still collected them, which was mad in itself, but the whole world was fucking mad now.

Maybe I can get a medical appeal for Marcus. Battle stress. Nobody wants to talk about it, admit they've got it, least of all Marcus. Stigma my ass. He doesn't have to prove himself to any bastard.

Dom took the medal out of its small leather box and rubbed it on his pants. The inscription was just his name and rank, and two simple words: FOR COURAGE.

Courage. It was every day, every hour, every minute. Dom couldn't see the line between what he did at Aspho Point and everything else he made himself do when he couldn't face the next second. Whatever Marcus was going through now would be a damn sight harder than taking on the Indies at Aspho Fields.

And he'd be doing it alone.

CHAPTER 7

Why would anyone want to escape from the Slab these days? It's probably the safest place in Jacinto now. There'll be people breaking in to hide there before too long, mark my words.

(Kennith Heugel, former warder at CPSE Hesketh—aka the Slab.)

LATRINE AND SHOWER BLOCK, THE SLAB: GALE, 11 A.E.

Niko checked each toilet stall, pushing the waist-level swing doors open, as if anyone could possibly hide behind them. Reeve waited. It had to be important for a screw to risk coming down here on his own.

"So he keeps his nose clean," Niko said at last. He seemed satisfied they wouldn't be overheard and pressed a small paper-wrapped package into Reeve's palm. "He's not looking terrific, though, is he?"

Reeve squeezed the package and estimated there were five roll-ups in it, not bad pay for keeping an eye on Marcus Fenix. "He's not eating much."

"See that he does."

"He's built like a brick shithouse. I can't make him eat his greens."

"But that's what I'm paying you for."

It was simplicity itself to kill someone. Adequate planning and a steady hand, that was what it took, and Reeve could have written a textbook on it. Keeping someone alive when they'd lost the will was much harder. Niko gave Reeve that warning look, chin lowered. A faucet dripped somewhere. The place smelled less like a lavatory than D Wing. It was easier to keep clean.

Niko tapped his pocket. "I've got two letters from his girlfriend."

"So?"

"So I need to know if it's going to tip him over the edge. Some guys, it keeps them going. But some just go mental. Can't bear to be separated, can't bear to think what she's getting up to with someone else, whatever."

"So put him on suicide watch."

"We don't *do* a suicide watch."

"Yeah, half the guys in here aren't exactly the relationship kind. And then there's the guys who prefer dead ladies anyway."

"Just tell me. Is this going to help or make things worse?"

Prisoners were allowed a letter a week or one visit a month. Reeve couldn't recall ever getting either, but his customers didn't make house calls. One of the arsonists had a couple of visits from his mom some years ago, but then she'd stopped coming and everyone assumed she was dead. Most people in the outside world were.

The whole world. Wonder what it looks like out there now?

"Let me find out." Reeve held out his hand for the letter. "You want to leave it with me?"

"No." Niko narrowed his eyes. "It's personal."

"Oooh . . ."

"The governor's checked it for security shit. You can take that look off your face."

"Come on, what could anyone possibly write in a fucking letter to a lifer that would compromise *security*? We're safer in than out. And not just for ourselves."

"Rules," Niko said. "I don't make 'em."

He turned and walked off. Reeve waited for his footsteps to fade on the broken floor tiles, taking the opportunity to liberate a frayed floorcloth from one of the buckets before ambling back to the main floor, laughingly known as the recreation area, as if everyone enjoyed a piano recital and cocktails there of an evening. Normally, he could predict who'd be where at any given time and what they'd be doing. There was only so much time that the guys who weren't in solitary could spend tending the gardens or trying to keep this glorified hovel clean. The mycoprotein vats in the east wing were automated and only needed shutting down and cleaning every couple of months when somebody got a seriously bad dose of shits from food poisoning.

Busy was good in this place, though. Busy meant you were still alive instead of wide awake in your coffin, Reeve decided, and stopped the more antisocial residents from slicing you up out of boredom.

You noticed that yet, Marcus? Have you noticed how different we all are?

Prison's like the army, despite the dirt. It has ranks and rules. Every society's like that.

Everything happened on the main open floor of D Wing. The screws could see most of what was going on from the safety of the gallery or the gantry, if they gave a damn, and the lags had the illusion of privacy, at least from above.

But not from your fellow guests, of course.

"Hey, Chunky," Reeve called. The little guy was sitting in his cell cross-legged on the bed, working away at that damn blanket with a single needle. He'd blagged some more scraps off someone, then. "Can we see what it is yet?"

"Patience, son," Chunky said. "It's a map."

"Now, if you were in here for knocking over a bank, I'd be interested . . ."

"And if I'd buried the stash somewhere, it'd be worth shit now. But a rug, that's another thing." Chunky tucked the needle in the top pocket of his overalls and held up the chaotic mass of cloth, about the size of a big bath mat. "Getting there, a square at a time. Nearly done."

"Bit small for a blanket."

"It's a *rug*," Chunky said, as if he was teaching Reeve a new word. "And it's *crochet*. Not goddamn knitting."

Reeve couldn't make out any detail in it. It was a steadily growing raft of all kinds of stuff—thin strips of cloth, bits of wool, thick thread, even dog hair, or at least Reeve *hoped* it was dog. If there was a rag or anything remotely weavable being thrown out, Chunky would pounce on it. Still, it made sense to have a good thick rug even if it didn't look much like anything. The floors here were either poured concrete or granite slabs. In winter it was cold enough to freeze the balls off Embry's statue.

Reeve fished around in his pocket and took out the frayed floorcloth. The knitted cotton yarn was already unraveling so all Chunky had to do was finish picking it apart. "Compliments of the house," he said.

Chunky grinned. "I bet your momma always told you what a good boy you were, Reeve."

So there was another neighbor who'd owe Reeve a small favor one day. Life in the Slab was mostly a delicate balance of favors and diplomacy, occasionally interrupted by unpleasant things that Reeve could forget had ever happened if he tried hard enough. The rules weren't the same ones the outside world was used to but if you followed them long enough, they seemed perfectly normal. Even a shithole like this was quiet routine most of the time. Violent offenders—he loved that word, *offenders*, like they all belched in public or something—couldn't keep it up all day, every day, any more than a thrashball player could.

But it was unnaturally quiet today. Reeve could see a row of asses ahead as a dozen or more guys leaned over the checkers table in a huddle, looking as if they were studying something. The Indie guy everyone ignored as if he didn't exist, Edouain, hovered on the fringes like he usually did. When Reeve got close up he could see everyone was jostling for a newspaper, which were pretty thin on the ground these days.

"So how old is *this* one?" he said, trying to get a look in. He cast around to check where Marcus was but couldn't see him. There was no sign of Merino, either. "Six months? Three?"

"A week." That was Leuchars. His nose was almost touching the paper. The guy hadn't had a new pair of glasses in years. If the cops had only had the sense to take his specs away the first time they'd arrested him, they might have saved a few lives. "It's even got an up-to-date map."

"Of what? Somewhere else none of us are ever going to go?"

Reeve spread his shoulders a little to ease his way into the pack without starting a fight. Now he could see it. It was a mauled copy of the *Jacinto Daily*, which was now more like an occasional weekly sheet because they didn't have enough newsprint and everyone relied on the state radio or Ephyra World Service anyway. And it was a map, all right. It was one of those graphics things that journos loved, a map of the Ephyra plateau centered on Jacinto with all the grub front lines drawn in and marked by almost cartoonish images of drones. Reeve had only seem them on the TV news in shaky, badly lit recon footage, but they didn't look funny at all.

The other thing that didn't look funny was the lines.

"They're getting fucking *close*," said Leuchars. "Look."

He traced his finger along what would have been contour lines or something. Reeve could see the granite areas marked out in black, the places where volcanoes had erupted millions of years ago and been eroded by time, leaving the plugs of lava as granite and basalt. The Slab stood on one of the smaller ones, things they called side vents, cut from the granite itself. The boundary of the granite wasn't a smooth line, though. It had lobes, almost like petals of a flower, narrow bits that stuck out into the softer ground, and the Slab was on one of those. For a moment, Reeve felt the place was stuck on a pier and that it could be surrounded and cut off at any time.

"They've got to get in first," he said. Yeah, that was right, wasn't it? "Remember why they put this place here. So nobody could tunnel their way out. If we can't get out, they can't get in."

Leuchars straightened up and took off his glasses. He looked more like a bank manager than a bank robber. "You ever heard of climbing over walls, Reeve? Or flying? Those assholes have Reavers. And ladders."

"They've had ten years to fly in and fuck us up. Why now?"

"Why ten years ago? Because they're grubs and they just kill humans. It's what they do."

Most of the huddle broke up and wandered away, leaving Leuchars leaning on the table and staring at the map as if he was planning a raid. Reeve looked up and saw two of the warders, Gallego and Campbell, leaning on the gantry rail and just watching. Reeve snatched the paper from under Leuchars's hands and held it up like laundry.

"So, have we got an evacuation plan?" he called.

Gallego shrugged without moving his arms. "I'll ask the Department."

They didn't even have a fire drill. There was a muster point in the gardens if the fire alarm went off, but they'd still be stuck inside a locked maze with fifteen-meter walls until someone found another secure place to take them, and he wasn't sure that the COG had anything like that left.

If he'd been Chairman Prescott, he would have had everyone quietly shot by now. It was the only sensible thing to do.

But if they just opened the doors—how much difference would that really make? I mean, the world's up to its ass in homicidal monsters already, and maybe they'd take out a few of the human ones too.

The public address system whistled with feedback for a second or two before a metallic, nasal announcement made Reeve's fillings rattle. *"Prisoner Alva, report to the infirmary for your appointment, Prisoner Alva . . ."* Well, the medic was still paying the occasional visit, so at least somebody cared. Reeve wandered slowly back down the broad hall, glanced into Marcus's cell—army-tidy, the crabby blanket and threadbare sheets tucked so straight and tight on the metal bed that you could bounce a coin off them—and wondered if he was in the east wing. That was where the kitchens were. A guy could have accidents in there unless someone was around to look out for him. Reeve speeded up discreetly and started composing a good reason for going there that didn't make him look like he was kissing Marcus's ass. It would raise questions, and then everyone else would find out about the smokes, and he'd be hassled for them. A quiet life, that was all Reeve wanted.

He was heading for the far end of the hall when he heard Chunky's raised voice. Someone was giving him a hard time. The trouble with long, straight halls was that you had to get pretty close to be at the right angle to see who was inside the cells, and Reeve couldn't hear the other voice yet.

"Hey, c'mon, why pick on me?" Chunky was saying. He wasn't any trouble to anyone, at least not the other inmates. "Don't, you asshole, you're gonna rip it—"

Then someone stepped backward out of the cell, not paying any attention to who was behind him because he didn't have to. It was Merino, and he had the rag rug in one hand. Just stupid, childish bullying, beneath Reeve's contempt in the real world, but in here it was a much bigger deal because this was all they had, the only pecking order they would know until the day they died, because for the COG, life meant life, and a sentence often meant life even when it wasn't.

But this was Merino, and Reeve picked his battles.

"It's a real nice rug," Merino said, laughing his ass off. He wasn't looking behind him. The boss wolf didn't need to watch his back. "You can make another."

Chunky was on his feet now at the cell door, almost in tears. "It took me three fucking years to collect the cloth, man."

"Well, we're none of us going anywhere, so—"

That was the moment when Reeve saw Marcus appear behind Merino like he'd stepped clean out of the granite wall. Merino must have realized he was there a second later. Marcus just reached out, expression completely blank, and the next moment Merino's face was slammed against the bars and Marcus twisted his arm up behind his back. The first thing Merino did was to look up, checking who was watching. A sprained arm was nothing compared to a bruised reputation.

"You're going to wish they stuck you up against a wall, Fenix," Merino grunted. He was doing his best to look casual about it, but there really was no dressing it up. "Time to start looking over your shoulder."

"Shouldn't argue over your knitting, ladies," Marcus said. "He'll give you the pattern if you ask nicely."

He peeled the rug out of Merino's hand and tossed it into Chunky's cell, then walked on, back turned on them. But his fists were balled. For a moment Reeve expected the confrontation to erupt into a full-scale fight. Heads popped out of the other cells to watch, and he could have heard a rat fart if the rats hadn't already abandoned the place.

Don't look at Merino. Don't make eye contact.

"You want to finish this, Fenix?" Merino called. "Then we can all settle down and get back to normal."

Reeve risked looking up behind him for a second, just to see where

Campbell and Gallego were. They were just watching. It was what the warders always did.

Marcus got to his cell door and turned around. "Yeah, why not?" he said, like he'd been invited for coffee and cake. "You've probably got nothing to lose. And I've got *less* than nothing." Then he went inside and sat down.

The longer the silence went on, Reeve thought, the more Merino would feel he had to assert his authority. Now it was a coin toss, a gamble as to whether he could take Marcus or not. And Marcus had his back to the wall, quite literally.

I can't just stand here. Can I?

Everything told Reeve to let them get on with it. Merino started walking from the far end of the hall, a casual stroll for a few paces, then speeded up. The guy didn't exactly have a choice now. There were rules in here, the things that kept the place stable. Someone had to be top of the pile. Merino obviously wasn't so cocksure of his position that he could laugh off Marcus, though, and he paused at the cell door for a split second to reach into his back pocket. That was a mistake.

Marcus was on his feet instantly. There was a loud crack like a chicken wishbone snapping and Merino stumbled backward from the door. He might have fallen: maybe he tripped. Either way, he scrambled to his feet as Marcus came at him, pulled his blade from his pocket, and lunged upward. Reeve didn't see if it connected or not. He just watched Merino headbutt Marcus, knocking him back a pace, and then Marcus just went for him. Shit, the blow didn't slow him down at all. He landed a hell of a punch in Merino's face and followed it up with his elbow. Merino fell flat on his back and Marcus just jumped straight on him, on his knees, fist raised again. That was the moment when Reeve found a reflex he didn't even know he had and dived in to grab Marcus's arm.

It was a good way to lose some teeth. Reeve braced. Marcus seemed to snap out of it instantly and stood up, flexing his hand. Merino got to his feet, blood streaming from his nose, just as the barking started and the wooden door flew open.

Parmenter came out with a crazy, snarling Jerry almost standing upright on the end of his leash. "Right, you assholes, break it up." Jerry took a lunge at Merino first. "Everybody back in their cell. Fenix—hands behind your head and face that fucking wall. Merino—get out of here. And you, Reeve—what are you gawping at? Piss off."

Marcus just meshed his fingers behind his head and turned around.

Merino looked stunned, possibly because nobody had seen a warder come down to deal with a fight before, even when it was pretty well over. Parmenter didn't even mention the blade. Maybe he hadn't seen it, but he wouldn't have cared if he had. Reeve dodged around Jerry's snapping jaws—he was still sure that dog was all mouth, like his handler—and took a slow walk back, looking over his shoulder while Merino completely ignored Parmenter and watched.

"Okay, it's solitary for you." Parmenter grabbed Jerry by his collar and held him at arm's length while he shoved Marcus in the back, a sort of half-hearted attempt at being a hard case. "You hear me, Fenix? If it was up to me, I'd just let the damn dogs have you. But I've got orders not to do that, so I'm going to think up some other ways to make your stay here memorable. Move it."

Marcus walked out ahead of Parmenter and didn't look back. Reeve watched the door close and glanced up at the gantry. Campbell, a pretty quiet kind of guy, was still leaning on the rail. Just as Marcus passed under the gantry, Campbell spat over the side.

"Bastard," he said. His son was a serving Gear. He pushed himself off the rail and walked away. "You're going to get yours."

It could have been an empty threat, a prediction, or a promise. Whatever it was, Reeve could do nothing, and he was worried, and it was nothing to do with losing his payment of smokes.

STAFF OFFICES, THE SLAB.

Niko shoved his time card in the machine outside the deserted staff room and wondered if he was the only bastard left on Sera who could be bothered to work.

Ospen had called in sick—busy drinking, more like—and Niko had given up his day off to cover, with the promise of extra food rations for his trouble. But Campbell, Gally, and Lasky should have been here.

He couldn't see them. He leaned over the stairwell and took advantage of the echoing acoustics. "Gally? If you bone-idle assholes are playing cards again, I swear I'm going to swing for you."

Niko didn't like 1400 to 2300 shifts at the best of times. He got up in the morning, cleared the chores if his wife was working days at Jacinto Medical Center, and then the whole day was suddenly gone. He'd get back home just after 2400 to find nothing on the TV or radio, and Maura waiting to tell him what a shitty day she'd had, because every day was shitty at the hospital

now—rustlung, burns, simple infections turning fatal because they were running out of antibiotics, and occasionally Gears with terrible wounds when the
military medics were overwhelmed.

Those seemed to upset Maura the most.

Niko stuck his head into the staff room—deserted, cold cups of coffee sitting on the table, plates stacked in the sink—and paused to listen for signs of
activity elsewhere. All he could hear was the general burble of conversation
and occasional raised voices as prisoners gossiped and argued. If he'd recorded
that and played it to folks without telling them the location, they would have
thought it was just a regular bunch of guys in a warehouse or big, echoey
workshop, not a garbage can for the most dangerous criminals in the COG.
He couldn't even hear the dogs, just the murmur of voices and the clank of tin
mugs and cell doors, the usual sound of a few dozen men rattling around in a
space built for a thousand.

Great. Leave me to fill out the handover sheets, why don't you?

He took the clipboard off the hook by the range—how many goddamn
times did he have to warn these guys about not leaving paper near a heat
source?—and walked out onto the gantry above the main floor. All he had
to do was tick the roster to say all prisoners were present, alive, and relatively
healthy. He could do that easily from up here. Nobody had stabbed anyone
else for a good couple of years; the place had found its own equilibrium. He'd
go check on the psychiatric block later.

"Hey, Edouain." The Indie looked up from the grimy mop he was pushing
around the main floor. The inmates were on cleaning duties, which was going
to make the headcount harder. "Any guest checked out since oh-six-hundred?"

Edouain cocked his head as if he was counting. "Alva went to see the medic
some time ago. The COG's in solitary."

It took Niko a second to connect *COG* with Marcus. Damn, what had he
done? "Get Reeve. Know where he is?"

"Cleaning the urinals, I think."

"So go pull him out." Niko pointed at a spot on the floor next to the checkers table. His stomach was starting to knot. "Tell him to wait *there* until I get
back."

By now, a small crowd had started to gather on the floor. They all looked
up at Niko, accusing and grim. This was the other world; his was up here on
the gantry. The inmates weren't out of control, not lately anyway, but Niko was
suddenly conscious of the numbers again. Four warders—even all twelve—
couldn't make forty men do what they wanted unless they shot them from the

gantry and even then the staff still wouldn't win. The doors were locked, but this control was all based on an understanding, on consent. Humans looked for the normal in life, a way of getting along as a group: just as the inmates couldn't behave like criminals every day, all day, the warders couldn't maintain disgust every minute. Eventually there was always a glimpse of the person within. Niko didn't have the energy to hate strangers permanently.

One of the longest-serving inmates, Seffert, looked up with his arms folded. He'd done kidnaps with big ransoms and he hadn't tolerated late payment. "Fenix got in a fight with Merino," he said. "Campbell was shooting his mouth off."

That wasn't Campbell's style. Niko's mental alarm bell went off. He gave the growing crowd of prisoners a *wait* gesture like a traffic cop and headed for the solitary block.

It had to be for Marcus's own safety. Merino wouldn't let up until he'd won and proved he was the biggest frigging baboon in the troupe. Solitary wouldn't be a lot of fun for Marcus, but it would keep him out of harm's way, and that was what the Chairman's office wanted—and maybe Marcus wanted to sit and fester on his own anyway. He wasn't remotely sociable. Yes, that was it. Niko had constructed the whole explanation and was halfway down the flagstone corridor of the secure wing before he heard the noise.

The acoustics of the rambling granite fort were unpredictable. A few meters away, all he could hear was the echo of his own boots, but as he passed the janitor's store room it leapt out at him—the staccato of wet thwacks, punctuated by grunts, as if someone was pounding a steak but couldn't maintain an even rhythm and was struggling for breath. And then a terrible voice, a man gasping but still roaring defiance: "Is that all you got? *Is that all you fucking got?* Go on! Just fucking *do* it! Finish it—"

It was cut short by another dull crunch. "Had enough yet, you bastard? Come on, asshole, you going to just stand there and take it?"

One voice was Marcus Fenix; the other was Bradeley Campbell. Niko took a few slow seconds to work out that he was listening to Marcus getting the shit kicked out of him. He tried to pull back the sliding bolt, but the room was locked from the inside.

That was why they were in there. They didn't want interruptions.

Niko started pounding on the steel panel. "Hey, what the hell's going on in there? Open up." There was a second of silence, but the thwacking and grunts started up again. "Campbell? I said *open this fucking door.*"

He was about to go and grab a set of keys when the lock rattled and the door swung open. Gally stood in the doorway for a second before Niko pushed past him and found Lasky watching Campbell, who was poised with his baton drawn back, lining up for a swing. And there was Marcus, just standing there half-turned away, knees sagging and making no attempt to defend himself. The baton hit Marcus in the lower back at kidney level with a sickening thud, once, twice. He swayed. But he didn't fall.

Campbell steadied for another swing. Niko had a heartbeat to grab it or block him. His first reaction was to use his bodyweight and ram Campbell sideways to break it up, and the two of them almost fell. Campbell turned, face red with fury. Niko jerked his thumb over his shoulder at Marcus.

"You want him? Then you'll have to drop me first." Niko took a step back to shield Marcus, drawing his own baton without thinking. It just happened. He didn't plan it and he didn't have any control over it. He just had to do it. "You heard me. Don't think I won't give you a frigging smack in the mouth."

Gally and Lasky froze. It was like they'd sobered up in a heartbeat. Campbell just seemed to be getting his breath back. Niko was looking at buddies he now didn't know at all, reduced to animals and strangers, people he wouldn't turn his back on again. They didn't say a word.

No, just ordinary humans. I know that, don't I? Seen it before. One kicks it off, and we all fall into line and do the unthinkable.

"My boy's been wounded three times and he's still at the front," Campbell said. "But this asshole decides to piss off in the middle of the battle because he's got better things to do."

Niko resisted argument. "Did he start this?"

"Got in a ruck with Merino." Campbell was still watching Marcus, looking like he was waiting for another chance. "You know the rules."

"We don't *have* any damn rules. I said, did he start *this*?"

Campbell still gripped the baton. He wasn't going to give up. "My boy could be dead tomorrow, and this prick's just sitting on his ass in here."

"We're not the fucking judge and jury, okay?"

Campbell finally holstered his baton, visibly running out of steam. He'd always been such a nice, calm guy. It was scary to see that person peel away and reveal the primal savage. "Like you've never taught any of these shits a lesson."

"Yeah, but he's not some frigging nonce. He's damn well *sick*."

"Sick my ass."

Niko wasn't squeamish; he'd thumped a few inmates in his time. They pushed their luck. They were lippy. They needed a lesson. But he'd never ganged up on one guy and beaten the shit out of him. This was a Gear, for fuck's sake. Whatever the guy had done to end up in here, he'd spent at least ten years at the front defending Tyrus, and that meant he'd earned some respect. Niko decided it was safe to take his attention off Campbell and see to Marcus, who still seemed to be concentrating hard on just standing up, staring at the wall like he'd collapse if he blinked. It was hard to tell how badly hurt he was. A trickle of blood ran down his chin into the patch of beard, and a cut above his eyebrow was starting to swell, but everything else was hidden by his singlet. He looked like he was having trouble breathing. Then he turned his head slowly to look at Niko, and that did it. He tottered, then sank to his knees and pitched to one side on the floor like a felled tree.

"Shit." Niko struggled for half-remembered first aid procedures. *Facial trauma: blood, inhaling the stuff, turn him on his side, stop him choking.* He tried to turn Marcus into a recovery position but the guy lashed out almost like a reflex. Niko ducked. The swing didn't connect. "Whoa, fella—Campbell, you got a cover story for this? Because if he dies, I'll turn you all in. Count on it. Now get a frigging doctor in here. Get an ambulance."

"You call an ambulance, and it's official," Gally said.

"Do it. Because the Chairman's office is going to have our asses. You want to be drafted to the front, do you?"

Whatever crazed mob mentality had taken over now evaporated. Gally glanced back at Niko as he walked out, that chin-lowered, it-wasn't-my-fault look, but Niko just mouthed *fuck you* at him and went back to work on Marcus. If the guy died, they'd all be in the shit.

"Fenix, can you hear me? Come on, fella, talk to me." Marcus was lying on his side now, eyes open, as if he was trying to focus on something on the wall. Niko kept a wary eye on those fists. "Okay. I'm not going to touch you. We'll get the doctor to take a look."

Marcus tilted his head back like he was struggling to focus. "Just fucking finish it," he said hoarsely. "Go on. Kill me. Do me a favor."

So he was still coherent, but that didn't mean a damn thing if he had a head injury. Niko had learned that much from his wife. These things took hours to show. Marcus tried to sit up.

"Don't move until the medic gets here," Niko said.

Marcus struggled to his knees. "If you haven't got the balls to kill me, then there's no point in me hanging around."

"You want to die, is that it?"

"You're catching on."

"Lots of guys think that way at first. But they deal with it. They manage."

Marcus put his hand out to steady himself on a rusty filing cabinet as he tried to stand, but he missed and almost tipped over. Niko caught his arm and hauled him upright. For a second their eyes met and he got another glimpse of something terrible and anguished within.

Got to remember how he ended up here. His dad's been killed. That isn't helping.

"The sooner I'm gone," Marcus said, "the sooner people outside can forget me and move on with their lives."

So it was about his girlfriend, then. Niko understood that, too. "You know I've got to put you on suicide watch now you've said all this shit, don't you?"

"Sorry to mess up your paperwork."

"Can you make it to the infirmary?" Niko started worrying how he was going to keep Campbell away from him. "The doc might be some time."

"I'm fine," Marcus said. He wasn't. It was pretty damn obvious. He held his hands out to be cuffed but Niko shook his head. "Yeah. Okay. Whatever."

Niko checked outside to make sure Campbell was gone, but he could hear someone heading their way. Gally appeared around the corner, shaking his head.

"They're swamped with casualties again," he said. "They've even got Stranded at the checkpoints trying to get medical help. Things are going to shit out there. No ambulances and they're not willing to fly out a doctor."

"Bullshit." Niko caught Marcus by the biceps and steered him. "They did a house call for Alva, didn't they? Where is he, anyway?"

"They took him in."

"What?"

"Took him into JMC for tests. Personally, I didn't think he was that ill, but then the slimy bastard can charm anyone."

That didn't make sense. JMC didn't even scramble for heart attacks in here. "You signed him over to the hospital? They know he's category A, don't they?" Too bad: losing Marcus would land them all in even deeper shit than Alva going on the run. "Well, you can take the crap if he does some kid. Now piss off while I sort Fenix out."

"Look, I know you're mad. It wasn't how it looked."

"You're a cowardly shit. You joined in."

"I didn't touch him."

"Yeah, but you stood back and watched, didn't you? Just get out of my face."

Gally had the sense to clear off. Niko steered Marcus down the metal stairway to the ground floor on the other side of the main security zone, no

easy task given the state of the guy. Condensation dripped off the metal gratings above them like the aftermath of a storm. Still, the infirmary wasn't a bad
place to be for a while. Despite the peeling paint, there were clean sheets,
quiet, and some privacy to take a piss. The small four-bed ward smelled of
damp and disinfectant.

"Sit down." Niko pointed at the unforgiving steel-framed chair next to the
bed. "I'll do my best, but it's first aid, that's all. I'm sorry."

Marcus couldn't even sit down properly. He waved away Niko's attempt to
help him and settled with his elbows braced on his knees, head in his hands,
taking shallow, ragged breaths. Niko took a risk and pulled up the back of his
blood-flecked singlet to check out the damage.

"Oh *shit*," he said.

Marcus was a mess. All Niko could see from his waistband to halfway up his
back was purple bruising with red streaks that looked like broken blood vessels.
The swelling must have come up fast. And that breathing bothered him.

"Okay, just relax," Niko said. "What's stopping you breathing?"

Marcus looked up very slowly as if he was stunned by the stupidity of the
question. "Pain," he growled.

"He's busted your ribs."

"Maybe." Marcus pushed himself off the chair and unfurled himself cautiously until he was almost upright. He must have been in a hell of a lot of
pain. "I need to take a leak."

"In there." Niko gestured to the toilet. "You going to be all right?"

Marcus gave him a don't-even-think-about-it look. "I don't want any help to
hold it, thanks."

"I wasn't offering. Look, if you die on me, I'm in the shit."

Marcus just shrugged and hobbled into the toilet. Niko checked the drugs
cabinet, not that it was stocked with much these days, just salicylic acid painkillers and basic out-of-date antibiotics. Any drugs still being manufactured
tended to end up at JMC, where there were nice innocent patients who
needed them. This was the first time that had been a concern to Niko. He
was reading the label and wondering how many tablets a guy of Marcus's size
would need when he heard him murmur, then the john flushed.

"You okay?" Niko called. *Dumb question.* "What is it?"

Marcus came out, zipping up his pants, and almost fell against the door
frame. "I'm pissing blood. Kidneys."

"You'd know that."

"Basic combat first aid."

"Okay, you wait here. Sit down or something."

Niko never called Maura at work, but this was an emergency. He picked up the phone in the orderly's cubicle and dialed.

"ER," the voice said. "Can I put you on hold? We're busy."

"Honey? It's me. Can you talk me through something?"

"Nik? Are you okay?"

"I've got an injured inmate and we can't get help." Niko tried to use the jargon. "Some facial injury. Punch in the face, probably. Blunt trauma to the lower back. Bruising, trouble breathing, peeing blood."

"Kidney damage," Maura said wearily.

"Yeah, he said that. What do I do?"

"Keep an eye on the blood and give him complete bed rest. The head injury—if he hasn't lost consciousness, he'll probably be okay."

"Drugs?"

"No, his kidneys have got enough work to do as it is. Maybe mild painkillers, and antibiotics in case he gets an infection. So watch his temperature too."

"Is that it?"

"Just about. Anything more serious and he'll need surgery." Maura paused. In the background, Niko could hear the hospital PA paging someone, the clatter of trolley wheels, and an alarm chirping. "Nik, are you in trouble? Did you hit him?"

Niko felt oddly indignant. "Look, I stopped someone beating him to death. He's a Gear who cracked up. He shouldn't be in here."

"Oh God, you're not getting involved, are you? Never helps, Nik. Take it from me. Just steer clear."

"Yeah, I'm doing what I have to. Thanks, honey. See you later."

When he came out of the cubicle with the tablets, Marcus was sitting on the edge of the bed, eyes screwed up in obvious pain. He seemed to realize Niko was there after a few seconds and snapped back to that blank I'm-okay expression too late to convince him.

"You better lie down, Fenix," Niko said. "I got some advice from my missus. She's an ER nurse. Bed rest, painkillers, and antibiotics. That's all I can do, buddy. Sorry."

Marcus just stared at him, then blinked slowly. "It's okay." He seemed to be building up to asking something, licking his split lip. "Why me? Why give a shit?"

"You're a Gear. You put it on the line, whatever else happened."

"I refused an order. Guys died because of that. Save your sympathy for someone who's worth it."

It could have been a rebuke, but he sounded matter-of-fact, almost apologetic. Niko had never bothered to put a prisoner on suicide watch before because the average inmate was generally nicer dead, and he knew Maura was right: he was getting involved, and there were people who could never be saved no matter how hard you tried. Maybe Marcus had nothing left to live for, and forcing him was cruel. But he *did* have something outside to cling to. Niko still had the letters in his pocket, the ones from his girlfriend. It might have been just what the poor bastard needed right then.

"Well, there's someone else who gives a damn," Niko said.

He reached into his jacket and took out one of the letters. He held it up so Marcus could see the handwriting on the battered COG military envelope. The reaction was instant, silent, and utterly broken. Campbell had beaten the shit out of Marcus without getting so much as a whimper from him, but the sight of that neat, methodical handwriting had brought tears to his eyes. He stared, then shook his head.

"She needs to forget me."

"You have to read them."

"No." Marcus shook his head again, lips compressed as he drew in a painful breath. "I don't."

He heaved himself onto the bed, rolled onto his stomach and buried his face in his folded arms. Niko had a response for every damn thing in this prison except that—a man who quietly gave up on life, a man who looked as if he'd never walked away from anything.

"I'll keep them for you anyway," Niko said, and slipped the envelope back in his jacket before leaving Marcus to it and locking the door as per regulations. Once he was outside in the passage, he took the letter out again. It wasn't his to read, but if this was a Dear John letter then maybe it was best left undelivered. It had already been opened and resealed by the admin office. When he eased the flap open again, he found a photo inside and sheet of paper. The photo stock was so thin that he hadn't even felt it in there. On the back was penciled YOU LOOKED AWAY and when he flipped it over, the image made him hold his breath.

It looked like something snapped in passing in an army office. There was Marcus, wearing armor and a black do-rag with a sergeant's stripes on the front, standing in front of a desk and caught as he turned around to look at something off-camera. Sitting at the desk was a really lovely woman—blonde, classy, effortlessly glamorous even in a gray COG uniform—and she was looking at Marcus with an expression that clearly said he was the center of her whole damn world.

So that was what he'd lost. Not just his father, his buddies, and his honor, but a woman who loved him. Niko felt like a pervert for reading the letter. He unfolded the single sheet and the first line was all he could manage.

Marcus, I'm always going to be here, waiting, no matter how long it takes. Because you're mine. And Mom taught me never to take no for an answer.

Well, damn it, Marcus Fenix was going to read that letter, and he'd reply to it. Niko would make sure of it. He'd even find him some paper. Sometimes women did wait for men a very long time indeed, although few men had ever left the Slab alive.

Marcus will. He deserves better.

Niko realized he was now thinking of him as Marcus, not Fenix, or even Prisoner B1116/87. He put the letter and the photo back in the envelope and made a note to check on Marcus in an hour.

D WING, THE SLAB: TWENTY-SIX HOURS LATER.

"Two MIA," Chunky said. He was still engrossed in his rescued crochet mat, cross-legged on his bunk like an old-fashioned tailor. "Normally we seen the bodies by now, but maybe they just dump 'em in the trash these days."

Reeve parked the food cart outside the cell. Chunky was a human security camera. He was getting on now and none too fit, so he tended to spend his time in his cell just watching and doing odd jobs that didn't need any muscle. He repaired stuff. The position of his cell meant he also saw everything that came and went, so he traded information, and Reeve was a regular customer.

"Marcus is in the infirmary." Reeve ladled out some mycoprotein casserole and a few extra potatoes. They were still some of the tasty yellow-fleshed ones at this time of year, grown in any spare patch of soil within the walls and sometimes no bigger than grapes. "Not MIA. We know where he is."

"How do *you* know?"

"Because I'm going to get my ass kicked for letting him get into a fight."

"Didn't think Merino hurt him that bad."

"He didn't. The screws beat seven shades of shit out of him."

Chunky stopped looping the scraps of fabric and frowned at the pattern, almost looking through it. "All 'cause of me. I owe the guy." He tugged at a stubborn knot. "Assholes. Parmenter?"

"Campbell."

Chunky stopped completely and looked right at Reeve. "Now that's a surprise. Never had him down for a shithouse." He shook his head. "So what we gonna do for Fenix?"

Reeve knew the outside world wouldn't have believed it, but even in a cess-pit, there was community, *brotherhood.* Inmates would shiv one another when society's rules were broken, but they would also close ranks, and he got the feeling that was happening now. *Polarizing.* That was the word for it. He'd read it in a very old management magazine in the latrines, its paper too stiff and shiny to be much use as toilet paper. If there was an uneasy truce between two groups, then an incident like this would draw battle lines and tribalism would take over. And as this place shrank year after year—as the numbers of inmates slowly fell, and more parts of the prison were shut down—the closer and more volatile the community became.

Smaller territories. Stresses any animal, they say. And that's what we are, right?

The enemy's enemy thing kicked in, too. Marcus was one of their own now, whether he liked it or not. If the warders beat him, the whole prison took it as a personal affront. They didn't have to like him or even know him to feel that way.

"If he survives, then he's got to come back in here," Reeve said. "So maybe we reach a deal with Merino to back off him."

"How are we gonna do that?"

"I'll think of something."

"If he's so well-connected and all that, how come this is happening?"

"It's the army. Go figure. Anyway, better finish my rounds or Merino will slap me senseless for serving up cold chow."

Reeve kicked the brake off the cart and pushed it to the next cell, clattering over ridges in the broken tiles. He wondered what his former associates would have thought to see him playing cook and delivery boy, a professional assassin reduced to household help. But he was still alive, and they were probably grub fodder by now. Prestige was measured differently inside these walls. Kitchen duties meant control of the food supply in a starving world, and Reeve liked that. It gave him much the same status as his ability to liquefy a target's brain with a single well-placed high-velocity round from three hundred meters.

And the food waste, the peelings . . . that had value too. *Moonshine.* This joint was an ecosystem with its own economy, a self-contained world. Even the glucose nutrient for the mycoprotein came from photosynthetic bacteria in their own little sealed globe, the only thing in the Slab that basked in sunlight.

Merino was still in overall charge down here. It was a gangland environment.

Reeve felt comfortable with the familiarity, but still wondered if things might have been better under Marcus.

But he doesn't want to play. He wants to die. He's stuck here and he's shut himself in his own world.

So where's Alva? Maybe he's got some seriously bad shit they don't want us catching.

And I ask again . . . why keep us alive here? What's the fucking point? Habit?

"Reeve, for fuck's sake, we're starving here," Leuchars yelled. The voices echoed for everyone to hear, but privacy in the Slab was a thing you created in your own mind. "Get a move on."

"You brewing?"

"Maybe."

"I'll tell you where I stashed the potato peelings . . ."

"Okay, asshole, *one liter*. But no more."

"Deal."

That was binding. Everyone had heard him agree on a price. Liquor stills had to be kept hidden from the screws in the old days, but they were an open secret now because nobody gave a damn and the staff didn't venture down here very often. They were as reliant on an uninterrupted supply of hooch as anyone else. It was currency. Reeve glanced up at the gantry and checked out Jarvi and Gallego. Normally they'd stand side by side, but they were at opposite ends of the walkway now like they'd had a bust-up. Jarvi gave Reeve an almost-invisible nod—*I want to see you later*—and looked away. He'd want his cut of that liter.

"Hey, Reeve? You frigging wanked yourself *deaf*?" That was Vance. "He said dish out the chow already."

It was just noise to reassure themselves. Reeve moved at his own pace because he could afford to. Like Merino, nobody was really going to risk fucking with him. "You better clear your plates, or I'm going to force-feed you the painful way."

"Yeah. Just get the fuck on with it."

Some guys ate in their cells and some preferred the table. Edouain, the Indie whose folks came from Pelles, still kept to himself in his cell at the south end of the floor. He'd sabotaged a munitions supply train in the Pendulum Wars and taken out half of Dormera with seven hundred civilians in the explosion, which put him in the same league as either a really prolific serial killer or a half-hearted grub. Reeve wasn't sure if that made Edouain a terrorist or a successful enemy agent. He didn't fit in here any better than Fenix did.

He was the last to get fed, always. There was no reason for it except for the position of his cell. Reeve leaned on the rusting iron door frame. Edouain was poring over a piece of paper laid out on his bunk, or at least a patchwork of paper scraps that had been stuck together somehow like some kind of quilt.

"The choice is casserole, casserole, or casserole," Reeve said. "What's that?"

"Map." Edouain turned it carefully so that he could see, holding it up by the corners like a delicate piece of lace. "My *worry* map."

Reeve filled the bowl and placed it on the small rickety table in the cell. Edouain needed keeping sweet, because he had skills that would be useful in an emergency—if he could blow up a train, he could do plenty. There weren't many technically minded killers left in here.

"You want to worry me too," Reeve said. "Is that it?"

Edouain indicated lines drawn on the map. Pieces of it were actually torn out of the copy of the *Jacinto Daily* that had been doing the rounds, the map graphic that showed how far the grubs had advanced. Edouain must have thought the detail was pretty important to forgo wiping his ass on it.

"This is how far they've come in the last five years." He indicated another very old scrap of newsprint right on the edge of the map. "If they carry on at this rate, then we'll be overrun."

Reeve stared at the paper. Damn, the guy must have saved odds and ends from the newspaper over the years and stashed them away. But he was an agent, a guy who was trained to operate behind enemy lines: this was the way he thought and worked, always keeping an eye out, always assessing the risk.

"Surrounded, maybe. This place is solid granite."

"But the sky *isn't*." Edouain rolled up the map with slow care, like it was some ancient parchment in the National Museum of Ephyra. "They have Reavers. And Brumaks almost as tall as the walls. And on that day, we'll be fish in a barrel. We're trapped here."

He looked up at Reeve for a few moments, almost smiling, as if he enjoyed seeing the penny drop so slowly. They'd had ten years to obsess about this, but somehow Reeve, like everyone else here, thought in terms of grubs being beneath them, the literal monster under the bed. They didn't really do air-raids. They didn't have paratroopers.

They didn't need to. *Not yet.*

"Well, shit," Reeve said. "If they haven't done it yet . . ."

"They have a very long list of targets, I imagine. You want to wait to find out?"

"You suggesting we do something?"

"Oh yes. I am."

"Over or under?"

"I think we can tunnel."

"Come on, that's the whole reason this place was built where it is. You can't."

"We can. It's just going to take a long time." Edouain stood and picked up the bowl of casserole. "I'm getting out, even if the rest of you want to wait for those things to come and get you. A prison where people are too scared to try to escape. Only the COG could be so blindly *obedient*."

But the government would move us out before then. Surely. And this place is . . .

. . . shit, maybe nowhere near as safe as we thought.

No, they might not, and they might not even be able to when the time came. Blindly obedient: Edouain had a point. Reeve realized that he was getting just as dumb and soft after so many years in here. "Okay," he said. "Are you telling me to be conversational, or telling me because I can get resources?"

Edouain just raised one eyebrow and dug into the brown slurry, jabbing his fork around to find solid lumps. "When did any of you COG ever have a conversation with me?"

"Okay. I'm in." Reeve leaned out of the cell door to check the rusting tin-faced clock on the wall at the far end of the floor. Niko Jarvi was still leaning on the gantry rail, ignoring Gallego, but he stared in Reeve's direction and tapped one finger discreetly on his wrist. "Got to go. I'll be back later."

Jarvi was probably going to go apeshit at him for letting Marcus run into trouble. Reeve parked the cart in the passage outside the kitchens and headed back to the latrines. If the Slab had the equivalent of a DMZ, of a no-man's land, of a diplomatic neutral zone, then the latrine block was it, a place where scores were settled, deals were done, and the unwary or weak discovered in the hardest way of all what it meant to be the bottom of the pile in a men's prison.

Jarvi was waiting for him, arms folded, ass resting on one of the washbasins. Somewhere in the building, the dogs started barking again. Sound traveled through conduits and vents and emerged in misleading places.

"Okay, what did you expect me to do?" Reeve said, deciding to get his shot in first. "You were the assholes who pulled him out and beat him up."

"I was off shift," Jarvi said quietly.

"Is it my fault your buddies can't read the memo?"

"Didn't say it was."

"He started it with Merino. Okay, he was defending Chunky, but he should have known better."

Jarvi was still very quiet, almost preoccupied. He had his keys in his hand

and was staring at them as if one was missing and staring would bring it back somehow. "Well, he's pissing blood now. Campbell busted his kidneys. When he comes back onto the wing, you're going to look after him like he was your virgin little sister, you understand?"

"That means protecting him from himself, basically."

"Whatever it takes. I can't be here twenty-six hours a day. You want the smokes—you play sheepdog. That's the deal."

"You want the liquor, though."

"Y'know, I think I'd prefer Fenix in one piece."

"I get it." Jarvi had to be on some kind of payola to look after him. "You're getting a lot more than smokes for this."

Jarvi looked at his keys again and shook his head. That frown wouldn't go away, the kind of frown you got when you were looking at something that upset and disgusted you. "No, you *wouldn't* get it. Just keep him alive. The man's not well. And go get him something to eat. Come and knock on the security door when you're ready."

The trouble with the Slab was that there was nothing to do in here but obsess over a small amount of information. Reeve tried to keep things in proportion but the place was cut off from reality and the rest of the human race, and for all he knew the rest of Ephyra might have been charcoal by now except for a charade maintained by the warders. He fished around in the vat of casserole with a ladle to find as many decent chunks of vegetable and protein as he could, then headed for the security door that would let him into the next block.

If Marcus is that important, just ship him out of here. Simple.

Reeve rapped the door and listened for the long sequence of jangling keys and sliding bolts. The door swung open and Jarvi gestured him through. As he followed the warder up the passage to the infirmary, he looked up through the grating that formed the gantry level walkway and saw Gallego and Campbell staring down at him.

It was hard to imagine Campbell belting anybody. Of all the staff here, he was about the mildest. Reeve thought that all the way down the passage until Jarvi opened the infirmary door and he caught sight of Marcus standing at one of the basins with his back to the door. For a moment, Reeve thought he was wearing some discolored purplish tank top. Then it all suddenly made sense: he wasn't. That was his *skin*, for fuck's sake, and the color was one vast bruise. No . . . it was a mass of overlapping welts and bruises. Reeve felt his stomach starting to churn.

How the hell was Marcus even standing up?

"Fenix, *bed*," Jarvi barked. "Bed rest. Orders."

Marcus half turned, hands still in the sink. Reeve, transfixed by that terrible bruising, could see what he was doing now. Marcus was washing his singlet. A couple of wrung-out pieces of fabric, socks or briefs maybe, sat in the soap holder. Seeing a guy like that—and in that state—doing his laundry just stopped Reeve in his tracks. But he was a soldier. They had their routine, Reeve knew, and they had to keep their kit clean and tidy.

"I'm fine," Marcus said. His face didn't look too bad, apart from a swollen lip and a black eye, but the rest of him was another matter. He was breathing like it hurt. Shit, it had to. "I'm done here."

"You're not *fine*."

"Urine's clear." Marcus wrung out the singlet, whipcord muscles knotting in his forearms. "Can't stay here forever."

He shook out the singlet and frowned at it for a few seconds as if he was trying to work out which way was up. Then he started to try to put it on over his head, but as soon as he raised his arms Reeve saw him flinch. He couldn't manage it.

"Hey, leave that, we got some work shirts that do up at the front," Jarvi said, holding out his hand for the wet singlet. He walked up to Marcus and looked up at him like a worried dad. "Reeve's brought food. Sit down and eat it."

Marcus took a few moments to think about it, then sat down on the edge of the bed with elbows braced on his knees. He hung his head and ran his hands over his face for a moment like a guy waking up after a heavy night's drinking.

Jarvi squatted to look him in the eye. "Look, Fenix, I've told Reeve here that if you get so much as a splinter in your ass in the future, I'll have his guts for garters." He gestured to Reeve to bring the bowl of food, then took something out of his inner jacket pocket, a few sheets of folded paper that he placed on the bed cover. "It's his job to look out for you. Now damn well read this letter, eat the sodding food, and write back to your girl. I've even got the paper for you. Understand? I'm going to get that shirt."

Marcus's jaw was set but Reeve could see embarrassment getting the better of him. He blinked a few times. "Okay."

Jarvi gave Reeve a scowl as he left. *Get on with it, or else.* Reeve handed Marcus the casserole and a spoon. Marcus tried a mouthful or two, but gave up pretty fast and put the bowl down on the cabinet next to the bed. Reeve waited to see if he was going to open the letter but he just stared at it, *through* it, expressionless. Reeve had never felt a damn thing for any stranger and made sure he kept things that way. But this unlucky bastard wasn't a stranger now, and Reeve struggled to work out why.

"Just read it," Reeve said. "Write back. I know it's tough, but you've got to survive somehow. You've got to hang on to something. Maybe she'll visit."

Marcus looked up at him, now completely unreadable. "If she came in here," he said slowly, "it'd break her heart. And if any of you assholes looked at her, I'd know what you were thinking, and then I'd have to fucking kill you."

He said it very quietly, very matter of fact, as if it was some necessary thing he really didn't want to do but would have to. It wasn't even a threat. It was a prediction. Reeve wasn't easily intimidated in his line of work, but Marcus was something far outside his daily experience. It took Reeve some time to work out what was bothering him. Damn it, he felt *wrong*. It was *wrong* to upset Marcus, not because he was perfectly capable of snapping someone's neck if they pissed him off, but because he radiated some kind of unshakeable decency.

Holy fuck. Am I finally going nuts in here? What the hell's that all about?

Reeve could switch off guilt and remorse with a single thought. He'd never given a rat's ass about what his targets felt, because that didn't do anybody any good and it didn't change what he had to do. But this was like tormenting a caged lion in some rundown zoo, pointless and demeaning because the creature just didn't belong there and couldn't use its lethal power. Marcus radiated a kind of battered nobility. There was no other word for it. Reeve didn't need to know he had the Embry Star to see he was a hero.

"Okay," Reeve said. "You get in any more fights, I get stomped. Do we have an agreement? Think of my ass even if you don't care about your own."

Marcus had shut down again. There wasn't a flicker on his face now and that odd light had gone out of his eyes. "Hoffman."

"You keep saying Hoffman. Who's Hoffman?"

"Colonel."

"Oh. Right. You think he's asked for special treatment for you. Actually, this came from the Chairman's office."

"Yeah. Hoffman." Marcus stood up and cast a shadow, a sure indication that the conversation was over. But he had that letter and the blank paper clutched in one hand, which Reeve took as a good sign. "Okay, I'm done. Where's that shirt?"

He walked to the infirmary door and rapped on it. Jarvi came back a few moments later and thrust a threadbare gray shirt at him. Reeve helped him put it on and he shoved the letter and paper inside before straightening up and doing a credible impression of someone who wasn't in pain at all as he walked back down the passage toward D Wing.

Jarvi selected a key from the bunch chained to his belt and caught Reeve's arm as Marcus walked ahead.

Not one scratch, he mouthed. *Not one fucking scratch, okay?*

Reeve nodded. Yeah, he got it. Marcus paused at the next set of locked doors and Jarvi opened and re-locked them behind him one at a time. Maybe it was an army thing, but Marcus never moved his head when he walked into any space, just raised his eyes or stared straight ahead. When the inner doors to the main floor opened, it took maybe twenty seconds for the buzz to run along the cells and get the inmates to come out and watch.

Merino was standing there too, leaning against the wall at the far end and just telegraphing unfinished business. Reeve's heart sank. Marcus was going to be bounced back to solitary in seconds. The silence was awful, and the dogs had started up again. Whatever the hell was making them bark was suddenly irrelevant.

"Here we go," Reeve sighed.

Then Merino pushed away from the wall and ambled back to his cell. Leuchars, still staring at Marcus, started clapping, then Vance picked it up, and then Chunky, and in seconds Marcus was getting an ovation like some goddamn concert pianist. From the look on his face, he would probably rather have taken a punch in the mouth. Reeve could only describe it as baffled dismay.

And Merino . . . is he biding his time?

"Shit," Marcus grunted, then nodded and headed for his cell, walking a little stiffly, but walking at all was a massive show of strength. In Slab terms he'd acquired a battle honor. Everyone knew by now what had happened to him, even if Reeve would still have to update them on just how bad a beating Marcus had taken. Whether he liked it or not, he was a goddamn hero all over again.

Reeve got the feeling that was the last thing Marcus would ever accept that he was.

CHAPTER 8

I insist that you check on Fenix personally at least once every three months, and I want a phone update every week. I know how easily the Slab loses inmates. And if you can't manage it, I'll do it myself.

(Chairman Richard Prescott to Dr. Jay Assandris, senior MHO, COG DoH.)

COG RESEARCH STATION AZURA: LATE GALE, 11 A.E.

Adam realized how few pictures of Marcus he'd salvaged when he tried to arrange them on the wall by his workstation in the main laboratory.

He had eight: Marcus aged four with Elain, Marcus at ten when he'd started at Olafson Intermediate School—damn, he came home with a black eye the very first day—and then six of Marcus from enlistment to the day he'd received his Embry Star. Adam tended to think of those as Marcus the man, but he'd been an unsettlingly adult little boy from the time he'd turned five, when Adam had returned from deployment to Kashkur. He'd become a little adult while Adam's back was turned. Marcus decided he had to be the man of the household because Daddy was away fighting the war and saving people. He'd asked why Daddy had to go to war, and Adam had told him he couldn't let the other Gears down.

They're my friends. They're the people who'll look out for me so I don't get hurt. We take care of one another.

Adam would never forget the rapt look on Marcus's face when he told him that, and how this small child had declared that he was going to be a Gear too. He never wavered from that day onward. He kept his word, even at five years old.

And I wondered why he defied me to enlist, did I? I made it sound worth leaving your family for, so much loyalty and love and devotion in it. I never gave

*him enough of that at home. He had to find it somewhere. He found it with the
Santiago family and 26 RTI.*

Adam held two pictures of Marcus side by side, the one taken in his Olafson school uniform and the one in Royal Tyran Infantry number two service
dress on the day of his passing out parade, and was struck yet again by how
old and serious Marcus looked in both. *Yes. I remember how he got that black
eye. Defending Carlos Santiago when he hardly knew him. Even then, instantly
loyal, willing to do anything for his comrades.* Adam ran his thumb gently over
the parade photo, wondering if it would fade in the bright tropical sun slanting
through the window, and decided not to risk it. He'd have nothing left of his
son if he lost those pictures. He paused and touched the photo to his lips, so
proud of Marcus that it hurt.

*I wasted all those years. And now I'll probably never see him again. My boy.
My wonderful boy.*

Did I ever tell him that I loved him?

"Sir?"

The voice made him jump. It was Captain Dury. Adam turned around,
embarrassed, and slid the photos into his inside jacket pocket. "I'm sorry, I was
miles away."

"We found it." Dury held out a perfume bottle with amber liquid slopping
around in it. "I found it when we offloaded today. It must have fallen down a
gap in the Raven's deck when we transferred your effects."

It was a nice euphemism for kidnap, but what else did Adam deserve? This
was a kindness he hadn't earned. The bottle was the last remnant of Elain's
perfume. He folded his fingers around it and almost let tears overtake him,
and wondered what kind of man went to all that trouble to find something so
apparently trivial for a traitor, for someone who'd failed to warn humanity of
approaching genocide. Dury was a battle-hardened veteran with something of
the look of Hoffman about him, not so much his actual appearance but the
clenched jaw and visible disapproval of old money and ancestry. Adam tried
not to mistake Prescott's orders to placate him for actual sympathy.

"Thank you, Captain," he said, pocketing the bottle. "This means a great
deal to me."

Dury pulled up a chair and sat opposite Adam with his elbows braced on
his knees and fingers meshed as if he had a pep talk to give him. Adam was
getting used to the Onyx Guard wandering around Azura as casually as infantry. He used to think that 26 RTI, his own regiment, was the sole elite that
defended the heart of Tyrus, but how wrong he'd been. The guardsmen were

now the defense force for Azura as well as personal security for the Chairman, complete with artillery and an air wing. They weren't ceremonial and they weren't just black ops.

This was where all the senior command and best scientific minds had been relocated after being declared dead or MIA. Adam was struggling to get used to this parallel world, this afterlife of elite souls in their well-fed, well-equipped, hidden heaven.

No, not souls. Ghosts. I am, anyway. A ghost. I'm truly dead.

And he'd caught sight of Julian Bissell: Bissell, whose memorial service he'd attended, Bissell the Octus Medal pharmacologist, Bissell who hadn't been missing presumed dead at all, but was strolling around the grounds with his wife. His wife was *alive*. Elain was not. Adam found himself still looking, still hoping that he'd been wrong about the remains he'd found in the Hollow and that this was another one of Prescott's elaborate cover stories, but it wasn't. Elain was gone forever.

"The Chairman's going to call you later," Dury said, jolting him out of his fermenting anger. "I don't want you to worry, because everything's all right now, but your son had a spot of trouble at—"

"Oh God." Adam's stomach plummeted. "No."

Dury raised a forefinger without unmeshing his hands. "Hear me out. He's okay. He got in a fight, and one of the guards assaulted him."

"*Assaulted* him?" Adam's worst expectations rocketed from idling to overdrive. "What the hell do you mean?"

"I'm not going to bullshit you, sir. One of the guards has a son at the front and he laid into Marcus with his baton. Put him in hospital, basically. But he's up and about now."

Adam felt physically sick. All he could think of was Marcus, utterly alone, utterly without hope, being brutalized by thugs and perverts in that stinking hole. He'd fight back and get himself killed. Would they even tell him if Marcus was dead? Adam had no way of verifying anything. He wanted to run to Marcus and get him out of there. But he was on the other side of Sera, a prisoner himself.

"Why are you telling me this?" he asked. He caught a movement in his peripheral vision. He must have raised his voice, because some of the technicians had turned around to see what the commotion was. He lowered his voice to a hiss. "Is this the game you're playing? You let my boy be abused and tortured, and then tell me all about it to ensure I *behave*? Because if you think that's an effective way to motivate me, you've *failed*." Adam leaned as close to Dury as he dared without letting his own rage tip him into grabbing the man's collar. "Do *not* touch my son. Don't even *think* about it. Do you understand? If I save Sera, then I do it solely for him. For the day he's released. This is all about *him*."

Adam realized he'd said much the same to Myrrah and that he *meant* it. Sera was worth nothing if he lost Marcus. It was just a ball of rock and assorted organisms without him, not a living world. No wonder Marcus had dropped everything to try to save him. This was the example he set his son—to abandon duty for family, perhaps set too late but better than not at all.

And that's how it should be. I see that now. I should have seen it long ago.

Dury didn't even blink. "I was just telling you everything, sir. If I was threatening you, you'd know all about it."

"Prove to me that he's alive."

"I'll see what I can do." Dury leaned back in the seat, hands on his knees now. "Look, the Chairman rarely gives his word. But in my experience, when he does, he keeps it. And you and your son aren't exactly blameless, are you? So I think we're all going to have to learn to trust one another."

"Marcus served frontline for nearly fifteen years. He's not a coward. You *know* he's not a coward."

"Oh, I don't doubt your son's got guts, sir. He's probably just like too many other poor bastards—he's finally succumbed to the stress. But as things stand, he's escaped a firing squad and you should be grateful for Prescott's intervention."

Adam found himself sliding down into the abyss, searching for a deal, a bargain, a threat, anything to get Marcus out of there before it was too late. The prospect of his getting killed in combat was a nightmare enough. But that prison would be a slow, agonizing torment that would be far worse.

"You could bring him here," Adam said. "If he's going to be in his seventies before he's released—if he lives that long—then he could serve his sentence here. I'd be a damn sight more motivated."

Dury gave him a long look, and then stood up. Adam knew they had an audience but he didn't care now. He had no dignity left.

"When you talk to the Chairman, you can raise that," Dury said. Now he looked awkward, folding his arms as if he didn't know what to do with them when he wasn't holding a rifle, just like Marcus. "We have a new resident. Might be of interest to you. They've just flown him in from the Slab."

For one blissful moment, the crushing tension in Adam's chest relaxed and he expected the next word to be *Marcus*. The relief perished instantly because he could see from Dury's grim expression that it wasn't, and he hated him for getting his hopes up and then dashing them even though the man hadn't said a word or even implied it. It was delusion born of futile fear, grief, and self-loathing.

"Who is it?" Adam asked.

"A prisoner. William Alva. A volunteer."

"A volunteer for what?"

Dury shrugged. "I'm not a doctor, sir. That's up to you and Dr. Bakos. Anyway, I imagine anything beats getting glass and turds in your food and a broom handle up your ass. He's a pedophile, sir. Three murders. Little boys."

The captain was a strange blend of the erudite and the profane, and seemed to know how to balance the mix for maximum impact. He gave Adam a polite nod and walked out of the lab, boots clicking on the polished cream terrazzo floor.

Something had now numbed Adam. He tried to work out if it was what happened to pedophiles, or what might be done to Marcus, or what this Alva thought he'd volunteered for. He turned around in his chair to see where Jerome—one of the senior geneticists—had gone.

"Rex, was this Esther's idea?" It wasn't what Adam was thinking at all. *Marcus, what the hell have they done to you?* "Did she ask for volunteers?"

Jerome stepped out of the alcove where he was prepping slides. "No idea, Professor."

"Well, he can't possibly know what he's volunteered for, so I'll be damned if I'll take advantage of him."

"Who?"

Adam couldn't tell if Jerome was playing dumb or genuinely so absorbed in his work that he hadn't heard the conversation. It was hard to ignore an Onyx Guardsman and an angry discussion in a quiet lab, but Jerome might well have been the man to manage it. He gave Adam a baffled frown as he walked out and went in search of isolation.

Ironically, Adam felt physically better than he had in a long time. His ribs weren't fully healed, but he was getting more exercise simply walking from office to office around the Azura complex, and the food was better. Back home he'd been able to get hold of the best that Jacinto had to offer, even when supplies were running low, but the menu in the island's many facilities brought home to him just how desperate things really were back on the mainland and how low his expectations had sunk. *And they say they're having to make cutbacks.* The tower where his quarters were located rivaled the best hotels he'd known before Sera had been ripped apart and burned.

By me. I made the burning possible. Didn't I?

And the Maelstrom. Damn, they even used my power generation research. I'm complicit in everything, whether I realize it or not.

He walked through the plush lobby, all mahogany and jacquard hangings, and thought he recognized the figures in a few of the niches. Yes: it was from the Ushayev collection that his father had given to the National Museum on permanent loan. Adam thought of the ancient silver Kashkuri horse figurine he'd found himself in the looted ruins of Shavad's museum, and finally put to rest the regret about lost art just as Helena Stroud had told him to.

Marcus. Adam stepped onto the elevator, an open platform that allowed residents to take in the full majesty of the vast, vaulted lobby with its glass dome and slanted sunlight playing on ceramic containers of rare plants. *Oh God, Marcus, what have I done?* He took a slow step to the edge of the platform and looked down. Various people milled around with no apparent sense of urgency, and apart from the housekeeping staff who moved unnoticed in the shadows, not one of them was an ordinary human being. *Elain, can you forgive me? I've let you down. I didn't look after Marcus.*

He had to stop this. He had to focus. He was no use to Marcus in this state. He strode down the wide carpeted corridor, boots almost silent on the thick pile, and shut himself in his apartment to sit at his desk with his head in his hands, just trying to center himself enough to come up with a plan.

He'd had what felt like five minutes' peace when there was a tap at the door. He could release the lock from his desk. There was no point pretending he was out of town, after all.

"Come in," he said, pressing the release button.

Esther Bakos stood in the doorway, looking irritated. "You know you've switched your phone off, don't you, Professor?"

Adam didn't. He looked at the buttons on the handset and tried to work out when he'd pressed the wrong one. "I'm sorry. It's not been a good day."

"I need to talk to you. Rex said you were concerned about something."

I don't have time for this. Go away. "Apart from what's happening to my son?" Adam knew the gossip would be circulating faster than a particle accelerator. He allowed himself a little display of acid. "Yes, I'm told we've brought in a *volunteer* for tests."

"I find myself in the position of having to come to a physicist to ask for permission to make a clinical decision." Bakos made it sound like consulting a leper on manicure techniques. "We know this organism jumps the species barrier somehow. We absolutely have to do human tests as soon as possible."

"He's a prisoner, and he can't possibly give informed consent for something like this. We don't have the information to advise him. We're floundering ourselves."

"He rapes and kills children."

"Is this some kind of high school ethics debate?"

"He's not being forced. He might not be harmed at all." Bakos looked like a perfectly pleasant, reasonable woman. She wasn't a monster. "He can repay his debt to society."

"This isn't ethical."

And neither was the Hammer of Dawn. Go on, say it. Go on, let's tie ourselves in knots again. Just because I did one terrible thing it doesn't mean I can breeze straight into another.

Bakos looked fed up with him, arms folded. "This world will die of ethics, Professor. I don't like decent but dead. I prefer alive and remorseful. As do you, obviously."

This was the thin end of the wedge, easy to embark on when the victim was stereotypically repellent, but Adam feared the slide along the continuum to the moderately antisocial through the undesirable and disenfranchised and ultimately to the helpless who simply couldn't defend themselves.

But the world's being poisoned. Not just humanity. Everything. The situation's different.

No, this is exactly what ethics were designed for. The tough times. The extreme times.

Adam sat back in his chair, scarcely able to believe he was taking this stand for the lowest form of human life when his own son was suffering and the entire world was under threat. It was the right thing to do. But he didn't trust his motives, and he struggled to work out whether he just wanted to persuade himself he was a good man who'd made some bad choices. In the end, it made no difference to William Alva.

"You will *not* use that prisoner," Adam said quietly. "But I'll find you a human tissue alternative."

"Oh, it's a case of teach yourself molecular biology in a weekend, is it?"

Some things became very clear, very fast. The lightning bolt of clarity over big issues had hit Adam more than once in his career, simpler than choosing between tea or coffee, instant in the panoramic and perfect view of the crisis that it gave him.

"I'll do it," he said. "I'll be the test subject. Use *me.*"

HOUSE OF THE SOVEREIGNS, EPHYRA.

"Colonel? I'd like five minutes."

Prescott's voice cut through the hubbub of conversation in the crowded corridor outside CIC. There wasn't really enough room for HQ personnel in the building, but all Hoffman had to do was to wait a few more months and the grubs would grind the COG down to the right size to fit. He debated whether to pretend he hadn't heard and just stride out the door. But the corridor was now lined with trestle tables for relocated personnel who didn't have workstations, and it was a classic choke point for an ambush. He was stuck in the kill zone. At least Prescott had learned something in his brief time as a Gear officer, then.

"Chairman," Hoffman said, turning. "Here or in your office?"

Prescott beckoned to him to follow and headed for the men's bathroom. *Great, a pisspot parliament. Maybe he thinks I'll respond better to the common touch.* But it was closer than walking back to Prescott's office. Hoffman followed him in, cast a wary eye around for boots under the stall doors, and leaned against the green and gold tube-lined tiling with his Lancer over his shoulder. Saw-teeth clinked against the ceramic.

"I can't help but notice a general depression settling in HQ," Prescott said. "I need to know if it's about the situation generally or a reaction to Fenix's sentence that's lingering rather too long."

Hoffman held Prescott's gaze for a few beats while he worked out what the hell the man was actually driving at. Prescott knew damn well what the state of play was. He had that politician's radar, that ability to taste the air like a cobra and work out where the despair, weakness, and hope was trying to hide before he uncoiled and sank his fangs in it.

"You want me to order them all to cheer the fuck up, then, Chairman?" Hoffman *hurt.* As the weeks went on, he felt worse about Marcus and less able to understand either his own reactions or Marcus's behavior. Dom and Anya weren't exactly ignoring him—nothing so hostile—but the looks on their faces said he'd cut their hearts out and that nothing would ever be the same again. A desperate thought went through his mind. "Look, if you said the word, Fenix could be out of there tomorrow. Call it what you like—stick him in a penal battalion, a suicide squad, however you want to dress it up, but he could be back on the front line in twenty-six hours."

"And what message does that send to the other Gears?"

"That we need every man we can get?" Hoffman had once thought he could guess where Prescott was heading but he'd been left in his dust for the last few years. "I did it by the book, Chairman, because that's exactly what Sovereign's Regulations are for. They save us from not knowing what to do when guys we like and admire break the rules. No favor, no prejudice, no argument. Fenix did it. I wish to God he hadn't. We miss him—hell, *I* miss him. But what do I do?"

"That's my point. If he returns . . ." Prescott was staring at something on the tiles just above eye level. He reached out and rubbed at the gleaming ceramics with his forefinger and then inspected whatever had come off on his fingertip. "If he returns, it causes offense to the comrades and families of the men who died. It signals a breakdown of discipline. It may even look as if we care more about the sons of the elite than about the average Gear."

"So you're actually telling me no change, then. Have I missed something?"

"No, I plan to reassure Fenix's comrades that he isn't being starved and violated in prison, which might be something of a compromise. He's already getting into fights and he's been beaten up by the warders. I've asked for a regular medical report on him with proof of current welfare."

Goddamn. Does Anya know? Maybe Marcus had really cracked up after all, whatever the medics had said about his mental state. He had a hell of a temper. But it had always been channeled into the right places until now. "Is he okay?"

"He's a tough man to kill."

It wasn't an answer. "Are you ordering me to release him or not, sir?" Ah, Hoffman finally got it, or so he thought. Prescott *did* want Marcus freed, but he didn't want the responsibility if there was a backlash. "If so, you have to order the Judge Advocate's office to do it under the Fortification Act. I don't have authority over a civilian prison."

Hoffman struggled to work out Prescott's strategy. The JA's office was a twenty-two-year-old asthmatic admin clerk with terminal acne who'd failed the fitness requirements to enlist frontline, so he wasn't going to put up a fight, and the judiciary was reduced to magistrates' courts that handed out fines for petty crime in the shape of reduced rations or a firing squad for the really serious offenses. A dying world didn't have the resources to waste on trials, ordinary prisons, or appeals. So whatever Prescott wanted, Prescott could simply have. One Gear, even a guy like Marcus, couldn't possibly have any political value for him. Adam Fenix had been a man Prescott liked to keep sweet, but he was dead. Nobody seemed to be running the technical side of the war effort now. For a moment, Hoffman tried to imagine what Adam's reaction would have been to his son's disgrace. It was painful.

"No," Prescott said. "I'm just going to monitor the situation, and I want you to keep me apprised on general morale."

Like I don't do that every chance I get anyway. Hoffman was now too confused and busy to worry about Prescott's agenda any longer. And he had to see Anya with the bad news. *Great.*

"Very good, sir," he said flatly. "I'll update you later."

Hoffman escaped while he could and wove his way through the congestion in the corridor to the ops room. There were two captains ahead with their backs to him, lost in conversation as they ambled along. Regimental cap badges were now largely sentimental rather than organizational in an army shrunk to almost nothing by the war, and even rank didn't work the way it used to, but Hoffman clocked the officers almost subconsciously as Sovereign's Hussars.

Then he caught a waft of the conversation. "*. . . makes a change for Two-Six to deal with their miscreants instead of pinning medals on them . . .*" And that was it. That was just what he needed to press the button after weeks of two-hour naps instead of real sleep and with the weight of guilt crushing the breath out of him. He took four fast strides and almost tailgated the two Hussars.

"Yeah, Captain, but my *miscreant* gave every drop of goddamn sweat he had for *fifteen years* before he disobeyed me, so I'll thank you to keep your fucking opinions about my boys to *yourself*," Hoffman snarled. The two officers turned around, stunned by the outburst, and even took a few paces back. "You got somewhere else to be?"

"My apologies, sir," one of them said, but it didn't look like he meant it. "Won't happen again."

The busy corridor was completely silent for a few seconds too long as the officers walked off, double-time. Hoffman wanted to vanish into the carpet. But he would have felt far worse if he hadn't spoken up. Okay, he knew 26 RTI's reputation, earned over *centuries*: too much influence on policy, too much of the defense budget, too cocksure of itself, and he knew his own reputation, too, an over-promoted grunt who would never have an officer's polish or judgment as long as he had a hole in his ass.

But I got the job done. Until now.

He strode into Ops with his head down, wondering how the hell he would get his Gears back on task if he couldn't move on himself. Anya still smiled when she saw him, but it looked like an effort. Her face was a lot thinner. The gray shadows around her eyes said she'd spent last night either crying or lying awake in utter misery.

"When did you last eat, Lieutenant?" he asked quietly.

"I'll get something later, sir."

"I'll make sure you do." Hoffman should have done this over a coffee, but he hated keeping anything from her. He just had to package it right. "Prescott's decided to keep more of an eye on Marcus's welfare. Seems he got in a scrap or two, but he's okay now. Has he written back?"

Anya tried to put on her coping face but she wasn't doing a very good job of disguising that fear in her eyes. "No. Dom's still trying to get a visit arranged. Everything takes so damn long."

"Is the goddamn prison dicking with him?"

"No. I think Marcus is refusing to see him. Dom thought he might." Anya suddenly looked down and took an unnaturally keen interest in the papers on her desk. "Wants us to forget him."

Shit, that was something Hoffman should have seen coming. Marcus always got unswerving loyalty without even trying but he didn't want it. *Maybe I should have handled him. Sat on it. Dealt with it inside the tent.* But it was way beyond too late now, and veering between remorse and justification wasn't going to resurrect the Gears who died at Chancery.

"I'll see what I can find out," Hoffman said.

"Anyway, sir." Anya looked up again, freshly composed. Aigle walked by just behind her and glanced at Hoffman with that look that said *bastard.* "Guess who showed up? Private Salton's back. Do you want to see him?"

"Pad? Where is he?" The sniper hardly ever came back to base, living like a feral cat far outside the wire for months at a time, watching and waiting, just a voice on the radio. The Stranded didn't come in to volunteer intel. Pad went out and got it. "I'd better debrief him."

"Gone out to the Unknowns for a smoke."

"Okay, Lieutenant, keep me in the loop. I'll be on the radio."

Hoffman went out the back entrance to the vehicle compound, an open space that had once been rose gardens but had been leveled to create space for the draw-down from Ephyra. Some things were sacred, though, and nobody was going to dig up the gardens that continued beyond the retaining wall—the Tomb of the Unknowns, the cemetery for the COG's fallen war heroes. The gravestones mostly had names, except for the one genuinely unknown with the eternal flame set in a plain black marble chalice on the chipped gravel surface.

Hoffman wouldn't allow so much as a single pebble to be touched. But then nobody had asked. He made sure he walked through the cemetery at least once a week to pay his respects. As soon as he turned left at the end of the wall and walked through the archway, he could see Pad's red hair like a beacon, albeit a fading one now. He was looking down at one of the headstones with his Longshot sniper rifle and a couple of Locust weapons slung across his back. Judging by his position, he was at Carlos Santiago's plot. Okay, fine: Hoffman could guess how today was going to go.

He walked slowly up to Pad and stood beside him. The man's hair was now streaked with white, lightening into a sandy orange in that way that redheads often did as they aged, but the South Islander facial tattoos on his pale skin were as intensely dark blue as ever. He'd shaved. Sometimes he'd come back unexpectedly from some godforsaken shithole and the mix of stubble and tattoos made him look like a scarecrow whose stuffing had burst out, his COG-issue chest plate and boots the only indication that he was a Gear and not some Stranded hermit.

Hoffman waited for him to turn his head. He never expected Pad to snap to attention when he was lost in thought—or maybe prayer—at a graveside. Eventually, Pad let out a breath and his shoulders relaxed.

Prayer, then. Say one for me.

"Sir," Pad said quietly.

"Good to see you, Pad." Hoffman would normally have slapped him on the shoulder but these weren't normal times. Instead he leaned over and placed a fragment of dark green granite on the headstone. All he could see at that moment was a twenty-year-old Marcus Fenix digging a small hole in the chippings on that grave with his knife and burying his Embry Star within an hour of receiving it from Chairman Dalyell. "Damn, you're looking thin. What the hell are you living on out there?"

Pad fumbled in his belt pouch and took out some tissue paper and what looked like tobacco, then began rolling a smoke. "You know us Islanders. We can always live off the land. Found something else to smoke, too. The grubs can't detect this stuff as easily, either."

That hinted at times when they'd spotted him. Hoffman would enquire later. "Come on, let's go to the mess. Fill your boots. Proper food, not dead rats."

"Later, sir." Pad lit up and inhaled. He was right. Whatever he'd dried for that smoke smelled faintly like silage, nothing pungent at all. "I need to ease myself back to being around people again."

He jerked his head at Hoffman to follow and they walked off in the direction of the vehicle compound. Pad was now probably his oldest friend, his last buddy from the old days, the only one left from the men who had served with him at Anvil Gate. It was easy to tell him things. Pad had his own troubles, of course. He'd never been the same since his spotter, Baz, had been killed, and then he slid a little more after the Hammer strikes, but when everyone expected him to do a Bardry and blow his brains out, he just slogged on. Eventually he'd found some sort of peace alone out there on long-range surveillance duties in the wastelands.

Islanders were quietly tough, both the tribal guys like Tai and the white co-
lonial stock like Pad. Hoffman had never known any of them to give in to the
shit life dealt them.

Pad motioned Hoffman into the Packhorse, a smoke dangling from his lip.
"Okay, tell me what I've missed while I was off camp, sir."

"It's Vic." Nobody else was left to call him Vic anymore. He needed to hear
his own name. "Vic who used to be a regular Gear like you. Not the CDS."

The Packhorse was a little haven of sanity once Hoffman shut the driver's
door and turned the key. Pad rested his Longshot on the open window as they
rumbled over the carpet of debris that was now the highway into the southern
boroughs of Ephyra. For Hoffman, it was almost like old times, long before the
grubs emerged, a precious connection to the sergeant he'd once been, blissfully uncomplicated days when all he had to do was survive a contact, make
sure the enemy didn't survive his, and RTB with all his platoon intact.

"I suppose this is about Marcus," Pad said at last.

"Just talk some sense to me."

"I haven't had a conversation for months. Don't even talk to myself much
now. You forget how to, eventually."

"So consider this avoidance of skills fade." Hoffman scanned for movement
in the rubble. "No other officer loses this much sleep over busting one single
Gear."

"Well, there you have it." Pad leaned on the passenger door and tried to
brace his elbow to scope through with the Longshot. "You're not an Academy
boy. You never started out seeing Gears from the other end of the telescope.
It's the sergeant in you. Paternal. You know?"

"Yeah."

"And tribal. Two-Six. We *Unvanquished* don't do that kind of shit. That's for
other regiments." Pad lowered his Longshot and leaned back a little. "Blimey
fucking O'Reilly, Vic, if Anya hadn't been the one to tell me, I'd never have
believed Marcus would do that. He must have cracked. Poor sod. Never
thought he would, but there but for the grace of God and all that."

"Medics say not."

"They would," Pad said. "Nobody wants to admit everyone's getting totally
fucked up. Bad for morale." He held the smoke out to Hoffman. Hoffman
took a deep drag for the first time in many years, a habit he'd given up to
keep Margaret happy. "But if he is, what do you do with him? Have we got
any psychiatric hospitals left that aren't worse than the Slab? No. Does he
need to be in one? Probably not. What if you put him back on the front

line and he does something even worse? See, this is what you forget, Vic, all those other scenarios besides the should-I-or-shouldn't-I-have-busted-him. There's no good outcome whichever way you cut it. He did it, and everything flowed from that."

"I don't want to, but I think I'm in danger of focusing on his bad side to make me believe I was justified."

"Yeah, but you'll never be able to hate him. He's a bloody good bloke. Never gives a shit about himself. Part of you won't forget that."

"I wish I could."

"Anyway, you realize this is all academic, don't you? Because he'll never serve ten years, let alone forty."

"Life expectancy in there is about *two* years. Best average I've ever heard is five."

"I meant the grubs are going to be all over the plateau long before then. He's tough enough to survive in the Slab, so he'll still have to get out years before his sentence is finished. Have you thought about that?"

Hoffman hadn't. It bothered him that such a simple, logical thing hadn't occurred to him. Yeah, that would be a great comfort for poor Anya.

Don't worry, sweetheart. Your man's going to endure years of total animal degradation, then the grubs will invade, and he'll end up in a penal squad. It'll all work out fine. Go right ahead and plan for a happy ever after.

The conversation was distracting Hoffman but he still had his subconscious tuned to the road. The Packhorse vibrated slightly every few seconds. It might have been the effect of the shifting rubble beneath the tires, or even a resonance from a misfire or something. But ten years of surviving Locust attacks told him to assume the worst first.

"What are those assholes excavating out there, Pad?"

"Well, without the utility guys' seismometer network, I'm guessing, but they're definitely busy. Lots of spoil heaps. Suggests small pockets of soft material being dug out because they've hit so much granite. That's slowed 'em down a lot." The Packhorse was five or six kilometers outside the wire now. If Hoffman had swung right, he would have been able to see the forbidding outline of the Slab perched on the top of the granite cliff. "How the hell did you evacuate all the civvies?"

"We didn't. We lost a lot. Still doing the head count."

"Bugger." Pad suddenly slapped the dashboard like a driving instructor making a pupil do an emergency stop. "Whoa, *stop.*"

Hoffman slammed on the brakes. Pad was out of the Pack in a second and crouching by the door, Longshot aimed to the left. Hoffman grabbed his Lancer from the back seat and worked his way around to Pad.

"What is it?"

Pad held his breath for a few moments, pointing slowly into the rubble. "Thirty meters," he whispered. "Practically right on top of it."

Hoffman suddenly caught the slightest movement, something small and close to the ground like a rat, and then he realized he was looking at the tips of a Corpser's legs as it tried to emerge from a hole almost dead ahead. Like a spider making its way out of a plug-hole, it felt around gingerly for a while, blindly tapping and probing. It was impossible to tell how big the thing was until more leg appeared. Stones and dirt kicked up as it shoved more debris out of its way, and then the first joints of two of the legs became visible. Hoffman guessed it was much smaller than he'd expected, maybe two or three meters tall. They were normally huge bastards, bigger than a Centaur.

Pad sighted up. "Ever used one of those mini excavators in the garden?"

"I never had a garden," Hoffman whispered, raising his Lancer. "Why?"

"Doesn't matter." Pad dropped slowly onto his right knee and braced his left elbow on the other to steady his aim. "Leave this one to me."

It was a very close shot for a sniper, ludicrously easy. At this range, though, it was just a case of hitting the thing before it burst out and jumped. They could cover a lot of ground before they dropped.

More legs unfurled from the hole, six tapping feet scrabbling for purchase. The second joints were visible. Yes, a small one, relatively. Hoffman prepared to empty a clip into it whether Pad stopped it dead or not. The thing almost bounced for a moment like a swimmer trying to get a bit of momentum going to heave himself out of a swimming pool. Then it lunged.

Crack.

Hoffman saw the carapace shatter and fluid jet into the air almost before he realized Pad had squeezed one off. The single Longshot round could stop a truck and it had to, because the chamber only held one bullet. The Corpser managed to heave itself clear but then flopped down onto the hole again, legs sticking out at bizarre angles. Hoffman laid down a few short bursts to make sure it wasn't getting up again, but by then Pad had reloaded and put a second round into it. It crumpled in slow motion like a collapsing building.

They waited, listening. Corpsers were usually the pathfinders for grub insertions, tunneling through the ground ahead of the drones. After a long minute it didn't sound as if it had company.

"Okay, let's test a theory," Pad said.

He stood up and trotted over to the dead Corpser. Hoffman covered him, still not convinced that he wasn't going to find himself on top of another e-hole. Pad prodded the body with his boot.

"There you go," he said. He squatted and tried to get a grip on the body, but there was nothing to grab hold of. He gave up and pulled out his fighting knife to poke at the soil around it. "Bloody hell, imagine finding this in your bathtub."

"Just tell me, Pad."

"I've been keeping a log of Corpser sizes for the last couple of years."

"Well, there's not much entertainment where you are."

"You can tell by the size of Corpser what the geology's like." Pad managed to shift the Corpser about half a meter. A chunk of carapace and flesh fell away like a steel drum full of jelly. "The smaller the ones they deploy, the narrower the fissures in the granite. And it means they can get a lot further into the plateau than we thought. If they can't get a grub through a hole, I bet they'll send in Tickers now. *Anywhere.*"

Hoffman walked back to the Packhorse. He felt better for having discharged his weapon, as if he had some control of the situation again. The reality was that he had no goddamn handle on it at all.

"Well, shit, Pad," he said. "We're fresh out of good news, aren't we?"

Pad kicked the chunk of Corpser around like he was warming up for thrashball, apparently oblivious of the fact they were in grub territory, but then that was where he now lived his life, a hybrid of Stranded and Gear. "Hey, I ran into a Four-ELI patrol a couple of months ago. First time I've ever seen that Cole Train guy. Hell, he's *big.* They've got this mouthy little gob-shite corporal called Baird, though. He needs a good kicking."

He walked back to the Packhorse, rolling another smoke, and flopped into the passenger seat.

"Come on, Vic," he said. "I'm ready to face people again. Let's eat. And just accept there's not much you could have done differently for Marcus."

COG RESEARCH STATION AZURA.

William Alva was a really charming man. Out of his prison overalls, he looked like a kindly grocer on his day off, and he was clearly both stunned and happy to be on Azura.

Nevil watched him strolling along the cliff pathway between the headlands as he paused to admire the bobbing lavender heads of wildflowers. It was like walking a potentially boisterous dog, keeping an eye on him in case he went off worrying sheep and upsetting the locals.

"So we're taking our pet nonce for a walk." Dury ambled beside Nevil, one hand resting on the sidearm in his holster. "Aren't you supposed to have vivisected him by now?"

"No, I'm a physicist," Nevil said. "We bang bits of metal together and do sums."

"I'm serious, Dr. Estrom. If he isn't going to be kept locked up in the hospital, I've got a serious security problem. And a public confidence issue."

Azura had everything except a prison. Nevil wondered if that was sheer naivete about the capacity of people with high IQs to commit crime, but when the COG built this facility in the Pendulum Wars a prison was probably the last thing it thought it would need. One thing it did have was a school with nearly a hundred pupils, because this was where the COG planned to rebuild civilization. The chosen elite had families; at least one generation had already grown up on Azura.

And word was now getting around that they not only had a convicted pedophile in their civilized paradise, but a homicidal one at that.

"See Adam about it," Nevil said. "He says he's taken all the samples he needs for the time being. Can't they lock the guy in the isolation ward?"

"That's not exactly secure. He's not just a nonce, he's a nonce who's been in the Slab for twenty years and learned a lot of extra bad habits."

And that was where Adam's son was right now. Nevil had met Marcus a few times and never known quite what to make of him, but he knew every damn thing about him—or at least as much as Adam did, and Nevil wasn't convinced how much that actually was. The two of them didn't seem to talk anywhere near enough. When they did, it wasn't always frank. Nevil knew because Adam had the conversations with him that he should have had with Marcus.

He told me he lied to Marcus as a kid, lied by omission about why Elain went missing. Didn't tell him he found she was still going on expeditions to the Hollow. The whole Fenix family's built on silence.

Alva stopped at the cliff edge and gazed out to sea, probably marveling at the Maelstrom, the impossible artificial storm that should never have been there on such a lovely day. Dury ground to a halt with Nevil. It was as if they were maintaining a cordon sanitaire to avoid breathing anywhere near a pervert.

"How's the working relationship with Professor Fenix?" Dury asked, taking a twist of rag paper out of his pocket and flipping it into his mouth. It was a bag of nuts or something. "Can't have been easy for you, putting the knife in him like that after all those years."

Ouch. But Dury was right, if brutal. "Don't you already know the answer?"

"Look, I'm special forces, not the intelligence services. Which we haven't got now, and they were useless farts anyway. It's a genuine question."

"Well, we're certainly not as close as we used to be," Nevil said sourly. "And I don't want to be here anyway."

"Well, you're stuck, Doctor Estrom. Your brother was Duke of Tollen's, wasn't he?"

"Yes."

"I know you kept trying to enlist. I respect that." Dury, chewing thoughtfully, watched Alva, eyes scanning without moving his head. "Now, I've got to try to rub along with you brainiacs and boffins on a day-to-day basis, and I can't always tell if you're bullshitting me about what needs doing or not. If you say something has to happen, and from a security point of view I don't agree, then I have to make the call. In this case, you've got a nonce to do experiments on, but he's swanning around doing nothing. I was expecting him to be shot full of pathogens and too buggered to be a danger to anyone."

"You watch too many movies."

"Prescott had him brought here, and that's one guy who definitely knows the difference between reality and fiction, so what's going on?"

"I honestly don't know, Captain. I'm not a biologist." Nevil realized Dury had a point. "I know biologists do some research on tissue samples, but for other things they need to observe the results in a whole organism."

"Well, let me put it this way." Dury shoved the paper bag back in his pocket and started walking again. Alva had moved off. "If that whole organism up ahead ends up raping or killing a kid here, I'm not going to be amused. So I'm going to have to lock him up somewhere, and preferably not one of the hospital wards."

"Okay," Nevil said. It didn't seem unreasonable; why did he need to ask? Maybe he was more worried about upsetting the scientific community here than he let on. "Go ahead."

"Is he a biohazard?"

Nevil had the feeling they didn't even know yet. "If Dr. Bakos hasn't quarantined him, he has to be safe to handle. In a manner of speaking."

Dury seemed to be considering that. Then he frowned, dropped his shoulders, and let out a parade ground yell that made Nevil's spine stiffen. "*Mr. Alva!* Time's up. Let's get you back to your presidential suite, shall we?"

Alva turned around like a man used to being told where to go and what to do. He walked back toward them, frighteningly normal and pleasant. Nevil found himself backing off, more because he was repelled by the idea of the man than by the chance of being contaminated by him—if he was infected, anyway.

"This is really, really nice," Alva said, all smiles. "What a lovely place."

"And how are you feeling?" Dury asked. "What have they done to you so far?"

"Oh, just blood tests and skin samples." Alva patted Nevil on the arm as he passed him to walk ahead of Dury. It made his flesh crawl for no sensible reason. "Small price to pay for being out of *that* place."

Nevil had to ask. He knew damn well that Adam would have already. "Did you see Marcus Fenix?"

Alva nodded. "The Gear? Oh yes."

"How is he?"

"How do you expect him to be? It's a vile place. Do you know him?"

It would be old information anyway. Nevil found himself peeling back onion layers of motive and double-dealing, and just gave up. Maybe it was simply just as it looked—Bakos had wanted a live human subject, and nobody would miss a pedophile or shed a tear for him if it ended badly.

"Sort of," Nevil said.

"Not very nice to tell him his dad's dead, though, is it? I mean, that poor professor. But I understand. And it's not as if I can ever go back, is it?"

"Very true." Dury motioned Alva to move on. "You certainly won't be leaving Azura for the foreseeable future."

"Suits me," said Alva. "Thank you."

Dury took a few paces and then turned to look back at Nevil as he unslung his Lancer. "You going to see the Prof?"

"Yes." Nevil's eyes were suddenly on the rifle. It wasn't so much that Dury looked as if he was worried that Alva would slip away to prey on some kid. It was the rifle itself. Nevil had seen Lancers hundreds, thousands of times, so much part of the Gears around him in Jacinto that sometimes he didn't even notice them. But now he did, and there was something he needed to do. "Captain, can I ask a favor of you?"

"I'll do my best."

"Would you train me to use a Lancer, please? For whatever favor you want in return."

Dury took a few seconds to nod. "Certainly. Every man should know how to handle a firearm these days."

Civilians in Tyrus weren't routinely armed. That was how much faith the citizens put in their Gears. "And—well, think of something by way of payment."

"Reach Gear proficiency," Dury said, almost smiling. "That'll be my reward."

Nevil pondered that as he watched him walk away, then carried on up the cliff path to the observation point. He cut through the water gardens with their tinkling streams trickling over gold stone and headed back to the Landa Tower. He tried hard to care about Alva, but he was still tormented by the what-ifs of alerting the world to the existence of the Locust before E-Day. The platform elevator to the top floor rose at a leisurely pace, giving him time to marshal his thoughts.

I need to thrash this out with Adam. I can't spend the rest of my life being cooked by my own anger.

It was surprisingly hard to stay angry. Nevil knew people who kept grudges for years, polishing them to a perfect hateful brightness, but he didn't have the stamina for that. Anger was an animal, he decided. At some point it became detached from its source, a creature in its own right that needed care and feeding, and then it became like a pet that had outlived the first few days of novelty for a spoiled child. It was a source of guilt. You had to take it for walks, while all the time you wished someone would take it off your hands. Nevil felt he had to be outraged by Adam's arrogant irresponsibility because the man had done some appalling things, but what he'd done was so vast that it was impossible to connect to the human scale of it.

Like the Hammer of Dawn. I suppose I killed millions too. Billions, maybe. My calculations. My work. Yet I never so much as threw a punch at another human being.

If he had to work on being outraged, then it probably wasn't the feeling that was tearing him apart. Maybe it was being excluded. Adam had been a mentor, a friend, almost a father for fifteen or sixteen years, and that had to count for something.

But he confided in me. It was years too late, yes, but he told me. He couldn't tell Marcus. He couldn't tell his own son. Either he thought I'd understand better, or my anger and disappointment was easier to take than Marcus's.

Only the people you truly cared about had the power to hurt you.

The Landa Tower became more of a maze on the top floors. Nevil left the main lift and worked his way up smaller elevators to the penthouse suite. No wonder Esther Bakos was so pissed off about Adam's arrival. He hadn't even been on the must-take personnel list, but he ended up with the best apartment and effective control of the Lambency project. A damn physicist, too. Feathers were ruffled, and there was no terror and destruction outside to focus minds on the real issue as there was in Jacinto.

Nevil walked down the corridor and rapped on the door of the penthouse. It opened remotely, because when it slid open, Adam was sitting at his antique mahogany desk shuffling papers. Nevil had never been up here before.

"Hi, Adam." It was easier to plunge in on an impersonal note. "Why the sealed door?"

"I have a small lab up here," Adam said. "It's all designed for containment of some kind. I don't think it was meant for a physicist." He managed a sad smile, then stood up. "Come in, Nevil. Coffee machine's working. Just like the DRA, isn't it?"

Nevil sat down on one of the sumptuous leather sofas. The suite of rooms reminded him more of Haldane Hall than the office, and he wondered if Prescott had moved Adam here like a kindly zookeeper because it was similar to his natural environment, or if it was simply the easiest place to keep an eye on him. "Are they keeping you up to speed about Marcus?"

Adam disappeared into another room and came out with a silver coffee pot and two porcelain cups. "Yes."

"And?"

"He's not thriving. He ended up . . . well, getting a thrashing."

Nevil had already heard the gossip but it didn't make that any easier to hear straight from Adam. It was hard to express his genuine sympathy without making Adam feel even worse. "They're taking it out on him, are they?" Nevil said. "I'm really sorry. Honestly."

"Should be me in there, shouldn't it?"

"I didn't say that."

"No. I did. Look, proper brown sugar lumps. No saccharine." Adam plopped the sugar into the cups. "I can't complain about being confined here when he's going through that. So, are we talking again?"

"I suppose we are. Look, you're in trouble, and you probably spent more time and effort on me than you did on Marcus, and I can't just forget all that." Nevil said it sincerely, but he saw Adam wince. "I'm not going to pretend I'm not . . . well, disgusted. Hurt. Shocked. I've still not worked it all out. I still can't believe you did it. But we're both prisoners, and we can do more to solve problems if we're not embroiled in some feud."

The silence hung there. Adam probably needed to feel he wasn't alone, and this was maybe the first time that his self-sufficiency had buckled in his adult life. Nevil felt for him. It was impossible not to. He wasn't malicious, just surprisingly naive for a man with such a prodigious intellect and real combat experience.

"The interesting thing about being a traitor among scientists," Adam said, "is that they don't resort to a lynch mob. We're all so very *civilized*. Sometimes I wish people would just punch me and get it over with."

"Sometimes I feel like I could oblige you."

"I have no defense other than naïve overconfidence."

"You know how hard I'm trying to come to terms with what you did?" Nevil asked. "I started thinking that if you'd sounded the alarm as soon as you knew about the Locust, then perhaps we'd have launched an early strike and actually wiped them out before they emerged. But then we wouldn't have found out about the Lambent. So there might have been purpose to this."

"Or we might have cooperated with the Locust on research and found a solution."

"If you'd believed that was possible, you'd have done it."

"I would."

"Is there anything you're still not telling me about this? Like the Sires?"

"I knew nothing about that. I know almost nothing now."

Nevil realized he was grasping at anything that might vindicate Adam. He'd heard the gossip about the Sires. The COG had its own mucky research. That might have been enough to justify keeping the existence of the Locust—and the Lambent—from Adam's political masters. But life wasn't that simple, and Nevil accepted that there would never be a neat, clear-cut answer that would put things right for him again.

"I just ran into our resident pervert," he said, forcing himself to change the subject. They both knew where they stood now. "Alva. Seriously, Adam, are you really using him for research?"

Adam sipped his coffee in silence for a while, glasses sliding down to the tip of his nose. The gilt clock on the mantelpiece clicked with a slow, steady heartbeat.

"No," he said at last. "I'm not. Enough secrets, Nevil. I've told Esther this, and I'm telling you, but I'd rather that was as far as it went. Prescott mustn't know."

"Know what?"

"I've done enough morally dubious things in my life and I don't need any more on my conscience. I've forbidden Esther to use the prisoner. I'm inoculating myself with the Lambent pathogen—"

"No, no. Hold it." Nevil's scalp tightened. "Stop right there. I'm not a biologist, but I know that's not inoculation. That's *infection*. Are you insane? You don't know a damn thing about this organism."

"I need to provide Esther with data on how it reproduces in a whole organism. We can't do this with tissue samples alone. We *have* to know what this thing does before it jumps the species barrier to us."

"You have *no idea* what it'll do to you. *No goddamn idea* at all. And you're just helping it jump, haven't you? What the hell are you thinking?"

Adam held up his hand for silence, doing that little dismissive head shake that he always used to trash a suggestion. "There's a long tradition in medicine of self-experimentation among doctors. We wouldn't have a cure for gastric ulcers or half of our anesthetics without their taking that risk."

"*Doctors*, Adam. Not people with doctorates. *Medical* doctors. Men and women who knew what they were doing."

"But they didn't. That's what experimentation is."

"You've already done it, haven't you?"

"Yes."

"Oh my God . . ."

Nevil found himself looking into Adam's face for signs of symptoms. He had no idea what form Lambency might take in a human, but Adam looked worried and tired, nothing more than that. He'd been looking that way for a long time, so he was fine by Adam Fenix standards.

"It's a wonderful incentive for finding a cure, anyway," Adam said.

"That's not funny." Nevil gestured to his coffee cup. *What if this is airborne, or spread by contact?* He tried hard to stay rational, but the primal fear of contagion was hard to keep in check. "How the hell do you know you're not going to transmit this to everyone else?"

"I handled it without full biohazard procedure for years and I never developed symptoms. That's why I had to inject it."

"So how are you going to hide this? I think you should come clean with Prescott. Don't you ever learn?"

"Esther simply passes off my results as Alva's. He has no idea what we're doing. He gets vitamin shots and gives tissue samples. Simple."

"He raped and murdered small boys. Someone's sons. Forgive me for going out on a limb, but if you don't know if this is lethal, and you tell him so, what's unethical about doing it? And shouldn't he pay for what he did?"

Adam stared into his cup, frowning. Then he looked up. "And shouldn't *I*?"

That was it. Nevil was incensed. Adam was getting his science confused with his piety. "Is that it? Atonement? How does that help us? How does risking the life of our leading weapons scientist make sense when we're losing a war? Damn it, Adam, that's *selfish*."

It was the first time Nevil had dared say that they were losing. He hadn't even realized he believed it until the words erupted from him. But it was just a matter of doing the math; the human population was now less than 0.1 percent of the total it had been before E-Day, even on the most generous estimate. They needed a miracle, and science didn't do those.

And yes, he thought Adam was being a martyr.

Adam cradled the empty cup in both hands like a fortune teller reading the grounds. "I'm just a bomb-maker, Nevil," he said, "who happened to have a brilliant wife who left some valuable notes. But I was also an officer in the Royal Tyran Infantry. And I never asked my Gears to do anything I wasn't ready and willing to do myself."

Nevil had never served. It ate at him. It was hard now to get through the day without thinking of Emil and how that was what it meant to do the right thing. Sacrifices had to be made.

"Okay, you can infect me as well," he said. "More test subjects, better data. I'll do it."

"No," Adam said. It was a voice he rarely used, his Major Fenix persona. "You will *not*. And that's an order."

CHAPTER 9

Fenix won't cooperate, end of story. I've examined him, and he's obviously under a great deal of stress, not really surprising given the state of the prison, but he's not presenting as mentally unfit on tests. I suspect he's giving me the answers he knows will fall in the normal range. He knows how to sound perfectly fine, because he's probably been living behind that facade for years, and he's highly intelligent. This is a man typical of his social group—the archetypal stiff upper lip of the founding families, and the unwillingness of the Gear to admit what he sees as weakness. He wants to be punished. He feels he's failed his comrades, and disgraced his family name and regiment. And the thought of being set free but relegated to a civilian on top of that ignominy, and a mentally ill civilian at that, is almost worse than the prospect of death or a life sentence for him. That, unfortunately, makes him NFT—Normal For Tyrus. By the way, who's Carlos?

(Dr. Monro Alleyn, consultant psychiatrist, in an informal note to the Judge Advocate's office.

Copy to Chairman Prescott: check before adding to redacted file.)

THE RUSTY NAIL, KALONA STREET, JACINTO: BOUNTY, 11 A.E.

Everyday, routine places had gaping voids in them now, and not just because the grubs had destroyed them. Everywhere that Anya looked, Marcus was *not* there, and he would not be there again.

She walked into the Rusty Nail, usually her last port of call when looking for him when he was off-duty and not answering his radio. It wasn't as if he took much downtime anyway, but when he went to ground—and it was almost always when yet another Gear he knew well had been killed—this was where he ended up. He'd park himself on a bar stool, order a shot, and sit there staring into the glass for hours.

It was usually only one or two drinks, the bar staff told her. Once, though, they said he'd worked his way through a whole bottle of Maranday apple brandy and walked out six hours later, still remarkably steady on his feet.

I know. He showed up in my quarters, fell asleep on the bunk as soon as he took off his jacket, and I had to leave him there when I went on watch. The only time he ever stayed the whole night, and I wasn't even there.

Curzon. That was all he'd said by way of explanation, Roland Curzon. He said he'd hit him once. It took Anya some time to work out that the fight with Curzon had been when they were kids, and that the grown-up Curzon had just been killed on foot patrol.

Marcus never forgot a damn thing: not a name, not a callsign, not a detail on a map, or anyone he felt guilty about.

"You going to come in?" the barman called. It was Chas. He put a small beer on the counter for her, slopping it from a glass jug. "Haven't seen you in here for ages."

Anya stood in the doorway, looking instinctively for a battered tan leather flying jacket hunched over the bar, but knew she wouldn't find it. She walked to the counter and picked up the glass, conscious of the looks she was getting, but then it was always like that. She was usually the only woman in the bar. That didn't normally bother her because most of the guys who drank in there were Gears, HQ support staff, or medics from JMC, and she knew plenty of them by sight. But this time she felt exposed and . . . *resentful.* That was the word. She resented anyone drinking there when Marcus couldn't. It was a strange mix of emotions.

"I'm waiting for Dom," she said.

"Hasn't come in yet." Chas leaned on folded arms. "Hey, I'm really sorry about Marcus. Don't worry. He's as tough as old boots, and that place is going to have to shut down anyway when the grubs get there. They won't wait forty years. And if they do, then we won't have a problem anymore, will we?"

It was an interesting thought, but the kind of dumb, dishonest but well-meaning reassurance people gave each other when there was no real hope. Anya looked for a spare seat at the bar. If she sat at a table, she'd be inviting company that she didn't want. One of the brand-new second lieutenants, Donneld Mathieson, was at one of the tables but he seemed to be getting up to go, probably on his way to play thrashball again. He was a nice kid, always cheerful, always volunteering, always on the go. He'd have his own platoon in a month or two.

Kid. God, I'm thirty.

Even if things work out, I'll be pushing seventy when Marcus is released.

It didn't matter. He was hers, and she was willing to wait forever if that was what it took. She'd made up her mind twelve years ago after the medal investiture, with her mother's posthumous Embry Star in her hand and the loss still so raw that it almost stopped her breathing. Carlos was dead, too; Marcus was in pieces under his I'm-just-fine shell. Unfamiliar alcohol, a desperate need for comfort when the world hurt so much, and then he walked her back to Helena Stroud's silent, empty apartment, and their hormones and shared misery took over.

We shouldn't be doing this, he said, not an enlisted man and an officer. Okay, I said, we'll just have to be discreet. Sneaking time together was a thrill at first. Then it got to be a habit, a dirty little secret, and that wasn't what I wanted at all. What's the opposite of a platonic relationship, where you've got the guy's body but you never lay a finger on his soul? There's got to be a word for it.

Anya took a few pulls at the beer—they must have been brewing wheat this time, oddly sweet stuff—and swirled the dying foam around the sides of the glass. She'd never known Marcus's mother. But she'd known his father well enough to understand how fixated both of them had been with their research. Marcus had every possible comfort as a child except time and attention.

Their concern was always for his future. It was never for his here and now.

Chas rattled an empty jug on the counter in front of her. "You want a top-up?"

Anya was caught out by her empty glass. She'd been sitting here longer than she realized. There was still no sign of Dom. Well, it was just beer. It wasn't as if she was in here every night getting hammered. She hardly drank.

"Why not?" she said. "Thanks, Chas."

Come on, Dom.

She had bad news for him anyway, but it wasn't as if he didn't know it was coming. The JA's office confirmed that the only appeal possible had to be against sentence, and as it had already been commuted from the death penalty, the only route left was medical.

Why the rules? Why do we still have damn rules? The whole world's been reduced to one city, we're under martial law, and we cling to rules that aren't relevant any longer. She checked her watch: 1805 hours. *What are you doing now, Marcus? Did you get my letters? Are you reading them? What are those animals in there doing to you? Why won't you let me visit?*

"Hey, Anya." Someone slid up onto the stool beside her. She heard the whisper of fabric and caught the scent of carbolic soap with a top note of liquor. "You okay?"

It was Barry, one of the trauma surgeons from JMC. She couldn't recall his surname or if she even knew it. There was a kinship between doctors and CIC Gears because they worked in the same meat-grinding operation. Anya deployed men, listened to them getting hit and yelling for casevac, and men like Barry tried to put the pieces back together again in ER. This was the nearest bar for the medics to flee to after their shift and find some oblivion.

Man down. Man down. She must have heard that thousands of times over the last thirteen years and it still turned her gut over every time. The call would go down the line, and she'd hear it over the RT, just as she'd heard her mom. *Man down. T-Four. T-One. T-damn-well-dead or crippled.*

"I'm waiting for Dom," she said.

"Oh. I see."

"No, not *oh*. It's not like that." Anya bristled more at the idea that Dom had given up on looking for Maria than the suggestion she'd hopped beds now that there was no more Marcus. "He's been in town trying to raise funds for Marcus's appeal."

Barry just looked at her.

"You get prisoners in from the Slab occasionally, don't you?" she said. Her glass was empty again. Damn, she *had* been here a long time. "What state are they in when you see them?"

Anya knew she was putting him on the spot. She watched him blink. She watched him put his glass to his lips to buy time while he found the kindest way to tell her what she already feared she knew.

"What do you want?" he said at last. "What you want to hear, or the truth?"

It had to be done. "The truth."

"Shit. I thought you might." Chas appeared like a ghost and topped up Anya's glass as if she was going to need it. Barry held his out as well. "Well, the biggest cause of mortality is other inmates. A knife in the back . . . blunt force trauma . . . look, we don't get many. Really. Three since I started at JMC. Normally they sort their own crap, and there aren't that many men there now anyway. It's been distilled down to the hardcore ones who are too evenly matched to get a result." He paused as if he realized he'd worded that a little too brutally. "Two years' life expectancy was about right in the past, but the fittest have survived. We had one come through the other day, but—well, he was shipped out again, nothing wrong with him, so I imagine he's back inside now."

Anya didn't know what kind of look she had on her face. She knew that she felt weepy, but she'd always been good at gritting her teeth and hiding it, or so she thought. Barry twisted on the stool a little and looked into her face.

"Have you heard from Marcus?"

"He won't see me and he hasn't replied to my letters."

"Might not be getting them."

"He told Dom that we both had to forget him and that's the last thing he said." *Why the hell am I telling him this? To hear it out loud, so that I finally believe it?* "How am I ever going to do that?"

"Come on," Barry said. "How long have any of us got? I could be dead tomorrow and so could you. How old are you? Thirty-five? You're still young."

"*Thirty,*" Anya said, teeth gritted and suddenly feeling unreasonably pissed off.

"Well, you're gorgeous. You could have any man you want."

Anya couldn't look away from the beer. She was angry, but it was a formless, vague resentment. It wasn't explosive. It was just simmering. It was about everything: Mom pulling that crazy stunt, grubs, Marcus being gone, Marcus doing insane, stupid things, Marcus throwing away what little they had, Hoffman doing what he had to—but mainly Marcus.

How could you do it to me? How could you leave me alone like this?

"I *know* I could," she said, daring to admit for once that she knew she was beautiful. She'd never felt this *acid* before. "Which is why I want Marcus. The alpha female has a right to the alpha male in the pack. Right?"

Barry put his hand on her elbow. Somehow it slid to the top of her thigh. She froze.

It was the kind of thing Marcus would never, ever do in public. And that was why it pissed her off—not because Barry was groping her, but because she wished that Marcus would at least have held her hand in public, just acknowledged their relationship and not pretended he wasn't sleeping with her. There were too many dead for anything else to matter, too few chances to live.

"Sweetheart," Barry said, "if you wait for him, that damn thing's going to heal over before you get laid again."

So she hit him.

It came out of nowhere. Tempers always did. Even as she felt her fist connect, she was off the stool and nose to nose with Barry, somehow both grieving and furious at the same time. She didn't know how hard she'd hit him. He was just sitting there with his hand to his jaw, wide-eyed, but her right hand was one white-hot ache for a moment.

"Yes, I'm saving it for *him,* okay?" Everyone turned. "It's him or nobody. That's what I'm going to do. Keep your hands to your damn self."

The adrenaline ebbed so fast that she felt as if a plug had been pulled. Her instinct was to apologize, but Barry had already slid off his stool and was backing away.

"I'm sorry," he said. "Look, I know. I was out of line. Okay? Forget I said it. I'd better go."

Anya had to get a grip. And she still had to wait for Dom. She climbed back on the stool as the doors closed behind Barry and tried not to meet anyone's eye. Chas managed it, though.

"I'd better stick to soda now," she said quietly.

Chas nodded, polishing a glass on a grubby rag. "Uh-huh."

Her knuckles were starting to hurt. When she checked them out, the skin was broken and weeping watery blood. She sucked the joint ruefully just as a hand touched her shoulder, and she swung around ready to lash out again.

"Whoa," Dom said. "What's wrong?"

Anya was just relieved to see him. "Sorry. I made a fool of myself. Had a beer too many. Barry—you know, the surgeon, the one with the blond sideburns. He felt me up. I hit him."

Dom was all instant indignation, an outraged brother ready to defend his sister's honor. "Right, I'm going to go break his fucking legs. *Asshole.* Where did he go?"

"Dom, just leave it." She gripped his forearm. He hadn't even changed out of his combat rig, just taken off the armor plates and put on a jacket. "It wasn't like that. He's a nice guy. I just lost it. It's Marcus. I'm just angry all the time."

"You're going through a kind of mourning thing," Dom said. "When Bennie and Sylvie got killed, me and Maria had bereavement counseling. They tell you all kinds of useless shit, but some of it's true. Like getting angry with the person who's gone, feeling they've run out on you. All kinds of crazy mood swings. It passes."

"I know. Remember?"

"Yeah, sorry. Shouldn't have said it like that. But just remember this is sort of like . . ." Dom trailed off. He didn't get as far as saying *death.* "But if that guy's hassling you—"

"He isn't."

"Okay, but if he *does,* you tell me, okay?" Dom stared into her face for a few seconds, waiting for the kill order. She couldn't have wished for a better friend. Then he settled down next to her, apparently satisfied that gutting Barry could wait until tomorrow, and folded his arms on the counter. "Well, I did it. Took goddamn months, but I *did* it."

"What?" Anya grasped at every straw and felt a fool for it. "What have you done?"

Dom took out an envelope. When he folded back the flap, it was stuffed with ration coupons, the real hard currency in Jacinto. The only way to build up a pile of those was illegal—the black market, or even claiming rations for people who were dead but had somehow missed being recorded as deceased. Either way, Dom was on thin ice.

"I sold my Embry," he said.

That broke her heart. What made it worse was looking into Dom's face. He shone with pure devotion. He never once asked her what she'd done with her mother's medal. It appalled her that she hadn't volunteered it, and she wasn't even sure why she hadn't.

"God, Dom. I'm sorry."

"Hey, don't be. Some dick's prepared to starve a neighborhood because he wants a medal he didn't even win. Works for me."

"Look, I've still got Mom's." She was complicit now, offering to get involved in his coupon deal. "Take it back to him and swap it."

Dom smiled sadly to himself and put the envelope back in his jacket. "No. That's all you have left of your mom. Marcus buried his in Carlos's plot as soon as they pinned it on him. Mine's mine to give for *him*."

He took off his jacket and laid it on the counter, then nodded at Chas for a drink. Anya always found it hard now to take her eyes off the tattoo on his arm, the heart-shaped one that said *Maria*. Dom knew exactly what it meant to love one person and never want another. Yet he still gave up time that he could have been searching for Maria to help Marcus. Tears pricked at Anya's eyes.

"Okay, the JA says the only appeal we can possibly lodge is on medical grounds, but it's a long shot," she said, wiping her nose discreetly on the back of her hand. "If they find he's not responsible for his actions, then the guilty plea can be set aside. But then he'll end up discharged from the army anyway. He won't be pleased about that. Or being labeled mentally unfit."

"I don't care if I've got to paint him green and tell everyone he thinks he's a goddamn tree," Dom said. "We get him out, *then* we worry about what to do next."

"So what do we do now?"

"What?"

"We can't make contact with him. No visits, and we don't know if he's getting letters or just ignoring them."

"So I'll get Hoffman to talk to Prescott. He'll get things moving. Then we hire a proper lawyer, not some clerk from the JA's office." He must have seen the expression on her face change. "Hey, Hoffman's wife was a lawyer. He said she was a frigging *demon* with judges. Damn shame she's not still around." He took a swig of beer. "He'll put some pressure on 'em. The old man feels bad about Marcus, Anya. You know that. We'll sort it, okay?"

Dom said it all with confidence. Any man who could spend so many years looking for his wife in the wastelands outside the wire wasn't going to be daunted by a prison system or red tape. Anya felt he wouldn't even be put off by a whole Locust army if it meant saving Marcus.

Be alive for him, Maria. Please. I want to see Dom happy again. He deserves it.

"So, what do you want to do tonight?" she asked. It wasn't a matter of taking in a movie or a meal, even if such civilized refinements still existed. There were only two things on their agendas, either worrying about Marcus or worrying about Maria. "Patrols said some new Stranded moved in to Lower Jacinto. I'll drive."

Dom drained his beer. "No, bike," he said. "Less fuel, less hassle." He ran his hand over his Maria tattoo again, a desperately sad caress. "You and me, Anya, we're both in the same boat. They're out there, Marcus and Maria, and we have to bring them home. No matter how long it takes."

Yes, it was *we*. It was very much *we*. She had a brother by default, and that made things a little easier to take.

"I always said you were one in a million." She patted his back. For a moment he felt like Marcus, the T-shirt warm and slightly damp down his spine, and that comfortingly solid feel of muscle and bone. "Better make that one in a billion."

THE SLAB, SOUTHWEST JACINTO CITY LIMITS.

Dury brought the car to a halt twenty meters from the entrance and stared up at the prison's granite facade. It looked like a lonely fort set on a finger of rock that jutted out from the core of the plateau, separated from the nearest buildings by a broad no-man's land of scrubby heath that had been the Wenlau Heath park when there were staff still around to maintain it.

The gold lettering on the peeling board mounted to the side of the gate said CPSE HESKETH. Dury appeared to be troubled by it. He frowned.

"I never knew it was called that," he said, ducking his head back inside the car. "I thought it was just Jacinto Maximum Security Prison."

"There was more than one in my father's day." Prescott gathered his thoughts. He had never needed to visit Coalition Prison Service Establishment Hesketh on any fact-finding missions in his early career, and he had certainly never expected to be personally acquainted with anyone serving time in there. "Expensive things, prisons. They divert our resources simply to keep men idle. Not a luxury we can afford, although in this case it's probably a necessity."

"Are you ready, then, sir?"

"I think so."

"Permission to speak freely?"

"As always."

"They're going to shit themselves when they see you. They're only expecting me and a minion."

"Yes, I imagine it'll have a laxative effect." Prescott's father had taught him that the best fertilizer for a farm was the master's boot on the soil, although David Prescott had never actually farmed. He'd simply owned a number of them. "They'll never know if the next inspection will be a personal one, so a very cost-effective long-term deterrent."

Dury got out and opened the rear passenger door of the staff car. Prescott stepped out into an overcast day to feel the spittle of light rain on his face. It was going to turn into a downpour soon. At this moment, as he strode up the short path with Dury beside him in anonymous COG armor—just a cavalry unit insignia stenciled on his plates, no indication of which guards regiment that was—he knew someone inside the prison had spotted them. They'd have to be monitoring the exterior.

Dury rapped on the small door set in the huge twin gates, once painted gloss black and now simply faded and matte. It took some time for it to open. Prescott wondered if he was wrong about monitoring. The uniformed warder who appeared at the door looked at Dury, then at Prescott, and the show started.

Yes, officer. I'm Chairman Richard Prescott.

"Oh . . . sir?"

Prescott just inclined his head politely and let Dury do the introductions, now clearly unnecessary. "Chairman Richard Prescott to see prisoner Fenix," Dury said. He held his helmet tucked under one arm, the better to look the crew-cut, hard-faced bastard who got results. "He's a busy man, so can we crack on with this, please?"

Prescott stifled a smile. It was good to see someone with a talent for political theater. Dury was naturally easy-going, except when he needed to be otherwise, and had he come from the right family and gone to the right school, then he would have had a fine career: perhaps he might even have been a political rival. For a moment Prescott felt that thrill, that beginning of an adrenaline rush, at the thought that Dury might have given him a run for his money or even trounced him.

We find what pleasure we can in the jobs we do. That's the secret to doing them well. Especially the more unlovely work.

"Sorry, sir, come in," the warder said. "We weren't expecting you, or else we'd have had someone here to meet you." Prescott followed Dury through the inset door, ducking his head slightly to step in, and the warder walked ahead while talking to someone on his radio in an anxious whisper. "Niko . . . no, it's the Chairman, as in Prescott . . . yes, *Prescott* . . . how the hell should I know? . . . okay . . . yeah."

The place was typical of the institutions built before the Coalition of Ordered Governments had been formed, classic Tyran architecture, military and utilitarian—high walls, an open courtyard for vehicles just inside the double gates, with the accommodation and office floors looking down onto a central parade ground that housed a statue of Nassar Embry in armor, with the uplifting inscription: I AM RESPONSIBLE FOR MYSELF AND MY ACTIONS. It was the opening line of the Octus Canon, the affirmation of citizenship sworn by every man and woman in the COG.

Yes, Embry. I fully understand my responsibilities. Were things simpler in your day? More black and white?

The windows—ceiling height, arched at the top, mullioned—were falling apart and one on the east wing was minus most of its leading, but the overall grandeur hadn't been diminished. Prescott caught a glimpse of solid, square archways leading off like undercrofts in the buildings with smaller courtyards beyond. The granite paved path, setts missing and grass growing in the cracks, led up to main entrance doors that had seen better days. When he looked right, he could see greenery, and realized the complex actually had gardens.

"What's that?" he asked, pointing.

The warder followed his finger. "That's where we grow food, sir. We're pretty self-sufficient. We have to be."

Dury caught Prescott's eye accidentally as they waited for the doors to be unlocked. The captain was looking up at the impossibly high, slippery walls made of solid granite blocks. Prescott could read the man easily. No, nobody was going to escape from this place anytime soon. Then the doors swung open, and Prescott felt he had walked into the underworld.

It was hard to say which hit him first, the darkness or the smell. A ceiling of skylights, many of them cracked or broken, cast pools in the gloom and old tungsten lightbulbs struggled to illuminate the hallway ahead. The smell hit him in waves: first mold, decay, and damp, and then the inhabitants. He'd expected the institutional aromas—stale cooking fat, urine, disinfectant—and the sheer *maleness* of it, more so even than in an army barracks, where some of the residents were still women. But there was also a bitter smell of feces, not the usual drains smell that pervaded a shattered city, but something else. It was *different*. He assumed it was poor cleaning or broken plumbing until he heard the dogs barking.

Of course: they had guard dogs here. The smell was their waste. By the sound of it, there was a good-sized pack of them. Then a siren started up, a single, steady note every few seconds, and a countdown began on the public address system: "*One minute to lockdown . . .*"

It was almost a dark parody of the ever-present public address system on Azura, not the soothing tones of long-dead Niles Samson but a gruff, bored voice of someone who didn't much like his job.

"Just getting the prisoners back in their cells, sir," the warder said. "Officer Jarvi will be with you soon. He's . . . well, he's the senior officer. We don't have a governor. Just a dozen of us, and we run the place ourselves."

"How? You have some very dangerous men in here."

"Oh, we found a way, sir. We're locked off from the inmates. They have to run their own daily routine, cook, and clean the place, and if we need access to them, then we've got secure separation zones. And the dogs." The man nodded as if he was talking about a much-loved elderly gun-dog rather than what the frantic barking and snarling suggested to Prescott. "They're really scared of the dogs, sir. Cheap and effective."

Other than the dilapidation, the smell of dog feces, and the sliding metal bars across every door, this place could have been Prescott's old preparatory school as it might have looked after decades of neglect. The ornately carved moldings, wooden paneling, and tiled floors reminded him of the alien place where he'd found himself one day just after his fifth birthday, clutching a small suitcase and ready to be turned into a little gentleman. He cried himself to sleep every night in the dormitory for weeks, until he accepted that his life wasn't going to be like that of little boys whose daddies were ordinary men. His duty would be the service of the nation. He would learn his father's trade and become a statesman.

And so I did.

Prescott followed the warder up creaking metal stairs, Dury close on his heels, to an office that seemed more like a store cupboard. It was probably easier to keep the smaller rooms heated. He accepted a seat and the offer of a cup of coffee, and the door closed. Dury pulled out a chair and sat down. The dark walls were depressing and a threadbare oriental rug dotted with dark stains did nothing to soften the impression of a decaying mausoleum.

"I'd top myself if I was stuck here, for sure, sir," Dury murmured.

"Yes. Mr. Alva must be relieved to be out of it."

Dury was about to reply when the door opened again and a different warder appeared, a slight man in his forties who looked as if he hadn't slept in a long time. No, he wasn't actually slight. He was just *average*, a normal man on normal civilian food rations, not a frontline Gear. Prescott adjusted his mental scale accordingly.

"Mr. Chairman, sir," the man said, taking off his dark blue cap. "Officer Niko Jarvi. I'm sorry. We were expecting a clerk to visit Fenix. You want to see him yourself, yes?"

Prescott made a snap judgment on Jarvi. *A regular man who does what's asked. Tries to be fair. Struggles to make ends meet with rations.* Dury's background check said Jarvi's wife was an ER nurse, and like too many couples on Sera they'd never had children. "Yes, thank you, I would," Prescott said. "I know Fenix socially. I knew his father very well." The past tense wasn't a clever act, because the Adam Fenix that Prescott had discovered this year was one he really hadn't known at all. "May I see him here?"

"Of course, sir. We're fetching him now."

"No handcuffs, by the way. I find that distasteful, and as you can see, I do have my close protection officer."

"Understood, sir."

Jarvi darted away. Dury sat watching the door like a cat staking out a mousehole. Yes, Prescott did know Marcus socially: not well, of course, but he'd met the tall, awkward, painfully skinny nine-year-old Adam had introduced at the opening of the Allfathers Library extension that the Fenixes had funded, and later the young Gear who'd enlisted rather than accept the vast privilege and automatic army commission that men of Prescott's and Adam Fenix's class were born into. He'd shed his well-spoken, well-heeled, well-connected upbringing and taken on the mantle of an ordinary working-class Gear.

Prescott expected to see Marcus a little the worse for his time in prison, but he wasn't prepared for what walked through the door.

Marcus came to a halt in at-ease position, hands clasped behind his back and boots apart, as Jarvi stepped to one side and tried to disappear. Prescott had only ever seen Marcus in armor and that black bandanna headgear he seemed to prefer to a helmet. Without those trappings, in just pants and singlet, he was a different creature.

"Marcus." Prescott stood up. The display of courtesy and the familiarity had its calculated purpose, including stopping short of holding out his hand for shaking, but he was genuinely shocked by the state of the man. Marcus was powerfully built and it would take a prison years to erode that frame. But there wasn't a scrap of fat visible on his arms or face, and his skin looked wasted and dry. He seemed to have lost at least ten kilos. Prescott was sure it wasn't just an illusion from seeing him out of armor. "Before we start, may I say how sorry I am about your father."

Sorry. Yes, I am: but not in the way you think, of course. On the other hand, I'm not going to lie to you. I've never actively lied in my career. I've just omitted details. Every word I say is technically true.

And you're not a player in this, are you? You're collateral damage. Just a Gear, an unlucky Gear, the poor damned infantry. I'm not going to add to your misery.

"Chairman," Marcus rasped. He looked Prescott straight in the eye. He had that permanent look of weary disbelief, as if he didn't believe a damn word anyone told him, and that it saddened rather than angered him. He had his father's eyes, but what dwelt behind them seemed very different. One thing was clear: he'd finally given up. "What do you want?"

Prescott glanced past him at Jarvi. "You don't have to feel inhibited by the staff. Are you being treated well now?"

Marcus blinked. "They haven't ruptured any of my internal organs this week, if that's what you mean, Chairman."

"Yes, I'm sorry about that incident." Prescott could see a few old, yellowing bruises on Marcus's shoulder, but that could have been anything. "That's why I'm here personally, to make sure that doesn't happen again."

He got the silent response. It didn't look like insolence and if anything Marcus seemed baffled. Then he morphed into the Marcus that Prescott always suspected was still there, the son of the Fenix dynasty. His voice took on its patrician vowels again.

"Tell Hoffman," he said, "to stop atoning. *I did it.* It doesn't even matter why. I deserve my sentence. It's not his problem anymore."

"I'm sorry to disappoint you, but this has nothing to do with the Colonel."

"I'm sure."

"Like it or not, Marcus, your service record means your sentence was commuted for a reason." *Not that I can tell you the primary one, of course.* "It was better for troop morale that you weren't executed, and one day the COG may have need of you again. You know the situation out there better than anyone."

Prescott thought it was worth dropping that lure in front of him. It happened to be true: there would inevitably come a time when a Gear with his exceptional skills was needed for a suicide mission, and Prescott could keep him alive in here awaiting that day rather than risk him dying on the front line, but he skipped that detail. The effect of those few words was fascinating. Marcus's eyes changed immediately. The light came on again. His blink rate increased and he seemed to have some color back in his face. In any other man, Prescott thought, it would have been the prospect of release, but this was Marcus Fenix, and his motives were very different.

He wanted to atone. He wanted to sacrifice himself, to die for the COG—no, for his comrades, more likely, penance for all the men who'd died because of him. That was why he thought Hoffman was atoning. That was why he chose that emotional, almost religious word, because that would have been his response had he been Hoffman. It was pitifully innocent. Prescott squirmed behind his facade of concerned calm.

"I do," Marcus said at last. He switched back again to the voice he'd adopted, rough and uncultured, matching the tattoos and stubble that seemed to be a defensive facade of his own. "Will you do something for me, Chairman?"

"If I can." It would soothe Adam. Adam needed to focus on his research. "What is it?"

"Tell Private Santiago and Lieutenant Stroud to get on with their lives and forget that I exist. If they see me like this, it'll just . . ."

He trailed off. Prescott nodded. "Very well. But I suspect they won't listen."

Marcus nodded as if a spell had been broken, then turned his head slowly and looked pointedly at Jarvi. He wanted to go. Prescott wasn't used to being dismissed, but he was too unsettled by the meeting to take offense, and Marcus was just an unlucky bystander caught in the blast, of no individual political importance beyond securing Adam's cooperation. Jarvi looked to Prescott, and Prescott nodded. Marcus walked out. Prescott could have sworn his spine was a little straighter than when he'd walked in.

"Officer Jarvi," Prescott said, "I'll be going now, but can you assemble your colleagues at the exit, please?"

Timing was everything. Word would go around this small community in minutes, and now was the time to reinforce the message. By the time Prescott had taken a slow walk down the stairs with Dury, four warders were lined up by the door, and Dury had already ensured that this shift contained two of the men who'd assaulted Marcus.

Prescott smiled at them. When accompanied by harsh words, his father had told him that always chilled the blood more than a display of temper.

"Understand this," Prescott said. "You will treat Fenix humanely. If you don't, and I see the slightest hint that he's been mistreated again, I'll personally ensure that you're all conscripted and given a hazardous deployment alongside Fenix's comrades, who will be told who you are and that you abused him. They're Royal Tyran Infantry. They're *very* loyal to their brothers, and they're not squeamish. Do I make myself clear? I'll include inmates in that, too."

Jarvi didn't blink. Prescott respected that. Campbell, the one Dury had identified as bearing the grudge, looked sullen. The other two warders just stood and took it.

"Yes, sir," Jarvi said. "Understood."

"Very good. I'll see you next time, then."

Prescott swept out and didn't look back. He probably would never need to visit in person again. He waited until Dury shut the car door behind him and took a deep breath. Dury started the engine and headed back to what they both knew simply as *Sovereigns*.

"Never seen you rattled before, sir," Dury said. "Unless you *wanted* to be seen that way, at least."

Prescott wondered why he'd dropped his guard even by a fraction. Sometimes he found it hard to distinguish between accidental displays of emotion and those deliberate ones so practiced that they'd become unnoticed, automatic.

"Yes, it's hard to see a man with that pedigree reduced to such squalor," he said. "So I'm only letting my class prejudices show, Paul. Don't mistake me for a kind man."

"Wouldn't dream of it, sir. Just not callous. Or sadistic."

"Necessity, Paul. Necessity."

When it came to saving what was left of Sera — of Tyrus — Prescott was willing to do anything, and nobody could doubt that after the Hammer strikes nine years ago. Marcus Fenix was just collateral damage.

But at least it would make talking to Adam on the phone tonight that much easier. Marcus would survive. Prescott was certain of that.

THE SLAB: LATE FALL, 11 A.E.

"Did you hear?" Leuchars said. "Campbell's son's been killed. Grubs ambushed his patrol."

He was on his hands and knees on the flagstones next to the boiler room,

taking his turn to move the spoil from the tunnel while Vance did some digging below. The distant thump of artillery and the occasional noise of a Raven
high overhead penetrated from the outside world.

"Oh, shit." Vance's voice wafted up from the hole. "Campbell's going to be
Fenix-hunting to make himself feel better, then."

Campbell had backed off Marcus since he put him in the infirmary, or at
least Reeve hadn't seen any attempt at physical violence. The verbal abuse
was pretty consistent, but words never killed anybody. Maybe it was because
Marcus had changed. Reeve wouldn't have described it as perking up, because
Marcus still looked as miserable as sin, but he definitely had something on
his mind, and it had all followed Prescott's visit. Maybe he'd been promised
parole. Maybe it was nothing at all. For all Reeve knew, Prescott might have
been his dad's best buddy. Whatever it was, it seemed to have lifted the guy
just a little.

"Well, Jarvi's going to have to keep Campbell on a leash," Reeve said. "I
only signed up to keep *you* assholes from killing our soldier boy." He paused.
He didn't want to look like he'd gone sentimental on Marcus. "Smokes available in return for reading material."

"Does Fenix know something we don't?" Leuchars knelt back and looked
toward the door that led out to the kitchen gardens. That was where Marcus
spent his work time when he wasn't on the cleaning roster. When he couldn't
dig or rake or weed another square centimeter of soil, or when it got too dark to
work, he'd quit, take a shower with his back to the wall, and shut himself in his
cell until it was time to start all over again. "He's eating and doing his exercise.
What did they do, threaten to shove that half-assed feeding tube up his nose
and make him eat?"

Vance nodded absently. "Yeah, maybe he heard what happened to poor old
Brendan. Get that tube wrong and those fucking things *kill* you."

Edouain kept looking toward the door to the gardens. "So go ask the COG
if he'd like to contribute to the effort now."

Reeve knew the old war hadn't gone away for Edouain. He still called Gears
"COG" like it was their rank. He regarded himself as a political prisoner, as if
what was in his mind when he blew the shit out of Dormera made him better
than Reeve, who didn't have his mind on anything at all when he squeezed the
trigger except getting paid and not getting caught.

"He doesn't want to escape," Reeve said. "He's doing his penance."

Edouain watched the debate, calculating something on the back of a piece
of cardboard. Reeve loaded the soil and stones into a small bucket and walked

them out casually via the latrines and into the lean-to toolshed by the exit to the gardens. From there, it was simply a matter of scattering the soil on the vegetable beds. Few of the closed-circuit TV cameras still worked, and the guards didn't give a shit anyway.

The trees were busy dumping their leaves in the yard and the air smelled of damp decay. It was only outside that Reeve connected with time and was reminded that it wasn't the same day he was experiencing over and over again, but the unstoppable procession toward death. He could do without all this connection to the seasons shit, thanks.

The artillery noise was a lot louder today. It was so frequent, such a part of the daily soundtrack of life, that Reeve didn't pay much heed. Sometimes he really didn't even notice it. It was only the way Marcus reacted to it that made him take an interest; those sounds said something different to him. That was his old life, his buddies, his family, and he stopped digging to watch. Reeve could almost see him filling in the gaps and reading information from the sound that Reeve never could. He looked up in the direction of the noise as he broke up the soil, lips slightly parted as if he was going to say something to himself, a different man from the one who'd walked in looking like everyone's worst nightmare. He still looked intimidating in a bar-brawl kind of way, but the pants that had been a proper fit were now loose, and his belt—yeah, he could have ended it for himself any time—was several notches tighter. He'd lost a lot of muscle. The end drooped from the buckle, ten centimeters at least.

"Hey, Marcus?" Reeve called, but Marcus didn't look up. Maybe he hadn't heard him. He went on digging, occasionally bending down to fish something out of the soil, brush the dirt off with his thumb, and put it in his pocket. Reeve had found his own blade that way, a broken kitchen knife that could still be honed and used defensively. "Marcus?"

Marcus finished turning over the soil and stood staring at it like he'd dug a grave. Then he stepped back and leaned on the shovel, looking up into the sky. A lot of guys did that, but not in the way Marcus did. Reeve saw what had grabbed his attention. A Raven helicopter chattered overhead and Marcus tracked it, slowly and sadly, watching it until the sound faded and it was gone. Maybe he had a way of recognizing individual choppers and realized he knew the pilot or something. Then he wiped his hands on his pants, shouldered the shovel like a rifle, and looked across the garden at Reeve.

"What?" he called.

"You done?"

"Maybe."

"You want to join us?"

"Yeah, cocktails on the terrace." Marcus stabbed the shovel in the dirt again and went back to digging. "Sorry. No tux."

"We're doing some home improvements. Plumbing."

"I know."

"Come on, Marcus. For fuck's sake, buck up. Or at least help us out."

Marcus froze with the shovel just above the soil and gave Reeve that look, the one where he turned his head really slowly as if he was daring him to repeat some insult before ripping his head off. Reeve could read bits of him now—not the whole man, because this guy was an expert at keeping the shutters drawn, but enough to understand the landscape of where he could and couldn't tread.

"What do you want from me?"

"You shouldn't be in here. You of all people. They need you outside whether they admit it or not." Maybe provoking him, pressing that machismo button, would put some fight back in him. He had a temper. He just had to harness it. "Don't let the motherfuckers win."

It didn't work. Marcus looked unmoved, not galvanized. "Thanks for the concern but don't try to psych me up."

Okay, I tried. "And when are you going to read your goddamn letters?"

Marcus went on digging like a machine and didn't respond.

"You ought to know," Reeve said. "Campbell's boy's been killed. Try and stay out of his way and don't piss him off."

Marcus's rhythm faltered for a second. "Poor bastard," he said.

Reeve wandered off and watched from the door, waiting for Marcus to give in out of boredom, but he just finished digging and walked over to the carp pond to stare into the murky water and lob small things to the fish. He was probably feeding them leatherjackets or other pests he'd dug up. Reeve gave up and went back into the maintenance area, working out another tack to try later.

"So the COG sends his regrets, does he?" Edouain said. He held out his hand to help Vance out of the hole. "Pity. Everybody needs a hobby."

Reeve shoved the buckets into the janitor's closet, not that anyone was going to be checking. "The screws must know we're up to something. Nobody spends this much time cleaning the place."

"Yeah, yeah, you keep saying that, but they're not going to rock the boat." Vance squeezed out of the hole like a gopher. "If they weren't here, they'd be cuddling a Lancer with a bunch of drones up their asses. And so would we."

And so would everyone who got out of here, probably. Escaping was the less suicidal of two options, but it still meant walking straight out into a war zone. Reeve kept trying to recall the routes and safe houses he used in the city, but that had been before E-Day and everything he saw from the outside world told him that once he got beyond the Slab's walls, there'd be nothing left that he recognized except the landmark buildings in the center of Jacinto, like the Octus Tower, the Ginnet Mausoleum, and not much else. He'd be like a paratrooper dropped into enemy territory without a map. They all would, except Marcus, and he didn't look as if he was planning to come along for the trip.

Gallego and Parmenter were up on the gantry when Reeve walked back into the cell block. Parmenter had Jerry with him on a leash. That was unusual in itself, because the dogs normally stayed on the ground floor. Reeve could see the mutt shifting unhappily from foot to foot on the metal grid, probably because his pads kept slipping between the gaps. Or maybe he didn't like heights: that was interesting. Reeve was watching for Campbell. He was definitely back, despite losing his son, because Reeve had seen him walk past the security doors.

Merino sidled up beside Reeve and stood watching too. "We're all back to normal again, are we?"

"No. Campbell's son bought it."

"Oh. He'll want to express his feelings to Fenix, then."

"Fenix is the Chairman's anointed. Campbell can't touch him now."

"Chairman's an hour away in heavy traffic and only knows what he gets told. Takes a minute to settle a score."

"He hasn't got a score."

"Got to take it out on someone."

Reeve was still watching Jerry, trying to work out how to make use of the dog's weakness. It might come in useful one day. The animal was standing still, ears pricked forward and staring down through the grid, but then he threw his head up and looked around as if someone had yelled at him.

Parmenter put out a hand to steady him. "You okay, boy? What is it?"

The other dogs started barking somewhere behind the wooden shutter. Reeve looked around to see who was coming in, but the main security doors stayed shut. Jerry started whining.

Marcus stepped out of his cell and took slow, careful paces down the hall with his eyes fixed on the paving slabs as if he was looking for lost keys or something. Reeve watched him. He tilted his head slightly, not focusing on anything. The dogs were still barking. It wasn't their usual crazed frenzy sound, more sporadic and hesitant, a kind of whistling in the dark for dogs.

Marcus pointed down at his boots. "You can't feel that?"

"No." Merino had suddenly taken an interest. "What is it?"

"Grubs." Marcus shrugged and turned back to his cell. Reeve realized he had something in his hand, a strip of metal or something that he was fiddling with. "Must be excavating something big."

"Goddamn it, *underneath* us?"

"No. A few klicks away, probably."

Merino wasn't easily rattled. Reeve wondered if Marcus was just winding him up, but the dogs seemed to be able to sense it too. Maybe Gears were more attuned to small vibrations because they had to react to them. Nobody in the Slab had ever had to learn and read the danger signs for real. They were still cocooned in granite.

"Is he fucking with me?" Merino demanded.

"No, he's just being a Gear," Reeve said. "Another reason to get off his case. You think the screws are going to hang around and evacuate us if those things show up? Watch Marcus. He'll know before we do."

He left Merino to ponder that and wandered across to Marcus's cell. Marcus was sitting on his bunk, holding that damn envelope at its corners between thumb and forefinger. Reeve could see what the metal thing was now. It was sitting on the bunk, a broken knife or a piece of metal strap from a crate. It was the first time Reeve had actually seen him with a blade, another subtle hint of a changing attitude.

Reeve decided to give him another nudge along the path. "What's this, one of those cabaret acts where you guess what's written on a piece of paper without looking at it?"

"I'm wondering how I get back to solitary, since you ask," Marcus said.

Reeve ignored the piss-off message. "Ah, come on. Read it. How long have you been incubating that letter under your mattress?"

Marcus would have punched him out or walked off by now if he'd really been offended, Reeve decided. Marcus stared at him for a few seconds. His expression had upgraded from the usual just-fucking-kill-me look in his eyes to grim distraction, which was progress of a kind. Then he peeled back the flap of the envelope, took out the folded paper, and carefully extracted a photo while keeping it face-down.

He must have spent forever feeling that envelope and being too scared to look at the photo. And he still is. Poor asshole.

It would have been good manners to turn away while Marcus read, but Reeve needed to see his reaction. He wanted to watch it transform him. Dumb and sentimental, maybe, but seeing other guys find a way to hang on helped Reeve keep going himself. But Marcus wasn't transformed, at least not in the right direction. He clenched his jaw, suddenly expressionless again, but his eyes were brimming.

So she'd either dumped him or *not* dumped him. It was hard to work out what he really wanted. Then he did the unexpected and held the photo out to Reeve, not even glancing at it. So it had to be one of *her*.

Or maybe her now getting married to his best buddy . . .

"You going to look at it?" Reeve asked.

"Are you?"

Wow. Weird. I thought he'd punch the shit out of anyone for gazing on her frigging sacred countenance. "Okay, but what do you want me to do then?"

"Just *understand*," Marcus said.

Reeve wasn't expecting her to be a complete dog, but he wasn't expecting her to look like *that*, either. She was the kind of woman that heroes got issued with. It was a strange snapshot in an office, as if that was all she had to send him, or maybe it was a day that had some special meaning for them.

"Okay, I can see why you're cut up," Reeve said. "But I'd keep going if a terrific piece of ass like that was waiting for *me*."

There was every chance that he'd given the wrong answer and that Marcus was now going to break his neck in a couple of efficient seconds, but the guy just held out his hand for the photo and put it back in the envelope without looking. Then he stuffed the envelope in his pants pocket. Reeve bunched his fingers into a pen grip and mimed scribbling. *Go on, reply to her.* Marcus shrugged. But there was a definite change in him: the reminder of the world he'd lost had upset him, but he was obviously thinking something over, and maybe that had given him the nerve to finally open the letter.

"I've got KP duty," he said, standing up. Ah, he hadn't used that term before. The army in him was seeping out again, which might have been a good sign. "Aren't you supposed to be nursemaiding me in case I drown in the goddamn soup?"

"Yeah, I need to guarantee my smokes," Reeve said. "Is it the Chairman going to drop by again to chew the fat with you? Wow, for a social outcast, you still move in some fancy circles."

Marcus grunted, walked out, and glanced up at the gantry, Reeve right behind him. Campbell was up on the metal walkway all on his own, elbows resting on the rail, head down, and when he looked up again it was pretty clear that his mind wasn't on the prison or anything happening inside the walls. All the little tics and gestures that the world outside might miss were magnified here, where there was nothing else to do except focus on the tiny community that Reeve was now stuck in.

Then Campbell seemed to notice Marcus and spat over the side again.

Reeve expected Marcus to just ignore it like he'd done before, but he stopped and turned square-on to Campbell.

"I'm sorry about your son," he said. "I really am."

Campbell looked at him for a second, then just turned his head away. It was hard to tell if that had made things worse or not. Marcus walked off and Reeve thought nothing more of it. They had to pass through a stretch of corridor with open security gates at either end that closed top to bottom, and Marcus was a couple of meters ahead of Reeve when one started to slide down.

Marcus glanced over his shoulder at the noise. "Shit—"

Reeve darted forward and scraped under the gate. It was a simple reflex, nothing calculated, just catching up with Marcus and not getting separated from him, but then the next gate at the far end dropped down and the metal clips slammed closed with a clunk. Marcus looked around, checking out what was now a cage. All the exits leading off the passage were kept locked, keeping the inmates' territory separated from the staff's. Reeve's gut knotted.

"Hey, open the goddamn gates, will you?" Reeve yelled. Only the warders could operate these gates and they almost never came down here. This wasn't going to turn out well, he knew it. "Yeah, funny, Campbell. It's you, isn't it? Stop jerking us around. We've got work to do."

"Shit." Marcus looked from door to door. "I think this is for me, Reeve."

"Well, I'm stuck in here with you. Great."

"He's just going to come in and smack me around." Damn, Marcus took it as a minor inconvenience. He was watching the side doors. That was the only way Campbell could come in without Marcus getting out. "Don't get involved. Stand back. I know how crazy losing someone can make you."

"Campbell?" Reeve didn't know if he could hear him because he didn't know where he was. "Campbell, just stop this shit, okay? You're not an asshole. Just fucking stop it, okay?"

"Leave it," Marcus said. "Just stand back."

"He better have some back-up." Reeve wasn't going to do *any* damn standing back. "Because he's not built to take *me* on his own, let alone you."

Marcus was watching the end door. There were two on the right, one on the left. They all led out to the main lobby by one route or another. Marcus spun around to the door nearest him like he could hear something, then Reeve heard a thud and the sound of a latch swinging back.

Suddenly he was looking straight at two charging Pellesian guard dogs, a split-second, a blur of black and tan and white. He hadn't even heard them bark.

They hadn't. It was silent and instant. One cannoned into his chest and knocked the breath out of him. He hit the floor, cracking the back of his head, and the next thing he felt was red-hot searing pain in his raised arm, then in his leg. Maybe he shrieked: it was all noise and slow motion pain as if his arm was pulling apart like cooked meat, hot and wet. One dog's muzzle was right in his face. Reeve felt its teeth sink to the bone of his forearm as it shook him like a rag. He could feel his leg being ripped apart, too, but the sensation was somehow a long way away and happening to someone else.

Marcus was yelling at him. "Curl up, Reeve! Goddamn it, *curl up!*" Shit, he was *trying* to. Then the light above him was blotted out and all he could see past his arm was Marcus astride the dog. Its bite started slackening off. It took Reeve a moment to work out that Marcus was throttling the animal. He was twisting something one-handed, then brought his fist down hard on the dog's snout. The pain shook through Reeve from arm to spine to leg and the dog slid off him like a heavy sack of potatoes. Reeve raised his head, suddenly aware of the other dog again. It broke off from him and went for Marcus.

Marcus was on one knee when it sprang. He ducked but it caught him full in the face. For a moment Reeve thought it had him by the throat, but Marcus gripped its scruff in one hand, stopping it from pulling away, holding it so tight to him that Reeve wondered if he was trying to crush its windpipe the hard way. For a moment it looked like he was punching it in the gut. He was yelling his head off like he was bayonetting an enemy. By the time Reeve had dragged himself clear, the dog was yelping and twitching on the floor between Marcus's knees. Reeve tried not to look at his own arm.

"Is that piss?" Reeve asked. There was a puddle. It was a dumb question but the first one that came into his head. "Fuck, Marcus, are you okay?"

Marcus knelt back with his hand pressed hard against the right side of his face. He was clutching a short strip of metal in his other hand. The spreading puddle wasn't piss. It was blood, and both Marcus and the dog were covered in it. *His blood? Mine? The dog's?* Someone was yelling and arguing behind the door. One of the security gates lifted, clanking and squeaking.

"Yeah, the bastard's bitten me, that's all." Marcus took his hand away and looked at his palm. A *bite?* Shit, it was way more than that. There was a jagged rip from his right eye all the way down through his lip, raw and bloody, but he didn't seem to realize the mess he was in. "If I ever see a frigging dog again it'll be too soon."

"It's ripped your face open."

Marcus didn't seem to be taking any notice. "You just got to keep your head. Don't let them pull away. That's how they tear flesh . . ."

"Nice plan, but it didn't do you much good."

"Have you seen the state of your arm, Reeve?"

Reeve tried not to look. He knew it was shredded but as long as he didn't *look*, it wouldn't hurt. Then he looked, couldn't work out what was shredded flesh and what was torn shirt, and felt his gut start rolling.

Boots clattered down the passage and Reeve found himself looking up at Jarvi and Chalcross. "Holy shit," Chalcross said. "Parmenter's going to do his nut about the dogs."

"Just shut it, Dan. Get Reeve on his feet." Jarvi hauled Marcus upright. "Bollocks. This is all we need. Come on, Fenix. Press your hand on it. Come on, *hard.*"

So this was shock, was it? Reeve was losing chunks of time. He couldn't remember stumbling down the passage and through another set of security doors, but he was in the infirmary now, lying on a bunk and trying to look at his ripped arm while Chalcross kept pushing it down and swabbing it with a wet rag. Reeve twisted his head as far as he could and saw Marcus sitting with his arms folded tight across his chest while Jarvi did something to his face.

Jarvi was putting in stitches. Marcus took it with a slight twitch each time the needle went in.

"Keep still." Jarvi finished stitching. He tried to stick a dressing over the whole length of the wound, but it wouldn't adhere. "You need to go to JMC, Fenix."

"What, so they can do this all over again? Just give me some antibiotics."

"Yeah, and what am I going to tell Prescott?"

"Your problem. How about Reeve? He's lost blood. Get *him* to JMC." Marcus got up and walked over to Reeve, leaning over him and ignoring Chalcross. God, his face was a mess. He was lucky he hadn't lost an eye. His speech sounded slurred. "How do you feel, Reeve?"

"I think I've lost my smokes for this week, Marcus. Anyway . . . hey, I could have bled to death back there. Thanks."

"No sweat. Sorry you got caught up in it."

Chalcross stepped back. "I'm going to call a medic. Both of you, damn well shut up and lie down. You're still losing blood."

Chalcross disappeared. Jarvi took a look at Reeve's leg, shook his head, and went after Chalcross without comment, slamming the orderly station door behind them. No wonder they were shitting themselves if what Jarvi had told him about Prescott was true.

"Well, that gets me off kitchen roster." Reeve felt his stomach shaking as if he was going to laugh, but he wasn't. "You're going to have a hell of a scar, Marcus."

"Yeah." Marcus looked different now, and it wasn't just the blood still trickling down his face. He looked *lit up*. It was the only way to describe it. It was like he'd forgotten how good adrenaline felt, but now he remembered and he was on top of the world. "So, when Jarvi lets us out of here, you need some help digging. I'm in."

Did I hear him right? Reeve couldn't work out what had turned him around so fast. Maybe he'd misunderstood him. "I thought you wanted to rot here for your sins, all noble and shit."

"I can rot later." Marcus straightened up with a real set to his shoulders. He was talking to himself now. Reeve realized he must have been through a lot worse than this on a pretty regular basis, because he now seemed absolutely calm, completely focused on the next thing he had to do. "I need to get out of here. I need to kill some fucking *grubs*."

CHAPTER 10

The patient sustained a serious laceration to the right side of his face, approximately 11 centimeters in length and extending from the lower right orbit to the upper lip, the result of an animal bite. I was asked to treat him approximately two days after the wound was sustained. There was no damage to the eye. The laceration was relatively superficial with no damage to the bone, but the buccinator and orbicularis oris muscles required dissolving sutures. The nerves of the zygomatic and buccal branches were undamaged, so he should regain full facial movement when the wound heals, although he may experience permanent loss of sensation. Scarring will be conspicuous but discoloration and depth may reduce over time. Early intervention by the prison staff with oral antibiotics appears to have prevented infection, always a considerable risk with animal bites. I have enclosed a series of photos of the wound for your records. May I remind you that treating such injuries within a facility like CPSE Hesketh is unsatisfactory and all future incidents should be handled by JMC ER.

(Dr. Jay Assandris, senior MHO, COG DoH, in a report to Chairman Richard Prescott regarding Prisoner B1116/87 Fenix, M.M. Archive note from Ms. J. Beston, Secretary to Chairman Prescott: not to be included in redacted file.)

THE SLAB: GALE, 12 A.E.

"There's a word for you," Reeve said. "Obsessive."

"*Forty*." Marcus grunted under his breath, hauling himself up again with an overhand grip. "Forty-*one*, forty-*two* . . ."

Marcus was doing chins from the exposed steel joist in the ceiling. The joist ran through every cell on the main floor and should have been boxed in, but maybe the governor who supervised the last half-assed refurbishment fifty years ago had decided the inmates would appreciate a nice sturdy beam to hang themselves from. Reeve found it handy for drying laundry. It was in the right position to hang a sheet for some privacy, too, but if he put up a screen it only encouraged some bastard to find out what he was doing behind it. The screws hadn't been down on the floor to check inmates at lights-out for years, anyway.

"Forty-*four*, forty-*five* . . ."

The dogs started barking somewhere else in the building, a noise that was routine to Reeve but always seemed to put Marcus on alert. This time, he barely broke his rhythm. The fight was back in him and Reeve could trace it back to an exact moment. He'd watched it ramp up: a little more steel in Marcus's spine after Prescott spoke to him, enough to make him read the letters from his girl, and then the clincher, the dog attack. Looking back, it was like Marcus needed to convince himself that he could still fight and that he had a reason to, and then the adrenaline of fighting for his life and winning had thrown that switch again and made him realize what he did best. He was a Gear. His purpose was to kill grubs, and he could probably do it with his bare hands, if only he could get out of here.

And that seemed to be what he was working toward now. The guy wouldn't let himself off the hook, though. He was only keeping himself combat-fit and helping dig the tunnel because he was planning to get out and kill as many Locust as he could before they finally killed him. It was slowly starting to make sense to Reeve, but only because he'd finally managed to see the world as Marcus saw it.

Or a glimpse of it. Nobody really gets inside his head, I'll bet. Not so sure I'd want to, either.

Reeve could set his watch by Marcus. He had the zeal of a guy with a deadline to meet. He finished his set, dropped back onto the floor, shook out his arms, pulled his elbow across his chest a few times to stretch out, right then left, then stepped up onto the bunk to reach the joist again. It was an underhand grip this time. He did another fifty chins, then dropped down and took a breather, hands braced on his thighs. The big scar from his run-in with the dogs was still a canyon across his face, a deep gouge with ragged edges, but somehow he made it look like an accessory instead of a disfigurement. They said your life story showed on your face. Reeve was pretty sure he could read Marcus's.

"I'm charging admission," Marcus said, straightening up. He still sounded slightly slurred. His mangled cheek was going to be stiff and numb for a long time. "You should try it. Physio for that arm of yours."

"I can't fucking grip now and you know it." Yeah, the arm was a mess and some of Reeve's fingers still had no feeling in them. He'd have been an out-of-work assassin now. "We've got bigger problems."

"What?"

"They're shutting the psych wing. We're going to be down to six warders soon."

Marcus just looked at him, then swung onto the joist again, one-handed this time. "Why?"

"Jarvi says they've drafted some screws."

Marcus's face fell as much as an already unsmiling guy's ever could. It was one of the few times Reeve was certain he knew what he was thinking: it should have been *him* going back to the front line, a proper Gear, a man who wanted to fight again and knew exactly how.

"Campbell?" Marcus asked at last, grunting with effort.

"Nah."

Marcus went silent for a moment, probably counting. Reeve waited for him to finish his set and drop down.

"Shit." Marcus dusted off his hands with more concentration than was necessary. "Can't be their reward for taking chunks out of me, then."

That didn't mean anything to Reeve. "He's backed off you, hasn't he?"

"Yeah. So who's left?"

"Jarvi, Parmenter, Ospen, Chalcross, Campbell, and the nightshift guy. What's his name—Ling."

Marcus seemed to be checking the list mentally, frowning. Then he shrugged. "This shithole runs itself. They just watch. Why's it a big deal?"

"Do the math, Marcus. It takes twelve of them to run this place, and that's because they need to wrangle the loonies in the secure wing. Two guys per shift can't do that. So they're either going to let 'em mix with us—"

Marcus looked around like he'd heard something and went to the cell door to look up in the direction of the gantry. He always seemed to pick up sounds Reeve missed. Maybe it was all that practice at listening for grubs.

"Yeah, that'll pass the time," Marcus said, distracted, and walked out onto the central floor. He called out. "Officer Jarvi? Any mail?"

Reeve stepped back to watch. It was the first time he'd ever heard Marcus raise his voice by even a fraction. Jarvi, scarf wrapped around his neck and arms folded tight against the cold, looked down over the rail with an apologetic expression.

"Nothing today, Fenix."

Marcus just nodded at him and looked lost for a moment. It was the kind of exchange that would have earned a few catcalls—at the very least—for anyone else. But Marcus had somehow managed to step outside the pecking order of the prison.

In the world, but not of it. Who said that? Ah, can't remember. But true.

Merino ambled down the hall like an NCO coming to see what all the noise was about. Marcus never made eye contact with him now. Reeve studied their body language with the eye of an expert, because there wasn't much else to do except watch other people. Merino walked like he owned the place, as he pretty well did, but he never stood too close to Marcus, blocked his path, or crossed the invisible line that marked the boundary of his open cell door. For his part, Marcus didn't do that square-on gesture, the way he'd sometimes stand with his shoulders set and fists clenched at his side as if he was spoiling for a fight. The agreement was silent. Marcus wasn't going to kiss Merino's ass, but he wasn't interested in being top dog either. He had other things on his mind.

That didn't stop guys treating him as if he had some authority, though. Merino was still visibly edgy about that. Marcus seemed to be reassuring him that he could keep his poxy job as King of Turd Hill.

"You got a problem, Fenix?" he asked.

It was the sort of question that could erupt into a fight without the slightest effort. Reeve's arm was too damaged now to be useful in breaking up a brawl so he just prayed that Marcus wouldn't take the bait.

"Yeah, I'm not getting any letters from . . ." Marcus skipped half a beat. "My girlfriend."

Reeve realized it was the first time he'd actually used the word. He hadn't even said her name, not once. If Merino had been working up to try to put Marcus in his place once and for all, the answer had totally disarmed him.

"Shit, man," Merino said. He shook his head. "Ah, they take time to get used to it. She'll write. And if she doesn't—you can forget her."

So it was Marcus's turn to be taken aback. He blinked a couple of times. "Yeah." Then he went back into his cell and carried on with his exercise routine.

Merino looked at Reeve and tilted his head slightly. *What's up with him?*

Reeve did a discreet head jerk for Merino to follow and walked a little way down the hall. There was an argument going on somewhere. It sounded like Seffert and Van Lees going at it in the kitchens over that goddamn radio and who had broken it. The kitchens were the warmest place in the Slab and it attracted too many volunteers for the space available. Tempers frayed.

But shit, no radio. That was their last independent link with the outside world.

"Look, all Marcus is interested in is getting out and killing grubs," Reeve said. "He's made it his mission."

"Yeah, he's unhinged, I know. I feel kind of sorry for him. Still loyal to the assholes who put him in here."

"I don't think it's that simple."

"Maybe not," said Merino. "Now let's get down to the real problem in here. Not that we have any formality going with the screws, but what are we going to do when our new guests arrive from the psych wing, as they surely will?"

"Your call, Dan."

"Who've we got in there?"

Reeve tried to remember. It hadn't seemed important to know who the criminally insane were, except out of idle curiosity and something to gossip about, because everyone had assumed they'd never have to rub shoulders with them. They had to be kept separate.

"Well, there's Ruskin, the guy who chopped up mailmen and ate bits." Reeve recalled newspaper headlines. "Then there's the serial rapists . . . Beresford, Tasman . . . the guy who went nuts with the automatic in the Tollen supermarket . . . that arsonist they took years to catch . . . yeah, picking the most sociable out of that bunch is going to be tough. Are they going to let them out with us?"

"It isn't going to happen," Merino growled. "Or if it does, it won't be a situation that lasts more than a few hours."

"We're kind of picky, considering, aren't we?"

"We're the ones at risk here, buddy," Merino said. "Not the public, and not the screws. If the nutters end up killing half of us, it's a result for them."

It wasn't as if any human rights do-gooders were going to rise up and object. Reeve wasn't sure that there were any left. "Wouldn't they have done it by now if that's what they wanted?"

"No prisoners, and the screws end up at the front."

"Yeah, but Campbell probably *wants* that."

"But some others don't." Merino didn't so much shove Reeve in the chest as tap him in the sternum in a way that said he could have used a knife instead if he'd felt like it. "You're the one who's matey with Jarvi. Go sort it out. I'm going to make sure everyone else is prepped for a little self-defense."

Merino walked away, hands in his pockets, and disappeared into the kitchens, probably to secure blades and anything else that might come in useful, or at least to make sure the psych wing inmates couldn't get their hands on them. Reeve felt threatened for the first time in years. The Slab wasn't the nicest resort on Sera, but once the worst excesses had passed and folks had generally settled down, it had been far safer to be inside its walls than out since E-Day. Now that was all starting to change again. He looked around to see if Jarvi had returned to the gantry, but Campbell was up there now, looking like a ghost next to Chalcross. Shit, so Chalcross was going to be handed a Lancer and told to do the business, was he? It was a shame the warders didn't have a better working relationship with Marcus. He had to have a whole stack of tips on how not to end up dead.

Campbell was looking down at the main floor. He didn't seem to be focusing on anything at the moment. Reeve found it hard to think of him as a poor bastard because his arm was never going to be right again after the dog attack, and he had a chunk out of his calf big enough to put a fist in, but Campbell looked utterly fucked. Losing an only son had to be goddamn hard. So many folks couldn't have kids at all. It made things that much harder.

But Campbell wasn't a bad guy. Funny, Marcus had just accepted that fear and eventually bereavement made Campbell take it out on him. He didn't think it was sadistic at all, just desperate. Not that being understanding made a goddamn difference to Marcus. He still had a slice ripped out of his face that was going to give him trouble for years to come.

"Hey, Marcus?" Reeve went back and stuck his head into the cell. Marcus was doing crunches on the floor now, boots up on the bunk. Reeve waited for him to finish. He took a damn long time. "You done? Tunnel time. We might need it sooner rather than later if we end up sharing the floor with our crazy colleagues."

Marcus got to his feet, picked up his prison-issue jacket, and strode after Reeve in the direction of the boiler room. "Maybe they'll be really tolerant."

"Shit, it's not funny."

"We'll be okay with the rapists."

"They're not all in for doing ladies, Marcus."

"Terrific."

"You still got your blade?"

"Yeah. Hate messy cuticles."

"Wow, you've perked up some lately."

"Sooner we finish this tunnel, the sooner I get to kill grubs. Motivational."

"Not down to your girl, then. Has she got a name?"

"Yeah."

"It's Anya, isn't it?"

Marcus slowed and turned, all frozen menace. Reeve almost tripped over

him. "I don't want to see that name scrawled on the latrine wall with any interesting comments. I'm guessing you'll keep it to yourself."

"Course I will."

Marcus picked up his pace again. "You know it's going to take a year to dig
beyond the walls, don't you?"

"What do you call her? Anya, I mean."

"Lieutenant."

"Oh, I get it."

"No. You don't." They were in the boiler room corridor now. Marcus
seemed not to understand that a bunch of people stuck in jail, with their contacts outside either dead or keen to forget them, found his personal soap opera
enormously interesting. "I said a year."

"We better dig faster than the grubs, then."

Reeve looked over Leuchars's head and peered down into the hole. He
couldn't see anyone down there now, so they'd turned a corner. All he could
hear was quiet scraping and the occasional rainfall sounds of soil falling.
Edouain hauled soil across the floor on an old sack and began piling it into
buckets.

"You know you're going to hit granite any minute now," Marcus said. He
got on his knees and stuck his head down the hole. "If you carry on digging
a shallow shaft, you won't get under the walls. You're going to have to dig
down first."

"Exactly," Edouain said. "That's why we're going for the utility conduit."

"That's not a good idea."

"You got a better one?"

"No."

"So I suggest you follow orders, then, COG."

Marcus stood with his hands on his hips, feet apart, and just stared at Edouain without blinking. Edouain didn't look away. Reeve began to worry that
this might go on for hours.

"Give it a rest, Indie, will you?" Reeve said. "Just let the guy dig."

Edouain took it with a raised eyebrow. "Get Vance out."

Marcus called Vance and the guy eventually shuffled out of the hole, holding a small trowel. No wonder it was taking forever. But there was no point
using the shovel when there was so little soft soil to excavate anyway. Vance
handed Marcus the trowel and clambered out.

"I think I've found it," he said. "I can't tell how big it is from the exposed
section, but it's that rigid plastic they used to use."

The grubs had made Marcus the buried infrastructure expert, Reeve reckoned. He must have seen more ripped-up foundations, smashed pipes, and soil than anyone in here.

"I'll check it out," he said. "If it's the composite I think it is, then we'll need to shatter it to get in. We'll need a hammer. Not a cutting tool. Where are you planning on coming up, anyway?"

Edouain took a folded sheet of rag paper out of his back pocket and unfurled it in front of Marcus, standing over him. "Here," he said. "About seven hundred meters out. There should be an inspection hatch. Or at least there was one when I was first briefed."

"What do you mean, briefed?"

"Back in the war both you and I remember, COG. A hundred useful facts for a saboteur about the enemy and its heartland. Your electricity company built inspection plates every kilometer inside the borough limits."

Marcus looked up for a moment, shoved the trowel in the waistband of his pants, then swung his legs into the hole and lowered himself in. Reeve heard him slither around the curve of the tunnel. There was no headroom to stand up, and he'd have to turn himself around in the shaft to go head first along the opening to dig flat on his stomach or side. It wasn't a job for the claustrophobic, and it wasn't easy for a guy as tall and broad as Marcus. He was just determined to do it. Reeve wondered how the hell they'd pull him out if he got stuck down there. It got hotter than a steam bath after a few minutes' sweaty work even in this freezing weather, and passing out from dehydration was a real danger. Short sessions were the only way.

"You still think we're going to be safer outside than in?" Vance asked, wiping his face on his sleeve.

"If they open up the psych wing—for sure," Reeve said. He stuck his head down the hole. "Ten minutes, Marcus, then we swap, okay?"

He heard a growl that might have been agreement and turned to keep an eye on the old tin-face clock behind a locked glass scuttle high on the wall. Eight . . . nine . . . ten . . . eleven minutes passed. There were still chunking, scraping sounds coming from the hole.

"Hey, Marcus, come on, time's up," Reeve called.

"Found something," Marcus said.

It was another couple of minutes before the digging noises stopped and were replaced by shuffling and heavy breathing. Marcus squeezed his upper body out of the hole, glazed with sweat and looking even more pissed off with life than normal, and folded his arms on the edge.

"What is it, then?" Edouain asked.

"I've exposed the conduit."

"So now we can start making an opening into it. It's going more smoothly than I expected."

"You might want to revise that. What size aperture did you think it was?"

Edouain shrugged. "Two and a half meters. That's standard."

Marcus heaved himself out of the hole and stood up. "Make that a shade under one meter," he said. "I can see the degree of curve. We're going to have to crawl out of here like cavers, single file. Not walk."

"We can do that," Edouain said, not missing a beat. "Any other little down-beat messages for us?"

"Yeah," Marcus said. "Did I ever tell you how the grubs got into the center of Ephyra?"

STAFF ADMIN OFFICE, THE SLAB.

"Fuck him," Campbell said, squatting in front of the wood-burning stove in the staff room. He opened the glass-fronted metal door and threw something in, making the flames lick up the front. *"Fuck him."*

The flames roared and then died down while Campbell stared into them. Niko only half-glanced his way to see what had caused the surge of heat in the small room. He was lost in accounts paperwork for the meager supplies from Jacinto and waiting for a phone call back from the Health Department.

"Fuck who?" he asked.

"Oh, forget it."

Niko never pushed Campbell lately. In a world where everyone was be-reaved, he was handling his son's death worse than average. He hardly spoke and when he did he was a negative, quarrelsome guy Niko didn't recognize. But he'd backed off Marcus Fenix after setting the dogs on him, and that was all that mattered. For some reason, he'd expected to be conscripted into the army with the others and seemed upset that he hadn't. Niko was still trying to work out if that was part of Chairman Prescott fulfilling his promise to punish them if Marcus was mistreated again, or something else entirely.

"What're you burning?" Niko asked.

"Paper. I'm damn well freezing."

"Yeah, well, you know we can't turn the heating on yet, so don't blow all our combustible waste at once, will you?"

Campbell went on tidying up the office. Niko bent back over the

paperwork. He had no idea which prisoners were safe to move out of the secure unit or what to do with the ones who weren't. He was waiting for a call
back from a psychiatrist with guidance on who was most dangerous, as if any
shrink still working there had any goddamn idea about that, and the call still
hadn't come.

*When did the ones who need medicating last get their drugs? I can't even re-
member. We haven't had any psych drugs for years.*

"We could just leave them in there," Campbell said. "Okay, they don't get
any exercise. They have to wash in the basin in their cell. So frigging what?
We've got the death sentence for any number of crimes now, but we're wasting
time and resources on prisoners who'd be shot today."

"Well, there's your answer," Niko said. "There was no martial law in force
when they were sentenced."

"We're still pretending the world's nice and normal out there. Laws and
regulations, my ass."

"Yeah, because the more we cut corners on this stuff, the less civilized we
let ourselves become."

"Where do you pick up this bullshit?"

Niko wasn't sure. Something at the back of his mind said that he had to
hang on to some rules, however pointless they seemed, because they were all
that was left of normal COG life as he knew it. If they tossed everything over
the side, things would descend into anarchy. Even the Stranded had rules.

Campbell mooched around the office, lifting stacks of paper and dusting
under them with a cloth that might once have been white. He moved Niko's
half-full coffee cup complete with the spoon resting in it and wiped under
that, too, then put it back down again on the ring-stained desk. The spoon
tinkled gently against the porcelain.

He walked away and it tinkled again. Niko's first thought was floorboards,
but it went on tinkling when Campbell stood still. Niko stared at it. The spoon
shivered for about fifteen seconds before it stopped.

"Grubs," he said.

Campbell stared at the cup for a few moments. "How much digging are
they doing if they can shake a building on granite bedrock?"

"Who knows?"

"We should shut this place down."

Everyone said it, and it always begged the question—why a government
that could and would take the most extreme steps to survive the grub onslaught
would draw the line at wiping out a handful of pariahs. Perhaps the only reason

was the same as Niko's own, that throwing all the laws and rules to the wind brought the world too close to a place they wouldn't recognize and wouldn't be worth saving any longer. They always said terrible things crept up on you a slice at a time, but even when moral corruption approached by slow stealth, a man could sometimes still see the line in the sand. Maybe Prescott did.

"We'll shut it down when we're told to," Niko said, and checked his watch. If the shrink didn't ring back in an hour, he'd have to leave the call to Parmenter, who couldn't take an accurate note of a phone call to save his life. "Until then, we do the business. Okay? Come on, there's a supply drop later today. Canned meat, possibly."

"Any ammo? We're almost out."

"Don't think so." They had a couple of rifles and four boxes of ammo, and each warder had a sidearm with enough for one reload each. So far they hadn't needed to use it except to shoot pigeons for the pot and it was hoarded like the imperial jewels of Kashkur, just in case. "We *never* get ammo. Powdered milk, though. They promised."

"Better keep Ospen out of that. He had the last consignment."

"You know what? I'll unload it myself and hand it to Merino. That's the only way the goddamn inmates stand a chance of getting any of it."

"Why does that matter to you if you think they're all scum?"

"Because it's my job to ensure they're treated humanely. Doing the right thing when I don't want to is called *being a fucking adult*, okay?"

Niko wished he hadn't snarled at the guy, but then reminded himself what he'd done to Marcus, who still worried him. The man wasn't moping around waiting to die these days, but he still wasn't the full buck. He'd switched into a grim, obsessed, focused state as if he knew something the rest of them didn't and was waiting for an order.

"Are those bastards up to something down there?" Campbell asked. "It's all a bit too quiet."

"Keep your fingers crossed that they're trying to escape."

Campbell seemed to find some more waste paper to burn. Niko glanced at him, distracted from the phone for a moment, just to check that there wasn't any space left on the back of any of it that could be written on. It looked heavy with ink, airmail paper or something flimsy. It occurred to him that it might have been letters from his son. He didn't dare ask. There was no telling why a bereaved father might do that, and why he might do it here rather than at home.

"You should send that stuff for repulping," Niko said carefully.

Campbell tossed the last of the pile into the stove. It flared again. "I can't be assed. Just burn it. Use the ash on the gardens."

The phone rang and the wisdom of recycling was forgotten. If it wasn't the Department of Health, then it would be the Justice Department or Prescott's office, and neither was going to have anything uplifting to say. Niko picked up the handset.

"CPSE Hesketh, Officer Jarvi speaking."

"Dr. Wilsen here. You wanted a risk assessment on your psychiatric inmates."

Niko fumbled for a pencil and flipped over the pad of requisition forms to use the blank backs. There was nothing much to requisition now. "That's it. I need to know who the risks are if I transfer them into the main cell wing. We're down to fifty percent staffing levels. I'm worried about whether they can be let out to mix with the regular inmates."

"Well, you say they're not medicated. So your big risk is Ruskin, because we've got him down as a schizophrenic as well as his other issues. But then you probably already know that if he hasn't been on his tabs for a while."

"I just need information. I have to clear the wing and shut it down."

"There's no guarantee they won't harm each other or themselves."

"I don't think any of their families are going to sue us somehow."

"Okay, keep Ruskin on his own, and if you can keep him locked up all day, that's good. The rest—the arsonist will probably be worth keeping an eye on. The others are probably more danger to themselves."

I waited hours for that professional opinion?

Would anyone notice or even care if we shot them? Not that we've got enough ammo to spare for that. If they knew . . . ah, we lost control of this place years ago.

"Terrific," Niko said. "Thanks, Doc."

He put the phone down, resigned to leaving Merino to sort out the mess. Campbell looked at him expectantly. "So?"

"Ah, total waste of time. Come on, let's go prep Ruskin to move." It was a baton and handcuffs job. It was bad enough taking him out of the cell to let him use the showers, because that meant shutting off the main floor to stop him getting access to the regular inmates and taking him down there personally. That wouldn't get done now. "Might as well get it over with."

"Okay. Who's doing it?"

"You and me."

Campbell closed the stove door and reached for his baton, hanging on the back of the chair from a leather strap. "Parmenter better let the dogs out, then. Lockdown."

The solitary cells—the psychiatric wing, out of necessity—were pretty good accommodation compared to the main floor, at least in the summer. The cells were dark, but they were cool and quiet. Niko sometimes wondered how he'd cope in here and decided that he'd do better with privacy than living on the main floor like a mannequin in a shop window.

"Hey, screw!" a voice yelled from down the corridor. That was Beresford. "Jarvi, is that you? There's water in my goddamn cell. Look. It's damn well *freezing.*"

Niko gestured to Campbell to stay put while he checked it out. "What do you mean, *water?*" He walked along the row of doors. "Where?"

"On the floor. It's been seeping up through the flagstones."

Niko made sure he had his baton ready with the leather loop firmly around his fist. He'd never had any crap from Beresford, not for a few years anyway, but he never felt easy around the guy even though he wasn't violent toward men. Niko opened the door and motioned Beresford to stand at the back of the cell.

He was right about the water. Niko could see the shimmering reflection in the light from the overhead grille. The floor wasn't awash, but there were small, glittering puddles in the indentations, the deeper ones showing reflections. His first thought was that the toilet or washbasin was leaking. But he checked the U-bends and the seals, and they were bone dry.

"I see little bubbles sometimes," Beresford said. "It's coming up from underground."

"I don't think we're on a stream or spring or anything."

"So? Where's it coming from?"

"Well, you're moving upstairs anyway, so you won't have to worry about it." Niko shut the door behind him. "We'll move you out next."

"It's probably condensation," Campbell called.

"No, there's water seeping up through the floor," Niko said. "And don't say call maintenance." It wouldn't have been the first time they had to shut down an area because the wiring had perished or something structural had collapsed and there was nobody to fix it. "Must be recent."

Campbell yelled out. "Anyone else got water in their cell?"

"Me, sir." That was Slupinski. His cell was on the same side of the passage as Beresford's. "Just a bit under the sink this morning."

"I bet it's the goddamn grubs," Campbell muttered. "They've shifted a watercourse or something when they've been digging."

"Don't let them in!" Ruskin whimpered. "Don't let them in here! Please!"

"It's okay, the grubs don't have keys." Niko would have felt sorry for the guy if he hadn't known what he was in for. "They'll have to put in for a visiting pass."

Ruskin didn't have *crazy mailman-eating cannibal* tattooed on his forehead. He was a thick-set, chubby guy in his fifties, all dark curly hair shot with gray, someone Niko would have taken for a short-order cook if he hadn't known he'd been a teacher. The lack of exercise in solitary showed. All Ruskin cared about was that no strangers came to his door. Niko could piece that one together, just about.

"Promise?" Ruskin said.

"Come on, Ruskin." Niko stood at the open door, shaking the handcuffs. He'd never had a problem with Ruskin. Most of the time, he just seemed terrified of noises and voices, but there was no point getting careless. "We're moving you."

Ruskin backed away a couple of paces. "Where?"

"Somewhere nice and dry." Campbell was right behind Niko, probably looking menacing by Ruskin's standards. Niko didn't look over his shoulder. "The water's leaking up from the bedrock. You'll have your own cell, don't worry."

Ruskin edged around the walls of the cell like a rat laying down a scent trail. He knew the drill. He held his hands out for the cuffs. His breath made little clouds on the cold air.

"I don't want anyone calling at my door," he said. "You promise me, okay?"

"No strangers," Niko said. He'd work it out once that door was locked behind him. "Come on, buddy."

The dogs were barking their heads off behind the wooden door as the countdown siren sounded. Once outside the relative soundproofing of the secure wing's thick granite walls, Ruskin caught the full impact of it. Niko had a grip on his right elbow while Campbell flanked him on the left. They stopped in front of the door and waited.

"Three . . . two . . . one . . . *lockdown*," the PA system said.

The barking was manic. In a way, Niko was glad that Marcus had managed to kill some dogs because it had taken away a little of their bogeyman status. Parmenter was worried he'd lose some more of his precious puppies now that Marcus had proved they weren't unbeatable, so if he set them loose, he now released the whole pack. Nobody, not even Marcus, could deal with that unarmed, but Parmenter was still worried that *somehow* he would. For a quiet guy who was actually no trouble, Marcus managed to scare the shit out of everyone.

Niko got on his radio. "Dogs back in yet?"

"Clear," Parmenter said.

Campbell opened the door and the two of them shoved Ruskin inside to start the long walk. Niko knew it would have been a little easier if he'd moved Ruskin at night after lights out, because now he had to run the gauntlet of the inmates watching balefully from their cells. The mood on the floor was sullen: no catcalls or barracking, just a wall of silent stares that said not-in-my-back-yard. Niko understood. Okay, it was dumb for one bunch of killers and worse to look down on another bunch of killers and worse, but that was humanity in a nutshell, and prison was no different.

The slightly more decent folk of Slab society did have a practical point, though. Niko really didn't know what the psych wing guys would do, and two warders per shift wouldn't be able to go through the secure routine with them in here any more than they would in the solitary wing. He'd worked it out. They'd have to time it all to coincide with dogs-out time.

Niko turned his head. Merino was just watching, leaning on the horizontal panel, arms folded through and around the bars. A few cells along, Marcus wasn't taking any notice at all. He was doing crunches, boots up on the bunk, arms crossed, as if he had an upcoming fight he needed to be fit for. Reeve said it was all harmless military stuff that kept him busy and not to worry about it, because it beat getting into scraps with Merino. Ruskin didn't stop to stare at Marcus, but he certainly gave him a worried look as he passed.

"Nothing to worry about there, Ruskin," Niko said, pushing him along a little faster. He opened the cell door manually with the key and shoved him in. "I'll bring your blankets and bedding up in a minute, okay?"

"Lock it," Ruskin said. "Please."

Poor sod. Niko turned the key and rattled the bars to reassure Ruskin that nobody was going to get in. Sometimes he felt guilty for having any sympathy, but he judged the men by how they treated him in here. It was impossible to think of the crime and not react to the human being standing in front of him. He just couldn't keep up any disapproval or anger because there was nothing going on to refuel it, at least not with Ruskin. The kiddie fiddlers were another matter. It was hard to look at a guy who did that kind of shit and not be reminded of it, but what really kept his loathing fresh and sharp-edged was that none of the ones here seemed at all sorry for what they did, and they still tried to connive and manipulate every chance they got. They were the creepiest, most worthless bunch of fuckers he could imagine. A cannibal was a peach by comparison.

Campbell paused and looked around the floor, then up at the gallery. From down here, the place was an amphitheater. Niko caught a whiff of his mood. This was how it would be from now on, except on shift handover: two warders on their own, surrounded by a bunch of men with nothing to lose, absolutely nothing at all, an island in a shrinking world under siege beyond the walls. Somewhere in a passage beyond the wing, the dogs were barking. It seemed to be a constant soundtrack for life these days.

"Let's go," said Campbell.

Niko passed Marcus's cell again and paused. There was always some laundry strung in a neat line from the faucet on the basin to a peg Marcus had managed to hammer into the wall between the blocks. That army discipline hadn't left him.

"So you wrote at last," Niko said. Reeve had passed him an envelope a couple of weeks ago to stick in the outgoing mail to Sovereigns, painstakingly addressed in small, precise letters. Niko had had no direct conversation with Marcus since his last keep-Prescott-happy medical examination. "Good call."

Marcus took a few more crunches to react. "Thanks for the paper."

The Slab wasn't much of a kingdom, and Niko was only the senior warder because nobody else wanted to take responsibility. But he was god here, and a god had choices, a menu of thunderbolts and blessings. He decided to use his omnipotence for a change. He opened the cell door.

"Come on, Fenix."

"Now what have I done?"

"Just move it."

Marcus got to his feet and the first thing he did was look at Campbell, arms at his sides but fists clenched. Niko read that more as a self-conscious guy not knowing what to do with his hands more than getting ready to swing, although Marcus was more than capable of that. Campbell read it another way entirely. The rest of the wing seemed to get the same idea. The yelling started as Marcus stepped out.

"You give as good as you get, Gear," someone yelled.

"Yeah, how many of you is it gonna take to put him down *this* time?"

"Assholes . . ."

"Hang in there, Fenix."

It was inevitable, Niko supposed. It hurt. It shouldn't have, but it did. But he couldn't start justifying himself to inmates or bargaining with them about why he was taking Marcus out of his cell. They'd fixed on Marcus as some kind of touchstone, their guy, their champion, and while they would probably have yelled for any other guy they thought was going to get a good hiding, Marcus had become symbolic.

They thought he didn't belong here. Maybe they thought none of them belonged here, either.

Campbell locked the door behind Niko and let rip.

"What the hell are you doing?"

"Mind your own business." Niko shoved Marcus ahead of him toward the stairs. "I mean it. Thin out. Me and Fenix need a talk."

Campbell stood in Niko's way for a moment and then seemed to work out something. He probably thought Niko was doing a deal to use whatever value Marcus had for Prescott to squeeze some supplies or other advantage out of the system. That was fine. He could go on thinking that. It wouldn't piss him off, whereas knowing that Niko was treating Marcus like a stray in need of scraps definitely would. Campbell shrugged, ran up the stairs ahead of them, and disappeared through the door that led out onto the next gallery.

Niko steered Marcus to the staff room, pulled out a chair, and sat him down at one of the desks. He dragged the phone across the scratched and varnished wood. Then he slopped some coffee into a mug and put it in front of him.

"I'm going to take a walk," he said. "Ten minutes. Call your girl. Dial eight to get an outside line. Drink the coffee. Then I'll take you back."

Marcus looked up at him as if he was mad. "Can't do that."

"Can. Do it."

Marcus would change his mind about ten seconds after the door closed. Niko shut it behind him and made a deliberately noisy exit down the passage to sit out the ten minutes on the battered leather sofa outside the staff toilet, where he could also keep watch to stop Campbell coming back. The dogs started barking again. The sound drifted through a grating in the wall. Sometimes they barked like they were having a noisy conversation, sometimes the barking was frantic and let-me-at-'em. At other times it was just sporadic, a kind of what's-going-on or where-is-everybody. Parmenter seemed to know what they said. He was the only guy willing to get down among them.

Ten minutes . . .

Time was up. Niko went back, rattled the door handle by way of warning, then opened the door. Marcus was still sitting at the desk. The phone was exactly where Niko had left it, but so was the mug, and Marcus had finished the coffee. He was staring at the desk.

"So is everything okay?" Niko asked. "She got your letter?"

"Didn't call," Marcus said. "Thanks anyway. Appreciate it."

"Why the hell not?"

"I can't do that to her."

"She damn well needs a call, man."

Marcus just raised his eyes, not his head. He was suddenly the sergeant explaining something to a dumb recruit. "She's stopped writing. If she's found someone else, the last thing she needs is some fucking pathetic call from me making her feel guilty for getting on with her life."

Niko just didn't get it. "But you *wrote*."

"You don't censor the outgoing mail, do you?" Marcus had that I-get-it look. "You don't read it."

"No. I just put it in the admin box for Sovereigns and one of us drops it off every week."

"Then you don't know what I wrote."

"What do you want, Marcus?" He didn't call him Fenix. It just slipped out. "What do you really want at this moment?"

Marcus rarely faced people when he spoke to them, not that he talked much. He normally looked somewhere else but never gave the impression he wasn't listening. In fact, his focus seemed a bit too intense on whatever he *wasn't* looking at. Niko wondered if there was anyone he looked full in the face and had a proper conversation with. He stared straight past Niko through the arrow-slit window that gave a small, mean-spirited view of Jacinto's ornate towers.

"I want to pay for what I did," he said. "I want the people I've hurt to be happy again. And I want to use whatever I've still got left in me to kill grubs."

There was no answer to that. Niko wondered whether to walk away again and see if he changed his mind, but it didn't look likely. He picked up the cup and tilted it at Marcus to ask if he wanted a refill, but Marcus shook his head and got up. He always decided when the conversation was over, nobody else. And he wanted his punishment. Niko was surprised he'd accepted any coffee at all.

"We're all allowed one slip, Fenix," Niko said.

Marcus walked ahead of him down the metal stairs and waited patiently at the door to D Wing as Niko unlocked it and gripped the bolt.

This time he turned around and looked Niko right in the eye, almost too close to be comfortable. But he seemed less focused on him than ever. His mind was definitely on something or someone else. Niko could see that distance in his eyes.

"No, Officer Jarvi," Marcus said. "I'm not."

ESCAPE TUNNEL, THE SLAB.

"You still wasting your time?" Merino wandered past the excavations outside the boiler room. "You ever thought this through? Like where you're going to go when you get out?"

"Out," Edouain said.

Reeve watched the theater between Edouain and Merino as he dragged more buckets of gritty mud out of the tunnel on the end of a rope. Vance was down there at the moment, scooping out cupfuls in a session rather than bucketfuls. The utility conduit had leaked and filled up with gravel and silt over the years, so it saved them no time, but at least it gave them some kind of reinforcement for the tunnel roof. It was heavy going. Two years of patient digging hadn't got them to the line of the wall yet, according to Edouain's map. Leuchars was waiting his turn with the digging.

"*Out* means rejoining COG society," Merino said. "Terrific plan. No papers. No ration book. So they'll treat you as Stranded—if you're lucky. And you know what they do with Stranded guys who show up inside the wire? They conscript them."

"So maybe we head the other way," Leuchars said. "They say the Stranded survive okay. Can't be much different from being in here, except you can run away from the grubs. But anything beats being in here when those things break through."

"Not showing much faith in our brave Gears, are we?"

"Yeah, speaking of which, where's our certified hero?"

Reeve looked up. He was Marcus's minder, and everyone knew it, so he felt he had to defend his absence from the dig. "Maybe Jarvi's holding Campbell while Marcus gets his own back."

"Nah, he's Mr. Clean," Merino said. "He'd insist on sporting odds. Well, can't stay here all day chatting to you ladies. You might want to think about your long-term future in Jacinto, though."

Edouain snorted. "If Jacinto has one itself."

"So you'll be catching the fast train back to Pelles, then. First class?"

"I'll be finding whatever the COG's left of my own people somehow, yes."

"I'll wave you goodbye, Indie boy."

Merino chuckled and walked off. He had a point. Once they were outside, then there was a whole new social order, and Reeve had been doing the math. Small population, much smaller space, strict food rationing . . . it would be hard to disappear in the city like he'd once been able to. Maybe the Stranded route was the more sensible one. Marcus would know. His intel was the most current, although Merino still seemed to have his communications channels running somehow, probably via Artur Ospen. If any of the screws could be described as bent in the good old-fashioned way, it was him.

Reeve thought of all that propaganda bullshit on the radio about how civilians were sucking it up like the Gears as part of the war effort. The hell they were. Plenty would, of course, but many would be just the same as they were in the last war: there'd always be black marketeering, hoarding, and not giving a shit about neighbors or even the Gears at the front. Humans were humans. The Slab was distilled essence of mankind, the stuff you had to dilute in the outside world to make the species tolerable.

"Here he comes," Leuchars said, holding up a finger. "Listen."

Marcus had a distinctive gait, the stride of a man used to moving in formation and at speed. He didn't walk: he marched. It was thud, thud, thud on the flagstones and there he was at the doorway, looking somewhere between troubled and impatient. Reeve gave him a discreet once-over, just in case he'd guessed wrong and Campbell had taken another pop at the guy. No external marks, as far as he could tell, so maybe it was just Jarvi slipping him some more notepaper.

Asshole. He should trust me to get that stuff to Marcus. Okay, fine.

"So what did Jarvi want, COG?" Edouain asked.

Marcus frowned at the mess on the floor. "Just needed to reassure somebody I wasn't dead yet."

"Well, you're alive, so you can dig." Edouain yelled down the hole. "Vance? *Out.*"

Vance was using a small trowel now. The space was tight and the power cable was buried in the sludge. Nobody wanted to put a shovel through it and get fried, so it had become more like an archaeological excavation, removing a little spoil at a time. Vance scrambled out, soaked and shivering. Marcus took the tool and the wind-up flashlight from him and eased himself halfway into the hole. He paused, taking his weight on his hands.

"What are you going to do if you meet a grub coming the other way?" he asked.

"What are *you* going to do?"

"Yeah, I know how to fight these assholes." Marcus grabbed the empty bucket and tugged on the knotted rope to check it. "I mean that I keep telling you we're making an ingress point for them. And you think they can't detect vibrations?"

"So why are you digging, then?"

"Because we might just beat them to it. But the next problem we hit—we better have a rethink."

Marcus dropped down into the hole and Reeve handed the bucket down to him. After a few moments of crunching noises it all went quiet. He was making his way down the shoulder-width pipe to the face of the excavation, which was getting further underground and more difficult to work in every day. Reeve wondered whether this was the time to simply stop him doing this and call it quits. Trying to keep him in one piece in the cell block was a waste of time if he ended up dying down there.

"We should put a line on him too," Reeve said. "In case we need to pull him out."

"We don't have another rope long enough." Edouain kept fetching pails of water from the boiler room. The one thing they seemed to have an abundance of was buckets. "Come on, Vance, rinse yourself. I know the warders don't give a damn, but let's not advertise what we're doing."

Reeve stuck his head down the hole and listened anxiously to make sure Marcus was still digging. The pipe funneled the sound. He could still hear the rhythmic *chuk chuk chuk* of the trowel blade hacking into the silt. So far, so good. After a few minutes, Marcus tugged on the line, the signal to haul up the bucket. He'd follow behind to grab the next empty one, because there was no way to drop it down the shallow gradient of the pipe. They needed to build a pulley.

"That's damn fast, Marcus," Reeve called. "Pace yourself."

"The mud's getting softer."

"What?"

Marcus's voice was louder. "I said—the mud's getting softer." He seemed to be able to crawl up and down the pipe a hell of a lot faster than the others despite his size. "I'll do one more."

"Don't push it."

Reeve lowered the bucket and Marcus reached out for it. Reeve was now at the point where he wasn't keen to go any further into the tunnel himself. He'd been more or less okay as long as he could see some dim light from behind to reassure him that there was an opening, but they were so far in now that it was almost pitch black and horribly like being buried alive. That was always a possibility, of course.

He slid into the hole and stuck his head through the opening in the pipe. The smell of decay, a bit like rotting wood, was mixed with faintly sulfurous odors and something chemical, maybe the plastic coating on the power cables.

"Ah—goddamn," Marcus grunted. He was a long way down the pipe, but sounded a lot closer. "Shit."

"You okay?"

"We've got a problem . . ."

Reeve heard a silence, and then a loud glopping sound like oatmeal boiling and throwing up exploding bubbles. The rope on the bucket went taut. Marcus called out.

"I'm coming up."

"Marcus?"

"For fuck's sake—it's *flooding*."

Reeve could hear exactly what was happening now. There was gurgling and bubbling, and the sound of boots scrabbling for purchase on the sides of the pipe.

Oh shit.

"Grab the rope!" Reeve yelled. "Go on, *grab it*."

He pulled. The rope came free in his hand, hauling nothing at all.

The bastard thing had broken loose from the handle, or maybe it hadn't, but Marcus hadn't got a grip on it and he was down there in rising mud. He was still scrabbling around, still moving up the pipe as far as Reeve could tell, but the mud sounded like it was overtaking him.

"*Marcus!* Marcus, talk to me! You there?"

"Of course I'm still fucking *here*." Marcus was breathless. "Goddamn it—"

Reeve did think twice, but he hated himself for hesitating. He squeezed into the pipe head first. It wasn't the smartest move either for him or for Marcus, but there wasn't another damn thing in his brain and all he could do was take a chance. He was about five meters in when he suddenly found Marcus right in his face. For a second they both froze.

"Back out," Marcus barked. Reeve could see the mud below reflecting the faint light. "*Now*."

Reeve could only push back on the floor of the pipe with his hands as fast as he could while the mud welled up. Marcus rammed into him. He kept going until his boot hit something—the cut edge of the opening—and scrambled out up the access hole. He didn't have a choice. The hole was only wide enough for one man at a time. All he could do was clear the way for Marcus and then reach down to try to haul him out.

Reeve turned to Edouain and Vance. "Grab my legs. Don't let me fall in." He stuck his head down the hole again and slid in as far as he could. "Marcus?" He could hear the other guys clustered behind him, going nuts, but he just shut them out automatically. "*Marcus?* Give me your goddamn arm! *Now!*"

Reeve couldn't see him and he couldn't hear him. The heavy, oily sound of the mud muffled everything. He could see it spilling out of the pipe, not a torrent, but fast enough to trap and kill. Silence: one, two, three, four, five seconds, way too long. And then there was a slow-motion splashing, and Marcus corkscrewed out of the cut section of pipe, almost headbutting Reeve and gasping for breath.

Now Reeve realized just how much damage the dogs had done to his forearm. He reached for Marcus and caught his wrist, so cold it felt like a corpse's, but he couldn't keep a grip. Then someone jerked him backward.

"Fuck, I haven't got him, you hear? I can't reach him." He skidded on his chest, face-down on the flagstones, and for a moment he thought Marcus had slipped back down the pipe. Then he heard the coughing, and a column of misshapen mud rose slowly out of the hole.

It was Marcus. He managed to get his elbows far enough out for Edouain and Vance to grab him and haul him clear. For a few moments he flopped onto all fours, retching and spitting. Then got his breath and stood up, completely caked in gritty, dark brown mud. Shit, it wasn't funny at all. It would have been a god-awful way to go.

"You got a plan B?" he wheezed.

"Where's the flashlight?" Edouain asked.

Marcus had a habit of getting quieter as he got madder. Reeve knew the warning signs. "How about *you* go find it?"

"Whoa, *shit*." Vance was standing over the hole, hands braced on his knees. "What the hell's *that*?"

The mud had reached the top of the hole and was starting to spread across the floor, looking exactly like a blocked toilet discharging backed-up shit. Marcus took a few steps back. Reeve got to his feet to take a cautious look.

"How much do you reckon is down there?" Reeve said.

Vance stepped back as the mud spread out. "Are we just going to stand here admiring it?"

"Unless you've got a frigging big cork, smartass, that's about all we *can* do."

The pool was now a meter and a half across, as smooth and glossy as chocolate sauce. If it kept going it would flood the whole floor, then the whole wing. There had to be some limit to it. Reeve prayed for one. Nobody said a word for a long time, maybe a minute, because there was absolutely nothing to say and there was no emergency service they could call to fix it. But at some point, they'd have to hit an alarm or call the guards.

"Maybe they'll evacuate us," Leuchars said quietly.

Marcus took a step forward. The look on his face said he'd seen this before and that he'd never wanted to see it again. His whole body braced. His right hand began moving as if he was reaching for something on his back. Then he stopped dead. Reeve worked that out in a second. Marcus's reflex was to go for a rifle that no longer existed. He felt in his pocket instead and slipped out the short blade he always kept on him these days.

"Better check that out," he said.

Reeve watched the mud shiver for a moment. Something terrible was going to burst out. He could see what was coming written on Marcus's face. Small bubbles were forming and popping on the surface of the mud, and then a dull rumbling began like a train some way off.

"Get clear," Marcus said quietly. He didn't move. Reeve had no idea what he thought he could do to stop a grub with half a knife. "You heard me. Go."

But they didn't have time to do more than duck. A fountain of water jetted out of the hole, showering them with debris. The plume of muddy liquid crashed back down on the floor, followed by a loud sucking noise and then a long gurgle like someone pulling a plug in a bathtub. The mud vanished. Reeve stared, arm still half-raised to shield himself.

"Wow." Vance peered into the hole. "That did the trick. Some asshole's used a damn big sink plunger somewhere down the line. Hey—look."

They gathered around the hole and looked down. It had now cleared completely and was almost clean. The toilet comparison seemed spot-on now. Surprisingly, the power was still on; the boilers were chuntering away. Either the utility company had managed to make the cables watertight, or the power supply in the conduit fed somewhere else.

"At least we know where the water in the solitary wing's coming from," Edouain said.

Marcus stared at him, coated in gritty mud. "No shit."

"So what now?" Reeve asked.

Edouain shrugged. He looked shaken, but so did Marcus. "There's got to be another way out."

"Call me when it's done," Marcus said, and stalked off.

Reeve went after him. "Hey, Marcus, okay, it could have been grubs, I know—"

"You *don't* know," Marcus growled, not looking around. He was heading for the showers, leaving a trail of muddy prints. "You haven't been outside since before E-Day. You've got no damn idea at all."

Marcus strode straight into the showers and turned the hand-wheel. The first shower made strangled noises but no water came out. The next shower-head rattled before spewing a torrent, and Marcus stepped under it, boots and all. The showerheads were clogged with all kinds of shit from the deteriorating pipes and the perforated plates were breaking up, so it was more like a jet of water from a garden hose than a decent shower. He stood there, jaw clenched, staring at the mud spiraling down the drain. The grit settled in the ridges of the shower tray. He gulped a mouthful of water from the jet and swirled it around his mouth like he was cleaning his teeth, then spat a few times. He didn't look at Reeve once.

Reeve leaned against the wall, feeling like he'd almost let him die. Chunky and a couple of other guys appeared in the doorway, probably wondering what the noise was.

"Shit, I thought you were gone," Reeve said. "Look, I did my best, buddy. I tried to pull you out."

"I know." Marcus spat and wiped his mouth on the back of his hand again, then looked past Reeve toward the door. "Beat it, Chunky. Show's over."

Reeve didn't look to see if they'd left. He didn't need to. For a moment he thought Marcus was shaking, but he was just shivering. There was never hot water in the washrooms; even in the summer, it was cold enough to stop your goddamn heart. "You okay now?"

"Lost a guy a while ago," Marcus said. "Drowned in cement."

Shit. It was an explanation of sorts. Maybe he was shaking after all. Reeve didn't ask for details. "Look, why didn't you run if you thought it was grubs? What the hell did you think you could do without a rifle?"

Marcus took off his boots to rinse them. Reeve was only just starting to understand just how much the guy ran on hard-wired reflexes. He'd never had time to think things through. He just had to rely on stuff he'd been drilled to do so often that he did it without thinking, and got it right first time because if he hesitated he'd be dead. That wasn't the kind of killing Reeve had been used to. He'd always had time to plan, to perfect his shot.

"I don't like confined spaces," Marcus said at last. "I don't like the dark. And I don't get on with dogs. So I make myself face it."

That was some admission. "Yeah, but grubs . . ."

"It's what I'm for. I kill grubs."

"You've never chickened out of anything in your life, have you? Never lost your bottle."

Marcus shook out both boots and tossed them onto the dry floor. He frowned like he was genuinely trying to remember something. "Never heard that one before," he said, rubbing his fingers through his hair. "Yeah, I've *lost my bottle*. Lost it today, in fact."

He didn't elaborate. Reeve decided not to press it. Marcus switched off the water and shook himself, then went to go back to the boiler room.

"What are you doing?"

"Got to check out that pipe again."

"Marcus, there's a fine line between facing down fear and being a total fucking idiot," Reeve said. "You're well across it."

"You got a better idea?"

"Not yet."

"How do we get hold of a geological survey map?"

"Why?"

"We need to know where that water's coming from."

"We need to find another way out. We've just blown a year's work."

"Well, I've got another thirty-odd left. And my diary's clear."

The dogs were still barking somewhere. They just didn't stop now. Marcus didn't seem bothered that he was putting on wet boots, but maybe he was used to a lot worse in the field. Reeve had only seen the war on the news and then tried to follow it on the radio when the television broke down for good, but it didn't tell him a damn thing. Marcus hadn't exactly spent his time telling tales from the front line, but just watching how he behaved told Reeve everything he needed to know.

"You've beaten the odds," Reeve said.

Marcus checked in his pocket for his blade. "What?"

"Two years." It was journo bullshit, Reeve was sure, but everyone quoted it. "That's what they always say is the average life expectancy of a guy in here."

For a moment, he thought Marcus was going to smile. No, that wasn't going to happen now, and maybe the wound to his face meant it never would. But he nodded.

"Imagine that," he said.

CHAPTER 11

This isn't like the Pendulum Wars. This isn't a case of whether we'll be occupied and whether we'll all end up speaking Pellesian or Ostrian. It isn't a case of how we'll handle being swallowed up by an enemy empire. This is a war of survival. We win or we die. There's no middle ground. No surrender. No terms. This is a war for survival of the human species, and that changes all the rules, people.

(Colonel Victor Hoffman, reminding his junior staff of the stakes post E-Day.)

BASTION ROW, CENTRAL JACINTO: BLOOM, 12 A.E.

"Hey, Dom. You missed Pad again."

Sorotki's voice boomed in Dom's earpiece, complete with loud engine noise in the background. He flinched and turned the volume down. That was the problem with wearing a radio off-duty: the background noise wasn't there and it was easy to leave the earpiece on max. Damn, he was going to be deaf by the time he was forty.

And he'd missed Pad Salton yet again. The guy had become a ghost. Dom was beginning to wonder if he'd just gone UA a step at a time over the years and Hoffman didn't have the heart to have him arrested. He'd never been quite right after the Hammer strikes, those god-awful patrols just after the fires died down and the entire landscape was shrouded in thick, dark gray ash like filthy snow.

"Goddamn, you know when I last saw him?" It wasn't Sorotki's fault. The guy was just passing it on. Dom carried on walking along Bastion Row, picking his way between piles of brick rubble. "Eight years ago. Maybe more."

"Look, if we run into him again, you want me to pass on a message?"

"Just tell him to get his ass back into HQ more often and have a beer with his buddies."

"Will do. Two-Three-Nine out."

Dom had no idea where Sorotki was. He could have been flying recon or just standing next to his Raven in the maintenance bay while the ground crew were running engine tests. Not knowing precisely where people were was starting to trouble Dom at a level he knew wasn't healthy. He knew what caused it. He just couldn't stop himself doing it, that was all.

Bastion Row had been one of the most expensive pieces of real estate in Jacinto before E-Day. It was the sort of place Dom would take Bennie and Sylvie for walks when Maria needed a bit of peace and quiet to get on with the chores, playing tourist in his own city by staring at the homes of the wealthy. The properties were a couple of hundred years old, four-story ashlar-fronted town houses or office conversions with tall windows and ornate black iron railings in front of a small forecourt basement. Sylvie was always fascinated by that. On dark winter afternoons, the basement rooms were always lit up and Sylvie loved to peer down into them. She called them dolls houses. Dom could see the resemblance if he tried hard enough.

He stopped to look down at a potted plant pushed up against one of the basement windows, a succulent of some kind. Most of its leaves were gone but a couple were hanging on to life with grim determination, dusty and stunted. Like most of the other windows that hadn't already been blown out by the blasts, the panes were cross-taped from the inside to reduce shattering.

Sylvie would be what, fourteen or fifteen now? I'd be worrying about her dating boys. I got Maria pregnant at sixteen. Yeah, I'd be a real overprotective dad . . .

Dom buried the pang of memory and moved on. He wasn't killing time here today. He was looking for an office. Some of the houses were missing doors, blown out by direct hits from Reavers, and it was hard to work out the numbering. Half the properties had unhelpful names like *Oaks Villa* or *Tyr House* because they were too posh to have ordinary numbers. The lawyer had said his office was at number 86.

Dom kept checking and counting, peering at the doors. A face loomed up at one of the windows, blast curtain drawn back, and startled him so much that he jumped back. He wasn't wearing uniform or armor: he must have looked like a looter on the prowl.

"It's okay," he said, holding his hands up. The guy behind the glass couldn't hear him. "Number eight-six." Dom mouthed the words again, exaggerating. "Number *eighty-six. Where's number eighty-six?*"

The blast curtain twitched and fell back into place. The front door opened.

"This is fifty-three," the guy said, looking him up and down. Civvies in Jacinto didn't usually have firearms, but Dom didn't take anything for granted and was ready to draw his sidearm if he had to. "Other side of the road, and down there."

"Thanks. Just passing through."

"You a Gear?"

"Yeah."

"Okay."

So maybe he didn't take me for a looter. Even in civvies, Gears were conspicuously different, bigger and healthier-looking than the general population because they got the extra rations. Dom carried on down the other side of the road where the buildings were mostly intact, and counted the doors until he found the one with a small engraved brass plate screwed to it: B. L. AMBERLEY, ADVOCACY SERVICES. The short path was swept clear of debris. He tried the door, pushed it open, and stepped into the hall. The place was crammed with piles of box files, books, and brown card folders stacked against the walls.

"Anyone home?"

"On your right," a voice called.

Dom followed the voice through the obstacle course of filing and found a guy sitting at a desk surrounded by even more files. He looked like a Gear dug into a sangar. All that was missing was the machine gun.

"Dom Santiago," Dom said. "You Mr. Amberley? Sorry if I'm late. Hard to find the house."

"You're not that late." Amberley was about fifty, balding, dressed in a sweater and casual pants rather than the office suit Dom was expecting. He gestured at a battered chair among the files. "Take a seat. Sorry about the clutter, but I had to salvage everything from the offices when we evacuated. There's nowhere else to work now."

Dom eased himself into the chair and waited while Amberley rummaged through a cardboard box. Officialdom terrified him. He felt helpless and insignificant. Anya would have handled this much better, but it wasn't fair to ask her. No, this was his responsibility.

Why didn't I just ask Marcus why Hoffman diverted us to extract his dad? He wouldn't have lied to me. I know he wouldn't. Then I could have stopped him and we could have sorted this out ourselves, no court-martial.

Dom had turned the what-ifs over in his mind for month after month, all the things he could and should have done. Anya did, too. It was all if-only; if only she'd radioed the pilot and grounded the Raven, if only Dom had queried the new orders, if only . . . and Adam Fenix would probably still have died. The rescue attempt had been doomed either way.

"Ah, here we are." Amberley opened a folder and took out a sheaf of papers. "I'm sorry this has dragged on so long, but processing Justice Department admin isn't a priority these days. That's the problem with the Fortification Act being in force—almost every crime's dealt with by summary courts. The appeal system's pretty well fallen apart."

"I know, sir, but you've got a response, yes?"

"Yes. But it's not good news, I'm afraid." Amberley held out a sheet of paper to him. Dom found he was looking at the typed words without being able to take them in. All he saw was the COG Justice Department seal printed on the top of the letter. "The JD's ruled that there aren't any grounds for appeal on mental health grounds, even if Mr. Fenix agrees to one."

"What do you mean, *agrees*?"

"You can't force the subject of an appeal to agree to it. It's not something you can force on an unwilling person."

"But he's not . . . normal. Sane. Whatever. Can't I lodge an appeal for him?"

"You need power of attorney to act for him, and you'd only get that if he agreed to it, which seems unlikely given his response to the idea of an appeal, or if he was sectioned by a doctor under the Mental Competence Act. But you won't get any doctor to certify him because the medical report says he's fine. You're stuck in a loop, Mr. Santiago. There's no action you can take."

"But Marcus—*normal* Marcus would never have done that. He's Mr. Perfect. He never put a foot wrong. *Ever.* He's got to be unbalanced." It felt like betrayal to talk about Marcus like that, but it had to be done. "How the hell can they say he's normal? Have they had a doctor look at him?"

"He's examined regularly." Amberley cleared a space on his chaotic desk. "But read that report—okay, let me summarize it for you. Mr. Fenix reacts like a normal, sane man. There's no reliable medical evidence that he suffers from any traumatic disorder or that his judgment was impaired by it."

"Marcus always sounds perfectly normal. But he isn't."

"There's nothing you can do."

"There has to be."

Amberley looked at Dom for a few moments, frowning, like he was racking his brains for another answer. "You want to know my personal opinion, rather than my professional one?"

"I'll take anything you've got."

"Mr. Fenix has already had his sentence commuted, and that's very unusual. He's also being examined regularly, which is unheard-of for Hesketh."

"That's no real comfort, sir."

"My point is that he's already being treated with exceptional leniency, so whatever favors his family is due appear to have been called in. If he's in jail, then that's because the Office of the Chairman wishes it, probably to set an example to any other Gear who's finding life a little trying at the moment." Amberley held out his hand for the report. "They're making an example of him. Which is why you can do nothing. And the fact that he won't see you or his young lady, and isn't responding to letters, simply reinforces what I've been told—that he believes he belongs there. And I can't say if that reaction's sane or insane, but it's certainly logical given the facts."

Dom was crushed. It wasn't the lawyers and the doctors who'd destroyed his hopes, though. It was Marcus. The stubborn bastard was martyring himself. This do-the-honorable-thing bullshit would kill him.

"I've got to get him out," Dom said, realizing he sounded like a dumb asshole for repeating that when the guy had just told him pretty damn clearly what the situation was. His face prickled and burned with sudden sweat. "I have to."

"Well, you've exhausted all the legal avenues."

The words were out of Dom's mouth before he'd even thought to the end of the sentence. "What about *illegal* avenues?"

Amberley just stared at him for a while. Dom wasn't even sure what he meant, but now he was suddenly thinking how anyone got out of the Slab if it wasn't with the government's blessing or in a coffin.

"We shouldn't really be having this conversation," Amberley said. "I'm obliged to advise you that planning to extract a prisoner from jail is conspiracy. But as you're my client, mentioning that unadvisable course of action remains between you and me."

Dom wasn't sure what he meant by that either. It could have been a straight warning not to talk to him about breaking the law, or something else Dom didn't quite understand. He reached inside his jacket and took out the ration coupons that he'd counted before he left the barracks, a month's supply of meat, cheese, and beer—an amount that Dom could have saved up perfectly legally, but trading them for other things was definitely an offense. It took food out of the mouths of those who needed it. Amberley took the bundle and counted it, then slipped it into his desk drawer.

So he was fine with illegal. That was the only way anyone could lay their hands on extra food coupons.

"Is *that* covered by the client-lawyer confidentiality thing too, Mr. Amberley?"

Amberley shrugged. "Best I can do is give you a list of my former clients with a history of that kind of *arrangement*. Any conversation you might have with them—well, I wouldn't know anything about that. Hesketh does have a reputation for having employees willing to enter into unusual and informal agreements to look the other way at certain times."

Dom had to repeat all that to himself to get the meaning from it.

"You said a list."

Amberley took out a folder, thumbed through it, and then wrote something on a scrap of paper. "Here," he said. "Three possibles. Number one hangs out in the bar next to the ferry terminal. The other two both work in the imulsion depot on Dyrham Street. Just exercise some caution. They don't operate under Sovereign's Regulations."

Dom had been doing the rounds of Stranded camps for the best part of a decade. A few regular criminals weren't going to be any more risky to handle. "Thank you," he said. "I'll do that."

Amberley got up to see him out. "You're absolutely determined about this, aren't you?"

"He's my brother," Dom said. "Why wouldn't I be?"

Dom took the long way back to the barracks this time. He needed time to let it sink in that he'd done another immoral thing that would have really upset his dad. Eduardo Santiago had handed down his plain, honest code of right and wrong to his sons. No lying, no stealing, no cheating, and no picking on the weak: show everybody respect, take responsibility for your actions, and never let your friends down. It didn't need any fancy language. There was no bargaining to be done with any of it, no avoiding the spirit of its intention.

But I'm doing this for Marcus. This isn't some goddamn theory. Where there's a clash of rules, I have to choose, so I'll follow the one that saves the people I care about.

Dom ambled along the side of the highway, kicking small stones and brick fragments down the embankment. A few vehicles passed him in both directions, but it was a very quiet day, like everyone was in hiding and waiting for something to break. To his right, only a couple of kilometers away, he could see what was left of his old neighborhood, or at least where the last house he'd shared with Maria and the kids had been. It was just a house. Everything that made it a home had gone a long time ago, but it had still been hard to move out and let the government billet displaced families in it. One man didn't need a big place like that. And Dom didn't need to be cooped up with his memories. The things he couldn't bear to part with—toys, clothes, discs—were in storage at the barracks in a couple of big cardboard boxes.

When I find Maria, we'll start over. A nice little apartment, like the first one we rented in Lower Jacinto.

Smoke curled up in wisps right across the landscape. Some of it was cooking fires, and some was just fires still burning under the rubble. The body recovery teams were out there too, working through the debris to identify and dispose of remains. The areas they'd cleared were full of people returning to pick up the pieces of their lives and salvage what they could, supervised by civilian police or Gears. Dom hadn't seen any actual looting in years. That was dealt with instantly.

Could I pull the trigger? He'd had to police food riots and that still ate at him. Now he had a stash of illegally obtained ration coupons. *You know what? I don't give a fuck. A guy's only got so much nice in him, and if you spread it too thin it doesn't help anyone.*

He carried on, fingering the scrap of paper in his pocket and working up the courage to read it and *do* something about it. It took him a while. So this was the guy who might solve his problem—Piet Verdier. Dom put two and two together and decided this guy had to have transport access, delivery trucks or something, because the only other ways in or out of the Slab were tunneling out or using a helicopter to bypass the walls. Only the COG had helos. And nobody could tunnel out of the Slab—or into it.

Bent warders, like Amberley said. Paid to look the other way.

But Marcus has got to cooperate. Can't kidnap him. How the hell am I going to persuade him when I can't even talk to him?

Maybe Verdier had an answer to that, too.

Dom could hear a vehicle coming up behind him, slowing and crunching down through the gears. He knew the sound of a Packhorse. He stopped and turned. The Pack drew level with him and the passenger window opened.

"Hey, Dom." It was Rossi. Tai was driving. "What are you doing out here? You want a ride?"

There was no point fueling gossip or speculation. "Just been to see a lawyer. They blew out an appeal." He climbed into the back seat of the Pack. "Marcus isn't crazy. Official. They tested him and he just wasn't nuts enough to qualify."

"Assholes," Rossi said. Tai offered no comment and the Pack roared off. "So what now?"

Dom wondered whether to discuss it but decided that it wasn't fair to drag anyone else into this. "No goddamn idea."

The highway led into the center of the city. As the Pack got closer, the world looked deceptively normal except for the occasional missing building replaced by a shattered bomb site, and the razor wire and sandbags everywhere. People were out and about, repairing windows and queuing with their buckets and plastic bottles at supply tankers to get water. The engineers, poor overworked bastards, hadn't reached this part of Jacinto to restore the water supply yet.

"Might get a few days' peace," Rossi said.

Dom hoped so. He had business to do. He'd head down to the ferry terminal tonight and look out for this Verdier guy. Then the radio bolted to the dashboard came to life just as they were turning off for Wrightman.

"*All gun positions, Reavers inbound, range ten kilometers. Sectors Kilo and Lambda. Stand by.*"

Tai stepped on the gas and Dom was thrown back on his seat. There wasn't a whole lot that infantry could do on the ground when Reavers raided except pick up the pieces, but that was enough. Rossi grabbed the handset and called in.

"You are troubled, Dom," Tai said suddenly.

"You're a mind reader."

"I simply know you."

Tai was the guy who never let life touch him, who seemed to have a haven in his head that he could always retreat to. He treated the shit that life threw at him as having a purpose and a place in the chain of events rather than being random, unfair crap that made no sense.

"Got any wisdom for me, Tai?" He had to know it was about Marcus. The rest of Jacinto had settled down to life minus Marcus Fenix, but Dom never would. "You know what my problem is."

Tai nodded to himself. "There is a chain that connects all events, Dom. Our lives are all links in it. One day, at one moment, you will look back at the events in your life, and Carlos's, and Marcus's, and Maria's, and you will see that the chain could only ever have been made one way. You will see and understand the purpose of your life and death, and you will have perfect clarity and peace."

Dom's nape prickled slightly. Tai sounded certain, absolute concrete-sure. Rossi hung up the handset and chuckled to himself, not laughing at Tai but probably embarrassed by his sincerity. Pad Salton would have told him to cut the crap and drive. He was from another Islander culture entirely. He thought dead was dead, and that the only hand that guided anyone's destiny was pure fucking chaos.

"Yeah, some clarity would be good right now," Rossi said.

Dom couldn't answer. But he knew he'd remember Tai's advice, even if it made no sense right now, and hoped he'd recognize that peace when it came.

OFFICE OF THE CHAIRMAN, HOUSE OF THE SOVEREIGNS, JACINTO: BLOOM, 12 A.E.

Politics taught a man many lessons, but the most surprising one that Prescott had learned was just how much could be forgotten when it was absolutely necessary.

You can't just work with the people you like and trust, Richard. You have to learn to work with those who can give you what you need. And they may well be your enemies, or just hateful people. But you have to look beyond that at what they can do for you.

Richard Prescott sat back in his leather chair and tried to recall how old he'd been when his father had told him that. He'd been about ten, perhaps eleven. It sounded like an ugly, dishonest thing to do. He was at that age when friends mattered and friendships took on a deadly earnestness, and the thought of having to be nice to horrible people—not just the usual good manners— seemed awful. How did he square that with all he'd been taught about telling the truth and standing up for what he believed in? That was when he understood that he needed to be two people: the inner one who had his own rules and standards, and the outer functional shell that did what it had to, like one of those Silverback loaders the operator stepped into temporarily to become a different beast entirely. He found a bridge between the two personas in never letting himself tell a lie.

There was omission, yes. He would have been dangerously naive if he thought a statesman could always tell everyone the entire truth, even if he knew what it was—which, quite frequently, he didn't. Knowledge was never perfect. But he drew the line at falsehood. His language became precise, surgical, whole under scrutiny: not one word, not one syllable, was ever a lie. He was proud of the skill but also dependent on it, because it was the one lifeline that reassured him he understood where reality lay and that he had his own moral compass. He'd worked with so many colleagues who lied to the electorate, then lied to themselves, and then believed their own lies because they'd told them so often, so thoroughly, and so well.

In anyone else, that would be delusional behavior. A psychiatric problem. Truth—well, not lying—is the only sanity I can hold on to.

Human memory was malleable. Sometimes, though, it wasn't malleable enough. Prescott rehearsed his conversation with Adam Fenix, due to begin when the satellite window was available in fifteen minutes' time. His father would have defined Adam as one of those hateful or inimical people who had to be embraced, or at least kept under close scrutiny, because they were of use.

Prescott had evolved his own way of balancing those conflicting feelings. He willed himself to see Adam as a man whose genius he needed because the world depended on it, not a . . . a . . . actually, Prescott *didn't* have a word for it. Traitor? No, Adam hadn't backed Locust against humanity. He'd done something utterly inexplicable that transcended arrogance and shaded into destructive recklessness, and the dictionary had yet to catch up with the concept. But it was bad, and Prescott had found a way to put it to one side. It was simply too big to swallow. He could forget it for the time being.

Timing transmissions to Azura was tricky. The Maelstrom barrier blocked signals and the choice was either to disable the barrier or use an adapted Raven flying at its maximum altitude as a relay. Prescott always opted for the relay.

And now . . . how much can I withhold from Adam about his son and still feel comfortable with myself? How much is necessary?

Prescott slid open the top drawer of his desk and took out the medical file on Marcus. This was his own record, the full one with all the unhappy detail, not the redacted copy that was kept for transmission to Azura. Sensibly, Adam asked for proof of Marcus's health and welfare. He seemed to avoid the obvious issue—that such things were so easy to fake that Marcus could have been long dead anyway. Somehow he'd reached a tacit understanding with Prescott that they would behave like the gentlemen they were, leveling with one another as far as they could over a rather unpleasant business.

How would I feel if this were my only child, and I saw images like this?

Prescott tried to imagine. Sometimes he wondered how things might have turned out if he'd married a woman he cared about, instead of waiting for the right political wife who was the least risk to his career but who never came along. Power didn't mean choice. He grasped that far too late. He untied the folder's tag and took another look at the clinical photographs of the dog bite, the dispassionate record of the injury and the process of suturing it, and the progress of the scarring. No, he couldn't possibly show that to Adam, not even now. It still looked terrible. It was too distressing for a father. But he couldn't tell him that Marcus was enjoying the facilities of a country club, either. Nobody thrived in that prison. If Adam asked for photographic evidence of

Marcus's state of health, then some old ID photos would need to be adapted.

The mental health assessment, though . . . Adam should see that. There was nothing in it that a scientifically literate man couldn't have worked out for himself. The only other document was the simple physical exam—height, weight, blood count, the mechanical basics. Prescott selected the material he felt fulfilled the compromise between distracting Adam from his research and being frank with him about what life in the Slab was doing to his son. He switched on the scanner and fed the documents into the rollers. Then he sat back in front of the video camera, moved the mike stand across, and waited for Jillian to buzz him and tell him the link was live.

"The Professor's online, sir."

Nobody used the name Fenix. Apart from the Onyx Guard, Jillian was the only person in Jacinto who knew Adam was alive and where he was.

"Thank you, Jillian."

The feed from Azura was always a little grainy. Adam suddenly appeared in frame, arms folded across his chest, seated in front of his desk in the penthouse suite. Prescott knew the backdrop all too well by now.

"How are things going, Adam?"

"How's Marcus?"

It was always the same opening exchange. Prescott reached across and pressed the transmit button on the scanner. "See for yourself."

This was what ate the time on the transmission. Adam would insist on waiting for the copies of the documents to crank out of the printer at his end of the link, and then he would read them. He did it fast and knew what he was looking for, but it still took time. Prescott waited patiently and drained the last of his coffee. It was cold.

Adam was staring at one report, chewing his lip. "His . . . emotional state. Can I get him any help? Anything at all?"

"He won't accept it. You've seen the report."

"God, he's—" Adam let out an exasperated breath and looked down, rubbing his fingertips across his brow. "I know he can be resistant to suggestions. Please tell me he hasn't been assaulted again."

"No, I believe not." *True. I'm not lying. And Marcus does tend to swing first, doesn't he?* "No more scraps with the laboring classes."

Adam struggled. Prescott watched him literally squirm, shuffling in his seat. "We all know what happens in men's prisons, Richard."

Ah. I see. "If you're asking if he's been the unwilling subject of assertive male attention, I can assure you he hasn't."

Adam looked as if he was trying not to blink. "I see you're always sensitive to my parental anxieties, Richard."

"Don't underestimate your son. He's more than capable of defending himself. The main concern with the Slab is the conditions rather than the treatment, so I'll see what I can do about enhanced rations and extra blankets."

Prescott didn't actually intend that as a shake-down maneuver. He'd used it as a soothing concession to move Adam on to the more pressing business of the research program, but for once—and it *was* rare—he'd miscalculated the effect. Adam's slightly open mouth suggested he hadn't grasped some of the fine detail. Food worried him, yes, because he'd mentioned it: Marcus was used to maximum rations as a frontline Gear. But it seemed the simple mention of blankets, such a basic and invisible amenity, had shaken him. There he was, sitting in the balmy tropics, and Marcus was in a crumbling pre-Coalition ruin that was mostly unheated even in the harsh Tyran winter. Oddly, that seemed to bring Marcus's predicament home to his father even more forcefully than reports of injury.

"I don't know how he's going to last thirty-odd more years," Adam said quietly.

"I don't see how Jacinto can, either." Prescott had to move this on. Dury could do some diplomacy and hand-holding after the transmission. "Can you update me on your progress?"

Adam seemed to rush to that for refuge. He straightened up in his chair. "I'm sending over the latest results, but to summarize quickly—the samples we've grown in the lab are mutating spontaneously. That's making it very difficult to target the organism. In every batch, some cells—for want of a better word—survive, they mutate into a form that resists the current antigen, and then we have to start over."

"I've read the reports, Adam. I won't pretend to be a biologist, and neither are you, but are we missing something here? Are we helping it evolve into something stronger?"

"It's always a risk. We see it with antibiotics. Resistant strains of bacteria emerge, partly due to our use of the drugs. But the alternative is to do nothing and we know we daren't go down that path." Adam must have interpreted Prescott's silence as disbelief. "It's not a bacteria, Richard. If you examine the current form of it under the microscope, it still doesn't look like anything the biologists have seen before. That's why nobody realized imulsion was an organism for so long—it had no response to stimuli, no apparent reproduction, and no metabolic processes. It's changed. It seems to have a complex life cycle that spans decades, maybe even longer. All we have to go on is the data we've been gathering since it was discovered. We're probably looking at the tip of an iceberg in developmental terms. It could have been here since the beginning of life on Sera. We have no idea."

It was a pity, Prescott thought, that he had Adam Fenix here and not Elain. That was the intellect he needed.

"Well, at least we understand the scope of the problem."

"Biology might not solve it."

"The Hammer won't, either. But you know that." Prescott tried again. "The Locust must be pretty proficient at biotechnology in their own way, given the mutations they've bred for their own purposes. Is there nothing we can take from that?"

"Why do you think they wanted me? They were losing the battle long before us." Adam reached to one side of his screen and picked up another sheet of paper. "What we can't judge yet is whether this is a pathogen or actually a parasite."

"Does it matter?"

"Parasites generally evolve to preserve the life of the host. Pathogens have other reproductive strategies. We still don't know what Lambency's reproduction strategy is because we can't even tell what its final form might be, or even if it has one. We don't even know if every Lambent form self-detonates. This is going to be a case of observation—keeping an eye out for signs of Lambency in other life-forms." Now he wagged that piece of paper at the camera. "One interesting thing, though. Esther's got some striking results she wasn't expecting. Not good, but significant in the wider sense. The mice she's been using—when they're injected with Lambent cells, their fertility drops rapidly. Litter size fell to two or three pups and thirty percent of those offspring are sterile."

Prescott knew that imulsion, like so many other substances that Seran industry had depended on, caused its fair share of health problems, including birth deformities. Previous governments and imulsion producers had spent a lot of time and legal effort suppressing those findings. It was all slotting together like a horrific jigsaw puzzle.

"What are you suggesting?" he asked. "We know it's toxic one way or another. So are half the metals we mined."

"Esther says look at the declining family size in southern Tyrus alone. High proportion of only children and childless couples. Siblings aren't the norm. We don't have the data because we didn't investigate the motives, whether couples wanted fewer children or just didn't conceive and never sought medical help for it. We just recorded the numbers and assumed it was just increasing affluence reducing family size."

"So . . . she thinks Lambency might already have jumped the species barrier to humans."

"Hard to tell without testing whole populations, and most people will show traces of industrial contaminants in their tissues anyway. We might not be able to tell the difference between the pathogen and inert imulsion. But it's an area we have to consider. The priority is to kill it."

"Will that kill infected people as well?"

Adam blinked a few times, suddenly very still. "Let's hope not. We're still thinking in terms of pathogens."

"You can test it on Mr. Alva."

"That won't be necessary."

"Really?"

"We have all the tissue samples we need to carry out tests. We know what the problem is—fast mutation."

Prescott couldn't get any more out of this conversation without a Ph.D. of his own. "Well, Mr. Alva can't come back here, so what do we want to do with him?"

"I didn't ask for him, and that's not my decision," Adam said stiffly.

Moralizing bastard. No, don't get diverted. These are the people you must work with, the ones who have what you need.

"Very well, I'll consult Captain Dury, because your patient is now a security problem. How badly infected is he? Is he a biohazard?"

Adam always seemed to stop and chew things over as if there was a catch to the question. Part of that was simply the lag in the satellite signal, but Prescott had seen Adam dodging issues before—nine years ago, debating the options for stopping the Locust—and now he knew what he'd been avoiding. The signs were all there again. There was something he was holding back now.

"No, he's not," Adam said.

"So you've killed all the Lambent cells in him, or whatever the technical phrase is. If you can do it with him, why not everything?"

"I simply meant he can't transmit the pathogen. Things aren't that simple."

Adam might just have been a professionally vain man unable to simply shrug and say he didn't really know what these biologists were actually talking about. Prescott noted it as something else for Dury to keep an eye on.

"I'm sure they're not," Prescott said. A crumb needed to be tossed now, a little hope to keep Adam on his toes. "I'll see that Marcus gets some extras whenever it's practical. We'll talk again soon. Goodbye, Adam."

Prescott switched off the camera at his end and pushed the mike aside. The office door opened almost immediately and Jillian came in with another cup of coffee and a couple of cookies, probably cued by the line shutting down on her intercom. It was always the little things that made life bearable.

"You're a mind reader, Jillian."

"You haven't stopped for lunch, sir. Can't bear men fainting on me."

"Where did you get the cookies?"

"Oh, I'm resourceful . . ."

"Would it be presumptuous of me to ask if I might have a few extras to oil the wheels of diplomacy?"

"I think Sergeant Fenix is going to need more than a few cookies, sir." Yes, she had that special secretarial sixth sense, unnerving yet reassuring. And she still gave Marcus his old rank. "But yes, I'll see what I can acquire."

These were the people he did business with and placed his trust in. The people with the most power to make or break weren't always the ones with the conspicuous authority. Prescott reached into his tray, picked up the latest aerial recon images of Locust activity around Jacinto, and began calculating how long the city had to live.

JACINTO FERRY TERMINAL: REAP, 12 A.E.

"You sure you want to drop off here?" Jace asked. He nodded in the direction of the Fusilier bar with its partially boarded windows and flickering green neon sign behind flyblown, grimy glass. It was early evening, already getting dark. "Man, that place is rougher than a dog's ass. You ain't gonna get any leads on Maria there."

He slowed the Packhorse to a stop and turned around in the driver's seat to give Dom a you-must-be-crazy look. Tai, sitting in the front passenger seat, said nothing. Dom could feel his mouth going dry and his pulse beginning to speed up. He wasn't afraid of walking into a rough bar, but he was terrified of blowing what might end up being his last chance to get Marcus out of jail.

He put his hand on the door handle. "It's not about Maria. I'll be okay, Jace."

"Well, you ain't here for their elegant champagne cocktails. You wanna explain?"

Here we go. Dom didn't want to drag anyone else down into his deepening mire. Just knowing what he was up to put them in a difficult position, and it was bad enough compromising Anya by telling her about the illegal ration books. "It's for Marcus. I'm doing something iffy, and I don't want you involved."

Jace just hit the gas and drove off. "Okay."

"Hey, let me out." The Pack screeched around the corner, shaving past a couple of junkers and a dodgy-looking group of guys hanging around outside another bar. The place also seemed to be full of the roughest hookers Dom had ever seen. "Come on, Jace, quit pissing about."

"You go in there, whatever shit you're gonna pull, and we go in as backup. Right, Tai?"

Tai nodded, his crest of hair bobbing. "We share a path."

"I'll take that as a yes. Dom, I ain't lettin' you out until you level with us."

"Okay, we've run out of legal appeals. Now I'm down to paying a guy to spring him."

"Holy *fuck*."

"See? Now you're in the shit too because you know. Just drop me off and leave me to it."

"Dom, we were on that bird with you when Marcus went to get his dad. If that ain't involved, I don't know what is."

"You didn't know what he'd done."

"Neither did you. But we know now, and we're in. I told you we'd do whatever it took. Look, they might slit your goddamn throat in there, man. You need us there."

Dom now understood what people meant when they said events developed a life of their own. He couldn't step back. He couldn't rewind to the point where Jace and Tai knew nothing about this. But he couldn't suddenly decide that paying some guy to spring Marcus was a bad idea; he'd considered it, there was a chance it might work, and he'd made a promise to do whatever it took to get Marcus out. If he didn't go through with it, he'd always feel that he hadn't pulled out all the stops for him.

And he'd do it for me. He'd take a bullet for me without thinking, and I'd do the same for him. I know that for sure. I know what he tried to do for Carlos. He's family, and you don't give up on your brother while you've still got breath in your body.

"You realize how much shit you could be in if this goes wrong?" Dom asked.

Jace turned around the block and headed back to the Fusilier. "Compared to the shit we're all in generally? Maybe we all need a few more grubs up our ass to get our priorities straight."

Tai reached behind his seat and picked up his sidearm from the floor well. "We are off duty, yes?"

Dom nodded and checked his own pistol. This wasn't army business and they needed to keep the regiment's name out of this. The fact they had a COG Packhorse was an awkward detail, but this wouldn't take long, and it would be back in the vehicle pool before anyone started asking questions. Jace pulled up at a sensible distance from the bar and they shoved their sidearms under their jackets. Tai had his big fuck-off hunting knife too.

"Is that bloodstains, Tai?" Jace asked, indicating marks on his vest.

Tai nodded. "My craft leaves its signature."

"Okay, cool, I'll have whatever you're drinking, then."

They looked at each other. Now there was no turning back. Dom opened the rear door and slid out, heart in his mouth. If this failed—damn, he was already thinking about what he would need to do to commandeer a Raven and airlift Marcus out.

But he'd have to cooperate. And he won't even see me or answer letters. It'd be like an opposed boarding and extraction.

Screw it. If that's what it came down to, he'd do that, too.

Dom noted the dappling of blood spots on the paving outside before he pushed the door open and walked in, feeling his boots stick and peel off the carpet as he headed for the bar. The place smelled a lot more appetizing than it looked, a mix of rich meat stew, cigarette smoke, and a little graphite grease. The grease was oddly pleasant. It reminded Dom of his dad's workshop.

He glanced at Jace and Tai. "Take a seat over there," he said, jerking his head in the direction of an empty table.

Stevedores and truck drivers were leaning on the bar, some with their backs to the door and some watching who'd walked in. Just as Dom knew exactly what they did for a living simply by looking at them and their work clothes, they could see what he was, too. Tai and Jace took a seat and Dom went up to the widest gap along the bar.

He folded his arms on the counter, one boot on the old brass rail, and put his coins down. Bars were one of the few places where hard currency still counted for anything. Dom never quite understood how that worked, but alcohol wasn't rationed. If a bar or a brewery ran out of raw materials, it was too bad, so customers tended to contribute whatever brewable scraps they had to ensure a steady supply. The barman took his time finishing his chat with a regular before ambling across to Dom.

"What can we do for you, soldier?"

"Three halves of whatever you've got on draft." There was all kinds of shit behind the bar: old photographs, parts of a shotgun, Sharks' thrashball scarves, and even part of a Brumak's skull. The mirror that formed a backdrop to the optics of mostly half-empty liquor bottles was cracked at one edge and the silvering was flaking off. "I'm looking for Piet."

The barman poured a glass with slow care. "Piet who?"

"Verdier." Dom had to make it clear that his business was as murky as Verdier's. "His lawyer's my lawyer."

"Ah."

"Is he around?"

The barman just looked at Dom without blinking. Dom only realized something was happening when he heard movement at Jace's table, glanced over his shoulder, and saw a tubby middle-aged man in overalls slide off one of the bar stools. Jace and Tai looked ready to intercept.

"I am," said the man. "What do you want?"

Dom turned to the barman. "Make that four halves," he said, then gestured to the table. "I want to know if you can do a job for me."

The only thing that gave away Verdier's real business was the look in his eyes, nothing else about his face at all. If he'd been wearing shades, Dom might have taken him for a regular working joe who did nothing more sinister than divert a few cans of processed meat from his delivery truck each week. But those dull gray eyes were completely devoid of warmth or compassion. The faint smile didn't do anything to soften the effect. He sat down, just glancing at Tai and Jace like he was checking if they were worth anything, and waited for Dom to put the beer down in front of him.

"So you know Benjamin," he said. "Why would he be giving you my name? And what's yours?"

"I'm Dom Santiago." He was in the shit anyway, so using his real name wasn't going to make it any worse. "My brother's in the Slab and I want him out. The appeal system isn't quite doing it for me."

Verdier turned and looked at Tai for a few moments. Tai looked back at him, unfazed and unmoved. Tai's spectacular facial tattoos had a sobering effect on most people because everyone knew what South Islanders were like once they *got a strop on*, as Pad put it, and staring at them was one way to start it. It didn't matter to the outside world which island they came from, although it mattered a lot to the individual Islander. They were grade A psychos in combat, all of them, and wouldn't stop unless someone put them down permanently.

"You got a problem, pal?" Verdier asked.

"My friend's problem is my problem also," Tai said mildly, not breaking eye contact. "Can you help us?"

Verdier actually looked away first. Dom wondered if they were ahead on points now because Tai was so far outside Verdier's experience and he really didn't know how to take him.

"Okay," Verdier said. "What's he in for? Because if it's about kids or old folk, I won't spring him for any amount. He can fucking rot."

Dom adjusted his moral compass to Verdier's. "Court-martial for disobeying orders."

"Okay. It's going to cost you. My payment has to cover the guard's take and the driver's look-the-other-way fee too. And it could take a damn long time. There isn't traffic in and out of there on any kind of regular basis, let alone frequently."

"So you think it's doable," Dom said.

"Eventually. But think the best part of five, six, seven months—a year, maybe. I'm serious. These things take a lot of planning and luck when there's a war on. And they get called off at the last minute, like military ops, but then you'd be used to that. Can your guy hold out that long?"

"Probably." Could he? Dom thought Marcus could take anything, but the guy he'd last seen wasn't that Marcus at all. "How would you do it?"

"If you've got a handful of guards and half of them would pimp their grannies for a packet of smokes, it's not hard to get one of them to shove a guy on a truck. Just got to pick the right shift, get word to your guy, and he's out. It's getting the delivery and the shift to coincide that's the tough bit. The chief screw's an honest type. Tries to keep the beating and starving of inmates down to a minimum. Regular girl scout."

Dom's stomach knotted. He worried his guts out about what was happening to Marcus in there, and that just confirmed the worst he could imagine. If Marcus hadn't been such a stubborn, self-sacrificing bastard, Dom could at least have visited him and reassured himself that he was doing okay—or as okay as anyone could be in there.

But if it was me, and I thought I was never coming out—how would it feel to have my old life dangled in front of me and know I would never get it back again?

"Okay," Dom said. "What if the guy we're extracting is reluctant to go?"

"Oh, I see. Family feud." Verdier seemed to take *brother* literally. As far as Dom was concerned, it was. "Hey, you want him dead? That's a lot cheaper, unless you've got some reason for wanting to do it yourself."

"No, I want him out alive. But I might have to go in to persuade him." *Punch him out and drag him, probably.* It was too complicated to explain. *Just lie.* "He'd find it hard to accept being on the run as opposed to pardoned."

"Persuade a guy he doesn't want to spend the rest of his life ankle-deep in shit and defending his ass? Yeah. Tough sell."

"Okay, then if you can't get me in, find a way to get him on a truck even if he doesn't want to go."

"What can you put on the table?"

This was the hard bit. If the plan was going to crash anywhere, it would be about price. "Ration books."

"It's going to cost more than that, kid."

Kid. Okay . . . "I'm talking about a *neighborhood kitchen's worth* of books. Mass catering for two thousand for four months. High value. Meat, dairy, eggs, that kind of stuff. Half on the table, half when you bring Marcus back."

"That's his name, is it?"

"Marcus. Yeah. Marcus Fenix."

Verdier stared into his beer for a while. Dom hardly dared look at Jace. He seemed to be watching what was going on at another table, or at least glancing past Dom with that deliberate slowness that said he was trying to be discreet. Tai just stared at Verdier like he was some new kind of grub, frowning slightly.

"That's a lot of ration books," Verdier said at last. "You been pilfering from COG HQ? Am I going to get a bunch of angry guys in black armor trampling all over my business?"

"No." Dom felt suddenly and inexplicably pissed off. It was a weirdly unpleasant situation because he wasn't sure he liked his reasons for feeling offended. "I was awarded the Embry Star. I sold it to some asshole collector because my brother means more to me than a medal. And he won the Embry Star too. He deserves better than he got."

It shut Verdier up, which Dom wasn't expecting. He looked at him for a while. The dead gray eyes changed just a fraction: surprise, pity, contempt? Dom couldn't tell. But Verdier nodded, held out his hand for shaking, and Dom took it.

"Half now," he said.

"Deal." Dom shook his hand, appalled that he felt no guilt whatsoever and wondering again what the hell Mom and Dad would have thought of this. He took the long brown envelope out of his shirt and laid it on the table. It was hard to trust anyone these days, but he had no way of checking this guy out, although he could certainly make sure that the bar got a direct hit by accident one day if Verdier stiffed him. *Shit—listen to me. What am I becoming?* "How are you going to get in touch with me?"

"You can use this bar, or Amberley's office."

"Okay. When are you going to check back with me?"

"I'll touch base with you once a month until it's set up. Starting next week."

Verdier drained his beer in one pull, pocketed the envelope, and went back to the bar. Nobody seemed to be taking any notice of him. It was that kind of place, though. They were probably all into some scam or other. It was the kind of small-scale civilian corruption that would normally have outraged Dom, but right then he didn't give a shit. He was perfectly comfortable with his morality. He couldn't weep over people he didn't even know going hungry when Marcus was in jail, especially as his mental image of the place had been completely confirmed by Verdier.

A year. Marcus might be in there for another damn year. He's going to be a wreck when he gets out.

It was when, not if. Dom went on drinking his beer. Tai sipped his like a duchess, which made him look as if he was messing around, but that was just the way he drank everything. Jace seemed more focused on the door.

"I don't want to worry you," he said, "but four assholes were watching you and Mr. Wonderful there doing business. I think we need to go check that the Pack's still out there."

"Okay, drink up."

That was all Dom needed, to have to explain to Hoffman why they'd lost a Packhorse in the red-light district. He checked his watch. Yeah, it was time they left. He got up and walked out of the door as casually as he could, steeling himself for the worst. But the Packhorse was still parked there. The street lighting was patchy, one light in three kept on despite the power shortages to deter kryll, but it looked like it was in one piece.

He paused on the curb, feeling his life had reached a watershed. So it was done. He'd taken the plunge. Now he had to let the thing run its course. Jace and Tai could deny all knowledge if they had to, even though he knew damn well they never would.

"Hey, it's got all its tires," Jace said, right behind him. "Still some respect for the uniform, then. I'm gonna break the speed limit getting out of this shithole, believe me."

Jace walked around to the driver's door and Tai went the other way. Normally Dom's situational awareness was pretty damn sharp even in the relative safety of the city, but for some reason he just didn't see it coming. Someone cannoned into him from the side and knocked him flat. He hit the ground hard, winded. His first instinct was to ram his elbow in the guy's face—it was a young blond guy, right on top of him—but then he saw someone's boot coming and curled up in a ball. The kick caught him in the shoulder. Jace was yelling at someone to get the fuck on the floor. Dom was now pinned by two guys, and he realized when they made a grab inside his jacket that it wasn't the Packhorse they wanted.

That'll teach me to hand over an envelope in a public place.

Oh shit . . .

He couldn't reach his sidearm. He was going to get knifed. He knew it. Worse than that, he was about to lose the second half of the payment. One of the guys was flat on him, almost face to face and trying to press his arm across his throat, and Dom didn't even think: he sank his teeth into the first flesh in range. It was a blind animal moment. His teeth hit something hard and his mouth was suddenly full of blood. His attacker screamed and tried to jerk free. What had he bitten down on—a hand, an ear, a wrist? He didn't know and he didn't care. He hung on like a dog. In one of those weird suspended seconds when every sound, every movement, every smell became crystal clear. He could hear the thwock-thwock-thwock sounds of someone getting punched shitless and Jace yelling at someone that he had plenty more where that came from, *motherfucker*. Then a shot rang out and everything stopped dead. The pressure eased off his right arm.

"You can release him now, Dom," Tai said. "Let him go."

Sanity and rational thought flooded back. Dom still had his teeth in the blond guy's wrist. *Oh god. Terrific.* That explained the blood. Tai pulled the two guys off him and by the time he rolled over and knelt up, spitting blood and feeling sick, one was flat on the ground and not moving. Tai had the blond one across the hood of the Pack with his arm twisted up his back.

Piet Verdier was standing over another guy Dom hadn't even seen, a handgun aimed between his eyes while he tried to sit up. Jace was kneeling on the fourth guy's chest, shaking his right hand like he'd broken a bone or something. There had been four of them, then. It must have looked like reasonable odds when it started.

"Just so we're clear," Verdier said, "this is nothing to do with me. Okay?" He rested the muzzle against the forehead of the guy on the ground, who was clearly shitting his pants. "Son, you need to learn something. Don't fuck with my customers, and don't fuck with my income. Got it?"

For a moment Dom thought that would be it, just a frightener to make his point. Then Verdier cocked the weapon, and Dom realized he was going to pull the trigger. *Shit, not here. Not in front of us.* He was going to witness a murder. That wasn't part of the plan at all.

"We didn't mean to," the guy said. "Honest, Mr. Verdier."

Verdier paused for a moment, then moved the muzzle to the guy's left kneecap and fired. The scream echoed all over the goddamn street. Jace and Tai froze. The kneecapped guy was writhing on the pavement, shrieking, and Verdier had to put his boot on his shoulder to hold him in position. Calm and slow, he put the pistol to the guy's other knee and fired again. The screaming was off the scale now. Nobody came out of any of the buildings nearby. The regulars at the Fusilier watched casually from the doorway, smoking and probably comparing points of technique. Dom just stared. It was only a few seconds but he felt like he'd been standing there for hours.

"There," Verdier said. The guy was rocking back and forth on his side now in a pool of blood. Dom had never heard anyone scream that much, not even on the battlefield. "Now, the rest of you get to walk, because I want you to run away and tell the rest of your fuckwit kiddie gang what happens if you try to piss up my lamppost. Who's it going to be? You? Yeah, you, ginger. Come on. Up you get."

The ginger kid couldn't have been more than twenty and there was a big wet patch down the leg of his pants. He hesitated. Then he scrambled to his feet and ran for it. Dom expected Verdier to shoot him. Instead he just watched him go and checked his clip.

"You okay?" he asked.

Dom had no idea what to say. "We're fine."

"Okay, you boys go and leave me to tidy up." Verdier went over to the two remaining guys and frowned like he couldn't make up his mind where to shoot them for effect. "I'll be in touch. You've got my word, Mr. Santiago. An Embry Star still counts for something, you know."

Dom couldn't work out if Verdier was making the point that he would use violence without a second thought if he didn't get his other payment, or if he really did simply object to half-assed gangs operating on his turf. Maybe he meant it about the Embry Star. It was hard to tell. Verdier waved Tai aside, pulled the third guy off the Packhorse, and grabbed his wrist to straighten his arm. Dom didn't want to see what was coming next.

"Off you go, Gear," Verdier said, jerking his head in the direction of the city center. He shoved the handgun into the crook of the guy's elbow. "You don't want to see this. Elbows. Even harder to fix than kneecaps, not that I want to burden JMC any more than I have to. Poor assholes. Always working flat out."

Jace got into the Packhorse and started the engine. Dom hadn't even seen what had happened to the guy he was kneeling on. "Dom, move it. You too, Tai."

Yeah, that was good advice. Dom slammed the rear passenger door behind him and tried to focus on why he was getting sucked into all this. Jace hit the gas hard. But the roar of the accelerating engine couldn't drown out the sound of another gunshot, then the shrieking that carried on the air and didn't seem to fade with the distance.

Nobody spoke until they were a kilometer from Wrightman. Jace let out a breath.

"Now there's a man of his word," he said.

Dom was sure he could still hear the scream. It was never going to go away. But in this world, a man had to save who he could and screw the rest.

CHAPTER 12

I understand if you don't want to write back. But I'll keep writing every week,
because something's got to get to you sooner or later, and I'll keep writing until the
day you're released. I will be there, Marcus. I swear I'll be waiting.

(Lieutenant Anya Stroud to Prisoner B1116/87, Fenix M.M. Letter not delivered.)

HOUSE OF THE SOVEREIGNS, JACINTO: FROST, 12 A.E.

Hoffman rarely watched the news these days because he already knew what
the headlines were going to be.

He didn't need some half-assed parasite at Tyran State Broadcasting trying
to convince him it was all under control. The hell it was: he knew exactly how
bad things were, but he couldn't tell how much worse they'd get, or how fast,
because grubs hadn't been to strategy classes at the Academy. They didn't follow COG doctrine. They didn't have any other kind of military logic as far as
he could see.

But they weren't stupid, and they were winning.

He studied the recon imaging coming in from the Ravens and tried to make
sense of the composite map that was forming on the CIC wall. The noise
wasn't making that any easier. Drilling and hammering around the building as
the maintenance teams repaired damage was making his back teeth ache. In
the room itself, printers chattered and radio operators collated reports from pilots and artillery positions. Hoffman concentrated on the red line that marked
the city limits of the sprawl of Ephyra. It was now mostly in grub hands or laid
waste, and to the east, right on the coast, lay the last district that the COG had
managed to hold—or hold most of, anyway: the port of Jacinto and a small
slice of Ephyra beyond its boundaries. It wasn't a clear line. Grubs made

sporadic incursions across it. The arrogant gray bastards even got as far as the Tomb of the Unknowns.

That's the last place I'll let them take. Even if I have to stand there on my own with just a fucking knife to defend it.

He'd been waiting for the big push every day since Chancery Bridge. The grubs had been attacking in small waves, but nothing like what he'd been expecting after their assault on Ephyra.

What are they waiting for? What's next? Why don't they use all the assets they've got?

He was so focused on shutting out the noise that he didn't even hear Prescott walk up behind him. That was piss-poor situational awareness in this job.

"Here's what I don't understand." Prescott's polished vowels made him jump. "They never press home their advantage. Is it *won't* or *can't?*"

"If we knew that," Hoffman said, "we'd be halfway to beating the bastards."

Sometimes Hoffman found common ground with Prescott, and sometimes he loathed him, but he could never find a concrete reason for that. This was his head of state, a man tasked to take the cold, high-level decisions. He wasn't supposed to be his best buddy. But Hoffman could never read him and knew somehow that Prescott made sure nobody ever would. He felt shut out of something and couldn't even define what it was.

"I think they lack capacity and have to keep restocking their menagerie, for want of a better word," Prescott said.

"Is that a guess, sir?"

Prescott hesitated for a fraction of a second. Hoffman noted that and wondered how calculated it was. "An *educated* guess, I suppose," Prescott said. "What kind of force launches a global assault that takes out a quarter of the population in a few days, and then spends more than a decade unable to finish it off despite overwhelming numbers?"

"An enemy with its own supply problems, running out of steam." None of this was news. Hoffman had just become used to the idea that nobody knew what the grubs were, where they'd come from, or what they wanted, beyond the annihilation of every human on the planet. "Or an enemy that's dicking with us for some reason and hasn't contacted us with terms for our surrender. But we're fighting flat out with all we've got, so we don't have that many strategies at our disposal. We fight until we win or die. That's all we've got."

Prescott was standing right next to him now, almost touching shoulders as he studied the map on the wall. "I'm not going to ask you how long we can hold out."

"Good, because I have no goddamn idea from one day to the next."

"I know, Victor. I'm sorry."

And he sounded it, too. Hoffman decided to take that at face value. "We're seeing more of those kryll things at night. The only good news is that the grubs don't seem to like them either, so it looks like it's cut down on their incursions after dark. But that means the things are either one of their own engineered creatures gone wrong, or something else entirely."

"I don't want to get your hopes up, Victor, but I'm really pushing the DRA team on the Lightmass bomb."

"Yeah, Adam Fenix never did finish that, did he?" Damn: Hoffman had said the name, and suddenly it all came rushing back, the stuff he'd had to make himself forget just to get the job done. He glanced around to make sure Anya wasn't in earshot. "If we could get the bastards while they were still in their tunnels, it'd make all the difference."

"As soon as they get the targeting device working properly, we'll deploy it," Prescott said. "Deal with those kryll nesting sites, too."

"Yeah." Hoffman studied the map again, out of ideas and resigned to firefighting. "I'm going to let the artillery deal with Reavers for a while. We can't keep dogfighting with Ravens. The assholes are just degrading our air capability."

"I agree."

Then Prescott did an odd thing. He actually patted Hoffman on the shoulder before he walked away. It had to be calculated, because Prescott definitely wasn't one of life's back-slappers, but Hoffman felt both oddly comforted and taken in by the probably fine calculation of it.

Fenix. He tried to put Marcus out of his mind again, but couldn't. There were days—weeks, sometimes months—when he never even thought about his own dead wife. He needed to get back to that same state of oblivion with Marcus.

Damn, he missed Margaret so badly some days that he felt actual pain in his chest. He needed someone to unburden himself to, if nothing else. He also needed to matter to someone beyond being the guy in charge who was supposed to have all the answers.

"Sir?" Aigle appeared at his side. "Sir, it's Mathieson. His patrol's been hit."

And there's my wake-up call. Self-pity.

That kind of news always felt the same. A familiar name, a kid who deserved better, and his gut turned over. "Oh, for fuck's sake, not Donneld."

"He's alive, sir, but he's lost both legs. They've airlifted him to JMC. Two of his Gears are dead, though, Witmann and DeVere. The others are okay. Just minor blast injuries."

Okay was a relative term. Hoffman ran his hand across his chin and switched off just to get through the day. Even if he tried to get angry and grieve these days, the feeling was ripped away from him by the reflex he'd cultivated over the years. He didn't have a conscious choice about it any longer. All he could do was go through the intellectual process of reminding himself that Mathieson was a nice kid and that it wasn't fair. Everybody liked him. But he wasn't going to be playing thrashball again, even if he survived.

"I hope they've got a half-sober trauma surgeon on duty today."

"It's Hayman," Aigle said. "I always check. That'll increase his chances."

"I'll have to meet her one day. Next best thing to an army surgeon." *Got to get on with it. Come on. Do something useful.* Hoffman defaulted to what he always did when he'd had that kind of news. He wanted to go out and face it all personally. "I'm going to check out the arty positions. Time they saw my face again. Back in an hour or two."

"You want a car, sir?"

"I'll take a Pack. No point tying up a driver."

"Lieutenant Stroud's back on watch at fifteen hundred."

Anya usually pulled double watches. Hoffman understood that completely. She wanted to saturate every second in the day with work, work that stopped her thinking beyond the events right in front of her. He tried to do that, too. It didn't always work. He knew Anya went out on Dom's endless trawls for his wife, but he didn't have that option, so any downtime was best spent asleep. And that meant staying busy until the moment he couldn't keep his eyes open any longer and he collapsed on his bunk in the officers' quarters.

Hoffman never recalled his dreams when he woke these days. He simply knew he'd had them from where the sheets ended up or how soaked with sweat his pillow felt when his eyes jerked open. Nature could be merciful when it felt like it.

"Do me a favor, Aigle," Hoffman said, pulling on his gloves. "Make sure she's had something to eat, will you?"

"Will do, sir."

The Packhorse parked outside was one of the old wrecks converted to run on reclaimed cooking oil. It had taken one close blast too many. Its panels and chassis—welded, hammered, straightened, riveted—didn't stand much chance of withstanding another blast on patrol. Hoffman fumbled for the keys left in the ignition and started it up, catching a pleasant whiff of fries from the exhaust as he leaned out of the window to reverse out of the parking space.

There wasn't much traffic about in Jacinto now, just military traffic or municipal vehicles. Each fuel station he passed was either closed and converted to an observation post or field kitchen, or had notices scrawled on A-boards on the forecourt: NO GAS UNTIL NEXT WEEK. They rarely specified the week by date. It seemed more like a hope than an announcement. Nobody sane was going to be driving far anyway, certainly not outside the wire when they knew no Gears would be sent to rescue them. The sign at the vehicle checkpoint on Timgad Bridge meant what it said: ALL JOURNEYS PAST THIS POINT AT YOUR OWN RISK.

People walked a lot now. Jacinto wasn't that big. Hoffman slowed down to check out the AA gun position on the site of the old cinema, a maze of sandbags, concrete blocks and canvas. He got a casual salute from the Prince Ozore's Artillery sergeant sitting behind the gun. The man was obviously feeling the cold. Shoulders hunched, chin buried in his upturned collar, he thrust his hand back in his pocket right away. Waiting for Reavers was a miserable and tedious job. Hoffman stopped the Pack and got out.

"Morning, sir." The gunner's voice was muffled by his collar. "Embry weather, innit?"

The army was small enough now for everyone to know Hoffman by sight and not to be thrown into a panic when he showed up in person. He preferred it that way. The men on the ground knew him for what he was, too. "Yeah, I'm countersunk too, Sergeant. How's it going?"

"No trade yet."

"I'm pulling back the Ravens for a few days for maintenance and to rest the crews. You'll get some action later, I expect."

"Fine by us, sir."

Another gunner appeared from beneath a canvas awning with a steaming tin mug in each hand. He saw Hoffman, did an about-face, and emerged again with an extra mug. Hoffman curled his fingers around it. The metal was blissfully hot even through his leather gloves.

"That's decent of you, Gunner."

"It's only beef tea, sir. Well, if you're flexible on the definition of beef."

"Beats that barley coffee."

"What do they want, sir?"

"What?"

"The grubs. Why come up and trash the place if they don't set up camp on the surface?"

It was a good question, but it was just one of many that didn't look likely to be answered and was less pressing after so many years than are-we-going-to-survive-the-night. People always forgot why wars were fought and just went on fighting them.

"Maybe they're scared to," Hoffman said. "Or maybe they've got problems we don't even know about."

The three of them sipped in silence for a while, looking up at the gray sky. The city was the quietest he'd ever known it. Were the grubs finally grinding to a halt? No, it was too much to hope for, and if they were, it was too late for the likes of Mathieson anyway. Hoffman wondered if he'd ever recognize the end of the war if he saw it. There certainly wouldn't be a formal surrender with treaties signed and speeches made, like the Pendulum Wars.

It might never end. Or he might not live to see the end of it.

"Anything you boys need?" he asked, draining his mug. "Other than the usual."

"Toilet paper, sir. Any kind, really."

"I'll see what I can do."

Hoffman got in the Pack and drove off again. He passed food stores with long lines outside as civilians queued for their supplies, clutching their ration books in their hands. One young woman was chatting with a guy standing behind her, clearly flirting if all that fiddling with her long hair was any guide. People waited in line for so long that they now treated it as a social event for catching up with the neighbors or checking out newcomers. Humans coped, one way or another. Hoffman detoured to three more artillery positions to be seen and to chew the fat, then found himself waiting at a red light.

There was no traffic. The lights were still on automatic settings, and he just waited, hands clasped on the steering wheel, not so much at a loose end as unable to think of a single positive thing he could do today except try to boost morale. Random thoughts hit him. *Marcus Fenix.* He wasn't going to go away today, was he? Hoffman would forget him for months and then the court martial would suddenly bounce back time and time again like one of those annoying kid's toys, a bat with a ball on the end of a piece of elastic. The worst thing was that Hoffman hated himself, and now he was getting flashes of something else—hating Fenix for making him hate himself more than he already did.

How long had Marcus been in prison? Two and a half years? Three? Hoffman couldn't remember. But in the growing pile of shit he had to deal with, personal guilt was way down the bottom of the list.

Dom never mentions him. But I know damn well Anya hasn't stopped thinking about him. I catch her writing letters. She thinks I don't see her, but she's always making envelopes and takes waste paper from the recycling dumpster, so who else is she going to be writing to? Goddamn, that's some devotion after all these years. Not a damn word from him, and she's still waiting.

And if Anya hadn't forgotten Marcus, then neither had Dom. Hoffman didn't have to ask him to know that.

Life went on, though. One man didn't make an army. The casualty list was full of men—and women—whose families and friends missed them and whose lives had been torn apart. The void that Marcus had left was of his own making.

You asshole. How dare you make me feel guilty.

The lights changed through amber to green and Hoffman slipped the Pack into first to pull away. If he turned right at the next intersection, he could call in at JMC and make nice with the medical staff, seeing as they were picking up the pieces when the army surgical unit at Wrightman was swamped. He could tell how close he was getting to the place by the sudden increase in traffic. The roads went from near-deserted to moderately busy. As soon as he turned into Florenz Place, he could see vehicles parked anywhere and everywhere—ambulances, Packhorses, junkers, police cars, so many that the road was suddenly choked to a single lane. He found a spot a hundred meters away and walked up to the building, ignored by the civvies on all sides because he was just another Gear to them. The main doors opened and he found himself in another world of weird smells, chirping alarms, and a crush of people, injured, sick, or clearly distraught about someone else who was, trying to find seats or waiting at the reception desk. A constant background of paging over the public address system let him know just how overwhelmed the place was. He stood and watched for a few moments, mainly because he didn't feel able to muscle his way to the front of the line and demand attention when the place was packed with people who needed to be here more than he did. But he also took it all in, and was glad the emergency response stuff was Royston Sharle's job. It was another war in its own right.

"Can I help you, Colonel?" said a voice.

Hoffman turned. A very young woman in a white coat was frowning at him, clutching a tattered clipboard. She obviously recognized rank insignia. That impressed him, given that he had a scarf obscuring most of the stars on his collar.

"I'm Colonel Hoffman," he said. "I was going to ask to see your chief of ER, but I've caught you at a bad time."

"There's never a good time, sir," she said. "Problem?"

"Just wanted to say thanks."

"Oh." She didn't seem to be expecting that at all, judging by the quick frown. Her name badge said DR. J. ADEMI. She crooked her finger at him to follow her. "It's Dr. Maryon-Hayman today," she said, then lowered her voice. "She prefers *Hayman*. We think she ate her last husband after mating."

Hoffman thought the kid was just putting him at ease until he followed her into a side ward full of oxygen bottles and stacks of cardboard boxes marked STERILE. A woman in scrubs, fists on hips, was bawling out some lad still wearing a surgical cap and gloves as if she'd hauled him out of theater. When she paused for breath, she realized someone was behind her and turned. She was past retirement age—thin, white-haired, deeply lined—but it didn't seem to have affected her lung capacity one bit.

"Have you washed your hands, soldier?" It wasn't kindly meant. "What do you want?"

"Colonel Hoffman, ma'am. Chief of the Defense Staff."

She pointed at the ceiling with a nicotine-stained forefinger. "Your boys are on the fourth floor."

"Just called in to thank you, Dr. Hayman." *My mistake, obviously.* "We appreciate the care you're giving our Gears. Perhaps you could pass that on to your team, too."

Hayman looked surprised for a moment, but it didn't last. "You're welcome, Colonel. Can I continue coaching my goddamn useless staff now?"

Hoffman knew he was short on charm but he could usually get a better response from women than from men. With any luck, he wouldn't have to run into this bitch again. "Carry on, ma'am."

He retreated to the corridor, duty done. Dr. Ademi caught his arm.

"You want to visit your Gears? We've got about six surgical cases at the moment."

Hoffman nodded. "Is Donneld Mathieson out of theater yet? Double amputation."

"I'll check." She herded him into the elevator and stood staring at the indicator panel as the car creaked its way upward floor by floor. "I deal with rust-lung, basically," she said. "I'm a medical registrar. I'm glad I don't get many trauma cases because I'd probably end up like Dr. Hayman."

She didn't elaborate. The lift reached the fourth floor and she left him sitting in a reception area, staring down a brightly lit corridor lined with swing doors. From the sign on the wall, he guessed the operating theaters were on this floor. What did he say to Mathieson? Would he even be conscious? And why him, out of all the Gears who ended up dead or crippled? Everybody liked Mathieson. Maybe that was it. He was irrepressibly positive about every damn thing even in the face of evidence that would have convinced any sane man to put a gun to his own head. He was a Gear because he wanted to be, not a conscript, and he loved army life.

It was another ten minutes before Dr. Ademi came back, time enough for Hoffman to realize that he was sitting here because Mathieson was his personal touchstone for the course of the war. If that kid didn't survive, then nobody would.

"He's in recovery," Ademi said. "They'll be keeping him heavily sedated so you can't talk to him, but he might well be aware you're there."

"Do I have to scrub up or anything?"

"No, just don't touch him."

Recovery was a small side room off one of the operating theaters, whitewashed and tiled, and as brightly lit as the corridors. It took Hoffman a second longer than he expected to spot Mathieson. There were various steel trolleys standing around the room and a long counter against the wall on one side. Then he realized one of the trolleys was a gurney of sorts, and the drips, oxygen line, and old-fashioned monitor trailing from it were plugged into a human being. He simply hadn't registered the fact that it was Mathieson, not because he couldn't see much of his face under the oxygen mask but because he expected to see a man who was nearly two meters tall. The guy on the trolley was a lot shorter than that.

Oh God.

It was hardly the first time that Hoffman had seen terrible injuries. But for some reason the clean, white environment made this all the worse. He stared for a moment. A theater nurse came out and glared at him over the top of her surgical mask.

"He can't talk to you," she said.

Dr. Ademi nudged Hoffman. "But he's going to make it, yes?"

The nurse shrugged. "He shouldn't have made it this far, but he has. So maybe."

"Mathieson, it's me," Hoffman said, edging forward as far as he dared. "It's Colonel Hoffman. You hang in there, Donneld. Soon as you're out of here, we'll have you back at work, okay? Don't you worry."

"Terrific," said the nurse, unimpressed. Hoffman always checked out names instinctively, and hers was stenciled on her scrubs: M. JARVI. "Now we've got to get him to a ward. Off you go, Colonel."

Hoffman had worked out that his rank counted for nothing here, but he didn't care. He backed out of the recovery room. Dr. Ademi led him down the corridor. It was good of such a busy girl to spare him the time, he thought.

"You meant that about having him back as Gear?" she asked. "Does that matter to him? What's he going to do in a wheelchair?"

"Plenty of support roles need filling," Hoffman said. "And now I've made a promise to him, I intend to keep it whether he heard it or not."

Dr. Ademi didn't comment. They walked in silence toward the elevator, but halfway down the corridor the lights went out and the whole floor was plunged into gloom and sudden silence, broken a second later by a muffled chorus of swearing from behind doors. A nurse burst through a set of doors to the right of Hoffman, looking around like she was checking if the power was out on all floors.

"Damn outage," she called to someone through the doors. "Get the generators going."

It happened. There were rolling power cuts throughout Jacinto all the time to save fuel at the generating stations, but JMC was one of the places the utility company kept operational. Hoffman hoped this wasn't a sign of even worse to come. He made his way down the almost pitch-black stairwell with Dr. Ademi, feeling for each step with his boot.

"You'll be calling to check on that young man, won't you?" she asked. "You don't have to see Dr. Hayman again."

"Count on it," Hoffman said. "Hayman or no goddamn Hayman."

D WING, THE SLAB.

Reeve heard the yelling and cursing start up just after breakfast.

Baiting Ruskin or one of the other psychiatric cases had been a big sport when they were first transferred into the main wing, but soon it got to be just too much effort, and nobody could be assed to keep it up unless they were really bored. Boredom set in winter along with the freezing weather, though. Seffert was standing outside Ruskin's locked cell, raking a tin plate up and down the bars. Reeve just wished he'd shut the fuck up. For once, the dogs were relatively quiet. It was humans making the racket for a change.

"Special delivery!" Seffert hammered on the bars. "Hey, fucknugget, I got a parcel for ya . . ."

Ruskin yelled his head off. "Warder? Warder! Get this bastard away from me! You hear me? *Get him out!*"

The noise was really grating on Reeve now. His hands were so cold that he could barely hold the needle he was darning his socks with, icy water was seeping up through the floor in the shower block, and the kitchen supplies were down to canned pork, kale, and barley. He didn't need one more pain in the ass right then.

"Seffert, you asshole." He stuck his head out the cell door. The floor seemed to be empty, which meant most of the inmates had moved to the kitchen block for warmth. "Shut your yap, will you?"

Seffert blithely gave him the finger. Then Reeve realized what he was doing. He was slinging shit into the locked cell, human shit, chuckling to himself in a malicious schoolboy kind of way and lobbing it at Ruskin with a roll of newspaper like some perverted game of scoop-ball. Reeve tossed the darning onto his bunk and stormed up the hall.

"What the hell are you doing?" Ruskin was flattened against the far wall of his cell, cowering from the barrage, screaming at Seffert to stop. "You better clean that up. We've got to live in here twenty-six hours a day, buddy."

"Ah, it'll dry out," Seffert said. "Besides, I can't get in there."

"You hear me? Pack it in. You think if we fuck up the place enough that the screws will come down here and clean it for us?"

"How are we gonna notice either way?" Seffert seemed to have run out of ammo. He crushed the newspaper into a ball and took aim at Ruskin. "Look at the state of it, man. The plaster's falling off the goddamn walls and the wood's rotting."

"Yeah, great, so why not make things worse, then? Frigging great idea. Just wait until Merino gets hold of you. Chunky's going to go nuts, too. He's downwind."

"Yeah, whatever." Seffert ambled away. "Maybe you better start digging another tunnel. Because this place is going to collapse before the goddamn grubs get here."

Reeve turned to go back to his cell but then stopped to take another look at Ruskin. The guy was now crouched in the far corner of the cell, blanket over his head, sobbing quietly. The psychiatric cases were in the five end cells on each side of the floor with a couple of empty units to separate them from the sane residents. Reeve wasn't sure if the psychological dividing line was that clear-cut any longer, though. Nobody ever looked like a murderer or a rapist, and the nutters didn't all look mad either. Ruskin was the only one who had the decency to give the world a clue that he was crazy by huddling under that blanket. The other assholes looked as normal as the next guy, but normal—no, there was nothing normal in the Slab. There never had been. Nobody was getting out and it changed everything inside a guy's head. Reeve suddenly realized he wasn't holding on to anything. He'd abandoned it all. He'd reached the stage where a guy pelting another guy with shit like a demented monkey was a minor annoyance.

And I feel sorry for a guy who kills and eats mailmen.

The smell of shit was too much for him. He went into the yard and the cold air stung his eyes. Marcus was squatting by the fishpond, messing around with the surface of the ice. Reeve hovered in the shelter of the doorway.

"What are you doing?" he called.

"Got to let the pond gases escape." Marcus was busy pouring boiled water around a float stuck in the ice. "Gets messy down there."

"How do you know all this stuff?"

"Used to watch the gardener when I was a kid."

"Oh, yeah, you had a gardener. You had staff. I bet you had a fucking *lake*."

"Yeah. Big estate." Marcus tilted his head to one side, watching the float bobbing in the small hole. "I was on my own a lot. Got bored."

Reeve looked up. The helicopters were always passing overhead, pretty well on the same flight path most days, and the artillery sounded like it was getting closer. But it was hard to tell if it was just the wind direction today. The grubs still hadn't come.

Marcus stood up and looked over his shoulder as if he'd heard something. For a guy who'd spent all his adult life around deafening noise, his hearing seemed pretty sharp. Reeve followed his gaze and saw Officer Jarvi leaning out of one of the sash windows in the admin block. The screws didn't come into the yard very often these days, not even Jarvi.

"Fenix," he called. He held something out of the window, a brown paper rectangle about the size of a small shoebox. "Parcel for you. A Packhorse just showed up with it."

Marcus almost looked hopeful. His eyebrows raised a fraction. "Cake with a file in it?"

"From the Chairman's office. Come on, I can't stand here all day."

Marcus looked slightly crestfallen, probably still expecting something from his precious goddamn Anya, but she hadn't written in years. He jogged over to the wall and Jarvi dropped the parcel for him to catch before shutting the window again. Reeve decided to poke his nose in. Marcus squatted in the lee of a bush and unwrapped the package carefully, pocketing the string and smoothing out the paper. He examined both sides like he was looking for a message somewhere. Reeve squatted next to him but all he could see over his shoulder was the words PRISONER B1116/87 FENIX M. M., ES written on it in thick black letters. Reeve had often wondered if they'd stripped him of his medal, the thing that entitled him to have the initials ES after his name. It seemed that they'd let him keep it. The army had never made sense to Reeve and he knew it never would.

"Cookies," Marcus growled. "Again."

The *again* threw Reeve. How had he missed that windfall before? "What?"

"Someone in Prescott's office sends me cookies once in a while."

"Oh . . . Anya?" Reeve dared say the holy name aloud. "You think it's her?"

Marcus paused for a few moments, staring at the plain cardboard packet, then just shook his head. He opened it in a resigned kind of way and took a couple of cookies before holding it out to Reeve. Nobody shared anything in this place. You *traded*, yes, but handing over something that rare for nothing was unthinkable. Reeve took one cookie. It was richly dark, scented with treacle and vanilla. He couldn't recall the last time he'd had anything like that.

"What do you want for it?" he asked.

"It's a cookie," Marcus said. "Just eat the frigging thing."

"You're still not getting the hang of prison economics, are you?" God, that cookie smelled like heaven. "You don't get something for nothing."

"*Army* economics," Marcus said, crunching slowly. "Share ammo. Share rations. Stay alive."

Reeve bit into his cookie. The slightly bittersweet molasses taste burst on his palate and he almost wished he hadn't tasted it. It reminded his mouth that he'd forced it to get used to stuff no sane man should ever have had to eat. His mouth remembered the best restaurants in Jacinto, because Reeve's services hadn't come cheap.

"Here." Marcus tore a careful strip off the sheet of brown paper, folded a pile of cookies in it, and tucked the rest of the box inside his jacket. He held the small packet out to Reeve. "Don't go flashing them around. I'd hate to see grown men shivving each other over goddamn *cookies*."

Reeve calculated how long the cookies would last in the damp environment and mentally rationed himself to three a day. It was a banquet. He lingered over the one clutched in his hand.

"How are we going to get out of here?"

"Won't be a tunnel."

"How long do you think we've got, then?" Reeve asked. "You being the grub expert."

Marcus squatted back on his heels and looked up at the sky. "No idea."

"Lots more Ravens now."

"Fewer Ravens doing more sorties."

"Well, you'd know that. You can recognize them."

"They're under pressure."

"But the grubs have been dicking around on the border for years now."

Marcus just looked at him. He didn't do that much. He was always staring at something or looking past the person he was talking to, not that he talked much. It was odd to look into his eyes and see the thought behind them plain as day: *you naive asshole.* Reeve could tell he knew what was coming. Marcus still had one foot in the world beyond the walls.

"They don't dick around," he said at last.

He got up and wandered off to the pond again. Reeve was debating whether to go back to the cells and face the stench when the fire alarm went off. It rang for a few seconds, then stopped.

"Better see what that is," Marcus said, heading for the doors.

For a man who spent most of the day avoiding all contact with other inmates, he was quick to plunge in when there was trouble. Reeve wondered if that sergeant's sense of responsibility was so ingrained that he couldn't just mind his own business like any regular guy. Reeve followed him back inside, clutching his precious stash of cookies inside his coat, and found himself in a near pitch-black corridor. The dogs were barking somewhere, that scared, uncertain, yappy bark this time.

"Power outage," Marcus said. "Must have tripped the alarm."

Reeve couldn't recall the power failing before. They walked toward the faint light from the kitchen, which had plenty of skylights to keep the glucose vat operating. "We've got a backup generator. It should have kicked in by now."

"Where is it?"

"Staff side. It's to keep the security systems powered—you know, the lockdown system."

"Shit. What about the dogs?"

"Never mind the dogs. What about the nutters?"

Marcus did an about-turn and jogged back down the passage, but Reeve was pretty sure he wasn't running away. The outer door squeaked on its hinges. A few moments later, Marcus came jogging back with a meter-long stave of wood in one fist.

"You really don't like dogs, do you?" Reeve said.

"I don't like getting my face ripped off."

Marcus strode down the corridor, looking like he meant business. The Slab was so badly lit that it was hard to tell if the lights were out or not, but when Reeve got to the kitchen, fifteen or so guys were clustered around the range, the best source of warmth in this freezing shithole.

"We go back in there *carefully*." Merino leaned against the brick lining of the warm alcove next to the range, giving instructions to Leuchars and his other lieutenants. He gestured with a large serrated kitchen knife. "Check the locked cells. I'm going to get Jarvi to sort this out. We'll freeze to death once this goddamn range cools down." He looked past Leuchars at Marcus. "You going to make yourself useful, soldier boy?"

Marcus never rose to the bait. In fact, he always looked as if he hadn't even noticed it. He didn't so much as blink, and indicated the internal doors with a jerk of his head. "I notice you're not in there checking it out. Want me to do it?"

Okay, maybe he wasn't ignoring it after all. Merino stared at him. Marcus stared back. This time Merino looked away first and pushed himself away from the nice warm wall with a show of weary boredom. "Let's you and me go take a look."

Reeve always stuck close to Marcus now. It wasn't just a need for smokes in payment, or even that guilty obligation he felt to a misplaced and maybe even misjudged man, but a sense that Marcus was the only guy in here who knew anything about what was coming and who stood a chance of dealing with it.

Even before they reached the end of the passage, Reeve could hear the growing noise of a mob. When the doors onto the main floor swung open, the inmates were standing in the middle of the floor like angry workers at a union meeting, yelling up at the gallery while Parmenter looked down from the edge and Jerry barked his head off. The combination of the dark, the noise, and the stench of shit suddenly seemed freshly depressing, like seeing the Slab in an awful and even worse new light. Reeve hoped no bastard had stolen his socks and darning kit.

Seffert seemed to have taken over as convenor in Merino's absence. "Come on, get the frigging power back on, you assholes!"

"What about the heating?"

"Wassamatter, can't you let the fucking dogs out?"

Then someone lobbed something. Reeve saw it arc through the air, catching what little daylight there was, and Jerry yelped. Parmenter jerked the dog back from the gap in the balustrade.

"We're in the same boat as you!" Parmenter yelled back, almost drowned out by the abuse. "No frigging phones or anything. Just shut up and let us deal with it."

Merino shouldered his way to the front. "What about the generator? We've got an emergency backup, right? Always had that."

"No fuel," Parmenter said. "We've got sweet FA, buddy. Get used to it. We're the lowest priority in the COG. Just watch the goddamn psychos, okay?"

Parmenter dragged Jerry away by his lead and vanished into the gloom. Without the pumps, fans, and other background electrical noises that were always there but unnoticed, the place was unnaturally quiet. Marcus walked over to the wooden door that let the dogs loose. It opened from the top like a hatch, so it was hard to tell if it was locked down or not.

"What happens when the power comes back on?" he asked.

Seffert walked along the row of cells, checking the doors. "Can't rely on any of these systems working—oh, *shit.*"

Reeve turned at the sound of sliding metal. Seffert was at the end of the row now, backing away from something. "Whoa," he said. "Okay."

It took Reeve a couple of seconds to realize that the doors had opened, and by then it was too late. Ruskin burst out of the cell and thudded into Seffert, shoving him backward. He staggered and fell. Reeve thought Ruskin had just hit him, but then he saw the blood and the short length of rusty pipe jutting out of the base of Seffert's throat. Everyone froze for a fraction of a second. Marcus and Merino broke first and ran for the two men, almost like they'd drilled for this.

"Somebody get a warder." Marcus dropped his chunk of wood and knelt beside Seffert, trying to stop the blood. Merino shoved Ruskin back into the cell. "I said *get a fucking warder.* Check the other goddamn cells, too, in case they're all going to go apeshit."

The floor was now sheer chaos. Reeve made sure he had his blade in his hand as he ran to check the other cells with Leuchars and Edouain, but the guys in those were being sensible and just staying well back from the bars. They could hear what was going on: there were a couple of screams from Ruskin's cell that stopped almost immediately, then grunting as if Merino was punching the shit out of him. Marcus was still bent over Seffert.

Shit, that was a mess. Seffert was making a gargling noise, eyes staring and looking down as if he was trying to focus on what was sticking out of him. There was nowhere near as much blood as Reeve expected, but there was a damn big chunk of pipe rammed right into his throat and it didn't look like Marcus had a hope in hell of doing anything about it.

"Reeve, come on. Press here." Marcus indicated a point on Seffert's throat. Seffert was an asshole, a kidnapper, but somehow Marcus was treating him like a wounded Gear. "Hey, Reeve, *buck up*! Press it, or there's going to be blood every-fucking-where."

Reeve obeyed. It was pointless, though. "And what are you going to do if you take it out?"

Marcus peered into the wound and eased the pipe a fraction. Blood welled up. Seffert thrashed around weakly. "Ah, *shit*." He knelt back on his heels, looked up at the gallery, and yelled loud enough to make Reeve flinch. "Warder? *Officer Jarvi!* We need a medic."

Merino came out of Ruskin's cell with the kitchen knife held down at his side. "Yeah, good luck with that. The phones are out and even if they had a radio, we're on our own."

Seffert was starting to have a fit or something. He shuddered uncontrollably, made a few wheezing, sucking sounds, and then stopped. Reeve was left with his fingers jammed into the neck of a guy who was just staring up at the ceiling. He knew what dead looked like. Marcus looked defeated. Whatever was going on in his head had little to do with the reality in front of him. His hands were covered in blood.

"That solves one problem," Reeve said. "He's gone."

"Okay, we better start stacking the stiffs outside." Merino seemed to take it in his stride. "Hey, *you*." He jabbed a finger in the direction of Vance, who was standing guard outside Beresford's cell as if a rapist was going to give him any trouble. "Get that damn cell cleared. The body *and* the shit. It's bad enough in here as it is."

"What about the nutters?"

"I'll deal with them." Merino inspected his knife with mild disgust. It was covered in blood. "The screws aren't going to do a damn thing for us."

Marcus must have been more distracted by his efforts to save Seffert than Reeve thought. He looked at Merino as if he'd just noticed him. "You knifed Ruskin."

"Yeah, that's the idea." Merino didn't back down when Marcus got that look in his eye, and Reeve had to admire that. "You got a problem with summary justice, Mr. War Hero? Maybe you should ask Seffert."

Marcus looked down at the body, then did that slight roll of the head as if he was shaking it very slowly, unable to believe the state the world had come to.

"Yeah," he said at last. "So what are you going to do about the rest of them?"

Merino looked past Marcus at something behind him. That was when

Reeve realized things weren't going quite as he'd expected, and Marcus turned a little too late.

"And what the hell do you—"

Leuchars, Vance, Van Lees, and a guy called Warrick—one of Merino's casuals, but still a big, thick-set lad—jumped him. Marcus was fast, a big, aggressive target to take down, but he'd just dropped his guard for a second too long and that gave them the edge they needed. They grabbed him, one on each arm, one with a headlock, just as he was shifting his weight. Merino dived in too. Marcus hit the flagstones with a thud. Vance got a hefty kick in the balls trying to pin his legs, and it took all five of them to hold him face-down, but he wasn't superhuman, and he wasn't armed or prepared. He had a pretty foul mouth on him for landed gentry. Vance eventually got his wrists tied behind his back. It was just a takedown, no kicking or settling scores. Reeve didn't have to decide whether to defend Marcus and get his own teeth kicked in.

Merino dusted himself off and squatted to look at Marcus. "Fenix, we're not going to give you a smacking," he said. "You're an okay guy, even if you're as mad as a fucking hatter. Just sit this out and don't be such a frigging boy scout."

"Sit *what* out, asshole?"

"Pest control," Merino said. He jerked his thumb over his shoulder and nodded at Leuchars. "Go on, stick him in his pit. This isn't going to take long. Then he can write a long and well-educated complaint to his buddy the Chairman."

"You better think what you're going to do when you frigging *untie me*," Marcus snarled.

"It's not your problem, soldier boy. Just look the other way for once." Merino looked at Reeve. "Go on. You too. You'll think it's sloppy and amateur."

"Are you doing what I think?" Reeve asked.

"How long's this power going to be out?" Merino asked. "And how long do you want to wait for one of the loonies to come and get you? No nasty stuff, mind. Just putting 'em down, fast as we can. Only chance we're going to get."

Merino walked over to the secure cells, each of which now had a bunch of regular inmates like a picket line at the door. Leuchars, Vance, and Warrick managed to shove Marcus onto his bunk and slide the door shut with a belt around the locking mechanism before he rolled off onto the floor to get to his feet.

"It's for your own good," Reeve said. "Merino must respect you, buddy, or else he'd have cut your throat."

Marcus stared at the lynch mob gathering around the psycho cells. He just didn't get it. He didn't understand that there were things a guy had to walk away from, things that just weren't his problem.

"You're not even frigging animals," Marcus said, more to himself than anything. "Animals don't do that."

"Don't start wanking on about human decency, for fuck's sake."

"So what have I been fighting for? What have my buddies died for?"

"Not to save some asshole who'd kill 'em as soon as look at 'em," Reeve said. "That I know."

Reeve stood in his way so he couldn't see, but of course the whole damn building could hear. Leuchars slid back the first door and the guy inside— Tasman, serial rapist, serial strangler—was begging for his life. He was lucky he still had one, anyway. He'd have been shot these days. Right now, he probably wished he had been.

"You can't do this," he said. "I'm not going to hurt anybody."

"That's what they all say." Merino hefted his knife. "Now, who's first?"

THE SLAB: STAFF OFFICES, TWENTY MINUTES INTO POWER OUTAGE.

The phone was still dead, absolutely dead, the generator was out of fuel, and the radio hadn't worked in years. It hadn't needed to. Niko was stuck in a dead building, with two choices: to sit it out until the power came back on, or to take the Slab's elderly Packhorse and drive to the nearest location with power and phones.

He had no way of knowing where that might be until he started driving, of course.

And then the screaming and yelling started.

The acoustics of the Slab were weird at the best of times. Sound traveled along conduits and through gratings, sometimes making things in the next wing sound closer than those in the next room. But the dogs were barking again, and Parmenter burst into the office with Jerry.

"They've gone nuts down there, and I can't let the dogs out. The gate system's dead."

Niko wondered whether to drain the Pack's fuel tank and use it to run the gennie for a couple of hours while he got the situation under control. But it was a gamble. If this outage dragged on, he didn't want to be stuck here without transport, and he damn well wasn't going to drain his own bike. It was hard enough to get gas even with a government priority pass. He abandoned the phone and braced himself to appeal for a bit of common sense among a bunch of people who had absolutely nothing to lose and who knew he wouldn't go down on the floor in person.

"If they wreck the place, it's their problem, and anyway, what's left to wreck?"

"The cell locks failed, and Ruskin attacked Seffert," Parmenter said. "They're killing the psych ward guys."

Shit. Shit, shit, shit. How the hell can I put the lid on that?

Should I even try?

"You find a way to sort out the dog runs," Niko said. "Go get Campbell and Ospen. There's got to be a way to override that manually."

Niko flipped to autopilot and took the rifle and a box of thirty rounds from the cupboard he called an armory. That meant he had two reloads left. The weapon was based on the old army-issue Lancer, a lighter and more basic version for police use, and as soon as he started jogging down the passage he knew that all he could do was target whoever was in range on the floor. He couldn't put a man down with every shot, so he was going to run out of ammo long before he ran out of inmates.

Then what do I do if things get worse?

The Slab was less than half an hour into a power cut and the place had already boiled over into anarchy. The floor of the main wing looked like a bare-knuckle fight, with most of the inmates in a broad arc waiting and watching with their hands deep in their pockets, jackets buttoned to the neck against the cold. Niko leaned over the gantry to look for Merino, and then for Marcus Fenix, but there was no sign of Marcus and he could only hear Merino. He was barking orders: "Come on, come on, *come on.*" Then he emerged from a cell, and Niko realized he wasn't giving orders but dragging Carew, the guy who'd machine-gunned the Tollen branch of QuikiMeal because the voices told him it was the only way. Merino had a knife. Just about every inmate did, but it was one of those things Niko had had to turn a blind eye to because he couldn't run this place any other way.

He wasn't a good shot. He hadn't used a rifle for years. He remembered his drill, slid the safety catch off, and aimed. Carew was whimpering.

"Don't, please, please . . ." Carew was trying to make eye contact with Merino. He didn't seem to realize that it wouldn't change a damn thing. "I won't hurt anyone. I won't. I swear."

Niko couldn't get a clear shot at all. He stared down the sights. "Come on, Merino, pack it in," he called. "Let him go."

There was a drain grating in the floor, one of the sluices that let water drain away when the floors were cleaned, not that the place was scrubbed out often. Merino shoved Carew down on his knees over it and wrangled him into position like a sheep-shearer. "Yeah? I *told* you not to dump these assholes on us." He pulled Carew's head back by the hair, ignoring the rifle completely. He must have seen it. The place was gloomy, not pitch black. "If you can't do your goddamn job, then I'll do it for you."

It happened so fast that Niko couldn't have stopped it even if he'd been a better shot. He didn't squeeze the trigger anyway. Merino just drew the blade across Carew's throat in a quick, short motion and let him slump over the drain. Carew would bleed out by the time Niko got down there, if he could get down there at all with the automatic locks jammed. All he could do was watch helplessly. It was suddenly very quiet, no jeering and no threats, just a kind of resignation that had spread across all the inmates until things seemed almost normal again.

But there was a guy on the floor bleeding out like a pig in a slaughterhouse. No, that wasn't normal, not even for the Slab.

Merino looked up at Niko, shaking blood off the blade. "What did you expect me to do, stab 'em? Way too slow. You put down a dangerous dog, you do it as humanely as you can."

"I should fucking well shoot you, Merino."

"Yeah, go ahead. But you don't know when the power's coming back on, and what we'll be able to do between now and then, do you?" He squatted to check on Carew. "Okay, we're done. Let's get the body moved and then we clean this place up, okay?" He turned his back on Niko and faced the inmates. "Go on. *Move.* Hey, Reeve? Has Fenix calmed down yet? Let him out when he has."

Well, at least that answered one question. Marcus was in one piece and the Chairman's office would be placated. Niko couldn't imagine Marcus standing by and letting Merino get on with it. Niko wasn't sure how he felt about it himself. Merino had certainly solved a few problems for him, and what was he going to do about it anyway? He could either shoot Merino, if he could get in a position to do it, or he could revoke parole or privileges, but as neither existed in the Slab the only option was to be grateful that Merino had a handle on the situation and to just fill in a report in due course.

God Almighty. Listen to me. I watch a guy slaughtered—I mean literally slaughtered, abattoir style—and I'm going to fill out a form and hope the problem's gone away.

"Whoa, steady! It's not my goddamn fault, okay?" That was Reeve's voice. Merino saw him back out onto the floor from the direction of Marcus's cell, hands held out in a don't-hit-me kind of way. "Look after number one. We're none of us any use to anyone if we try to save the whole damn world. They were just sick fucks, okay? Kindest thing."

Marcus stalked out, rubbing his wrists, shoulders set for a fight. "You don't get it, do you? You just *don't get it.* You think we're any better?" Then he looked up. "Officer Jarvi? What the fuck do they pay you for?"

Nearly three years in the Slab hadn't changed Marcus. He might have buried most of himself, but the core erupted occasionally like a volcano, the red-hot bit that was all duty and doing the right thing even though it was obvious to anyone that there wasn't anything right left to do except stay alive. Maybe he'd understand that one day. Niko felt a little dirty at being bawled out over morality. Marcus had hit a nerve.

"What else do you expect me to do, Fenix?" he said. "You think I can do any more than you did?"

Marcus just stared back in silence for a few moments. "You don't even know what's caused the outage, do you?"

"No."

"Then you better find out. Because there's sub-station faults, and then there's grub incursions."

"I'm going to take a drive out. The phones are down."

"Take a look from the roof first. You've got no idea what's out there yet. Got any field glasses?"

"Somewhere." Niko felt the need for some expert advice, but the inmates were now completely separate from the staff areas for the duration of the outage. If he grabbed a ladder and let Marcus climb up to the gallery, he'd have the rest of the prisoners up here too, and that was one extra problem he didn't need. "It'd be handy if you'd take a look."

Marcus gave him that yeah-very-funny stare. "How?"

"Can you get up to the windows via the yard? Then you can get access to the roof."

"If anyone could, then you'd know already." Marcus paused, then nodded as if he'd decided to accept the challenge. "Okay, might as well try."

"I'll open the window."

"And keep the goddamn dogs under control."

Niko went to collect the binoculars from the office, and by the time he opened the third story window overlooking the yard, he could hear branches breaking below. He leaned out and looked down. Marcus was shinning up the rusty iron drainpipe, making for the barred sash window on the floor above. Damn, that pipework wasn't going to take his weight. The drain fed through a spiked collar at window height, designed to stop inmates from doing just what Marcus was doing now, but a smaller pipe ran at a slight horizontal slope above it. Marcus reached out to grab the vertical window bars and froze there for a moment.

"Now you're stuck, yeah?" Jarvi said. "I'll find a rope."

"Wait." Marcus repositioned his left hand. He gripped one of the cross-bars welded to the backs of the verticals, just a hand-width wide, and seemed to be taking a deep breath. "Nearly done."

He hauled himself up with his right arm, a straight chinning movement, then swung his left leg up and jammed his boot into the small gap at sill level. Niko couldn't see how he was going to get out of that. But he did: he took another deep breath and pushed off from his toe-hold in an explosive movement like a rock-climber, catching the bars with one hand. It was more of a leap than a climb. Now he was clinging to the grid and looking up for his next hand-hold. Niko held his breath. Marcus took his time getting the fingers of his left hand into a gap that Niko couldn't even see, then looked up at him.

"When I say so," Marcus growled, "you grab my damn arm, okay?"

Niko nodded. *Easier said than done.* He laid down his rifle, braced his knees against the inside wall, and prayed that he didn't drop him.

"One, two . . ." Marcus pulled up with his left arm and reached for the windowsill with his right. "Come on, Jarvi, give me a hand."

Niko got an overhand grip on Marcus's arm and pulled. It was still a scramble to get him over the ledge, but once his shoulders were through the frame, he tipped forward and Niko grabbed the back of his belt. Marcus rolled onto the floor, got up, and dusted himself off without a word.

"You would have made a good burglar," Niko said. "Come on. Access is this way."

A flight of narrow wooden stairs led up to a roof space full of header tanks. Niko climbed the metal ladder to the roof hatch and trod carefully on the flat section of the roof that ran behind the parapet. On a good day, the visibility was twenty-five kilometers, but even on an overcast afternoon, he could still see far enough to know that the outage hadn't just affected the prison. Smoke hung in the air about five klicks away as an artillery piece boomed in the distance. He could hear the sound of Centaur tanks grinding but the area around the prison was completely still and deserted.

Marcus leaned on the parapet and adjusted the binoculars. "This would be easier at night."

"Yeah, we might still be cut off by then."

"No street lights or illuminated signs that I can see. But that doesn't mean anything."

Niko pulled out his street map, looking for landmarks that might give him a clue. There was an electricity sub-station a kilometer north, but there was no line of sight with it. How long could he leave it before he fueled the generator or went out and got some help? He decided to give it a couple of hours. When it started to get dark, then he'd split the fuel between the generator and the Packhorse, secure the cells, let the dogs out into the runs, and drive for the nearest checkpoint.

Yeah. Two hours.

It was freezing. He slung his rifle and shoved his hands under his arms to keep warm. Marcus wandered up and down the parapet for a while, checking out the full panorama, then sat on the parapet with his legs dangling over the edge. He didn't seem to have any fear of heights.

"When did this place start looking normal to you?" he asked.

Niko shrugged. "I don't remember. That's what scares me."

"It's all wrong."

"What is?"

"Killing the psychos. I don't know where the line is anymore."

Niko waited for him to go on but he'd just ground to a halt. *What would happen if I just gave him the keys to the Pack and told him to get lost?* Niko could guess. He'd go find a rifle somehow and finish his war, either with his buddies or without them. He wouldn't go back to see his girl or his best friend. Marcus's line was more clearly drawn than he realized.

"Would you do it again?" Niko asked.

"What?"

"Try to save your dad. Tell your CO to fuck off."

"Probably." Marcus was still looking out over the heath toward the city center, binoculars pressed to his eyes. "So I'm in the right place after all."

"You know there's no right answer to it, don't you? Damned if you do, and damned if you don't." Everyone forgot Marcus wasn't just jailed and disgraced. He was still grieving, too. Most people were, but that didn't make it any easier. "How would you feel now if you'd left him to face the grubs alone?"

Marcus just grunted. Niko wondered how bad things would need to be before he'd decide to abandon the Slab, go grab Maura, and get out of Jacinto, but he knew that point would come and that he wouldn't lose sleep over it. He sat back and checked his watch: forty-five minutes. The sky was getting darker with clouds that would probably spit sleet, rounding off a perfect bastard of a day, and he didn't dare try to go home until this place was sorted. Maura would be worried sick if he wasn't back when she left for her night shift. When the power came back on, he was going to get a radio transmitter from Sovereigns even if he had to walk in and rip it out of somebody's office personally.

He waited in silence with Marcus. From time to time there was automatic fire that sounded much closer because of the wind direction, and a couple of Ravens circled over a position on the other side of the highway. When he leaned back against the pitched roof next to the hatch, sound wafted up from the floor beneath—dogs still barking, someone still hammering on metal, isolated sounds in a silent building. Damn, it was bitterly cold up here.

One and a half hours. Okay, we'll split the gas and that'll give us three hours of power on the gennie. I take the Pack, find a patrol, get word to Sovereigns, and call Maura. Then I come back.

He found himself thinking that if the grubs were in town, then maybe Maura would be safer here, but she'd have to travel into town every day for her shift, so there was no getting away from a city that felt more under threat every day.

"You think this place is safe?" Niko asked.

Marcus, still sitting on the edge of the parapet, took a long time to answer. For a moment Niko wondered if he'd heard him. Then he shrugged.

"They'll have a hard time getting in here," he said. "Unless they dig into a sewer like they did a few years ago. But yeah, this is as safe as anywhere. Just more vulnerable to a siege."

"I don't know how we'll defend the place if that happens. A couple of rifles and a hundred rounds."

"Shit. Is that all you've got?"

"That and an evacuation plan."

"Surprised you've got one."

"Well, in the absence of a bus, which we don't have now, I'll just open the goddamn doors and everyone can take their chances."

Marcus turned his head slowly and looked at him. "You know how long you'll last unarmed against grubs?"

"What else can I do?"

Marcus looked like he was going to make a suggestion when the fire alarm went off again. In the gray and brown haze of the city in the distance, pinpoints of light appeared.

"Hey!" It was Campbell, yelling up the ladder. "Niko? We got lights. It's back on."

"Thank god for that." Niko got to his feet, his ass numb with cold. "Saved by the bell, Fenix. Come on."

"Don't get too excited until you find out what happened," Marcus said, climbing down the ladder ahead of him.

The corridor was just as grim and dark when Niko walked down it to the staff office, but the place was alive with the humming and ticking of pumps, motors, and fans. For a ruin, it still had systems that hadn't yet failed. He motioned Marcus to wait outside—probably the only prisoner he would trust to do that—and tried the phone. The dialing tone was back. Parmenter stuck his head around the door.

"Still no cell locks, or heating," he said. "The circuits must have fried when the power came back on. Smell it? The wiring in here's at least fifty years old. It's a death trap."

"Does *anything* work?"

"Well, there's access to D Wing. And hot water. The dog runs are open, but we can't shut the individual gates, so we're just letting them run around the circuit."

"Okay. Check what's happening on the floor."

There was a definite smell of burned rubber. That worried Niko more than the access issues. He picked up the phone again and dialed the Justice Department, not really expecting to get through or for anyone to pick up, but he got an answer after a few rings.

"JD," said a voice. "Admin office."

"Hesketh, Officer Jarvi here," he said. "We lost power for a couple of hours. What happened?"

"You and the whole south and west of the city. The Locust hit the power sub-station on Ginnet Drive."

"Wow, they got that far inside the wire?"

"They dug through a conduit. I don't know all the details."

"Well, we've still got problems. The cell door system's screwed. It's an electrician job."

"You might have to wait."

"How long?" Niko asked. "We kind of need locked doors. And some heating."

"Can the prisoners get out?"

"No. They're locked in, more or less."

"Then you're going to have to wait your turn."

"But what about the heating? If we get another cold snap, we're going to have guys freeze to death."

"They're lifers," the clerk said. "So what?"

There was no point debating that delicate moral issue. Niko gave up. Maybe he could get Edouain to take a look at the wiring, given his technical skills, and make himself useful for a change. Niko went outside to find Marcus leaning against the wall with his arms folded, chin down.

"I heard," he said.

"What?"

"The grubs. They dug through again."

"Yeah. Come on. Let's get you back to your cell."

"You should be worried."

"Why?"

"Because nobody thought they could get as far as Ginnet Drive," Marcus said. "They're finding ways into the city, granite or no granite. And that means they could come up in here."

It was only a matter of time. Niko knew that, had *always* known it, but time could be ten weeks or ten years. All anyone could do was wait.

"So what do we do now?" Niko asked.

"The only thing we can," Marcus said. "When the day comes, we fight."

CHAPTER 13

I will forsake the life I had before so I may perform my duty as long as I am needed.
(From the oath sworn by recruits to the army of the Coalition of Ordered Governments.)

COG RESEARCH STATION AZURA: LATE GALE, 13 A.E.

Adam gazed at the backs of his hands and tried to recall what they'd looked like last week, last month, last year.

He noted every hair, pore, and scar, but there was no visible change. He checked the calendar on the wall of his study. The best part of three years had slipped away since he'd regained consciousness on an island he'd never known existed and realized he was far from the only man on Sera weighed down by vast secrets, and he had nothing to show for it except understanding a little more of what Lambency had been a month or a year ago, but not what it was right now.

In my blood. In my tissues. Look at me. It's time that's changing me. Not the pathogen. Time, and worry about Marcus.

Despite injecting himself with the ever-evolving Lambent pathogen, sometimes every week, sometimes not for months, nothing seemed to have happened. He was perfectly well. Apart from the endlessly mutating proteins in his blood, there was no evidence that the organism had any adverse effect on him. Esther Bakos said she wasn't sure if it was mutating to try to infiltrate his immune system, or if it was reacting to the steady assault of antigens that she'd developed. DNA research was in its infancy. She kept saying that one day, understanding genomes would transform Sera, and if previous Chairmen hadn't been so ignorantly prejudiced against genetic engineering, then the world wouldn't have been in this mess now.

Adam wondered how much she knew that she still kept from him. He never assumed that he had the full picture, not even now.

Well, would I trust me? Perhaps not.

He dragged the razor carefully down to the line of his beard and watched his hand in the mirror.

And you're still unkillable, you little bastards. Just when we think we've finished you off . . . you come back. What do you want? What's your plan? Blow me up and disperse your genetic material like a fungus? Mutate me into something to serve some other purpose? Just give me a clue. Any clue.

He looked out of the bathroom window onto another perfect tropical day—perfect except for that permanent, static curtain of storm clouds—and tried to cling to the knowledge that this was all utterly abnormal. The rest of Sera was turning into a wasteland, a world on borrowed time. Myrrah knew it. So did he. For a moment he let himself hope that Lambency had finally found a species it couldn't colonize and that it would never become active in humans. But the toll it would take on other life-forms was still an unknown threat to human survival. It wasn't much good being immune if every food species on Sera died.

And imulsion *did* cause mutations in humans. He knew that all too well now, as the COG had known for years. But the process by which it changed from an apparently biologically inactive fuel to a live pathogen remained unclear, as did finding parallels between imulsion's teratogenic effects and its behavior as a pathogen. Adam suspected they weren't linear stages of the same thing but evidence that imulsion was evolving, diversifying just like the first life on Sera had done. He'd been slapped down by Bakos once too often for taking intuitive leaps without the foundation of proof, though. He merely suggested routes she might explore.

It's not as if I haven't been wrong before. But I'm right far more often than I'm wrong.

Adam settled on humility for the day and checked himself again in the mirror, straightened his collar, and noted that his age was showing rather unkindly. Stress and insomnia had shaved kilos off him. His hair was thinning. He wondered if that was why the other scientists gave him a wide berth, as if anyone who worked with the pathogen was a leper, but it was probably just the fact that he was poor company these days.

We know it's not airborne. We know from animal studies that it isn't transmitted by simple contact. So I shall have breakfast like a civilized human being for a change. I shall go out.

He checked his overnight messages on the computer and bristled at Bakos's request for another sperm sample, which had begun to feel more like a ritual humiliation than a routine lab test. *Which might prove of little use in determining loss of fertility,* she wrote, *as men in their late fifties have low sperm motility and up to 80 percent of their sperm show abnormalities anyway.* The bitchiness of scientists was more elegant than the lay variety. He toyed with the idea of taking a physicist's revenge and reminding her of the cruel effects of gravity on connective tissue in females.

And there was still no word on Marcus. He'd have to chase Prescott on that.

Breakfast could be taken in a number of places on Azura, but Adam wanted to sit outside and look at the sky, which struck him as a rather prisoner-like wish and one that made little sense to him. Escape for humans meant lateral movement, not flight. It was one of those rare cliches with no basis in fact. But did Marcus spend any time staring up at the clouds over Jacinto? Did his cell even have a window? Perhaps it was more about fresh air and sunlight. Marcus probably had neither. Sometimes it was almost too painful to think about him. Adam picked up coffee and pastries from the restaurant, nodded politely to colleagues whose obituaries he'd read years ago—damn, there were some he'd even *written*—and went to find a secluded seat overlooking the bay. Gray and yellow seabirds he'd never seen anywhere else wheeled in the air before diving into the waves to snatch fish.

As he chewed and thought, the rattle of automatic fire drifted on the breeze. It was a sound he'd grown so used to over the years, even in the city, that it almost didn't register on him. It took a few moments to break into his thoughts and make him look around to see where it was coming from.

It didn't sound like a firefight. At first it was single, evenly timed shots, then controlled bursts five seconds apart. Someone was doing Lancer drill. Adam finished his coffee, tipped the dregs out onto the grass, and ambled off in the direction of the noise. If someone was using live rounds there'd be a red pennant flying somewhere conspicuous to stop people wandering onto the range.

The interior of Azura was unspoiled tropical forest with a few farms to support the research center's population. In all the time he'd been here, Adam had rarely ventured out of the main complex to go on the field trips because it had seemed like a shameful indulgence, and it also meant being social with a group of people he'd still not come to terms with. Was his deception any worse than theirs? He still didn't know. By now, he should have known everyone on the island. He suspected he was on name terms with only a quarter of them, and some of those were the housekeeping staff.

The Lancer fire grew louder as he reached the top of the headland. On the close-cropped turf at the bottom of the long slope, someone had set up a couple of wooden targets, the old Pendulum Wars kind in the form of a UIR infantryman painted in thick black lines on a flimsy softwood sheet. Adam looked for the range warning flag, but couldn't see one. He recognized the two men lying prone and squeezing off bursts, though. It was Dury and Nevil.

Nevil was drilling neat clustered shots in the thoracic triangle just as Adam himself had been trained to. Adam watched for a while, surprised to see his assistant handling a rifle like a seasoned Gear. It was rather touching. Nevil had always longed to serve. Adam waited until Dury knelt back on his heels and took the magazine out of his rifle before venturing any closer.

"You kept that quiet," Adam said, walking down the slope. Dury turned. "And shouldn't you be wearing ear protectors?"

"What do you think, then, Professor?" Dury asked. "Dr. Estrom's up to Onyx Guard standards. I'm damn impressed. Are you?"

"Absolutely. Why didn't you tell me, Nevil?"

Nevil slung his rifle and stood looking like an embarrassed teenager. "Because you're not very forgiving of failure."

Adam cringed. Nevil, like Marcus, had never failed at anything. It was sobering to think that either of them might have been too scared to do less than excel. *Is that how Marcus saw me?* Adam was mortified. All he could do was hold out his hand for shaking. Nevil took it and smiled, still embarrassed.

"Any word from Jacinto, Captain?" Adam asked.

"I thought the Chairman called you last week."

"He did. I want to know how my son is *this* week."

"Well, the prison's still having power supply issues with some of its systems, but Marcus is okay. Still safer inside than out at the moment. Have you been reading the CIC briefings?"

Marcus wouldn't want *safe*. He would want to be out there on the front line, dealing with it. Adam imagined the pain of his frustration on top of everything else. "Yes."

"Then you'll know Jacinto's taking a pounding. East Barricade's almost permanently cut off."

Well, that was one way to break the news that his ancestral home was in ruins. Adam thought of all the paintings and antiquities that he should have had the sense to place in government storage years ago, but suddenly found he didn't care at all. Dury started walking back toward the complex and Adam and Nevil followed him, lost for conversation.

"By the way," Dury said. "If either of you have anything useful to contribute on the Lightmass bomb and the resonator, the DRA team would be really grateful."

"And I'm supposed to be dead, so how are you going to give them the information?" Adam asked. "Say you had a wonderful idea over coffee and would they mind checking your calculations?"

Dury looked back over his shoulder, faintly amused. Nevil gave Adam a discreet elbow in the ribs.

"I'm just an ignorant grunt, Professor," Dury said, smiling. "I'm expecting someone with your crackerjack IQ to come up with a brilliant plan. Would you like to see their latest efforts?"

"I suppose Prescott's asking for full reports from them and they've absolutely no idea why a layman would want all that detail."

"They think he's an interfering pain in the ass, yes. But he's willing to live with that to get you the data you need."

"Why do they tell you what they think of him?"

"They don't. I find out."

Adam followed him down the path in silence, sobered. Dury never made threats. He was obviously a hard man and unafraid of violence, but he never needed to throw his weight around. Adam understood perfectly what he was capable of from his few plain, undecorated words. *How long was I under surveillance myself?* Was his phone tapped or his mail intercepted? How much had the Onyx Guard now recovered from his home?

"I'll certainly take a look," Adam said. He might have been an annoying hobbyist to the biology team, but nobody could touch him on weapons physics. He needed to feel positive about his skills again, and Nevil probably did too. "But they'll need better mapping of the tunnels before they deploy it. There may well still be some data in my archives at Haldane Hall."

"Yes, we're recovering what we can. Good of you to leave that for the grubs."

"They don't need to be told what their own tunnels look like, Captain. And they'll have excavated many more since then."

"You still feel sorry for them, don't you?"

"No, but I do respect the extraordinary understanding of genetics it takes to create living weapons that bring global powers to their knees."

"Not extraordinary enough to sort out the Lambent, though."

"Unfortunately not."

"But if they did get lucky without your help, then we'd still be exterminated, wouldn't we?"

Adam gave up and conceded defeat. He found himself almost liking Dury.

It was that inexorable logic, that ability to come back instantly with an argument that put Adam on the spot. Prescott actually seemed fond of him. It must have been a comfort to have the company of a competent, loyal aide who was also smart. Adam suspected that Prescott not only missed the cut and thrust of politics, but also felt increasingly lonely and starved of decent conversation. It was the curse of the intellectually able.

They were back in the main complex now, strolling through well-tended borders and catching the light spray of water as the breeze whipped through the fountains. It was going to be another balmy day. That was the only kind that Azura had. Dury peeled off to the right to head for the admin center, turning to give them a nod. Adam and Nevil carried on toward the labs.

"I'll do the number crunching if you like, Adam," Nevil said. He still had his Lancer slung over his shoulder, which was getting a few odd looks from passing residents, but he carried it as if it was a seamless part of him just as any Gear did. "I need to polish my self-respect. Make myself useful for a change."

"At least you're young enough to be post-apocalyptic breeding stock."

"God, tell me it won't be with Erica Marling. I'm looking for a girl with a healthy dose of guilt."

"I'm glad you've still got your sense of humor."

"I wasn't joking, actually."

"I don't want to sound avuncular, Nevil, but don't make my mistakes. Have a family if you can, a big one."

"But you've *got* a family. You've still got Marcus. He's going to be released, trust me on that."

"But he's the last of the Fenix line," Adam said.

If only we'd had a brother or sister for him. All those awkward talks he'd had with a teenaged Marcus, all the times he'd told him to *be careful* with girls because he was wealthy and privileged and had to make the right marriage, not accidentally impregnate some gold-digger and ruin his life. Adam had never imagined that Marcus would take that advice so literally and then devote himself faithfully to an infertile woman like Anya. Was that why he hadn't married her, because Adam had made him believe that continuing the Fenix line was more important than his happiness? Or had Elain's distance and disappearance dented his attitude toward women, his willingness to trust them?

We made him what he is.

The officer-enlisted barrier could have been made to go away, but Marcus had never been willing to discuss his private life with his father. It was some-thing far more fundamental that held him back. Either way, the Fenix name would die with him.

"And I'll be the last of the Estrom line," Nevil said.

"You might need to learn to look for Erica's better points."

"I better see the ophthalmologist, then."

Esther Bakos was already at her desk when Adam and Nevil stepped out of the elevator. She looked at Adam over her glasses and indicated his desk with a slow nod.

"You've got a visitor," she said.

Adam couldn't see the far side of his desk from there, and Bakos obvi-ously wasn't going to volunteer a name. Yet again, as foolishly optimistic as a child believing in magic, Adam's thoughts jumped straight to Marcus even though he knew damn well that Prescott wouldn't and couldn't have had him released. Perhaps it was Salaman Bardry. Adam found it hard to talk to him, knowing how everyone had pitied him for blowing his own brains out after deploying the Hammer strikes, as if he was the only one with the decency to do it when Adam, Prescott, and Hoffman had the affront to go on breathing as if nothing had happened. Sometimes Adam wondered how Hoffman—com-pletely charmless, but straight as a die—would react if he heard Bardry was alive and well, living in a lovely apartment with his wife.

I was with Hoffman. I was with him when he turned the key, knowing his own wife was out there in the strike zone. He did his duty. No wonder he couldn't cut Marcus any slack.

It wasn't Bardry sitting opposite Adam's desk, though. It was a woman in a navy blue business suit. She had her back to him, reading something, and then she turned: late thirties, perhaps forty, very well groomed but not glamorous, a no-nonsense kind of woman. He knew her from somewhere. He couldn't recall where, though.

"Professor Fenix," she said, getting up to hold out her hand. "It's been a long time. Interesting here, isn't it?"

There was a distinctive bulge under her jacket, and that was what prodded his memory, not her jaw-length brown bob or those sharp features he couldn't quite place, but the fact she had a pistol in a shoulder holster under her jacket.

She was a COGIntel agent. She'd been in all the meetings to plan the raid on the UIR facility at Aspho Point, but the name eluded him. He recalled her being rather terse with him when he'd tried to split ethical hairs over the fate of the UIR scientists.

"I'm very bad with names at my age," he said, shaking her hand. "My apologies."

"Louise Settile," she said. "COG Intelligence. Aspho. Remember?"

"Oh, yes, I do." He found it hard to let go of her hand, as if it had been a happy memory. It hadn't. If nothing else, it had marked the time when Marcus had retreated behind his defenses for good, devastated by Carlos Santiago's death. "You look very well indeed, Agent Settile. Have they given you coffee?"

"Yes, I'm fully caffeinated, thanks, Professor. How are you?"

"I *have* been better." God, did she know what he was doing with the pathogen? No. She was just being polite. *And here I am, embroiled in yet another deceit. I don't like myself at all.* "Do call me Adam, please. What can I do for you?"

"Nothing specific. I just wanted to say hello."

"You're rather polite for an intelligence agent who must know why I was brought here."

"I know you've been a very naughty boy, Adam, but my job's prevention, not punishment. You're cooperating on the Lightmass and resonator, aren't you?"

"Of course. Why wouldn't I?"

"I have to be sure. I don't want to send men into Haldane Hall to risk being killed if you're not leveling with me."

"Dr. Estrom and I will give you every cooperation. How are you going to present our work to the DRA, though?"

"I'm going to say we've recovered discs from your home and we're gradually reconstructing the data. They're still having problems processing the resonator imaging."

"Yes, that was as far as we'd got when I was detained."

"This won't take you away from your Lambency research, will it?"

I only need to stand here and metabolize to do that.

"I'm just a physicist, as Dr. Bakos keeps telling me." He sat down at his desk and logged into the computer system. A new folder had appeared on his drive, the Lightmass project data. "So you've known about Azura for years, I assume."

"Yes, since I joined the service nineteen years ago."

"Am I the only one who didn't know? A little surprising to keep this from the Director of the DRA."

"Nothing personal, sir, but you'd been identified as a potential risk while you were still a serving Gear."

"Too argumentative with the top brass."

"Too vocal about defense policy. And your wife was, too."

Adam had never realized how *observed* he'd been for his whole adult life.

But then given his line of work, he could hardly object. "Well concealed, though. This is an awfully big project to make invisible."

"It's been a long, slow process. But in a war like this, removing people is much easier than in the Pendulum Wars. By the way, you don't mind us taking away your pet pedophile, do you? I understand there have been objections from the residents to having him here with so many unsupervised children around."

"He's part of a research project."

"I spoke to him yesterday when I flew in. He says he hasn't given tissue samples for a year, at least."

William Alva was Adam's cover. The samples could have been from any man, and Bakos made sure she was the only person who dealt with him: but if Alva was removed, then the obvious question would be to ask who was providing them now. "Well, that doesn't mean anything." Would Settile know he was bluffing? "Who else do you suggest we inject with a live pathogen?"

"I must admit I'm surprised that you'd tolerate experimentation on human beings, Adam." Settile smiled. "You gave us hell about neutralizing UIR weapons scientists because they were civilians. It's much easier for me. I have no moral line except ensuring the survival of the maximum number of COG citizens by any means necessary."

Adam tried to feign interest in the file on his screen. It really was quite absorbing. The Lightmass team, or what now passed for it, had gone down a complete dead end in the imaging trials. It was blindingly obvious to him, a correction that would take him and Nevil a week at most with the processing power of the Azura mainframe.

She knows. Or at least she knows how to make me think she does and start me sweating. That's her job.

"I'm afraid I must insist on keeping Alva," he said at last. "Even if he's getting undeservedly fat for contributing little to society. You can have him when we're done with him."

"I admire a realist, Adam," she said. "The stakes are too high, after all." She got up to go. "I'll be around pretty frequently if you need anything. If I get the chance when I'm in Jacinto, I'll look in on your son."

There was nothing that COGIntel didn't know about Adam. They also had access to Marcus any time and could do with him as they pleased. Settile—very competent, very forthright as he recalled—might have been making that point, or simply being kind to a man who was worried about the nightmarish existence his son was enduring. Adam couldn't decide on her motives, though, and cursed himself for falling into the game of doubt and self-doubt so far and so fast.

No, she wouldn't lay a finger on Marcus, if *that* was what she meant. Prescott needed his cooperation. *Sera* needed it. The price of that was Marcus's life and welfare.

Like Settile said, everyone had their line, their nonnegotiable limit. And Adam's was Marcus.

THE SLAB: EARLY RISE, 13 A.E.

"For fuck's sake," Ospen said. "I've been drafted."

He tried to put the phone down but the handset missed the cradle, and it took him a couple of fumbling attempts before he managed it. Yeah, Niko could understand that reaction. Nobody in their right mind would expect a jail to run on a handful of staff. And things weren't pretty outside the prison walls lately.

"Sorry," Niko said. In the background, all he could hear was muffled yapping. Those goddamn dogs just wouldn't stop barking. "You, Chalcross, and Ling."

Ospen rounded on him. He was young enough to be useful at the front, pretty fit even if he wasn't built like a Gear really needed to be to lug all that armor. It had to happen sooner or later. The grubs were moving further across the plateau every day.

"You *knew?*"

Here we go. "Yesterday. They told me I was going to get cut to half staff. I told them what a bad idea that was, but it was like pissing in the wind, as always."

"Why don't you send Parmenter?"

"I didn't get a choice, and anyway, I need someone to look after the dogs."

Ospen stood staring at him as if that would change everything. Chalcross had taken it a lot better; he let life bounce off him and got on with things. Now that the Slab was starting to seem less of a safe haven every day, getting a Lancer and the chance to run for it was starting to look like a better bet. Ospen obviously didn't think so. Ling hadn't been told yet. He wouldn't know until he came on shift tonight.

"I've still got stuff to do here," Ospen said.

"Oh, I'll just let the Chairman know you're declining the invitation, shall I?"

"I mean it. I'm going to get killed out there."

"Gears survive. Talk to Fenix. He'll tell you how it's done."

"No, I mean I'm going to get killed *for sure*." Ospen sort of shook his head, looking past Niko at the wall like he was imagining something terrible being drawn on it, and pinched the tip of his nose. "I mean I took a payment from a guy outside to do him a favor and I haven't had the chance to do it yet."

Niko was almost afraid to ask. Ospen liberated a fair few supplies meant for the inmates and sold them on the black market, but the supply drops were so few and far between that the impact on the general shortages here was academic. Now it had come back to bite him in the ass. Too bad: he'd have to sort out his own shit now.

"What, exactly?" Niko asked.

"You don't want to know. But when this guy finds me, I'm dead. I mean he's going to have me fucking *killed*."

"What the hell have you done?"

"I can't possibly be in deeper shit than I already am, can I?"

"No. I think that's a fair assessment. Other than me calling the JD and turning you in, and then they'll probably shoot you anyway."

"Okay, I said I could get a guy out."

"Who?" Ah, it had to be Merino. He was smart, a survivor. He always knew when trouble was coming. Niko wondered whether that was a sign to ask the JD to shut down the prison altogether. The inmates had been okay with staying in what seemed to be one of the few safe places left in Jacinto, but now they looked like they were having doubts. "Let me guess. Merino."

"No. Fenix."

"Wow." Niko wasn't expecting that at all. A guy like Marcus had friends with titles and ranks who could corner the Chairman at lunch. If they were going to pull Marcus out to do a suicide mission or something, they had a dozen other discreet ways to do it. "Who's behind that? Do you know?"

"One of his buddies."

"Shit, you've taken a bribe from a Gear to spring him?" he asked. "No wonder you don't want to play soldiers. They'll skin you alive when they find out."

"It's worse than that. I took the payment from Piet Verdier."

The name rang a bell, all right. Niko took a few seconds to dredge up the memory and Ospen's fear started to make perfect sense. Verdier had been running rackets for years before E-Day, and just like Merino, he was unforgiving in a lose-your-fingers-or-worse kind of way.

"You really picked the wrong guy to piss off," he said.

"Is that all you've got to say?"

"I reckon."

"I thought you were Fenix's guardian angel."

"I was told to make sure he survived," Niko said. What would Fenix do outside? How would Prescott react if he went over the wall? "If the Chairman wanted him out, they'd tell me. Just give the guy his bribe back. Coupons again, was it?"

"I can't. I exchanged it all for food."

"Well, then you're *really* in the shit." Niko got up from the desk and prepared to do the unthinkable because that was very nearly the last option he had left. Ospen was the least of his problems. "You'd better think of something before you have to hand in your keys."

He walked along the gallery, rehearsing his lines. He'd have two officers now to keep a lid on fifty high-risk inmates in a prison that was perched on the edge of disaster, and it just wasn't going to work without taking extreme measures.

What the hell do I do?

How long do I try to hold this together? When do I cut and run?

Niko had never wanted to be a prison officer, but once he became one he decided that he'd do his best. He couldn't look Maura in the eye if he didn't take his job as seriously as she took hers, and the poor woman came home shattered most days. That was when their shifts coincided. He didn't see her for a week at a time.

We all have to hang on to order. All of us. Once we think our little bit of it doesn't matter and we let go, the whole thing unravels and takes the world with it.

Niko walked onto the gantry, braced his hands on the iron rail, and looked around the floor at the inmates below.

"Merino and Fenix," he yelled. He didn't even need to use the PA system now. "Merino and Fenix. Get 'em for me."

Leuchars looked up. "Fenix is digging the vegetable beds."

"Well, damn well *get* him, then. And find Merino. I want to see both of them."

The cell locking system had been down since the power outage in the winter. Niko was seething, but the clerk at JD kept reminding him that the city had more important maintenance jobs to do than his. Edouain had fixed a couple of simple things like the fuses to the heating system, but the doors were now on manual only. Turning the hand-wheels was a slow, heavy job. Niko didn't bother to let the dogs out into the runs as a precaution because it was just too much work for two men. He waited, checking his watch. Maura would be leaving for work now.

"Got 'em!" Leuchars yelled.

"Okay, tell them to wait at the main door."

By the time Niko got downstairs and opened the gates, Marcus was standing behind the mesh inner door, arms folded, staring at the wall but not seeing it. He always had that don't-interrupt-me-I'm-thinking look on his face these days. Merino ambled up to him, not making eye contact. That was the way those two coped. Merino didn't provoke him, and Marcus wasn't playing, just watching the game from the sidelines.

If I want some guys to manage and enforce order down there, then it's those two.

Niko didn't have a choice. He couldn't cover three shifts now. If anything went wrong—if another system failed, if an officer had to go down there for any reason—then one man on his own could end up dead. It took another guy to operate the doors remotely.

And it was always a risk opening that main door on his own. He felt less confident coming down off the gantry every time.

Merino walked through first. "Wow, you must trust us, Officer," he said. "No backup?"

"We're all in the same shit, Merino." Niko waited for Marcus to clear the door and locked it again. If Merino decided to turn around and have a crack at him, Niko was dead, armed or not. "Let's help each other out."

Marcus walked ahead of him. He didn't look back. "You want to define the shit for us?"

"In a minute. Come on, keep moving."

They came to a dead end at the portcullis that opened onto the lobby. It was as far from D Wing as Niko could be, as far out of anyone's earshot as he could get. It was going to be hard enough breaking it to Campbell and Parmenter, let alone some of the inmates. Marcus and Merino turned to face him, probably now wondering if they'd walked into some set-up and were about to get a very hard time. Marcus was definitely tensed for a fight. The constant goddamn barking in the background didn't help.

Niko blocked their way back to the cells, whatever good that was going to do. "Here's the deal," he said. "I've been fucked over again by some pen pusher at Sovereigns. They're drafting more warders, so I'm down to three staff."

"What, you want us to do your filing?" Merino asked. "Make the coffee?"

"The only way I'm going to run this place with two staff and three shifts is either to lock everyone down, all day, every day, or you help me out."

Marcus shrugged. "Or you could just shoot us. You think anyone would give a shit?"

"*I'd* give a shit," Niko said, tapping his CPS badge. "*I* would. I've got a job and I'm going to do it. Look, there'll be three warders on duty during the day. At eighteen hundred, we hand the place over to you. Merino, you run that wing anyway, and Fenix can be your deputy. You got a problem with that?"

Merino just looked at him, probably calculating the advantage. Marcus frowned.

"How are we supposed to notice the difference?" Merino asked.

"I give you the internal keys. You manage the silent hours access. If you piss me around, we've always got the dogs."

Marcus didn't say a word. Niko couldn't tell if he'd mentally checked out again or if he just disapproved. Merino shrugged.

"Why?" Merino asked. "We're locked down overnight anyway."

"Yeah, but if there's an emergency, air strike, fire—"

"We'd *love* a fire. We're freezing our balls off half the time. And if we can't get out of the building anyway, what's the point?"

"Buys you time." He had a point. But all Niko could think of was guys being trapped in their cells like caged chickens. Scum or not, he just couldn't stomach that. "It's a big place."

"Yeah, like the fire and rescue guys are going to turn out if our alarm goes off."

Marcus was now looking at Niko like he was crazy. "You know none of this makes any frigging sense, don't you?"

"Tell your buddy Prescott that. As long as this jail's here, I've got a job to do. Somehow."

Merino just smiled. "We'll manage."

"What's prompted the draft anyway?" Marcus wasn't giving up. This had thrown his switch again. "We haven't had a working radio for over a year— maybe two. Is it that bad outside now?"

"Yes. It is. The grubs are moving in to the north of us now. That means we could be cut off any time."

Predictably, Marcus didn't ask what that meant for the jail. He always seemed to be focused on the bigger picture beyond the walls. "If we can't hold that line, then we're basically down to central Jacinto and not much else."

"Who's *we*?" Merino asked. "They kicked you out, soldier boy. You're *us* now. And we're still safe in our bunker, right?" He nodded at Niko. "Okay, you let me manage it how I see fit down here, and we don't give you any hassle. As before."

"Okay." Niko handed him the ring of keys. They only opened the cells and the service areas like the kitchens, not the staff areas. Nobody was going to be walking out the front door, although if they were given enough time and put their minds to it they'd probably find a way. "Come on, about turn. Back you go."

Niko had to flatten himself against the mesh to let them pass. Marcus was right. It was a dumb situation from start to finish. But the COG was a mass of contradictions, a crumbling city under siege still pretending it could carry on as before, just an army and a bunch of terrified civilians waiting for the inevitable end but too scared to admit it was coming. The Slab was just a miniature version of that.

Denial wouldn't stop the grubs. Niko knew denial wouldn't save the Slab, either. He opened the door and waved Marcus and Merino through.

Merino glanced back at him. "We can take care of ourselves okay," he said. "But if I were you, I'd start working out a plan B for when your bosses abandon you completely. Because what happens to us then?"

Niko didn't answer and began closing the bolts, heaving the hand-wheel until the metal clunked into place. As he walked along the mesh run back to the stairs, some of the dogs shot past him in the adjacent passage, barking again. The noise never seemed to stop. All the dogs did was eat, shit, and yap. Niko wondered if they were worth the hassle now because deploying them was so much time and effort, and Merino was going to keep things under control anyway.

Can I trust the word of a gang boss?

He's never really been in the business of lying, though. Just strong-arming people.

And how am I going to unload a pack of dogs? We only need to keep a couple.

He went back to the offices and checked what was left in the fridge and the store cupboard. Ospen usually had the sense not to touch the staff supplies. There was enough powdered milk to last for a decent time, something labeled *tea* that could have been anything from herbs to the clippings from the hedges at Sovereigns, a fifteen-kilo sack of rice that was four years past its use-by date, and a meter of spicy dried sausage that made a half-decent soup when fried with kale. That would see them through any emergency. He turned on the radio and waited for the news on the hour.

It wouldn't help if I got the inmates another radio, even if I could. It's only bad news and shitty music these days.

Ospen stuck his head around the door. "Niko, you better take a look outside. The shelling's getting really close."

Niko turned down the volume on the radio and listened for a moment. There was the usual sporadic artillery noise, nothing exceptional, but it did sound louder.

"Okay, but what do you expect me to do about it?" The spoons resting in the coffee mugs rattled for a couple of seconds. That bothered him, because the movement could only come from the fissures in the bedrock, and that meant grubs. "Keep an ear on the news for me, will you? And if you touch anything in the larder, I'm going to chop off your fingers personally."

It was quicker and safer to climb up to the roof and take a look than venture out of the gates. Niko learned the lessons Marcus taught him. The parapet had become a little observation post in recent weeks, and Niko was sure that when he looked across Wenlau Heath to the city, there was a glint of field glasses from rooftops looking back at him. The first thing he checked for was the smoke from artillery, then he'd scan for Ravens. He could hear them long before he saw them.

What he could hear now was Centaurs, though, the steady grinding noises of a column of tanks, but for a moment it was hard to get the direction. He had to put down the binoculars and just look for movement. And there they were: three Centaurs were rumbling north up the Andius highway with a couple of Armadillo APCs behind. He watched as they turned off the road and came down the ramp before disappearing from sight. Where the hell had they gone?

The 'Dills reappeared first, bouncing up from a culvert onto the heathland and taking up position on the far side, hatches open and gunners on top cover. Niko waited for the Centaurs to reappear, but the noise of a Raven coming in fast from behind made him look around. It was only when the Raven swept past at roof height, so close that he could see the door gunner feeding in an ammo belt, that he paid attention to the ground.

The scrubby gorse bushes were shivering but there was almost no wind. The ground shook visibly. Then a plume of soil and grass ripped up like someone was strafing in a precise line, and something exploded out of the heath about four hundred meters away, sending bushes tumbling and soil spewing into the air. A Corpser stumbled out of the hole followed by more than a dozen gray, scaly grubs. The Raven opened fire.

All Niko could do was stand and stare, horrified. The damn things had never tunneled this far through the layer of soil before and there was now a firefight going on right outside the Slab. The 'Dills came screaming in with guns firing. The Centaurs roared up behind them, bouncing across the rough ground, and opened fire on the Corpser. The second shell was a direct hit. Half of the Corpser's legs were blown off but it kept moving for a while until another Centaur finished it off.

Ospen thudded onto the roof next to Niko and nearly made him crap himself.

"Fuck, they're right outside," Ospen panted. "What are we going to do?"

"Sweet FA, unless you've got an artillery piece hidden away."

"I'm going to call JD."

"I think they'll know soon enough." *Yeah, what* are *we going to do? What use are a few rifles going to be?* "But grubs can't get under the walls. They can't."

The grubs were still coming out of the e-hole, though, and the 'Dill crews kept picking them off as they came up. It went on for about five minutes that seemed more like five hours. Niko wondered whether to go and get Marcus, but he wasn't in any position to do anything either. Ospen watched, open mouthed, as the grubs kept boiling out of the hole into the tank barrage.

"They're dumb," Ospen said. "They're just walking into it. What's wrong with the assholes?"

Niko had one eye on the 'Dills. He saw one of them turn its turret around 180 degrees to face back toward the city, and when he followed its line of sight he suddenly saw why. On the highway behind the armored vehicles, movement caught his eye, steady movement like a flow of lava. He looked through the binoculars.

"Oh *shit*," he said. "The grubs. There's a column of grubs on the highway."

The other 'Dill broke off and headed for the road. One of the Centaurs hung back and kept shelling the e-hole, but it was pretty clear now that the emergence was a distraction while the main grub advance took the highway. After a couple of minutes all the tanks headed back to the road, shelling as they went, and the few grubs left on the heath trotted toward the city, leaving Ospen and Niko gaping.

"Shit, they'd waste all those troops deliberately to divert us from the road?" Ospen said.

"Better make a note of that." Niko climbed down through the access hatch. "You'll be a Gear this time next week."

This was too damn surreal. Niko was used to Reaver attacks and the hit-and-run nature of grub raids in the city outskirts, but the Slab had always seemed immune from all that. He went back to the office and dialed the JD number.

"What are you going to tell the prisoners?" Ospen asked. "They must have heard it."

"I don't know until I work it out myself," Niko said. "But I'll be damned if we're going to sit here with a couple of pointed sticks and harsh words if those things are right at our gates now. I want goddamn weapons."

"You can't give prisoners weapons."

"Oh, for fuck's sake, Artur, go make yourself useful. Find Merino or Fenix and tell them what's going on outside."

Ospen shot off and Niko waited for the phone to be answered. Niko got the same helpful clerk he usually did.

"Buddy, we've got grubs right outside the gates," he said. "I've got a hundred rounds and two rifles. I might as well not bother with the sidearms. Arm us properly. Send us enough weapons for the inmates and I'll make sure we hold this damn prison."

"Dream on," said the clerk.

"What do you expect me to do? Set the dogs on them? Come on, we're in the shit. We need arms."

"Well, it'd be possible," the clerk said. "I could get the CDS to approve the issue. But that's not your biggest problem."

Tell me about it. "What is, then?"

"The grubs have taken the Andius highway. So you'd better dig in for a long wait."

"Can't help noticing we've still got helos."

"Yeah, and they'll be fighting grubs. So don't expect supply drops. How many staff have you got?"

"There's just two of us on duty at the moment."

"Well, dig in for a long wait, buddy. Nobody's going in or out until the area's been retaken. *If* it's retaken. You're cut off."

BRAVO SQUAD: SOUTHWEST JACINTO.

"What do you mean, it's *off* again? I've waited nearly eight, nine goddamn months for this, and you tell me it's fucking *off?*"

Dom made his calls from public phones these days. COGIntel might have been long gone, but he wasn't taking any chances. It was maybe the sixth time they'd had to call off Marcus's extraction because of grub attacks or a lack of vehicles or some other shit, and he'd had enough. Sure, he'd been warned it was going to take time, and a few more months was just a drop in the ocean compared to a forty-year sentence, but even so, it was the final straw.

Tai and Jace watched him from the Packhorse as he tried to look discreet in the booth on the corner of Dalyell Street. He kept in line of sight with them so they could warn him when Drew Rossi was heading back to the vehicle. It was bad enough having two buddies who knew too much about the jailbreak to deny it without adding any more.

"In case you haven't noticed," Verdier said, "the goddamn prison's cut off. Now, I'm thinking that's more of a problem for the army to solve than for me. So why don't you get your armored ass on the case, shift the grubs, and then we can get on with springing your guy? Okay? Great."

The phone slammed down on the other end. Dom was left staring helplessly at the buzzing receiver, fresh out of abuse to hurl at Verdier anyway. He walked back to the Pack and slid into the rear seat next to Tai.

"He says the extraction's on hold again because the Slab's cut off," Dom said.

"Fate is beyond our control," Tai said. "But we have a choice whether to embrace it, or waste time resisting it."

Dom gritted his teeth and tried to remember that Tai didn't just mean well. Sometimes he actually made sense. But right now he was talking shit, and Dom concentrated on calming down before Rossi returned. He could see the sergeant ambling down the road with a grubby but well-filled checkered cloth tied in a bundle. He always knew where to get hold of snacks in exchange for favors that Dom didn't ask too many questions about, although they usually involved women.

"He bounced back pretty good after Laurie," Jace murmured. "Never thought he would. Now look at him."

Dom always wondered how Rossi had managed to stop grief paralyzing him completely. He was eating something as he walked, a pastry or a cake. He'd gone apeshit when his paramedic girlfriend—Laurie—was killed in a grub raid when she was recovering bodies, but after a year of plunging down to rock bottom, Rossi seemed to decide he was going to thwart the grub assholes by living well. He screwed everything that moved. Women liked him and didn't seem to feel at all used by him, but there was a war on, and that did strange things to people's inhibitions. Dom kidded himself it wasn't like that in the

Pendulum Wars, but he thought of how young most people were when they got married, and how soon they had kids, let alone all the desperate, last-ditch flings that went on. *I had a wife, a son, and another baby on the way by the time I was eighteen.* Ever-present, random death reminded you what you were brought into this world to do.

Rossi could move on because he'd seen Laurie's body. There was no crazy hope to hang on to.

He opened the driver's door and put the bundle on the seat, then untied it to reveal a shiny brown loaf. The heady aroma of freshly baked bread filled the compartment as he tore the bread into chunks. "Okay, who's up for a nice bit of sourdough?" he asked. "I had to trade my virginity for this again, so I hope you assholes are grateful."

"Baby, you're supposed to pay *her*," Jace laughed.

"She's not like that. Is it my fault that women always want to exploit my affectionate and trusting nature?" Rossi chewed contentedly. "Now, Dom, are you going to tell me what the problem is, or do I have to beat it out of you?"

"What problem?"

"Don't give me that bullshit. I'm a sergeant. I've got eyes in my ass. I know your every thought. Look at you."

I just have to brazen this out. "I'm okay," Dom said.

"Yeah, and you've stopped at every working public phone we've passed for the last month or two, so I'm guessing you've got trouble." Rossi licked his fingers and wiped them on his pants before brushing the crumbs off the seat. "Which means it's a lead on Maria, or it's about Marcus. Am I right?"

Dom just sat staring at the back of Jace's head. Rossi started the engine and took the radio handset off the dash, thumb resting on the button.

"Okay, that's three-stripes-right, then," he said. "Maria? Is there money involved? I can always get intel out of Stranded, Dom. For free."

Dom found himself shaking his head purely out of reflex. "Look . . ."

"It's Marcus, then. Smuggling stuff into jail for him?"

Rossi never gave up. A couple of Reavers streaked overhead, pursued by a Raven, and he didn't move a muscle. The explosion and fall of debris was so close that small fragments rattled on the Packhorse's roof. Jace and Tai said nothing. It was a long, awkward moment.

"Getting him out," Dom said at last. "Which is why I never said."

"I'm not going to stop you."

"No, but if you know, then—"

"I'm just pissed off that you didn't ask me if I wanted in." Rossi slipped the gear lever and pulled out from the curb. "So, while we're on our way, you can bring me up to speed."

They were heading for the Andius highway. Nobody except Gears patrols ever ventured past the wire to Andius these days, but the road was a handy defensive position to set up mobile artillery and air defenses on the western side of the city. Now the grubs had taken a kilometer of road and a corridor of the suburbs next to it.

They'd been sitting there for days, just blocking the road and driving off counterattacks.

Dom tried to work out what they were stalling for. Were they waiting for reinforcements? Did they know something else was coming, and just wanted to stop the COG moving heavy armor for a while?

Nobody could afford to wait and find out. The grubs had to be beaten back. They'd almost reached West Barricade to the south of the highway, and they were already in control of East Barricade. There was now just a strip between the two districts that the COG still held.

And that was why the Slab was cut off on its isolated spur of granite. Dom was clear what he was fighting for today.

"Okay, I paid a guy to spring Marcus, but it depends on a supply truck making a drop to the Slab," he said at last.

Rossi didn't bat an eye. "And what are you going to do with him when you get him out? Hide him in someone's attic? Yeah, he'll love that. He'll just wait it out, good as gold."

"I'll worry about that when I have to." Dom knew that was going to be tough, but it'd be far easier to think of something when he was face to face with Marcus and could talk some sense into him. "All that matters is I get him out of that shithole."

"Is he still refusing to take phone calls?"

"Yeah. He's working hard on not existing."

"And someone's going to stroll in and kidnap him. Because that's what it's going to take."

"Yeah."

Rossi turned the corner past a temporary soup kitchen, where families driven out of the suburbs during the last grub assault were having lunch doled out to them. Dom found it easy not to worry about where they slept and how they got through the day. But then he'd wonder where Maria was right now, and who was making sure she got fed, and seeing the displaced folks suddenly became too much for him. Maria had hardly been able to put a meal on the table before she walked out of the house and never came back.

"I'd bet that if you asked any pilot to do an extraction, they'd have said yes," Rossi said. "You've had years to ask us. We could have come up with a scam to walk Marcus out of there with forged papers or some admin shit that Anya could—"

"No, there's no Anya in this," Dom said. "She doesn't know. Keep her out of it."

Rossi shrugged. "Okay, but if this doesn't work, I reserve the right to come up with a better idea. Like when they have to evacuate the prison. Because they will, sooner or later. You ever think of that?"

The Packhorse rolled past the old city walls that ran parallel to the north of East Barricade, passing a column of 'Dills heading the other way. Rossi switched radio channels so they could hear the voice traffic on the open net.

"*KR-Six-One to Control, we've got eyes on six or seven Brumaks in position.*"

"*Roger that, Six-One. Any movement?*"

"*Breaking off, Control, Reavers on my six.*"

"How's Mathieson doing?" Jace asked, as if none of that was happening.

"Having physio now," Rossi said. "Hoffman's promised him a job in Ops or CIC once they get him a wheelchair."

"Can't keep that guy down." Jace shoved a few more clips into his belt. "So, we still goin' into the sewer?"

"That's the idea. If that's how they're moving around between East Barricade and the road, we burn 'em out."

"Without blowing up the city."

"They've trashed the whole sector anyway," Rossi said. "Worst we can do is blow up grub-held areas."

Dom started thinking about accessing the Slab through the sewer system and made a mental note to ask Staff Sergeant Parry for a look at the utility company's plans. They'd had a thousand prisoners inside at one time, so there still had to be a fair-sized sewerage network under there.

No, that's never going to work. Forget the commando stuff. You're ignoring the big problem. Marcus isn't going to cooperate with any of this unless he absolutely has to. Rossi was right.

Maybe Verdier would have somewhere outside the wire where he could stash Marcus for a while. The guy did business with everyone. Dom would check that out as soon as he got back.

If I get back.

"Okay, pegs on noses, lads," Rossi said. "It's shit-kicking time."

He brought the Packhorse to a halt on the embankment opposite East Bar-ricade, where the sappers were drilling test bores. The terraces, redoubts, and sloping banks were the remnants of Jacinto's ancient fortifications from an era when Tyrus had a monarchy and the COG was still centuries away. There'd always been a Haldane Hall here. Sometimes Dom thought about just how long the Fenix family had lived there, and reminded himself that the guy he thought of as an older brother was actually part of the history of the state, with all kinds of responsibilities and expectations that Dom couldn't really begin to imagine. He looked down at the ruined mansion half a kilometer away and found it hard to make the connection. Lennard Parry wandered up to Rossi and held up a tattered blueprint.

"Change of plan," Parry said. He indicated a route on the plan with his fin-ger. "I think they're getting in through the western outfall sewer and tunneling across into the next one. But we've sampled the air down there and it's not just sewer gas. It's full of manufactured methane too."

"What, they've ruptured some gas pipes?"

"Got it in one. They're pretty careless diggers, Corpsers."

"So we can't operate down there."

"I wouldn't recommend starting a firefight unless you want to be the first man in space."

"Okay, so we just lay some charges and press the button."

"I've spoken to Hoffman. He says if it stops them bringing up reinforce-ments for a few weeks, then he'll live with the damage. It's not like we can use the sewer now anyway. The utility company won't shut off the gas until we ask them to. They've accepted we're going to shove a nice big fireball through the system."

"We'll take care of that for you, then. Might as well, seeing as we're here."

"Very decent of you, Drew. I'd love to spend an hour *not* up to my knees in other people's crap for a change."

"Okay, start clearing your guys out and get the utility company to shut down at their end." Rossi beckoned to Dom and the others. "My lovely commando-trained assistant here will rig some charges. Jace, you ever done this? Watch Dom and learn."

"This really *is* blowing shit up, right?" Jace said.

"Very witty." Parry handed out flashlights and a hand-drawn map that looked like the Jacinto metro. "Crack on with it. Because once we do this, we've got to run like hell."

Dom took the canvas rucksack of charges and wires and lowered himself through the manhole to climb down the metal ladder. The sewer was one of the grand old Age of Silence wonders, an amazing construction project for its time, but it was showing its age. The brick lining of the vaulted ceiling had crumbled away in various places. At times like this, Dom regretted not wearing a helmet. He stepped down into the water—calf-high, nothing too deep—and switched on the flashlight.

"Wow." Jace dropped down after him, followed by Tai and Rossi. "Look at all that damn *carving*. Why'd they bother, when there's only turds and rats gonna see it?"

The pillars and walkways along the length of the sewer were beautifully decorated with stylized flowers and rope-edged borders. It did seem a waste of effort. "Because they *could*," Dom said. "Kind of proving how rich and sophisticated they were."

"And we're gonna blow it up."

"Don't get all cultural on me," said Rossi. "Just think of the plastic pipe guys and all the paying work they'll have one day."

The air smelled like the city after a grub strike—the strong sulfur odor that the utility company added to gas so they could detect leaks. That got Dom's attention much more than the sewage smells. He listened for grubs, hearing only trickling water.

"Okay, lay charges every ten meters," he said. "Mount 'em on the walls with a thirty-second delay, because if we can't get a radio signal down here, then we need to detonate before we climb out. Should be easy to jam a spike in the pointing and keep them clear of the water."

"How far are we gonna go in?" Jace asked.

"We've got enough charges for five hundred meters. That's more than enough to collapse the sewer, let alone ignite the methane."

Tai and Rossi went ahead to check out the tunnels, flashlight beams bouncing off the walls and the surface of the water. That meant using their Lancers one-handed or dropping the flashlights. Parry wouldn't thank them for that. Dom stopped a couple of times to make sure Jace was wiring the dets properly as they waded further down the tunnel.

Splashing made Dom look up. Tai was jogging toward him. Rossi appeared a few seconds later.

"We hear them," Tai whispered. He put his finger to his lips. "The grubs are down here."

"How close?"

Rossi aimed his flashlight at a point on the map. "Hundred, two hundred meters from about here, possibly. Hard to tell with the acoustics."

"You want us to keep laying more dets?"

"Another fifty meters, then we get out and blow the place. Can't risk a fire-fight down here."

"Unless we have to."

"Dom, suicide missions make terrific movies, but I'd rather keep trained guys for another day. Let's do it."

They waded on and placed more charges at the next ten-meter interval, and the next three, and then waited for a moment in silence. Dom was unsettled both by what he could see and *not* see. As he shone his light on the water, he watched it shiver like a cup of coffee on an unsteady table. And there were no rats. He'd expected the sewer to be full of them, but they'd gone a long way into the sewer and seen nothing at all. The grubs were excavating somewhere. The rats were too smart to hang around.

"I think we'd better go now," he said.

Rossi edged up to a junction with another tunnel and peered around the corner. "Yeah," he said. "Good time to clock off, I reckon. I can hear splashing."

If the grubs were coming their way and wading through the water, then they probably wouldn't hear over the sound of their own splashing if anyone broke into a run. Dom was willing to risk slipping on some shit and falling in. They'd have thirty seconds to get out of the manhole and put as much distance as they could between them and the sewer. It seemed to take forever to get back to the ladder and for a moment Dom thought they'd taken the wrong turn. Then the light levels rose and he spotted the shaft of light that marked the open manhole. The sound of grubs somewhere behind them—grumbling animal sounds and steady splashing—meant they had even less time than they'd planned.

"Okay," Rossi said. "Everybody out."

Dom waited for Tai and Jace to clear the opening, then shoved Rossi. "You first. I'll detonate when I'm halfway up the ladder, okay?"

"Don't piss around."

"I won't. Go on, get going."

Thirty seconds. How far he could run in that time? It wasn't a bad head start. He positioned the det in one hand so that he could operate it with his thumb and climbed nine rungs up the ladder, still beneath the level of the roof and metal reinforcement. Another three would take him to the top. Rossi peered down the hole.

"Ready?"

"In three . . ."

Two.

One.

Dom pressed the button and threw the detonator up to Rossi to leave both hands free to scramble out of the hole. He found himself sprinting across the short turf and wondering who'd mowed it. Then he realized there must have been loads of grazing rabbits around, the dumbest and most irrelevant thing he'd ever thought when he was seconds from being minced to hamburger.

"Move it move it *move it!*" Rossi yelled.

Dom found himself thinking *fifteen seconds*, like he'd counted or anything. The engineers were nowhere to be seen. He kept going, neck and neck with Rossi, wondering why the hell the charges hadn't blown yet and thinking he'd screwed it and they'd wasted their time. Then the ground shook. A few seconds later, a loud explosion split the air a long way behind him. He turned—something he'd been warned never to do—and saw the weirdest sight imaginable. A disc was spinning in the air like a coin, falling toward land. Another loud boom sent something arcing high into the air. It wasn't until the disc hit the paving with a loud metallic clunk and shattered the concrete that he realized it was a manhole cover blown out by the detonating gases. The damn manholes were blowing all along the line of the sewer. It was almost comic.

"Well, *that* did the trick," Rossi panted, hands braced on his knees. "Bye-bye, grub boys."

The ground was still trembling. Dom didn't like the feel of it. He could see the line of a wall and some trees that ran along the earthworks between the redoubts, and the wall was starting to sag in the middle.

"Oh shit," he said. "There goes the sewer."

The trees tipped slowly at a crazy angle. Yeah, he was right about the rabbits: they appeared from nowhere, racing around in a panic and looking for cover. All Dom could focus on was the landscape changing as half a kilometer of ancient tunnels and brickwork caved in and dragged the landscape of the old barricades down with it. The rumbling, groaning noises went on for minutes like a slow earthquake. Birds abandoned trees that weren't even close to the blast zone.

Rossi got on the radio. Dom could hear the conversation in his earpiece. "Bravo to Three-E-E, over. Parry? Dom's made a dirty great hole in Jacinto."

"Parry here. Tell him he's an honorary sapper. Hope it damn well works."

Dom could still feel movement under his boots. Every Gear was hypersensitive to vibrations, the only early warning they usually got of a grub emergence. He couldn't move until it stopped. He kept his rifle trained on the ground, even though he knew what was causing the tremors.

"Come on, Dom," Rossi said. "Damage done. Grubs fucked. Rinse your boots off and let's go."

Dom had more personal problems on his mind now than how many grubs he'd char-grilled or buried in the sewer. Marcus was still stuck in the Slab, the grubs still held the Andius highway, and somewhere out there, way beyond the wire, Maria needed him.

Does she think about me? Does she wonder why I haven't come for her? Does she even remember me?

He had to believe she did. He jogged back to the Packhorse and looked over his shoulder at the dent he'd put in the map of Tyrus.

"Way to go, Dom," Jace said. "Damn, you're gonna sink the whole city one day."

CHAPTER 14

You have no understanding yet of the things that we in power must do to ensure the survival and welfare of the state. When you realize what you have to do, your life will change forever, and you can never be like other men again. This is a one-way journey.

(Chairman David Prescott, to his young son Richard.)

THE SLAB: FIRST WEEK OF BLOOM, 13 A.E.

It was a shitty situation, but it had its moments.

The Slab had now been cut off by the grub incursion for more than a month. Reeve had learned all the right words for it because he'd spent years learning Gearspeak from Marcus, not that the guy had been the most talkative of buddies. For the prisoners, a few weeks without supplies was business as usual, but for the two warders stuck here with them—well, role reversal was a beautiful thing.

Because the staff had left the inmates to fend for themselves and live largely off what they grew and produced, the prisoners now had a food supply and the warders didn't. And the screws were effectively imprisoned here with the rest of them. Reeve tried not to gloat, but he was in a minority. Jarvi and Ospen were stranded in the prison with only a phone line for company, and Merino had put a twenty-six-hour guard on the kitchens and the yard.

Ospen stood at the barred door that marked the divide between the worlds. Merino was leaning against the wall on the other side, beaming. Reeve watched with the other inmates. It was great theater.

"Good morning, Officer," Merino said. "And how are you?"

"I want to talk," Ospen said.

"Got all the time in the world, buddy."

"Let's trade."

Merino rattled the keys on his belt, warder-style. Boy, Jarvi's timing had been fantastic. "What have you got that we could possibly want?"

"Cut the crap, Merino. We're starving. We're living on a hundred grams of rice and five centimeters of sausage a day."

"Sounds like a *euphemism* to me, officer. The sausage, I mean. Yeah, I'd want more than five centimeters . . ."

That got a belly laugh from the inmates. Merino probably wouldn't have done it to Jarvi, but this was Ospen and everyone knew what the bastard had gotten up to over the years. Now they were making him pay. It was just too bad that Jarvi was collateral damage. Reeve wanted to do something about that. Behind the crowd of prisoners enjoying turned tables for once in their lives, the doors to the outer yard opened and Marcus walked in with a bucket brimming with greens, the early summer crops. He glanced at Ospen and tilted his head slowly to one side like the whole tableau fascinated him.

"Okay, Merino, what do you want?" Ospen asked.

Merino's smile faded a line at a time. "You're a thieving motherfucker," he said. "You've been skimming off our supplies ever since the day you started here, and as far as I'm concerned, watching you starve to death could be the proof I need that there *is* a god after all."

"A-fuckin'-*men!*" Chunky cheered, still busy with some goddamn crochet or hook-work or whatever the hell it was now. He roared with laughter. "Testify, brother!"

"Yeah, time you tried eating the dog food," Leuchars sneered.

Ospen wasn't the worst screw they could have been saddled with. The drafted prison guards were nothing like the handpicked career sadists who'd staffed the Slab when it was fully operational, because the older inmates recalled the last of those, and the stories they'd told Reeve about the regime made it sound like a Gorasni labor camp. Ospen was just rotten, like most humans were when they were given the opportunity to get away with something for nothing. But this was the wrong time to be the guy who stole supplies. Yeah, maybe there was a god after all.

Ospen's jaw tightened. "Remember this blockade isn't going to last forever. You're going to have to face us sooner or later."

Merino turned around slowly and began doing an exaggerated head count of the inmates. "One, two, three, four . . . stop me if I'm outnumbering you, Officer Ospen."

"I'm going to make you pay for this, you asshole."

"You could unlock that door, walk in, and try it right now. But you're too scared to. You won't let the dogs loose, either, because you're too scared of them as well." Merino looked in Marcus's direction. "Damn shame Campbell wasn't on duty instead of Jarvi. Would have been educational for him to stroll in here on his own, eh, Fenix?"

Marcus looked Ospen up and down. "I hear you got drafted," he said. "Don't worry. The army'll wait for you."

"Who asked your goddamn opinion?"

"That's no way to talk to the man with the cabbages."

"You're fucking enjoying this, aren't you?"

Merino laughed. "Payback."

"Just remember who's got the rifles."

Marcus sort of perked up at that. Reeve had a pretty good idea now of what would kick off his temper—boy, did he have one, however tightly he reined it in—and threats were close to the top of the list.

"You've got a hundred rounds," Marcus said. "I'm betting you couldn't make a fifth of them count. That'd leave you unarmed with twenty of us still standing."

Ospen was getting madder by the second. "Well, while you're feeling full of shit about that, asshole, I'm the guy who's supposed to be fixing your ticket out of here. You want to think about that?"

It all went quiet. Marcus froze for a moment and then shouldered his way forward through the small crowd. "You *what*?" he growled.

"You heard. Your buddy paid to spring you."

Marcus didn't seem to need to ask who that was. The blood really did drain from his face. It was hard to tell whether he was shocked or furious or both.

"Fucking *idiot*," he snarled. Reeve thought he meant Ospen, but maybe not. He slammed the bucket down and stood looking at the floor, arms at his side and fists balled. "Goddamn it."

He stalked off back to the cells. Nobody had any idea what was going on, but Ospen decided to get lippy. "I knew that'd shut you up." He looked at Merino. "So what about a deal? Some of the carp. You can spare some fish."

Merino pushed himself away from the wall and the inmates started dispersing. "Go fuck yourself, Ospen. Ask the Chairman for an air drop."

Reeve went after Marcus. He wanted to think it was concern for the guy, but the idea that someone was trying to get him out three years after he'd been convinced they'd all done as he'd asked and forgotten him was . . . compelling.

Gears could get in anywhere and do pretty well anything from what Reeve could gather. If they could take on grubs hand to hand, then breaking into the Slab was probably a piece of piss for them. When he caught up with Marcus, he was back in his cell giving himself a haircut with a razor, using a piece of broken glass propped at an angle for a mirror. He still kept his hair army-short and shaved every day while he waited for his personal war to resume. He didn't even look at Reeve.

"I take it you didn't know about that," Reeve said.

"Of course I didn't frigging know."

"So he's still got your back after all these years. That's some buddy you've got there. Dom, yeah?"

"I've only got one."

"He doesn't give up easy."

Marcus swung around, razor pointed like a finger to make his point. "How the hell has he paid for anything? He's got fuck all to sell, so what's he done to pay? Shit, maybe Anya's in this too. I *told* them. I told them to damn well *forget* me."

Reeve had to ask. "So what are going to do?"

"What do you mean, what am I going to do?"

"You didn't even ask Ospen what the plan was."

"That's because I'm not doing it."

"Aw, come *on*."

Marcus's temper was a weird, cold thing. He didn't rage and shout. It was more growling through gritted teeth, all simmering fury, and just occasionally it erupted in a silent, instant punch. He went back to his haircut. If he'd calmed down and thought about it, he could have asked Chunky to do it because the guy owned the one set of clippers in the Slab these days. He was using them to trim his rag mats.

"Marcus, you'd be more use out there than in here," Reeve said. "Admit it."

"I'm in here for a reason. I got guys killed."

"Do it for Dom, then."

Marcus did that slow turn that said he was low on patience. "I'd do *anything* for Dom. But I won't let him fuck up his life for me. They'll catch him, and they'll shoot him."

Reeve held his hands up in mute surrender and walked away. It was always the best thing to do, because there was no arguing with Marcus. Crazy bastard: he was throwing away a chance to get out of here. Reeve suspected that after all this time nobody would give a damn what he'd done as long as he could still shoot straight. The war wasn't exactly going well and that was obvious even inside the granite walls of the prison. Reeve could hear the steady pounding of guns and the drone of Ravens overhead. The grubs weren't giving way. When he went out into the yard—a little more risky these days because of the Reavers—he could see the smoke to the northeast, toward the city. But the Slab seemed to be forgotten by both humans and grubs.

Jarvi was leaning on the windowsill above the yard, staring up at the sky. Reeve thought he had to be missing his wife. He didn't know if Ospen was married, but if he was, his missus must have been grateful for the break.

Damn, this might go on for months.

"We should have stuck the psychos in the freezer." Edouain walked up and stood beside him. "Terrible waste of protein."

"Ruskin had all the recipes, though." The nutters had all been cremated in the far corner of the yard on a makeshift bonfire. Nobody from the JD had shown up and nothing had been said, so either Jarvi hadn't reported it—who was counting, after all?—or he had and nobody in authority gave a shit, which was more likely. "I hope Jarvi *didn't* tell the JD, actually. They'll only cut our rations when the supply drops resume."

"The water's flooding back through the old tunnel, by the way."

"So?"

"It started last month when there were all those explosions."

"Jarvi said he was told they collapsed the sewers to stop the grubs."

"Well, that worked a treat, didn't it?"

Two Ravens flew low overhead, drowning out all conversation for a few moments. All the rules had changed. Authority had lost control both inside the prison and outside, but there was nowhere worth escaping to, just as Merino had always said. Sitting here and waiting for the worst wasn't an option, though. It was a terrible limbo that Reeve could only stand the same way as everyone else—simply by focusing on surviving the day, which meant concentrating on the food supply.

The fighting went on the next day, and the next, and the day after that. Marcus went back to his daily round of exercise and endless damn digging in the yard, but he seemed to have stopped talking completely, like he was so angry about this Dom guy and his rescue that he couldn't stop rehearsing the argument in his head.

It was definitely getting to him. Everyone in this place had their bad days, their sleepless nights, and the goddamn dogs didn't help matters much with their barking and whining, but Marcus had nightmares. Reeve didn't sleep too

well and in a cell block with only forty guys in it, he heard pretty well everything some nights. He'd lost count of the times that he'd laid awake and heard
Marcus wake up with a yelp, panting like he'd run a marathon, or listened to
him pacing up and down or even doing his goddamn exercises at some ludi-
crous hour. Reeve could always hear the thud as he dropped down from doing
chins on the joist. Anya must have had the patience of a saint to put up with all
that. But maybe Marcus was a totally different guy when he was back among
the people he cared about.

Reeve doubted that, though.

Ospen didn't come back and try to do any more deals. For a few days, Reeve
didn't even see anything of Jarvi, although he was pretty sure that Marcus
slipped him some vegetables when nobody was looking. He was out in the
yard all day and Jarvi spent a fair bit of time at that window. Reeve didn't mind
as long as Jarvi didn't share any of the food with Ospen, because the bastard
deserved to choke.

Two men couldn't make their own supplies last forever, though.

One morning around the end of the month—Reeve had to check the days
marked off on someone else's cell wall, because he'd given up counting long
ago—Chunky came down the hall, slapping his hands to get attention and
summon everyone.

"Officer Jarvi wants to talk," he said. "Come on, folks, let's listen to the man."

Jarvi stood at the door, looking as threadbare and gaunt as any of the
inmates. He had a rifle slung on his back. It seemed more precaution than
threat, but he definitely looked resigned to something.

"Guys," he said. "This isn't going to end anytime soon. There's a kilometer
of wall-to-wall grubs out there, and we're in this shit together."

The small crowd of prisoners parted to let Merino through. Reeve couldn't
see Marcus. "Well, you're not going to offer us our freedom, obviously,"
Merino said. "Because we're not dumb enough to walk out there. So I'm en-
thralled. Do tell."

"I've got to shoot the dogs," Jarvi said. "We're running out of dog food, and
we might even need that ourselves, but . . . well, hungry dogs are too damn
dangerous for my liking."

There was a brief silence, then a ripple of cheers. "Fuck *yeah*," Leuchars
said. "If you think that's going to get you on our good side, great. But you can't
handle them without Parmenter around anyway."

"No, I meant that if you guys want any meat, I'll swap it for some mycoprotein or vegetables, and somewhere to store the carcasses."

Reeve had to give Jarvi points for presentation. He just said it and waited. Damn, the dogs were still barking out there somewhere, even howling. But the guys in here had probably eaten a whole lot worse over the years without realizing it or asking too many questions, and meat was meat.

"Including Jerry?" Chunky asked.

"Why, you fond of him or something?"

"No, but Parmenter's gonna go nuts."

"Parmenter's not starving," Jarvi said.

"Okay." Merino nodded, doing his I-can-be-reasonable act. "But you show us twelve dead mutts, or the deal's off."

"Done," said Jarvi.

Reeve just looked at Merino as the inmates wandered off, grumbling. "You're not that keen on filet of Pellesian, are you?"

"No," Merino said. "But I like the idea of evening up the odds."

About an hour later, the first shots rang out, two close together. Reeve was washing his smalls in a bowl in the yard, enjoying the sunshine and only taking the minimum notice of the ongoing firefight in the distance. Marcus, still messing around with the damn carp pond like it was his hobby, snapped to attention instantly and laid down the rake he was using to drag weed out of the water. He headed for the doors.

"It's the dogs," Reeve called. "Jarvi's shooting them for meat. All of them."

Marcus changed course and diverted to Reeve's position. "You're shitting me."

"Nope. If you'd shown up earlier, you'd have heard. He's splitting them with us. Course, everyone's going to argue over who gets the mastiff. You got any good dog meat recipes?"

Marcus just looked faintly disgusted. "You're not seriously going to eat that."

"Sure I am." Reeve rolled up his sleeve and reminded Marcus how much was left of his forearm muscles after the dog attack. "Don't you want to sink your teeth in something that sank its teeth in you? Have the last goddamn laugh?"

"I'll try vegetarian," Marcus muttered. "I'm a humorless bastard."

The shooting went on longer than Reeve expected, along with the frantic barking. Either Jarvi wanted to make sure he only expended one round per animal and was having trouble getting clear shots, or he was losing his nerve. Reeve counted the shots. The barking thinned out.

Eight . . . nine . . . ten.

Damn, it couldn't have been easy. Those damn things were loose in a pack, even if they were stuck between the mesh partitions. Reeve tried to think how he'd have tackled that scenario, just to make sure his skills weren't rusting too much.

Eleven.

The barking had stopped completely. Another shot rang out.

Twelve.

"Bye bye, Jerry," Reeve said, and started rinsing his socks.

OFFICE OF THE CHAIRMAN, HOUSE OF SOVEREIGNS: LATE REAP, 13 A.E.

"Sir? Sir, I'm sorry, but you need to hear this."

Jillian hovered in the doorway. Prescott leaned back in his seat, knowing that it had to be important for her to interrupt a transmission to Adam Fenix.

"Wait a moment, Adam," he said. Should he mute the audio? No, he had a pretty good idea what this might be about, and it did Adam no harm to be reminded of the stakes back home in Jacinto. "What is it?"

"The Colonel says they've suppressed the Reavers and they're going into West Barricade now. No promises, he says, but this may have turned the battle."

Prescott gave her a smile. "First good news I've had in weeks. Thank you, Jillian."

She had no choice but to glance at the screen. Wherever Adam sat to receive the video link, the daytime backdrop on Azura was inevitably a window with a view on some exquisite tropical landscape. Prescott watched the reaction on her face, just the merest hint of longing, and wondered when the best time might be to arrange for her to slip out of the city. It would be a shock for her sister, of course, but a knock on the door in the middle of the night and an order to grab a bag and ask no questions was a small price to pay for salvation. Every civilian kept a grab bag by the door anyway. It was part of the compulsory civil emergency drill for a population used to being evacuated time after time.

Jillian closed the door after her and Prescott swiveled in his chair to face Adam again. "Sorry. Where were we?"

"Am I supposed to ask what that was all about?" Adam asked. "You're too diligent to forget to mute the call."

"Perhaps." They knew one another far too well now. "We've been fighting a Locust incursion on the western side of the city for a couple of months, but Hoffman seems to have worn down their air assets. Which means ground forces stand a better chance of pushing into the area and clearing them off the Andius road."

"Ah, and the point being that the prison is in that sector."

"The prison's been cut off for some time," Prescott said.

Adam sat back in his chair and took off his glasses, laying them flat on the desk in front of him and gazing down as he moved the hinged arms back and forth like a child playing with a toy. It was his build-up to a burst of temper.

"And you never thought to mention that, Richard. The last few welfare reports on Marcus were fiction, then."

"No, they're genuine. He's fine. Well, a great deal better than the prison officers, anyway. The inmates seem to be running the place now, but the Justice Department is in regular touch with the senior officer by phone."

"And you're going to assure me that Marcus is safer inside than out."

"I am indeed. Because he is. I do have a vested interest in his welfare beyond guaranteeing your best behavior, Adam."

Sometimes the best way of muddying the waters and shifting Adam from his binary, linear mentality was to tell the whole truth. It wasn't simply a matter of do-this-or-else. It was about leveling with Adam, explaining why Marcus mattered, but in such a way that he understood that his son's life still depended on his cooperation.

Adam was lying again. Prescott knew it but couldn't pin it down. Louise Settile knew it, too. She'd shake it out of him eventually.

"You're dying to tell me," Adam said.

"He's an exceptional soldier. Perfect for small unit and one-man ops. I'll need him again one day, and when the risk to morale passes—when the Gears who thought he should have been shot are so beleaguered that they'll take whatever help they can get—then I'll have him released and deployed."

Adam looked as if he was mulling it over. Prescott hoped he did it fast, not that he needed his consent. The satellite window was brief.

"That's a very elegant threat," Adam said at last. "If I don't cooperate, you'll make him pay for it. But you'll keep him alive for suicide missions. I really have underestimated your capacity for managing complexity, Richard."

"I'm just a lateral thinker," Prescott said. "And I have nothing against your son. Now, is there anything else you want to tell me?"

Adam always paused a heartbeat longer than the satellite delay. Yes, there was something going on there. "No, other than that I'm going to be looking at physical means to destroy the pathogen while Dr. Bakos pursues a pharmaceutical approach. At the risk of repeating myself, if any more Lambent life-forms are found, we really do need samples to monitor its progress in the wild. We're very limited here and there's no guarantee that the organism behaves the same under laboratory conditions as it does in the environment. It's not even the same organism from week to week."

"Understood," Prescott said. "The Lightmass data's being put to good use, by the way, so thank you. And I hope I have some good news for you next time we talk."

Prescott switched off the video link and rolled his head a little to ease his stiff neck. Louise Settile, stretched out in the deep-buttoned leather library chair in the corner, raised her eyebrows at him.

"He's definitely up to something," she said.

"I know. The trouble with Adam is that secrecy is his default. It might not even be anything significant."

"Which is his view of us, of course."

"I didn't say I was blinded by the veil of irony, Lou." His father wouldn't have approved of her, but times had changed beyond his recognition, and she was the only woman Prescott could trust who also functioned on his level. She understood his professional burdens and he understood hers. No aristocratic home-making kind of woman could have risen to that challenge, not in the world he'd inherited, and he needed the kind of companion who would do more than just listen sympathetically. "Look, you *are* going to let Paul do what he does best, aren't you? Leave the intelligence gathering to him."

"I'll be fine. God, if I operated behind Ostri lines in the last war, I can certainly deal with a few Locust."

"But you don't have to."

"And I can't spend all my time on Azura, either. Adam and Nevil are the only remotely interesting challenges there." She bounced up and was suddenly sharp and breezy again. "Got to go, dear. You're sure I can't borrow Marcus Fenix?"

"I'm sure. If anything went wrong, what would I tell Adam?"

"You really *must* learn to lie properly. I mean tell complete, unashamed porkies. All these finely polished technical truths won't get you anywhere. This isn't politics. Nobody's going to discredit you or cause embarrassing headlines, not when we're heading for an apocalypse."

It was almost funny, a spy telling a politician that he needed to stop being so honest. She chuckled, ruffled his hair, and let herself out. Nobody had done that to him habitually since he was seven years old. It was comforting not to have to be Chairman Prescott every second of every day.

No. It's about sanity. Everyone needs someone to unburden themselves to.

Jillian, with all the silent discretion of a priest, opened the main door again two minutes later. "Will you be going over to CIC, sir? Colonel Hoffman's doing a briefing in half an hour."

"Oh, he's not leading the charge today, then?"

"I know he's rude, sir, but he means well."

Prescott made an effort to stop himself feeling sorry for Hoffman. He was there for a reason, like everybody else. *Like me, in fact.* David Prescott had always warned his son that as soon as he allowed one relationship in his life to become more than necessary utility, then he'd begin eroding the steel shell needed to take the kind of decisions that other men were too emotionally tied to countenance. His duty was to care generally, not specifically. It was the only way to survive the numbers game that statesmen were doomed to play: one life for many, one loss to gain more. Prescott had been the one kept in the dark at various times in his career, had accepted it, and now reminded himself that was happening to Hoffman for a good reason. But the steel was definitely beginning to pit. He'd have to keep an eye on that.

"At least I can cheer him up about the Lightmass project." Prescott fastened his tunic and picked up his leather folio. "Would you be a dear and procure me some more of those treacle cookies, by the way? If we're going to break through to Wenlau Heath again soon, I'd like to show up with some comforts for Adam's son. They're eating dogs now, you know."

"People do." Jillian shuddered. "*Worms.* They have worms."

It was a short walk from the office to CIC, something that had once been a pleasant stroll through courtyards and gardens to break up the day and breathe fresh air. The day was as sunny and fragrant as any had been, but the scent was overlaid by brick dust, charred varnish, and the resin odor of sawn wood as the repair teams patched up the House of the Sovereigns complex again. There was only the occasional Reaver strike and small raiding parties of drones, more psychological warfare than real destruction, but it sent a message: *we can get to you, to the heart of your city.* Repairing official buildings sent the riposte: *and we will carry on.* Prescott sent the message not to the enemy but to the citizens of Jacinto.

Only Adam Fenix had tried to speak directly to the Locust. That hadn't ended well.

Hoffman was in the briefing room to address the company commanders and senior NCOs, flanked by Anya Stroud and the young lieutenant who'd lost his legs. Mathieson, that was his name: Donneld Mathieson. It was his first week learning the ropes in CIC. Prescott walked up to him before anyone had a chance to snap to attention and just took the lad's right hand in both of his to shake it. It was an art as well as a courtesy, his father had said: *make people feel they matter, Richard, make them feel you've taken the time to find out their names and who they are.*

"Good to have you back, Donneld," Prescott said. He couldn't recall seeing him before, but that was academic. He might have passed him a hundred times and not seen his face under the helmet. He was terribly, unfairly, unsettlingly *young.* "Let me know if there's anything you need."

Mathieson beamed. "Thank you, sir."

Hoffman just looked at Prescott, nodded, and carried on talking. He looked as if he hadn't slept properly in weeks. Stroud looked exhausted too. Prescott stood back in an alcove and watched the briefing unfold, the charts and overhead projectors showing the Locust positions.

"Okay, people, as of two hours ago, the grubs have fallen back to this line here." Hoffman dragged his finger along the transparent sheet, casting a thick black shadow on the projection. "Mostly drones and Boomers. Three batteries from Six-POA are currently pushing them out of West Barricade, and Eight-Oh-Two Raven squadron is concentrating on the Brumaks. Time's of the essence. We don't know how long it'll be before they can deploy Reavers again. So I want every Gear from the northwest boundary and the East Barricade corridor pulled up to *here.*" He tapped his finger on Brodeau Square. "Alpha and Echo companies push through *here* and clear the area building by building, Connaught and Chevron divert either side *here* and close on the grub positions on the Andius highway. I want to see a carpet of dead grubs ten deep, people. Get to it. And Rossi?"

"Yes, sir?"

"Don't leave without me, you hear?"

Prescott watched officers and NCOs almost jog out of the briefing room, charged with determination. This was what Hoffman was born for. *This* was what made him far more valuable deployed in Jacinto than sitting around on Azura doing strategic planning with Bardry. He was a hands-on commander willing to share the hard graft with ordinary Gears. The troops loved that and would do anything for him. Prescott had once thought that it was astute leadership, but he'd discovered very quickly that Hoffman simply wanted to fight, get his wars over with, and keep the maximum number of his men alive, and he thought little beyond that. He was also willing to do whatever it took to win. His service record wasn't pretty, but by God it was *effective,* and one of

Prescott's first moves when Dalyell's death had thrust him into office was to make sure that Victor Hoffman was lined up to become his senior commander on the ground.

And I did pick the right man. I wish we could be more cordial, but that's not going to stop either of us from getting the job done.

"Did you want to see me, Chairman?" Hoffman asked.

"It can wait," Prescott said. "Just wanted to let you know that the Lightmass bomb will be ready to deploy within a few months. They've fixed their imaging problem. It's a manufacturing issue now."

Hoffman actually looked happier for a moment. "I won't open the champagne yet, but that's a welcome development."

He went out after Rossi, one of his pet NCOs from his old regiment, 26 RTI, which was more tribal than any other. Prescott got the feeling that if the COG ever collapsed, the Royal Tyran Infantry would just carry on and become its own little military state without a backward glance.

"Sir?" Anya Stroud hovered uncertainly at his elbow. "May I ask you a question?"

"Of course, Lieutenant."

Prescott had known her for years. She was reliable, uncomplaining, and shiningly loyal to Hoffman, not that Prescott didn't respect that. And he knew roughly what was on her mind now and had been every day since that court-martial. Perhaps this was an opportunity to consolidate an ally, given the tactical power that CIC staff could wield on his behalf.

"The prison, sir," Anya said. "It's very difficult to get information. They've been cut off for weeks."

"It's all right, I know why you're worried. You don't have to skate around the topic."

"Oh." Poor woman: she looked crushed. "I know I've broken Sov's Regs, sir, and I'll take whatever disciplinary action might be coming. But Sergeant Fenix doesn't deserve . . . sorry, I shouldn't have asked. Forget I mentioned it."

"No, speak your mind. It's an awful situation and it gives me no pleasure, believe me."

"He's never written back to me and he won't take calls. I'm concerned for his mental state, let alone his health."

"Does he get your letters?"

"I think so. I write every week. Sometimes I save them up for a month, but I send them in the internal mail. Some of them must have got through, surely."

Prescott knew Marcus's determination to make everyone forget him. This

wasn't the time to tell Anya that they'd discussed it. "I can't treat him differently from any other Gear, and he's already had his sentence commuted," he
said quietly. "But would it help if I took a letter there personally? I'm going to
take a look at the whole western sector when the Locust have been pushed
back. It'd be no trouble."

Prescott had planned to drop in anyway, to be able to update Adam
with some sincerity. He hadn't lied to her. He really hadn't. Anya's eyes
brimmed.

"You have no idea how much that means to me, sir."

Oh, I do. "Give the envelope to my secretary and I'll personally hand it to
Marcus. I promise you that." He lowered his voice even further. "Standing by
someone in these circumstances is admirable, Lieutenant. I don't think anyone will discipline you for an inappropriate relationship now."

He stopped short of patting her arm. She looked as if that might tip her over
the edge into tears, and he wanted to leave her with some dignity so that she
could appreciate he'd done her a favor rather than embarrassed her.

One day, he'd need her to do something for him. And he'd need Marcus
Fenix, too. People at the lower end of the pecking order could often make or
break plans far more effectively than those with the most apparent power.

This was no time to make new enemies, least of all among those who
handled information.

THE SLAB: TWO DAYS LATER.

"Fenix? Get up here and tell me what's going on."

Niko had nothing to lose now. There was nowhere to go, and his chances
of enforcing order on the Slab were close to zero. He settled into what he
hoped was an inconspicuous position on the roof and adjusted the binoculars.
Marcus climbed out of the roof hatch and squatted beside him, hand held out.

"Binos," he said impatiently. "Come on."

A long, slow whistling sound made Niko look up, but he couldn't see where
it was coming from. Then the world shook like he was being rattled around in
a glass jar. Something dropped past him, fizzing, and he dodged it, but when
he looked around there was nothing on the flat section of roof. It was still rain-
ing down on him. He couldn't even see it. It was just that hissing noise. Marcus ignored it. He wasn't even wearing his working shirt today, just a singlet,
but he didn't appear to feel at risk. Niko was certain he'd feel naked without
armor. Perhaps he was inviting a bullet.

"It's only tiny pieces of shrapnel," Marcus said. "There's nothing left when it lands. It just heats up the air."

"What's happening out there? I still can't get any answers out of the JD."

"You can't expect them to know what's going on."

"Just tell me who's winning."

Marcus spent a few moments watching the sporadic fire across the heathland. Niko could see plenty of grubs hunkered down behind rubble and logs they'd dragged into position over the last week, firing over the top of the barrier and getting plenty returned from the other side. They were clustered under the elevated section of the highway, shielded from the Ravens overflying the area. It seemed to be going on forever.

"Nobody can tell until it's over," Marcus said at last.

"Shit."

"You never did say what your emergency plan was."

"Evacuation."

"Yeah, without transport. I heard. But how do you ship out forty guys into a war zone anyway?"

"I have no idea."

"Exactly." Marcus seemed to have fixed on something to the southeast. "Lot of 'Dills out there."

Niko could now identify artillery down to the type of gun, and he could hear the slow, steady *pom-pom-pom* of an old Brader that sent palls of smoke rising into the air on the east side of the highway. The road obscured most of the fighting in the neighborhood. All he could do was guess what was happening. Suddenly he could see a lot of activity on the grub-occupied section of the highway as a couple of Troika guns swung 90 degrees and pointed south. The grubs under the elevated section looked up, straining for a sight of what was going on above them but trying to avoid stepping out into the open. Then Niko spotted what had grabbed their attention.

The biggest bulldozer Niko had ever seen was trundling up the center of the road with an arrow formation of 'Dills tight behind it like a skein of heavily armored, pissed-off geese. It was straddling the center divide with its blade mowing down the barrier. Grub rounds began pinging off the vehicle. Marcus grunted approvingly, but he was looking in the opposite direction. He'd really perked up. He looked like he was gagging to get down there and join in.

"Now that's going to *hurt*," he said.

Niko looked north. No wonder the grubs were going crazy. Another huge bulldozer was heading south, crushing the central barrier under its tracks,

dozer blade held up like a shield. He guessed there were more APCs in formation behind it. The two bulldozers were converging at a fair old lick and
anything between them on that bridge was going to be history pretty soon.
Makeshift barriers and gun positions were swept aside. The collisions sounded
like explosions. The bulldozers just kept coming.

"What the hell are those?" Niko asked.

"Mammoths," Marcus said. "They lay bridges and trackway on the battlefield. I didn't know we still had any running."

They seemed to come as a surprise to the grubs, too. The drones and Boomers held their ground until the Mammoths got within fifty meters, then the
drones parted and tried to slip around to the sides of the dozer blades. Either
they couldn't see what was bringing up the rear or they had nowhere left to
run, but whatever their reason, the wedge of 'Dills opened up as soon as the
grubs got past the Mammoths. The only escape was a sixty-meter drop over the
side of the highway. Some took it. The Mammoths kept trundling on, finally
slowing down as the Boomers refused to give way and went under the tracks.

Niko had never seen anything like it. He was transfixed. He looked at Marcus, expecting some reaction, but the guy was just shifting from foot to foot,
visibly frustrated. The Mammoths backed up and gave each other room to
maneuver. By now the grubs on the highway had simply been swept off it or
mown down, and Gears had dismounted from the 'Dills and were hosing the
grubs below.

That was when common sense seemed to get the better of the drones under
the highway, and they made a run for it. They were heading straight across the
heath.

"Goddamn." Marcus laid down the binoculars and held out his hand to
Niko again. "Give me the rifle."

"What?"

"Give me the frigging rifle."

"I can't."

"For fuck's sake, I'm going to *shoot grubs*." Marcus's voice had dropped to a
growl. "Cut the crap and hand it over. I'll give it back when I'm done."

"They can't get in here."

"I don't care about that. I don't want them surviving to kill more Gears. You
got that?"

Niko had eaten dog and handed keys over to inmates. Giving a trained
Gear a rifle seemed pretty sensible by comparison. Marcus took the weapon
from him, checked the magazine, slid the safety off, and sighted up. The grubs

were jogging across the open ground, dodging fire from the highway. Marcus waited, one elbow resting on the parapet, squinting down the sights.

Then he fired. Niko didn't even see the round strike, but a grub was on the ground and Marcus aimed again. *Crack.* Another grub went down. This time Niko saw the round take a chunk out of its skull. Marcus kept going, patiently picking off a grub every few seconds until one of them found the nerve to stop dead and return fire. Something zipped past Niko like a bee. It took him a few moments to realize he'd just missed getting his brains blown out. Nobody had ever shot at him before, and he wasn't sure if he was rattled by the close shave or indignant. Marcus seemed to take it in his stride.

That was what the guy been waiting for all these years: to kill more grubs. But he didn't seem to be glorying in it. He was absolutely silent and deliberate, simply taking shot after careful shot. Niko couldn't tell if he'd brought down a grub every time, but he was definitely ahead on points. Marcus was now almost leaning over the parapet, firing down at a tight angle. Then he stopped and knelt back on one heel.

"Lost 'em," he said. He put the safety catch on and handed the rifle back to Niko. "Happy now?"

A couple of 'Dills were hurtling at full speed toward the prison, presumably chasing the grubs. Niko took the rifle back and stared at it, sobered at what it could do in the hands of an expert.

"Are you?"

"Not until I kill every last one of those assholes."

Marcus hung around on the roof for a while, still looking out in the direction of the highway as if he was longing for a few more targets. The shelling had stopped. The automatic fire was coming from behind the Slab, as if the Gears had caught up with the grubs on the edge of the escarpment and were hosing them.

"Well, there goes the JD's excuse for not sending supplies," Marcus muttered, grabbing the handrail and stepping backward down the hatch. "Better call your clerk and tell him to pull his goddamn finger out."

"Hey, Fenix?"

"What?"

"You're pretty good at what you do."

Marcus's expression shifted for a second from his permanent frown to something like regret. "Yeah, I was," he said.

He could have shot me. Then picking off Ospen would have been simple. And then he could have just unlocked the doors, and everyone would be out. But he didn't.

If a dodgy delivery truck showed up, Niko was sure now that he'd help them shove Marcus in the back even if he had to truss him up to do it. Whatever Marcus's beef was with the army, he really shouldn't have been in this dump.

Niko now had to get the Slab back on what passed for a normal security footing. He unlocked the main doors and followed Marcus back into D Wing. But Campbell and the others would soon be back on duty, and Parmenter would have a blue fit about the dogs. Nothing else had changed, though. Niko still had to run this place with three warders, and now that the dogs were gone, maybe the JD would decide he didn't really need Parmenter either. It was like they were leaving him with no choice but to abandon the place, with or without the inmates inside.

Merino was sitting in the yard having a smoke. Niko decided to stay social now that everyone was behaving. He risked walking up to the door with Marcus, knowing the rifle wouldn't save him if the prisoners decided to get assy.

"You look almost cheerful, Fenix," Merino said. "Did we win?"

"He shot a few grubs," Niko said. Marcus didn't join in and just walked up the yard, hands shoved in his back pockets. "Made his day."

"But is the road open again?"

"Yeah."

"Thank fuck for that. They've got to send us some decent food now, right? If only for you guys."

"I'm going to insist on it," Niko said.

For a moment or two, their positions and the reason why each of them was in the Slab were forgotten. Things would improve now, at least for a while. Niko locked the door, more out of habit than fear that anyone would escape, and went up to the office to yell at the JD clerk. Once he'd vented his spleen on him—would it have killed them to do one air drop?—he'd see if he could get hold of Maura.

"You know they don't give a shit." Ospen was fidgeting with his keys, wide-eyed and shaky. It was hard to tell if that was because he'd now be heading for boot camp sooner than he thought, or because the immediate prospect of Piet Verdier's enforcement had made him crap his pants. He was probably safer fighting grubs. "We won't get anything. Hey, call Campbell and Parmenter. Tell them to get their asses in here so I can go home."

"Whatever," Niko said, and started dialing.

Maura was too busy in ER to come to the phone, the receptionist said, but at least she knew he was okay. The JD clerk said there'd be trouble about the dogs, seeing as they were COG property, which was fascinating because he'd never said a word when Niko submitted the report about inmates killing each other. Calls made, Niko went off to sit on the windowsill overlooking the yard and smoke his last cheroot. The sudden quiet was unnerving. The only sounds he could hear to remind him there was still a war going on were Ravens in the distance.

It was four hours before Ospen came to find him. "At frigging last," he said. "Just had a call. There's a supply truck and a few visitors heading our way. Prescott."

"Oh, *fuck*."

"I told you not to shoot the dogs. Don't expect me to cover for you."

"Yeah, thanks." Niko almost went into a pre-inspection panic and then remembered the place was a slum and there was nothing he could do to make it look nicer for the Chairman. He gave up on the idea of having a quick shave, too. "Is anyone coming in to relieve us?"

"Campbell. Parmenter's going to be along later. Probably with a pickax, to avenge Jerry."

Niko waited at the front gates with the door open, watching the weed-covered, crumbling road across the heath. Eventually a 'Dill came into view, wobbling in the heat haze like a mirage and kicking up a faint cloud of dust. As it got closer, he could see a Packhorse behind it and a small delivery truck bringing up the rear. Was that Verdier's driver? It couldn't have been, not with Prescott around.

Nobody got out of the 'Dill. The APC just parked at the gates with a Gear on top cover, gun aimed out across the heath. Prescott got out of the Packhorse with his bagman, that hard-faced guy with the captain's insignia on his collar, and walked in as if nothing had happened, rather modestly dressed in a light summer jacket and open-necked shirt. Campbell jumped out of the passenger door of the supply truck.

"I understand things got rather unpleasant inside," Prescott said. "And that you managed to kill a few Locust. Would that be your marksmanship?"

"No, sir," Niko said. "That was Fenix."

Prescott seemed to remember the way in. Niko found himself following him. Ospen appeared in the entrance and Niko gestured at him to let the truck in.

"That would explain it," Prescott said absently. "I'd like to see Fenix, please. No need to take me to an office. I can stomach reality pretty well."

Yeah, this is how we exist. This is the pointless frigging prison you like to keep open. Time you saw it all, maybe.

Niko didn't notice the smell these days but he could see that Prescott and his captain—Dury, that was it, *Dury*—definitely did. They both stopped breathing for a few moments, then looked like they couldn't work out if it was better inhaling through the nose or the mouth. Even Campbell looked taken aback by it. Niko stood at the mesh security gate and yelled.

"Fenix? Somebody get Fenix. It's the Chairman."

Niko wasn't sure if that would speed things up or not. Eventually, Marcus wandered up the passage and stood at the gate, completely expressionless.

"Chairman," he said. He did it again. His voice changed completely, back to the guy who had money and pedigree. "You've come all this way to see me."

"How are you, Marcus?"

"Alive."

Prescott definitely looked pained. It wasn't the general squalor. Niko could read men pretty easily now. It was one upper-class guy looking at another and feeling bad that one of his own kind had to share space with the worst of the plebs without even a butler to polish his silverware. Prescott reached inside his jacket and took out an envelope. He held it up for a moment, then slid it through the gate between the center bars.

"I promised the Lieutenant I'd deliver this personally," he said. Marcus's jaw clenched. "Loyalty's a rare and precious thing, Marcus. Be glad you receive so much of it."

He took the letter and stared at it. Then he opened it. Knowing how long he'd sat on the last two letters, Niko was surprised that Marcus started reading it there and then. His jaw was still locked, but his expression shifted slightly from I'm-not-going-to-react to I'm-going-to-blow-my-stack, and then he looked up right through Prescott as if he wasn't there. Prescott blinked a couple of times, then nodded.

"And you're sure you're well? In reasonable health, anyway."

The words came out more as a breath than a growl. "Never better."

"Very well. I'll see you again."

Prescott turned away to walk back down the corridor and Niko wheeled around to see him off the premises. He caught Campbell's eye for a second. The guy looked away. Niko's radar told him there was something up, but he'd have to worry about that later. The most important thing was to get that food unloaded—without Ospen—and then go home and see Maura. Dury walked beside Niko, checking his watch, then inhaled pointedly.

"Drains. Definitely the drains." Dury wrinkled his nose. "You really should get them fixed."

"Maybe your boys should stop blowing up the sewers. That'd help."

Yeah, it was probably drains. The whole place was a plumbing nightmare now. He hadn't checked on the flooding in the old psych wing for ages.

But it could wait. There was probably coffee and soap on that truck. Niko didn't let himself think one second beyond that.

CHAPTER 15

I hadn't had a letter from you in years. I know I asked you to forget me, so I can't complain, and I shouldn't be making life harder for you by writing now. But there are things I should have said to you while I had the chance, and right now I really need to say them more than ever.

(Prisoner B1116/87 Fenix M.M., writing to Lt. Anya Stroud. Letter undelivered.)

JACINTO: EARLY FROST, 13 A.E.

It was the longest lull between grub attacks that Hoffman had ever known, and that made him more worried than ever.

He felt like something out of an old Pendulum Wars movie as he stood next to the anti-aircraft gun on the roof of the House of Sovereigns. It was a crisp early winter day, with good visibility and the scent of woodsmoke from Stranded encampments on the air. The gunners sat with their backs against the sandbags, smoking. One of them was lying flat on his back with his fingers meshed behind his head, staring up into the blue sky and occasionally squinting one eye as if he was checking out something at altitude. From time to time a Raven wandered across the skyline as if it was in need of something to do.

Hoffman's radio crackled. "Control to Hoffman." It was Mathieson, now standing in for Anya on the few occasions she could bear to tear herself away from CIC. She didn't want time to sit and brood, something Hoffman understood all too well. He pressed his finger to his ear.

"Go ahead, Mathieson."

"It's Pad Salton, sir. He's on the radio."

Pad usually just showed up unannounced at a checkpoint and ambled into town. If he was calling in, then it was urgent. "Patch him through . . . Pad? Where are you?"

"I'm just outside Ilima," he said. "Been talking to the Stranded. They're starting to see Reavers again. So I had a look around and kept obs on a gorge about two klicks east. Took a few weeks, but I saw them coming out of a fissure. You know the way bats come out at dusk? Like that. Not sure if it's their Reaver factory or whatever they call it, but they're back again."

Pad thought nothing of living in a hedge for months at a time, one of the things that made him such a great sniper, so if he said that something took some time, then he'd put in some serious surveillance far beyond an ordinary man's endurance. It must have worried him.

"Are they still emerging?" Hoffman started thinking of the Lightmass device. If the DRA guys were that close to making it operational, then targeting the tunnels where the grubs bred their Reavers was the best way to test it for real. "Is it safe to go back and check?"

"What d'you mean, *back*? I'm still there. I'm looking at it."

Hoffman didn't want Pad sitting right under the grubs' noses a second longer than he needed to. If he sent a Raven to do a recon, though, the chances were that it would either tip off the grubs or expose Pad's position.

"Can you give me coordinates?"

"I've given them to the kid in CIC. But I've got to sit it out, sir. You'll need someone doing FAC, at very least."

"If the DRA have got their asses in gear, then it'll be a ground strike. They've got a new gizmo."

"Yeah, the boffins always have. Tell 'em to make sure they put new batteries in it, though. I hate it when toys don't work."

"You sure you're going to be okay out there?"

"I've been okay out here for years."

Hoffman tried to jolly him along. "Living on bats."

"Nah. The little bleeders are too fast. No bloody meat on 'em, either."

"Okay, Pad. I'll get back to you. Hoffman out."

The gunners were sitting up now, listening to the one-sided conversation. Hoffman debated whether to go down to CIC or drop by Prescott's office.

"Reavers," he said. "Stay sharp. They're going to be back."

"Just in time to stop skills fade, sir."

"Yeah, they're thoughtful like that."

Hoffman opted for CIC and a secure phone call. He didn't have an office. He didn't feel he needed one; it was a luxury they didn't have space for, and anything he needed to say was probably something Mathieson needed to hear anyway. The kid looked okay, all things considered.

"No Stroud?" Hoffman asked, picking up the phone.

"I told her to get some sleep, sir," Mathieson said. "I've gone down in history as the man who told Anya Stroud she looked rough. She can't punch a cripple."

"You're doing okay, Mathieson."

"You want some privacy, sir?"

"No, I just need to talk to Prescott to see if we've got some new kit to deal with that location." He pressed the internal code and waited. Mathieson put his headset over both ears rather than just one, his way of saying that he wasn't eavesdropping, and Hoffman waited for Prescott's secretary to pick up. "Hi Jillian. It's Hoffman. Is he in?"

"I'll check for you, Colonel."

She was camped outside Prescott's door like a frigging guard dog. *Of course* she knew if he was in. Maybe she just said that automatically, but it pissed Hoffman off and all he wanted was for her to say she'd check if he was *free*. It sounded less like a half-assed lie. Hoffman drummed his fingers on the desk, wondered who had scratched the initials "PBD" into the grain, and waited.

Prescott's voice made him start. "What can I do for you, Victor?"

"I've got a cave target, Chairman. Reavers. How close are we to getting the Lightmass deployable?"

"I'll check and get back to you. What do you mean by Reavers?"

"Report from FAC. Salton's spotted what might be a Reaver breeding area."

"Very well. Give me ten minutes."

Hoffman put the phone down and waited again. He didn't like waiting and he didn't like sitting at a desk, but it beat meetings. He was doing something tangible. He'd rather have gone out and joined Pad to stare down the sights of a Lancer and pull the trigger, but he had to make do with what his rank allowed. Mathieson wheeled himself away from the desk and went to the far wall to stick marker pins in the map. He was having trouble reaching a location north of the city, and Hoffman got up to help him, but the kid didn't make eye contact and heaved himself up on one arm to stretch. He got the pin in the board eventually, but it was a struggle.

"I'm okay, sir." He flopped back into the wheelchair. "I can do this."

"I'll get the carpenter to build a ramp," Hoffman said. "No point making this any harder than it needs to be. You've got your invisible medal for being a stubborn bastard. You don't have to prove yourself to anyone."

Mathieson didn't look convinced. He stabbed the remaining pins into the lower half of the board with some force and went back to his desk. It was almost deserted in CIC today, just the quiet ticking of printers and the occasional burst of radio chatter, and when the phone rang it seemed much louder than normal.

"Prescott here. I've spoken to Dr. Payne and he says his best estimate for the Lightmass going live is Gale at the earliest."

"That's the goddamn New Year, Chairman. I need it in days. Weeks, at most. What the hell's he been doing all this time?"

"They're having manufacturing issues with the resonator components."

"Tell Payne he's no Adam Fenix."

Prescott actually laughed, his posh ha-ha noise rather than proper laughter. "Adam would be surprised to hear that endorsement from you, however oblique."

"Yeah. Pity it's too late." Hoffman wasn't going to let the grubs carry on popping out Reavers, though. He'd find another way. "I'll call Pad in and we'll see what we can put together ourselves."

"We do have intelligence-trained operatives, Victor."

"I'd rather rely on an experienced Gear, thanks."

"Let me know if you change your mind."

Hoffman hated having an operation snatched away from him. He walked up to the wall map and took a look at the location outside Ilima, now marked by a neatly cut square of red paper on the end of a dressmaking pin. A Lightmass bomb wasn't the only way to destroy grubs in tunnels. There was good old-fashioned sabotage, the quiet stuff he'd done years ago in special forces, and he still had some of the men who knew how to do it, like Dom.

"Mathieson, get me Pad," he said.

Pad's callsign was Outlier these days, although he'd had quite a few over the years. Hoffman was trying to recall what his callsign was at Anvil Gate when Mathieson looked up and pointed to the receiver to indicate Pad was waiting. He must have been hanging on for the signal.

"Pad, it's time to come in," Hoffman said. "Get your ass back here so we can plan a raid on the tunnels. How long is it going to take you?"

"I can be back at CIC by nineteen hundred," Pad said. "I've seen a couple more Reavers emerge, so let's not piss about. We've got to hit them soon."

"Pull out, Pad."

"Okay, sir, but I'm going to make sure there's no other exit from that fissure. I've got a camera."

"You heard me. Call it a day and RTB."

"Okay. Nineteen hundred. Outlier out."

Hoffman wasn't sure what kit Pad had these days. He was forever trading stuff with the Stranded, so if he came back with some imaging, that would help. They had the geological data for the whole of Tyrus somewhere. With survey information and a little common sense, they might be able to get a reasonable idea of what kind of tunnel system they'd be dealing with. It had to be hangar-sized. Reavers were big and needed space to get airborne. Hoffman walked over to the DRA archive on the other side of the square and got one of the clerks to book out the geological survey of Ilima, and by the time he returned with the cardboard tube tucked under his arm like a grenade launcher, Anya was back at her desk and the imaging interpreters were at their table, poring over the latest batch of aerial recon pictures that had just been printed off from the morning sorties.

Mathieson stood his ground as control room skipper and carried on regardless of Anya's return. *Neither of 'em with a clue what to do with themselves when they're not in here.* Hoffman hoped there weren't going to be fights over who got the main desk.

Anya did look bad, though. Not tired, as Hoffman had expected: she looked like she'd been crying, and that wasn't Anya at all. He'd have a chat with her later. It didn't take a mind-reader to work out who she'd been crying over. It was just the timing that bothered Hoffman. Why now? Maybe Marcus had finally written back to her.

"Okay." He unfurled the survey chart, offered it up to the wall in various places to find the best fit, and rummaged in the nearest desk drawer for some thumbtacks. "Let's fix these bastards while they're still in the shop, shall we?"

Anya looked up from the clipboard of handover notes but didn't offer a comment, and a couple of Raven pilots wandered in with recon images and left them in the in-tray on her desk. The trouble with quiet days was that they hung somewhere between hope and waiting for what felt like the inevitable.

And then the firing started, and Hoffman was left in no doubt what kind of lull this had been.

The AA guns on the roof started up just as the voice traffic burst over the radios.

"*KR-Seven-Seven, six Reavers, inbound, bearing two-seven-zero, range five kilometers.*"

"Roger that, Seven-Seven." Anya dived straight in and didn't give Mathieson a chance to open his mouth. "All callsigns—Reavers inbound from the west, two-seven-zero, six identified."

Hoffman abandoned his chart and moved over to the main illuminated plot table. Dealing with Reavers was always a balance between committing Ravens—which seemed to be the action the assholes were trying to provoke—and letting them get close enough to the wire for the artillery to take them out. "KR-Eight-Zero to Control, we have eyes on one Reaver squadron coming in from the north as well."

Hoffman didn't have a choice now. He had to use whatever asset was free to engage them. He could take a few hits in the city more easily than losing Ravens, though. There was one place where he could get a better handle on the situation, and that was the artillery position on the roof.

"I'm just going up top," he said, but the moment he opened the door something hit him in the chest and knocked him backward. The blinding flash and the explosion felt like it came later. He was flat on his back, winded, and the light vanished. He could hear something like tinkling water a long way off.

Glass. It's glass. Been here. Done that. Oh shit.

His mouth was full of dust. He spat before trying to inhale. But he could move and he was pretty sure he was on his feet now, or at least on his knees and able to stand. The light was filtering back in again as if smoke was clearing. Something creaked and then hit the ground with a thud. He tried to make sense of what was left of CIC.

"Anya? Donneld? Come on, people, talk to me. Anyone hurt?"

"We're okay, sir." That was one of the photographic interpreters. "Hell of a mess."

"Me too," Anya called out. "Mathieson, too. Just checking we're not bleeding and don't know it."

Hoffman looked up, ears ringing. The AA guns were still pounding somewhere above him. Most of the ornate plaster ceiling had fallen in, leaving the central lighting rose hanging from the joists above, and the windows were shattered. The blast had ripped charts off the walls. He looked behind him and saw that the door to the corridor was hanging off its hinges at the top, revealing the destruction outside. The passage looked like it had taken a direct hit and it was a matter of sheer luck that CIC had only caught the tail of the blast. He could already hear voices from the other side of the rubble as a damage control party tried to get through to them.

"We're okay," he called. He turned and crunched over the carpet of shattered plasterwork to Anya's desk. Mathieson was still sitting in his wheelchair, fishing wires and paper out of the debris on his desk. Anya, covered in pale gray dust as if she'd been floured like a piece of fish, was testing the connections on the radios.

"Well, it's one of those goddamn days," she said to herself. She picked up a phone and Hoffman could hear the line buzzing. They were still connected to the exchange, which was something. "Can't get any worse."

Everyone took it pretty calmly. There was a recovery plan for all this. They knew where they had to go to set up the command systems again and restore power and comms, and there were responders tasked to drop everything and help them do it. A couple of off-duty Gears in their civvies and a medic picked their way into the room, ready to do what was necessary. There'd be more people along soon.

"Like we'd take your word that everyone's okay, sir," the medic said. "Can everyone walk? Come on, clear this place and get over to the first aid station. You don't know what else is going to collapse." He went over to Mathieson, couldn't find a clear path for the wheelchair, and beckoned to one of the Gears. "Sorry, lieutenant, we're going to have to lift you out and fetch the chair afterwards. You'll need a Centaur chassis if you're going to work in this place."

Maybe it was a lucky hit, nothing more. Hoffman was always surprised how lucid he managed to be after getting caught in an explosion, but he found himself stumbling through rubble with Anya, heading to the far side of Sovereigns and thinking that this was the first phase of a new push by the grubs. Maybe they thought taking out CIC was a good start. Maybe they didn't understand just how decentralized the COG had become and that most units could go on fighting without CIC anyway.

We'll be up and running again in a few hours. Fuck you, grubs.

When he looked up at the open sky in the courtyard, he could see the smoke hanging in the air from the artillery barrage. The guns were still pounding right across the city. He sat on the steps with Anya as they waited their turn to see the doctor. She was dusting off a field radio that had seen better days.

"Just checking, sir," she said, brushing back her disheveled hair to shove in an earpiece. She fiddled with the dials. "Control to all KR units, CIC comms are temporarily down and we're relocating." Hoffman could only hear one side of the conversation. "Roger that, Eight-Zero . . . yes, understood."

"Gettner's playing squadron sheepdog, is she?" Hoffman asked.

"You can always rely on her, sir."

"You okay? Because you looked pretty strung out before we got hit."

"Just the triumph of hope over experience, as they say." Anya took an unnaturally intense interest in the radio receiver to avoid meeting his eyes. "I finally worked up the courage to phone the prison and Marcus wouldn't take the call."

"Did he write, then?"

"I know he got my letter this time," she said. "Prescott delivered it personally. So I've been waiting."

Really? Damn, I didn't expect Prescot to tell me, but Anya's confiding in him now? Well, shit.

"And he didn't reply."

"Not yet."

Asshole. Hoffman felt like a father whose daughter had been wronged. But Marcus had no expectation of getting out of there alive, and he'd been typically straight about it from the first day: *forget me.* Anya had been hovering around Marcus for more than fifteen years but she still didn't get that this might have been as much of Marcus as anyone could ever have.

"I don't know what to say to you, Anya," Hoffman said quietly. He folded his arms on his knees. "I don't know how to ask you what shape your relationship was in before this happened. Just . . . he's not demonstrative. Wanted to keep it private. Is that what really hurt you?"

Anya swallowed hard and brushed the tip of her nose with the backs of her fingers. Her eye makeup had smeared into gray shadows that made her look even more exhausted and broken. Hoffman wanted to drive over to the Slab there and then and give Marcus the punch in the face he so richly deserved.

"He loves me in his own way," she said.

"Bullshit." Hoffman bristled. "If you love someone, you love them in the way *they* want to be loved. That's a lame excuse for being cold."

"No."

"Oh, it is. That's *me*, girl. I had a wonderful wife who stood by me and put up with all my crap, right to the end." Hell, this was painful; but he had to know he was doing this for the right reasons, and he had to give Anya advice that would make her happier one day. "I came back from Anvil Gate a different man. She still stood by me. *For twenty damn years.* Not the first good woman I lost through being an asshole, either. She should have left me when she could, just like you need to get over Marcus and move on."

Anya rubbed her nose again. "Easier said than done, sir. You can't stop loving someone even if you want to."

"Anya, forgive me for offering an opinion, but he should have married you years ago." *He wouldn't take her goddamn call. Might be noble, might be selfish.*

Either way—just look at her now. "If your mother had still been around, she'd have kicked that bastard's ass."

It was harsh and it was true. Sometimes people needed a wake-up call. Anya blinked a few times, then gave him a sad I'm-okay-now smile that didn't convince him much. "Okay, I don't want to offend you, but seeing as we're being frank . . ."

"Truth doesn't offend me. It might hurt, but it never offends."

"Sometimes I wonder if you're my biological father."

Hoffman hadn't been expecting that. Shock did weird things to folks, though. "What the hell makes you think that?"

"Because Mom would never tell me who my dad was, and you've always been so kind to me."

"Goddamn." Hoffman shook his head. "Sweetheart, I can tell you for sure that I'm not. I just served with your mom, that's all. But . . . look, you're a lovely, loyal, clever girl, so why *wouldn't* I treat you right? I've lost too many people I care about. I cherish the ones who are left."

"That's me, loyal to a fault." She sounded disappointed, and the loyalty thing seemed to grate. "Sorry, sir."

"I wish I could say I was, Anya."

"We're all going a bit crazy these days, aren't we?"

"Damn right we are. Hey, Pad's coming back into camp tonight. It's high time we all got rat-assed in the mess. You up for that?"

"Sure." It sounded like *no.* "Why not?"

The worst thing about days like this, Hoffman decided, was that things got said in the heat of the moment and then couldn't be taken back. He'd never realized that Anya worried about who her father might be. It hadn't struck him that she might have *wanted* to get over Marcus, either, although she might simply have been fending off a painful conversation. He decided to leave it alone for a while and let her immerse herself in re-establishing CIC in the ballroom of the House of the Sovereigns, because busy was good. He liked busy too. The ballroom was a strangely luxurious place with paneled walls and a slightly sprung floor that would also double as a morgue or a casualty center if needed. Hoffman felt like a vandal for using pins to mount the charts on the walls.

He checked his watch. *Busy* really worked. It was 1830 hours, nearly a day lost, and Pad was due any minute. Damn, he should have been back by now, but he'd said 1900. Hoffman left Anya, Mathieson, and the current CIC watch staff to tinker with the new setup and set off for the checkpoint on Timgad Bridge.

"Evening, sir," said one of the Gears, a corporal called Tebbit. "Hear you got a direct hit today."

"Usual grub bullshit." Hoffman ducked under the rear barrier. "No Ravens lost, anyway. Two civvies and a couple of buildings. I think they're just jerking our chains. The bastards are going to do another winter push to piss us off."

"Looks like it. So are you keeping us company, sir?"

"I'm waiting for Pad Salton."

"I'm glad he remembers where Jacinto is. I sometimes wonder."

Hoffman stood at the checkpoint for four hours, arms folded on the top row of sandbags, waiting. Neither of the Gears on duty said a word to him. From time to time they handed him a tin mug of something hot and heavily laced with alcohol and sugar. It might have been a fruit concentrate of some kind. It was too sweet and too dosed with liquor to tell. But his greatest comfort right then wasn't the generous amount of alcohol they'd added, but simply the fact that ordinary Gears still treated him like one of them. It made the job a lot less lonely.

Hoffman tried the radio again. "Red Zero Two to Outlier, over." It was just dead air. "Red Zero Two to Outlier, over."

Tebbit leaned on the top of the barrier with him and took a look through the binoculars. Derelict buildings still looked like a city, more or less, but beyond the road the destruction was more complete, and the whole shape and structure of civilization had gone. The heaps of rubble looked random and almost like natural landscaping. It seemed to stretch into infinity.

"He goes walkabout for months at a time, doesn't he?" Tebbit said.

"Yeah. Months." But if Pad said he'd be back, he'd be back. There was something wrong, and Hoffman knew it. South Islanders had an uncanny ability to go to ground and survive anything, and Pad was living proof of that reputation, but sometimes things went wrong and they got killed like everyone else. "I'll give him another couple of hours."

In the end, Hoffman gave him until 2530. The rubble-strewn road on the other side of the bridge remained steadfastly deserted with only the sound of some feral cats slugging it out to indicate there was anything left alive out there. He made a note on the back of his map to get a replacement bottle of liquor for the checkpoint and turned to walk back to Sovereigns.

"He'll be back sometime, sir," Tebbit said. "You know he will."

Hoffman found he was ambling as if he was expecting a movie ending, where Pad would come down that road in the nick of time and he'd turn and give him a suitably gruff greeting to disguise his relief, just like grumpy old bastards were supposed to. But it wasn't a movie, and Hoffman knew that Pad had run into trouble. He hadn't made it. He was the last of Hoffman's old gang from 26 RTI. They were gone, all of them, all dead or disappeared.

"Sure," Hoffman lied, willing at that moment to trade the rest of his life for an hour talking to someone he could still call a friend. "Sure he will."

THE SLAB: BRUME, 13 A.E.

The water was ankle deep in the psych wing, but it wasn't getting higher, so Niko took that as a bonus.

He waded through the abandoned wing in rubber boots, checking with a flashlight in case this was raw sewage and not just water again. The place hadn't been right since the army had blown up the sewers a couple of kilometers east during the summer. It sounded like it was too far away to make a difference to the prison but there was no telling how all the tunnels and sluices fitted together. They said it was a labyrinth down there, the kind of place you could use for bomb shelters if you didn't need it to carry away waste and surface water. It made sense to Niko that you could really screw things up if you messed around with such a complex network.

Like traffic jams. One intersection gets blocked—the chaos spreads. God, when did we last have traffic jams? When did we still have that much fuel and that many vehicles?

He bent down to scoop up some of the water in an old pickle jar. Once he got outside into the light he'd be able to see the condition of the water and work out where it was coming from. The little he remembered from geography class told him that granite was impervious to water except when it was fractured. Well, there was plenty going on to fracture anything these days, but he suspected it meant that granite had fissures and holes in it from when it cooled or something.

But we carve granite. Statues. Buildings. Gravestones. Doesn't even take modern technology, because I've seen pictures of those monuments in Kashkur, thousands of years old. Why the hell do we think we're going to be safe forever on this plateau? Can't the grubs do what we can?

Well, it had worked for the best part of fourteen years, and there was nowhere else to run, so it was academic. He waded out of the psych wing with his jar of water and trudged up the steps to the ground floor. He had to take the jar all the way out to the front door and hold it up to the sunlight to get a good look at what he'd collected.

It looked pretty clean to him.

He sniffed it like a wine expert getting a whiff of a vintage. It didn't smell of anything in particular: definitely not sewage, then. The water was clear except for some specks of debris in it that could have been anything from dirt on the floor to grit being washed up from below. It could even have been from a spring. That kind of stuff happened even in granite, although he'd never known there were any springs around here. Well, there was no pumping it out, and no need to, so he ruled out the prospect of dysentery or something spreading through the jail. He tipped the water out onto the path.

When he went back inside, Parmenter was sweeping dead leaves out of the hallway. The windows were never going to be fixed. With every storm, more debris blew in through the broken panes.

"Asshole," Parmenter muttered, not looking up from the broom.

"Up yours," Niko sighed. Parmenter was never going to forgive him for shooting the dogs. "How long are you going to keep this up? For fuck's sake, we've got to work together."

Parmenter didn't answer. Niko found himself missing Gallego and even Ospen, because he was stuck here with a dog nut who thought he was a murderer, and Campbell, who'd been a decent guy and reasonable company to work with until he'd lost his son. It was like working in a hostile morgue for ten hours a day, one where the corpses sat up to bitch and whine at you. If the Slab hadn't had so many places to get away from people, Niko was sure he would have gone nuts.

Damn, the inmates were better company these days. He still didn't feel safe walking through the security gates even carrying his rifle and sidearm, but he could have sensible conversations with Merino and sometimes even with Marcus. He leaned over the gallery and watched him for a while.

Marcus was sitting at the table on his own, jacket collar turned up, playing some game of solitaire with the cards. That was unusual in itself. Normally he spent most of his time outside or in his cell, never in the kitchens where the majority of the guys hung out, and even Reeve gave him plenty more space lately. He'd always been the kind that lived in his head but now he'd retreated inside it. And it wasn't in a passive kind of way, either. He looked like he was seething, building up a real head of steam about something.

Now he sat with his arms folded tightly across his chest, back to the gallery and facing the main doors, looking like he was trying to work out why he was stuck with a lot of cards left and nowhere to lay them. He moved them around. Then he sat back and pulled something out of his inside pocket.

It was a creased envelope. Niko didn't need to see what it was because he knew it had to be the letter that Prescott had handed him at the end of the summer, the one from Anya what's-her-name that the Chairman had made a show of delivering personally. *Loyal?* That's what Prescott had called her, *loyal.* Well, she'd called the other day for the first time in all those years, but Marcus wouldn't take the call.

Maybe she'd called because of whatever he'd written back. He'd handed Niko his letter ages ago, and Niko had to admit that he'd been waiting to see a reply come in, but until the phone call there'd been nothing.

I can piece this together. She tells him she's still crazy about him, it upsets him, he writes back to say it's all over, so she tries to talk to him direct, to beg him to stay in touch. Which is why he won't take the call. Ah, shit. He's right, I know, but . . . goddamn, after the woman's waited years? Yeah. Loyal.

Marcus had definitely reacted badly when Prescott gave the letter to him, and hadn't even spoken to Reeve for two weeks after he read it. Reeve was still a useful informant. He was also pretty protective of Marcus, still treating him like a big dumb older brother he wanted to keep out of fights.

Marcus was now reading the letter again. He held it in both hands in his lap, below the level of the table, as if he didn't want to be caught looking at it if anyone else walked up to him from the main doors. Eventually he lifted one hand and leaned his head on it. He still had the letter in his right hand. Then he raked his fingers through his hair and just sat there with his forehead resting on the heel of his hand. It seemed like a gesture of despair. He obviously hadn't heard Niko walk onto the gallery.

He wouldn't appreciate being watched like that. Niko backed up a little, then moved along the gallery making enough noise to get his attention.

"Hey, Fenix," he called. "What's the water like in the carp pond?"

The letter had been sharply creased and re-folded so often over the weeks that Marcus could fold it one-handed. He slid it into his jacket like a man who was used to hiding stuff, and that wasn't a habit he'd learned in here. He turned and looked over his shoulder.

"It's wet," he said helpfully.

"I mean is it *contaminated.* The water's topped up from a buried pipe, right?"

"Kind of hard to spot contamination when we feed the carp on shit."

"Yeah, point taken. I was just checking out the flooding in the psych wing. Clean water. Like a spring."

"What did you really want to ask me?"

"What's pissed you off these last few months?"

"Let me ask *you* a question."

"Okay."

Marcus hesitated as if he was trying to find the right word. "Anya," he said. Now there was a word he had trouble with. Most guys would have said "my girl" or something. He didn't seem to know what to call her. "She says she wrote every week since I was jailed and never got anything back from me. And I wrote to her after Prescott visited. So what's happened to my fucking mail?"

It's that spotty little bastard in the JD's office. Can't be assed to deal with the inmates' mail because he's got to fill in forms. It's probably sitting there in his filing tray.

There was no easy way to tell Marcus that. Niko didn't plan to, not yet. "Why wouldn't you talk to her on the phone?"

"What the hell could I say to her? We've been here before, Officer Jarvi, remember?"

Niko tried to imagine how fucked up things would need to be before he couldn't face talking to Maura. If he knew he'd never see her again—well, maybe that would tip the balance. A phone call could be worse than nothing at all. Maybe Marcus had a point, but even if he didn't, it was about what he could live with and still stay sane in here.

"I'll go check on your mail," Niko said. "But why the hell didn't you tell me sooner?"

"Because you're the guy I hand my mail to."

"And I put it in the internal mail. I damn well do, Marcus. It's not me."

Marcus stared at the cards again and nodded. "Yeah. I know."

Niko walked back to the office and wondered if the letters had gone the way of all the goddamn requisition forms he'd put in for maintenance, equipment, and consumables over the last few years. He was seriously thinking of paying the JD's clerk a personal visit and teaching the little shit a lesson. It was going to be a pointless argument on the phone anyway.

Maura would tell him not to get involved. It wasn't that simple in here. Patients came and went, but inmates were neighbors, as much a part of a warder's human landscape as family, no matter how crazy or violent or weird they were. Niko stared at the rosters and memos stuck on the wall in front of his desk and wondered what would finish this place first: the grubs, the building collapsing, or the COG deciding to draft him and his two miserable staff and shutting down the place completely.

And then what would they do with the inmates? Prescott could come and shoot them himself. It had been bad enough putting down the dogs and there'd been a life-or-death reason for that. It wasn't some noble moral stance, just a sense that he'd had enough and that was as far as he was ever going to go.

"You still here?" Campbell wandered into the office with a handful of fly-blown lightbulbs that rattled when he shook them. They hadn't made that type of bulb for years. "Thought you were checking the psych wing."

"Done that." Well, this was the guy to ask. "Hey, you do the mail drop. What happens to it at Sovereigns?"

"I put it in the JD pigeonhole and check if we've got anything in ours," Campbell said. "Why?"

"You don't see the clerk personally."

"No. What's he done?"

"I want to know what happened to Fenix's mail after he got the first couple of letters."

Campbell just looked at him for a few moments.

"It makes good kindling," he said calmly. "You've warmed your hands on it once or twice. I saved it up for a while, then I thought—why should he have that?"

"You *what?*"

"I burned the lot. Mostly incoming, mostly from that woman, some from someone else. But he sent a few out, and I tossed them too."

Niko was rarely shocked. He'd expected shit from Ospen and even Gallego, but not Campbell. But then Campbell had really taken against Marcus: Niko hadn't forgotten how he'd laid into him with his baton. But dumping Marcus's mail seemed too small, too petty, too *sly* for a regular guy like Campbell.

"You *bastard*," Niko said at last. "That's a fucking high school revenge, isn't it? You came *that* close to beating him to death, and the best you can think of is burning his girlfriend's letters?"

"Yeah, actually. Because he gets a buzz out of being the hard man who can't be knocked down. But when he thought his girl had abandoned him, that hurt a hell of a lot more and for a lot longer than breaking a few bones. You know it did."

Niko struggled to understand it. Lashing out was one thing, but the slow, calculated effort needed to keep up something like that was beyond him. He didn't know Campbell at all. He should have realized that a long time ago.

"What's the *point?*" he asked. "You think he's having a great vacation here? Why not just beat the shit out of him again and have done with it?"

Campbell jabbed his forefinger at Niko. "He's *alive* and the guys he abandoned aren't. He's *alive* and my son isn't. He's *alive* because his dad was rich. And I'll bet he'll be out of here and treated like some frigging hero when it all blows over. But he's had a taste of what it feels like to be alone and lose everyone he cares about, and that's going to have to be enough for me."

"I never realized how your goddamn sick brain works, buddy. You know what? I'm going to tell him."

Campbell turned to the door and walked off. "I'll do it myself. I've waited years to see the look on his face."

"And he'll break your goddamn neck the first chance he gets," Niko called after him. "What's he got left to lose?"

It was stupid shit, all of it. The guys banged up in here were the worst criminals the COG had, men who even slaughtered each other without turning a hair, and now the fight of the day was going to be over some *letters*. Niko went after Campbell, more worried about the effect on the relative calm that Merino had managed to maintain through some pretty difficult periods. Niko wanted a quiet life.

When he got to the gallery, he couldn't see Campbell. He thought he might have chickened out or just gone for a leak on the way, but then he heard the big main doors swing open on the floor below and saw the stupid bastard heading for the cells.

A dozen heads popped out of doorways. They knew what was coming. "Where's Fenix?" Campbell demanded.

Niko leaned over the rail. "Campbell, get up here. *Now*." He checked to see if Campbell was armed for a change, but he was only carrying his baton. "Just give it a rest, will you?"

Merino appeared from the direction of the kitchens. Campbell was casting around, working himself up for a showdown. Niko had to decide whether to risk going down there and intervening. If he didn't, then Campbell would have to face not only Marcus but the rest of the inmates. But he never got the chance. Marcus came out of his cell and walked slowly up to Campbell, arms at his side but not at all relaxed.

"You wanted to see me?" he said.

"Hey, you two, don't start it," Niko yelled. "Just grow the fuck up, will you?"

Campbell didn't even blink. He was right up in Marcus's face now. "Your mail," he said. "The letters your bitch sent you. *I burned the goddamn lot.* And the ones you sent her. I just wanted you to know that. I did it because you're a cowardly piece of shit."

The whole floor was silent, breath held. Niko could only see Marcus's back, not his reaction, but he *could* see the looks on the faces of the guys watching him.

Marcus did that very slow head shake. Then he just threw a punch, a really savage right hook that landed with a loud crack: not a word, not a shove to kick things off, nothing. He just knocked Campbell flat on the floor and jumped on him. Everyone started yelling and cheering. Merino gestured at them to stay back. Niko yelled but nobody could hear him. If he went down there now he'd be too late to stop Campbell getting creamed anyway.

Campbell got in a punch or two, but Marcus was much bigger and a hell of a lot angrier. He laid into Campbell so hard that Niko thought he was going to carry on until he killed him. Maybe it wasn't all about his girlfriend. Then he stopped dead as if an inner voice had said *That's enough, Marcus*. He dragged Campbell to his feet and shoved him back across the table, pinning him one-handed by his throat.

"That's for *her*," he said. "You say one more word about *her* and I'll fucking kill you."

Niko thought Marcus was going to start on Campbell all over again, but he stepped back and looked up at the gallery. Campbell struggled off the table, barely able to stand but still refusing to call it a day. Merino and Reeve stepped in and pinned his arms before he restarted something he really couldn't finish.

"Okay," Marcus called. "Do what you've got to do, Officer Jarvi."

Niko knew Marcus would now walk quietly into solitary but that wasn't the point. Prison discipline had ceased to exist a long time ago. This was just two heartbroken, damaged guys slugging it out over a personal grievance. There was no riot waiting to kick off. If there were any sides and lines drawn now, it was between the world within these walls and what was waiting for humanity outside.

But Niko had accidentally created some new social order in the Slab. Shit, how did he handle that now? Two of the worst gangland thugs that Tyrus had ever jailed were suddenly playing by Ephyra Yacht Club rules to stop two members indulging in fisticuffs in the lounge. It was bizarre.

"You think it's over, Fenix, but it's not." Campbell was mumbling through split lips, but he knew he'd done the damage he'd set out to do. If anything, he looked pleased with himself. "Your rich buddies can't watch your back forever."

Reeve and Merino, playing gentlemen, steered Campbell away to the security door. Marcus was still looking up, waiting for Niko to say something.

"Next time, take the goddamn call if she rings again," Niko said. "Count yourself lucky I'm not sticking you in the psych wing, flooding or no flooding. Now get back to work."

Niko didn't stop to watch Marcus's reaction, but he didn't hear any of the usual backchat from the other guys as he walked away. He hadn't joined the prison service to rehabilitate criminals and give them a second chance. He didn't get a kick out of brutalizing prisoners. He hadn't even chosen to work here. But somehow, through desperation, fear, and disinterest, he'd managed to make the Slab a little less savage than it had been in Ossining's day.

It wouldn't last, though. If the inmates were released now, the only one who'd become a useful member of society again was poor damn Marcus Fenix. But for the time being, that didn't matter at all. The Slab was under control.

Even if it's not under mine.

The prison's time was running out, and chaos was the last thing anyone in here needed.

COG RESEARCH STATION AZURA: GALE, 14 A.E.

"You've never been trained to use a hypodermic, have you?" Bakos asked. Her voice was muffled by the surgical mask. "It's a miracle you've never given yourself an air embolism. Let me do it."

Adam was as used to the procedure now as an addict. He could apply a tourniquet, angle the needle correctly, aspirate to check he'd hit the blood vessel, and release the pressure in a relatively smooth procedure that had once made him shake and come close to fainting. He wasn't accustomed to doing it in front of someone else, though. The vial filled with dark red blood.

"You're not a physician," he said. "Putting needles in rats doesn't count. You can't pinch my scruff."

"Very funny."

"Anyway, I *was* trained. All Gears had to know basic battlefield medicine."

"You never thought it through. Dose, method, any of it."

"Imagine I'm a large but charmless rat. Would you say I'm infected now?"

"Oh yes. Even if it appears to be dormant in you. You're a carrier if nothing else."

"Well then, objective achieved." He withdrew the needle, laid the vial on a sterile sheet of plastic, and clenched a wad of cotton wool in the crook of his arm. Bakos, gloved and masked, took the sample, wrote ALVA, W. on the label, and sealed it into a plastic bag. "Sloppy physicist though I am, I achieved the desired result. All I ever tried to do was to reproduce the conditions of exposure in the Locust tunnels. You tend to forget that the Locust had investigated much of this themselves."

"Well, nobody else is showing actual signs of infection," she said. "Although everyone shows low levels of imulsion and chemical contamination, but that's par for the course with urban populations. Sorry—*former* urban populations."

Bakos leaned against the edge of the filing cabinet and leafed through the latest screening results. The whole population of Azura had routine blood and urine tests once a month and never asked why, but a community of scientists was well aware they were sharing an island with a dangerous pathogen. They didn't need to be told that the man who now spent a little more time in the public areas was a live host. Bakos was sure that transmission was via body fluids or ingestion because that was the only way she'd managed to infect any laboratory animals. Adam doubted it would make anyone keen to shake his hand if they knew what he carried, though. Scientists could sometimes be as irrationally scared as laymen.

Adam lifted the cotton wool to check whether the bleeding had stopped. Bakos took off her mask and gloves and dropped them in a flip-top bin marked MEDICAL WASTE—DISPOSAL BY INCINERATION ONLY.

"You think I'm mad, don't you?" he said.

"I've given up trying to work that out, Adam. I do think you take too much responsibility on yourself, though, to the point of messianism."

"I prefer to think that I played a part in failing to avert this war so I'm obliged to pay the price to end it."

"Yes. Sorry. It's the other M-word. Martyrdom."

"Look, are my tissues any use to you or not?"

"You know they are."

"Then, Esther, if I might borrow a phrase from one of my old platoon sergeants—button it."

Bakos didn't bristle. She gave him a smirk—there was no other word for it—and raised the internal blinds that obscured the window between her office and the main laboratory. It wasn't necessary. Nobody would have thought it odd that Adam was giving samples like everyone else. He hadn't actually injected any pathogen for a long time: the organism was surviving efficiently on its own. He just needed to inject the antigens as and when they were developed, and without anyone except Bakos and Nevil knowing.

If they ever found another source of the pathogen with different characteristics, though, he'd definitely inject that. He was committed now, unable to turn back. No avenue could be left unexplored. So far, they still didn't know what Lambency did in the human body, if anything, and they also didn't know how to permanently destroy it. It just kept bouncing back, a new mutation each time. But as the biologists said—they had no idea what its life cycle and reproductive strategy might be. Adam still thought of it in military terms: until he knew what the enemy wanted and how it planned to get it, then defeating it would be a crude and potentially wasteful process of simple overkill.

Would Prescott really care if he knew I'd infected myself?

Bakos took the bagged, sealed sample and left. Adam didn't feel comfortable sitting in her office on his own and went back to his own desk to check out the transmissions from Jacinto—God, was Payne still dithering around over the resonator imaging equipment?—and try to think laterally about destroying Lambent cells, if *cell* was the right word for such a strange organism.

They used to irradiate biohazard containment areas at La Croix University. Elain had told him so. She didn't trust the technicians to run the machinery safely, she said, and always cited every case of radio oncologists who got therapeutic doses wrong at JMC. That was her bête noire.

But it was a solution that a weapons physicist could understand. Adam pondered on how he could irradiate the organism without killing the patient if the thing was in every cell. He'd give that thought more time once the Lightmass debacle was resolved. Prescott had added a little handwritten note on the print-outs from the DRA:

"Remember that Hoffman says Payne is no Adam Fenix. Ha. Thought that would amuse you. RP."

Better a compliment when officially dead than none at all, Adam decided.

And Esther wonders why I feel the need to do everything myself. No, I don't delegate well.

Adam wasn't sure how long his secret would hold out in this small, increasingly bitchy village, or even if it mattered, but he was locked again into the downward spiral where each day of not admitting the truth made it harder to come clean.

I should have told Prescott right away that I was self-experimenting. A fait accompli, not asking permission.

But then what would have happened to Alva? It was already too late. Adam fretted about Marcus for a while and decided that he'd demand a photograph with some proof of date on it next time. He wondered if Marcus was keeping any record of his time in prison, any kind of journal, but then he'd never kept one as a boy as far as Adam knew, never confided in a diary. Everything that went on in Marcus's head stayed there to ferment. Adam, a man required to keep notes of every thought, idea, and action as part of his profession, understood the absence of personal material because Fenix men had been forbidden to wear hearts on sleeves, but he now worried about the absence of any kind of tangible evidence of his son's existence and career. Apart from the impressions he'd left on those around him, there was almost nothing to show that Marcus had ever existed, except his army record. For all Adam knew, that could have been ash by now if any of Jacinto's government archives had been hit.

It was time to go and see Nevil to evaluate the Lightmass data. There was no point in Bakos coming up with an antigen for Lambency if Jacinto fell to a much more definable and killable enemy like the Locust. Time had to be bought. There was never enough of it for Adam, though, and the price kept going up. He diverted via the men's bathroom, where the mirrors were brutal and unforgiving witnesses, not the gently silvered antiques in his apartment that flattered with their imprecision. God, he didn't like what he saw these days—balding, the surviving hair more gray than ever, and the flesh beginning to melt from his shoulders. Age was cruel. He'd always had a good head of hair, thick and black like Marcus's, and broad shoulders. Now the distinctive slope of his trapezius muscles was flattening into a sharper angle like a bank clerk's. Academic or not, he'd been a Gear, athletic, proud of his physique, certain that he'd always look that way however many lines etched themselves into his face, but it simply wasn't to be.

I'm not even sixty yet. That's what comes of a sedentary lifestyle. He turned away, stood at the urinals, and unzipped. *Elain would have aged more gracefully.*

He was lost in thought, wondering whether his prostate was making emptying his bladder a slower process, when one of the stall doors opened. Out of habit, he kept his eyes on the tiles in front of him. But the sound of heels forced him to look around, and the last person he expected to see was Louise Settile. He found himself hunching up in embarrassment and focusing on the tiles again.

"Sorry." She washed her hands in the basin, lathering the soap with enthusiasm. "I never can remember where the ladies' is. It's all this shuttling back and forth with Dury. Don't worry, Professor, you've got nothing that could shock Intel."

Adam tried to zip up as fast as possible and it was only when he was washing his hands and she was walking out of the door that he saw all the meanings in that apparently harmless comment. He waited a few minutes until he couldn't hear her heels any longer and went in search of Nevil.

Nevil was usually in the physics lab because fewer people used it and nobody minded his leaving snacks and coffee on the work surfaces. He was engrossed in his computer screen with a pencil clamped between his teeth and needed interrupting.

"Have you seen the Lightmass data?" Adam asked.

"Yes, Payne's a dick, isn't he? We did all the number crunching for him and the optics guy here even slipped in a few fixes." Nevil shoved the pencil behind his ear. "And have you seen Settile? First thing she did when the Raven dropped her this time was make a bee-line for me."

"You've *pulled*, as Dom used to say."

"No, no, she's Prescott's squeeze."

"Oh God. Really?" Adam hadn't noticed. He really was getting old, damn it. But then Prescott was a single man, so . . . he just seemed to be above all that kind of thing, that was all. "Makes sense, I suppose."

"Must be a shark breeding program. But seriously, she's rather interested in what we're doing, not surprisingly, but she does still seem focused on you."

Adam's heart sank a little further. "I'm something of a known security risk, I suppose. She probably thinks I'm calling Myrrah for chats."

Nevil gave him a slightly odd look, tinged with a little of that disbelief and suspicion that had hurt so much when he first confronted Adam. *Does he think I'm still hiding things from him? Well, what would I think if I were him?* Then he shrugged.

"She seems to be more interested in why a physicist is involved with biological research, so I tried to steer her off the subject by talking about the Lightmass systems." Nevil retrieved his pencil from behind his ear. "But I think you should brace for scrutiny."

"Well, if she works out what we're doing, it's not a disaster, is it?"

"You hid an invasion force from the most advanced state on Sera for fifteen years," Nevil said. "That's got to worry her and make her wonder what else you haven't come clean about."

And you? Does it make you wonder too? "I'll have to deal with it as it comes," Adam said.

At least Dr. Payne's inability to get the Lightmass imaging adjusted correctly with the manufactured parts drove every other anxiety out of Adam's mind for a few hours. He sat down with Nevil, studied the equipment that Payne had to work with, and came up with new figures. Adam wasn't even going to worry about how Prescott would inject those into Payne's consciousness as long as he managed it.

It was late afternoon before Adam decided to go for a walk and stretch his legs, leaving Nevil to do some research into irradiation techniques. He was standing in the gardens, watching the hummingbirds busy in the trumpet-shaped blooms of a vine he couldn't name, when Paul Dury ambled up to him.

"Professor," he said, "would you mind coming with me? Agent Settile's a bit worried about William Alva, and she wants you to explain something to her."

Ah well. Prescott would give him the icy stare, and Settile would dog his every call and step or at least get one of the Onyx Guard to do it for her, but it was a minor transgression compared to his previous one. He really could rely on the moral high ground. This was his body to poison or cure as he chose. It did nobody any harm.

"You will let Nevil know where I am, won't you?" Adam said. "I think I'm entitled to one phone call."

Perhaps that wasn't the best joke to make, given the situation.

CHAPTER 16

Santiago, you're a pain in the ass. I'm going to keep trying, but every asshole knows
we've got a deal to spring Fenix now. Like that's going to work. My guy inside, you
see, he mouthed off. He's still mouthing off because now he's a Gear stuck with your
guys, the ones who feel sorry for your buddy. He's trying to buy some slack so they
don't break his legs or happen to accidentally frag him. But that's the least of his
problems, believe me. And you better hope your boss doesn't hear about it, too, or
you'll be seeing Fenix in person sooner than you think.

(Piet Verdier, explaining the difficulties of continuing with the
attempt to extract Marcus Fenix under current conditions.)

THE SLAB: GALE, 14 A.E.

"That's not going to hold," Reeve said. The water boiler had been leaking for a
week, and Edouain's attempts to patch it up with some automotive body filler
that Jarvi had scavenged weren't working. "It needs welding. Or brazing. Or
whatever it's called."

"Soldering," Marcus said. "It's the copper pipe."

"Well, whatever your butler told you it was, it's not going to hold out much
longer."

Marcus, Edouain, and Vance were lying on the floor, heads under the
boiler, which was a big cylinder sitting on half-meter concrete blocks. The air
reeked with that pungent chemical smell of the filler, so overpowering that
Reeve could taste it in his mouth.

"It's slowed it down, anyway," Marcus said. "We can still heat the water. It's
leaking out more slowly than it refills."

"All the plumbing's breaking down." Edouain got up and paced around a bit, rubbing his leg as if he had cramps. "Don't expect the Justice Department to do any repairs. We may find ourselves using wood fires to heat tin baths before too long."

Every time Edouain stepped on the rusted piece of car door covering the tunnel they'd tried to dig a couple of years back, it clanged like a loose manhole cover, a noisy reminder of failure. Reeve wondered what would have happened if they'd pulled it off and managed to escape. Would they be invisible now in the mass of refugees in the city, or out among the Stranded, or long dead after running into their first grubs? Maybe all this delay was meant to be.

"Jarvi says the water's getting deeper in the psych wing," Vance said. "I mean, we've got to be on a spring or a leaky water main or something. That place has been flooded like *forever* now."

"Is there any pipework down there?" Edouain asked. "Can we get down there?"

They all looked at Marcus. Merino still had the internal keys, but nobody had wanted or needed access to the solitary cells since the psychos had been moved out. Jarvi would probably hand them over to Marcus if he asked nicely. It wasn't like anyone was planning a breakout.

"Okay," Marcus muttered, and got up. "But we've still got to cut any pipe we find, and make it watertight somehow."

"Yeah, well, you find some pipe, and we'll see what we can do about the rest."

Marcus went back to the main floor and Vance watched him go. "Chunky's finally made him a mat," he said. "It's taken him so long that Marcus probably forgot why he's done it."

"What, when he first came in here?" Reeve remembered that, all right. "When he had that run-in with Merino?"

"That was it."

"That's kinda nice. It's the thought that counts, not the delivery date."

Every tiny comfort counted. Reeve wondered when the next box of treacle cookies was going to show up, but he could wait. He went out to the main floor to see how Marcus was getting on scoring the psych wing keys. He couldn't see him anywhere, so he assumed he'd either gone out to the gardens to see if Niko was hanging around having his smoke with the window open, or Jarvi had already thrown the keys to him from the gallery and he'd gone down into the basement.

He knew his way, after all.

Someone called out from the other end of the floor. It was Van Lees.

"Hey, Reeve, this is getting beyond a joke. What the hell's happening with the crappers?"

"What am I, the frigging emergency plumber?"

"They're blocked."

"Yeah, so try dumping less down 'em."

"No, I mean they're all backing up."

"Terrific. This is connected to the flooding, I'll bet."

Reeve had a hunch and went back to the old tunnel in the utility area to check the water level down there. When he dragged the cover plate off, he could see the muddy water lapping a few centimeters below the surface. Yeah, the whole place was flooding. Jarvi would have to do something about it now, maybe finally evacuate to another building or something.

Dream on. We're here because they didn't have any other garbage bin to throw us in. Remember?

He was walking back to the wing with the intention of yelling for Jarvi to come take a look when Van Lees came running after him, this time with Vance.

"It's spiders, man," he yelled. "The toilets. Full of frigging *spiders*."

"Ahhh, you big girl," Reeve sneered. "Stamp on 'em. They're more frightened of you than you are of them."

"Not these," Van Lees said. "I'm not joking. I've never seen these before. They're fucking *huge*."

Vance nodded. "They're gross."

Reeve didn't mind spiders. They didn't get that many in here, probably because spiders were as smart as rats when it came to knowing where not to waste their time. But Van Lees wasn't usually excitable about bugs, and Vance never turned a hair at anything. Reeve followed them into the toilet block and looked up at the walls and ceiling, expecting to see something dangling from a web.

"No, down there," Vance said. "Behind the toilet."

Reeve had his smartass lines ready. No spider could be that bad. The really deadly venomous ones were small, as far as he remembered, and anything big was just scary-looking. He followed Vance's finger, starting to laugh, and squatted to take a look behind the U-bend.

Oh shit . . .

It was charcoal gray, with big knuckles on its jointed legs, and it was twenty centimeters across.

It also had a mouth. Swear to god, the thing had a mouth and *fangs*.

"Holy *fuck*." Reeve jumped back. "What the hell *is* that?"

"I don't know, but they're coming up through the toilet bowls," Vance said. He looked around and grabbed the near-bald mop that was propped against the tiles. "Look."

Reeve pushed the next stall door open with his boot. One of the things was scrambling over the broken seat. In the next toilet, another was scrabbling around behind the pipework, flinging small chunks of broken concrete over the floor like it was digging for a bone.

"You better get Merino," Reeve said. Vance fended off one of the spiders with the mop. It went for the mop-head like a snappy little dog. "Tell you what, get Marcus. And Jarvi. Hell, just get someone to take a look."

The lavatory door swung wide open and Marcus walked in clutching a couple of short lengths of copper pipe, pants wet up to his knees. "Take a look at—*shit*."

He dropped one length of pipe on the tiles, took two strides forward with the other gripped tight in both fists, and brought it down hard on the nearest spider. It took him five or six blows to kill it. Then he seemed to spot the rest of them, and took a pace or two back like he was counting them.

"Are you going to stand there just goddamn *watching* them?" he growled. "They're Corpsers. Kill them. Grab something heavy and kill them before they get away."

Van Lees got the idea fast and grabbed the pipe Marcus had dropped. "You're shitting me."

"You've never seen a fucking Corpser before? Seriously?" Marcus smashed the pipe down on another one trying to climb out of the toilet and sent legs flying in one direction and chunks of cracked porcelain in the other. By now, the other inmates were showing up to see what the noise was about. "What is this, a nunnery? Come on, get on with it. *Kill 'em*."

Reeve grabbed the first thing he could find, an old tin dustpan, and battered one of the Corpsers trying to scramble behind the pipes. No, they weren't spiders at all. They fought back. This one wasn't giving up without a struggle and jumped at him. It sank its fangs into his pants and he had to smash the dustpan against his leg to get the thing to let go. There had to be two dozen of the bastards scuttling around the toilets now, dodging between the partitions and getting stomped, battered, and skewered. The shouts and noise of clanging metal was deafening. Eventually it ground to a halt. Marcus was the last man left beating the crap out of one of them and he didn't seem to be satisfied that it was dead until it was a greasy smear across the floor. Then he went from toilet to toilet, looking down each pan and waiting a few moments before moving on to the next. *Bang.* There must have been one last straggler trying to make it out of the crapper. Marcus brought the copper pipe down on it and knocked it onto the floor before finishing it off with his boot.

He stood staring at the mess, breathing heavily, and then looked up at the stunned faces around him.

"None of you have ever seen a goddamn grub or anything like this for real, have you?" he said, like it was their fault they'd been locked up in here for life since before E-Day. "Shit."

"We've seen Reavers." Chunky emerged from the knot of shell-shocked inmates. Armed robbery and arson was easy, and they'd take that in their stride, but giant spiders with teeth was something else entirely, something they really didn't have the measure of. "I thought Corpsers was real *big* things."

"They are." Marcus went straight into sergeant mode, giving them a pep talk as he paced up and down looking for more movement. "Corpsers excavate e-holes. They're five, six meters high, maybe more, and they'll tear your fuck-ing head off. But they've got to come from somewhere. These are probably babies. And they've *dug their way into this place.*"

"Glad I wasn't taking a dump when that happened," Merino said, wander-ing in. "Have we got trouble?"

"You bet," Marcus said. He walked out into the cell wing, clutching the pipe like a cosh. Reeve followed him. It felt like the safest thing to do. "Officer Jarvi? You there?"

Jarvi jogged out along the gallery and leaned over. "What the hell's going on down there? Anybody hurt?"

"Not yet," Marcus said. "We've got Corpsers. You need to call Sovereigns, make sure they put you through to Colonel Hoffman or CIC, and tell him we've got grubs digging their way in via the sewer system. Tell him it's twenty-centimeter Corpsers. Probably newly hatched. He needs to know in case it's the run-up to a big attack."

"Oh, shit," Jarvi said. "Okay. Got it."

Jarvi jogged off and Reeve could hear him yelling for Parmenter and Campbell. Forty inmates were now gathered on the main floor, silent and be-wildered, and this time they were all looking to Marcus, not Merino. He knew about grubs. They were going to hang on his every word.

"What do we do now?" Merino asked. "You got a plan, Fenix?"

"Grab whatever weapon you can find and watch every goddamn hole in this place," Marcus said. "And if you see something come up—you just kill it. And you keep killing until they stop coming up."

Marcus came to life in a way that Reeve had rarely seen in the last three or four years. This was what he was made for: but it was also what he'd intended to do, to go down fighting these things and take as many of them with him as he could because he couldn't go back to the life he had before. There was a disturbing finality about him. This was the closest he could come to wiping away his disgrace and atoning.

No, you've got to survive this. You've got to win. You've got to redeem yourself and go back to your girl and start again with a clean slate, because that's what heroes do. That's what we all need. Even guys like me. We need to know that real heroes exist and that they win in the end. Because we can't save ourselves without you.

"What else is going to come up?" Chunky asked.

"I don't know," Marcus said. "Anything that's going to dig its way in needs to be able to fit in the pipes and conduits. The granite won't keep them out forever, but they'll take the easiest route in, just like humans."

"So what can get in?"

It was all different on the TV. When the Slab had still been getting news, the footage was mainly recon images, all man-sized grubs and the big Brumaks like walking tanks and generally things that were two-legged and looked like some kind of weird human. Reeve couldn't remember even seeing a proper Corpser in the footage. He realized he didn't have a clue what else was out there.

"We could get Tickers, too," Marcus said. "Wretches, maybe. Drones would have to come in via the front door. But don't rule out anything."

"Drones are big bastards," Merino said. "What happens if they get in here?"

"Then you're going to die." Marcus was completely matter-of-fact. "Because even I need a Lancer or a fighting knife to put one down."

"Hey, we're mostly in here because we're really good at killing," Reeve said. "Maybe we stand a chance."

Marcus nodded. "Yeah. We do."

Reeve had been right about the caliber of guys in the Slab, though. Society might not have been too keen to have them as neighbors, but when it came to violence, they all had a use. Inmates went back to their cells and dismantled metal bed frames, grabbed knives and hand-made blades from under mattresses, and went to stand guard by windows and drains and conduits. Parmenter came out on the gallery with his rifle, looking like he'd never handled one before in his life, with Campbell beside him. Campbell looked around the floor of the wing. Reeve kept an eye on him to see if he was checking out where Marcus was. Marcus looked up at the gallery as if he had the same thought.

"You won't have time for that if the fucking grubs get in here," Marcus murmured. "Asshole."

Jarvi came onto the gantry and banged the butt of his rifle on the metal rail to get everyone's attention. "Okay, I've alerted the army that we've got Locust coming up in the building," he said. "We're late to the party. They're already under attack on the south side of the city and they say they're getting reports of grubs massing on the western side of the escarpment. Yeah, that's us. So we're on our own. But you all knew that anyway."

"Who did you speak to?" Marcus asked. "Hoffman?"

"Lieutenant Stroud," Jarvi said.

The name didn't mean a thing to Reeve but he watched Marcus's reaction, and suddenly it all made sense. That was her, his girl: Anya Stroud. It was a really personal war, so few people left now that guys like Marcus couldn't help but fall over people they knew all the time. Reeve almost envied that connection, however painful it had to be. There was nothing outside waiting for him. He was going to survive for himself, nothing else, because he didn't have anybody waiting.

Jarvi must have known who she was, though. Maybe it was his way of letting Marcus know he'd told her he was okay.

"Better stand by, then, guys," Jarvi said. "Parmenter—give Fenix your rifle. He'll make better use of it than you will."

"You're fucking joking," Parmenter said.

"I am *not*. Do it."

Parmenter looked pissed off but threw a box of rounds over the gantry and lowered the rifle to Marcus on the end of a line. Reeve felt instantly better for seeing Marcus check the weapon, shove the ammo in his jacket pocket, and look every inch the fighting Gear. Maybe that was all part of his sergeant thing too, that he could make a nervous, ramshackle group of men feel a lot more confident about a fight most of them probably wouldn't survive.

Reeve was almost embarrassed to ask. He scratched his chin. He had to try.

"I'm the other marksman in here," he said. "Mind if I have a sidearm or something?"

Jarvi shrugged. "I've done a dozen other crazier things." He drew his handgun from his belt and gestured toward the doors for Reeve to come and collect it. "Why not?"

"You're not going to let me down, are you, Reeve?" Marcus said quietly.

"No," Reeve said. "Because we're really in the shit now, aren't we?"

Reeve hadn't handled a weapon in years. He preferred a sniper rifle, but the pistol made a lot more sense in here. And then he waited, walking slowly around the floor, checking out the kitchen drains and the toilets, and even waiting by the old tunnel for a while.

He stood at the open door onto the yard. The distant boom of artillery started up and a Raven droned somewhere north of the walls. Marcus wandered up beside him and stood scanning the sky.

"It's started, hasn't it?" Reeve said.

Marcus nodded. They shut the doors and walked back through the toilets and showers. It was so quiet that Reeve could hear his own pulse in his ears. Then another noise made him turn around and cock his head.

It was distant gurgling, like someone had pulled the plug out of a bath. It was a sound he'd heard years ago when they were trying to dig that goddamn tunnel, except this time it had a new significance. The noise was coming from the toilet bowls. Marcus pushed open a door and looked down. Reeve checked the stall next door.

The water in the toilet bowls had gone. It must have drained out somewhere. For a moment he saw the whole plateau in his mind, a big lump of shiny, speckled rock that was hard as iron but shot through with nature's cracks and man-made drains, not a solid barrier at all. The sewers and pipes were part of a road network for things Reeve hadn't even got names for yet.

"Here they come," he said.

Marcus nodded, absolutely still, rifle resting in his hands as naturally as if he'd been born with it.

"Yeah," he said. "Here they fucking come."

GALLERY LEVEL, THE SLAB.

"You're crazy, giving those assholes guns." Parmenter checked his sidearm. Campbell was a few meters ahead, minding his own business. "You won't be able to put the lid back on this."

Niko gave him a shove in the back to keep him moving down the passage. "It's *two weapons,* and one of them's with a veteran Gear," he said. "We're all low on ammo, the assholes in here could have broken out or killed us ages ago, and in case you hadn't noticed—we're all in the same shit."

"Only takes one round to kill you."

"Only takes one frigging moron to not understand that you arm the guys best at shooting grubs."

Yeah, if the inmates had put their minds to it, they could have taken out a handful of guards years ago. What was the name for it? *Institutionalization.* They'd all been in here so long that the idea of getting out made as much sense as it did to a cage-raised chicken. Some guy had once told him that you could open the cage and the chicken didn't have a goddamn clue that it could just walk out and run away. It couldn't tell the difference between the artificial rules and reality.

The Slab did have a harsh reality outside the cage, though, and it was starting to tunnel its way in right now. The three guards reached the top of the stairs down to the ground level. It had been a lovely staircase once, the kind that should have been in a ballroom instead of a place designed to break and destroy people.

"Makes more sense to stay on the upper floors," Campbell said.

"Like grubs can't climb stairs."

"You know what I mean."

"Yeah, and when those things have finished ripping up the inmates, then they'll come and find *us*." Niko trotted down the stairs. "That's what they're here for, to kill humans."

"We could make a run for it now," Parmenter said. "Just open the gates and go."

"Yeah, and you know what's out there? Whatever gets in through the pipes here will at least be *small*."

"I meant just us. Three guys. We could hide."

"If you think I'm leaving human beings in here for those things to kill, you're an even bigger asshole than I took you for. They're our own. I don't care what they did, they're *us*, humans, not grubs."

But Niko knew he might have to consider abandoning the prison if more of the freak show broke in. There were Reavers—there were always Reavers. Maybe a Brumak could put things over the walls, too. They could certainly fire over them. It was a lot of trouble to go to for forty victims but they probably didn't know how many humans there were in a big place like this.

He opened the security gates and left them unlocked. It took a deliberate, conscious effort to do that because locking everything behind him was automatic after all these years. Some of the inmates were hanging around the toilet block with metal bars or kitchen knives in their hands, but he didn't feel threatened by it at all now. They all knew what they'd have to kill long before they settled any scores with the prison service.

"Still all clear?" Niko asked.

Merino appeared from the toilets. The most likely access points were the bathrooms, the kitchens, and service area drains around the boiler room. "We split everyone into teams," he said. "We've got people watching all the main areas."

"Where's Fenix?"

"Boiler room," Merino said. "Maybe now's the time to tell you there's a tunnel down there. Some guys were trying to dig their way out via the utility conduit a couple of years ago but they gave up."

"Well, shit." *Y'know, I'm not sure I would have cared, as long as it wasn't one of the sick weirdoes. A few armed robbers and gangsters on the loose—so what?* "So he's thinking the grubs might use that as a way in."

"Yeah, he says they're really good at sniffing out tunnels."

Niko turned to Campbell. Even now, he still didn't trust him not to start another ruck with Marcus. "You stay here, okay? You too, Parmenter."

There was a short flight of stone steps down to the boiler area. Niko could hear the scraping, sawing, and banging as soon as he went into the outer passage. For a moment he thought Marcus was beating the shit out of more Corpsers, but then he heard the voices, quiet and unpanicked, and realized there was a bit of fortification going on. When he turned the corner, he saw Edouain, Reeve, Vance, and Marcus stripped down to tank tops and sweating as they rigged drainpipes from the boiler room. It was a lot warmer in there than Niko remembered, not that he'd been down here for years. Somewhere inside the room, water bubbled and popped like a kettle being boiled.

Marcus dragged a metal plate across the flagstones, setting Niko's teeth on edge. Edouain and Vance looked up from cutting into a piece of plastic drainpipe with a bread knife. Niko could now see the missing flagstones and a damn big hole in the floor big enough to take a man. He stood at the edge and looked in.

"That was full of water earlier," Marcus said. Nobody seemed to feel the need to make excuses for the escape tunnel. "Now it's drained out, which probably means there's a tunnel somewhere else that's opened up."

"Smart move to dig a hole. Not."

"Yeah, that's what I said. But I've never been the told-you-so type."

"What are you doing? You can't even fill it in. They'll just dig right through."

"We're thinking of getting a little Silver Era on their asses."

"What, exactly?"

Edouain finished sawing through the drainpipe and laid the end into the hole. "Come and admire our ingenuity, Officer Jarvi." He beckoned to Niko to follow him into the boiler room, where the boiler tank was making angry rattling noises. "Behold the walls of the castle and the boiling oil that awaits the unwary invader."

Vance and Reeve looked pretty pleased with themselves. A jury-rigged length of pipes ran from the massive hot water tank to the hole.

"When they start coming up, we just flood the tunnel with a zillion liters of boiling water," Reeve said. "We've turned up the thermostat to max. You could cook shrimp in it."

"And then what?"

"Well, the tunnel's logjammed with boiled grubs for a while, the boiler reheats, and if the assholes are dumb enough to try again, we pour more boiling water down there. You ever cleared drains?"

"That's an electrical conduit down there."

"Like losing the lighting's our biggest problem."

"You'd lose the boiler too."

Marcus shrugged. "The wiring survived the last few floods."

"Better that I don't know about that," Niko said. "So you look like you're in charge, then, Fenix. Plan? Other than kill everything. Heard that one."

"Containment," Marcus said. He dusted his hands on his pants and picked up the rifle resting against the wall. "Choke points. Stop them at the point of entry. Whatever comes in, it'll be harder to corner it when it gets loose. The small things tend to move fast. If anything does get in, best option is to clear the area and lock it in. That's the handy thing about a prison—you've got doors to slam on them."

"You've spent years working this out."

"Not really. Just been in plenty of tight spots like this one."

"Lucky we got a resident expert," Reeve said, "or we'd be fucked into a tinker's bucket by now."

"So we just wait," Niko said.

Marcus checked his rifle and patted down his pockets like he was checking where he'd put his ammo. "That's about the size of it." He walked over to the foot of the steps and listened. "The arty's ramping up. And more Ravens. The grubs are already out there on the ground."

He ran up the steps and disappeared. Niko looked at Reeve.

"He's loving this, isn't he?"

"Well, I wouldn't say *loving it*," Reeve said. "Finally got a real job to do, more like. He's back in his comfort zone, which just happens to be hell."

Niko would have worded it differently but he didn't want to say it out loud. Reeve probably thought the same thing. He just gave him that look: *yeah, he deserves a better end*. Marcus was pumped up for his last stand. It was frightening because they were going to have to make that stand too, but it was also tragic and upsetting because neither of them thought Marcus belonged here. They were watching a decent guy who'd had to choose between two wrong answers, a guy who was still willing to put it on the line to the very end, long after the army had forgotten him, and nobody would ever know about it.

Niko left Edouain and Vance to it and went up to the yard with Reeve. Marcus was scanning the sky, hand shielding his eyes from the watery sunlight.

"Did you get your radio working?" he asked.

"Yeah."

"You can't patch into the CIC net, though. Hear the rest of the voice traffic."

Niko shook his head. "No, but I can call in."

"Probably just as well. Can't work out what's going on even with a full ops room plot."

"I spoke to her, you know. When I called CIC. She promised to pass a message to my wife."

"Yeah. I guessed you knew who she was."

"She sounds . . . well, as good as she looks."

"Yeah." Marcus just nodded. Niko knew he wouldn't look him in the eye this time. "Yeah."

"She told me to tell you she loves you."

Marcus paused for a few moments. "Shame I didn't give you a message to pass on."

"Yeah," Niko said. Marcus didn't seem the type who'd take kindly to other guys poking their nose in his strained love life, but it was the right time to tell him. "So maybe I took the liberty of telling her what you would have said anyway."

Marcus turned his head slowly, the way he did when he was pissed off and almost challenging someone to dare repeat what they'd just said. But he just gave Niko a very discreet nod, eyes shut for a second.

"Appreciate it," he said.

The artillery noise was getting louder, almost continuous booming like a rapid and irregular heartbeat. Niko could hear the rattle of Raven door guns but he couldn't see the helicopters themselves. There was a battle going on outside. As they waited for whatever shit was about to spray off the fan in their direction, the door crashed open and Vance burst out.

"They're coming," he said. "We can hear them down there. Stand by."

Marcus lit up like someone had plugged him into the mains. "Okay, everybody stand to. Runners—you make sure you report any movement to every position. We'll stop them in the basement. Might be a feint, so keep a goddamn eye on every ingress point. Got it?"

Everybody broke as if they knew where to go. Niko was as impressed as hell. Marcus headed for the basement at a sprint and Niko followed, not even sure where Parmenter and Campbell had gone, but when he looked back along the corridor to the kitchens he saw Campbell heading that way with Chunky and a few other guys. The line between jailer and jailed was completely irrelevant now. Down by the boiler room, Edouain and Vance knelt by the escape tunnel, listening.

"Can't tell how far down they are," Edouain said. "You know what the acoustics are like."

Marcus nodded, rifle aimed down into the hole. "Hold off until they're pretty well at the top. Otherwise it'll just be a nice warm bath by the time it reaches them. They need scalding water full in the face."

"Lovely," Niko said. He wondered how much use his sidearm would be against a grub when Gears needed a goddamn rifle and chainsaw to stop them. "What are they, anyway?"

"Not drones," Marcus said. "Too big to fit. I could hardly move down there. I'm guessing Wretches. Evil little shits about so high." He indicated waist height with his free hand. "If you can't boil them, shoot them or jump them with someone else. It'll take two regular guys to pull one down."

"But one Gear."

Marcus shrugged and took aim again. "That's why they fed us the extra calories."

Niko could hear them now. Scurrying, scuffing noises wafted up from the hole, and a weird kind of mumbling that sounded like old men leering and hacking up phlegm at somebody. He'd never seen a Wretch and he despised them already. Edouain held up his hand like a race steward at the start line of the Ephyra Steeplechase.

"Hold it . . . *hold it* . . ."

The scrabbling was much louder now. Reeve held the drainpipe steady with what looked like a pair of ancient, rusted coal tongs while Vance gripped the valve that let the water flood out. Edouain seemed to be timing, nodding to himself as he counted under his breath.

"I can see them—*now!*"

"Bomb gone," Vance said, and the boiling water shot down the pipe into the hole. Steam billowed everywhere.

The squeals and screams below told Niko what he needed to know. Edouain held up a hand to signal *stop*. "Hold it!" No wonder Reeve was using tongs to steady the pipe. The water was so hot that the plastic looked slightly buckled. "That's ruined their day."

He leaned over the hole to take a look. It was pretty damn brave, Niko thought, because there was no telling what was down there. Thrashball-sized spiders with teeth were bad enough. But Edouain had probably been a war hero back in Pelles, a guy much like Marcus, a man with the balls to operate behind enemy lines even if he was just a terrorist on the COG side of the border. Everyone held their breath. Steam still wafted out of the tunnel. Edouain leaned in a little further, hands flat on the ground on either side of the hole.

"Can't see any—*uhh!*"

A gray shape shot out of the hole, shrieking, and smacked Edouain full in the face. Marcus didn't even pull the trigger. He caught the thing square in the chest with an upward swing of the rifle and Niko heard the wet squelch, almost like he'd skewered it with a bayonet. The rifle didn't have one. The creature landed on the flagstones with a thud and Marcus was right on it, pounding its face with the stock of the rifle until it stopped screaming and thrashing. Niko aimed his pistol down the hole, expecting another thing to follow, but it was hard to look away from the skewered creature. Marcus stepped back and poked the body with his boot.

"That's a Wretch," he said. "Parboiled."

Niko stared. So did Edouain. Reeve and Vance were still focused on the hole, ready to open the sluices again. The creature was misshapen and monkey-like in a way, the flesh falling off its chest like overcooked chicken. Its face might have been a mess from the scalding water. It was hard to tell how pretty it might have been before.

"Why didn't you shoot?" Niko asked.

Marcus grabbed the Wretch by its arms and dragged it over to the hole before rolling it back in. Niko heard it slither down the side of the tunnel and then squelch to a stop.

"Saving ammo for something bigger," Marcus said. "But now I've got to clean out the goddamn barrel. Got a cleaning kit?"

"In the office. Somewhere."

"Go get it, will you?"

Marcus just looked irritated that the Wretch had messed up his rifle. Niko ran as fast as he could, amazed at his own turn of speed when he needed it, and passed through the kitchens on the way to the back stairs.

"What is it?" Campbell called after him.

"Wretches," Niko shouted back. "We're boiling them. Everybody keep their hair on, okay?"

Niko grabbed the radio handset when he reached the office and shoved it in his pocket. He tried to call the Sovereigns switchboard. All he got was the recorded message saying the exchange was busy and to try later. When he went back to the boiler room, Edouain and Reeve were keeping watch on the hole. Every so often, Edouain said "Pour!" and Vance loosed a ten-second burst of boiling water while Reeve cocked an ear.

"I'm not hearing anything now," Reeve said.

"They're not going to give up that easily." Marcus stripped down the rifle and pulled the cleaning rod through a few times. "Okay, Mataki would have kicked my ass for a sloppy clean like that, but we're out of time." He reassembled the rifle and looked down the hole for himself. "I miss bots. They're great for recons."

Niko could still hear the boom of guns outside. He took the radio out of his jacket and checked the settings so he didn't need to fumble for the channel if he needed to call CIC fast. But what good was that going to do? The army sounded like it had its hands full with the grubs too. In the background, he heard someone running down a corridor—human boots, but enough to make him start—and then Chunky raced into the boiler area.

"There's these monkey things coming in," he said, breathless. "They're in the main wing."

"There's no ingress point," Marcus said. But he was halfway to the steps, rifle ready. "Okay, we'll plug that hole, wherever it is. Officer Jarvi, call CIC and tell them we've got Wretches in here. Reeve, with me."

"They're not going to send backup, Fenix," Niko said.

"I know." Marcus looked back for a moment. "But you still need to tell them."

Niko flicked the switch and held the radio to his mouth, wondering if he'd get Anya Stroud again, and also wondering if she would be happier or not for knowing that Marcus was still the man she'd always thought he was.

COG RESEARCH STATION AZURA: GALE, 14 A.E.

Nevil wasn't afraid of the Onyx Guard, COGIntel, or even Richard damn Prescott himself. What was there to lose? Everything he cared about was gone: and he could never go home again, whatever home meant these days.

He waited in the comfortable, well-equipped sitting room that served the two top-floor laboratories in the main building. The problem with Azura was that every element of it, even the most sinister bits, was tasteful luxury. The padded opulence around him deadened sound and made him feel as if he was being swallowed and digested by the place. If he was going to be interrogated and roughed up, he wanted it to be in a setting that fitted the occasion, preferably with a single naked lightbulb hanging from a frayed cable above a table in a dark, lonely cell scented with the previous prisoner's terrified piss.

But Paul Dury didn't do things that way. Neither did Louise Settile, as far as he could tell. She looked the part in her blue suit—no spa-style casuals for her—but she struck him as a woman who'd rationalized the disturbing life an agent had to lead by reducing everything to the same dull level of necessity as her housekeeping. *Feed the cat, collect the dry cleaning, neutralize two foreign spies, tap a phone.* He tried to imagine her getting smoochy with Prescott, another creature of infinite self-control and unshockability, and completely failed. It was hard to believe there was any personal connection at all between them, let alone passion.

Dury stirred the cups of coffee and handed one to him. "Just waiting for Professor Fenix and Dr. Bakos," he said. "You okay?"

That was the only question Dury had asked him today. There'd been no pressure to tell him everything he knew about Adam, nor any subtle inquiries. Maybe that was Dury's technique, just being the honest guy who asked straight questions and only shot you if you gave the wrong answer. Nevil liked him. They were on chummy first-name terms, Nev and Paul. It was impossible to spend hours on the range with Dury and not get to know him too well to do anything but admire his professionalism and directness.

"I'd be happier if I knew what this was about," Nevil said.

"Agent Settile just wants to clarify a few things with your boss."

"You don't have to euphemize with me, Paul."

"Okay, she thinks your boss is a lying toad and she's going to find out what he's keeping from her so she can sleep at night."

"Thanks." *Oh shit.* "That's what I needed to know."

"And *you* know what he's up to, but you've already gone way beyond your own boundaries of loyalty by grassing him up to Prescott. So I'm not leaning on you to tell me, because if it was dangerous stuff, I'm pretty sure you wouldn't sit back and let him be a complete asshole again. So . . . something dumb and annoying. But you know about vetting, don't you? You've been vetted for your security clearances quite a few times. The questions. Every cough and spit about your family. What you've done. What you've done that you'd rather not have everyone know about. And you know that it's not the *answers* that matter, Nev, but whether you're prepared to *lie*. That's all. Any answer is the right one, except a lie."

Nevil understood that. "How about failure to mention things?"

"Well, I'd still say that's a lie, and so would COGIntel, but Prescott would judge it according to who was doing the withholding and what was being withheld."

Nevil had now worked out Dury's interrogation methodology. He'd tell you the absolute truth. In a calm, level voice, he'd tell you that he needed to know something, and that if you didn't tell him, he'd break your legs. There'd be no threats or posturing. He'd simply be describing a sequence of events, and it would be up to you if you set those events in motion or not, but they *would* happen if you did.

I could just tell him. But I don't think he really wants me to. Let's see.

"So you want me to tell you what I know about Adam."

"Not really," Dury said. "Settile likes to do things evidentially, because she's got different agendas to me, and I kind of like you the way you are, a pretty decent guy who's motivated by outrage and decency rather than approval-seeking or fear."

Yes, Nevil had absolutely nailed Dury's MO, and Dury seemed happy with the knowledge that he was so transparent to him.

"Okay. I'll just drink my coffee then."

"I got you about right." Dury sipped contentedly. That meant he wasn't going back to the mainland for a few days, time for the faintest trace of real, honest-to-god coffee to clear his system. "We understand each other."

"We do."

Nevil leaned back in the chair and wondered why Adam was so secretive.

He wasn't a dishonest or dishonorable man. He almost made a hobby of wrestling with his conscience. But a lot seethed inside, and there seemed to be a point where he refused to share as a point of principle. Maybe his father had never allowed him any privacy and he still had a need to keep some things to himself as a reassurance that he had any control at all. It was too easy to buy Prescott's Adam-always-knows-best theory, the idea that Adam was so in love with himself intellectually that he didn't think lesser mortals would understand what he was doing and would just spoil his brilliant science by chasing him from the village with burning torches and pitchforks. No, it was sadder and darker than that. Nevil had seen Adam's tormented, uncommunicative relationship with his own son, and he knew.

Eventually voices carried down the hall outside. No footsteps: the exquisite hand-knotted Furlin carpet was too sumptuously thick for that. Settile was chatting with Adam and Bakos but the words were just murmurs from all of them. She stuck her head in the doorway.

"Would you gentlemen like to join us in the biohaz suite?" she said. "No need to gulp. I think you can bring your coffee."

Nevil didn't even meet Dury's eyes. Yes, he knew exactly what was coming. Bakos might have blabbed, or something else might have tipped off Settile, but Adam was going to get a spanking. All Nevil could do was keep his end up and focus on what this was about: finding a way of killing Lambency before it devastated Sera. It wasn't even about killing Locust. It was strategic stuff. He drained his cup and followed Dury down the corridor. The lab was deserted for once, at this time of the day that meant everyone had been ordered to disappear and not come back until they were told to.

"Okay," Settile said. "This won't take long." She walked along the bench to the microscope and stood by it like a TV presenter opening a worthy documentary. "I'd like you to show me some blood samples, Dr. Bakos. First of all, show me a stabilized slide of a sample with Lambent contamination, and a control sample of uncontaminated blood."

Nevil couldn't tell if Bakos was privy to this or not. She didn't flinch. But then she was complicit too, because she knew who the *in vivo* research subject was. She took a pair of fresh latex gloves from the dispenser and opened the storage chamber to select the slides.

"Okay, now show me," Settile said. "Regular blood first, Lambent sample second."

Nevil had never been sure what Settile's background was. But she'd been one of the intelligence analysts who'd worked on the UIR's orbital laser project, the woman whose team had said the Indies had the research that would give them a working weapon in a very short time, and whose advice had led to the raid on Aspho Point and the use of that stolen research to speed up the Hammer of Dawn project.

And that's where I came in.

Everyone's lives were inextricably linked. Louise Settile had caused Dr. Nevil Estrom, in a way. There was now one degree of separation. He watched, finding himself oddly disappointed that even if Sera was saved from its environmental disaster, the extraordinary mesh of individual lives that underpinned it would never be known and marveled over.

"That's a regular blood sample," Bakos said, adjusting the focus and letting Settile look down the eyepiece. Settile took her time, then stood back to let Bakos load the next one. "And that's a sealed one with the Lambent pathogen. Perfectly safe."

Settile bent over the microscope again. "I can see the difference, and I'm not a hematologist," she said. "The speckling around the margins of the red cells is distinctive, isn't it?"

"Yes. It's not even necessary to add dye to be able to see it."

"Good. So I know what I'm looking at." She took a couple of steps back. "Now show me specimens from Dr. Fenix and William Alva."

Bakos went back to the storage chamber, but Settile held up both hands, an apologetic little girl.

"No, I mean prepare me some slides *now.* In front of me. Like a thrashball drug test, you know? The player has to urinate in front of the doctor so everyone knows he isn't dosed to the eyeballs and using his friend's untainted pee to beat the test." Settile looked at Adam. "You won't feel a thing, Professor, and I swear I won't make any little prick jokes."

Nevil almost looked at Dury but resisted. Settile loved her long shakedowns. Okay, she was going to do the big theatrical act, make Adam feel small and foolish—always more painfully effective with a brilliant man than breaking his fingers—and tell him not to do it again or else he'd find himself wired to the electricity supply by his balls or Marcus would end up as another mortality statistic in the Slab, some suitable deterrent or other.

Okay, dear, get it over with.

Adam stepped forward, expressionless, and rolled up his sleeve as if he was expecting Bakos to draw the blood. Settile shook her head and pulled down some latex gloves from the box.

"I started in narcotics," she said. "Chemistry grad. I also know how to do a quick blood sample, so perhaps you'll just prep the slide for me while I watch, Dr. Bakos. And I do know how to handle biohazards."

Nevil really thought Adam was just going to confess now because the outcome was inevitable and he wasn't known for his patience. But he seemed set on going through with it. Settile took a glass sharp and nicked the skin of his thumb to let a blob of blood well up. Bakos held the slide to it and prepped it on the bench as Settile watched. The agent didn't even blink until that slide was under the microscope and she could look down the eyepiece.

"There," she said. "That looks to me like a Lambent-contaminated sample. Just confirm that for me, Dr. Bakos."

Adam was still licking the cut to stop the bleeding. For a second, it looked faintly comical, as if he was sucking his thumb. But he'd had enough now.

"Yes, Agent Settile, I exposed myself to the pathogen," he said wearily. "It's a time-honored method in scientific discovery. Most of us in this room benefit from the fruits of such methods on a daily basis. Your point?"

"Why didn't you mention this? Why is it not in any of your notes?"

"Oh, laymen get worried about things that don't really warrant it," he said. He was playing up to Prescott's stereotype. "And Richard would start fretting about my dying prematurely before he'd had his money's worth from me."

"So the test results we've seen are based on your specimens, not Mr. Alva's."

"Yes."

"Do I need to test Mr. Alva to verify that he's not contaminated?"

At that moment, Nevil started to realize that the rather gentle confrontation was now heading in a slightly different direction. The worst thing about working with chess players like Settile and Prescott was that they . . . well, *contaminated* you. Nevil found his physicist's thought process—observe, theorize, test—was slipping into speculate, speculate, and second-guess. His mind was racing ahead of what he was observing, running down all the avenues to see where Settile might go and why. He tried to call it to heel.

"He's not contaminated," Adam said at last.

"Okay." Settile stepped back and motioned Bakos to deal with the slide, taking her gloves off and dropping them in the bin. "I'm glad we've established that. I'm sorry it took so much laborious theater, Adam, but I wanted to make it clear that I'm very motivated to find the truth and I don't need to rely on your answers to do so."

"Come on," Adam said irritably. "It's unconscionable. Pedophile or not, we can't test pathogens on human beings—not even with their informed consent, as far as I'm concerned. I'm willing to take the risk. That's the moral thing to do."

"I know, which is why I knew there was something wrong when I heard you were using a prisoner for tests. I think I know where you draw your line, you see. I remembered just how agitated you were when we were talking about whether to assassinate or kidnap UIR weapons scientists."

"Yes. You mentioned that before."

"Put a face on it, and you can't pull the trigger. Make it anonymous, and you can wipe it out along with a few billion others with the Hammer of Dawn. And I'm not moralizing, Adam, I'm explaining how I reach my conclusions. Scientific method."

"I'd give you a round of applause if I weren't still sucking my thumb."

"So . . . you lied. Again. Lied by omission."

Adam did seem stung by that. "I know. What are you going to do, ground me?"

"No, I just want you to come with me." She sidestepped Adam to look at Nevil and Dury. "You too. All of you. Come with me."

Nevil was now lost in the alleys of Settile's game with no idea what was coming next. That was when he recognized her as the expert interrogator that she clearly was. Uncertainty shook people down; fear of the unknown was even more powerful than pain. Nevil followed the procession along the corridor to the small library at the corner of the building, and Settile opened the door to usher them in. William Alva was sitting at a marble-topped table reading a book. The floor was beautifully inlaid parquet, red and black wood.

"Hello, Mr. Alva," she said. "How are you?"

"I'm fine, Louise," he said. It was creepily familiar to use her first name, but damn, he really did look like a nice guy. Nevil had never quite squared that with the reality. "Am I going to have some tests?"

"No, this is just a demonstration." The center casement window was slightly ajar. She pushed both panes fully open and secured the latch, letting the warm, fragrant air wash in, and beckoned to Alva. "Come on. Would you just stand exactly here, please?"

She was about half a meter from the window. Alva gave her a look. He didn't have to be Adam Fenix to work out the physics of an open window and a tall building, and he'd spent years in the Slab, so he was probably wary of ambushes. He smiled, pushed back from the table, and did as she told him.

God, no. She's not going to push him out the window, surely? Why? Nevil hit a moral brick wall. He didn't like Alva's kind but something told him to do something, anything, even though he had no idea what was required, or why. So he froze.

"Does it matter which way I face?" Alva asked.

"No." Settile had her arms folded. She stepped behind one of the tables, still facing him. "Whatever suits you."

Alva's smile got a little more *knowing*. He turned slightly sideways and gripped the windowsill with his left hand. "Just in case I slip and fall," he said, looking at Dury. The breeze ruffled his hair. "We wouldn't want that, would we?"

"Absolutely not," Settile said.

Then she drew her sidearm and put one round through his head.

He didn't fall through the window: he went down like a stone. The glass either side of the open window was instantly sprayed red with blood. Bakos didn't make a sound, but Adam gasped. Nevil couldn't even move. He was sure he was going to throw up. He'd never seen anything killed, not even an animal, and he hadn't known how fast and awful it was, nothing like the movies. Bakos simply stood there, staring and swallowing. Biologists weren't the fainting or screaming kind.

Adam shut his eyes and pinched the bridge of the nose. It seemed to take him a few moments to find his voice.

"You *bitch*," Adam said slowly. "What the hell was all that in aid of? You think I'm impressed by murder? Was that all for my benefit?"

Settile holstered her weapon and stepped around the table to squat and check the body. She straightened up, apparently satisfied that Alva was dead and not just malingering.

"I know you think the world pivots on you, Adam," she said. "But that was for all kinds of reasons. One, we don't want a homicidal pedophile wandering around Azura. Two, you didn't use him so he's surplus to requirements. And three, I did it by the window to minimize the spatter on fabrics. Look." She peered over the sill. "Oh, there's some on the stonework, but it's mostly dispersed. Never mind. The next rainstorm will clean it off." Now her voice hardened a little more. "Yes, I could have shot him on the ranges or dumped him from the Raven out at sea, but I think you all get my point now. It's not just how easily it can be done, but that the situation is so serious now that it *will* be done."

Adam went over to look at the body. Nevil didn't dare, but Adam had been a frontline Gear and he could probably cope with that kind of thing better than he could. Nevil still felt he was going to vomit. And he still thought he should have done something, *anything*, without knowing what. That was shock, he supposed. He'd expected to feel something more complicated and emotional, not this weird physical reaction and little else.

"You should know by now that I don't respond to threats," Adam said. "And I don't respect violence."

"And I don't care," Settile said. "I just want you—all of you—to remember that we can't have secrets on Azura. It's the one place where everyone has a need to know. Do you get it? This isn't Jacinto. The rules are different. We have to work together. You no longer have secrets, and you no longer have the cozy luxury of a conscience. Understand what we have to do to survive."

Settile looked as if the execution hadn't even raised her pulse rate. If anything, only Adam's stubbornness had. Nevil had always thought he knew how high the survival stakes were in this war, but now he realized that he hadn't understood them at all. He was only just beginning.

To save a world, everyone was potentially an acceptable loss.

CHAPTER 17

They're coming in from the western edge of the plateau as well, Colonel. They're going to take the Andius highway again in the next ten hours, and then you're going to have pull a whole battalion back from somewhere else to get them out. Right now, you've got one platoon sitting here waiting to be turned into Gear puree.

(Lt. Mel Sorotki, pilot of KR-239, reporting back from recon sortie over western Jacinto.)

THE SLAB: ONE HOUR AFTER THE START OF THE LOCUST ASSAULT, GALE, 14 A.E.

Reeve could see the size of the problem as soon as he stepped through the doors into D Wing with Leuchars, Warrick, and Van Lees. Marcus shouldered ahead of them and let out a weary breath.

Wretches were rooting around the cells and exploring the place as if they didn't have a pressing schedule. There were about a dozen of them, dark gray and a meter tall. One was scuttling along the balustrade of the gallery, bold as brass. More movement caught Reeve's eye and he looked up at the ceiling. Marcus followed his gaze, squinting along the rifle's sights.

"Shit, I didn't know the assholes could *climb*," Reeve murmured.

"Yeah, I should have said." Marcus squeezed the trigger, a Wretch crashed to the ground, and its buddies turned around to start a loping run toward Marcus. "They do that. You might want to start shooting them now."

"Can't we tackle them?" Leuchars asked.

"You've seen the claws on those things."

"You've never been out drinking in the docklands, have you? No worse than a guy with a knife and a broken bottle."

Reeve, distracted by the rush of holding a loaded weapon for the first time in years, squeezed off one careful shot just to get the feel for it again and sent a Wretch skidding across the flagstones with half a head. Another one broke off from the pack and made a feint to the left but Leuchars and Warrick jumped it and pinned its arms. It bucked around like a demented spring, spitting and cussing.

"I said *don't!*" Marcus barked. He dropped to one knee and started picking off the others one at a time as they came at him. "Save it for when you have to."

"Hey, Leesy, give us a hand." Leuchars ignored him. "Can't hold the asshole all day. Ow, *shit!*" The Wretch had slashed a chunk out of his arm. "Move it, Leesy!"

Van Lees moved in, trying to get a kitchen knife into it. He had a length of metal bed frame shoved down the back of his belt. "What are they, armor plated?"

"*Thick hide,*" Marcus yelled back. "Stab it somewhere *soft,* for fuck's sake."

Reeve fired once and took down another Wretch. His second shot only wounded one, but it was good enough to leave it howling and struggling on the ground. He was counting his ammo in a way he'd never had to before, suddenly debating whether to finish off the wounded one that was now shrieking its head off.

"How about the eyes?" Warrick said. "Just do it, man. It's going to get away."

"Ah . . . okay."

Reeve stepped back and looked just as Van Lees grabbed the thing's head and tried to hold it steady as he rammed the knife into its face. He managed to get the blade into its mouth. Leuchars cheered. Van Lees had another couple of tries before he lost patience, pulled the length of pipe from his belt, and clubbed it senseless. But damn, it took a lot of blows to put it down. This was going to be a long day. They'd probably be out of ammo long before they ran out of Wretches, because more seemed to be ambling along the gallery.

Campbell, Parmenter, and Jarvi ran up behind Reeve. "Where the hell are they getting in?" Jarvi asked. "We can't keep dropping them."

Marcus was still taking aim and firing with calm deliberation. The last three Wretches from the first batch backed off a few meters and seemed to be working out if they should run for it or try to jump Marcus, but Reeve solved the problem for them by shooting two in the back as they turned tail. Campbell aimed and shot the third one. The Wretches up on the gallery vanished into the darkness.

Jarvi looked around.

"I've got twenty-five rounds left," Marcus said, standing up. He didn't look at Campbell or comment on the shot. "It's a gamble. If we piss all our ammo on these things, then we'll be in real trouble if we get drones or worse. How do we seal off this wing? Where can we put everyone and keep the grubs out while I find where they're getting in?"

"The old A Wing," Parmenter said. "No plumbing. Doors on manual locks."

"What if they're getting in via the roof or something?" Reeve asked.

"They're all coming from the far end of this wing," Marcus said. "I'm guessing the basement again, the psych wing. It floods. So there's probably a route in of some kind."

Jarvi walked out into the center of the floor and looked around. It was so damn dark in this place that a black shape like a Wretch was next to impossible to spot if it wasn't moving. "Okay, so we lock ourselves in A Wing. Then what?"

"I plug the hole and wait for me give you the all-clear," Marcus said. "And you better start planning in case you need to let everybody out. It won't be a picnic out there, but if it's a choice between being trapped with Locust inside, and being able to run for it outside, you stand a better chance over the wall."

"I'd have to be authorized by Sovereigns."

"Yeah, terrific, but consider thinking of your own asses and do it anyway."

"I'm not happy leaving you to do this, Fenix."

"Too bad. I'm the only grub expert you've got." Marcus jerked his head at Jarvi to go and picked up a length of pipe. "Do it. You too, Reeve."

"No way." Reeve started walking toward the doors with the warders but he had other plans. "You want to cut around through the dog runs?"

Marcus started after him. "No, I want you to damn well listen to me and hold A Wing with the warders."

"You're not going down there alone. Spare me the heroics."

"Bullshit."

"You'll have to shoot me to stop me, and you can't spare a round."

Reeve stopped and turned, blocking Marcus's path. He really should have been far more worried about where the Wretches were, especially as they could climb pretty well like spiders, but he'd never move a muscle if he let that get to him. Marcus brushed past him, shaking his head, because he always had to lead the damn cavalry charge. But Reeve couldn't leave him to do this alone. It was starting to look like he wanted to force a suicide mission and get it all over with, just the way he had when he first walked into this place. Prisoners were standing at their allotted positions with their makeshift weapons as he approached.

"I said *get everyone into* A *Wing*." Marcus's voice echoed in the corridor. A guy called Manon came from the direction of the kitchens bouncing half a dead baby Corpser in one hand like a ball. "Shit, Manon, are they back?"

"Just a few. You want any help with the monkeys? I just saw one trying to climb the dog runs. They're stuck the other side of that wall."

"Great. But get everyone into A Wing and wait."

"You sure?"

"Yeah. Leave this to me."

Manon walked on. Reeve could hear whooping from the toilets. It sounded like guys were having a perverse kind of fun killing Corpsers, which beat screaming panic, he supposed. Marcus projected grim calm and let's-do-it, so everyone else had picked up on that and thought they could beat grubs too. *So that's the sergeant thing. Nice trick if you can do it.* Reeve caught up with Marcus and nudged him in the back with his elbow.

"You don't go anywhere without backup, hear?" Reeve said. "If you don't give a shit about yourself, at least worry about the rifle."

"I gutted grubs for ten years," Marcus muttered. "They're just Wretches. It could be worse."

"Yeah, but you had armor and a chainsaw rifle then. And what if they open the doors for their big buddies?"

"You want some advice?"

"You're going to give it to me anyway."

"Don't try to save me. I told you that before."

"You're not a one-man army, Marcus. Get over yourself."

"I've got to live with *me*." He tapped his chest as he walked. "And this is the only way I can do it."

"For fuck's sake . . ."

Campbell's voice carried down the passage behind them. "Fenix? How long are you going to be?"

Marcus didn't look back. There wasn't any hint of bad blood in Campbell's question, which was weird in itself. "An hour, maybe," Marcus said. "But if the grubs get into the wing first, run like hell."

Reeve thought it was a pull-it-out-your-ass kind of figure, but it might have been Marcus's way of trying to be polite to Campbell for reasons best known to himself. Marcus seemed the kind of guy who couldn't be assed to waste his time holding grudges. He exploded, he threw a punch or five, and that was it.

It didn't fit with the marathon-length brooding that went on over other issues, but the one thing he never seemed was vengeful. He'd never have made it in organized crime. A guy had to have a good memory for a slight in that business or else he just had a big target painted on his back marked WEAKLING.

They reached the doors to the basement. The outer door was dogged back by clips. Marcus stopped to listen, holding his rifle one-handed.

"Try the lights."

Reeve fumbled around for the switches. "They'll know we're here."

"They know already."

"Okay . . . there you go."

There was a dim light somewhere in the corridor ahead. Reeve could now see the long row of doors, either locked shut or dogged open. When he walked through the outer door, he realized that the light was actually coming from a passage with internal windows that ran parallel to the main one.

"These are external deadbolts, right?" Marcus asked. "Slam them and they lock you in. Key to get in, key to get out."

"Yeah. Probably because you need to be able to bang the nutters up fast in an emergency. Because while you're looking for your keys, some guy's eating your face off."

"Okay. Let's clear this place a cell at a time."

Reeve never worked in a team. When he went on a job, he had to do it alone. The targets he was given weren't always sitting in happy ignorance of the round that was about to turn their brain to mush, and quite a few of them had guys employed to stop guys like him, but this soldier stuff was a lot more systematic. He tried to use his common sense in working out what Marcus was signaling him to do and where he needed him to go. It was a case of thinking what he'd do if he was a Wretch or a grub watching them, and doing it to the Wretch before the Wretch did it to him.

Yeah, it all came down to the same thing. It was just technique.

"So some of these things have guns and some don't." Reeve covered Marcus's back as he stood to one side of each door and then stepped in with the rifle raised. "I've led a sheltered life, obviously."

"No wonder you guys didn't have much of an escape committee."

They moved down the passage almost back to back, checking the ceiling as well. Wretches could cling anywhere. That changed the game a bit.

"There's no water on the floors," Marcus said. "It's drained out somewhere."

"How long have we been down here?"

"No idea. Twenty minutes. Half an hour."

"Yeah, time flies when you're enjoying yourself."

Marcus aimed his rifle at the ceiling. Some of it was stone, but some was the metal grid that was installed just about everywhere in the Slab. Reeve had never worked out why they used it unless it was to make the place colder and more miserable, or to let the warders spy on or piss over the inmates. It certainly wasn't to keep fresh air flowing. But it did allow more light into places like this, and when Reeve looked up to see what had spooked Marcus, he was staring at a Wretch's ass, and the Wretch was staring down at him.

Reeve fired.

Shit, that was messy. Reeve ducked the spatter. The Wretch managed to scramble away for a few meters, shedding blood and all kinds of stuff over the corridor, then slumped dead. Marcus didn't turn a hair. "So where does that conduit they're using actually start?"

"Yeah, it *was* a good shot through a metal grating, wasn't it? Don't mention it."

"How do I get in there?"

"You don't."

"They're not coming in through the cells. They can't get into them." Marcus shook his head. "All the shit I took for granted. Radios. Lancers. Decent boots."

"And maybe we shouldn't have eaten the dogs after all."

"I didn't. Okay, what's behind this?"

The end of the passage was blocked off by what looked like a plastered brick wall, but when Marcus tapped it, it sounded more like hollow wood. That got his attention. He kicked it a few times and cocked his head to listen. Reeve could hear the Wretches skittering around above but it was impossible to pin down the direction. They could have been near the roof for all he knew. Maybe they were just coming in over the walls after all.

"Ever thought of just going back to A Wing and asking Jarvi if he knows what's behind that, rather than kicking it in?" Reeve asked.

Marcus shook his head and fished in his pocket for the blade he always kept on him. "Or I could just look." He started scraping away at the plaster with the blade and exposed wooden battens. It was plasterboard, a pretty useless material for a wall in a prison. "Reeve, you stand back and shoot anything that comes out past me."

Marcus began kicking at the plasterboard in a steady rhythm and opened up a small hole at the bottom. Between kicking, ripping with his hand, and cutting into the plaster with the blade, he made an inspection hole about a meter square. A flashlight would have been handy. He got on his knees to peer in, rifle still in one hand.

"I think I can see light," he said. "You got any matches?"

"I've got my fire-starter."

"What are you, an arsonist now?"

"Let me find something I can burn." Reeve backed away, reluctant to turn his back on the hole until he knew what was inside. He went through the cells looking for paper or bedding, not expecting to find anything after the floor had been flooded, but there was an old pillow that might burn for a while. He set it down by the plasterboard wall and started striking the fire-starter over it.

"Hey, I'm getting reflections off something." Marcus tore back more plasterboard. He was covered in pale gray gypsum. "Metal joists or bars or something."

The pillow smoldered. Then a small flame leapt up from the grimy fabric and the fire took hold.

"There you go," Reeve said. The heat was nice, too, but it smelled like burning hair. "What can you see?"

"Goddamn," Marcus said. "It's an old elevator shaft."

Reeve warmed his hands by the fire for a few moments while Marcus seemed to be working something out. "You know, we could still just all hole up in A Wing and wait, right?"

"Wait for what?" Marcus muttered. "The cavalry's not coming, Reeve. We either stop these assholes getting in and treat this like a siege, which we can't do in A Wing because it's got no water. Or we take our chances outside."

He started ripping at the plasterboard with renewed vigor. Reeve shoved his pistol in the back of his belt and gave him a hand. They ended up ripping out nearly the whole wall and found themselves looking at elevator machinery, the really fancy old variety with decorative metalwork. The pillow was putting out a lot of smoke now but it had done its job.

"Could have done with a damn mirror to take a look," Marcus said. "Okay, I'll stick my head in and check above. You check below at the same time. Might both get our heads ripped off. Might not."

"That's inspirational. I'll do it."

And they did it, right on cue. Reeve was getting used to working with this guy. Reeve aimed his sidearm down but couldn't see much apart from faint lights that could have been reflections. Marcus sighted up on something above.

"Clear," he said. "The shaft must be capped off at the roof, because I never saw any winch mechanism up there before. But whatever it's covered by, it's glass or mesh. I can see some light." He looked down. "What's below here? I thought this was the basement level."

"So did I." Reeve stood up and fanned the smoke away from his face, then kicked what was left of the pillow over to the wall. "You think they're coming up or down?"

There was a loud, heavy, metallic clang. Reeve couldn't place it for a moment. Then the reality hit him at the same moment it seemed to dawn on Marcus.

"Some bastard's locked us in," he growled, and started running down the passage. "Campbell, you fucker, is that you?"

Reeve was right behind Marcus, thinking the same thought. "Campbell? Open the damn door."

It was shut, all right. Marcus rattled it furiously but he wasn't going to shift it without a key. There wasn't a lot of point yelling, either. If everybody else was in A Wing now, nobody would hear a thing if the Hammer of goddamn Dawn struck the basement.

"Campbell?" Marcus hammered on the door. "Reeve's in here. You can fuck around with me all you want, but he's not involved. Open the frigging door. Let him go."

Reeve held his breath. It was hard to tell if there was any movement outside because the door was so damn thick and heavy. Then something scraped against it.

"Come on, Campbell. Joke over."

The narrow eye-level hatch started to slide. Reeve resisted the urge to shove his pistol through it and blow Campbell's brains out. And then it slid all the way back.

Marcus had his rifle in both hands. Maybe he was finding it tough to resist too. Reeve waited, trying to peek through without getting too close. Suddenly weird yellow eyes and a gray, scaly slash of a nose filled the opening and eye-wateringly bad breath wafted in.

"*Groundwalker . . .*" a voice rasped. "*Hur hur hur!*"

Marcus squeezed off a burst through the hatch and dropped to the floor. Shots spat back through the opening. Reeve flattened himself against the door and watched the rounds strike the granite walls and ricochet. No doubt about that, then: the big grubs had shown up.

"Okay, Campbell, I take it all back," Reeve said. "So what *is* that thing?"

"That's a grub," Marcus said. He kept looking around like he was planning a way out. "A drone."

"Well, we're in here, and they're out there, so . . . have they overrun the place? Are they in A Wing? Yeah, I get your point about missing radios."

"If they get in here, we can shut ourselves in a cell and just stay clear of the door."

"And starve to death."

"They're not that patient. Plus there's plumbed water."

"I'm not drinking out of the toilet bowl."

"You can last three weeks without food, easy."

"So you're not going to make some noble last stand that they'll toast in the officer's mess, then."

"Depends what comes through that lift shaft."

The grub was still taking pot shots through the hatch, making that hur-hur-hur noise, and Reeve finally realized the bastard was *laughing*. That pissed him off more than he could ever have imagined. He tried to think of something he could shove through the opening, because the passage was pretty well dead straight and that meant there was nowhere to take cover except the cells. It was like a fairground shooting gallery for grubs.

"Okay." Marcus jerked his head. "When I say *go*, crawl along the edge of the wall and into the first open cell. Then we work our way from cell to cell until we reach the shaft."

"At least I'm learning to think like you."

"I'd see a shrink about that. Ready?"

"Yeah."

"Go."

Reeve went first. It was amazing what a guy could crawl in and not care about if there was a grub firing over his head. But the good news was that all the time the drone had its rifle jammed through the hatch, it couldn't see where it was firing. Reeve scrambled into the cell and Marcus slid in behind him. The firing carried on for a while, then stopped.

"One cell at a time," Marcus said. "If he's looking through, he's not firing. He can't look and fire at the same time. Short runs. Got it?"

"Yeah."

"Then we check out the lift shaft. If it's not the ingress point, we try going up and out. If it is—then we've got the lock-in option."

"Okay." Reeve didn't like that much. *Out* sounded a lot better. "Ready?"

"Go."

The grub hadn't given up. Rounds spat off the walls and hit the floor ran-
domly, and Reeve settled for dashing, not crawling. There was a run of three
closed cells that made for a pretty pants-pissing run to cover, but eventually
they worked their way down to the end cell and sat with their backs against the
wall, sweating and panting despite the chill.

"Now you can cover me," Marcus said. He handed him the rifle. "I'm going
to check out that lift shaft. Distract him while I get in there. And unclip the
door in case we need to slam it in a hurry."

"You're going to break your neck."

"Better than letting a grub do it for me." Marcus indicated the wall outside.
"I don't have to tell you how to do it, do I?"

"I think I remember."

Reeve crawled out and squatted against the open metal door, reaching
up to dislodge the hooked bar that held it open flat against the wall. Then
he sighted up on the hatch at the far end, just a small letterbox of dim
light. He wished he hadn't switched on the light in the parallel corridor,
but it was too damn late now to do anything about it. Marcus darted out
from the cell.

Crack. A round struck short, about halfway down the passage. Reeve fired
twice.

"I'm in," Marcus said.

Reeve didn't dare take his eyes off the door at the far end. He could hear
Marcus sliding over stone, the rasp of material on a hard surface, and then a
faint noise that sounded like someone polishing wood.

"I can still see lights below." Marcus's voice was muffled and echoey. "And I
mean lights. Not reflections. Seen that way too often."

"More grubs."

"Yeah."

"Where are you, exactly?"

"Hanging on the cable."

"Holy shit, Marcus, get out of there."

"I'm going to climb up."

"You're okay with that?"

"Yeah."

The polishing noise started again, a slow regular rhythm until it faded.
Marcus must have been shinning up some cable. He took it all so casually. It
gave Reeve a brief insight into the kind of day a Gear had in a war like this.
Yeah, Marcus Fenix would never be a civilian. Nobody was going to take the

army out of him. The grub fired off a few more bursts from the door and Reeve checked his own magazine. Nineteen rounds left now: he was eking them out carefully.

Marcus seemed to have been gone for a long time but Reeve could still hear him moving and twanging the cable. Eventually the polishing noise started again. "Okay, Reeve, cover me."

"Ready."

The grub wasn't watching this time. Maybe it was reloading or calling its buddies to come and watch the show. Marcus darted across the passage and squatted in the open doorway behind Reeve.

"It's climbable," he said. "But the cap of the shaft is mesh. There's a gap between it and the flat roof. It isn't big enough for me to push through."

"You know that a mouse can squeeze through a hole the diameter of a pencil?"

"Well, that's fucking terrific news if you're a mouse."

"So . . ."

Reeve stopped. He could hear a noise, echoing and thudding, and Marcus looked at him. It was coming from the shaft. Whatever was down there was coming up, and even if it was Wretches and not the big armed bastards, that was very bad news.

"That'll be our guests for dinner," Reeve said, standing up very slowly.

Damned if I'm going to get my head torn off.

Damned if I'm going to let anyone lock me up again, either.

Marcus straightened up. They were just out of the line of fire if the grub decided to play shooting gallery again, with a small margin of error when they stuck their heads out to look forward or behind. The noise from the shaft was getting louder.

"Time to repel boarders," Marcus said. "Better shut the door."

No. I can't face that. I haven't been through all this shit to go back to square one. "You sure they can't break in?"

"As sure as I can be. Otherwise I'd be saving the last round for myself."

"Should have brought sandwiches."

"Let's do it."

No. You'll be okay, but not me.

Marcus was a really big guy, not designed for half the things a smaller man like Reeve could do.

"Sure, Marcus," Reeve said. He had the rifle and the pistol. He'd done what he promised himself he'd do, smokes or no smokes. He'd done the right thing

for a guy who'd done enough right things of his own to deserve a little forgiveness for one shitty decision. Now he was going to do what he needed to, and
without having to cause one more death to do it. "I watched your back okay,
didn't I?"

"Yeah. Thanks." Marcus was distracted, trying to keep an ear on the lift
shaft and an eye on the grub at the door. "Never thought any asshole in here
would."

Reeve kept his hand on the edge of the door. He didn't have weight on his
side, but damn it, he'd give it a go. "Good, because that means you won't kill
me and eat me if we get stuck in here longer than we planned," he said, and
pushed Marcus into the cell like he was joking with him.

Then he jumped back and slammed the door shut.

"Hey, what the fuck are you playing at, Reeve?"

"You'll be okay in there."

"Open the goddamn door."

"Come on, you know how it works. Can't. Now, I'm out of time, so you shut
up and wait there, okay?"

"I said *open the door.*"

"See you around, Marcus."

"Don't. *Don't do this.* Get in a cell. Lock yourself in, for fuck's sake, Reeve.
You won't make it out. *Reeve!*"

Reeve didn't answer. He aimed the rifle down the lift shaft and opened fire.
The grubs—whatever they were—had to climb up just like he did. He heard
thuds and roars as something fell. There were still lights moving below, but a
lot further down now. He knew two things for sure: he couldn't get out along
the passage, and he was never going to have a door slammed and locked behind him again, no matter what. He squeezed off a few more rounds, looked
down the shaft, and decided he had a few minutes' head start.

Marcus was still yelling. "Reeve? You crazy bastard, *I warned you!* I warned
you not to try to save me. Get your ass back here!"

Marcus *would* be okay, though. He had water and the grubs couldn't get at
him, and sooner or later, someone would come to see where he was. He mattered to too many people out there, like the idiot who was trying to spring him
and a woman who was prepared to wait for him when she could have had any
man in Jacinto. When Reeve got out, maybe he'd even call that Hoffman guy
himself.

But he had to do it now. He could hear the grubs coming.

"Hang in there, Marcus," he called, and jumped out to grab the cable, looking up at the square of light above. "And you were right. It was fucking terrific news for a mouse."

CIC, JACINTO.

The grubs never gave up.

It wasn't the first time they'd launched an assault this size on multiple fronts, but the last time it had happened, Hoffman had had more assets: more Gears, more artillery, and more Ravens. Now he had to choose between saving south Jacinto or the west of the city. The COG was stretched past breaking point. He looked at the map on the wall and the plot on the chart table, all the assets marked and numbered, and searched for answers, but there was only one. He had to make the call on the basis of where he could save the most, not just lives, but resources like the hospitals, food warehouses, utilities, and the heart of the COG's forces.

He could live without the Andius highway for a while. The whole area had been trashed anyway. There was nothing of strategic importance to lose apart from the road. But if the ugly gray bastards got into south Jacinto, then the COG was as good as finished.

The doors swung open and Prescott walked in. Hoffman braced for a pep talk but the man just looked at him. "Doesn't feel right sitting in my office at a time like this, Victor," he said. "But at least I've got some good news for you."

"It'd need to be very good news indeed, Chairman."

"Payne's promised that the Lightmass and the resonator will be deployable by eighteen hundred today."

That was a big surprise, let alone good news. Hoffman had thought it was weeks away. "It's ready?"

"No, it's *deployable*. He's not happy, and he says it hasn't even passed inspection, but I've explained that we're going to use it anyway. Otherwise he'll be tinkering with it for another month, and another."

"I'll live with it," Hoffman said. Damn, he would have been grateful for a box of sharpened stakes right then. "Because we're out of options."

Prescott studied the chart table. It was illuminated like a lightbox, all the assets shown as colored symbols alongside the latest enemy positions and troop strengths, but it would have been obvious to a smart ten-year-old that the grubs were sweeping up from the south in a V movement around the whole south and west of Jacinto. Prescott folded one arm across his chest and tugged at his top lip with his other hand, his I-don't-want-to-interfere-but-I'm-going-to gesture.

"What are you going to do about the prison?" he asked. "They've already had Locust breach the building, yes?"

"They have. Their senior warder called it in." No, Hoffman hadn't forgotten Marcus, and he hadn't forgotten that Anya was in earshot, either, right behind him in an ops room that was holding its breath. "But I've only got one platoon out there and I'm going to have to pull them back soon. You've seen the numbers. We've as good as lost the western perimeter already."

Prescott didn't look at him. "Then I think we should order the evacuation of the prison."

"Fine, but I can't commit transport, Chairman. They'll have to take their chances."

"If the platoon that's out there can direct that—we're only talking about forty or so prisoners now. We release them and conscript them. I imagine some of them are very proficient with firearms."

Hoffman could bet his life on one thing: if Prescott wanted something done and explained it that specifically, then he had a damn good reason for it, and Hoffman would never really know just what that was. But this time he could hazard a guess. Prescott was worried about Marcus. Half the army might have forgotten him, but 26 RTI hadn't, and there'd be a lot of Gears who'd be pretty demotivated if they thought Prescott hadn't tried to give him a fighting chance.

"I know at least *one* of them is," Hoffman said.

Prescott dropped his arms to his side, nodding to himself as he looked at the map on the wall. "Do it, please." In fact, he looked right past Hoffman and focused on Anya. "Lieutenant, contact the prison and order them to release the inmates into the custody of—whose platoon's out there, Colonel?"

"Lieutenant Schachter."

"And tell the Lieutenant she can arm any of them she deems fit. I'm sure the proximity of the enemy will focus them wonderfully."

"Yes, sir," said Anya.

Her voice didn't change, not the slightest hint that she had any personal interest in what happened to any of the prisoners. It was exactly the same way she'd dealt with being the ops room controller in *Kalona* when her mother was busy getting herself killed at Aspho Fields. Anya Stroud could keep her cool even when her world was falling apart. Hoffman met her eyes, more by accident than intent, and for a moment he felt guilty that she'd thought he was a better man than he actually was.

Prescott sat down at one of the unoccupied desks with his elbows braced on the arms of the chair, fingers steepled and legs crossed as he watched the radio operators collating reports and sticking pins in the map. Anya gazed at him with a lot more warmth than Hoffman expected. He'd made one ally, then.

"Okay, people, let's crack on with this," Hoffman said. He could forget the Slab now. He didn't have to feel like a complete shit every time Anya looked at him. That was a load off his mind. "Stroud, get hold of Lieutenant Kim and set up an RV with him so I can brief him on the Lightmass. I want you along for that. He's going to have to deploy the thing as best he can, so get whatever data the DRA has to hand. Mathieson—find Cox for me. I want every available Centaur that's not already deployed patrolling between Timgad and East Barricade. Get me Major Reid, too."

"He's at the refugee center on Corren Way, sir."

"Get him back here, then. He can't run an operation from the ground."

Hoffman always tried to do exactly that himself, but Mathieson was too diplomatic to point it out. The kid did smile, though. It was reassuring that he still could. Hoffman went up to the roof to comfort himself with the closest thing he had to an overall picture of the city and spent a few minutes just listening to the noise in the distance and smelling the smoke and aviation fuel. When he went back downstairs, Prescott was still sitting there in complete silence. He hadn't even uncrossed his legs. He'd now been parked there for an hour, just watching and not being a pain in the ass—which was better than the alternative—but he was definitely waiting for something. He kept looking at his watch.

"Sir, I'll let you know when Schachter calls in," Hoffman said. "You don't have to sit it out. But if you could put another rocket up Dr. Payne's ass, that would take a load off my mind. I want everything he's got that Kim's going to need."

"He's sent the briefing data already."

Anya looked up. "Yes, got it sir."

"All of it?"

"Well, just about."

"Can you chase him for me, Chairman?" Hoffman asked. "Shake everything out of him. He always holds something back."

Prescott frowned, then nodded. It was all an act, but Hoffman knew him well enough to realize he was waiting on news of Marcus and that he might not want to make that obvious. This was a convenient way to tell him to piss off and stop scaring the CIC team without either of them losing face. And Hoffman *did* want someone with more clout than him to go and grab Payne hard by the short and curlies. If this didn't work, they'd be back to worse than square one.

"Thank you, Colonel," Prescott said. "You'll call me, though."

"Of course."

Prescott left and Mathieson raised his eyebrows at Hoffman. Hoffman could only shrug and hope Anya wasn't reading anything into it. But ten minutes later, Schachter came back on the radio. Anya gestured at him, mouthed "Schachter" and indicated the earpiece.

He picked up his headset and held it to one ear. "Go ahead, Lieutenant."

"Sir, we've now extracted three staff and thirty-seven inmates. The grubs have overrun most of the prison but the staff were barricaded in with the prisoners in a disused wing, so we shoved them into the 'Dills. Tight fit, and not very fragrant, but they're in one piece."

"Where are you?"

"We've pulled back east of the Andius highway. The grub column's moving south now. That's it. Kiss goodbye to the western perimeter for the time being."

Hoffman wanted this over with. He had ten kilometers of the southern perimeter under threat and there was a limit to how long he could spend on this. He'd kept faith with Anya. He could see her watching him discreetly. "Move out, then." Hoffman now *had* to ask. "What shape is Fenix in? You've got him, yes? He was Two-Six RTI. Remember him?"

There was a long pause. "Someone will. Wait one." Schachter muted her radio. He heard the click but she didn't come back to him for three very long minutes. "No, sir. No sign of Fenix. We're looking for the chief warder. He'll know."

"*Shit.*" There was no hiding this from Anya. She could hear what was happening just from his side of the conversation. "Where the hell is he?"

"No idea, sir. We can go back in. There's a basement level, but the security gates are locked down." Schachter paused. Hoffman could hear the artillery in the background. "We're going to have to move now because we're taking fire. But we're willing to try and get across."

Hoffman didn't look at Anya. The math was simple. He had a platoon, thirty guys, and a grub brigade right on top of them. Marcus wasn't where he should have been. He could have been dead; he could have escaped under his own steam. Or he could have been any damn where in a big, sprawling empty maze of a place. *Time.* They just didn't have time or numbers on their side.

"Leave him," Hoffman said.

"Sir—"

It was an awful, silent three seconds. Hoffman floundered. There was a platoon out there that was safe now but wouldn't be if it tried to cross back over the highway through grub lines. He couldn't squander any more lives.

"No, screw it," Hoffman said at last. *Screw him. I'm going to have to leave him to rot. I could commit Schachter's men and find Marcus dead, and then lose them as well.* "Goddamn—you can't take on a battalion of grubs with a platoon. He's on his own. Get everyone out of the sector."

"We don't leave a man behind, sir."

One of the ops room radio operators looked up, Bacher or Baker or something. Hoffman had never heard the guy offer an opinion in his life. "Yeah, like Fenix didn't leave my brother behind at Chancery Bridge."

The ops room was suddenly silent except for the hiss of static on open radio channels and the faint chatter of a printer.

"Move out," Hoffman said. Not everyone thought Fenix was a straight-up hero. The comment bit Hoffman right in his regimental pride. "And that's an order, Schachter. Leave him. We'll check out the place if and when the heat's off." And now he had to do the hardest thing of all: to look Anya in the eye. "Lieutenant, is that RV with Kim set up?"

She had her hand to her headset, still apparently calm, but he could see she was biting her bottom lip. That wasn't an Anya kind of habit. He went over and tapped her on the shoulder. "Come on, Lieutenant. Time to move out. You need to brief Kim. Got your tech data?"

"Coming, sir." She didn't look at him. Breaking her heart felt even harder than turning that key to fry Sera's cities. "Just got to print this off. Five minutes."

"You want me to let the Chairman know Schachter . . . completed the extraction?" Mathieson asked.

Hoffman nodded. "Yeah. I know you'll be diplomatic, but don't feel obliged to lie for me."

"Okay, sir."

This was the harsh shit he had to do. If Prescott didn't like his decision, then his only option was to override his CDS and order Schachter back across grub lines, and if he did that—well, the working relationship was going to get tense.

I can't fucking bleed for Marcus Fenix. Would I risk a platoon for some poor asshole from the Tollens, or any other damn regiment?

It was one of those things that had to be done in a war, and it went with the rank. Hoffman knew he'd regret it for the rest of his life. But he couldn't change his mind, even if that platoon was willing to die to get Marcus out, because it wasn't their call. It was his. The numbers didn't stack up, not even for Marcus.

Hoffman headed for the door. Anya snatched up her folio and trotted after him in silence: no remonstration, no pleading, not even a tear.

Fuck you, Marcus. It had to be you, didn't it? I've sweated at night for four goddamn years over you and I'd just about come to terms with it. Now you start it all over again. I wouldn't want anyone to go back for me. We leave guys behind all the time. We go back for them later. Sometimes they hold out until we can get to them. Sometimes we don't.

And sometimes I'm left with just two guys on Chancery Bridge who hung on while the rest of their buddies ran out of time and luck.

CIC was all long corridors with noisy tiled or parquet floors, making it feel like an eternity to get outside to the helo pad, and that was a very long walk to take in silence. Hoffman waited for Anya to finally crack and beg him to go back for Marcus. He almost wanted her to, to give him some excuse to change his mind. But she didn't. She was like her mother, all duty and common sense, but without the crazy risk-taking. She knew the stakes.

When they got outside, Lieutenant Mansell was playing loadmaster for the Ravens. He beckoned Hoffman over and indicated KR-239.

"You okay without a crew chief, sir?" he asked. "I've had to put Mitchell on another bird for the day."

"We'll manage, Lieutenant." Hoffman held his cap on to stop the rotor wash from whipping it off. When he looked around, he saw Dom heading his way at a jog. "Anya?" Hoffman gestured to her to board the Raven. "Go ahead. I'll be two minutes."

She looked back at Dom but kept walking, tottering in those heels. Hoffman knew he now had some explaining to do. A sane colonel would have turned his back and got on with his job, but Dom deserved better. He deserved to be told.

"Sir?" Dom speeded up and came sprinting across the pad. Hoffman had no idea where he'd come from, but he had his finger to his earpiece as if he was talking to someone while he ran. "Sir!"

"I need to talk to you, Santiago."

"And I need to talk to *you,* sir." He came to a halt in front of Hoffman and completely ignored Mansell. "Did I hear right? We're leaving Marcus behind?"

"Who'd you hear that from?"

Dom looked down at the ground. He didn't need to say *Prescott*. Crafty asshole: he wouldn't do anything as blatant as countermanding Hoffman's orders, but he knew damn well all he had to do was call Dom on the radio, tell him Marcus was in the shit, and he'd do the job for him. Damn, Prescott really was fixated on Marcus for some reason. Was 26 RTI's opinion that important? It didn't make sense, but Hoffman didn't have time to worry about that now.

"Santiago, I'm waiting," he said.

"Can't say, sir."

"Okay, you heard right, then."

"But you let the other assholes out."

It was all falling apart fast. Dom's face was all wounded betrayal and—worse—shock, obvious shock at his old CO not being the man he'd always thought he was. "You can't abandon Marcus, sir. You *can't*."

"You want to tell me how I can divert a couple of companies plus support to take on a grub brigade on the off-chance that he's still alive in there? Because Schachter can't do it on her own." Hoffman couldn't bear it. It was bad enough hurting Anya, but crushing Dom was almost more than he could stomach. He was damn fond of that boy. If Hoffman had a favorite, it was Dom: mindlessly brave, dog-loyal, the man who'd take a bullet for you without a second thought. Hoffman was telling him to leave his brother behind, quite literally. Carlos was gone, his kids were gone, and if he ever saw his wife again, he'd probably only be ID'ing her corpse. "I'm sorry. When the heat's off, we'll go back and try to find him."

"Sir, no offense, but I'm damn well going back for him *now*."

What do I do?

What the fuck do I do now and how will I live with it?

Hoffman knew what he should have done, but his resolve was already giving way to something far more personal and dangerous, something he hadn't even let get the better of him for Margaret. He took a few paces toward the Raven. Then he stopped and turned, aware of his audience. "There's maybe five hundred, a thousand grubs around the Slab. You were a terrific commando, Santiago, but those aren't good odds even for you."

"I can get through on my own."

Mansell was watching. He pitched in unasked. "Santiago, move out."

"Goddamn it, sir." Dom rolled straight over Mansell's order. His voice was almost a sob. "How can you do this to him? How can you do this to *me*? I'm going back for him, and you'll have to frigging shoot me to stop me."

Dom turned away and started jogging toward the 'Dills parked on the edge of the landing pad. Mansell turned to Hoffman, visibly shocked.

"You're not going to let him do that, are you, sir?"

Yes. I am. I damn well am.

It was the best Hoffman could do. It would still never be enough.

Dom got a few meters, then turned, almost stumbling a few paces as he walked backward. His expression was one of disbelief. "I'm going to bring him back, sir. You hear me?"

Hoffman no longer knew if Marcus deserved what he'd got. It didn't change what Marcus had done, and it didn't mean it would have been right to send a willing platoon back there to find him and maybe lose them too. But Marcus was 26 RTI, regiment, *family*—and however angry and confused Hoffman felt right then, he wanted Marcus to live. Dom, like his brother Carlos, was ready to die to make that happen.

Would I do this for any other Gear, any other regiment? No. I'd do what it took to save most lives. But they always said I was overpromoted, and now I'll prove them right.

"I haven't got time to stop you, Santiago," Hoffman yelled. *You know me, Dom. We took Aspho Point. We fought at Gossar Pass. You know I'm just a regular guy, not a monster. Understand what I'm saying now.* "And if you go on this goddamn jaunt without an extra Lancer and a few spare plates and get yourself killed, then I'm going to kick your corpse's ass all the way back to Wrightman."

Dom stopped in his tracks. For a moment, he did that little frown that always made Hoffman think he was going to burst into tears, ambushed by an unexpected gesture. His lips moved but he didn't manage a word, and then he opened the 'Dill's side hatch. But he didn't take the vehicle. He just dismounted Jack, the on-board bot, one of the last few operational smart bots the COG had. The small machine unfurled its twin arms, ejected from its housing, and glided out to float beside him awaiting instructions. Dom glanced back at Hoffman, then ran off with Jack following him at head height.

Mansell looked dumbfounded. "What the hell are you doing, sir? He's taking the damn bot. The last prototype."

"Yeah, thieving little bastard." Hoffman turned away. Dom stood a better chance of slipping into the Slab unnoticed without a big noisy target like a 'Dill. He still thought like a commando. He'd take a rifle for Marcus, too, and that would also be overlooked one way or another. "Discipline's gone to ratshit lately. I'm going to write a stiff memo."

"*Sir*, he should be stuck on a charge. We can't just—"

"Yes, but you've gone blind, Lieutenant, and I've gone deaf, so who can safely say it even happened? Move out." Hoffman started walking toward the Raven. He made sure he was out of Mansell's earshot but hoped he was in range of the fates or God or whatever else might be eavesdropping and willing to lend Dom a hand. "Good luck, Dom," he said to himself. "You bring him back, you hear? You bring him back *safe*."

Hoffman would have to put on a show of outrage when Marcus finally showed up, but he could manage that. Part of him was furious with Marcus for starting this shit, and part of him was repelled by his own do-it-by-the-book reaction. It would have been bad for morale if he begged Marcus's forgiveness.

He climbed into the crew bay and looked down at Anya. It was hard for a lovely kid like that to look wretched, but she did. She wasn't so much clasping her hands in her lap as wringing them.

"Goddamn," Hoffman said mildly, sitting down beside her. "Dom's a disobedient asshole, isn't he? Pardon my language, Lieutenant."

"Sorry, sir?"

"He's just taken Jack and gone haring off to the Slab with a spare Lancer and some armor. Damn, I'm going to have to put him on latrine duty for a week when this war's over."

Anya just looked at him, then shut her eyes for a moment. "Oh."

He patted her arm. "I'm none too proud of myself, Anya."

"Even the best of us do terrible things sometimes," she said. "And we don't even know why."

"Amen."

"I meant Marcus."

"I meant me."

Marcus had done something shockingly out of character, and now Hoffman had too, but Hoffman wasn't sure which of his actions was going to prove worse—not going back for Marcus right away, or giving a favorite Gear more breaks than some other grunt. He wasn't sure if that made them even or if it was just one of life's harsh lessons in the sameness of all flesh, that even a man who sweated over his moral compass could do something unconscionable in a split-second's moment of weakness, even if he would never dream of living his entire life that way.

Me? Him? Damn you, Marcus. Look what you've done to me.

"Sorotki, are we going to hang around all frigging day?" Hoffman barked. "Turn and burn."

The Raven lifted clear. Anya reached across and squeezed Hoffman's hand. The chain of command was forgotten for a moment.

"Thank you, sir," she said. "He's paid for it. But I know he'll keep paying for the rest of his life."

And so will I. We all have our Anvil Gate.

"Debt paid," he said.

CHAPTER 18

It's been a few hours. I can't hear anyone else out there. Reeve hasn't come back. The grubs can't get at me now, but I'm trapped. So . . . everyone probably thinks I'm dead. Anyway, if they find me, then they'll find this letter, too, and if it's too late, at least you'll know what was on my mind at the end. It was you.

(Prisoner B1116/87 Fenix M.M., writing to Lt. Anya Stroud. Letter not sent.)

TWO KILOMETERS FROM THE SLAB: ONE HOUR LATER.

"Jack, cloak yourself, will you?" Dom said. "This is meant to be a covert op. And stay off the radio."

The bot was just under a meter across without his mechanical arms, a steel and composite egg-shaped unit with a propulsion system, one of the most expensive drones the COG had ever developed. Dom had worked with bots before in the last war, but Jack was the latest and the last of his kind. He could also disappear by literally bending light around himself. Dom didn't understand the physics behind the skin of carbon nanotubes that did the trick, but it was just what he needed right now.

And Dom had always talked to bots like they were Gears. It seemed rude not to. They were smart, independent, and aware of what was said to them, and that was good enough for him.

Jack blipped and the air around him shivered like a mirage on a sunscorched road as he faded into transparency. Dom could still hear the faint noises—the hum of his propulsion unit, the whirr of servos—but to any casual observer, Jack simply wasn't there any longer. Dom could look straight through him. They were now at the intersection of the main highway to Andius and the underpass that ran from West Barricade to the edge of Wenlau

Heath. Somehow, they had to get through the grub lines and then cross open ground to reach the prison.

Dom dropped onto his belly at the edge of the elevated section of the northbound highway and crawled forward to get a look at the grub traffic on the southbound carriageway slightly below. He could see the metal stairs that connected the pedestrian footpath to the underpass, but he could also see a steady trickle of drones with Brumaks. The Reavers seemed to be elsewhere. At least he could avoid being spotted from the air.

"Shit, Jack, I'm going to have to break a few track records," he said. "Any ideas for distracting the grubs?"

Jack was smart but not much good for conversation. It was a shame the research program had been cut short before they added speech to the system. But maybe that would have made Jack just a bit too human for Dom's sanity.

Yeah, remember Pad and his bot. Used to call it Baz, after his buddy who got killed. That can't be healthy. Bots are designed to take the risks humans shouldn't, maybe even take a bullet for a human. Just another way to feel like you've lost your buddy twice.

Dom checked his watch, feeling the sweat trickling down his spine. He'd kept up a steady jog all the way from CIC with an extra rifle and a kitbag of armor, with five klicks still to go. He had no way of knowing if Marcus was already dead. Now he found himself starting to rehearse the idea and how he'd react to it, just to make sure he didn't lose it completely and fall apart if that was what was waiting for him in the Slab.

His mind raced and tripped over itself, fretting about how he'd recover the body, how he'd break it to Anya, and how he'd cope with having both brothers dead. He almost had to punch himself to make it stop. He brought his right fist down hard on the back of his left hand, crushing it against his Lancer for a second.

Get a grip.

Plan it. Visualize it. Do it. Goddamn, I'm a fucking commando. Think like one, then. Believe it.

He pressed up onto all fours and rebalanced his load. Jack could have carried some of it, but that would have defeated the point of having a cloaked bot. It was just a matter of slogging on. He worked out a path of cover down to the stairs—crawl along behind the crash barrier, sprint for the concrete bridge support, then take five or six steps down the stairs before dropping onto the grass verge that hadn't been mowed short in years—and went for it. Jack brushed against him at one point and he almost crapped himself. He knew the bot was right on top of him because he could hear him and even feel the faint breath of air and warmth like an animal at his side, but just not being able to see what had touched him was disturbing. He rose to a crouch, pushed off on his hands like a sprinter leaving the blocks, and ran for the shelter of the stanchion.

Nobody took a potshot at him. He pressed as flat to the concrete as he could and watched a patrol of grubs pass beneath him before cycling through the radio channels to listen in case there was any sitrep on grub numbers in the area.

Hoffman knows I'm here. Is it going to make any difference if I call in? No, don't push it. Stay off the net. Don't rub his nose in it. If he wants to get hold of me, he can flash me.

To the north, Dom could see more grubs with a Brumak about a hundred meters away. This was the break in the traffic that he needed. He slid over the metal handrail and landed on the stairs. He was sure the clanging of his boots must have carried halfway to Andius, but in five seconds he was over the side and falling into long grass, the first fresh growth of spring. Soft or not, he hit his elbow so hard when he landed and rolled that his eyes watered.

Come on. A hundred meters down the underpass and I'm on the heath. Keep going. Just do it.

"Jack, you still there?"

A disembodied chirp confirmed it. Dom squatted and checked both ways before darting into the underpass and below the southbound carriageway, trying not to break into a run that might echo and alert the grubs on the road above. The *pomp-pomp-pomp* of artillery would probably have been enough to shroud the noise, but he didn't dare risk it. If he didn't go back for Marcus then nobody else would, not until it was too late.

You should have sent a Raven for him, sir. I know it's wrong, but most of the pilots would have volunteered.

Dom struggled with the idea that Hoffman had abandoned Marcus. Nobody did that. No Gear was left behind. He knew it was irrational and emotional, and that Hoffman wasn't allowed to think that way now that he was the senior commander with so many other lives at stake, but it still hurt.

But he let me take all this kit and go find him. Either he doesn't give a shit about me these days, or he's still the Hoffman I know. Everyone's going crazy lately. Marcus, Hoffman, and me.

Wenlau Heath loomed ahead of him. He stood in the opening of the underpass, one hand on the broken tiles that had once been a mosaic mural of folk art depicting Tyran nursery rhymes, all cheery-looking monsters and heroes with swords. This part of the heath had been a picnic site with a play area before E-Day but nobody ventured out here with their kids anymore. It seemed a weird place to site a family picnic area given that a prison overlooked it. Maybe it had been intended as one of those cautionary tales for kids, a friendly warning that if they didn't behave they'd end up in there.

The Slab could have passed for a country estate if it hadn't been for the razor wire along the top of the walls. Dom estimated he had seven hundred meters to cover, a few minutes' walk if he could just stroll in the open, but a potential killing ground if the grubs were still out there. He knelt in the cover of some thorn bushes and scanned the horizon. Warm air brushed his arm like a hair dryer on a low setting as Jack took up station beside him.

"Jack, go up ahead and scout for me. You've got the floor plans in your database, haven't you?" Dom looked over his shoulder to check whether he could see the bot's faint mirage. The city skyline shivered a little. "Get to the gates and bleep me when it's clear."

Dom felt the wash of warm air again as Jack flew away, and took out his field glasses to scan the heath again. *No grubs. No Brumaks. Nothing big.* He scanned upward and magnified the image to take in the top of the walls, and that was when he caught some movement. It wasn't big enough to be a grub. He thought it might have been a crow or something, but then it paused in a gap in the parapet. *Wretches.* They were goddamn Wretches. His gut flipped, but he kept telling himself that breaching a building wasn't the same as controlling it. The Slab was a big place. Just getting inside didn't necessarily mean they'd penetrated every cell.

"Come on, Jack," Dom said. "Can you hear me? Are we clear yet? One blip for yes."

Jack took a full minute to respond with a single chirp. Dom picked out a path across the heath, ten or twelve moves from the underpass to the gates, most of the gorse bushes so short that he'd have to cover the ground at a crawl with his Lancer resting on his arms, dragging the kitbag. He edged out and began the slow approach, pausing every so often to stick his head above the level of the gorse and check that he was still heading the right way. Shit, it was slow. Twigs snagged his face and he kept expecting to find himself staring at the boots of a grub and with nowhere to run.

Just keep going. Right elbow forward, left knee . . . left elbow, right knee . . .

He was sweating like a pig. But the next time he raised his head, he was almost in line with the small door set into the big black gates, and then he was suddenly crawling on sharp gravel across the width of a single-track road.

"Jack?" He was right in front of the gates now, close enough to ease himself to a squat and slip to one side of the granite buttress. "Let me in, Jack."

For some reason he thought Jack would decloak in front of the gate, but he didn't. The small door eased open. Dom stepped in and almost collided with Jack hovering in front of him. Right: he could ascend over walls, so he'd just dropped in and opened the gate from the inside. Useful things, bots. But now Dom had to search this place without a hint of where Marcus might be. All he could do was follow Jack into the building, checking around him at every step.

The Slab stank to high heaven, the most depressing place Dom had ever seen, so dark and decaying that he couldn't believe any human being could live there. How the hell had Marcus ever coped with this? It explained a lot. First Dom had been afraid of how he'd react if he found him dead, and now he was starting to worry about what a live Marcus would be like. Every few minutes, the metal grids set in the ceilings shivered and clanged as Wretches scuttled along them. Dom trained his rifle on the grids and gantries, looking for a clear shot or an excuse to drop some of the little bastards.

All the doors hung open. There were gates and passages made entirely of steel bars or wire mesh, and the original fabric of the building with its heavy, carved wooden doors and metal bolts. At one point a Wretch darted out in front of Dom and he opened fire, shredding it with a long burst. He didn't need to do that. He just wanted to. Now he found himself edging down a long corridor that looked like someone had built a giant chicken run in the middle of it. He could hear water trickling somewhere. Then he heard Wretches moving around again, and looked up. One of the things was right above him on another grid. He fired, risking a ricochet, and it squealed and ran off.

"Find me D Wing, Jack," Dom said. "Prescott said D Wing."

Jack knew where he was going. Dom stuck close and found himself walking through a series of doors into a big, empty hall with an upper gallery, a complete wreck of a place that made his stomach roll. The first thing he saw was the dead Wretches scattered around the floor. A table at the far end had been tipped over, and fallen masonry lay in piles at one end of the central hall.

"Jack, you sure this is the place? Shit, you sure this isn't one of the derelict wings?"

Jack bleeped once, then twice. Now Dom could make out the individual cells set in the walls on either side. He started looking into each one, wondering whether to risk calling out, but decided to carry on in silence. In the end, he checked every cell on that floor and found nothing. He'd been in here an hour.

How the hell did Marcus survive in here? Shit, what's it done to him?

He tried to put that out of his mind for the time being. "Jack, any other cells in recent use on your plans? How are we going to find Marcus now?"

Jack moved off and Dom followed. The bot bypassed a couple of locks on security doors and floated down a flight of stairs into almost pitch blackness.

"Hey, lights, Jack."

Jack's tactical lamp shot out an intense white beam and Dom could see a short corridor with a metal door half-open. For some reason he was expecting to trip over human corpses, but there was nothing on the floor. Jack slowed down and went into the corridor. The only working light Dom had seen since he walked in cast patches of cold, bluish light on the stone floor. He couldn't hear anything down here, not even a sound from outside or even from the floor above. Jack started sweeping his beam from right to left across the corridor and back again, then stopped at one of the cell doors.

Dom fought an urge to say "What is it, Jack?" like the bot was a dog. But Jack had sensors, and maybe he could detect body heat and exhaled CO_2, or even pick up sounds that Dom couldn't. Overhead, a couple of Wretches stopped on the grid to spit down at him. He aimed at them, and they scuttled off.

The door had a small metal hatch. All Dom could do was slide it open and try to see what had grabbed Jack's attention. He could have sworn he saw movement.

Okay. I can always shoot it if it's a grub. Got to check it out.

"Rip the door, Jack."

Jack burned his way through the lock and the door swung open. A squadron of flies buzzed out, skimming Dom's face, and for a moment he wondered if he was rescuing a corpse. He couldn't see a thing inside except a shaft of dim light filtering through from the gantry above. Then he heard movement—creaking bedsprings, the shuffle of boots, those fucking Wretches still moving around on the overhead gantries—and Marcus loomed out of the darkness.

Dom had imagined the worst, but not this.

Even in this light, Marcus looked pretty much the same as he went in, just thinner, but not the emaciated shell of a man Dom was expecting. Dom wanted to hug him because that was what regular guys did when they hadn't seen their brother for years and didn't know if they'd ever see him alive again, but this was Marcus, and some things about him never changed. His body language said *don't touch me*. His shoulders were squared and his arms were held stiffly at his sides.

But I've come for you, Marcus. I swore I would. I'll never let you down. Come on, man. React.

Marcus just stood there, his outline picked up by the faint light, holding a scrap of paper in his hand. He folded it with surprising care for a man with Wretches scuttling about on the gantry above and puking drool over him, then slipped it into his pants and stared past Dom for a moment at Jack. The overhead light suddenly caught his face and Dom almost flinched. Shit, something had ripped up his right cheek. Dom steeled himself not to ask, at least not yet.

"What are you doing here?" Marcus demanded.

It was like a slap in the face. "Getting you out." *Damn, I should know better by now.* Marcus had gone straight back to his default setting, pretending nothing had happened. *Cut him some slack. God knows what he's been through in here. And you know what he's like.* Dom dropped the kitbag on the floor. "Here. Put this on. You'll need it."

Marcus was still staring suspiciously through the open door like someone had called trying to sell him brushes. He seemed to have worked out that Dom didn't have anyone's orders to stroll off with Jack. Then he opened the kitbag and started putting on his armor.

"You could get into a lot of trouble for doing this," he muttered.

"Not anymore." Dom had heard that embarrassed false annoyance before. It was a lot like Hoffman's. "Things have changed. We better go."

"What about the other prisoners? We can't just leave them here."

"They're gone. Hoffman pardoned everybody."

Marcus jerked his head back a fraction like he didn't believe what he'd heard. Then his face fell into that familiar grim resignation. "Is that right," he rasped.

Oh shit. Here we go. Shouldn't have said it. It wasn't quite like that, was it? But Dom was in a hurry, scared shitless, and none of that crap mattered right now. "Yeah. Welcome back to the army, soldier."

"Shit." Marcus seemed to have erased four years from his memory instantly. It was like he'd never been shut away, never missed anybody, never thought he'd die in here.

And he didn't ask about Anya.

But that was Marcus. The worse things got, the more he locked into that stiff-upper-lip, Fenix-men-don't-feel-pain bullshit. Dom got the feeling that any Fenix caught losing his intestines on the battlefield would be told to get a grip and snap out of it.

"What's the paper for?" he asked.

"Sanity." Marcus gave his Lancer a fond look like this was the reunion he'd longed for the most. "Let's go."

Dom decided to let Marcus say what he wanted to say in his own good time. He was safe, he was getting out of the Slab before the place killed him, and that was all that mattered. Dom didn't know if he was now facing a a court-martial of his own, but it was way too late to worry about that and he needed to unload Jack.

"Go on, Jack, thin out," Dom said. "Get out of here. Some other squad needs you now."

Jack paused for a moment like he didn't trust Dom to complete the mission on his own, but he might just have been checking the radio net for instructions. *Come on, he's not a guy. He doesn't react like that.* Jack cloaked himself and Dom felt the wash of warm air as the bot moved off.

He turned to Marcus. "Which way out?"

"Cut through D Wing," Marcus said. "Have you seen anyone else in here?"

"No. The place is deserted. I told you."

Marcus pressed his lips into a thin, angry line. Dom wondered if the realization that Hoffman had left him there had now sunk in and was starting to fester, which wasn't like Marcus at all. He'd always said he deserved his sentence.

"Goddamn," Marcus said. "Okay, I've got some catching up to do with the grubs."

Dom now had to risk using the radio. They'd need a Raven to extract them, however pumped up Marcus was to fight his way out. Ah, shit, Hoffman knew he was here anyway. Dom would take what was coming to him. He took a deep breath and pressed his earpiece.

"All KR callsigns, this is Delta-Two," he said. "We're at the Slab. We need extraction."

"Six-Four here, Delta. Copy that. We're beginning our run."

"Run?" Marcus said. They moved out onto the main floor of D Wing, on the alert for grubs. "What's his target? Did he understand that?"

Dom heard the Raven coming but as it swept overhead, a single burst of fire spat through the shattered glass of the roof and blew chunks out of masonry. Dom dived for cover and Marcus dropped down beside him.

"Six-Four, this is Delta-Two, *hold your goddamn fire.*" Shit, that was all they needed, getting hit by friendly fire after making it this far. "We're *inside* the Slab. Repeat, *inside.*"

"Six-Four to Delta, roger that. Holding fire. Advise you relocate. The place is crawling with grubs."

Marcus scrambled to his feet. "So who else doesn't know you're here?"

This wasn't the time to try to explain a messy situation, least of all one with the word *Hoffman* in it. Dom just wanted to get Marcus out of here without being creamed. A half-lie would shut him up for a while. "If Command knew I was here to get you, I'd be in some deep shit."

"Yeah? So how are you going to explain *me* to them? You said *things have changed.*"

"Hey, just worry about getting out of here first, okay?"

Marcus went up to a side door and kicked it open. The place was a cesspit. Dom could see blood and bullet marks on the walls, some recent, some not.

"What the hell went on in here, Marcus?"

"You don't want to know. Come on. This way."

Dom followed him outside into a big courtyard scattered with more fallen masonry. He could hear the radio traffic between two Ravens and the ground, calling in grub positions. Marcus was still looking around like he was checking for snipers or something.

"There was a guy," Marcus said impatiently. He held his hand at chin height, fingers squared. "Black guy, this tall, thin. So you didn't see him or his body. You're *sure.*"

"No, nothing, and we've got to keep moving." Dom could hear the Ravens moving back in. "The grubs took the Andius highway. It's pretty hairy out there."

Right on cue, a shell hit a tower on the far side of the prison, sending chunks of granite down on the yard. The top of the tower shattered and then the whole thing started tipping over, falling, before crashing down on a colonnade about twenty meters ahead of them. The next thing Dom saw was the muzzle flash right in front of him as grubs came charging out of an alley. He took cover behind a low granite wall with Marcus, bobbing up every few seconds to fire. Movement on the top of the walls caught his eye. More grubs were making their way along a bridge connecting two buildings at roof height.

"Either we put those assholes down, or we have to cross back through D Wing and get out that way." Marcus took a breath and knelt upright to lay down a long burst before dropping down again to reload. "Get ready to run."

The grubs were still coming out of the alley, and the ammo wasn't going to last forever. Dom decided it was time to get back on the radio. "Delta-Two to KR units, requesting some support here. Grubs up on that bridge."

"Six-Four here, we see them." Raven fire raked the walkway, sending chunks of it spinning into the air along with the grubs. "We're clearing the area for extraction. Stand by."

"Okay," Marcus said. He checked his grenades. "*Run.*"

They sprinted to the door they'd come out of, back into D Wing. The grubs were waiting for them. Dom ran straight into a hail of fire from the floor level while more grubs came running along the gallery above. So much for using the debris for cover: for a moment Dom thought they'd both be picked off in seconds from the upper floor, but the dumb gray assholes rushed down to fight on the ground. Dom didn't understand that and he didn't need to. He just grabbed their stupidity with both grateful hands and blew the shit out of them, moving from cover to cover.

He hadn't fought alongside Marcus for years, but they snapped back together as if they'd never been apart, staggering their reloads, overlapping their arcs of fire, both knowing exactly what the other would do next. For a moment Dom could kid himself that the Slab had never happened and that it was just another ruined building they happened to be clearing. The incoming fire died away a grub at a time and Dom and Marcus just stood there, panting in the sudden silence. All Dom could hear was the faint click of shattered stonework that was starting to crumble and fall from the walls.

"I think we're done," he said. Then he heard scrapes against the steel door and a searing point of white light punched through the metal. "Shit, they're cutting their way through."

Marcus lined up with the door and started swinging a grenade on its chain. "Fine. Saves us the trouble."

Dom took up position behind a granite block and covered the door, now fringed by a red-hot line as the cutting tool crept around the edges. It was all a matter of timing. If Marcus let the grenade go before the door was down, it would just bounce off and detonate in front of the door. He had to wait for it to fall in. He stood there, eyes fixed on the glowing metal, swinging the frag like it was some kind of exercise and nothing urgent at all.

No, he hadn't lost it. Whatever this shithole had done to him—and Dom knew he'd changed—Marcus was back on top of his game.

The hiss of the cutting tool stopped. "Here they come," Dom said.

Boom. The door panel blew out from behind and crashed to the ground, and Marcus let go of the grenade. It was perfect timing. It caught the first rank of grubs starting to pour in.

"Okay, *go!*"

Marcus headed straight into the smoke. Dom could see more grubs behind but Marcus just plowed ahead, emptying clips into them like he'd been saving up for this all those years. Dom pushed through the mangled doorway beside him and now they were in what was left of the lobby, back in the sunlight, listening for Ravens above the noise of the shelling. A gaping hole yawned in one of the shattered perimeter walls. At least the way out was obvious now.

But the grubs weren't dumb, and they'd worked that out. They rose up from the rubble like range targets and opened fire. Ricochets sprayed everywhere. Marcus dropped behind a low wall with Dom on his heels.

"All we've got to do is get through that gap," he said. "Thirty meters. Come on. One last push. On three . . . two . . . *go.*"

They darted for the next cover, hosing whatever raised its head or ran at them. Dom had reached the blind instinct stage. At one point he wasn't even aware of where Marcus was. It was only when the grubs stopped popping up that his body handed the reins back to his brain and he was acutely aware of the deafening noise of Ravens coming in low.

The pilots had to be able to see what was going on. They wouldn't leave them here, not now. Dom hit the radio.

"Delta-Two here, ready for extraction," he said, finger pressed so hard to his earpiece that it hurt. He could hear the chatter between the pilots but he wasn't sure who else was up there. "Six-Two? Any KR unit?"

"I'm hit. I'm hit."

Dom heard the impact before he saw the black smoke. Then he heard the worst: someone saying he'd lost control, the signal breaking up, and then the *whoomp* of something crashing and exploding.

"Six-One is down. Repeat, Six-One is down."

"KR-Zero-Eight-Zero here—Kim to Santiago, we're seeing ground deformation outside the walls. There's something emerging. We're pulling you out."

Goddamn. It had to be Kim, didn't it? *Mr. Sovereign's Regs. By the book.* Now everybody knew. Was it Hoffman or Prescott who sent him? Dom looked up and saw the Raven loop around.

"Santiago receiving, sir. We're on our way."

"Move it before that e-hole opens, Private. We can't hang around."

"Understood, sir."

Kim wasn't joking. The Raven was waiting on the pavement a long way from the hole in the wall, engine whining, and as soon as Dom put his boot on the concrete slabs he felt the ground shiver.

Marcus broke into a jog. He gave Dom his dubious look, eyes slightly narrowed. "So Kim's going to be fine when you tell him you happened to be passing and found me here. With armor and a Lancer."

"Look, gift horses, mouths—just do it."

The jog turned into a run and then a sprint. Dom was ready for whatever was about to burst out in front of them, prepared to jink left or right, but it didn't happen. The concrete started cracking and then almost tipped him forward like the rolling deck of a ship as the pavement reared and broke open behind them. He didn't really need to look, but he did. It was a fucking *huge* Corpser, tank-sized, so vast and dangerous that it didn't need a load of grubs coming up behind it to take out everyone plus the Raven. Concrete and debris rained off it as Dom and Marcus scrambled for the open door. It was so close when they skidded across the deck that Dom felt the hail of grit and gravel fly off its legs.

The Raven lifted and banked like it was spring-loaded. Dom struggled to sit up on the tilting deck and found himself staring right into the Corpser's open maw, so close that he could see the line of pale tissue down the center of its tongue. He wasn't going to forget that image in a hurry. For a second he was sure he was going to slide down its gullet.

The crew chief stepped in and pulled Dom to his feet. "So we've got an extra passenger," he said. It was Nat Barber. Dom didn't know him that well, but Barber seemed to know Marcus a lot better. "Now *there's* a familiar face. Good to see you back, Fenix."

And wherever there was Barber, there was his pilot, Gill Gettner. Her voice came over the radio, an oddly reassuring blend of seen-it-all and pure acid. "And they say women keep guys waiting. You two okay?"

"Yes ma'am." Dom slid into a seat. "Sorry about Six-One."

"Yeah." She paused. The woman never reacted, at least not in public. "I'm losing them all today. Nobody else left down there?"

"Nobody," Marcus said, like it really pissed him off.

He settled into the seat next to Dom, facing Kim like a man on a train trying not to get into a conversation with a stranger. The lieutenant handed him his water bottle in silence and Marcus took a pull at it. Nobody seemed to know what to say to a disgraced hero. History had been put on hold, probably forever. The Gear on the door—CARMINE A., it said on his armor—fired sporadically at something on the ground that Dom couldn't see.

"Welcome to Delta Squad," Kim said at last.

Marcus seemed to have forgotten "sir" and salutes. "Where are we going?"

"Embry Square." Kim either didn't know that Dom had defied the Chief of Defense Staff and hijacked a bot, or he'd been ordered not to care about it. "Colonel Hoffman's waiting for us."

"*Hoffman.*" Marcus leaned back, looked up to the deckhead, and visibly gritted his teeth. "Shit."

Dom tried to jolly him along. The old firm was back together, Santiago and Fenix. Marcus should have been happy. "This is going to be awesome."

Carmine, kneeling at the open door, glanced back into the crew bay for a moment. Marcus couldn't have looked more badass if he'd taken lessons in it. He was simmering with some fresh anger and the new scar on his face just doubled the effect. Dom couldn't see Carmine's expression underneath the full-face helmet, but it was clear from the way he tilted his head to look up at Marcus that he was starstruck by machismo.

"Hey, are you *the* Marcus Fenix?" He sounded really, *really* young. "The one who fought at Aspho Fields?"

Marcus's shoulders sagged. Carmine couldn't have known what a painful subject the battle was. "Yeah."

"Wow! Cool!"

Marcus turned away and looked down out of the door on his side. "Not really."

Gettner circled over a patch of waste ground in the center of the city. Dom could see Sorotki's Raven on the ground with its rotors turning. Hoffman was pacing around just outside the range of the rotor wash, probably rehearsing a rant. Gettner brought the Raven in to land.

"Marcus, don't start it with the old man," Dom whispered. "Okay?"

"Yeah."

"I mean it."

"Yeah. Reality doesn't change. I still did it."

Marcus jumped down and ambled toward Hoffman, leaving Dom some way behind. It was a clash of stubborn bastards. Hoffman was a nice guy, a decent man for all his snarling and cussing, and he'd just turned an awful lot of blind eyes toward Dom's insubordination. He could have had him shot. But Hoffman had his bullshit barrier to keep up just like Marcus did, and his clenched jaw said he was digging in. What else could he do, burst into tears and say how sorry he was? No, Hoffman just stepped into Marcus's path— shoulders squared, boots apart, fists on hips—and looked him up and down like a piece of unwelcome shit.

"You traitor," he growled. "You're not fit to wear the uniform."

Marcus made a visible effort to resist a fight. He turned his head away for a moment, then just rolled right over the insult in that I-didn't-hear-you kind of way that he had. "Looks to me like you can use all the help you can get."

Testosterone had been sprayed and face had not been lost. *Stupid assholes, the pair of them.* Dom watched, wanting them to just shake hands and be the way they were, but that wasn't going to happen anytime soon, if ever.

"Step aside," Hoffman said.

Marcus did. Hoffman went over to Kim and started telling him about some great new plan to fuck the grubs for good with another fancy device the guys at the DRA had now developed. They were struggling without Marcus's dad. They were just digging up his old notes and half-finished projects and trying to make some useful weapons out of it all. Dom watched Hoffman head for KR-239, suddenly in a more bullish mood than he'd been in a long time. For all the crap, he had to be happy to see Marcus back. He *had* to.

Then Anya stepped out of the Raven's bay to relay a message or something. She must have known Marcus was there. Marcus wasn't expecting her, though. She stopped in her tracks and looked at him. He stared back. It was hard to tell if she could see that terrible scar, or if she was just so struck by seeing him after so long that she couldn't react, but Marcus's face sort of fell again and Dom couldn't work out why. *Dismay.* That was it. Maybe he thought she was checking him out and deciding he hadn't come out of jail as pretty as he went in. Maybe he was thinking she didn't look as good as he remembered, either. The strain had certainly taken its toll on her.

But Dom knew exactly what look Marcus should have had on his face right then: joy and relief. The love of his life had waited for him, and now things were going to be all right.

The moment hung there. Dom didn't expect Marcus to sweep her up in his arms, but he did want to see some thaw in that expression. Then the ground trembled. Rounds struck the paving, throwing gravel in the air, and suddenly they had bigger problems to worry about.

"*Locust!*"

"Get down!"

Dom caught a glimpse of Anya scrambling into KR-239. Rounds whizzed past his head as he sprinted for the cover of a wall of sandbags. Muzzle flash lit up the overcast day, the rattle of automatic fire numbed his ears, and the world had returned to its terrible kind of normal, everyone back to their old routine of fighting and running and dodging the next round. But Dom had his brother back. That was almost all he needed.

Marcus squeezed off a burst and ducked down again. He glanced up at the sky. Dom knew damn well that he was checking that Anya was clear.

"She waited," Marcus said.

"Yeah," Dom said. "She *waited*."

"And Maria?"

"Nothing yet."

The Raven was already a dwindling speck in the distance. Marcus reloaded and peered over the sandbags, sighting up on a doorway where grubs were taking cover.

"Thanks, Dom," he said at last, and carried on firing.

EPILOGUE

COG RESEARCH STATION AZURA: LATE RISE, 14 A.E.

DRIVE A
FOLDERS:
FENIX_E_COPY
PROJECT_NEW_HOPE
PROJECT_BNO
PROJECT_HOYLE
PROJECT_WHITTLE
AJF_PERSONAL
AJF_FOR_MMF
SELECT FOLDER: AJF_PERSONAL
SELECT FILE: JOURNAL

I don't know whether to laugh or cry. It's the good news, bad news joke. Prescott has been in touch to tell me that Marcus has been freed and he's back on the front line. As that's possibly the only place he'll ever be truly happy—or the least unhappy, if I'm honest—I should probably be relieved. Dom, as ever, stands by him whatever happens. Is Marcus grieving for me? The damage is done. The loss has scarred him, even if he finds out one day that I'm alive. I want to see him again so I can tell him all the things I made myself too busy to express, things that can't be left to a letter or this journal. That brings its own problems, however: I'll have to tell him the truth.

But he has friends. Not people he drinks with, or says hello to at the office, or who occasionally send him mail. I mean devoted, life-on-the-line friends. They give him what I never could.

Meanwhile, we carry on. Nevil is my anchor to sanity and we share a distaste for the menu to excuse our existence here. Everyone I thought was dead is walking around alive and well, except Elain. Couldn't there have been just one more miraculous lie, just *one*, for me? But it seems the price we pay for real knowledge is sacrifice. Elain was willing to make hers and so am I. The person I care most about in this world thinks I'm dead anyway.

So I carry on with the tests. Fifty-two hours ago, I took a new Lambent antigen. Twenty-six hours ago, the Lambency marker proteins were absent from my blood samples. This morning, they're back, and they've changed again.

This organism evolves. We're always one step behind it. I must find a way to get ahead of it, and if biochemistry is the answer, we have to find a wider range of its hosts to test. But biology may yet fail us, so physics must be ready to step into the breach. Nevil and I are carrying out a parallel program—yes, I've told Prescott—to look for a way of killing the pathogen with targeted radiation. Nothing is indestructible. And if there's one thing history will say I excelled at, it's destruction.

The hummingbird is back. I see it drinking from the blooms outside my window every morning. It's glorious. It's a living emerald.

You'd find it fascinating, Marcus. Take care of yourself, son. One day, I'll see you again, I swear, and I'll finally manage to tell you how proud I am of you, and—yes, how much I love you.

```
ENCRYPT? Y/N
Y
BACKUP TO MAINFRAME? Y/N
N
SAVE TO DRIVE A? Y/N
Y
FILE LAST SAVED: 1115/G10/14.
```